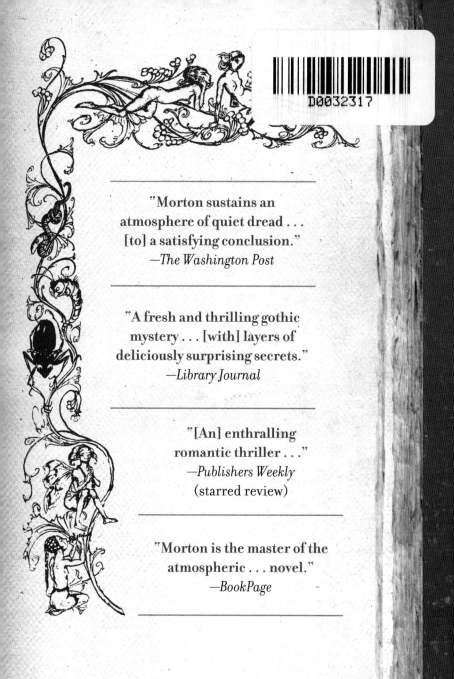

D0032317

More praise for Kate Morton

The Distant Hours

"Morton, as usual, deftly mixes all the necessary ingredients for a top-notch romantic thriller."

—Entertainment Weekly

"A rewarding, bittersweet payoff in the author's most gothic tale yet."

—Kirkus Reviews

"Morton has quickly established herself as a master of modern gothic."

—Library Journal

"An engrossing and suspenseful tale."

—The Historical Novels Review

"Morton is great at conveying a sense of slow-building gothic menace and hidden danger."

—The Onion's A.V. Club

"Morton takes writing a pastiche of the gothic novel a step beyond, grounding her story in historical reality and rooting it in relationships."

—The Columbus (OH) Dispatch

"Cast[s] a whispery spell."

—Marie Claire (UK)

"Shades of *I Capture the Castle* haunt Kate Morton's *The Distant Hours*."

—In Style (UK)

"A bewitching tale."

—Good Housekeeping (UK)

The Forgotten Garden

"Like Frances Hodgson Burnett's beloved classic *The Secret Garden*, Kate Morton's *The Forgotten Garden* takes root in your imagination and grows into something enchanting."

—Amazon.com

"A satisfying read. . . . Just the thing for readers who like multigenerational sagas with a touch of mystery."

—*Booklist*

"The puzzle is pleasing and the long-delayed 'reveal' is a genuine surprise."

—*Kirkus Reviews*

"A beautifully written and satisfying novel."

—*Daily Express* (UK)

"Simmers with secrets and strangeness."

—*Good Housekeeping* (UK)

The House at Riverton

"[A] stunning debut."

—*People*

"Morton triumphs with a riveting plot, a touching but tense love story and a haunting ending."

—*Publishers Weekly* (starred review)

"This novel will challenge your definitions of friendship, family and, most of all, trust."

—*Hallmark Magazine*

"An extraordinary debut . . . written with a lovely turn of phrase."

—*The Sunday Telegraph* (UK)

These titles are also available as ebooks.

Also by Kate Morton

The House at Riverton
The Forgotten Garden

THE DISTANT HOURS

A Novel

KATE MORTON

WASHINGTON SQUARE PRESS

New York   London   Toronto   Sydney

WASHINGTON SQUARE PRESS
A Division of Simon & Schuster, Inc.
1230 Avenue of the Americas
New York, NY 10020

Originally published in Australia in 2010 by Allen & Unwin.

Published by arrangement with Allen & Unwin Pty Ltd.

First Washington Square Press trade paperback edition July 2011

WASHINGTON SQUARE PRESS and colophon are registered trademarks of Simon & Schuster, Inc.

For information about special discounts for bulk purchases, please contact Simon & Schuster Special Sales at 1-866-506-1949 or business@simonandschuster.com.

The Simon & Schuster Speakers Bureau can bring authors to your live event. For more information or to book an event, contact the Simon & Schuster Speakers Bureau at 1-866-248-3049 or visit our website at www.simonspeakers.com.

Manufactured in the United States of America

10 9 8 7 6

The Library of Congress has cataloged the hardcover edition as follows:

Morton, Kate, date.
    The Distant hours : a novel / Kate Morton.—1st Atria Books hardcover ed.
        p.   cm.
    1. Mothers and daughters—Fiction.   2. Family secrets—Fiction.   3. World War, 1939–1945—Evacuation of civilians—Fiction.   4. World War, 1939–1945—England—Kent.   5. Domestic fiction.   I. Title.
PR9619.4.M74D57 2010
823'.92—dc22   2010033472

ISBN 978-1-4391-5278-2
ISBN 978-1-4391-5279-9 (pbk)
ISBN 978-1-4391-9934-3 (ebook)

*For Kim Wilkins, who encouraged me to start; and
Darin Patterson, who was with me to the last full stop*

CONTENTS

Hush . . . Can you hear him?

The trees can. They are the first to know that he is coming.

Listen! The trees of the deep, dark wood, shivering and jittering their leaves like papery hulls of beaten silver; the sly wind, snaking through their tops, whispering that soon it will begin.

The trees know, for they are old and they have seen it all before.

It is moonless.

It is moonless when the Mud Man comes. The night has slipped on a pair of fine, leather gloves, shaken a black sheet across the land: a ruse, a disguise, a sleeping spell, so that all beneath it slumbers sweet.

Darkness, but not only, for there are nuances and degrees and textures to all things. Look: the rough woolliness of the huddled woods; the quilted stretch of fields; the smooth molasses moat. And yet . . . Unless you are very unlucky, you won't have noticed that something moved where it should not. You are fortunate indeed. For there are none who see the Mud Man rise and live to tell the tale.

There—see? The sleek black moat, the mud-soaked moat, lies flat no longer. A bubble has appeared, there in the widest stretch, a heaving bubble, a quiver of tiny ripples, a suggestion—

But you have looked away! And you were wise to do so. Such sights are not for the likes of you. We will turn our attention instead to the castle, for that way also something stirs.

High up in the tower.

Watch and you will see.

1

Prologue

A young girl tosses back her covers.

She has been put to bed hours before; in a nearby chamber her nurse snores softly, dreaming of soap and lilies and tall glasses of warm fresh milk. But something has woken the girl; she sits up furtively, sidles across the clean white sheet, and places her feet, one beside the other, two pale, narrow blocks, on the wooden floor.

There is no moon to look at or to see by, and yet she is drawn to the window. The stippled glass is cold; she can feel the night-frosted air shimmering as she climbs atop the bookcase, sits above the row of discarded childhood favorites, victims of her rush to grow up and away. She tucks her nightdress round the tops of her pale legs and rests her cheek in the cup where one white knee meets the other.

The world is out there, people moving about in it like clockwork dolls.

Someday soon she plans to see it for herself; for this castle might have locks on all the doors and bars against the windows, but that is to keep the other thing out and not to keep her in.

The other thing.

She has heard stories about him. He is a story. A tale from long ago, the bars and locks vestiges of a time when people believed such things. Rumors about monsters in moats who lay in wait to prey upon fair maidens. A man to whom an ancient wrong was done, who seeks revenge against his loss, time and time again.

But the young girl—who would frown to hear herself described that way—is no longer bothered by childhood monsters and fairy tales. She is restless; she is modern and grown-up and hungers for escape. This window, this castle, has ceased to be enough, and yet for the time being it is all she has and thus she gazes glumly through the glass.

Out there, beyond, in the folded crease between the hills, the village is falling to drowsy sleep. A dull and distant train, the last of the night, signals its arrival: a lonely call that goes unanswered, and the porter in a stiff cloth hat stumbles out to raise the signal. In the nearby woods, a poacher eyes his shot and dreams of getting home to bed, while on the outskirts of the village, in a cottage with peeling paint, a newborn baby cries.

Perfectly ordinary events in a world where all makes sense. Where things are seen when they are there, missed when they are not. A world quite unlike the one in which the girl has woken to find herself.

For down below, nearer than the girl has thought to look, something is happening.

The moat has begun to breathe. Deep, deep, mired in the mud, the buried man's heart kicks wetly. A low noise, like the moaning wind but not, rises from the depths and hovers tensely above the surface. The girl hears it, that is, she feels it, for the castle foundations are married to the mud, and the moan seeps through the stones, up the walls, one story after another, imperceptibly through the bookcase on which she sits. A once-beloved tale tumbles to the floor and the girl in the tower gasps.

The Mud Man opens an eye. Sharp, sudden, tracks it back and forth. Is he thinking, even now, of his lost family? The pretty little wife and the pair of plump, milky babes he left behind? Or have his thoughts cast further back to the days of boyhood, when he ran with his brother across fields of long pale stems? Or are his thoughts, perhaps, of the other woman, the one who loved him before his death? Whose flattery and attentions and refusal to be refused cost the Mud Man everything—

Something changes. The girl senses it and shivers. Presses her hand to the icy window and leaves a starry print within the condensation. The witching hour is upon her, though she does not know to call it that. There is no one left to help her now. The train is gone, the poacher lies beside his wife, even the baby sleeps, having given up trying to tell the world all that it knows. At the castle the girl in the window is the only one awake; her nurse has stopped snoring and her breaths are so light now that one might think her frozen; the

3

birds in the castle wood are silent too, heads tucked beneath their shivering wings, eyes sealed in thin gray lines against the thing they know is coming.

The girl is the only one, and the man, waking in the mud. His heart splurting; faster now, for his time has come and it will not last long. He rolls his wrists, his ankles, he launches from the muddy bed.

Don't watch. I beg you, look away as he breaks the surface, as he clambers from the moat, as he stands on the black, drenched banks, raises his arms, and inhales. Remembers how it is to breathe, to love, to ache.

Look instead at the storm clouds. Even in the dark you can see them coming. A rumble of angry, fisted clouds, rolling, fighting, until they are right above the tower. Does the Mud Man bring the storm, or does the storm bring the Mud Man? Nobody knows.

In her bower, the girl inclines her head as the first reluctant drops splatter against the pane and meet her hand. The day has been fine, not too hot; the evening cool. No talk of midnight rain. The following morning, people will greet the sodden earth with surprise, scratch their heads, and smile at one another and say, What a thing! To think we slept right through it!

But look! What's that?—A shape, a mass, is climbing up the tower wall. The figure climbs quickly, ably, impossibly. For no man, surely, can achieve such a feat?

He arrives at the girl's window. They are face-to-face. She sees him through the streaky glass, through the rain—now pounding; a mudded, monstrous creature. She opens her mouth to scream, to cry for help, but in that very moment, everything changes.

Before her eyes, he changes. She sees through the layers of mud, through the generations of darkness and rage and sorrow, to the human face beneath. A young man's face. A forgotten face. A face of such longing and sadness and beauty; and she reaches, unthinking, to unlock the window. To bring him in from the rain.

Raymond Blythe, The True History of the Mud Man, *Prologue*

PART ONE

A Lost Letter Finds Its Way

1992

I⊤ started with a letter. A letter that had been lost a long time, waiting out half a century in a forgotten postal bag in the dim attic of a nondescript house in Bermondsey. I think about it sometimes, that mailbag: of the hundreds of love letters, grocery bills, birthday cards, notes from children to their parents, that lay together, swelling and sighing as their thwarted messages whispered in the dark. Waiting, waiting, for someone to realize they were there. For it is said, you know, that a letter will always seek a reader; that sooner or later, like it or not, words have a way of finding the light, of making their secrets known.

Forgive me, I'm being romantic—a habit acquired from the years spent reading nineteenth-century novels with a torch when my parents thought I was asleep. What I mean to say is that it's odd to think that if Arthur Tyrell had been a little more responsible, if he hadn't had one too many rum toddies that Christmas Eve in 1941 and gone home and fallen into a drunken slumber instead of finishing his mail delivery, if the bag hadn't then been tucked in his attic and hidden until his death some fifty years later when one of his daughters unearthed it and called the *Daily Mail*, the whole thing might have turned out differently. For my mum, for me, and especially for Juniper Blythe.

You probably read about it when it happened; it was in all the newspapers and on the TV news. Channel 4 even ran a special where they invited some of the recipients to talk about their letter, their particular voice from the past that had come back to surprise them. There was a woman whose sweetheart had been in the RAF, and the man

7

with the birthday card his evacuated son had sent, the little boy who was killed by a piece of falling shrapnel a week or so later. It was a very good program, I thought: moving in parts, happy and sad stories interspersed with old footage of the war. I cried a couple of times, but that's not saying much: I'm rather disposed to weep.

Mum didn't go on the show, though. The producers contacted her and asked whether there was anything special in her letter that she'd like to share with the nation, but she said no, that it was just an ordinary old clothing order from a shop that had long ago gone out of business. But that wasn't the truth. I know this because I was there when the letter arrived. I saw her reaction to that lost letter and it was anything but ordinary.

It was a morning in late February, winter still had us by the throat, the flower beds were icy, and I'd come over to help with the Sunday roast. I do that sometimes because my parents like it, even though I'm a vegetarian and I know that at some point during the course of the meal my mother will start to look worried, then agonized, until finally she can stand it no longer and statistics about protein and anemia will begin to fly.

I was peeling potatoes in the sink when the letter dropped through the slot in the door. The mail doesn't usually come on Sundays so that should have tipped us off, but it didn't. For my part, I was too busy wondering how I was going to tell my parents that Jamie and I had broken up. It had been two months since it happened and I knew I had to say something eventually, but the longer I took to utter the words, the more calcified they became. And I had my reasons for staying silent: my parents had been suspicious of Jamie from the start, they didn't take kindly to upsets, and Mum would worry even more than usual if she knew that I was living in the flat alone. Most of all, though, I was dreading the inevitable, awkward conversation that would follow my announcement. To see first bewilderment, then alarm, then resignation cross Mum's face as she realized the maternal code required her to provide some sort of consolation . . . But back to the mail. The sound of something dropping softly through the letter box.

"Edie, can you get that?"

This was my mother. (Edie is me; I'm sorry, I should have said so earlier.) She nodded towards the hallway and gestured with the hand that wasn't stuck up the inside of the chicken.

I put down the potato, wiped my hands on a tea towel, and went to fetch the post. There was only one letter lying on the welcome mat: an official post office envelope declaring the contents to be "redirected mail." I read the label to Mum as I brought it into the kitchen.

She'd finished stuffing the chicken by then and was drying her own hands. Frowning a little, from habit rather than any particular expectation, she took the letter from me and plucked her reading glasses from on top of the pineapple in the fruit bowl. She skimmed the post office notice and with a flicker of her eyebrows began to open the outer envelope.

I'd turned back to the potatoes by now, a task that was arguably more engaging than watching my mum open mail, so I'm sorry to say I didn't see her face as she fished the smaller envelope from inside, as she registered the frail austerity paper and the old stamp, as she turned the letter over and read the name written on the back. I've imagined it many times since, though, the color draining instantly from her cheeks, her fingers beginning to tremble so that it took minutes before she was able to slit the envelope open.

What I don't have to imagine is the sound. The horrid, guttural gasp, followed quickly by a series of rasping sobs that swamped the air and made me slip with the peeler so that I cut my finger.

"Mum?" I went to her, draping my arm around her shoulders, careful not to bleed on her dress. But she didn't say anything. She couldn't, she told me later, not then. She stood rigidly as tears spilled down her cheeks and she clutched the strange little envelope, its paper so thin I could make out the corner of the folded letter inside, hard against her bosom. Then she disappeared upstairs to her bedroom leaving a fraying wake of instructions about the bird and the oven and the potatoes.

The kitchen settled in a bruised silence around her absence and

I stayed very quiet, moved very slowly so as not to disturb it further. My mother is not a crier, but this moment—her upset and the shock of it—felt oddly familiar, as if we'd been here before. After fifteen minutes in which I variously peeled potatoes, turned over possibilities as to whom the letter might be from, and wondered how to proceed, I finally knocked on her door and asked whether she'd like a cup of tea. She'd composed herself by then and we sat opposite one another at the small Formica-covered table in the kitchen. As I pretended not to notice she'd been crying, she began to talk about the envelope's contents.

"A letter," she said, "from someone I used to know a long time ago. When I was just a girl, twelve, thirteen."

A picture came into my mind, a hazy memory of a photograph that had sat on my gran's bedside when she was old and dying. Three children, the youngest of whom was my mum, a girl with short dark hair, perched on something in the foreground. It was odd; I'd sat with Gran a hundred times or more but I couldn't bring that girl's features into focus now. Perhaps children are never really interested in who their parents were before they were born; not unless something particular happens to shine a light on the past. I sipped my tea, waiting for Mum to continue.

"I don't know that I've told you much about that time, have I? During the war, the Second World War. It was a terrible time, such confusion, so many things were broken. It seemed . . ." She sighed. "Well, it seemed as if the world would never return to normal. As if it had been tipped off its axis and nothing would ever set it to rights." She cupped her hands around the steaming rim of her mug and stared down at it.

"My family—Mum and Dad, Rita and Ed and I—we all lived in a small house together in Barlow Street, near the Elephant and Castle, and the day after war broke out we were rounded up at school, marched over to the railway station, and put into train carriages. I'll never forget it, all of us with our tags on and our masks and our packs, and the mothers, who'd had second thoughts because they came running down the road towards the station, shouting at the guard to let their kids off; then shouting at older siblings to look after the little ones, not to let them out of their sight."

She sat for a moment, biting her bottom lip as the scene played out in her memory.

"You must've been frightened," I said quietly. We're not really hand-holders in our family or else I'd have reached out and taken hers.

"I was, at first." She removed her glasses and rubbed her eyes. Her face had a vulnerable, unfinished look without her frames, like a small nocturnal animal confused by the daylight. I was glad when she put them on again and continued. "I'd never been away from home before, never spent a night apart from my mother. But I had my older brother and sister with me, and as the trip went on and one of the teachers handed round bars of chocolate, everybody started to cheer up and look upon the experience almost like an adventure. Can you imagine? War had been declared but we were all singing songs and eating canned pears and looking out of the window playing I Spy. Children are very resilient, you know; callous in some cases.

"We arrived eventually in a town called Cranbrook, only to be split into groups and loaded onto various coaches. The one I was on with Ed and Rita took us to the village of Milderhurst, where we were walked in lines to a hall. A group of local women was waiting for us there, smiles fixed on their faces, lists in hand, and we were made to stand in rows as people milled about, making their selection.

"The little ones went fast, especially the pretty ones. People supposed they'd be less work, I expect, that they'd have less of the whiff of London about them."

She smiled crookedly. "They soon learned. My brother was picked early. He was a strong boy, tall for his age, and the farmers were desperate for help. Rita went a short while after with her friend from school."

Well, that was it. I reached out and laid my hand on hers. "Oh, Mum."

"Never mind." She pulled free and gave my fingers a tap. "I wasn't the last to go. There were a few others, a little boy with a terrible skin condition. I don't know what happened to him, but he was still stand-ing there in that hall when I left.

"You know, for a long time afterwards, years and years, I forced myself to buy bruised fruit if that's what I picked up first at the green-grocer's. None of this checking it over and putting it back on the shelf if it didn't measure up."

"But you were chosen eventually."

"Yes, I was chosen eventually." She lowered her voice, fiddling with something in her lap, and I had to lean close. "She came in late. The room was almost clear, most of the children had gone and the la-dies from the Women's Voluntary Service were putting away the tea things. I'd started to cry a little, though I did so very discreetly. Then all of a sudden, *she* swept in and the room, the very air, seemed to alter."

"Alter?" I wrinkled my nose, thinking of that scene in *Carrie* when the light explodes.

"It's hard to explain. Have you ever met a person who seems to bring their own atmosphere with them when they arrive somewhere?"

Maybe. I lifted my shoulders, uncertain. My friend Sarah has a habit of turning heads wherever she goes; not exactly an atmospheric phenomenon, but still . . .

"No, of course you haven't. It sounds so silly to say it like that. What I mean is that she was different from other people, more . . . Oh, I don't know. Just *more*. Beautiful in an odd way, long hair, big eyes, rather wild looking, but it wasn't that alone which set her apart. She was only seventeen at the time, in September 1939, but the other women all seemed to fold into themselves when she arrived."

"They were deferential?"

"Yes, that's the word, deferential. Surprised to see her and uncer-tain how to behave. Finally, one of them spoke up, asking whether she could help, but the girl merely waved her long fingers and an-nounced that she'd come for her evacuee. That's what she said; not *an* evacuee, *her* evacuee. And then she came straight over to where I was sitting on the floor. 'What's your name?' she said, and when I told her she smiled and said that I must be tired, having traveled such a long way. 'Would you like to come and stay with me?' I nodded, I must have, for she turned then to the bossiest woman, the one with the list, and said that she would take me home with her."

"What was her name?"

"Blythe," said my mother, suppressing the faintest of shivers. "Juniper Blythe."

"And was it she who sent you the letter?"

Mum nodded. "She led me to the fanciest car I'd ever seen and drove me back to the place where she and her older twin sisters lived, through a set of iron gates, along a winding driveway, until we reached an enormous stone edifice surrounded by thick woods. Milderhurst Castle."

The name was straight out of a gothic novel and I tingled a little, remembering Mum's sob when she'd read the woman's name and address on the back of the envelope. I'd heard stories about the evacuees, about some of the things that went on, and I said on a breath, "Was it ghastly?"

"Oh no, nothing like that. Not ghastly at all. Quite the opposite."

"But the letter . . . it made you—"

"The letter was a surprise, that's all. A memory from a long time ago."

She fell silent then and I thought about the enormity of evacuation, how frightening, how odd it must have been for her as a child to be sent to a strange place where everyone and everything was vastly different. I could still touch my own childhood experiences, the horror of being thrust into new, unnerving situations, the furious bonds that were forged of necessity—to buildings, to sympathetic adults, to special friends—in order to survive. Remembering those urgent friendships, something struck me: "Did you ever go back, Mum, after the war? To Milderhurst?"

She looked up sharply. "Of course not. Why would I?"

"I don't know. To catch up, to say hello. To see your friend."

"No." She said it firmly. "I had my own family in London, my mother couldn't spare me, and besides, there was work to be done, cleaning up after the war. Real life went on." And with that, the familiar veil came down between us and I knew the conversation was over.

WE DIDN'T have the roast in the end. Mum said she didn't feel like it and asked whether I minded terribly giving it a miss this weekend. It seemed unkind to remind her that I don't eat meat anyway and that my attendance was more in the order of daughterly service, so I told her it was fine and suggested that she have a lie-down. She agreed, and as I gathered my things into my bag she was already swallowing two aspirins in preparation, reminding me to keep my ears covered in the wind.

My dad, as it turns out, slept through the whole thing. He's older than Mum and had retired from his work a few months before. Retirement hasn't been good for him: he roams the house during the week, looking for things to fix and tidy, driving Mum mad, then on Sunday he rests in his armchair. The God-given right of the man of the house, he says to anyone who'll listen.

I gave him a kiss on the cheek and left the house, braving the chill air as I made my way to the tube, tired and unsettled and somewhat subdued to be heading back alone to the fiendishly expensive flat I'd shared until recently with Jamie. It wasn't until somewhere between High Street Kensington and Notting Hill Gate that I realized Mum hadn't told me what the letter said.

A Memory Clarifies

Writing it down now, I'm a little disappointed in myself. But everyone's an expert with the virtue of hindsight and it's easy to wonder why I didn't go looking, now that I know what there was to find. And I'm not a complete dolt. Mum and I met for tea a few days later, and although I failed again to mention my changed circumstances, I did ask her about the contents of the letter. She waved the question away and said it wasn't important, little more than a greeting; that her reaction had been brought on by surprise and nothing more. I didn't know then that my mum is a good liar or I might have had reason to doubt her, to question further or to take special notice of her body language. You don't though, do you? Your instinct is usually to believe what people tell you, particularly people you know well, family, those you trust; at least mine is. Or was.

And so I forgot for a time about Milderhurst Castle and Mum's evacuation and even the odd fact that I'd never heard her speak of it before. It was easy enough to explain away; most things are if you try hard enough: Mum and I got on all right, but we'd never been especially close, and we certainly didn't go in for long chummy discussions about the past. Or the present, for that matter. By all accounts her evacuation had been a pleasant but forgettable experience; there was no reason she should've shared it with me. Lord knows, there was enough I didn't tell her.

Harder to rationalize was the strong, strange sense that had come upon me when I witnessed her reaction to the letter, the inexplicable certainty of an important memory I couldn't pin down. Something I'd seen or heard and since forgotten, fluttering now within the shadowy recesses of my mind, refusing to stop still and let me name it. It fluttered and I wondered, trying very hard to remember whether perhaps another letter had arrived, years before, a letter that had also made her cry. But it was no use; the elusive, granular feeling refused to clarify and I decided it was more than likely my overactive imagination at work, the one my parents had always warned would get me into trouble if I wasn't careful.

At the time I had more pressing concerns: namely, where I was going to live when the period of prepaid rent on the flat was up. The six months paid in advance had been Jamie's parting gift, an apology of sorts, compensation for his regrettable behavior, but it would end in June. I'd been combing the papers and estate agents' windows for studio flats, but on my modest salary it was proving difficult to find anywhere even remotely close to work.

I'm an editor at Billing & Brown Book Publishers. They're a small family-run publisher, here in Notting Hill, set up in the late 1940s by Herbert Billing and Michael Brown, as a means, initially, of publishing their own plays and poetry. When they started I believe they were quite respected, but over the decades, as bigger publishers took a greater share of the market and public taste for niche titles declined, we've been reduced to printing genres we refer to kindly as "speciality" and those to which we refer less kindly as "vanity." Mr. Billing— Herbert—is my boss; he's also my mentor, champion, and closest friend. I don't have many, not the living, breathing sort at any rate. And I don't mean that in a sad and lonely way; I'm just not the type of person who accumulates friends or enjoys crowds. I'm good with words, but not the spoken kind; I've often thought what a marvelous thing it would be if I could only conduct relationships on paper. And I suppose, in a sense, that's what I do, for I've hundreds of the other sort, the friends contained within bindings, page after glorious page of ink, stories that unfold the same way every time but never lose their joy, that take me by the hand and lead me through doorways into worlds of great terror and rapturous delight. Exciting, worthy, reliable companions—full of wise counsel, some of them—but sadly ill equipped to offer the use of a spare bedroom for a month or two.

For although I was inexperienced at breaking up—Jamie was my first real boyfriend, the sort with whom I'd envisaged a future—I suspected this was the time to call in favors from friends. Which is why I turned to Sarah. The two of us grew up as neighbors and our house became her second home whenever her four younger siblings turned into wild things and she needed to escape. I was flattered that someone like Sarah thought of my parents' rather staid suburban home as a refuge, and we remained close through secondary school until Sarah was caught smoking behind the toilets one too many times and traded in math classes for beauty school. She works freelance now, for magazines and film shoots. Her success is a brilliant thing, but unfortunately it meant that in my hour of need she was away in Hollywood turning actors into zombies, her flat and its spare room sublet to an Austrian architect.

I fretted for a time, envisaging in piquant detail the sort of life I might be forced to eke out sans roof, before, in a fine act of chivalry, Herbert offered me the sofa in his little flat below our office.

"After all you did for me?" he said, when I asked if he was sure. "Picked me up off the floor, you did. Rescued me!"

He was exaggerating; I'd never actually found him on the floor, but I knew what he meant. I'd only been with them a couple of years and had just started to look around for something slightly more challenging, when Mr. Brown passed away. Herbert took the death of his partner so hard, though, that there was no way I could leave him, not then. He didn't appear to have anyone else, other than his rotund, piggy little dog, and although he never said as much, it became clear to me by the type and the intensity of his grief that he and Mr. Brown had been more than business partners. He stopped eating, stopped washing, and drank himself silly on gin one morning even though he's a teetotaler.

There didn't seem to be much choice about the matter: I began making him meals, confiscated the gin, and when the figures were very bad and I couldn't raise his interest, I took it upon myself to door-knock and find us some new work. That's when we moved into printing flyers for local businesses. Herbert was so grateful when he found out that he quite overestimated my motivation. He started referring to me as his protégée and cheered up considerably when he talked about the future of Billing & Brown; how he and I were going to rebuild the company in honor of Mr. Brown. The glimmer was back in his eyes and I put off my job search a little longer.

And here I am now. Eight years later. Much to Sarah's bemusement. It's hard to explain to someone like her, a creative, clever person who refuses to do anything on terms that aren't her own, that the rest of us have different criteria for satisfaction in life. I work with people I adore, I earn enough money to support myself (though not perhaps in a two-bedder in Notting Hill), I get to spend my days playing with words and sentences, helping people to express their ideas and fulfill their dreams of publication. Besides, it's not as if I haven't got prospects. Just last year, Herbert promoted me to the position of vice chairman; never mind that there are only the two of us working in the office full-time. We had a little ceremony and everything. Susan, the part-time junior, baked a pound cake and came in on her day off so we could all three drink nonalcoholic wine together from teacups.

Faced with imminent eviction, I gratefully accepted his offer of a place to stay; it was really a very touching gesture, particularly in light of his flat's tiny proportions. It was also my only option. Herbert was extremely pleased. "Marvelous! Jess will be beside herself—she does love guests."

So it was, back in May, I was preparing to leave forever the flat that Jamie and I had shared, to turn the final, blank page of our story and begin a new one all of my own. I had my work, I had my health, I had an awful lot of books; I just needed to be brave, to face up to the gray, lonely days that stretched on indefinitely.

All things considered, I think I was doing pretty well: only occasionally did I allow myself to slip deep inside the pool of my own most maudlin imaginings. At these times I'd find a quiet, dark corner—all the better to give myself over fully to the fantasy—and picture in great detail those bland future days when I would walk along our street, stop at our building, gaze up at the windowsill on which I used to grow my herbs, and see someone else's silhouette fall across the glass. Glimpse the shadowy barrier between the past and the present, and know keenly the physical ache of being unable ever to go back.

I was a daydreamer when I was small, and a source of constant frustration to my poor mother. She used to despair when I walked through the middle of a muddy puddle, or had to be wrenched back from the gutter and the path of a hurtling bus, and say things like: "It's dangerous to get lost inside one's own head," or "You won't be able to see what's really going on around you—that's when accidents happen, Edie. You must pay attention."

Which was easy for her: never had a more sensible, pragmatic woman walked the earth. Not so simple, though, for a girl who'd lived inside her head for as long as she'd been able to wonder: "What if . . . ?" And I didn't stop daydreaming, of course, I merely got better at hiding it. But she was right, in a way, for it was my preoccupation with imagining my bleak and dreary post-Jamie future that left me so utterly unprepared for what happened next.

In late May, we received a phone call at the office from a self-styled ghost whisperer who wanted to publish a manuscript about his otherworldly encounters on Romney Marsh. When a prospective new client makes contact, we do whatever we can to keep them happy, which is why I found myself driving Herbert's rather ancient Peugeot hatchback down to Kent for a meet, greet, and, hopefully, woo. I don't drive often and I loathe the motorway when it's busy, so I left at the crack of dawn, figuring it gave me a clearer run at getting out of London unscathed.

I was there well before nine, the meeting itself went very well—wooing was done, contracts were signed—and I was back on the road again by midday. A much busier road by then, and one to which Herbert's car, incapable of going faster than fifty miles per hour without serious risk of tire loss, was decidedly unequal. I planted myself in the slow lane but still managed to attract much frustrated horn-honking and head-shaking. It is not good for the soul to be cast as a nuisance, particularly when one has no choice in the matter, so I left the motorway at Ashford and took the back roads instead. My sense of direction is quite dreadful, but there was a map in the glove compartment and I was resigned to pulling over regularly to consult it.

It took me a good half hour to become well and truly lost. I still don't know how it happened, but I suspect the map's vintage played a part. That, and the fact that I'd been enjoying the view—fields speckled with cowslips; wildflowers decorating the ditches by the side of the road—when I probably should have been paying attention to the road itself. Whatever the cause, I'd lost my spot on the map and was driving along a narrow lane over which great bowed trees were arched when I finally admitted that I had no idea whether I was heading north, south, east, or west.

I wasn't worried, though, not then. As far as I could see, if I just continued on my way, sooner or later I was bound to reach a junction, a landmark, maybe even a roadside stall where someone might be kind enough to draw a big red X on my map. I wasn't due back at work that afternoon; roads didn't continue on forever; I just needed to keep my eyes peeled.

And that's how I saw it, poking up from the middle of an aggressive mound of ivy. One of those old white posts with the names of local villages carved into arrowed pieces of wood pointing in each direction. MILDERHURST, it read, 3 MILES.

I STOPPED the car and read the signpost again, hairs beginning to quiver on the back of my neck. An odd sixth sense overcame me, and the cloudy memory that I'd been struggling to bring into focus ever since Mum's lost letter arrived in February resurrected itself. I climbed out of the car, as if in a dream, and followed where the sign-post led. I felt like I was watching myself from the outside, almost as if I knew what I was going to find. And perhaps I did.

For there they were, half a mile along the road, right where I'd imagined they might be. Rising from the brambles, a set of tall iron gates, once grand but listing now at broken angles. Leaning, one to-wards the other, as if to share a weighty burden. A sign was hang-ing on the small stone gatehouse, a rusted sign that read MILDERHURST CASTLE.

My heart beat fast and hard against my rib cage and I crossed the road towards the gates. I gripped a bar with each hand—cold, rough, rusting iron beneath my palms—and brought my face, my forehead, slowly to press against them. I followed with my eyes the gravel drive-way that curved away, up the hill, until it crossed a bridge and disap-peared behind a thick patch of woods.

It was beautiful and overgrown and melancholy, but it wasn't the view that stole my breath. It was the thudding realization, the abso-lute certainty, that I had been there before. That I had stood at those gates and peered between the bars and watched the birds flying like scraps of nighttime sky above the bristling woods.

Details murmured into place around me and it seemed as if I'd stepped into the fabric of a dream; as if I were occupying, once again, the very same temporal and geographical space that my long-ago self had done. My fingers tightened around the bars and somewhere, deep within my body, I recognized the gesture. I'd done the same thing be-fore. The skin of my palms remembered. *I* remembered. A sunny day; a warm breeze playing with the hem of my dress—my best dress—the shadow of my mother, tall in my peripheral vision.

I glanced sideways to where she stood, watching her as she watched the castle, the dark and distant shape on the horizon. I was thirsty, I was hot, I wanted to go swimming in the rippling lake that I could see through the gates. Swimming with the ducks and moorhens and the dragonflies making stabbing movements among the reeds along the banks.

"Mum," I remembered saying, but she didn't reply. "Mum?" Her head turned to face me, and a split second passed in which not a spark of recognition lit her features. Instead, an expression that I didn't understand held them hostage. She was a stranger to me, a grown-up woman whose eyes masked secret things. I have words to describe that odd amalgam now: regret, fondness, sorrow, nostalgia; but back then I was clueless. Even more so when she said, "I've made a mistake. I should never have come. It's too late."

I don't think I answered her, not then. I had no idea what she meant and before I could ask she'd gripped my hand and pulled so hard that my shoulder hurt, dragging me back across the road to where our car was parked. I'd caught a hint of her perfume as we went, sharper now and sour where it had mixed with the day's scorching air, the unfamiliar country smells. And she'd started the car, and we'd been driving, and I was watching a pair of sparrows through the window when I heard it: the same ghastly cry that she'd made when the letter arrived from Juniper Blythe.

The Books and the Birds

THE castle gates were locked and far too high to scale, not that I'd have rated my chances had they been lower. I've never been one for sports or physical challenges, and with the arrival of that missing memory my legs had turned, most unhelpfully, to jelly. I felt strangely disconnected and uncertain, and after a time, there was nothing for it but to go back to the car and sit for a while, wondering how best to proceed. In the end, my choices were limited. I felt far too distracted to drive, certainly anywhere as far as London, so I started up the car and proceeded at a crawl into Milderhurst village.

On first glimpse it was like all the other villages I'd driven through that day: a single road through the center with a green at one end, a church beside it, and a school along the way. I parked in front of the local church hall and I could almost see the lines of weary London schoolchildren, grubby and uncertain after their interminable train ride. A ghostly imprint of Mum long ago, before she was my mum, before she was much of anything, filing helplessly towards the unknown.

I drifted along the High Street, trying—without much success—to tame my flyaway thoughts. Mum had been back to Milderhurst, all right, and I had been with her. We'd stood at those gates and she'd become upset. I remembered it. It had happened. But as surely as one answer had been found, a host of new questions had broken free, fluttering about my mind like so many dusty moths seeking the light. Why had we come and why had she wept? What had she meant when she told me she'd made a mistake, that it was too late? And why had she lied to me, just three months before, when she'd told me that Juniper Blythe's letter meant nothing?

Round and round the questions flew, until finally I found myself standing at the open door of a bookshop. It's natural in times of great perplexity, I think, to seek out the familiar, and the high shelves and long rows of neatly lined-up spines were immensely reassuring. Amid the smell of ink and binding, the dusty motes in beams of strained sunlight, the embrace of warm, tranquil air, I felt that I could breathe more easily. I was aware of my pulse slowing to its regular pace and my thoughts stilling their wings. It was dim, which was all the better, and I picked out favorite authors and titles like a teacher taking roll call. Brontë—present; Dickens—accounted for; Shelley—a number of lovely editions. No need to slide them out of place; just to know that they were there was enough, to brush them lightly with my fingertips.

I wandered and noted, reshelved occasionally when books were out of place, and eventually I came upon a clearing at the back of the shop. There was a table set up at the center with a special display labeled LOCAL STORIES. Crowded together were histories, coffee-table tomes, and books by local authors: *Tales of Mystery, Murder and Mayhem, Adventures of the Hawkhurst Smugglers, A History of Hop Farming*. In the middle, propped on a wooden stand, was a title I knew: *The True History of the Mud Man*.

I gasped and picked it up to cradle.

"You like that one?" The shop assistant had appeared from nowhere, hovering nearby as she folded her dusting cloth.

"Oh, yes," I said reverently. "Of course. Who doesn't?"

The first time I encountered *The True History of the Mud Man* I was ten years old and home from school, sick. It was the mumps, I think, one of those childhood illnesses that keep you isolated for weeks, and I must've been getting whiny and unbearable because Mum's sympathetic smile had tightened to a stoical crease. One day, after ducking out for a brief reprieve on the High Street, she'd returned with renewed optimism and pressed a tattered library book into my hands.

"Perhaps this will cheer you up," she'd said tentatively. "It's for slightly older readers, I think, but you're a clever girl; with a bit of effort I'm sure you'll be fine. It's rather long compared with what you're used to, but do persevere."

I probably coughed self-pityingly in response, little aware that I was about to cross a tremendous threshold beyond which there would be no return, that in my hands I held an object whose simple appearance belied its profound power. All true readers have a book, a moment, like the one I describe, and when Mum offered me that much-read library copy mine was upon me. For although I didn't know it then, after falling deep inside the world of the Mud Man, real life was never going to be able to compete with fiction again. I've been grateful to Miss Perry ever since, for when she handed that novel over the counter and urged my harried mother to pass it on to me, she'd either confused me with a much older child or else she'd glimpsed deep inside my soul and perceived a hole that needed filling. I've always chosen to believe the latter. After all, it's the librarian's sworn purpose to bring books together with their one true reader.

I opened that yellowing cover, and from the first chapter, the one describing the Mud Man's awakening in the sleek, black moat, the awful moment in which his heart begins to kick, I was hooked. My nerves thrilled, my skin flushed, my fingers quivered with keenness to turn page after page, each thinning on the corner where countless other readers had taken the journey before me; I went to grand and fearsome places, all without leaving the tissue-laden couch in my family's suburban breakfast room. The Mud Man kept me imprisoned for days: my mother started smiling again, my swollen face subsided, and my future self was forged.

I NOTED again the handwritten sign—LOCAL STORIES—and turned to the beaming shop assistant. "Raymond Blythe came from around here?"

"Oh yes." She pushed fine hair behind each ear. "He certainly did. Lived and wrote up at Milderhurst Castle; died there too. That's the grand estate a few miles outside the village." Her voice took on a vaguely forlorn note. "At least, it was grand once."

Raymond Blythe. Milderhurst Castle. My heart had started to hammer pretty hard by now. "I don't suppose he had a daughter?"

"Three of them, actually."

"One called Juniper?"

"That's right; she's the youngest."

I thought of my mum, her memory of the seventeen-year-old girl who'd charged the air as she entered the village hall, who'd rescued her from the evacuee line, who'd sent a letter in 1941 that made Mum cry when it arrived, fifty years later. And I felt the sudden need to lean on something firm.

"All three of them are still alive up there," the shop assistant continued. "Something in the castle water, my mother always says; they're hale and hearty for the most part. Excepting your Juniper, of course."

"Why, what's wrong with her?"

"Dementia. I believe it's in the family. A sad story—they say she was quite a beauty once, and very bright with it, a writer of great promise, but her fiancé abandoned her back in the war and she was never the same again. Went soft in the head; kept waiting for him to come back, but he never did."

I opened my mouth to ask where the fiancé had gone, but she was on a roll and it was evident she'd be taking no questions from the floor.

"Just as well she had her sisters to look after her—they're a dying breed, those two; used to be involved in all sorts of charities, way back when—she'd have been packed off to an institution otherwise." She checked behind her, making sure we were alone, then leaned closer. "I remember when I was a girl, Juniper used to roam the village and the local fields; didn't bother anyone, nothing like that, just wandered sort of aimlessly. Used to terrify the local kids; but then children like to be scared, don't they?"

I nodded eagerly and she resumed: "She was harmless enough, though; never got herself into trouble she couldn't be got back out of.

And every village worth its salt needs a local eccentric." A smile trembled on her lips. "Someone to keep the ghosts company. You can read more about them all in here, if you like." She held up a book called *Raymond Blythe's Milderhurst*.

"I'll take it," I said, handing over a ten-pound note. "And a copy of the *Mud Man*, too."

I was almost out of the shop, brown paper bundle in hand, when she called after me, "You know, if you're really interested you ought to think about doing a tour."

"Of the castle?" I peered back into the shadows of the shop.

"It's Mrs. Bird you'll be wanting to see. Home Farm Bed and Breakfast down on the Tenterden Road."

THE FARMHOUSE stood a couple of miles back the way I'd come, a stone and tile-hung cottage attended by profusely flowering gardens, a hint of other farm buildings clustered behind. Two small dormers peeked through the roofline and a flurry of white doves wafted around the coping of a tall brick chimney stack. Leaded windows had been opened to take advantage of the warm day, diamond panels winking blindly at the afternoon sun.

I parked the car beneath a giant ash whose looming arms caught the edge of the cottage in its shadow, then wandered through the sun-warmed tangle: heady jasmine, delphiniums, and campanulas, spilling over the brick path. A pair of white geese waddled fatly by, without so much as pausing to acknowledge my intrusion, as I went through the door, passing from brilliant sunshine into a faintly lit room. The immediate walls were decorated with black-and-white photographs of the castle and its grounds, all taken, according to the subtitles, on a *Country Life* shoot in 1910. Against the far wall, behind a counter with a gold RECEPTION sign, a short, plump woman in a royal blue linen suit was waiting for me.

"Well now, you must be my young visitor from London." She blinked through a pair of round tortoiseshell frames, and smiled at my confusion. "Alice from the bookshop called ahead, letting me know I might expect you. You certainly didn't waste any time in coming; Bird thought you'd be another hour at least."

I glanced at the yellow canary in a palatial cage suspended behind her.

"He was ready for his lunch, but I said you'd be sure to arrive just as soon as I closed the door and put out the sign." She laughed then, a smoky chuckle that rolled up from the base of her throat. I'd guessed her age as pushing sixty, but that laugh belonged to a much younger, far more wicked woman than first impressions suggested. "Alice tells me you're interested in the castle."

"That's right. I was hoping to do a tour and she sent me here. Do I need to sign up somewhere?"

"Dear me, no, nothing as official as all that. I run the tours myself." Her linen bosom puffed self-importantly before deflating again. "That is, I did."

"Did?"

"Oh yes, and a lovely task it was too. The Misses Blythe used to operate them personally, of course; they started in the 1950s as a way to fund the castle's upkeep and save themselves from the National Trust—Miss Percy wouldn't have that, I can assure you—but it all got a bit much some years ago. We've all of us got our limits and when Miss Percy reached hers, I was delighted to step in. There was a time I used to run five a week, but there's not much call these days. It seems people have forgotten the old place." She gave me a quizzical look, as though I might be able to explain the vagaries of the human race.

"Well, I'd *love* to see inside," I said brightly, hopefully, maybe even a little desperately.

Mrs. Bird blinked at me. "Of course you would, my dear, and I'd love to show you, but I'm afraid the tours don't run anymore."

The disappointment was crushing and for a moment I didn't think I'd be able to speak. "Oh," I managed to say. "Oh dear."

"It's a shame, but Miss Percy said her mind was made up. She said she was tired of opening her home so ignorant tourists had somewhere to drop their rubbish. I'm sorry Alice misled you." She shrugged her shoulders helplessly and a knotty silence fell between us.

I attempted polite resignation, but as the possibility of seeing inside Milderhurst Castle receded, there was suddenly very little in life that I wanted more fiercely. "Only—I'm such a great admirer of Raymond Blythe," I heard myself say. "I don't think I'd have ended up working in publishing if I hadn't read the *Mud Man* when I was a child. I don't suppose . . . That is, perhaps if *you* were to put in a good word, reassure the owners that I'm not the sort of person to go dropping rubbish in their home?"

"Well . . ." She frowned, considering. "The castle is a joy to behold, and there's no one as proud of her perch as Miss Percy . . . Publishing, you say?"

It had been an inadvertent stroke of brilliance: Mrs. Bird belonged to a generation for whom those words held a sort of Fleet Street glamour; never mind my poky, paper-strewn cubicle and rather sobering balance sheets. I seized upon this opportunity as a drowning person might a raft: "Billing & Brown Book Publishers, Notting Hill." I remembered then the business cards Herbert had presented at my little promotion party. I never think to carry them with me, not in an official way, but they come in very handy as bookmarks and I was thus able to whip one out from the copy of *Jane Eyre* I keep in my tote in case I need to queue unexpectedly. I tendered it like the winning lottery ticket.

"Vice chairman," read Mrs. Bird, eyeing me over her glasses. "Well, indeed." I don't think I imagined the new note of veneration in her voice. She thumbed the corner of the business card, tightened her lips, and gave a short nod of decision. "All right. Give me a minute and I'll telephone the old dears. See if I can't convince them to let me show you round this afternoon."

WHILE MRS. BIRD spoke hushed words into an old-fashioned phone receiver, I sat in a chintz-upholstered chair and opened the brown paper package containing my new books. I slipped out the shiny copy of the *Mud Man* and turned it over. It was true what I'd said: in one way or another my encounter with Raymond Blythe's story had determined my entire life. Just holding it in my hands was enough to fill me with an all-encompassing sense of knowing precisely who I was.

The cover design of the new edition was the same as that on the West Barnes library's copy Mum had borrowed almost twenty years before, and I smiled to myself, vowing to buy a Jiffy bag and post it to them just as soon as I got home. Finally, a twenty-year debt would be repaid. For when my mumps subsided and it was time to return the *Mud Man* to Miss Perry, the book, it seemed, had vanished. No amount of furious searching on Mum's part and impassioned declarations of mystification on mine, managed to turn it up, not even in the wasteland of missing things beneath my bed. When all avenues of search had been exhausted, I was marched up to the library to make my barefaced confession. Poor Mum earned one of Miss Perry's withering stares and almost died of shame, but I was too emboldened by the delicious glory of possession to suffer guilt. It was the first and only thing I've ever stolen, but there was no help for it; quite simply, that book and I belonged to one another.

MRS. BIRD'S phone receiver met the cradle with a plastic clunk and I jumped a little. By the tug of her features I gathered instantly that the news was bad. I stood and limped to the counter, my left foot numb with pins and needles.

"I'm afraid one of the Blythe sisters isn't well today," said Mrs. Bird.

"Oh?"

"The youngest has had a turn and the doctor's on his way out to see her."

I worked to conceal my disappointment. There was something very unseemly about a show of personal frustration when an old lady had been taken ill. "That's terrible. I hope she's all right."

Mrs. Bird waved my concern away like a harmless but pesky fly. "I'm sure she will be. It's not the first time. She's suffered episodes since she was a girl."

"Episodes?"

"Lost time, is what they used to call it. Time she couldn't account for, usually after she became overexcited. Something to do with an unusual heart rate—too fast or too slow, I can't remember which, but she used to black out and wake up with no memory of what she'd done." Her mouth tightened around some further sentiment she'd thought better of expressing. "The older sisters will be too busy looking after her today to be bothered by disturbances, but they were loath to turn you away. The castle needs its visitors, they said. Funny old things—I'm quite surprised, to be honest; they're ordinarily not keen on guests. I suppose it gets lonely though, just the three of them rattling around inside. They suggested tomorrow instead, midmorning?"

A flutter of anxiety in my chest. I hadn't planned to stay, and yet the thought that I might leave without seeing inside the castle brought with it a profound and sudden surge of desolation. Disappointment darkened inside me.

"We've had a cancellation, so there's a room free if you'd like it," said Mrs. Bird. "Dinner's included."

I had work to catch up on over the weekend, Herbert needed his car to get to Windsor the following afternoon, and I'm not the sort of person who decides on a whim to stay for a night in a strange place.

"All right," I said. "Let's do it."

RAYMOND BLYTHE'S MILDERHURST

WHILE Mrs. Bird started on the paperwork, transferring details from my business card, I disengaged myself with a mumble of polite noises and drifted over to peek through the open back door. A courtyard had been formed by the farmhouse walls and those of other farm buildings: a barn, a dovecote, and a third construction with a conical roof that I would later learn to call an oast house. A round pool meditated at the center and the pair of fat geese had launched themselves across the sun-warmed surface, floating regally now as ripples chased one another towards the flagstone edges. Beyond, a peacock inspected the edge of clipped lawn separating the tended courtyard from a meadow of wildflowers that tumbled towards distant parkland. The whole sunlit garden, framed as it was by the shadowed doorway in which I stood, was like a snapshot of a long-ago spring day, come back somehow to life.

"Glorious, isn't it?" said Mrs. Bird, behind me suddenly, though I hadn't noticed her approach. "Have you ever heard of Oliver Sykes?"

I indicated that I hadn't and she nodded, only too happy to enlighten me: "He was an architect, quite well known in his time. Terribly eccentric. He had his own place in Sussex, Pembroke Farm, but he did some work at the castle in the early 1900s, soon after Raymond Blythe married for the first time and brought his wife here from London. It was one of the last jobs Sykes worked on before he disappeared, off on his own version of the Grand Tour. He supervised the creation of a larger version of our circular pool and did some tremendous work on the moat around the castle: turned it into a rather grand bathing ring for Mrs. Blythe. She was a terrific swimmer, they say, very athletic. They used to put . . ." She glued a finger to her cheek and wrinkled her forehead. "A chemical—oh dear now, what was it?" She removed the finger and raised her voice. "Bird?"

"Copper sulfate," came a disembodied male voice.

I glanced again at the canary, rummaging for seed in his cage, then the picture-hung walls.

"Yes, yes, of course it was," Mrs. Bird continued, unfazed, "copper sulfate to keep it azure blue." A sigh. "That was a long time ago now though. Sadly, Sykes's moat was filled in decades ago, and his grand circular pool belongs only to the geese. Full of dirt and duck mess." She handed me a heavy brass key and patted my fingers closed around it. "We'll walk up to the castle tomorrow. The forecast is clear and there's a beautiful view from the second bridge. Shall we meet here at ten?"

"You've an appointment with the vicar tomorrow morning, dear." That patient, wood-paneled voice drifted towards us again, however this time I pinpointed its source. A small door, barely visible, hidden in the wall behind the reception counter.

Mrs. Bird pursed her lips and seemed to consider this mysterious amendment before nodding slowly. "Bird's right. Oh now, what a shame." She brightened. "Never mind. I'll leave you instructions, finish as quickly as I can in the village, and meet you up at the castle. We'll only stay an hour. I don't like to impose any longer: the Misses Blythe are all very old."

"An hour sounds perfect." I could be on my way home to London by lunchtime.

MY ROOM was tiny, a four-poster bed squatting greedily in the center, a narrow writing desk huddled beneath the leaded window and little besides, but the outlook was glorious. The room was at the back of the farmhouse and the window opened out to look across the same meadow I'd glimpsed through the door downstairs. The second story, however, offered a better view of the hill that climbed towards the castle, and above the woods I could just pick out the tower's spire pointing at the sky.

On the desk someone had left a neatly folded plaid picnic blanket and a welcome basket filled with fruit. The day was balmy and the grounds were beautiful, so I picked up a banana, pinned the blanket beneath my arm, and headed straight downstairs again with my new book, *Raymond Blythe's Milderhurst*.

In the courtyard, jasmine sugared the air, great white sprays tumbling from the top of a wooden arbor at the side of the lawn. Huge goldfish swam slowly near the surface of the pool, listing their plump bodies backwards and forwards to court the afternoon sun. It was heavenly, but I didn't stick around; a distant band of trees was calling to me and I wove my way towards it, through the meadow dusted with buttercups, self-sown amid the long grass. Although it wasn't quite summer, the day was warm, the air dry, and by the time I'd reached the trees my hairline was laced with perspiration.

I spread the rug in a patch of dappled light and kicked off my shoes. Somewhere nearby a shallow brook chattered over stones and butterflies sailed the breeze. The blanket smelled reassuringly of laundry flakes and squashed leaves, and when I sat down the tall meadow grasses enclosed me so I felt utterly alone.

I leaned *Raymond Blythe's Milderhurst* against my bent knees and ran my hand over the cover. It showed a series of black-and-white photos arranged at various angles, as if they'd dropped from someone's hand and been photographed where they fell. Beautiful children in old-fashioned dresses, long-ago picnics by a shimmering pool, a line of swimmers posing by the moat; the earnest gazes of people for whom capturing images on photographic paper was a type of magic.

I turned to the first page and began to read.

CHAPTER ONE

Man of Kent

"There were those who said the Mud Man had never been born, that he had always been, just as the wind and the trees and the earth; but they were wrong. All living things are born, all living things have a home, and the Mud Man was no different."

There are some authors for whom the world of fiction presents an opportunity to scale unseen mountains and depict great realms of fantasy. For Raymond Blythe, however, as for few other novelists of his time, home was to prove a faithful, fertile, and fundamental inspiration, in his life as in his work. Letters and articles written over the course of his seventy-five years contain a common theme: Raymond Blythe was unequivocally a homebody who found respite, refuge, and ultimately religion in the plot of land that for centuries his forebears had called their own. Rarely has a writer's home been turned so clearly to fictive purpose as in Blythe's gothic tale for young people, *The True History of the Mud Man*. Yet even before this milestone work, the castle standing proud upon its fertile rise within the verdant weald of Kent, the arable farmlands, the dark and whispering woods, the pleasure gardens over which the castle gazes still, contrived to make of Raymond Blythe the man he would become.

Raymond Blythe was born in a room on the second floor of Milderhurst Castle on the hottest day of the summer of 1866. The first child of Robert and Athena Blythe, he was named for his paternal grandfather, whose fortune was made in the goldfields of Canada. Raymond was the eldest of four brothers, the youngest of whom, Timothy, died tragically during a violent storm in 1876. Athena Blythe, a poetess of some note, was heartbroken by her youngest son's death and is said to have descended, soon after the boy was laid to rest, into a black depression from which there would be no return. She took her life in a leap from the Milderhurst tower, leaving her husband, her poetry, and her three small sons behind.

On the adjoining page there was a photograph of a handsome woman with elaborately arranged dark hair, leaning from an open mullioned window to gaze upon the heads of four small boys arranged in order of height. It was dated 1875 and had the milky appearance of so many early amateur photographs. The smallest boy, Timothy, must have moved when the photo was being taken because his smiling face had blurred. Poor little fellow, with no idea he'd only months left to live.

I skimmed the next few paragraphs—withdrawn Victorian father, dispatch to Eton, a scholarship to Oxford—until Raymond Blythe reached adulthood.

After graduating from Oxford in 1887, Raymond Blythe moved to London, where he began his literary life as a contributor to *Punch* magazine. Over the following decade he published twelve plays, two novels, and a collection of children's poetry; however, his letters indicate that despite his professional accomplishments he was unhappy living in London and longed for the rich countryside of his boyhood.

It might be supposed that city life was made more bearable for Raymond Blythe by his marriage in 1895 to Miss Muriel Palmerston, much admired and said to be "the most handsome of all the year's debutantes," and certainly his letters suggest a sharp elevation of spirit at this time. Raymond Blythe was introduced to Miss Palmerston by a mutual acquaintance, and by all reports, the match was a good one. The two shared a passion for outdoor activities, word games, and photography, and made a handsome couple, gracing the social pages on numerous occasions.

After his father's death in 1898, Raymond Blythe inherited Milderhurst Castle and returned with Muriel to set up home. Many accounts from the period suggest that the pair had long wished to begin a family and certainly, by the time they moved to Milderhurst, Raymond Blythe was quite open in expressing concern in his letters that he was not yet a father. This particular happiness, however, was to elude the couple for some years and as late as 1905 Muriel Blythe wrote to her mother confessing the agonizing fear that she and Raymond would be denied "the final blessing of children." It must have been with tremendous joy, and perhaps some relief, that four months after her letter was sent, she wrote again to her mother advising that she was now "with child." With children, as it turned out: after a fraught pregnancy, including a lengthy period of enforced confinement, in January 1906 Muriel was delivered successfully of twin daughters. Raymond Blythe's letters to his surviving brothers indicate that this was the happiest time of his life, and the family scrapbooks overflow with photographic evidence of his paternal pride.

The next double page held an assortment of photographs of two little girls. Though they were obviously very similar, one was smaller and finer than the other and seemed to smile a little less certainly than her sister. In the last photo, a man with wavy hair and a kind face sat in an upholstered chair with a lace-clad baby on each knee.

There was something in his bearing—the light in his eyes, perhaps, or else the gentle press of his hands against each girl's arm—that communicated his deep affection for the pair, and it occurred to me, as I looked more closely, how rare it was to find a photograph from the period in which a father was captured with his daughters in such a simple, domestic way. My heart warmed with affection for Raymond Blythe and I continued reading.

All was not to remain thus joyous, however. Muriel Blythe was killed on a winter's evening in 1910 when a red-hot ember from the fireplace by which she sat escaped the bounds of the screen to land in her lap. The chiffon of her dress caught fire rapidly and she was aflame before aid could reach her; the blaze went on to consume the east turret of Milderhurst Castle and the vast Blythe family library. The burns to Mrs. Blythe's body were extensive and although she was wrapped in damp bandages and treated by the very best doctors, she succumbed within the month to her terrible injuries.

Raymond Blythe's grief following his wife's death was so profound that for some years after he failed to publish another word. Some sources claim that he suffered a crippling writer's block, while others believe he sealed up his writing room and refused to work, opening it again only when he began his now famous novel *The True History of the Mud Man,* born of a period of intense activity in 1917. Despite its widespread appeal to young readers, many critics see the story as an allegory for the Great War, in which so many lives were lost on the muddy fields of France; in particular, parallels are drawn between the titular Mud Man and the scores of displaced soldiers attempting to return home and reclaim their families after the appalling slaughter. Raymond Blythe himself was wounded at Flanders in 1916 and invalided home to Milderhurst, where he convalesced under the care of a team of private nurses. The Mud Man's lack of identity and the narrator's quest to learn the forgotten creature's original name and his position and place in history are also seen as a homage to the many unknown soldiers of the Great War and the feelings of displacement that Raymond Blythe may have suffered on his return.

No matter the large volume of scholarship devoted to its discussion, the truth of the *Mud Man*'s inspiration remains a mystery; Raymond Blythe was famously reticent about the novel's composition, saying only that it had been "a gift"; that "the muse had attended" and that the story had arrived whole. Perhaps as a result, *The True History of the Mud Man* is one of very few novels that has managed to capture and retain public interest, becoming almost mythic in its significance. Questions of its creation and influences are still vigorously debated by the literary scholars of many nations, but the inspiration behind the *Mud Man* remains one of the twentieth century's most enduring literary mysteries.

A literary mystery. A shiver crept down my spine as I repeated the words beneath my breath. I loved the *Mud Man* for its story and the way its arrangement of words made me feel when I read them, but to know that mystery surrounded the novel's composition made it just that much better.

Although Raymond Blythe had, to this point, been professionally well regarded, the enormous critical and commercial success of *The True History of the Mud Man* overshadowed his previous work and he would ever after be known as the creator of the nation's favorite novel. The production in 1924 of the *Mud Man* as a play in London's West End brought it to an even wider audience, but despite repeated calls from readers, Raymond Blythe declined to write a sequel. The novel was dedicated in the first instance to his twin daughters, Persephone and Seraphina, however in later editions a second line was added, containing the initials of his two wives: MB and OS.

For along with his professional triumph, Raymond Blythe's personal life flourished again. He had remarried in 1919, to a woman named Odette Silverman whom he met at a Bloomsbury party hosted by Lady Londonderry. Though

Miss Silverman was of unremarkable origins, her talent as a harpist gave her an entrée to social events that would most certainly have been closed to her otherwise. The engagement was short and the marriage caused a minor society scandal due to the groom's age and the bride's youth—he was over fifty, and she, at eighteen, only five years older than the daughters of his first marriage—and their different provenances. Rumors circulated that Raymond Blythe had been bewitched—by Odette Silverman's youth and beauty. The pair were wed in a ceremony at the Milderhurst chapel, opened for the first time since the funeral of Muriel Blythe.

Odette gave birth to a daughter in 1922. The child was christened Juniper and her fairness is evident in the many photographs that survive from the period. Once again, despite jocular remarks as to the continued absence of a son and heir, Raymond Blythe's letters from the time indicate that he was delighted by the addition to his family. Sadly his happiness was to be short-lived, for storm clouds were already gathering on the horizon. In December 1924 Odette died from complications in the early stages of her second pregnancy.

I turned the page eagerly to find two photos. In the first, Juniper Blythe must have been about four, sitting with her legs straight out in front and her ankles crossed. Her feet were bare and her expression made it clear she'd been surprised—and not happily—in a moment of solitary contemplation. She was staring up at the camera with almond-shaped eyes set slightly too wide apart. Combined with her fine blond hair, the dusting of freckles across her snub nose, and the fierce little mouth, those eyes created an aura of ill-gotten knowledge.

In the next photo Juniper was a young woman, the passing of years seemingly instant, so that the same catlike gaze met camera now from a grown-up face. A face of great but strange beauty. I remembered Mum's description of the way the other women in the village hall had stepped aside when Juniper arrived, the atmosphere she'd seemed to carry with her. Looking at this photograph, I could well imagine it. She was curious and secretive, distracted and knowing, all at the same time. The individual features, the hints and glimmers of emotion and intellect, combined to form a whole that was compelling. I skimmed the accompanying text for a date—April 1939. The same year my twelve-year-old mother would meet her.

After the death of his second wife, Raymond Blythe is said to have retreated to his writing room. Aside from a few small opinion pieces in *The Times,* however, he was to publish nothing of note again. Though Blythe was working on a project at the time of his death, it was not, as many hoped, a new installment of the *Mud Man,* but rather a lengthy scientific tract about the nonlinear nature of time, explicating his own theories, familiar to readers of the *Mud Man,* about the ability of the past to permeate the present. The work was never completed.

In the later years of his life, Raymond Blythe was subject to declining health and became convinced that the Mud Man of his famous story had come to life to haunt and torment him. An understandable—if fanciful—fear, given the litany of tragic events that had befallen so many of his loved ones over the course of his life, and one that has been gladly adopted by many a visitor to the castle. It is a prevailing expectation, of course, that a historic castle should come replete with its own spine-chilling stories, and natural that a well-loved novel like *The True History of the Mud Man*, set within the walls of Milderhurst Castle, should provoke such theories. Raymond Blythe converted to Catholicism in the late nineteen-thirties and in his final years refused visits from all but his priest. He died on Friday the 4th of April, 1941, after a fall from the Milderhurst tower, the same fate that had claimed his mother sixty-five years earlier.

There was another photograph of Raymond Blythe at the end of the chapter. It was vastly different from the first—the smiling young father with the pair of plump twins on his knees—and as I studied it my conversation with Alice in the bookshop came rushing back. In particular, her suggestion that the mental instability that plagued Juniper Blythe had run in the family. For this man, this version of Raymond Blythe, had none of the satisfied ease that had been so remarkable in the first photograph. Instead, he appeared to be riddled by anxiety: his eyes were wary, his mouth was pinched, his chin locked by tension. The photograph was dated 1939, and Raymond would have been seventy-three years old, but it wasn't age alone that had drawn the deep lines on his face: the longer I stared at it, the more certain I was of that. I'd thought, as I read, that the biographer might have been speaking metaphorically when she referred to Raymond Blythe's haunting, but now I saw she was not. The man in the photograph wore the frightened mask of prolonged internal torment.

DUSK SLUMPED into place around me, filling the depressions between the undulations and woods of the Milderhurst estate, creeping across the fields and swallowing the light. The photograph of Raymond Blythe dissolved into the darkness and I closed the book. I didn't leave, though. Not then. I turned instead to look through the gap in the trees to where the castle stood on the crest of the hill, a black mass beneath an inky sky. And I thrilled to think that the following morning I would step across its threshold.

The characters of the castle had come to life for me that afternoon; they'd seeped beneath my skin as I read and I now felt that I had known them all forever. That although I'd stumbled upon the village of Milderhurst by accident, there was a rightness to my being there. I'd experienced the same sensation when I first read *Wuthering Heights* and *Jane Eyre* and *Bleak House*. As if the story were one I'd already known, that it confirmed something I'd always suspected about the world: that it had sat in my future all along, waiting for me to find it.

Journey Through a Garden's Bones

If I close my eyes now, I can still see the glittering morning sky on my lids: the early summer sun simmering round beneath a clear blue film. It stands out in my memory, I suppose, because by the time I next saw Milderhurst, the seasons had swung and the gardens, the woods, the fields, were cloaked in the metallic tones of autumn. But not that day. As I set off for Milderhurst, Mrs. Bird's detailed instructions loosely in hand, I was enlivened by the stirrings of long-buried desire. Everything was being reborn: birdsong colored the air, bee buzz thickened it, and the warm, warm sun drew me up the hill and towards the castle.

I walked and I walked, until, just when I thought I was in danger of losing myself forever in an unending wooded grove, I emerged through a rusted gate to find a neglected bathing pool laid out before me. It was large and circular, at least thirty feet across, and I knew it at once as the pool Mrs. Bird had told me about, the one designed by Oliver Sykes for when Raymond Blythe brought his first wife to live at the castle. It was similar in some ways, of course, to its smaller twin down by the farmhouse, yet I was struck by the differences. Where Mrs. Bird's pool glistened blithely beneath the sun, manicured lawn reaching out to tether itself to the sandstone surround, this one had long been left to its own devices. The edging stones were coated in moss and gaps had appeared between them, so the pool was fringed now by kingcups and ox-eye daisies, yellow faces vying for the patchy sunlight. Lily pads grew wild across the surface, one tiled over the other, and the warm breeze rippled the entire skin like that of a giant scaled fish. The sort that evolves unchecked; an exotic aberration.

I couldn't see the bottom of the pool, but I could guess at its depth. A diving board had been installed on the far side, the wooden plank bleached and splintered, the springs rusted, the whole contraption held together, it appeared, by little more than good luck. From the bough of an enormous tree a wooden swing seat was suspended on twin ropes, stilled now by the host of thorny brambles that had plaited their way from top to bottom.

The brambles hadn't stopped at the ropes either: they'd been having a lovely time thriving unchallenged in the odd, abandoned clearing. Through a tangle of greedy greenery, I spied a small brick building, a changing room, I supposed, the peak of its pitched roof visible at the top. The door was padlocked, the mechanism completely rusted, and the windows, when I found them, were laminated thickly with grime that wouldn't wipe off. At the back, however, a pane of glass was broken, a gray tuft of fur impaled on the sharpest peak, and I was able to peer through. Which, of course, I wasted no time in doing.

Dust, so dense I could smell it from where I stood, decades of dust, blanketing the floor and everything else. The room was unevenly lit, courtesy of skylights from which several wooden shutters had been lost, some still hanging by their hinges, others discarded on the floor below. Fine flecks sifted through the gaps, spiraling in streamers of strangled light. A row of shelves was stacked with folded towels, their original color impossible to guess, and an elegant door on the far wall wore a sign that read DRESSING ROOM. Beyond, a gossamer curtain fluttered pinkly against a set of stacked lounging chairs, just as it must have done for a long time unobserved.

I stepped back, conscious suddenly of the noise of my shoes on the fallen leaves. An uncanny stillness permeated the clearing, though the faint lapping of the lily pads remained, and for a split second I could imagine the place when it was new. A delicate overlay insinuated itself atop the present neglect: a laughing party in old-fashioned bathing suits laying down their towels, sipping refreshments, diving from the board, swinging out low and long over the cool, cool water . . .

And then it was gone. I blinked, and it was just me again, and the overgrown building. A vague atmosphere of unnameable regret. Why, I wondered, had this pool been abandoned? Why had the last long-ago occupant washed their hands of the place, locked it up, walked away, and never come back? The three Misses Blythe were old ladies now, but they hadn't always been so. In the many years they'd lived at the castle surely there had been steaming summers ideal for swimming in just such a place . . .

I would learn the answers to my questions, though not for some time yet. I would learn other things too, secret things, answers to questions I hadn't begun to dream of asking. But back then all that was still to come. Standing in the outlying garden of Milderhurst Castle that morning, I was easily able to shrug off such musings and focus instead on the task at hand. For not only was my investigation of the pool getting me no closer to my appointment with the Misses Blythe, I also had a niggling feeling I wasn't supposed to be in the clearing at all.

I reread Mrs. Bird's instructions closely.

It was just as I thought: there was no mention of a pool. In fact, according to the directions, I was supposed to be approaching the south front right about now, making my way between a pair of majestic pillars.

A small stone of dismay sank slowly to the pit of my stomach.

This was not the south lawn. I could see no pillars.

And while it was no surprise to me that I was lost—I can get in a muddle crossing Hyde Park—it was intensely annoying. Time was pressing and, other than retrace my steps and start again, there seemed little choice but to keep heading higher and hope for the best. There was a gate on the other side of the pool and, beyond it, a stone staircase carved steeply into the overgrown hillside. At least a hundred steps, each sinking into the one beneath as if the whole construction had heaved an enormous sigh. The trajectory was promising, though, so I started climbing. I figured it was all a matter of logic. The castle, the Sisters Blythe, were at the top: keep going upwards and I'd have to reach them eventually.

THE SISTERS Blythe. It must've been around this time that I started thinking of them that way; the "Sisters" jumped in front of the "Blythe," somewhat like the Brothers Grimm, and there was little I could do to stop it. It's funny the way things happen. Before Juniper's letter I'd never heard of Milderhurst Castle, now I was drawn to it like the dusty little moth to the big, bright flame. In the beginning it was all about my mum, of course, the surprise news of her evacuation, the mysterious castle with the gothic-sounding name. Then there was the Raymond Blythe connection—the place where the Mud Man came to life, for goodness' sake! But now, as I drew closer to that flame, I realized there was something new making my pulse all thrilled and spiky. It might have been the reading I'd done, or the background information Mrs. Bird had pushed upon me over breakfast that morning, but at some point I'd become fascinated by the Sisters Blythe themselves.

I should say that siblings interest me generally. I'm intrigued and repelled by their closeness. The sharing of genetic ingredients, the random and at times unfair distribution of inheritance, the inescapability of the tie. I understand a little of that tie myself. I had a brother once, but not for long. He was buried before I knew him and by the time I'd pieced enough together to miss him, the traces he'd left behind had been neatly put away. A pair of certificates, one birth, one death, in a slim file in the cabinet; a small photograph in my father's wallet, another in my mum's jewelry drawer: all that remained to say, "I was here!" Along with the memories and sorrows that live inside my parents' heads, of course, but they don't share those with me.

My point is not to make you feel uncomfortable or sorry for me, only to express that despite having almost nothing material or memorable left with which to conjure Daniel, I've felt the tie between us all my life. An invisible thread connects us just as certainly as day is bound to night. It's always been that way, even when I was small. If I was a presence in my parents' house, he was an absence. An unspoken sentence every time we were happy: *If only he were here*; every time

I disappointed them: *He wouldn't have done so*; every time I started a new school year: *Those would be his classmates, those big kids over there.* The distant look I caught in their gazes sometimes when they thought they were alone.

Now I'm not saying my curiosity about the Sisters Blythe had much, if anything, to do with Daniel. Not directly. But theirs was such a beautiful story: two older sisters giving up their own lives to devote themselves to the care of the younger; a broken heart, a lost mind, an unrequited love; it made me wonder what things might have been like, whether Daniel might have been the sort of person I'd have given my life to protect. I couldn't stop thinking of those sisters, you see, the three of them tied together like that. Growing old, fading, spinning out their days in their ancestral home, the last living members of a grand, romantic family.

I CLIMBED carefully, up and up, past a weathered sundial, past a row of patient urns on silent plinths, past a pair of stone deer facing off across neglected hedges, until finally I reached the last step and the ground flattened. A pleached alley of gnarled fruit trees racked before me, drawing me onwards. It was as if the garden had a plan, I remember thinking that first morning; as if there were an order, as if it had been waiting for me, refusing to leave me lost, conspiring instead to deliver me to the castle.

Sentimental silliness, of course. I can only suppose that the steep incline had left me light-headed and subject to wildly grandiose thoughts. Whatever the case, I felt infused. I was intrepid (if rather sweaty). An adventurer who'd slipped from my own time and place and was going forth now to conquer . . . well, to conquer something. Never mind that this particular mission was destined to end with three old ladies and a country house tour, perhaps an offer of tea if I was lucky.

Like the pool, this part of the garden had long been left untended, and as I passed through the tunnel of arches I felt myself to be walking within the ancient skeleton of some enormous monster, long dead. Giant ribs stretched above, encasing me, while long linear shadows created the illusion that they also curved beneath. I skipped quickly to the end but when I reached it I stopped short.

There before me, cloaked in shade though the day was warm, stood Milderhurst Castle. The back of Milderhurst Castle, I realized with a frown, taking in the outhouses, the exposed plumbing, the distinct lack of pillars, entrance lawn, or driveway.

And then it dawned on me, the precise nature of my lostness. Somehow I must've missed an early turn and I had ended up winding right around the wooded hillside instead, approaching the castle from the north rather than the south.

All's well that ends well, though: I'd made it relatively unscathed and I was quite sure I wasn't yet offensively late. Even better, I'd spied a flat strip of wild grass wrapping its way around the walled castle gardens. I followed it, and finally—a triumphant trumpet flourish— stumbled upon Mrs. Bird's pillars. Across the south lawn, just where it ought to be, the front face of Milderhurst Castle rose tall and taller to meet the sun.

THE QUIET, steady accumulation of years I'd felt on the garden climb was more concentrated here, spun out like a web around the castle. The building had a dramatic grace and was decidedly oblivious to my intrusion. The bored sash windows gazed beyond me, looking towards the English Channel with a weary permanence of expression that emphasized my sense that I was trivial, temporary, that the grand old building had seen too much else in its time to be bothered much by me.

A clutter of starlings took flight from the chimney tops, wheeling through the sky and into the valley where Mrs. Bird's farmhouse nestled. The noise, the motion, was oddly disconcerting.

I followed their progress as they skimmed the treetops, skirling towards the tiny red-tiled roofs. The farmhouse looked so far away,

I was overcome by the strangest sense that at some point during my walk up the wooded hill I'd crossed an invisible line of sorts. I'd been *there*, but now I was *here*, and something more complicated was at work than a simple shift in location.

Turning back towards the castle, I saw that a large black door in the lower arch of the tower stood wide open. Strange that I hadn't noticed it before.

I started across the grass, but when I reached the stone front stairs I faltered. Sitting by a weathered marble greyhound was his flesh and blood descendant, a black dog of the type I would come to know as a lurcher. He'd been watching me, it seemed, the whole time I'd been standing on the lawn.

Now he stood, blocking my way, assessing me with his dark eyes. I felt unwilling, unable to continue. My breathing was shallow and I was suddenly cold. I wasn't afraid, though. It's difficult to explain, but it was as if he were the ferryman, or an old-fashioned butler, someone whose permission I needed before I could proceed.

He padded towards me, gaze fixed, footfalls noiseless. Brushed lightly beneath my fingertips before he turned and loped away. Disappeared without a second glance through the open door.

Beckoning me, or so it seemed, to follow.

Three Fading Sisters

Have you ever wondered what the stretch of time smells like? I can't say I had, not before I set foot inside Milderhurst Castle, but I certainly know now. Mold and ammonia, a pinch of lavender, and a fair whack of dust, the mass disintegration of very old sheets of paper. And there's something else, too, something underlying it all, something verging on rotten or stewed but not. It took me a while to work out what that smell was, but I think I know now. It's the past. Thoughts and dreams, hopes and hurts, all brewed together, fermenting slowly in the fusty air, unable ever to dissipate completely.

"Hello?" I called, waiting at the top of the wide stone staircase for a return greeting. Time passed and none came, so I said it again, louder this time. "Hello? Is anyone home?"

Mrs. Bird had told me to go on in, that the Sisters Blythe were expecting us, that she'd meet me inside. In fact, she'd been at great pains to impress upon me that I was not to knock or ring the bell or otherwise announce my arrival. I'd been dubious—where I came from, entrance without announcement came pretty close to trespassing—but I did as she'd bid me: took myself straight through the stone portico, beneath the arched walkway, and into the circular room beyond. There were no windows and it was dim despite a ceiling that swept up to form a high dome. A noise drew my attention to the rounded top, where a white bird had flown through the rafters and hovered now in a shaft of dusted light.

"Well then." The voice came from my left and I turned quickly to see a very old woman standing in a doorframe some ten feet away, the lurcher by her side. She was thin but tall, dressed in tweeds and a button-up collared shirt, almost gentlemanly in style. Her gender had been brittled by the years, any curves she'd had sunken long ago. Her hair had receded from her forehead and sat short and white around her ears with a wiry stubbornness; the egg-shaped face was alert and intelligent. Her eyebrows, I noted as I moved closer, had been plucked to the point of complete removal then drawn in again, scores the color of old blood. The effect was dramatic, if a little grim. She leaned forward slightly on an elegant ivory-handled cane. "You must be Miss Burchill."

"Yes." I held out my hand, breathless suddenly. "Edith Burchill. Hello there."

Chill fingers pressed lightly against mine and the leather strap of her watch fell noiselessly around her wrist bone. "Marilyn Bird from the farmhouse said you'd be coming. My name is Persephone Blythe."

"Thank you so much for agreeing to meet me. Ever since I learned of Milderhurst Castle, I've been dying to see inside."

"Really?" A sharp twist of her lips, a smile as crooked as a hairpin. "I wonder why."

That was the time, of course, to tell her about Mum, about the letter, her evacuation there as a girl. To see Percy Blythe's face light up with recognition, for us to exchange news and old stories as we walked. Nothing could have been more natural, which is why it came as something of a surprise to hear myself say: "I read about it in a book."

She made a noise, a less interested version of "ah."

"I read a lot," I added quickly, as if the truthful qualifier might somehow lessen the lie. "I love books. I work with books. Books are my life."

Her wrinkled expression wilted further in the face of such an innocuous response, and little wonder. The original fib was dreary enough, the additional biographical tidbits positively inane. I couldn't think why I hadn't just told the truth: it was far more interesting, not to mention honest. Some half-cocked, childish notion of wanting my visit to be my own, I suspect; for it to remain untinged by my mother's arrival fifty years earlier. Whatever the case, I opened my mouth to backtrack but it was too late: Persephone Blythe had already motioned for me to follow as she and the lurcher started down the gloomy corridor. Her pace was steady and her footfalls light, the cane, it seemed, paying mere lip service to her great age.

"Your punctuality pleases me, at any rate." Her voice floated back to me. "I abhor tardiness."

We continued in silence, deep and deepening silence. With each step, the sounds of outside were left more emphatically behind: the trees, the birds, the distant chattering of the somewhere brook. Noises I hadn't even realized I was hearing until they were gone, leaving a strange airy vacuum so stark my ears began to hum, conjuring their own phantoms to fill the void; whispering sounds, like children when they play at being snakes.

It was something I would come to know well, the odd isolation of the castle interior. The way sounds, smells, sights that were clear outside the walls seemed somehow to get stuck in the old stone, unable ever to burrow their way through. It was as if over centuries the porous sandstone had absorbed its fill, trapping past impressions, like those flowers preserved and forgotten between the pages of nineteenth-century books, creating a barrier between inside and out that was now absolute. The air outside may have carried rumors of buttercups and freshly mown grass, but inside it smelled only of accumulating time, the muddy held breath of centuries.

We passed a number of tantalizing sealed doors until finally, at the very end of the corridor, just before it turned a corner and disappeared into the further gloom, we came to one that stood ajar. A sliver of light smiled from inside, widening into a grin when Percy Blythe prodded it with her cane.

She stepped back and nodded bluntly, indicating that I should enter first.

IT WAS a parlor and it stood in great welcoming contrast to the shadowy oak-paneled corridor from which we'd come: yellow wallpaper that must once have been fiercely bright had faded over time, the swirled pattern settling into a tepid languor, and an enormous rug, pink and blue and white—whether pale or threadbare I couldn't tell—stretched almost to reach the skirting boards. Facing the elaborate carved fireplace was an upholstered sofa, oddly long and low, that wore the imprints of a thousand bodies and looked all the more comfortable for it. A Singer sewing machine fed with a swathe of blue fabric stood alongside.

The lurcher padded past me, arranging himself artfully on a flattened sheepskin at the base of a great painted screen, two hundred years old at least. A scene of dogs and cockerels was depicted, the olives and browns of the foreground faded to form a muted meld, the background sky eternally in the gloaming. The patch behind the lurcher had worn almost completely away.

At a rounded table nearby a woman the same age as Percy sat with her head bent close over a sheet of paper, an island in a sea of scattered Scrabble pieces. She wore huge reading glasses that were fumbled off when she noticed me, folded into a hidden pocket in her long silk dress as she stood. Her eyes were revealed as gray-blue, her brows a rather ordinary affair, neither arched nor straight, short nor long. Her fingernails, however, were painted a vivid pink to match her lipstick and the large flowers in her dress. Though dressed differently, she was as neatly packaged as Percy, with a commitment to outward appearance that was somehow old-fashioned even if the clothes themselves were not.

"This is my sister Seraphina," said Percy, going to stand beside her. "Saffy," she said in an exaggeratedly loud voice, "this is Edith."

Saffy tapped the fingers of one hand against her ear. "No need to shout, Percy dear," came a soft singsong voice, "my earpiece is in place." She smiled shyly at me, blinking for need of the glasses her vanity had removed. She was as tall as her twin, but through some trick of dress or the light, or perhaps of posture, she didn't seem it. "Old habits die hard," she said. "Percy was always the bossy one. I'm Saffy Blythe and it's really, truly, a pleasure to meet you."

I came closer to take her hand. She was a carbon copy of her sister, or she had been once. The past eighty-odd years had etched different lines on their faces and the result was somehow softer on Saffy, sweeter. She looked just as an old lady of the manor should and I warmed to her immediately.

Where Percy was formidable, Saffy made me think of oatmeal biscuits and cotton-fiber paper covered with a beautiful inky scrawl. It's a funny thing, character, the way it brands people as they age, rising from within to leave its scar.

"We've had a telephone call from Mrs. Bird," said Saffy. "I'm afraid she's been caught up in the village with her business."

"Oh."

"She was in a frightful flap," Percy continued flatly. "But I told her I'd be happy to show you round myself."

"More than happy." Saffy smiled. "My sister loves this house as other people love their spouses. She's thrilled to have a chance to show it off. And well she might. The old place is a credit to her: only years of her tireless work have kept it from falling into disrepair."

"I've done what was necessary to stop the walls collapsing around us. No more."

"My sister is being modest."

"And mine is being stubborn."

This chiding was evidently a normal part of their repartee, and the two paused to smile at me. For a moment I was transfixed, remembering the photograph in *Raymond Blythe's Milderhurst,* wondering which of these old ladies was which little twin, and then Saffy reached across the narrow divide to take Percy's hand. "My sister has taken care of us all our long lives," she said, before turning to look with such admiration at her twin's profile that I knew she had been the smaller, thinner of the two girls in the photo, the one whose smile wavered uncertainly beneath the camera's gaze.

The additional praise did not sit well with Percy, who scrutinized her watch before muttering, "Never mind. Not much further to go now."

It's always difficult to know what to say when a very old person starts talking about death and its imminence, so I did what I do when Herbert hints about my taking over at Billing & Brown "one day": I smiled as if I might have misheard and gave the sunlit bay window a closer inspection.

And that's when I noticed the third sister, the one who must be Juniper. She was sitting statue-still in an armchair of faded green velvet, watching through the open window as the parkland spilled away from her. A faint plume of cigarette smoke rose from a crystal ashtray, smudging her into soft focus. Unlike her sisters, there was nothing fine about her clothing or the way she wore it. She was dressed in the international costume of the invalid: an ill-fitting blouse tucked in firm and high to shapeless slacks, her lap marked by greasy spots where things had spilled.

Perhaps Juniper sensed my gaze, for she turned slightly—just the side of her face—towards me. Her eye, I could see, was glassy and unsteady in a way that suggested heavy medication and when I smiled she gave no sign that she had seen, just continued to stare as if she sought to bore a hole right through me.

Watching her, I became aware of a soft press of sound I hadn't noticed before. A small television set perched on a wooden occasional table beneath the window frame. An American sitcom was playing and the laugh track punctuated the constant hum of sassy dialogue with periodic stabs of static. It gave me a familiar feeling, that television set, the warm, sunny day outside, the still, stale air within: a nostalgic memory of visiting Gran in the school holidays and being allowed to watch television in the daytime.

"What are you doing here?"

Pleasant memories of Gran shattered beneath the sudden icy blow. Juniper Blythe was still staring at me but her expression was no longer blank. It was distinctly unwelcoming.

"I, uh . . . hello," I said. "I—"

"What do you think you're doing here?"

The lurcher gave a strangled yelp.

"Juniper!" Saffy hurried to her sister's side. "Darling girl, Edith is our guest." She took her sister's face gently in both hands. "I told you, June, remember? I explained it all: Edith's here to have a tour of the castle. Percy's taking her for a lovely little walk. You mustn't worry, darling, everything's all right."

While I wished fervently that I could somehow disappear, the twins exchanged a glance that sat so easily in the different lines of their matching faces that I knew it must have passed between them many times before. Percy nodded at Saffy, tight lipped, and then the expression dissolved before I'd worked out what it was about that glance that gave me such a peculiar feeling.

"Well then," she said with an affected cheeriness that made me wince, "time is wasting. Let's get on, shall we, Miss Burchill?"

I FOLLOWED gladly as she led us out of the room, around a corner, and down another cool, shadowed passage.

"I'll walk you past the back rooms first," she said, "but we won't stop long. There's little point. They've been under sheets for years."

"Why is that?"

"They all face north."

Percy had a pared way of speaking, a little like the way wireless commentators used to sound, back when the BBC was the last word on all matters enunciative. Short sentences, perfect diction, the hint of nuance concealed in the body of each full stop. "The heating in winter is impossible," she said. "It's just the three of us so we hardly need the space. It was easier to close some doors for good. My sisters and I took rooms in the small west wing, near the yellow parlor."

"That makes sense," I said quickly. "There must be a hundred rooms in a building this size. All the different levels—I'd be sure to get lost." I was babbling; I could hear it but I couldn't stop it. A basic lack of facility with small talk, excitement at finally being inside the castle, lingering discomfort from the scene with Juniper . . . whatever, it proved a lethal combination. I drew a deep breath and, to my horror, continued: "Though of course you've been here all your life so I'm sure it's not a problem for you—"

"I'm sorry," she said sharply, turning to face me. Even in the gloom I could see that her skin had whitened. *She's going to ask me to leave,* I thought; *my visit is too much, she's old and tired, her sister isn't well.*

"Our sister isn't well," she said, and my heart plunged. "It has nothing to do with you. She can be rude sometimes, but it isn't her fault. She suffered a great disappointment—a terrible thing. A long time ago."

"There's no need to explain," I said. *Please don't ask me to leave.*

"Very kind, but I feel I must. At least a little. Such rudeness. She doesn't do well with strangers. It's been an awful trial. Our family physician died a decade ago and we're still battling to find another we can tolerate. She gets confused. I hope you don't feel unwelcome."

"Not at all, I understand completely."

"I hope so. Because we're very pleased you could visit." That short hairpin smile. "The castle likes to be visited; it needs it."

CARETAKERS IN THE VEINS

ON the morning of my tenth birthday, Mum and Dad took me to visit the dolls' houses at the Bethnal Green Museum. I don't know why we went to see dolls' houses, whether I'd expressed an interest or my parents had read a newspaper article about the collection, but I remember the day very clearly. One of those few shining memories you gather along the way; perfectly formed and sealed, like a bubble that forgot to pop. We went in a taxi, which I remember thinking very posh, and afterwards we had tea at a fancy place in Mayfair. I even remember what I wore: a diamond-patterned minidress I'd coveted for months and finally unwrapped that morning.

The other thing I remember with blinding clarity is that we lost my mum. Perhaps that event, rather than the dolls' houses themselves, is why the day didn't fade for me when it was tossed in among the crushing constellation of childhood experiences. It was all topsy-turvy, you see. Grown-up people didn't get lost, not in my world: it was the province of children, of little girls like me who made a habit of following their daydreams and dragging their feet and generally Failing to Keep Up.

But not this time. This time, inexplicably, earth-joltingly, it was my mum who'd slipped through the cracks. Dad and I were waiting in a queue to buy a souvenir booklet when it happened; we were shuffling forward, following the line, each of us keeping silent company with our own thoughts. It wasn't until we reached the counter and both stood mutely, blinking first at the shop assistant, then at one another, that we realized we were somehow without our traditional family mouthpiece.

I was the one to find her again, kneeling in front of a doll's house we'd already passed. It was tall and dark, as I recall, with lots of staircases, and an attic running along the top. She didn't explain why she'd returned, saying only, "There are actual places like this, Edie. Real houses with real people living in them. Can you imagine? All those rooms?" A twinge at the edge of her lips and she continued, the soft, slow lilt of recitation: *"Ancient walls that sing the distant hours."*

I don't think I answered her. For one thing there wasn't time— my dad turned up right then looking flustered and somehow personally wounded—and for another I wasn't sure what to say. Although we never discussed it again, it was a long time before I let go completely of the belief that somewhere out there in the great, wide world stood real houses with real people living in them and walls that sang.

I mention the Bethnal Green Museum here only because, as Percy Blythe led me down darkening corridors, Mum's comment came back to me, bright and brighter, until I could see her face, hear her words, as clearly as if she were standing right next to me. It might have had something to do with the odd sense that pressed upon me as we explored the enormous house, the impression that I'd fallen victim somehow to a shrinking spell and been transported inside a house for dolls, albeit a doll's house that was rather down at heel. One whose child owner had grown beyond the point of interest and moved on to new obsessions, leaving the rooms with their faded wallpapers and silks, the rush-matted floors, the urns and stuffed birds, the heavy furniture waiting silently, hopefully, for reoccupation.

Then again, perhaps all that came second. Perhaps it was Mum's comment that came to mind first because of course she'd been thinking of Milderhurst when she'd told me about the real people in their real houses with lots of rooms. What else could have inspired her to say such a thing? That unreadable expression on her face had been the result of remembering this place. She'd been thinking about Percy, Saffy, and Juniper Blythe and the strange, secret things that must have happened to her as a girl when she was transplanted from south London to Milderhurst Castle. The things that had reached across fifty years with a grasp strong enough that a lost letter could make her cry.

Whatever the case, as I took Percy's tour that morning, I carried my mum with me. I couldn't have resisted her if I'd tried. No matter that I'd become inexplicably jealous that my exploration of the castle be my own—a small part of Mum, a part I'd never known, certainly never noticed, was anchored to this place. And although I wasn't used to having things in common with her, although the very notion made the earth spin a little faster, I realized that I didn't mind. In fact, I rather liked that the curious comment at the doll's house museum was no longer an oddity, a mosaic piece that didn't fit the whole. It was a fragment of Mum's past, a fragment that was somehow brighter and more interesting than those surrounding it.

So it was, as Percy led, and I listened and looked and nodded, that a small ghostly Londoner stepped silently beside me: wide-eyed, nervous, glimpsing the house for the first time, too. And it turned out I liked her being there; if I could've, I'd have reached down across the decades to take her hand in mine. I wondered how different the castle must have been in 1939, how much change had occurred in the past fifty years. Whether even then Milderhurst Castle had felt like a house asleep, everything dull and dusty and dim. An old house biding its time. And I wondered whether I'd have the chance to ask that little girl, if she was still at large somewhere. If I'd ever be able to find her.

It is impossible to recount everything that was said and seen that day at Milderhurst, and, for the purposes of this story, unnecessary. So much has happened since, subsequent events have bowed and bent and mixed in my mind so that it's difficult to isolate my first impressions of the castle and its inhabitants. I will stick, then, in this account, to the sights and sounds that were most vivid, and to those events pertinent to what came after, and what came before. Events that could never—will never—fade from memory.

Two important things became clear to me as I took the tour: first,

Mrs. Bird had been underplaying matters when she'd told me Milderhurst was a little shabby. The castle was distressed, and not in a glamshackle way. Second, and more remarkably, Percy Blythe was blind to the fact. No matter that dust smothered the heavy wooden furniture, that countless specks thickened the stagnant air, that generations of moths had been feasting on the curtains, she continued to speak about the rooms as if they were in their prime, as if elegant literary salons were staged, and royalty mingled with members of the literati, and an army of servants bustled unseen along the corridors doing the Blythe family's bidding. I'd have felt sympathy for her, caught as she was in a fantasy world, except that she wasn't at all the sort of person who engendered sympathy. She was resolutely un-victimlike and therefore my pity was transformed into admiration, respect for her stubborn refusal to acknowledge that the old place was falling apart around them.

Another thing I feel compelled to mention about Percy: for an octogenarian with a cane she set a cracking pace. We took in the billiard room, the ballroom, the conservatory, then swept on downstairs into the servants' hall; marched through the butler's pantry, the glass pantry, the scullery, before arriving finally at the kitchen. Copper pots and pans hung from hooks along the walls, a stout Aga rusted beside a sagging range, a family of empty ceramic pots stood chest to chest on the tiles. At the center, an enormous pine table balanced on pregnant ankles, its top scored by centuries of knives, flour salting the wounds. The air was cool and stale and it seemed to me that the servants' rooms, even more than those upstairs, bore the pallor of abandonment. They were disused limbs of a great Victorian engine that had fallen victim to changing times and ground to a final halt.

I wasn't the only one to register the increased gloom, the weight of decline. "Difficult to believe, but this place used to hum," said Percy Blythe, running her finger along the table's crenellation. "My grandmother had a staff of over forty servants. Forty. One forgets how the house once gleamed."

The floor was littered with small brown pellets I took at first for dirt but recognized, by their particular crunch underfoot, as mouse droppings. I made a mental note to refuse cake if it was offered.

"Even when we were children, there were twenty or so servants inside and a team of fifteen gardeners keeping the grounds in order. The Great War ended that: they all enlisted, every last one. Most young men did."

"And none came back?"

"Two. Two made it home, but they weren't the men they'd been before they went. There were none returned in quite the same shape they'd left. We kept them on, of course—to do otherwise would have been unthinkable—but they didn't last long."

Whether she referred specifically to the length of their employment or, more generally, to their lives, I wasn't sure, and she didn't leave me pause to inquire.

"We muddled along after that, employing temporary staff where possible, but by the second war one couldn't have found a gardener for love nor money. What sort of a young man would be content to occupy himself tending pleasure gardens when there was a war to be fought? Not the sort we cared to employ. Household help was just as scarce. We were all of us busy with other things." She was standing very still, leaning on the head of her cane, and the skin of her cheeks slackened as her thoughts wandered.

I cleared my throat, spoke gently. "What about now? Do you have any help these days?"

"Oh, yes." She waved a hand dismissively, her attention returning from wherever it had been. "Such as it is. We've a retainer who comes in once a week to help with the cooking and cleaning, and one of the local farmers keeps the fences standing. There's a young fellow, too, Mrs. Bird's nephew from the village, who mows the lawn and attempts to keep the weeds in check. He does an adequate job, though a strong work ethic seems to be a thing of the past." She smiled briefly. "The rest of the time we're left to our own devices."

I returned her smile as she gestured towards the narrow service staircase and said, "You mentioned that you're a bibliophile?"

"My mother says I was born with a book in my hand."

"I expect, then, that you'll be wanting to see our library."

I REMEMBERED reading that fire had consumed the Milderhurst library, the same fire that had killed the twins' mother, so although I'm not sure what I expected to see behind the black door at the end of the somber corridor, I do know that a well-stocked library was not it. That, however, is precisely what lay before me when I followed Percy Blythe through the doorway. Shelves spanned all four walls, floor to ceiling, and although it was shadowy inside—the windows were cloaked by thick, draping curtains that brushed the ground—I could see they were lined with very old books, the sort with marbled endpapers, gold-dipped edges, and black cloth binding. My fingers positively itched to drift at length along their spines, to arrive at one whose lure I could not pass, to pluck it down, to inch it open, then to close my eyes and inhale the soul-sparking scent of old and literate dust.

Percy Blythe noticed the focus of my attention and seemed to read my mind. "Replacements, of course," she said. "Most of the original Blythe family library went up in flames. There was very little salvageable; those that weren't burned were tortured by smoke and water."

"All those books," I said, the notion a physical pain.

"Quite. My father took it very badly indeed. He dedicated much of his later life to resurrecting the collection. Letters flew hither and yon. Rare-book dealers were our most frequent callers; visitors weren't otherwise encouraged. Daddy never used this room, though, not after Mother."

It might have been merely the product of an overactive imagination, but as she spoke I became certain that I could smell old fire, seeping from beneath the new walls, the fresh paint, issuing from deep within the original mortar. There was a noise, too, that I couldn't place; a tapping sound, unremarkable under normal circumstances but noteworthy in this strange and silent house. I glanced at Percy, who had wandered to stand behind a leather chair with deep-set buttons, but if she heard it at all, she didn't show it. "My father was a great one for letters," she said, gazing fixedly at a writing desk within a nook by the window. "My sister Saffy, too."

"Not you?"

A tight smile. "I've written very few in my life and those only when absolutely necessary."

Her answer struck me as unusual and perhaps it showed on my face, for she went on to explain.

"The written word was never my métier. In a family of writers it seemed as well to recognize one's shortcomings. Lesser attempts were not celebrated. Father and his two surviving brothers used to exchange great essays when we were young, and he would read them aloud in the evenings. He expected amusement and exercised no restraint in passing judgment on those who failed to meet his standards. He was devastated by the invention of the telephone. Blamed it for many of the world's ills."

The tapping came again, louder this time, suggestive of movement. A little like the wind sneaking through cracks, blowing grit along surfaces, only heavier somehow. And, I felt certain, coming from above.

I scanned the ceiling, the dull electric light hanging from a graying rose, a lightning-bolt fissure in the plaster. It struck me then that the noise I heard might well be the only warning we were to get that the ceiling's collapse was forthcoming. "That noise—"

"Oh, you mustn't mind that," said Percy Blythe, waving a thin hand. "That's just the caretakers, playing in the veins."

I suspect I looked confused; I certainly felt it.

"They're the best-kept secret in a house as old as this one."

"The caretakers?"

"The veins." She frowned, looking up, followed the line of the cornice as if tracing the progress of something I couldn't see. When she spoke again, her voice was slightly changed. A hairline crack had appeared in her composure, and for a moment I felt that I could see and hear her more clearly. "In a cupboard in a room at the very top of the castle there lies a secret doorway. Behind the doorway is the entrance to an entire scheme of hidden passages. It's possible to crawl along them, room to room, attic to vault, just like a little mouse. If one goes quietly enough, it's possible to hear all manner of whispered things, to get lost inside if one isn't careful. They're the castle's veins."

I shivered, overcome by a sudden and pressing image of the castle as a giant, crouching creature. A dark and nameless beast, holding its breath; the big, old toad of a fairy tale, waiting to trick a maiden into kissing him. I was thinking of the Mud Man, of course, the Stygian, slippery figure emerging from the lake to claim the girl in the attic window.

"When we were girls, Saffy and I liked to play pretend. We imagined that a family of previous owners inhabited the passages and refused to move on. We called them the caretakers, and whenever we heard a noise we couldn't explain, we knew it must be them."

"Really?" Barely a whisper.

She laughed at the expression on my face, a strangely humorless *ack-ack* that stopped as suddenly as it had started. "Oh, but they weren't *real*. Certainly not. Those noises you hear are mice. Lord knows we've enough of them." A twitch at the corner of her eye as she considered me. "I wonder. Would you like to see the cupboard in the nursery that holds the secret door?"

I believe I actually squeaked. "I'd love to."

"Come along then. It's quite a climb."

The Empty Attic and the Distant Hours

SHE was not exaggerating. The staircase turned in upon itself, doubling back again and again, narrowing and darkening with each flight. Just when I thought I was going to be plunged into a state of utter blindness, Percy Blythe flicked a switch and a bare lightbulb fired dully, swinging on a cord suspended from the ceiling high above. I could see then that at some point in the past a rail had been attached to the wall to assist with the final steep assault. Sometime in the 1950s, I guessed; the metal cylinder had a dull utility feel about it. Whomever and whenever, I saluted. The stairs were perilously worn, all the more so now that I could see them and it was a relief to have something onto which I could clutch. Less happily, the light meant I could also see the webs. No one had been up those stairs in a long time and the castle spiders had noticed.

"Our nurse used to carry a tallow candle when she took us to bed at night," said Percy, starting up the final flight. "The glow would glance against the stones as we went and she'd sing that song about oranges and lemons. You know it, I'm sure: *Here comes a candle to light you to bed.*"

Here comes a chopper to chop off your head: yes, I knew it. A gray beard brushed my shoulder, sparking a wave of affection for my plain little shoebox bedroom at Mum and Dad's. No webs there: just Mum's biweekly dusting schedule and the reassuring whiff of disinfectant.

"There was no electricity in the house back then. Not until the midthirties, and then only half voltage. Father couldn't abide all those wires. He was terrified of fire, and understandably so considering what happened to Mother.

66

"He devised a series of drills after that. He'd ring a bell, down on the lawn, and time us on his old stopwatch. Shouting all the while that the place was about to go up like a mighty pyre." She laughed, that glass-cutting *ack-ack,* then stopped again suddenly when she reached the top step. "Well," she said, holding the key in the lock a moment before turning it. "Shall we?"

She pushed open the door and I almost fell backwards, bowled over by the flood of light that came rolling towards me. I blinked and squinted, gradually regaining my vision as the room's contrasting shapes sharpened into view.

After the journey to reach it, the attic itself might have seemed an anticlimax. It was very plain, with little of the Victorian nursery about it. Indeed, unlike the rest of the house, in which rooms had been preserved as if the return of their inhabitants was imminent, the nursery was eerily empty. It had the look of a room that had been scrubbed, whitewashed even. There was no carpet, and the twin iron beds wore no covers, jutting out from the far wall each side of a disused fireplace. There were no curtains, either, which accounted for the brightness, and the single set of shelves beneath one of the windows was naked of books and toys.

A single set of shelves beneath the attic window.

I needed nothing more to make me thrill. I could almost see the young girl from the *Mud Man*'s prologue, woken in the night and drawn to the window; climbing quietly onto the top shelf and gazing out across her family's estate, dreaming of the adventures she would one day have, utterly unaware of the horror that was about to claim her.

"This attic housed generation after generation of Blythe family children," said Percy Blythe, her eyes making a slow sweep of the room. "Centuries of peas in a pod."

She made no mention of the room's bare state or its place in literary history and I didn't press her. Since the moment she'd turned the key and led me in, her spirits seemed to have sunk. I wasn't sure whether it was the nursery itself that was having such an enervating

67

effect, or whether the increased light of the stark room simply allowed me to see her age writ clearly within the lines of her face. Whatever the case, it seemed important to follow her lead. "Forgive me," she said finally. "I haven't been upstairs in a time. Everything seems . . . smaller than I remember."

That I understood. It was strange enough for me to lie down on my childhood bed and find that my feet had grown past the end, to look sideways and see the unfaded rectangle of wallpaper where Blondie had once been pasted and remember my nightly worship of Debbie Harry. I could only imagine the dissonance for someone standing in a bedroom they'd outgrown some eighty years before. "All three of you slept up here as children?"

"Not all of us, no. Not Juniper; not until later." Percy's mouth contorted a little, as if she'd tasted something bitter. "Her mother had one of the rooms off her own chamber converted to a nursery instead. She was young, unfamiliar with the way things were done. It wasn't her fault."

It seemed an odd choice of words and I wasn't sure that I understood.

"Tradition in the house was that children were permitted to move downstairs to a single room when they turned thirteen, and although Saffy and I felt very important when our time finally came I must confess to missing the attic room. Saffy and I were used to sharing."

"I suppose that's common for twins."

"Indeed." An almost smile. "Come. I'll show you the caretakers' door."

The mahogany cupboard stood quietly against the far wall, in a tiny boxlike room that opened out beyond the twin beds. The ceiling was so low that I had to duck to enter, and the fruity smell entrapped within the walls was almost suffocating.

Percy didn't seem to notice, bending her wiry frame to pull at a low handle on the cupboard, creaking the mirrored door open. "There it is. Right in there at the back." She eyeballed me, hovering near the doorway, and her blade-thin brows drew down. "But surely you can't see; not from all the way over there?"

Manners forbade me actually covering my nose so I took a deep breath, holding it as I moved quickly towards her. She stepped aside, indicating that I should come closer still.

Suppressing the image of Gretel at the witch's oven, I climbed, waist-deep, into the cupboard. Through the grim darkness, I spotted the small door cut into the back. "Wow," I said on the last of my breath. "There it is."

"There it is," came the voice from behind me.

The smell, now I had no choice but to breathe it, didn't seem so bad and I was able to appreciate the Narnia thrill of a hidden doorway in the back of a cupboard. "So that's where the caretakers get in and out." My voice echoed around me.

"The caretakers perhaps," said Percy wryly. "As to the mice, that's another story. The little wretches have taken over; they don't need a fancy door like that one."

I climbed out, dusted myself off, and couldn't help but notice the framed picture hanging on the facing wall. Not a picture: a page of religious script, I could see when I went a little closer. It had been behind me on the way in and I'd missed it. "What was this room?"

"This was our nurse's room. When we were very small," said Percy. "Back then it seemed like the nicest place on earth." A smile flickered briefly before failing. "It's little more than a closet, though, isn't it?"

"A closet with a lovely outlook." I'd drifted towards the nearby window. The only one, I noted, whose faded curtains remained.

I drew them to one side and was struck immediately by the number of heavy-duty locks that had been fitted to the window. My surprise must have shown because Percy said, "My father had concerns about security. An incident in his youth that had stuck with him."

I nodded and peered through the window, experiencing, as I did so, a frisson of familiarity; I realized that it wasn't for something I'd seen, but for something I'd read about and envisaged. Directly below, skirting the footings of the castle and spanning twenty feet or so, was a swathe of grass, thick and lush, an entirely different green from that beyond. "There used to be a moat," I said.

"Yes." Percy was beside me now, holding the curtains aside. "One of my earliest memories is of being unable to sleep and hearing voices down there. It was a full moon and when I climbed up to look out of the window our mother was swimming on her back, laughing in the silvered light."

"She was a keen swimmer," I said, remembering what I'd read about her in *Raymond Blythe's Milderhurst*.

Percy nodded. "The circular pool was Daddy's wedding gift to her, but she always preferred the moat, so a fellow was engaged to improve it for her. Daddy had it filled in when she died."

"It must have reminded him of her."

"Yes." Her lips twitched, and I realized I was exploring her family's tragedy in a rather thoughtless way. I pointed at a stone protrusion that cut into the moat's petticoat and changed the subject. "Which room's that? I don't remember noticing a balcony."

"It's the library."

"And over there? What's that walled garden?"

"That's not a garden." She let the curtain fall closed again. "And we should be getting on."

Her tone and her body had stiffened beside me. I felt sure I'd offended her in some way but couldn't think how. After scrolling quickly over our recent conversation, I decided it was far more likely she was just upset by the press of old memories. I said, softly, "It must be incredible to live in a castle that's belonged to your family for so long."

"Yes," she said. "It hasn't always been easy. There have been sacrifices. We've been forced to sell much of the estate, most recently the farmhouse, but we've managed to hold onto the castle." She very pointedly inspected the window frame, smoothed a piece of flaking paint. Her voice, when she spoke, was wooded with the effort of keeping strong emotion at bay. "It's true what my sister said. I do love this house as others might love a person. I always have." A glance sideways. "I expect you find that rather peculiar."

I shook my head. "No, I don't."

Those scarlike eyebrows arched, dubious; but it was true. I didn't find it peculiar at all. The great heartbreak in my dad's life was his separation from the home of his childhood. It was a simple enough story: a small boy fed on fables of his family's grand history, an adored and moneyed uncle who made promises, a deathbed change of heart.

"Old buildings and old families belong to one another," she continued. "That's as it's always been. My family lives on in the stones of Milderhurst Castle and it's my duty to keep them. It is not a task for outsiders."

Her tone was searing; agreement seemed to be required. "You must feel as if they're still around you"—as the words left my lips, I had a sudden image of my mum, kneeling by the dolls' houses—"singing in the walls."

A brow leaped half an inch. "What's that?"

I hadn't realized I'd spoken the last aloud.

"About the walls," she pressed. "You said something just now, about the walls singing. What was it?"

"Just something my mother told me once"—I swallowed meekly—"about ancient walls that sing the distant hours."

Pleasure spread across Percy's face in stark and brilliant contrast to her usual dour expression. "My father wrote that. Your mother must have read his poetry."

I was sincerely doubtful. Mum had never gone in much for reading, and certainly never for poems. "Possibly."

"He used to tell us stories when we were small, tales of the past. He said that if he didn't go carefully about the castle, sometimes the distant hours forgot to hide." As she warmed to recounting the memory Percy's left hand drifted forth like the sail of a ship. It was a curiously theatrical movement, out of character with her thus-far clipped and efficient manner. Her way of speaking had altered, too: the short sentences had lengthened, the sharp tone softened. "He would come upon them, playing out in the dark, deserted corridors. Think of all the people who've lived within these walls, he'd say, who've whispered their secrets, laid their betrayals . . .'"

"Do you hear them, too? The distant hours?"

Her eyes met mine, held them earnestly for just a moment. "Silly nonsense," she said, breaking into her hairpin smile. "Ours are *old* stones, but they're still just stones. They've no doubt seen a lot but they're good at keeping secrets."

Something crossed her face then, a little like pain: she was thinking of her father, I supposed, and her mother, the tunnel of time and voices that must chatter to her down the ages. "No matter," she said, more for her own sake than mine. "It doesn't do to brood on the past. Calculating the dead can make one feel quite alone."

"You must be glad to have your sisters."

"Of course."

"I've always imagined that siblings must be a great comfort."

Another pause. "You haven't any of your own?"

"No." I smiled, shrugged lightly. "I'm a lonely only."

"Is it lonely?" She considered me as if I were a rare specimen deserving of study. "I've always wondered."

I thought of the great absence in my life, and then of the rare nights spent in company with my sleeping, snoring, muttering cousins, my guilty imaginings that I was one of them, that I belonged with somebody. "Sometimes," I said. "Sometimes it's lonely."

"Liberating, too, one would expect."

I noticed for the first time a small vein quivering in her neck. "Liberating?"

"There's none like a sister for remembering one's ancient sins." She smiled at me then, but its warmth fell short of transforming her sentiment to humor. She must have suspected as much, for she let the smile fall away, nodding towards the staircase. "Come along," she said. "Let's go down. Careful, now. Make sure you hold the rail. My uncle died on those stairs when he was just a boy."

"Oh, dear." Hopelessly inadequate, but what else does one say? "How awful."

"A great storm blew up one evening and he was frightened, or so the story goes. Lightning sliced open the sky and struck right by the lake. The boy cried out in terror, but before his nurse could reach him, he leaped from his bed and fled the room. Silly lad: he stumbled and fell, landed at the bottom like a rag doll. We used to imagine we heard him crying in the night sometimes, when the weather was particularly bad. He hides beneath the third step, you know. Waiting to trip someone up. Hoping for someone to join him." She pivoted on the step below me, the fourth. "Do you believe in ghosts, Miss Burchill?"

"I don't know. Sort of." My gran had seen ghosts. A ghost, at any rate: my uncle Ed after he came off his motorbike in Australia. *"He didn't realize he was dead,"* she'd told me. *"My poor lamb. I held out my hand and told him it was all right, that he'd made it home and that we all loved him."* I shivered, remembering, and, just before she turned, Percy Blythe's face took on a cast of grim satisfaction.

THE MUD MAN, THE MUNIMENT ROOM, AND A LOCKED DOOR

I FOLLOWED Percy Blythe down flights of stairs, along gloomy corridors, then down further still. Deeper, surely, than the level from which we'd climbed initially? Like all buildings that have evolved over time, Milderhurst was a patchwork. Wings had been added and altered, had crumbled and been restored. The effect was disorienting, particularly for someone with no natural compass whatsoever. It seemed as if the castle folded inwards, like one of those drawings by Escher, where you might continue walking the stairs, round and round, for eternity, without ever reaching an end. There were no windows—not since we'd left the attic—and it was exceedingly dark. At one stage I could have sworn I heard a drifting melody skating along the stones—romantic, wistful, vaguely familiar—but when we turned another corner it was gone, and perhaps it had never been. Something I certainly did not imagine was the pungent smell, which strengthened as we descended and was saved from being unpleasant by sheer virtue of its earthiness.

Even though Percy had pooh-poohed her father's notion of the distant hours, I couldn't help running my hand against the cool stones as we walked, wondering about the imprints Mum might have left when she was at Milderhurst. The little girl still walked beside me but she didn't say much. I considered asking Percy about her, but having gone this far without announcing my connection to the house, anything I thought to say carried the stench of duplicity. In the end I opted for classic passive-aggressive subterfuge. "Was the castle requisitioned during the war?"

"No. Dear God. I couldn't have borne it. The damage that was done to some of the nation's finest houses—no." She shook her head vehemently. "Thank goodness. I'd have felt it as a pain to my own body. We did our bit though. I was with the Ambulance Service for a time, over in Folkestone; Saffy stitched clothing and bandages, knitted a thousand scarves. We took in an evacuee, too, in the early years."

"Oh?" My voice trilled slightly. Beside me the little girl skipped.

"At Juniper's urging. A young girl from London. Goodness, I've forgotten her name. Isn't that a pip? Apologies for the smell along here."

Something inside me clenched in sympathy for that forgotten girl.

"It's the mud," Percy went on. "From where the moat used to be. The groundwater rises in summer, seeps through the cellars, and brings the smell of rotting fish with it. Thankfully there's nothing down here of much value. Nothing except the muniment room, and it's watertight. The walls and floor are lined with copper, the door is made from lead. Nothing gets in or out of there."

"The muniment room." A chill rippled fast up my neck. "Just like in the *Mud Man*." The special room, deep within the uncle's house, the room where all the family's documents were lodged, where he unearthed the moldy old diary that unraveled the Mud Man's past. The chamber of secrets in the house's heart.

Percy paused, leaned on her cane and turned her eyes on me. "You've read it then."

It wasn't a question exactly, but I answered anyway. "I adored it growing up." As the words left my lips I felt a stirring of old deflation, the inability to express adequately my love for the book. "It was my favorite," I added, and the phrase hung hopefully before disintegrating into specks, powder from a puff that drifted unseen into the shadows.

"It was very popular," said Percy, starting again down the corridor. No doubt she'd heard it all before. "It still is. Seventy-five years in print next year."

"Really?"

"Seventy-five years," she said again, pulling open a door and issuing me up another flight of stairs. "I remember it like yesterday."

"The publication must have been very exciting."

"We were pleased to see Daddy happy." Did I notice the tiny hesitation then, or am I letting things learned later color my earliest impressions?

A clock somewhere began its weary chime and I realized with a stab of regret that my hour was up. It seemed impossible, I'd have sworn black and blue that I'd only just arrived, but time is an odd ungraspable thing. The hour that sagged between breakfast and my setting out for Milderhurst had taken an age to pass, but the sixty brief minutes I'd been granted inside the castle walls had fled like a flock of frightened birds.

Percy Blythe checked her own wristwatch. "I've dallied," she said with mild surprise. "I apologize. The grandfather is ten minutes fast, but we must get on nonetheless. Mrs. Bird will be here to collect you on the hour and it's quite a walk back to the entrance hall. There'll be no time to see the tower, I'm afraid."

I made a gasping noise, a cross between "Oh!" and a sharp reaction to pain, and then I recovered myself: "I'm sure Mrs. Bird won't mind if I'm a little late."

"I was under the impression you had to be back in London?"

"Yes." Though it seems unfathomable, for a moment I'd actually forgotten: Herbert, his car, the appointment he had to make in Windsor. "Yes, I do."

"Never mind," said Percy Blythe, striding after her cane. "You'll see it next time. When you visit us again." I noticed the assumption, but I didn't think to query it, not at the time. Indeed, I gave it little thought other than to pass it off as a rather fun and meaningless rejoinder, for as we emerged from the stairwell I was distracted by a rustling sound.

The rustling, like the caretakers, was only very faint and I wondered at first if I'd imagined it, all that talk of the distant hours, people trapped in the stones, but when Percy Blythe also glanced around, I knew that I had not.

From an adjoining corridor, the dog lumbered into view. "Bruno," said Percy, surprised, "what are you doing all the way down here, fellow?"

He stopped right beside me and looked up from beneath his droopy lids.

Percy leaned forward to scratch him behind the ears. "Do you know what the word 'lurcher' means? It's from the Romany for thief. Isn't that right, boy? Terribly cruel name for such a good old boy as you." She straightened slowly, one hand in the small of her back. "They were bred by the Gypsies originally, used for poaching: rabbits and hares, other small creatures. Pure breeds were forbidden to anyone who didn't belong to the nobility and the penalties were severe; the challenge was to retain the hunting skills whilst breeding in sufficient variation that they didn't look like a threat.

"He's my sister's, Juniper's. Even as a small girl she loved animals specially; they seemed to love her too. We've always kept a dog for her, certainly since the trauma. They say everyone needs something to love."

As if he knew and resented being made the topic of discussion, Bruno continued on his way. In his wake, the rustling came again faintly, only to be drowned out when a nearby phone began to ring.

Percy stood very still, listening the way people do when they're awaiting confirmation that someone else has picked up.

The ringing continued until disconsolate silence closed around its final echo.

"Come along," said Percy, a note of agitation clipping her voice. "There's a shortcut through here."

THE CORRIDOR was dim, but no more so than the others; indeed, now that we'd emerged from the basement, a few diffuse ribbons of light had appeared, threading their way through the castle knots to spill across the flagstones. We were two-thirds of the way along when the phone began again.

This time Percy didn't wait. "I'm sorry," she said, clearly flustered. "I can't think where Saffy is. I'm expecting an important telephone call. Will you excuse me? I shan't be a moment."

"Of course."

And with a nod she disappeared, turning at the end of the corridor and leaving me stranded.

I blame what happened next on the door. The one right across the hall from me, a mere three feet away. I love doors. All of them, without exception. Doors lead to things and I've never met one I haven't wanted to open. All the same, if that door hadn't been so old and decorative, so decidedly closed, if a thread of light hadn't positioned itself with such wretched temptation across its middle, highlighting the keyhole and its intriguing key, perhaps I might have stood a chance, remained, twiddling my thumbs, until Percy came to collect me. But it was and I didn't; I maintain that I simply couldn't. Sometimes you can tell just by looking at a door that there's something interesting behind it.

The handle was black and smooth, shaped like a shin bone and cool beneath my palm. Indeed, a general coldness seemed to leach from the other side of the door; though how, I couldn't tell.

My fingers tightened around the handle, I started to twist, then—

"We don't go in there."

My stomach, I don't mind saying, just about shot through the roof of my mouth.

I spun on my heel, scanned the gloomy space behind. I could see nothing, yet clearly I wasn't alone. Someone, the owner of the voice, was in the corridor with me. Even if she hadn't spoken I'd have known: I could feel another presence, something moving and hiding in the drawing shadows. The rustling was back now, too: louder, closer, definitely not in my head, definitely not mice.

"I'm sorry," I said to the cloaked passage. "I—"

"We don't go in there."

I smothered the panicky surge in my throat. "I didn't know—"

"That's the good parlor."

I saw her then, Juniper Blythe, as she stepped from the chill darkness, and slowly crossed the corridor towards me.

Say You'll Come Dancing

Her dress was incredible, the sort you expect to see in films about wealthy debutantes before the war, or hidden on the racks of upmarket charity shops. It was organza, the palest of pink, or it had been once, before time and grime had got busy, laying their fingers all over it. Sheets of tulle supported the full skirt, pushing it out as it fell away from her tiny waist, wide enough for the netted hemline to rustle against the walls when she moved.

We stood facing one another across the dull corridor for what felt like a very long time. Finally, she moved. Slightly. Her arms had been hanging by her sides, resting on her skirt, and she lifted one a little, leading from the palm, a graceful movement as if an unseen thread stitched to her inner wrist had been plucked from the ceiling behind me.

"Hello," I said, with what I hoped was warmth. "I'm Edie. Edie Burchill. We met earlier, in the yellow parlor."

She blinked at me and tilted her head sideways. Silvered hair draped over her shoulder, long and lank; the front strands had been pinned rather haphazardly with a pair of baroque combs. The unexpected translucence of her skin, the rakelike figure, the fancy frock: all combined to create the illusion of a teenager, a young girl with gangly limbs and a self-conscious way of holding them. Not shy, though, certainly not that: her expression was quizzical, curious, as she took a small step closer into a stray patch of light.

And then it was my turn for curiosity, for Juniper must have been seventy years old and yet her face was miraculously unlined. Impossible, of course; ladies of seventy do not have unlined faces, and she was no exception—in our later meetings I would see that for myself—but in that light, in that dress, through some trick of circumstance, some strange charm, it was how she appeared. Pale and smooth, iridescent like the inside of a pearl shell, as if the same passing years that had so busily engraved deep imprints on her sisters had somehow preserved her. And yet she wasn't timeless; there was something unmistakably olden days about her, an aspect that was utterly fixed in the past, like an old photograph viewed through protective tissue in one of those albums with the sepia-clouded pages. The image came to me again of the spring flowers pressed by Victorian ladies in their scrapbooks. Beautiful things, killed in the kindest of ways, carried forward into a time and place, a season, no longer their own.

The chimera spoke then, and the sensation was compounded: "I'm going in to dinner now." A high, ethereal voice that made the hair on my neck stand to attention. "Would you like to come too?"

I shook my head, coughed to clear a tickle from my throat. "No. No, thank you. I have to go home soon." My voice was not itself and I realized I was standing very rigidly, as if I was afraid. Which, I suppose, I was, though of what I couldn't say.

Juniper didn't seem to notice my discomfort: "I have a new dress to wear," she said, plucking at her skirts so that the top layer of organza pulled up a little at each side, like the wings of a moth, white and powdery with dust. "Not new exactly, no, that isn't right, but altered. It belonged to my mother once."

"It's beautiful."

"I don't think you ever met her."

"Your mother? No."

"Oh, she was lovely, so lovely. Just a girl when she died, just a girl. This was her pretty dress." She swirled coyly this way and that, peered up at me from beneath her lashes. The glassy gaze of earlier was gone, replaced by keen blue eyes, knowing somehow, the eyes of that bright child I'd seen in the photograph, disturbed while she was playing alone on the garden steps. "Do you like it?"

"I do. Very much."

"Saffy altered it for me. She's a wonder with a sewing machine. If you show her any picture you fancy she can work out how it's made, even the newest Parisian designs, the pictures in *Vogue*. She's been working on my dress for weeks but it's a secret. Percy wouldn't approve, on account of the war, and on account of her being Percy, but I know you won't tell." She smiled then, and it was so enigmatic that my breath caught.

"I won't say a word."

We stood for a moment, each observing the other. My earlier fear had dissipated now, and for that I was glad. The reaction had been unfounded, an instinct only, and I was embarrassed by its memory. What was there to fear, after all? This lost woman in the lonely corridor was Juniper Blythe, the same person who had once upon a time chosen my mother from a clutch of frightened children, who had given her a home when the bombs were falling on London, who had never stopped waiting and hoping for a long-ago sweetheart to arrive.

Her chin lifted as I watched her, and she exhaled thoughtfully. Apparently, as I'd been reaching my conclusions she'd been drawing her own. I smiled, and it seemed to decide her in some way. She straightened, then started towards me again, slowly but with clear purpose. Feline, that's what she was. Her every movement contained the same elastic mixture of caution and confidence, languor that masked an underlying intent.

She stopped only when she was close enough that I could smell the naphthalene on her dress, the stale cigarette smoke on her breath. Her eyes searched mine, her voice was a whisper. "Can you keep a secret?"

I nodded, which made her smile; the gap between her two front teeth was impossibly girlish. She took my hands in hers as if we were friends in the schoolyard; her palms were smooth and cool. "I have a secret but I'm not supposed to tell."

"Okay."

She cupped her hand like a child and leaned in close, pressing it against my ear. Her breath tickled. "I have a lover." And when she pulled away her old lips formed a youthful expression of lustful excitement that was grotesque and sad and beautiful all at once. "His name is Tom. Thomas Cavill, and he's asked me to marry him."

The sadness I felt for her came upon me in a rush, almost too great to bear, as I realized she was stuck in the moment of her great disappointment. I longed for Percy to return so that our conversation might be ended.

"Promise you won't breathe a word of it?"

"I promise."

"I've told him yes, but shhh"—a finger pressed against her smiling lips—"my sisters don't know yet. He's coming soon to have dinner." She grinned, old-lady teeth in a powder-smooth face. "We're going to announce our engagement."

I saw then that she wore something around her finger. Not a ring, not a real one. This was a crude impostor, silver but dull, lumpy, like a piece of aluminum foil rolled and pressed into shape.

"And then we're going to dance, dance, dance . . ." She started to sway, humming along to music that was playing, perhaps, in her head. It was the same tune I'd heard earlier, floating in the cold pockets of the corridors. The name eluded me then, no matter how tantalizingly close it came. The recording, as it must have been, had stopped some time ago, but Juniper listed regardless, her eyelids closed, her cheeks colored with a young woman's anticipation.

I worked on a book once for an elderly couple writing a history of their life together. The woman had been diagnosed with Alzheimer's but was yet to begin the final harrowing descent, and they'd decided to record her memories before they blew away like bleached leaves from an autumn tree.

The project took six months to complete, during which time I watched her slip helplessly through forgetting towards emptiness. Her husband became "that man over there" and the vibrant, funny woman with the fruity language, who'd argued and grinned and interrupted, was silenced.

No, I'd seen dementia, and this wasn't it. Wherever Juniper was, it wasn't empty, and she'd forgotten very little. Yet there was something the matter; she clearly wasn't well. Every elderly woman I've known has told me, at some point, and with varying degrees of wistfulness, that she's eighteen years old on the inside. But it isn't true. I'm only thirty and I know that. The stretch of years leaves none unmarked: the blissful sense of youthful invincibility peels away and responsibility brings its weight to bear.

Juniper wasn't like that, though. She genuinely didn't realize she was old. In her mind the war still raged and, judging by the way she was swaying, so did her hormones. She was such an unnatural hybrid, old and young, beautiful and grotesque, now and then. The effect was breathtaking and it was eerie and I suffered a sudden surge of revulsion, followed immediately by deep shame at having felt such an unkind thing—

Juniper seized my wrists; her eyes had reeled wide open. "But of course!" she said, catching a giggle in a net of long, pale fingers. "You already know about Tom. If it weren't for you, he and I would never have met!"

Whatever I might have said in reply was swallowed then as every clock within the castle began to chime the hour. What an uncanny symphony it was, room after room of clocks, calling to one another as they marked the passing time. I felt those chimes deep within my body and the effect spread icy and instant across my skin, utterly unnerving me.

"I really do have to go now, Juniper," I said, when finally they stopped. My voice, I noticed, was hoarse.

A slight noise behind me and I glanced over my shoulder, hoping to see Percy returning.

"Go?" Juniper's face sagged. "But you've just arrived. Where are you going?"

"Back to London."

"London?"

"Where I live."

"London." A change came over her then, swift as a storm cloud and just as dark. She reached out, gripping my arm with surprising strength, and I saw something I hadn't before: spider-web scars, silvered with age, scribbled along her pale wrists. "Take me with you."

"I . . . I can't do that."

"But it's the only way. We'll go and find Tom. He might be there, up in his little flat, sitting by the windowsill . . ."

"Juniper—"

"You said you'd help me." Her voice was tight, hateful. "Why didn't you help me?"

"I'm sorry," I said. "I don't—"

"You're supposed to be my friend; you said you'd help me. Why didn't you come?"

"Juniper, I think you're confusing me—"

"Oh, Meredith," she whispered, her breath smoky and ancient. "I've done a terrible, terrible thing."

Meredith. My stomach turned like a rubber glove pulled inside out too fast.

Hurried footsteps and the dog appeared, followed closely by Saffy. "Juniper! Oh, June, there you are." Her voice was drenched with relief as she reached her sister's side. She wrapped Juniper in a gentle embrace, drawing back at length to scan her face. "You mustn't run off like that. I've been so worried; I looked everywhere. I didn't know where you'd got to, my little love."

Juniper was shaking; I expect I was too. *Meredith* . . . The word rang in my ears, sharp and insistent as a mosquito drone. I told myself it was nothing, a coincidence, the meaningless ravings of a sad, mad old woman, but I'm not a good liar and I had no chance of fooling myself.

As Saffy brushed stray hair from Juniper's forehead, Percy arrived. She stopped abruptly, leaning on her cane for support as she surveyed the scene. The twins exchanged a glance, similar to the one I'd witnessed earlier in the yellow parlor that had so perplexed me: this time, however, it was Saffy who broke away first. She'd managed, somehow, to penetrate the knot of Juniper's arms and was holding her little sister's hand tightly in her own. "Thank you for staying with her," she said to me, voice quavering. "It was kind of you, Edith—"

"E-dith," Juniper echoed, but she didn't look my way.

"—she gets confused and wanders sometimes. We watch her closely, but . . ." Saffy shook her head shortly, the gesture communicating the impossibility of living one's life for another.

I nodded, unable to find the right words to reply. *Meredith.* My mother's name. My thoughts, hundreds of them, swarmed at once against the current of time, picking over the past few months for meaning, until finally they arrived en masse at my parents' home. A chilly afternoon in February, an uncooked chicken, the arrival of a letter that made Mum cry.

"E-dith," said Juniper again. "E-dith, E-dith . . ."

"Yes, darling," said Saffy, "that's Edith, isn't it? She's come to visit."

I knew then what I'd suspected all along. Mum had been lying when she told me Juniper's message was little more than a greeting, just as she'd lied about our visit to Milderhurst. But why? What had happened between Mum and Juniper Blythe? If Juniper was to be believed, Mum had made a promise that she'd failed to keep; something to do with Juniper's fiancé, with Thomas Cavill. If that was the case, and if the truth really was as dreadful as Juniper suggested, the letter might have been an accusation. Was that it? Was it suppressed guilt that had made my mother cry?

For the first time since I'd arrived at Milderhurst I longed to be free of the house and its old sorrow, to see the sun and feel the wind on my face and smell something other than rancid mud and mothballs. To be alone with this new puzzle, so that I might begin to unpick it.

"I hope she didn't offend you . . ." Saffy was still speaking; I could hear her through my own reeling thoughts as though she was far away, on the other side of a thick and heavy door. "Whatever she said, she didn't mean it. She says things sometimes, funny things, meaningless things . . ."

Her voice tapered off but the silence left behind it was unsettled. She was watching me, unspoken sentiments in her eyes, and I realized that it wasn't concern alone that weighted her features. There was something else hiding in her face, particularly when she glanced again at Percy. Fear, I realized. They were frightened, both of them.

I looked at Juniper, hiding behind her own crossed arms. Did I imagine she was standing especially still, listening carefully, waiting to see how I'd answer, what I'd tell them?

I braved a smile, hoping against hope that it might pass for casual. "She didn't say anything," I said, then shrugged my shoulders for good measure. "I was just admiring her pretty dress."

The surrounding air seemed to shift with the force of the twins' relief. Juniper's profile registered no change, and I was left with a strange, creeping sensation, the vague awareness that I'd somehow made a mistake. That I ought to have been honest, to have told the twins all that Juniper had said, the cause of her upset. But having failed thus far to mention my mum and her evacuation, I wasn't sure that I could find the necessary words—

"Marilyn Bird has arrived," said Percy bluntly.

"Oh, but things do have a habit of happening all at once," said Saffy.

"She's come to drive you back to the farmhouse. You're due in London, she says."

"Yes," I said. *Thank God.*

"Such a shame," said Saffy. Through sterling effort and, I suppose, many years of practice, she managed to sound completely normal. "We had hoped to offer you tea. We have so few visitors."

"Next time," said Percy.

"Yes," Saffy agreed. "Next time."

It seemed unlikely, to say the least. "Thank you again, for the tour . . ."

And as Percy led me back along a mysterious route, to Mrs. Bird and the promise of normality, Saffy and Juniper retreated in the opposite direction, their voices skirting back along the cold stones.

"I'm sorry, Saffy, I'm sorry, sorry, sorry. I just . . . I forgot . . ." The words broke then into sobs. A weeping so wretched I wanted to slam my hands against my ears.

"Come along now, dearest, there's no need for all that."

"But I've done a terrible thing, Saffy. A terrible, terrible thing."

"Nonsense, little dear, put it out of your mind. Let's have our tea, shall we?" The patience, the kindness in Saffy's voice made a small chamber within my chest clench tight. I think that's when I first grasped the interminable length of time that she and Percy had been making such reassurances, wiping the confusion from their younger sister's aging brow with the same judicious care a parent gives their child, but without the promise that the burden would someday ease. "We'll get you back into something sensible, and then we'll all have tea. You and Percy and I. Things always look better after a cup of nice, strong tea, don't they?"

MRS. BIRD was waiting beneath the domed ceiling at the entrance to the castle, puffed up with apologies. She fawned on Percy Blythe, grimacing dramatically as she lambasted the poor unwitting villagers who'd held her up.

"It is of no matter, Mrs. Bird," said Percy in the same imperious tone a Victorian nanny might use to address a tiresome charge. "I enjoyed leading the tour myself."

"Well of course you did. For old times' sake. It must be lovely for you to—"

"Indeed."

"Such a shame that the tours were ended. Understandable, of course, and it's a credit to you and Miss Saffy that you managed to keep them going for so long, especially with so much else on your—"

"Quite." Percy Blythe straightened and I became aware suddenly that she didn't like Mrs. Bird. "Now if you'll both excuse me." She bowed her head towards the open door, through which the outside world seemed a brighter, noisier, faster place than when I'd left it.

"Thank you," I said before she could disappear, "for showing me your beautiful home."

She eyed me a moment longer than seemed necessary, then re-treated along the corridor, cane beating softly beside her. After a few paces she stopped and turned, barely visible in the cloaking dim. "It *was* beautiful, you know. Once upon a time. Before."

ONE

ONE thing was certain: there'd be no moon tonight. The sky was thick, a roiling mass of gray, white, and yellow, folded together like victims of a painter's palette knife. Percy licked the tobacco paper and tamped it shut, rolling the cigarette between her fingertips to seal it. An airplane droned overhead, one of theirs, a patrol plane heading south towards the coast. They had to send one, of course, but there'd be nothing to report, not on a night like this, not now.

From where she leaned, her back against the van, Percy followed the plane's progress, squinting as the brown insect grew small and smaller. The glare brought on a yawn and she rubbed her eyes until they stung pleasantly. When she opened them again the plane was gone.

"Oi! Don't you go marking my polished hood and wings there with your lounging."

Percy turned and rested her elbow on the van's roof. It was Dot, grinning as she loped from the station door.

"You should be thanking me," Percy called back. "Save you twiddling your thumbs next shift."

"True enough. Officer'll have me washing tea towels otherwise."

"Or giving another round of stretcher demonstrations to the wardens." Percy cocked a brow. "What could be better?"

"Mending the blackout curtains, for one."

Percy winced. "That is dire."

"Stick around here much longer and you'll be needle in hand," warned Dot, arriving to lean beside Percy. "Not much else doing."

"He's heard then?"

"RAF boys sent word just now. Nothing on the horizon, not tonight."

"Guessed as much."

"Not just the weather, neither. Officer says the stinking Boches are too busy marching for Moscow to bother much with us."

"More fool them," said Percy as she inspected her cigarette. "Winter's advancing faster than they are."

"I suppose you're planning on hanging about anyway, making a nuisance of yourself in the hopes Jerry gets confused and drops a load nearby?"

"Thought about it," said Percy, tucking the cigarette into her pocket and swinging her bag over her shoulder. "Decided against. Not even an invasion could keep me here tonight."

Dot's eyes widened. "What's this then? Handsome fellow asked you to go dancing, has he?"

"No such luck; good news all the same."

"Oh?"

The bus arrived and Percy had to shout to be heard over its motor as she climbed aboard. "My little sister's coming home tonight."

PERCY HAD no greater lust for warfare than the next person—indeed, she'd had more occasion than most to witness its horrors—which was why she never, ever, acknowledged aloud the strange kernel of disappointment that had festered deep inside her since the cessation of nightly raids. It was utterly absurd, she knew, to feel nostalgia for a period of abject danger and destruction; anything other than cautious optimism was damn near sacrilege and yet an appalling temper had kept her awake these past months, ears trained on the quiet night skies above her.

If there was one thing on which Percy prided herself it was her ability to exercise pragmatism in all matters—Lord knew, someone had to—thus she'd determined to Get to the Bottom of Things. To find a way to still the little clock that threatened to tick away inside her without opportunity ever to strike. Over the course of weeks, taking great care never to reveal her inward state of flux, Percy had evaluated her situation, observing her feelings from all angles before finally reaching the conclusion that she was, quite clearly, several shades of crazy.

It was only to be expected; madness was something of a family condition, as surely as the gift for artistry and the likelihood of long limbs. Percy had hoped to avoid it, but there you are. Inheritance was a damn good shot. And if she was honest, hadn't she always supposed it a mere matter of time before her own unhinging?

It was Daddy's fault, of course, in particular the terrific stories he'd told them when they were girls, small enough to be lifted, green enough to curl themselves perfectly within his wide, warm lap. Tales from his family's past, about the plot of land that had become Milderhurst, that had starved and flourished, twisted and turned throughout the centuries, been flooded and farmed and fabled. About buildings that had burned and been rebuilt, rotted and been sacked, thrilled and been forgotten. About the people who had called the castle home before them, the chapters of conquest and sublimation that layered the soil of England and that of their own beloved home.

History in the storyteller's hands was a potent force indeed, and for an entire stretch of summer after Daddy left for the Great War, when she was a girl of eight or nine years old, Percy's dreams had been vivid with invaders storming the fields towards them. She'd coerced Saffy into helping establish forts in the treetops of Cardarker Wood, building stockpiles of weapons, and beheading the saplings that displeased her. Practicing, so that when the time came for them to do their duty, to defend the castle and its lands from the invading hordes, they'd be ready . . .

The bus rattled round a corner and Percy rolled her eyes at her own reflection. It was ridiculous, of course. Girlish fancies were one thing, but for a grown woman's moods still to hinge on their echo? It really was too sad. With a huff of disgust, she turned her back on herself.

It had been a long trip, far longer than usual, and at this rate she'd be lucky to make it home for pudding. Whatever that might be. The storm clouds were amassing, darkness threatened to drop on them at any moment, and the bus, with no headlights to speak of, clung to the verge in readiness. She checked her watch: already half past four. Juniper was expected at six thirty, the young man at seven, and Percy had promised to be back by four. Doubtless the Air Raid Precautions fellow had acted on good authority when he'd waved the bus over for random inspection, but tonight of all nights she had better things to be doing. Lending temperance to the preparations at Milderhurst, for one.

What were the odds that Saffy *hadn't* worked herself into a state during the day? Not good, Percy decided. Not good at all. No one submitted so willingly to the tumult of occasion as Saffy, and ever since word had arrived from Juniper that she'd invited a mysterious guest to join them, there'd been little chance of the Event, as it was thereafter known, being spared the full Seraphina Blythe treatment. There'd been talk at one stage of unpacking Grandmother's leftover coronation stationery and writing out table places, but Percy had suggested that a party of four, three of whom were sisters, made such fuss unnecessary.

A tap on her forearm and Percy realized that the little old lady beside her was holding an open tin, gesturing that she should take something from within. "My own recipe," she said in a bright, piping voice. "No butter to speak of but not bad at all, even if I do say so myself."

"Oh," said Percy. "No. Thank you. I couldn't. You keep them for yourself."

"Go on." The lady rattled the can a little closer to Percy's nose, nodding approval at her uniform.

"Well, all right." Percy selected a biscuit and took a bite. "Delicious," she said, with a silent lament for the glorious days of butter.

"You're with the FANYs then?"

"Driving an ambulance. That is, I was during the bombing. Cleaning them for the most part lately."

"You'll be finding yourself some other way to help the efforts now, I don't doubt. There's no stopping you young folk." An idea dawned, making saucers of her eyes. "But of course, you should join one of those sewing bees! My granddaughter belongs to the Stitching Susans, back home in Cranbrook, and oh, but they do a mighty job, those girls."

Needle and thread aside, Percy had to concede the notion was not a bad one. Perhaps she should channel her energies elsewhere: find a government official to chauffeur, learn how to defuse bombs, pilot a plane, become a salvage adviser. Something. Maybe then the ghastly restlessness would abate. Much as she hated to admit it, Percy was coming to suspect that Saffy had been right all these years: she was a fixer. No instinct for creation, but a habit of restoration and never happier than when she was put to good use, patching up holes. What a thoroughly depressing thought.

The bus lumbered around another corner and at last the village came into view. As they drew nearer, Percy spied her bicycle, leaning against the old oak by the post office, where she'd left it that morning.

Giving thanks again for the biscuit and solemnly promising to look into the local sewing bee, she disembarked, waving at her old lady as the bus trundled on towards Cranbrook.

The breeze had picked up since they'd left Folkestone and Percy shoved her hands into her trouser pockets, smiling at the dour Misses Blethem, who drew collective breath and gathered their string shopping bags close, before nodding a greeting and scurrying away home.

Two years of war, and there were still some for whom the sight of a woman in trousers heralded the dawn of the apocalypse; never mind the atrocities at home and afar. Percy felt a welcome resurrection of spirits and wondered whether it was wrong to adore her uniform all the more for the effect it had on the Misses Blethem of the world.

It was late in the day, but every chance remained that Mr. Potts hadn't yet made his delivery to the castle. There were few men in the village—across the country, Percy was willing to bet—who had taken to the office of Home Guard with a zest to match that of Mr. Potts. So zealously did he seek to protect the nation that one was liable to feel quite neglected if not stopped at least once monthly for an identity check. That such dedication left the village without a reliable postal service, Mr. Potts seemed to regard as an unfortunate but necessary sacrifice.

The bell tinkled above the door as Percy entered, and Mrs. Potts looked up sharply from a pile of papers and envelopes. Her manner was that of a rabbit caught unawares in a gardener's patch, and she obliged the image further by giving a little sniff. Percy managed to conceal her amusement beneath stern congeniality, which was, after all, something of a speciality.

"Well, well," said the postmistress, recovering herself with the speed of one well practiced in mild deception. "If it isn't Miss Blythe."

"Good afternoon, Mrs. Potts. Anything to collect?"

"I'll just have a look now, shall I?"

The very notion that Mrs. Potts wasn't intimately acquainted with every piece of correspondence that had come or gone that day was laughable, but Percy played along. "Why, thank you," she said, as the postmistress repaired to the boxes on the back desk.

After much officious riffling, Mrs. Potts pulled free a small clutch of assorted envelopes and held them aloft. "Here we are then," she said, making a triumphant return to the counter. "There's a parcel for Miss Juniper—from your young Londoner, by the looks; happy to be back home, is she, young Meredith?" Percy nodded impatiently as Mrs. Potts continued. "A letter hand-addressed to yourself and one for Miss Saffy alone, typed."

"Excellent. One hardly needs bother reading them."

Mrs. Potts lined the letters up neatly on the countertop but didn't release them. "I trust all is well up at the castle," she said, with rather more feeling than such an innocuous query seemed to warrant.

"Very well, thank you. Now if I—"

"Indeed, I hear congratulations are in order."

Percy let out an exasperated sigh. "Congratulations?"

"Wedding bells," said Mrs. Potts, in that irksome manner she'd perfected, managing both to crow at her ill-gained knowledge while greedily digging for more. "Up at the castle," she repeated.

"I thank you kindly, Mrs. Potts, but alas I'm no more engaged today than I was yesterday."

The postmistress stood a while computing, before breaking into pealing laughter. "Oh! But you are a one, Miss Blythe! No more engaged today than yesterday—I must remember that." After much mirth she sobered, pulling a small lace-trimmed handkerchief from her skirt pocket to dab beneath her eyes. "But of course," she said between blots, "I never meant *you*."

Percy feigned surprise. "No?"

"Oh no, for heaven's sake, not you or Miss Saffy. I know neither of you have any plans to leave us, bless you both." She wiped her cheeks once more. "It was Miss Juniper I was speaking of."

Percy couldn't help but notice the way her little sister's name crackled on the gossip's lips. There was electricity in the very sounds, and Mrs. Potts a natural conductor. People had always liked to talk about Juniper, even when she was a girl. The little sister had done nothing to help matters; a child with a habit of blacking out at times of excitement tended to lower people's voices and get them talking about gifts and curses. So it was throughout her childhood, that no matter what strange or unaccountable situation arose in the village— the curious disappearance of Mrs. Fleming's laundry, the consequent outfitting of Farmer Jacob's scarecrow in bloomers, an outbreak of mumps—just as surely as bees were drawn to honey, loose talk turned itself eventually to Juniper.

"Miss Juniper and a certain young fellow?" Mrs. Potts pressed. "I hear there've been quite some preparations up at the castle? A fellow she met in London?"

The very notion was preposterous. Juniper's destiny lay elsewhere than marriage: it was poetry that made her little sister's heart sing. Percy considered having fun with Mrs. Potts's eager attention, but a glance at the wall clock made her think better of it. A sensible decision: the last thing she needed was to be drawn into a discussion about Juniper's removal to London. The chance was all too real that Percy might inadvertently reveal the trouble Juniper's escapade had caused at the castle. Pride would never allow such a thing. "It's true that we're having a guest to dinner, Mrs. Potts, but although it is a *he*, he is nobody's suitor. Merely an acquaintance from London."

"An acquaintance?"

"That is all."

Mrs. Potts's eyes narrowed. "Not a wedding then?"

"No."

"Because I heard it on good authority that there's been both a proposal and an acceptance."

It was no secret that Mrs. Potts's "good authority" was obtained by careful monitoring of letters and telephone calls, the details of which were then cross-referenced against a healthy catalogue of local gossip. Though Percy didn't go so far as to suspect the woman of steaming envelopes open before sending them on their merry way, there were those in the village who did. In this case, however, there had been very little mail to steam (and not of the sort to get Mrs. Potts excited, Meredith being Juniper's only correspondent) just as there was no truth to the rumor. "I believe I would know if that were the case, Mrs. Potts," she said. "Rest assured, it's just a dinner."

"A *special* dinner?"

"Oh, but aren't they all at a time like this?" said Percy breezily. "One never knows when one might be sitting down to eat one's last." She plucked the letters from the postmistress's hand and as she did so spied the cut-glass jars that had once stood on the counter. The acid drops and butterscotch were all but gone, but a small, rather sad pile of Edinburgh rock had solidified in the base of one. Percy couldn't stand Edinburgh rock, but it was Juniper's favorite. "I'll take what you have left of the rock, if you don't mind."

With a sour expression, Mrs. Potts broke the mass free from the jar's glass base and scooped it into a brown paper bag. "That'll be sixpence."

"Why, Mrs. Potts," said Percy, inspecting the small, sugary bag, "if we weren't such firm friends, I'd suspect you of trying to fleece me."

Outrage suffused the postmistress's face as she spluttered a denial.

"I'm joking, of course, Mrs. Potts," said Percy, handing over the money. She tucked the letters and the rock into her bag and donated a brief smile. "Good afternoon, now. I shall inquire after Juniper's plans on your behalf, but I suspect when there's anything to know, you'll be the first to know it."

Two

ONIONS were important, of course, but that did nothing to alter the fact that their leaves brought absolutely nothing to a flower arrangement. Saffy inspected the feeble green shoots she'd just cut, turned them this way and that, squinted in case it helped, and applied whatever creative power she could muster to imagining them in place at table. In Grandmother's heirloom French crystal vase they stood a fleeting chance; perhaps with a splash of something colorful to disguise their origin? Or else—her thoughts gathered momentum and she chewed her lip as was her habit when a grand idea was breaking—she might surrender herself to the theme, throw in some fennel leaves and marrow flowers, and claim it a humorous comment on the shortages?

With a sigh she let her arm drop, hand still clutching the flagging fronds. Her head shook sadly, seemingly of its own accord. Onto what mad thoughts did a desperate person latch? Clearly the onion shoots would never do: not only were they hopelessly ill suited to the task, but the longer she held them the more potently their odor struck her as remarkably similar to that of old socks. A smell the war, in particular her twin sister's occupation in it, had given Saffy ample opportunity with which to become familiar. No. After four months in London, mixing in the smartest Bloomsbury circles, no doubt, braving the air raid warnings, sleeping some nights in a shelter, Juniper deserved better than *eau de* filthy laundry.

Not to mention the guest she had mysteriously invited to join them. Juniper was not one to gather friends—young Meredith being the single surprising exception—but Saffy had an instinct for reading between the lines, and despite Juniper's lines being squiggly at the best of times, she'd gathered that the young man had performed some act of gallantry to earn Juniper's good favor. The invitation, therefore, was a show of the Blythe family's gratitude and everything must be perfect. The onion sprouts, she confirmed with a second glance, were decidedly less than perfect. Once picked they mustn't be wasted though—such sacrilege! Lord Woolton would be horrified. Saffy would find a dish to take them, just not from tonight's menu. Onions and their aftereffects could make for rather poor society.

Sounding a disconsolate huff, then doing the same again because the sensation so pleased her, Saffy started back towards the house, glad as always that her path didn't take her through the main gardens. She couldn't bear it; they'd been glorious once. It was a tragedy that so many of the nation's flower gardens had been abandoned or given over to vegetable cultivation. According to Juniper's most recent letter, not only had the flowers by Rotten Row in Hyde Park been flattened beneath great piles of wood and iron and brick—the bones of Lord only knew how many homes—the entire southern side was given over now to allotments. A necessity, Saffy acknowledged, but no less tragic for it. Lack of potatoes left a person's stomach growling, but absence of beauty hardened the soul.

Directly before her a late butterfly hovered, wings drawing in and out like the mirrored edges of a set of fireside bellows. That such perfection, such natural calm, should continue while mankind was bringing the world's ceiling down around it—why, it was nothing short of miraculous. Saffy's face lightened; she held out a finger but the butterfly ignored her, lifting, then falling, darting to inspect the brown fruits of the medlar tree. Completely oblivious—what wonder! With a smile, she continued her trudge towards the castle, ducking beneath the knobbled wisteria arbor, careful not to catch her hair.

Mr. Churchill would do well to remember that wars were not won by bullets alone and to reward those who managed to sustain beauty when the world was being blasted into ugly pieces around them. The Churchill Medal for the Maintenance of Beauty in England had a lovely ring to it, Saffy thought. Percy had smirked when she'd said so at breakfast the other morning, with the inevitable smugness of one who'd spent months climbing in and out of bomb craters, earning her very own bravery medal in the process, but Saffy had refused to feel foolish. Indeed, she was working on a letter to *The Times* on the subject. The thrust of it: that beauty was important, as were art and literature and music; never more so than when civilized nations seemed intent upon goading one another into increasingly barbarous acts.

Saffy adored London, she always had. Her future plans depended upon its survival and she took each bomb dropped as a personal attack. When the raids had been in full swing and the crump of distant antiaircraft guns, the screaming sirens, the miserable explosions had been nightly companions, she'd chewed her nails feverishly—a terrible habit and one whose blame she laid squarely at Hitler's feet—wondering whether the lover of a city might suffer its plight all the more for being absent when disaster struck, in the same way a mother's anxiety for a wounded son was magnified by distance. Even as a girl Saffy had glimpsed that her life's path lay not in the miry fields or within the ancient stones of Milderhurst, but amid the parks and cafes, the literate conversations of London. When she and Percy were small, after Mother was burned but before Juniper was born, when it was still just the three of them, Daddy had taken the twins up to London each year to live for a time at the house in Chelsea. They were young; time hadn't yet rubbed away at them, polishing their differences and sharpening their opinions, and they were treated—indeed they behaved between themselves—as a pair of duplicates. Yet when they were in London, Saffy had felt the early stirrings of division, deep but strong, within herself. Where Percy, like Daddy, pined for the vast, green woods of home, Saffy was enlivened by the city.

An earthy rumble sounded behind her and Saffy groaned, refusing to turn and acknowledge the heavy clouds she knew were gloating over her shoulder. Of all the war's personal privations, the loss of a regular wireless weather forecast had been a particularly cruel blow. Saffy had faced the shrinkage of quiet reading time with equanimity, agreeing that Percy should bring her one book a week from the lending library instead of the usual four. On the matter of retiring her silk dresses in favor of practical pinafores she'd been positively sanguine. The loss of staff, like so many fleas from a drowning rat, and the consequent adjustment to her new status as head cook, cleaner, laundress, and gardener, she'd taken in her stride. But in Saffy's attempts to master the vagaries of the English weather she had met her match. Despite a lifetime in Kent, she had none of the countrywoman's instincts for weather: she had discovered, in fact, a curious antithetical knack for hanging out washing and braving the fields on the very days rain was whispering in the wings.

Saffy marched faster, almost at a canter, trying not to mind the odor of the onion leaves, which seemed to be gaining strength as she gained pace. One thing was certain: when the war ended, Saffy was giving up country life for good. Percy didn't know it yet—the timing must be right before the news was broached—but Saffy was going up to London. There she intended to find herself a flatlet, just for one. She had no furniture of her own, but that was a small impediment: such matters Saffy trusted to providence. One thing was certain, though, she'd be taking nothing with her from Milderhurst. Her accoutrements would all be new; it would be a fresh start, nearly two decades later than she'd initially planned, but that could not be helped. She was older now, stronger, and this time she wouldn't be stopped no matter how overwhelming the opposition.

Though her intentions were secret, Saffy made a habit of reading the letting pages in *The Times* each Saturday so that when opportunity presented itself, she'd be ready. She'd considered Chelsea and Kensington but decided in favor of one of the Georgian squares in Bloomsbury, in walking distance of both the British Museum and the shops of Oxford Street. Juniper, she hoped, might also remain in London and set up in a place nearby, and Percy would, of course, come to visit. She'd stay no longer than a single night though, due to strong feelings about sleeping in her own bed and being on hand to prop up the castle, bodily if need be, should it begin to crumble.

In the privacy of her own thoughts, Saffy visited her little flatlet often, especially when Percy was stalking up and down the castle corridors, raging about the flaking paint, the sinking beams, decrying each new crack in the walls. Saffy would close her eyes and open the door to her very own home. It would be small and simple, and very clean—she'd take care of that herself—and the overriding smell would be one of beeswax polish. Saffy clenched her fist around the onion sprigs and walked even faster.

A desk beneath the window, her Olivetti typewriter at its center, and a miniature glass vase—an old but pretty bottle would do at a pinch—in the corner, with a single flower in the prime of its bloom, to be replaced daily. The wireless would be her only companion, and throughout the day she'd pause in her typing to listen to the weather reports, leaving briefly the world she was creating on the page to gaze through the window at the smokeless London sky. Sunlight would brush her arm, spilling into her tiny home and setting the beeswax on the furniture to sparkling. In the evenings, she'd read her library books, write a little more of her own work in progress, and listen to Gracie Fields on the wireless, and no one would grumble from the other armchair that it was a load of sentimental rubbish.

Saffy stopped, pressed her palms to her warm cheeks, and gave a sigh of deep contentment. Dreams of London, of the future, had brought her all the way back to the rear of the castle; what was more, she'd beaten the rain.

A glance at the henhouse, and her pleasure was curdled somewhat by regret. How she'd live without her girls she didn't know; she wondered if it would be possible to take them with her. Surely there'd be space in her building's little garden for a small run—she would just have to add this necessity to her list.

Saffy opened the gate and held out her arms. "Hello, darlings. How are you this afternoon?"

Helen-Melon ruffled her feathers but didn't shift from the roosting bench, and Madame refused even to look up from the dirt.

"Chin up, girls. I'm not going anywhere yet. Why, there's a whole war to win first."

This rallying call did not have the cheering effect Saffy had hoped for and her smile staled. It was the third day in as many that Helen had been downcast, and Madame was ordinarily nothing if not vocal. The younger hens took their cue from the older two, so the mood in the coop was decidedly gray. Saffy had become accustomed to such low spirits during the raids; chickens were every bit as sensitive as humans, just as susceptible to anxiety, and the bombers had been relentless. In the end, she'd taken all eight down into the shelter with her at night. The air had suffered, it was true, but the arrangement had suited all concerned: the hens returned to laying, and with Percy out most nights, Saffy had been glad of the company.

"Come now," she cooed, scooping Madame into her arms. "Don't be stroppy, my lovely. It's just a storm gathering, nothing more." The warm feathered body relaxed, but only briefly, before wings flapped and the hen staged a clumsy escape, back to the dirt she'd been scratching.

Saffy dusted off her hands and set them on her hips. "As bad as that, is it? I suppose there's only one thing for it then."

Dinner. The only move in her arsenal guaranteed to brighten their spirits. They were greedy, her girls, and that was no bad thing. Would that all the world's problems were solved with a tasty dish. It was earlier than usual, but these were critical times: the parlor table was still not set, the serving spoon was missing in action, Juniper and her guest would be at the door in no time at all—with Percy's spirits to manage, the last thing she needed was a clutch of cranky hens. There. It was a practical decision, to keep them sweet, and nothing whatever to do with Saffy being a hopelessly soft touch.

THE STEAM of a day spent conjuring dinner from what could be found in the larder or begged from the adjoining farms had collected in the upper nooks of the kitchen and Saffy tugged at her blouse in an effort to cool down. "Now," she said, flustered, "where was I?" She lifted the saucepan lid to satisfy herself the custard had gone nowhere in her absence, guessed by the oven huffing that the pie was still cooking, then spotted an old wooden crate that had outlived its original purpose but would suit her current one perfectly.

Saffy dragged it into the furthest corner of the larder and climbed aboard, standing on tiptoes right at its edge. She spider-walked her hand along the larder shelf until her fingers grazed the darkest patch and a small can reached out to meet them. Wrapping her hand around it, Saffy smiled to herself and clambered back down. Months of dust had settled, grease and steam had formed a glue, and she had to wipe the top with her thumb to read the label beneath: sardines. Perfect! She grasped it tightly, relishing the thrill of the illicit.

"Don't worry, Daddy," sang Saffy, digging the can opener from the drawer of clunky kitchen utensils, shutting it again with a bump of her hip. "They're not for me." It had been one of her father's ruling tenets: canned food was a conspiracy and they were to submit themselves to willing starvation sooner than allow a spoonful to pass their lips. A conspiracy by whom and to what effect Saffy did not purport to know, but Daddy had been forceful on the matter and that had been enough. He wasn't one to brook much opposition and for a long time she'd possessed no desire to give him any. Throughout her girlhood he had been the sun that shone for Saffy, and the moon at night; the idea that he might ever disappoint her belonged in a counter-realm of ghouls and nightmares.

Saffy mashed the sardines in a porcelain bowl, noticing the hairline crack in its side only after she'd rendered the fish utterly unrecognizable. It was of no consequence as far as the hens were concerned, but along with the wallpaper she'd discovered peeling away from the chimney in the good parlor it was the second sign of decline in as many hours. She made a mental note to check carefully the plates they'd put aside for tonight, to hide any that were similarly marred; it was just the sort of wear and tear to get Percy fuming, and although Saffy admired her twin's commitment to Milderhurst and its maintenance, her ill mood would not be conducive to the atmosphere of convivial celebration she was hoping for.

A number of things happened then at once. The door creaked ajar, Saffy jumped, and a remnant of sardine spine dropped from the fork's tine onto the flagstones.

"Miss Saffy!"

"Oh, Lucy, thank God!" Saffy clutched the fork against her staccato heart. "You shaved ten years off my life!"

"I'm sorry. I thought you were out fetching flowers for the parlor . . . I only meant . . . I came to check—" The housekeeper's sentence broke into tatters as she drew closer, took in the fishy mash, the open can and she dropped her train of thought completely when she met Saffy's gaze. Her lovely violet eyes widened. "Miss Saffy!" she said. "I didn't think—"

"Oh-no-no-no—" Saffy flapped a hand for silence, smiling as she lifted a finger to her lips. "Shh, Lucy dear. Not for *me*, certainly not. I keep them for the girls."

"Oh." Lucy was visibly relieved. "Well, that's different, isn't it. I wouldn't like to think of Himself"—her eyes raised reverentially towards the ceiling—"being upset, even now."

Saffy agreed. "The last thing we need tonight is Daddy turning in his grave." She nodded at the first-aid box. "Pass me a couple of aspirin, will you?"

Lucy's brow rumpled with concern. "Are you unwell?"

"It's the girls. They're nervous, poor darlings, and nothing smoothes a frazzled temperament quite like aspirin, except perhaps a sharp swig of gin, but that would be rather irresponsible." Saffy used the back of a teaspoon to grind the tablets to powder. "You know, I haven't seen them so bad since the raid on May the tenth."

Lucy paled. "You don't think they sense a fresh wave of bombers?"

"I shouldn't think so. Mr. Hitler's far too busy marching into winter to trouble much about us. At least, that's what Percy says. According to her, we should be left alone until Christmas at least; she's terribly disappointed." Saffy was still stirring the fishy concoction and had drawn breath to go on when she noticed that Lucy had moved away to the stove. Her posture gave no indication that she was listening anymore and all of a sudden Saffy felt silly, like one of her hens when they were in the mood for clucking and the garden gate would do for company. After an embarrassed little cough she said, "Anyway, I'm prattling. You didn't come to the kitchen to hear about the girls and I'm keeping you from whatever it was you were doing."

"Not at all." Lucy closed the range door and stood tall, but her cheeks were a deeper pink than the oven alone might cause and Saffy knew that she hadn't imagined the previous moment's discomfort; something she'd said or done had spoiled Lucy's good humor and she felt beastly about it. "I was coming to check on the rabbit pie," Lucy continued, "which I've now done, and to let you know that I didn't find the silver serving spoon you wanted but I've put another at table that should do just as well. I've also brought down some of the records Miss Juniper sent back from London."

"To the blue parlor?"

"Of course."

"Perfect." It was the good parlor, and therefore they would entertain Mr. Cavill there. Percy had disagreed, but that was to be expected. She'd been in a temper for weeks, stomping along the corridors, forecasting doom and gloom about the coming winter, grumbling about the shortage of fuel, the extravagance of heating another room when the yellow parlor was already warmed daily. But Percy would come round; she always did. Saffy tapped the fork on the side of the bowl with determination.

"You did very well with your custard. It's lovely and thick, even without the milk." Lucy was peeping beneath the saucepan lid.

"Oh, Lucy, you're a darling. I made it with water in the end, a little honey as sweetener so I could save my sugar for marmalade. I never thought I'd thank the war for anything, but I wonder that I might have lived my entire life without knowing the satisfaction of creating the perfect milkless custard!"

"There's many in London would be grateful for the recipe. My cousin writes that they're down to two pints each a week. Can you imagine? You ought to jot down the steps to your custard in a letter and send it to the *Daily Telegraph*. They publish them, you know."

"I didn't know," said Saffy thoughtfully. It would be another publication to add to her little collection. Not a particularly salubrious addition, but a clipping nonetheless. It would all help when the time came to send off her manuscript, and who knew what else might come of it? Saffy quite liked the idea of a regular little column, "Sew-a-lot Saffy's Advice to Ladies" or some such, a small illustrated emblem in the corner—her Singer 201K, or even one of her hens! She smiled, as pleased and amused by the fantasy as if it were a fait accompli.

Lucy, meanwhile, was still talking about her cousin in Pimlico and the single egg they were allowed each fortnight. "Hers was rotten the other week, and can you imagine—they wouldn't replace it for her."

"But that's just mean spirited!" Saffy was aghast. Sew-a-lot Saffy, she suspected, would have much to say on such matters and wouldn't be afraid to make magnanimous gestures of her own as recompense. "Why, you must send her some of mine. And take half a dozen for yourself."

Lucy's expression could not have been more delighted had Saffy begun handing out lumps of solid gold, and Saffy felt embarrassed suddenly, forcing the specter of her newspaper doppelgänger to dissolve. It was with an air of apology that she said, "We've more eggs than we can eat, and I've been looking for a way to show you my gratitude—you've come to my aid so often since the war began."

"Oh, Miss Saffy."

"Let's not forget I'd still be laundering in caster sugar if it weren't for you."

Lucy laughed and said, "Well, thank you kindly. I accept your offer most gratefully."

They started wrapping the eggs together, tearing small squares from the salvaged newspapers stacked by the stove, and Saffy thought for the hundredth time that day how much she enjoyed their former housekeeper's company and how unfortunate it was that they'd lost her. When she moved into the flatlet, Saffy decided, Lucy should be given the address and encouraged to call for tea whenever she came up to London. Percy would no doubt have something to say about that—she had rather traditional ideas about the classes and their intermingling—but Saffy knew better: companions were to be valued, wherever one found them.

A grumble of thunder menaced from outside and Lucy ducked her head to spy through the grimy windowpane above the small sink. She took in the darkening sky and frowned. "If there's nothing else, Miss Saffy, I'll finish up in the parlor and be on my way. The weather looks like settling in and I've a meeting to attend this evening."

"WVS is it?"

"Canteen tonight. Got to keep those brave soldiers fed."

"That we do," Saffy said. "Speaking of which, I've stitched some children's dollies for your fund-raising auction. Take them tonight if you're able: they're upstairs, as is"—a pause for theatrical effect—"the Dress."

Lucy gasped and her voice dropped to a whisper, even though they were alone. "You finished it!"

"Just in time for Juniper to wear tonight. I've hung it in the attic so it's the first thing she sees."

"Then I shall certainly pop upstairs before I go. Tell me—is it beautiful?"

"It's divine."

"I'm so pleased." A moment's hesitation and Lucy reached out to take Saffy's hands lightly in her own. "Everything's going to be perfect, you see if it isn't. Such a special night, having Miss Juniper back from London at last."

"I just hope the weather doesn't hold up the trains too long."

Lucy smiled. "You'll be relieved to have her home safe and sound."

"I haven't slept a single night through since she's been away."

"The worry." Lucy shook her head sympathetically. "You've been a mother to her, and a mother never sleeps easy when she's worried for her babe."

"Oh, Lucy"—Saffy's eyes glazed—"I *have* been worried. So worried. I feel like I've been holding my breath for months."

"There haven't been any episodes, though, have there?"

"Mercifully not, and I'm sure she would have told us if there had. Even Juniper wouldn't be untruthful about something so serious—"

The door blasted open and they each straightened as sharply as the other. Lucy squealed and Saffy almost did, remembering this time to swipe the can and hide it behind her back. It was only the wind picking up outside, but the interruption was sufficient to sweep away the pleasant atmosphere inside and take Lucy's smile with it. And then Saffy knew what it was that had Lucy on tenterhooks.

She considered saying nothing, the day was almost over and sometimes least said really was soonest mended, but the afternoon had been so companionable, the two of them working side by side in the kitchen and in the parlor, and Saffy was eager to set things to rights. She was allowed to have friends—she *needed* to have friends—no matter what Percy felt. She cleared her throat gently. "How old were you when you started here, Lucy?"

The answer came quietly, almost as if she'd expected it: "Sixteen."

"Twenty-two years ago, was it?"

"Twenty-four. It was 1917."

"You were always one of Father's favorites, you know."

Within the oven, the pie filling had begun to simmer inside its pastry casing. The former housekeeper's back straightened and then she sighed, slowly and deliberately. "He was good to me."

"And you must know that Percy and I are both very fond of you."

With the eggs all bundled, Lucy could find no further occupation at the far bench. She crossed her arms and spoke softly. "It's kind of you to say, Miss Saffy, and unnecessary."

"Only that if you ever changed your mind, when things are more settled, if you decided you'd like to come back in a more official—"

"No," Lucy said. "No. Thank you."

"I've made you uncomfortable," Saffy started. "Forgive me, Lucy dear. I wouldn't have said a word, only I don't like to think of you misunderstanding. Percy doesn't mean anything by it, you see. It's just her way."

"Really, there's no need—"

"She doesn't like change. She never has. She almost died pining when she was sent away to hospital with scarlet fever as a girl." Saffy made a weak attempt to lighten the mood: "I sometimes think she'd be happy for we three sisters to remain together here at Milderhurst forever. Can you imagine? All of us old ladies with hair so long and white we could sit on it?"

"I should think Miss Juniper would have something to say about that."

"Quite." As would Saffy herself. She had a sudden urge to tell Lucy all about the flatlet in London, the desk beneath the window, the wireless on the shelf, but she suppressed it. This wasn't the time. Instead, she said, "Anyway, we were both sorry to see you leave us after so many years."

"It was the war, Miss Saffy, I needed to be doing something to help, then with Mother passing as she did and Harry—"

Saffy waved her hand. "There's no need to explain; I understand completely. Affairs of the heart and all that. We all of us have lives to lead, Lucy, particularly at a time like this. War makes one see what's important, doesn't it?"

"I should get on."

"Yes. All right. And we'll see each other again soon. Next week perhaps, to make some piccalilli for the auction? My marrows—"

"No," said Lucy, a fresh note tightening her voice. "No. Not again. I shouldn't have come today, only you sounded beside yourself."

"But, Lucy—"

"Please don't ask me again, Saffy. It isn't right."

Saffy was at a loss for words. Another gust of angry wind and a distant rumble of thunder sounded. Lucy gathered up the tea towel of eggs. "I should get on," she said, more gently this time, which was somehow worse and brought Saffy to the brink of tears. "I'll fetch the dollies, take a look at Juniper's dress, and be on my way."

And then she was gone.

The door swung shut and Saffy was alone again in the steaming kitchen, clutching a bowl of mushy fish and racking her brains, wondering what had happened to drive her friend away.

THREE

PERCY coasted down the slope of the Tenterden Road, across the rattle of stones at the base of the driveway, and jumped off her bicycle. "Home again, home again, jiggety jig," she recited under her breath, gravel crunching beneath her boots. Nanny had taught them the rhyme when they were very small, decades ago now, yet it always came to mind when she crossed from the road onto the driveway. Some tunes, some chains of words were like that; they lodged and refused to dislodge no matter how a person might wish it. Not that Percy cared to rid herself of "Jiggety Jig." Dear Nanny with her tiny, pink hands, her certainty in all things, the clickety needles as she sat by the attic fire at night, knitting them to sleep. How they'd wept when she celebrated her ninetieth birthday by retiring to live with a great-niece in Cornwall. Saffy had gone so far as to threaten a death plummet from the attic window in protest but, alas, the pronouncement had been dulled by previous deployment and Nanny was not swayed.

Even though she was already late, Percy walked rather than rode her bicycle up the drive, letting the familiar fields welcome her home as they fanned out on either side. The farm and its oast houses to the left, the mill beyond, the woods to the distant right. Memories of a thousand childhood afternoons roosted in the trees of Cardarker Wood blinking at her from the cooling shadows. The exhilarating terror of hiding from the white slavers; hunting for dragon bones; hiking with Daddy in search of the ancient Roman roads . . .

The driveway wasn't particularly steep and it wasn't for lack of ability that Percy chose to proceed on foot, rather that she enjoyed walking. Daddy had been a first-rate walker, too, particularly after the

Great War. Before he published the book, and before he left them to go up to London before he met Odette and remarried and was never really theirs again. The doctor had advised that a daily walk would help his leg and he'd taken to roaming the fields with the stick Mr. Morris had left behind after one of Grandmother's weekends. "You see the way the end swings out before me with each stride?" he'd said as they strolled along Roving Brook together one autumn afternoon. "That's as it should be. Good and solid. It's a reminder."

"Of what, Daddy?"

He'd frowned at the slippery bank as if the right words might be hidden there, between the reeds. "Why . . . That I, too, am solid, I expect."

She hadn't understood his meaning then, had only presumed him enamored of the stick's weight. She certainly hadn't probed further: Percy's position as walking mate was tenuous, the rules governing its continuation firm. Walking was, according to the doctrine of Raymond Blythe, a time for contemplation; on rare occasions, when both parties were amenable, for the discussion of history or poetry or nature. Chatterboxes were certainly not tolerated and the label once given was never lost, much to poor Saffy's chagrin. Many was the time Percy had glanced back towards the castle as she and Daddy set off on their ramble, to see Saffy scowling from the nursery window. Percy had always twinged in sympathy with her sister, but never sufficiently to stay behind. She figured that the favor was just reward for the countless times Saffy held Daddy's ear, making him smile with amusement as she read aloud the clever little stories she'd written— more recently it was for the months they'd spent together, the two of them, immediately after his return from war, when Percy had been sent away with scarlet fever.

Percy came to the first bridge and stopped, resting her bicycle against the railing. She couldn't see the castle from here, not yet; it remained hidden in the clutch of its woods and wouldn't appear fully until she reached the second, smaller bridge. She leaned over the edge and scanned the shallow brook below. The water swirled and whispered where the banks widened, hesitating a little before continuing on towards the woods. Percy's reflection, dark against the white-reflected sky, wavered in the smoother, deeper middle.

Beyond was the hop field in which she'd smoked her first cigarette. She and Saffy together, giggling over the stolen case, pinched from one of Daddy's more pompous friends while he roasted his hammy ankles by the lake on a stifling summer's day.

A cigarette . . .

Percy felt the breast pocket of her uniform, the firm cylinder beneath her fingertips. Having rolled the damned thing, it was as well to enjoy it, surely? She had a feeling that once she entered the castle's fray a quiet smoke would be but a distant dream.

She turned, resting against the railing, struck a match, and inhaled, holding her breath for a moment before letting go. God, how she adored tobacco. Percy sometimes suspected she would be happy to live alone, to never speak another word to a single living soul, on condition she could do so here at Milderhurst with a lifetime's supply of cigarettes for company.

She hadn't always been so wretchedly solitary. And even now she knew the fantasy—though certainly not without its comforts—to be just that. A fantasy. She could never bear to be without Saffy, not for long. Nor Juniper. It had been four months since their little sister took herself to London, and the two of them left at home had behaved in the interim like a pair of handkerchief-twisting old dearies: speculating as to whether she had sufficient warm socks, sending fresh eggs to London with whomever they knew was making the journey, reading her letters aloud over the breakfast table in an attempt to discern her mood, her health, her mind. Letters, incidentally, in which no mention—veiled or otherwise—was made of the possibility of marriage, thank you very much, Mrs. Potts! The suggestion was laughable to anyone who knew Juniper. While some women were formed for marriage and prams in the hallway, others, most decidedly, were not. Daddy had known that, which is why he'd arranged things the way he had, to ensure that Juniper would be taken care of after he was gone.

Percy huffed with distaste and flattened her spent cigarette beneath her boot. Thoughts of the postmistress reminded her of the items she'd collected and she pulled them from her bag, an excuse to linger in the calm of her own company a little longer.

There were three pieces in total, just as Mrs. Potts had advised: a parcel from Meredith to Juniper, a typed envelope addressed to Saffy, and another letter with her own name written across its front. The script, with its dizzy loops, could belong to none other than Cousin Emily, and Percy tore open the envelope eagerly, angling the top page so it caught the remaining light and she could make out the words.

With the exception of the time she'd dyed Saffy's hair blue, Emily had borne the esteemed title of Favorite Cousin throughout the Blythe twins' childhood. That her only challenge came from the pompous Cambridge cousins, the strange, thin cousins from the north, and her own younger sister, Pippa, whose unfortunate tendency to weep at the slightest provocation earned her immediate disqualification, rendered the honor no less heartfelt. A visit from Emily had been cause for great celebration at Milderhurst and without her the twins' childhood would have been a rather more stagnant place. Percy and Saffy were very close, as twins couldn't help but be, but they were not the sort whose bond excluded all others. Indeed, they were a pair whose friendship was improved by the incorporation of a third. Growing up, the village had been full of children with whom they might have played if not for Daddy's suspicion of outsiders. Darling Daddy, he'd been a terrible snob in his way, only he'd have been shocked to be labeled as such. It wasn't money or status that he admired, but brains; talent was the currency with which he sought to surround himself.

Emily, blessed with both, had received the Raymond Blythe stamp of approval and had thus been summoned to stay at Milderhurst every summer. She'd even earned inclusion in the Blythe Family Evenings, a semiregular tournament instituted by Grandmother when Daddy was a boy. The call would go out on the auspicious morning—"Blythe Family Evening!"—and anticipation would animate the household all day. Dictionaries were located, pencils and wits were sharpened, and finally, when dinner was done with, everyone would gather in the good parlor. Contestants would take up position at the table or in a favorite armchair, and finally Daddy would make his entrance. He always withdrew from general activity on tournament day, secreting himself away in the tower to produce his list of challenges, and their announcement was something of a ceremony. The specifics of the game varied, but at its most general a location, a character type, and a word would be supplied, then Cook's largest egg timer flipped, and the race would be on to craft the most entertaining fiction.

Percy, who was bright but not a wit, who loved to listen but not to tell, who wrote slowly and punctiliously when she was nervous and made everything sound impossibly starched, had dreaded and despised these evenings until, quite by accident, when she was twelve years old, she discovered the amnesty accorded to the game's official scorekeeper. While Emily and Saffy—whose devotion to one another only fueled their competition—sweated over their stories, furrowed their brows, bit their lips, and raced their pencils across pages, vying hotly for Daddy's praise, Percy sat serenely awaiting entertainment. For written expression they were evenly matched, Saffy perhaps a little stronger in vocabulary; however, Emily's wicked humor gave her a distinct advantage and for a time it had been clear that Daddy suspected the family's gift of flowering specially in her. That was before Juniper was born, of course, with a precocious talent that swept all other claims aside.

If Emily felt the chill when Daddy's attention shifted orbit, her recovery had been swift. Her visits had continued happily and regularly for many years, long beyond childhood, until that last summer in 1925, the last before she was married and it all ended. It was to Emily's great advantage, Percy had always supposed, that despite her talents she'd never possessed the artist's temperament. She was too even-tempered, too good at sports, too jolly and well liked to walk the writer's path. Not even the merest whiff of neuroses. Much better for Emily the fate that had found her after Daddy's focus waned: marriage to a good sort, a clutch of freckle-nosed sons, a grand house overlooking the sea, and now, according to her correspondence, a pair of amorous pigs. The entire letter was little more than a collection of anecdotes from Emily's Devonshire village: news about her husband and boys, adventures of the local ARP officers, her elderly neighbor's obsession with her stirrup pump, yet Percy laughed as she read it. She was still smiling when she reached the end, folded the letter neatly, and tucked it back into its envelope.

Then she tore it in half and in half again, pushing it deep within her pocket as she continued up the driveway. She made a mental note to remove the shreds to her wastepaper bin before her uniform found its way into the laundry pile. Better yet, she'd burn the pieces that very afternoon and Saffy would be none the wiser.

Four

THAT Juniper, the only known Blythe not to occupy the nursery in childhood, should wake on the morning of her thirteenth birthday, toss a few valued possessions into a pillowcase, then head upstairs to stake her claim on the sleeping attic had surprised no one. The perfect contrariness of the event was so in keeping with the Juniper they knew and loved that whenever anyone spoke of it, in years to come, the progression seemed utterly natural and they found themselves debating the very suggestion that the whole thing hadn't been planned in advance. For her part, Juniper said very little on the subject, either at the time or later: one day she slept in her small annexed room on the second floor, the next she presided over the attic. What more *could* one say?

More telling than Juniper's removal to the nursery, Saffy always thought, was the way in which she'd dragged an invisible cape of curious glamour after her. The attic, an outpost in the castle, the place to which children had traditionally been banished until by age or attribute they were deemed worthy of adult regard, a room of low ceilings and feisty mice, skull-freezing winters and simmering summers, the outlet through which all chimneys passed on their way to freedom, suddenly seemed to hum. People with no reason at all to subject themselves to the climb began to gravitate to the nursery. "Just going to pop my head in," they would say, before disappearing up the staircase, only to reappear somewhat sheepishly an hour or so later. Saffy and Percy would exchange an amused glance and entertain one another with guesses as to what on earth the poor unwitting guest had been doing up there when one thing was certain: Juniper had not been playing hostess. It wasn't that their little sister was rude, only that she wasn't particularly affable either, and there was no company she enjoyed as much as her own. Which was a good thing, given that she'd been afforded very little opportunity to meet anyone else. There were no cousins her age, no family friends, and Daddy had insisted she should be educated at home. The best Saffy and Percy could figure out was that Juniper ignored her visitors completely, leaving them to potter unfettered in the busy chaos of her room until finally they tired sufficiently and took it upon themselves to leave. It was one of Juniper's strangest, most indefinable gifts and one she'd possessed all her life: a magnetism so strong it was worthy of study and medical categorization. Even people who didn't like Juniper wanted to be liked by her.

The last thing on Saffy's mind, however, as she climbed the uppermost staircase for the second time that day, was unraveling the mysteries of her little sister's charm. The storm was gathering faster than Mr. Potts's Home Guard patrol, and the attic windows were wide open. She'd noticed them when she was sitting in the henhouse, stroking Helen-Melon's feathers and fretting over Lucy's sudden sternness. A light's ignition had drawn her attention and she'd glanced up to see Lucy collecting the hospital dollies from the sewing room. She'd followed the housekeeper's progress—a shadow as she passed the second-floor window, the spill of lingering daylight as she opened the hallway door, then a minute or so's passing before a light flickered in the upper staircase that led to the attic. And that's when Saffy had remembered the windows. She'd opened them herself that morning in the hope that a day's fresh air might clear away months of stagnation. It had been a fond hope and one whose fulfillment Saffy doubted, but it was better, surely, to try and fail than to throw one's hands in the air. Now, though, with the smell of rain on the breeze, however, she needed to get them shut. She'd watched for the light to be extinguished in the stairwell, waited another five minutes, then, judging it safe to venture upstairs without fear of meeting Lucy, headed inside.

TAKING GREAT care to avoid the third step from the top—the last thing Saffy needed tonight was the little uncle's ghost making mischief— she pushed open the nursery door and switched on the light. It glowed dully, as did all the Milderhurst electrics, and she paused a while in the doorway. Murky light aside, it was her custom when considering a foray into Juniper's domain. There were few rooms on earth, Saffy suspected, where it was as prudent to plot a course before attempting entry. Squalor was perhaps going a little too far, but only a little.

The smell, she noticed, remained; the blend of stale tobacco smoke and ink, wet dog and feral mouse, had been too stubborn for a single day's breeze. The doggy odor was easily explained—Juniper's mutt Poe had languished in her absence, splitting his moping between the top of the driveway and the end of her bed. As to the mice, Saffy wasn't sure whether Juniper had been feeding them on purpose or if the little opportunists were merely benefiting from her slatternly oc- cupation of the attic. Either was possible. And, although she wouldn't confess it too widely, Saffy quite liked the mousy smell; it reminded her of Clementina, whom she'd bought from the Harrods pet depart- ment on the morning of her eighth birthday. Tina had been a dear lit- tle companion, right up until the unfortunate altercation with Percy's snake, Cyrus. Rats were a much-maligned breed, cleaner than people gave them credit for and truly companionable, the nobility of the ro- dent world.

Having glimpsed the clear-ish passage to the far window—a leg- acy of her previous expedition—Saffy started gingerly through the jumble. If Nanny could only see the place now! Gone were the clean, clear days of her reign, the supervised milky suppers, the little broom- ette pulled out at night for crumbs, the twin desks against the wall, the lingering scent of beeswax and Pears soap. No, Nanny's epoch had been ended well and truly; replaced, it seemed to Saffy, by anarchy. Paper, paper everywhere, inked with odd instructions, illustrations, questions Juniper had written to herself; clusters of dust gathering contentedly, lining the skirting boards like chaperones at a dance. There were things stuck to walls, pictures of people and places and oddly assembled words that had, for some inexplicable reason, captured Juniper's imagination; and the floor was a sea of books, articles of clothing, cups with dubiously grimy insides, makeshift ashtrays, favorite dolls with blinking eyes, old bus tickets with scribble around their edges. The whole made Saffy light-headed and decidedly queasy. Was that a bread crust beneath the quilt? If so, it had hardened by now into a museum piece.

Though tidying up after Juniper was a nasty habit and one against which Saffy had long ago waged war and won, on this occasion she couldn't help herself. Mess was one thing, comestibles quite another. With a shudder she reached down, wrapped the granite-hard crust in the quilt, and hurried to the closest window, releasing the crust and listening for the dull thud as it hit the old moat grass below. Another shudder as she shook out the quilt, then she pulled the window closed and sealed the blackout curtains.

The tatty quilt would need washing and patching, but that was for another day; for now Saffy would have to content herself now with giving it a thorough folding. Not too neatly, of course—though Juniper, it was safe to assume, would neither notice nor care—just enough to restore to it some semblance of dignity. The quilt, Saffy thought fondly, drawing the corners to arm's length, deserved better than a four-month furlough on the floor playing shroud to a stale lump of bread. It had been a gift originally; one of the estate farmers' wives had sewn it for Juniper many years before, that being the sort of unsolicited affection Juniper tended to inspire. Although most people would be touched by such a gesture, bound by it to take special care of the item, Juniper was not most people. She placed no greater value on the creations of others than she placed on her own. This was one of the aspects of her little sister's character Saffy found most difficult to understand, and she sighed as she took in the autumn of discarded papers on the floor.

She looked for a place to leave the folded quilt and settled on a nearby chair. A book lay open atop a pile of others and Saffy, pathologically literate, couldn't help flicking back to the title page to see what it was. *Old Possum's Book of Practical Cats,* inscribed to Juniper by T. S. Eliot after he came to visit and Daddy showed him some of June's poems. Saffy wasn't sure about Thomas Eliot; she admired him, of course, as a wordsmith, but there was a pessimism in his soul, a darkness in his outlook, that always left her somehow more aware of hard edges than she had been before. Not so much with the cats, who were whimsy itself, as with his other poems. His obsession with ticking clocks and passing time, it seemed to Saffy, was a recipe for depression, and one she could quite do without.

Juniper's feelings on the matter were unclear. This was not a surprise. If Juniper were a character in a book, Saffy often thought, she'd be the sort whose evocation was best limited to the reactions of others, whose point of view was impossible to enter without risk of turning ambivalence into absolutes. Words like "disarming," "ethereal," and "beguiling" would be invaluable to the author, along with "fierce" and "reckless," and even on odd occasion—though Saffy knew she must never say so aloud—"violent." In Eliot's hands, she'd be Juniper, the Cat *au Contraire.* Saffy smiled, pleased by the notion, and dusted her fingers on her knees. Juniper *was* rather catlike, after all: the wide-apart eyes with their fixed gaze, the lightness of foot, the resistance to attention she hadn't sought.

Saffy began wading through the sea of papers towards the other windows, permitting herself a brief detour past the cupboard where the Dress was hanging. She'd brought it upstairs that morning, as soon as Percy was safely out of the house, pulled the dress from its hiding place and draped it over her arms like the sleeping princess of a fairy tale. She'd had to bend a coat hanger out of shape so that the silk might swathe against the outside of the wardrobe, facing the door, but it was necessary. The dress must be the first thing Juniper saw when she pushed open the door that evening and switched on the light.

Now the dress: there was the perfect example of the unknowable Juniper. The letter, when it arrived from London, had been such a surprise that if Saffy hadn't witnessed a lifetime of her sister's abrupt about-turns, she'd have believed it a prank. If there was one thing

123

about her sister she'd have put money on, it was this: Juniper Blythe did not give two hoots about clothing. She'd spent her childhood in plain white muslin and bare feet and had a curious knack for reducing any new dress, no matter how smart, into a shapeless sack within two hours of wear. Although Saffy had held out some hope, maturity had not changed her. Where other girls of seventeen longed to go up to London for their first season, Juniper hadn't even mentioned it, shooting Saffy a stare of such withering intensity when she so much as hinted at the possibility that the afterburn had pained for weeks. Which was just as well, seeing as Daddy would never have allowed it. She was his "creature of the castle," he used to say; there was no need ever for her to leave it. What would a girl like her want with a round of debutante balls anyway?

The hurried postscript in Juniper's letter, then, asking whether Saffy minded putting a dress together, something a person might wear to a dance—wasn't there an old frock of her mother's somewhere, something she'd worn to London, just before she died, perhaps it could be altered?—had been utterly bemusing. Juniper had made a point of addressing the letter to Saffy alone, so although she and Percy usually worked in partnership where Juniper was concerned, Saffy had pondered the request privately. After much consideration she'd come to the conclusion that city life must have changed her little sister; she wondered whether Juniper had been changed in other ways, whether she'd want to move to London for good after the war. Away from Milderhurst, no matter what Daddy had wanted for her.

Regardless of *why* Juniper had made the request, it was Saffy's delight to fulfill it. Along with her typewriter, Saffy's Singer 201K—undoubtedly the finest model ever made—was her pride and joy and although she'd done copious sewing since the war began, all of it had been practical. The opportunity to set aside the stacks of blankets and hospital pajamas for a time and work on a fashion project had been thrilling, particularly the project that Juniper had suggested. For Saffy had immediately known the dress of which her sister spoke; she'd admired it even then, on that unforgettable night in 1924 when her stepmother had worn it to the London premiere of Daddy's play. It had been in storage ever since, down in the muniment room, which was airtight and therefore the one place in the castle where moths and rot couldn't find it.

Saffy ran her fingertips lightly down the sides of the silk skirt. The color really was exquisite. A lustrous almost-pink, like the underside of the wild mushrooms that grew by the mill, the sort of color a careless glance might mistake for cream, but which rewarded close attention. Saffy had worked on the alteration for weeks, always in secret, and the duplicity, the effort, had been worth it. She lifted the hem to check again the neatness of her handiwork, then, satisfied, smoothed it. She took a small step backwards, all the better to admire the full effect. Yes, it was glorious; she'd taken an item that was beautiful but dated and, armed with favorite editions from her collection of *Vogue* magazines, turned it into a piece of art. And if that sounded immodest, so be it. Saffy was well aware that this might be her last opportunity to see the dress in all its glory (the sad truth: once Juniper took possession there was no telling what dreadful fate awaited it); she wasn't about to waste the moment by adhering to the dreary strictures of false modesty.

With a glance behind her, Saffy slipped the gown from its hanger and felt its weight in her hands; all the best dresses had a pleasing weight. She inserted a finger beneath each of the shoulder straps and held it up in front of her, chewing her bottom lip as she regarded herself in the mirror. There she stood, head tilted to the side, a childhood mannerism she'd never managed to shed, and from this distance and in this half-light, the passage of the years might never have been. If she squinted a little, smiled more broadly, she might still be the nineteen-year-old who'd stood beside her stepmother at the London premiere of Daddy's play, coveting the pale pink dress and promising herself that one day she too would wear such a wondrous thing, maybe even at her own wedding.

Saffy put it back on the hanger, tripping on a discarded glass tumbler in the process, one from the set Daddy and Mother had received from the Asquiths on their marriage. She sighed; Juniper's irreverence really knew no bounds. Which was all well and good for Juniper, but Saffy, having seen the tumbler, couldn't very well ignore it. She bent to pick it up and was halfway to standing again when she glimpsed a Limoges teacup beneath an old newspaper; before she knew it she'd trespassed all over her own golden rule and was down on all fours, cleaning. The pile of crockery she'd assembled within a minute didn't make a dent in the clutter. All that paper, all those scribbled words.

The mess, the impossibility of ever reasserting order, of reclaiming an old thought, was almost a physical pain for Saffy. For while she and Juniper were both writers, their methods were quite opposed. It was Saffy's habit to set aside precious hours each day in which to sit quietly, her only companions a notebook, the fountain pen Daddy had given her for her sixteenth birthday, and a freshly brewed pot of strong tea. So arranged, she would carefully, slowly, craft her words into pleasing order, writing and rewriting, editing and perfecting, reading aloud and relishing the pleasure of bringing her heroine Adele's story to life. Only when she was absolutely happy with the day's work would she retire to her Olivetti and type up the new paragraph.

Juniper, on the other hand, worked like someone trying to write themselves free of entanglement. She did so wherever inspiration found her, writing on the run, spilling behind her scraps of poems, fragmented images, adverbs out of place, but somehow the stronger for it; all littered the castle, dropped like bread crumbs, leading the way to the gingerbread nursery at the top of the stairs. Saffy would find them sometimes when she was cleaning—ink-splotched pages on the floor, behind the sofa, under the rug—and she'd surrender herself to the conjured image of an ancient Roman trireme, sail hoisted, wind beating it full, an order shouted on deck while in the bows the secreted lovers hid, on the brink of capture . . . only for the story then to be abandoned, victim of Juniper's fleeting, shifting interest.

At other times, whole stories were begun and completed in wild fits of composition; manias, Saffy sometimes thought, though that was not a word any of the Blythes used lightly, certainly not in relation to Juniper. The littlest sister would fail to appear at table and light would be found streaking through the nursery floorboards, a hot strip beneath the door. Daddy would order them not to disturb her, saying that the needs of the body were secondary to the demands of genius, but Saffy always sneaked a plate up when he wasn't looking. Not that it was ever touched; Juniper just kept scribbling all night long. Sudden, burning, like those tropical fevers people seemed always to be getting, and short-lived, so that by next day all would be calm. She would emerge from the attic: tired, dazed, and emptied. Yawning and lounging in that feline manner of hers, the demon exorcised and quite forgotten.

And that was the strangest aspect of all for Saffy, who filed her own compositions—drafts and finals—in matching lidded boxes that were stacked prettily for posterity in the muniment room, who had always worked towards the thrill of binding her work and pressing it into a reader's hands. Juniper had no interest whatsoever in whether or not her writing was read. There was no false modesty in her failure to show her work to others; she simply couldn't have cared less. Once the thing was written, it was no longer of any interest to her. Percy, when Saffy mentioned it, had been nonplussed, but that was to be expected. Poor Percy, without a creative bone in her body—

Well, well! Saffy paused, still on hands and knees; what should appear beneath the underbrush of papers but Grandmother's silver serving spoon! The very thing she'd spent half the day looking for. She sat back on her haunches, pressing her hands flat against her thighs, forcing the kink from her lower spine. To think that all the while, as she and Lucy had turned drawers inside out, the spoon had been tucked beneath the rubble in Juniper's room. Saffy was about to pluck it from its resting place—there was a curious stain on the handle that would need attention—when she saw that it had been acting as a bookmark of sorts. She opened the notebook—more of Juniper's scratching handwriting, but this page was dated. Saffy's eyes, trained by a lifetime of voracious reading, were faster than her manners, and within the split second it took to blink she'd discerned that the book

127

was a journal, the entry recent. May 1941, just before Juniper left for London.

It was simply dreadful to read another person's journal and Saffy would be mortified if her own privacy were invaded in such a fashion, but Juniper had never cared for rules of conduct and in some way that Saffy understood but couldn't formulate into words, that fact made it all right for her to take a peek. Indeed, Juniper's habit of leaving personal papers lying flagrantly in the open was an invitation, surely, for her older sister, a mother figure really, to ensure that all was in order. Juniper was almost nineteen, but she was a special case: not responsible for herself like most adults. How else were Saffy and Percy to act as Juniper's guardians other than by making it their business to know hers? Nanny wouldn't have thought twice about leafing through diaries and letters left in view by her charges, which was precisely why the twins had gone to such great lengths to rotate their hiding spots. That Juniper didn't bother was evidence enough to Saffy that her baby sister welcomed maternal interest in her affairs. And she was here now, and Juniper's notebook was lying right there in front of her, open to a relatively recent page. Why—it was almost uncaring, wasn't it, not to take a tiny little peek?

FIVE

THERE was another bicycle leaning against the front steps, where Percy had taken to leaving her own when she was too tired, too lazy, or too plain rushed to put it in the stables. Which was often. This was unusual—Saffy hadn't mentioned guests other than Juniper and the fellow, Thomas Cavill, each of whom would be arriving off buses and definitely not by bicycle.

Percy climbed the stairs and dug about in her satchel, searching for the key. Saffy had become very particular about keeping the doors locked since war started, convinced that Milderhurst would be circled in red on Hitler's invasion map and the Blythe sisters marked out for arrest, which was fine with Percy except for the fact that her front-door key seemed always intent on hiding from her.

Ducks spluttered on the pond behind; the dark mass of Cardarker Wood quivered; thunder grumbled, closer now; and time seemed to stretch like elastic. Just as she was about to give up and start pounding on the door, it swung open and Lucy Middleton was there, a scarf over her hair and a weak-beamed bicycle lamp in her hand.

"Oh my!" The former housekeeper's free hand leaped to her chest. "You frightened me."

Percy opened her mouth, but finding no words closed it again. She stopped rummaging and swung her satchel over her shoulder. Still no words.

"I—I've been helping in the kitchen." Lucy's face was flushed. "Miss Saffy gave me a ring. On the telephone, earlier. Neither of her dailies was available."

Percy cleared her throat and regretted the action immediately.

129

The resulting croak connoted nervousness, and Lucy Middleton was the very last person before whom she wished to seem uncertain. "Everything's set then, is it? For tonight?"

"The pie's in the oven and I've left Miss Saffy with instructions."

"I see."

"The dinner will cook slowly. I'd be expecting Miss Saffy to boil over first."

It was a joke, an amusing one, but Percy left it too long to laugh. She sought something else to say, but there was too much and too little and Lucy Middleton, who had been standing, waiting for something further, must have realized that it wasn't coming because she moved now, somewhat awkwardly, around Percy to retrieve her bicycle.

No, it wasn't Middleton anymore. Lucy Rogers. It had been over a year since she and Harry had wed. Almost eighteen months.

"Good day, Miss Blythe." Lucy climbed onto her bicycle.

"Your husband?" said Percy quickly, despising herself as she did so. "Is he well?"

Lucy didn't meet her eyes. "He is."

"And you too, of course?"

"Yes."

"And the babe."

Almost a whisper: "Yes."

Her posture was that of a child expecting to be scolded, or, worse, thrashed, and Percy was overcome with the sudden, hot desire to fulfill the expectation. She didn't, of course, adopting instead a casual tone, less precipitate than before, almost light, and saying, "You might mention to your husband that the grandfather in the hall is still gaining. We arrive at the hour ten minutes sooner than we should."

"Yes, ma'am."

"I don't think I imagined that he bore some special sentiment towards our old clock?"

Lucy refused to meet her eyes but uttered a vague reply before mounting her bicycle and pushing off towards the top of the driveway, lamplight scribbling a shaky message on the ground before her.

AT THE shudder of the front door downstairs Saffy clapped the journal shut. Her blood thrummed warm beneath her temples, her cheeks, the skin stretched taut above her breasts. Her pulse beat faster than a small bird's heart. Well. She stood shakily, pushing herself up from the ground. That certainly took away some of the guesswork: the mystery of the evening ahead, the alteration of the dress, the young male guest. Not a gallant stranger at all. No. Not a stranger.

"Saffy?" Percy's voice cut sharp and angry through the layers of floorboards.

Saffy pressed a hand to her forehead, steeling herself to the task ahead. She knew what she had to do: she needed to get herself dressed and downstairs, she needed to assess how much cajoling Percy was going to require, then she needed to make sure the evening was a great success. And there was the grandfather chiming six o'clock so she had to do it at once. Juniper and her young man—whose name, Saffy was sure she remembered correctly, was the same as that she'd glimpsed in the journal entry—would be arriving within the hour, the strength with which Percy had slammed the front door foretold a dark mood, and Saffy herself was still dressed like someone who'd spent the day digging for victory.

Pile of liberated crockery forgotten, she waded hurriedly through the paper so she could close the remaining windows and draw the blackout curtains. Movement on the driveway caught her eye—Lucy crossing the first bridge on her bicycle—but Saffy looked away. A flock of birds soared across the distant sky, way over by the hop fields, and she watched them go. "Free as a bird" was the expression, and yet they weren't free at all, not as far as Saffy could tell: they were bound to one another by their habits, their seasonal needs, their biology, their nature, their birth. No freer than anyone else. Still, they knew the exhilaration of flight. What Saffy wouldn't give sometimes to spread her wings and fly, right now, drifting from the window to soar above the fields, over the top of the woods, following the planes towards London.

She'd tried once, when she was a girl. She'd climbed out of the attic window, walked along the ridge of the roof, and scrambled down to the ledge below Daddy's tower. She'd made herself a pair of wings first, the most glorious pair of silken wings, bound with twine to fine, light sticks she'd salvaged from the woods; she'd even sewn elastic loops on the back so she could wear them. They'd been so beautiful—neither pink nor red but vermilion, gleaming in the sun, just like the plumage on real birds—and for a few seconds after she'd launched herself into the air she'd really flown. The wind had buffeted her from beneath, whipping up through the valley to push her arms behind her, and everything had slowed, slowed, slowed, briefly but brilliantly, and she'd glimpsed what heaven it was to fly. Then things had begun to speed up, her descent had been rapid, and when she'd hit the ground, her wings and her arms had been broken.

"Saffy?" The shout came again. "Are you hiding from me?"

The birds disappeared into the swollen sky and Saffy pulled the window shut, sealing the blackouts so not a chink of light would be seen. Outside, the storm clouds rumbled like a full stomach, the gluttonous belly of a gentleman who'd escaped the frugalities of a rationed pantry. Saffy smiled, amusing herself, and made a mental note to jot down the description in her journal.

IT WAS quiet inside, too quiet, and Percy's lips tightened with familiar agitation; Saffy had always been the sort to hide when confrontation reared its bitter head. Percy had been fighting her twin's battles all their lives, something she excelled at and actually quite enjoyed, and which worked very well indeed until dispute arose between them and Saffy, woefully out of practice, was ill equipped to meet it. Incapable of fight, she was left with only two options: flight or abject denial. In this instance, judging by the emphatic silence that met Percy's attempts to find her, Saffy had chosen the former. Which was frustrating, exceedingly frustrating, for there was a fierce, spiky ball inside Percy, just waiting to get out. With no one to scowl at or take to task, however, Percy was stuck nursing it, and the fierce, spiky ball wasn't the sort of affliction to shrivel of its own accord. With nowhere to fling it, she would need to seek satisfaction elsewhere. Whisky perhaps would help; it certainly wouldn't hurt.

There was a moment each afternoon at which the sun reached a particular low point in the sky and light vanished, immediately and drastically, from within the castle. That moment passed as Percy went down the corridor from the entrance hall. When she emerged in the yellow parlor it was almost too dark to see her way across the room, which might have been hazardous had Percy not been able to navigate the castle blindfolded. She edged around the sofa into the bay window, pulled the blackout curtains across the glass and switched on the table lamp. As usual it made no practicable dent in the gloom. She pulled out a match to light the paraffin lamp's wick but found, with mild surprise and strong annoyance, that after the encounter with Lucy her hand was shaking too much to strike it.

Ever the opportunist, the mantel clock chose that moment to step up its ticking. Percy had never liked that damned clock. It had been Mother's and Daddy had insisted it was dear to him; thus its tenure was secure. There was something in the nature of its tick, though, that set Percy's teeth on edge, a malicious suggestion that it took far more joy than a china object should at sweeping aside the passing seconds. This afternoon her dislike verged on hatred.

"Oh, shut up, you stupid bloody clock," said Percy. Forgetting about the lamp, she tossed the unspent match into the bin.

She'd pour herself a drink, roll a cigarette, and then she'd head outside before the rain came—make sure there was sufficient firewood in the pile; see if she couldn't rid herself of that spiky ball in the process.

SIX

DESPITE the turmoil of the day, Saffy had left a small portion of her brain free to devote itself to wardrobe rummaging, sorting through the options in her head so that come evening she wouldn't be waylaid by indecision and forced to make a careless choice. Truthfully, it was one of her favorite pastimes even when she wasn't hosting a special dinner: she visualized first this dress, with those shoes and that necklace, and then started again, cycling blissfully through the countless permutations. Today, combination after combination had presented itself only to be dismissed because it didn't meet the final, essential criterion. Which was probably where she ought to have started, only it would have limited so direly the options. The winning outfit was always going to be the one that worked best with her finest nylon stockings: that was, the only pair whose six darned holes could happily be concealed by careful selection of the right shoes and a dress of the right length and persuasion. Cue the peppermint silk Liberty gown.

Back in the order and cleanliness of her own bedroom, as Saffy climbed out of her pinafore and did battle with her underwear, she was glad she'd already made the difficult decisions. She had neither the time nor the focus to make them now. As if deciphering the implications of Juniper's journal entry wasn't enough to contend with, Percy was downstairs and she was angry. As always, the whole house glowered with her; the slam of the front door had traveled all the way along the house's veins, up four stories, and into Saffy's own body. Even the lights—never bright—seemed to be sulking in sympathy, and the castle cavities were dirty with shadows. Saffy reached into the very back corner of the top drawer and retrieved her best stockings. They were tucked inside their paper packaging, wrapped inside a piece of tissue paper, and she unfolded them carefully, running her thumb lightly over the most recent repair.

The problem, as Saffy saw it, was that the nuances of human affection were lost on Percy, who was far more sympathetic to the needs of the walls and floors of Milderhurst than to those of her fellow inhabitants. They'd both been sorry to see Lucy go, after all; and it was Saffy who was more apt to feel her absence, alone in the house all day, washing and scrubbing and patching meals together with only Clara or half-witted Millie for company. But while Saffy understood that a woman, given the choice between her work and her heart, would always choose the latter, Percy had refused to accept the changed household with any grace. She'd taken Lucy's marriage as a personal slight and there was no one like Percy for holding a grudge. Which was why Juniper's journal entry and what it might portend was so disquieting.

Saffy slowed in her inspection of the stocking. She wasn't naive and she wasn't a Victorian; she'd read *Third Act in Venice* and *Cold Comfort Farm* and *The Thinking Reed,* and she knew about sex. Nothing she'd read before, though, had prepared her for Juniper's thoughts on the matter. Typically frank; visceral, but lyrical too; beautiful and raw and frightening. Saffy's eyes had raced across the page, taking the whole lot in at once, an enormous glass of water tossed at her face. It was unsurprising, she supposed, given the pace at which she'd read, her confusion at meeting such vivid sentiments, that she couldn't now bring to mind a single line; only fragments of feeling, unwanted images, occasional forbidden words and the hot shock of having met them.

Perhaps it hadn't been the words themselves that had so astonished Saffy as much as to whom they belonged. Not only was Juniper her far younger sister, but she was a person who had always seemed emphatically sexless; her burning talent, her eschewal of all things feminine, her just plain oddness—all seemed to elevate Juniper above such basic human desires. What was more, and perhaps it was this which stung most, Juniper had never so much as hinted to Saffy that she was contemplating a love affair. Was the young male guest this evening the man in question? The journal entry had been penned six months ago, before June went to London, and yet the name Thomas had been mentioned. Was it possible that Juniper had met him earlier, at Milderhurst? That there had been more to her leaving than met the eye? And if so, were they still, after all this time, in love? Such a brilliant and exciting development in her little sister's life, and not a word had been shared. Saffy knew why, of course: Daddy, if he were alive, would be furious—sex too often led to children, and Daddy's theories on the incompatibility of art and child-rearing were no secret. Percy, as his self-elected emissary, must therefore remain none the wiser; Juniper had been right in that. But not to tell Saffy? Why, she and Juniper were close, and as secretive as Juniper was, they'd always been able to talk. This matter should be no different. She rolled the stocking off her hand, resolving to rectify matters as soon as Juniper arrived and they could snatch a few private moments together. Saffy smiled; the evening wasn't merely a welcome home, or a show of gratitude. Juniper had a *special* friend.

Satisfied that the stockings were in good order, Saffy hung them on the bedrail and prepared to take on the wardrobe. Good Lord! She stopped still, turned her underwear-clad self this way and that, glancing back over her shoulder to get a rear view. Either the mirror had developed some sort of reflection disorder or she'd gained a few more pounds. Really, she ought to donate herself to science: to gain weight despite the grave state of England's pantries? Saffy couldn't decide whether it was downright un-British or a clever victory against Hitler's U-boats. Not worthy perhaps of the Churchill Medal for the Maintenance of Beauty in England, but a triumph nonetheless. Saffy pulled a face at herself, cinched in her stomach, and opened the wardrobe door.

Behind the selection of dull pinafores and cardigans hanging at the front was a wonderland of vibrant neglected silks. Saffy clapped her hands to her cheeks; it was like revisiting old friends. Her wardrobe was her pride and joy, each dress a member of an esteemed club. It was a catalogue of her past, too, as she'd once thought during a fit of maudlin self-pity: the dresses she'd worn as a debutante, the silk gown she'd worn to the Milderhurst Midsummer Ball of 1923, even the blue frock she'd made to attend Daddy's play's premiere the following year. Daddy had maintained that daughters should be beautiful and they'd all continued to dress for dinner as long as he was alive; even when he was confined to his chair in the tower they'd made the effort to please him. After his death, however, there hadn't seemed much point, not with the war. Saffy had kept it up for a time, but once Percy joined the ambulance service and started spending nights on duty they'd agreed, wordlessly, to let the custom slip away.

One by one, Saffy swept the gowns aside, until finally she glimpsed the peppermint silk. She held the others clear a moment, taking stock of its lustrous green front: the beading on the décolletage, the ribbon sash, the bias-cut skirt. She hadn't worn it in years, could barely recall the previous occasion, but she could remember Lucy helping to mend it. It had been Percy's fault; with those cigarettes and her careless manner of smoking them she was a menace to fine fabrics everywhere. Lucy had done a neat repair job though; Saffy had to hunt along the bodice to find the singe mark. Yes, it would do nicely; it would have to. Saffy drew it from the wardrobe, draped it across the bedspread, and took up her stockings.

The biggest mystery, she thought, spidering her fingers down the sides of the first stocking and easing her toes in, was how someone like Lucy could possibly have fallen in love with Harry the clock man in the first place. Such a plain little man, not at all a romantic hero, scuttering about the passages with his shoulders hunched and his hair always a little longer, a little thinner, a little less kempt than it should be—

"Oh Lord, no!" Saffy's big toe caught and she began to topple sideways. There was a split second in which she might have righted herself, but her toenail had snagged in the fiber and to plant her foot would have risked a new ladder. Thus, she took the fall bravely, whacking her thigh painfully on the dressing-table corner. "Oh dear," she gasped. "Oh dear, oh dear, oh dear." She slid onto the upholstered stool and scrambled to inspect the precious stocking: why, oh why, hadn't she concentrated better on the task at hand? There would be no new stockings when these ones tore beyond repair. Fingers trembling, she turned them over and over, running her fingertips lightly across the surface.

All seemed in order; it had been a narrow escape. Saffy let out the sigh she'd been holding, and yet she wasn't wholly relieved. She met her pink-cheeked reflection in the mirror and held it: there was more at stake here than the last remaining pair of stockings. When she and Percy were girls they'd had plenty of opportunity to observe adults up close and what they saw had mystified them. The ancient grotesques behaved, for the most part, as if they'd no inkling at all that they were old. This perplexed the twins, who agreed that there was nothing so unseemly as an old person who refused to acknowledge his or her limitations, and they'd made a pact never to let it happen to them. When they were old, they swore, they would jolly well act the part. "But how will we know?" Saffy had said, dazzled by the existential knot at the question's core. "Perhaps it's one of those things, like sunburn, that can't be felt until it's too late to do anything about it." Percy had agreed on the problem's tricksy nature, sitting quietly with her arms wrapped around her knees as she gave herself over to its consideration. Ever the pragmatist, she'd reached a solution first, saying slowly, "I suppose we must make a list of things that old people do—three ought to be enough. And when we find ourselves doing them, then we'll know."

Gathering the candidate habits had been simple—there was a lifetime's observation of Daddy and Nanny to consult; more difficult was limiting their number to three. After much deliberation they'd settled on those leaving least room for equivocation: first, professing strong and repeated preference for England when Queen Victoria was on the throne; second, mentioning one's health in any company other than that which included a medical professional; and third, failure to put on one's undergarments whilst standing.

Saffy groaned, remembering that very morning when she'd been making up the bed in the guest chamber and caught herself detailing her lower-back pain to Lucy. The conversation's topic had warranted the description and she'd been prepared to let it slide, but now this: felled by a pair of stockings? The prognosis was dismal indeed.

PERCY HAD almost made it safely to the back door when Saffy finally appeared, gliding down the stairs as if she had nothing in the world to answer for. "Hello there, sister mine," she said. "Save any lives today?"

Percy inhaled. She needed time, space, and a sharp swinging implement in order to clear her head and exorcise her anger. Otherwise, she was as likely as not to hurl it. "Four kittens from a drain and a clump of Edinburgh rock."

"Oh, well! Victory all round. Marvelous work indeed! Shall we have a cup of tea?"

"I'm going to chop some wood."

"Darling"—Saffy came a step closer—"I think that's rather unnecessary."

"Better sooner than later. It's about to pour with rain."

"I understand that," said Saffy, with exaggerated calm, "but I'm quite sure we've sufficient in the pile. Indeed, after your efforts this month, I estimate we're set until approximately 1960. Why don't you take yourself upstairs instead, get dressed for dinner"—Saffy paused as a loud noise sheeted from one side of the castle's roof to the other—"there now, saved by the rain!"

Some days even the weather could be counted on to take the other side. Percy pulled out her tobacco and started rolling a cigarette. Without looking up she said, "Why did you ask her here?"

"Who?"

A hard stare.

"Oh, that." Saffy waved her hand vaguely. "Clara's mother was taken ill, Millie's as daft as ever, and you're always so jolly busy: it was simply too much for me on my own. Besides, there's no one who can sweet-talk Agatha quite like Lucy."

"You've done all right in the past."

"Darling of you to say so, Percy dear, but you know Aggie. I wouldn't put it past her to cut out tonight, just to spite me. Ever since I let the milk boil over she's held a mighty grudge."

"She's—*it's*—an oven, Seraphina."

"My point exactly! Who'd have thought her capable of such a ghastly temperament?"

Percy was being managed; she could feel it. The affected lightness in her sister's voice, being cut off at the pass on her way to the back door, then shooed upstairs where she was willing to bet a dress—something wretchedly fancy—had already been laid out for her: it was as if Saffy feared she couldn't be trusted to maintain civility in company. The suggestion made Percy want to roar, but such a reaction would only confirm her sister's concerns, so she didn't. Swallowing the urge, she dampened her paper and sealed the cigarette.

"Anyway," Saffy continued, "Lucy's been a darling, and with nothing decent to roast I decided we needed whatever help we could get."

"Nothing to roast?" said Percy breezily. "Last I looked there were eight contenders fattening up nicely in the birdhouse."

Saffy drew breath. "You wouldn't."

"I *dream* of drumsticks."

A gratifying tremor had insinuated itself into Saffy's voice, traveling all the way down to the tip of her pointed finger: "My girls are good little providers; they are not dinner. I will not have you looking at them and thinking of gravy. Why, it's . . . it's barbarous."

There were a great many things Percy wanted to say, but as she stood there in the dank corridor, rain pounding the earth on the other side of the stone wall, her twin sister standing before her, shifting uncomfortably on the stair—hips and stomach stretching her old green dress in all the wrong places—Percy glimpsed the thread of time and all their various disappointments along it. It formed a block against which her present frustration slammed, concertinaing behind. She was the dominant twin, she always had been, and no matter how angry Saffy made her, fighting subverted some basic principle of the universe.

"Perce?" Saffy's voice still trembled. "Do I need to put my girls under guard?"

"You should have told me," Percy said with a short sigh, snatching the matches from her pocket. "That's all. You should have told me about Lucy."

"I wish you'd just put the whole thing behind you, Perce. For your own sake. Servants have done worse to their employers than leave them. It's not as if we found her with her fingers in the silver drawer."

"You should have told me." Percy's throat ached as she spoke. She fumbled a single match from the deck.

"If it matters so much, I won't ask her back. For what it's worth, I can't imagine she'll put up much argument; she struck me as rather keen to avoid your society. I think you frighten her."

A snap as the matchstick broke between Percy's fingers.

"Oh, Perce—now look, you're bleeding."

"It's nothing." She wiped it on her trousers.

"Not on your clothing, not blood, it's impossible to clean." Saffy held up a crumpled item of clothing she'd brought with her from upstairs. "In case you failed to notice, the laundry staff left us some time ago. I'm all that's left, boiling and stirring and scouring."

Percy rubbed at the bloodstain on her leg, smudging it further.

Saffy sighed. "Leave your trousers for now; I'll see to them. Go on upstairs, darling, and make yourself tidy."

"Yes." Percy was looking at her finger in mild surprise.

"You put on a nice party frock and I'll put on the kettle. Make us a pot of tea. Better yet, I'll fix us a cocktail, shall I? It is a celebration, after all."

Celebration was taking it a bit far, but Percy's fight had left her. "Yes," she said again. "Good idea."

"Bring your trousers down to the kitchen when you're done; I'll put them in to soak right away."

Percy clenched and unclenched her hand as she started slowly up the stairs, and then she stopped and turned. "I almost forgot," she said, taking the typed envelope from her bag. "A letter for you in today's mail."

SEVEN

SAFFY hid inside the butler's pantry to read the letter. She'd known immediately what it would be and it had taken all her efforts to conceal her excitement from Percy. She'd snatched at the envelope, then stood watch at the bottom of the stairs, making sure her sister didn't suffer a last-minute change of heart and head for the woodpile instead. Only when she'd heard Percy's bedroom door close behind her had she finally allowed herself to relax. She'd all but lost hope that a reply would ever come, and now that it had, she almost wished it hadn't. The anticipation, the tyranny of the unknown, was nearly too much to bear.

Downstairs in the kitchen, she hurried into the windowless butler's pantry, which had once swollen with the indomitable presence of Mr. Broad but now contained little more to evidence his reign of terror than the desk and a wooden cabinet of old, impossibly tedious daily records. Saffy pulled the string that fired the lightbulb and leaned against the desk. Her fingers turned to thumbs as she fumbled with the envelope.

Without her letter opener, which was sitting in its cradle on her writing desk upstairs, Saffy had to resort to tearing the envelope open. Which she didn't like doing and therefore did as neatly as possible, almost enjoying the prolonged agony such extreme caution brought. She slipped the folded paper from within—very fine paper, she noted; cotton fiber, embossed, warm white—and, with a deep breath, opened it out flat. Eyes scanning quickly, she drank in the letter's meaning, then went back to the beginning again, forcing herself to read more slowly, to believe what she was seeing, as incredible joyous lightness of being spread from deep within her body, turning even the outer-most tips of her fingers to stardust.

She'd first glimpsed the advertisement in *The Times* when she was leafing through the lettings. *Female companion and governess sought to accompany Lady Dartington and her three children to America for the duration of the war,* it had read. *Educated, unmarried, cultured, experienced with children.* The advertisement might have been written with Saffy in mind. Though she had no children of her own, it was certainly not for lack of desire. There had been a time when her future thoughts had been filled—surely like most women's?—with babies. It seemed they were not to be had, however, without a husband, and therein lay the sticking point. As to the other criteria, Saffy was quite confident she could claim without immodesty to possess both education and culture. So, she'd set out immediately to win the position, composing a letter of introduction, including a pair of splendid references, and putting together an application demonstrating Seraphina Blythe to be the ideal candidate. And then she'd waited, trying as best she could to keep her dreams of New York City to herself. Having long ago learned that there was no point ruffling Percy's feathers unnecessarily, she hadn't mentioned the position to her twin, allowing her mind to fill privately, and vividly, with possibilities. She'd imagined the journey in rather embarrassing detail, casting herself as a sort of latter-day Molly Brown, keeping the Dartington children's spirits buoyed as they braved the U-boats en route for the great American port . . .

Telling Percy would be the hardest part; she wasn't going to be pleased, and as to what would become of her, marching the corridors alone, mending walls and chopping wood, forgetting to bathe or launder or bake—well, it didn't bear thought. This letter, though, this offer of employment Saffy held in her hand, was her chance and she wasn't about to let a bad habit of sentiment stop her from taking it. Like Adele, in her novel, she was going to "seize life by the throat and force it to meet her eyes"—Saffy was very proud of that line.

She closed the pantry door quietly behind her and noticed immediately that the oven was steaming. In all the excitement she'd almost forgotten the pie! What a thing! She'd be lucky if the pastry weren't burned to a cinder.

Saffy slid on her oven mitts and squinted inside, breathing a great sigh of relief when she saw that the pie's top, though golden, was not yet brown. She shifted it into the bottom oven, where the temperature was lower and it could sit without spoiling, then stood to leave.

And that's when she saw that Percy's stained uniform trousers had joined her own pinafore on the kitchen table. Why, they must have been deposited when Saffy was in the pantry. What luck that Percy hadn't discovered her reading the letter.

Saffy gave the trousers a shake. Monday was her official washing day, but it was just as well to leave the clothes to steep a while, especially where Percy's uniform was concerned; the number and variety of stains Percy managed to collect would've been impressive if they weren't so jolly difficult to remove. Still, Saffy enjoyed a challenge. She stuck her hand into first one pocket, then the other, in search of forgotten odds and sods that would spoil her load. And it was just as well she did.

Saffy pulled out the pieces of paper—goodness, such a number!— and laid them beside her on the work top. She shook her head wearily; she'd lost count of how many times she'd tried to train Percy to clear her pockets before putting clothes out for laundering.

But how strange—Saffy shifted the shreds about with her finger, located one with a stamp. It was, or had been once, a letter, torn now into pieces.

But why would Percy do such a thing? And who was the letter from?

A slamming noise above and Saffy's gaze swung to the ceiling. Footsteps, another slam.

The front door! Juniper had arrived. Or was it him, the fellow from London?

Saffy glanced again at the tattered pieces of paper, chewed the inside of her cheek. Here was a mystery, and one she needed to resolve. But not now; there simply wasn't time. She needed to be upstairs, to see Juniper and to greet their guest; Lord only knew what Percy's state was now. Perhaps the torn letter would shed some light on her sister's foul mood of late.

With a short nod of decision, Saffy concealed her own secret letter carefully down the front of her dress, and stashed the pieces she'd pulled from Percy's pocket under a saucepan lid. She would investigate properly later.

And, with a last check of the rabbit pie, she straightened her dress about the bust, discouraged it from clinging quite so closely to her middle, and started upstairs.

PERHAPS PERCY only imagined the rotting odor? It had been an unfortunate phantom lately; it turned out there were some things, once smelled, that could never be escaped. They hadn't been in the good parlor for over six months, not since Daddy's funeral, and despite her sister's best efforts a musty edge still clung. The table had been pulled into the center of the room, right atop the Bessarabian rug, then laid with Grandmother's finest dinner service, four glasses apiece, and a carefully printed menu at each place. Percy picked one up for closer inspection, noted that parlor games were scheduled, and put it down again.

A jolt of memory took her back to a shelter she'd found herself in during the first weeks of the Blitz, when a planned visit to Daddy's solicitor in Folkestone had been scotched by Hitler's fighters. The forced gaiety, the songs, the horrid, acrid smell of fear . . .

Percy shut her eyes then and saw him. The figure dressed all in black, who'd appeared midway through the bombing and leaned, unnoticed, against the wall, speaking to no one. Head deeply bowed beneath his dark, dark hat. Percy had watched him, fascinated by the way he stood somehow outside the others. He'd looked up only once, just before he gathered his coat around him and walked out into the blazing night. His eyes had met her own, briefly, and she'd seen nothing inside them. No compassion, no fear, no determination; just a cold emptiness. She'd known then that he was Death and she'd thought of him plenty since. When she was working a shift, climbing into bomb craters, pulling bodies from within, she'd remember the ghastly, otherworldly calm he'd carried wrapped around him as he strode from the shelter out into the chaos. She'd signed up with the ambulances soon after their encounter, but it wasn't bravery that drove her, it wasn't that at all: it was simply easier to take one's chances with Death on the flaming surface than to remain trapped beneath the shaking, moaning earth with nothing but desperate cheer and helpless fear for company . . .

There was an inch or so of amber liquid in the bottom of the decanter and Percy wondered vaguely when it had been put there. Years ago, certainly—they used the bottles in the yellow parlor for themselves these days—but it hardly mattered, liquor was the better for aging. With a glance over her shoulder, Percy dropped a shot into a glass, then doubled it. Rattled the crystal stopper back into place as she took a swig. And another. Something in the middle of her chest burned and she welcomed the ache. It was vivid and real and she was standing here right now feeling it.

Footsteps. High heeled. Distant but ticking rapidly along the stones towards her. Saffy.

Months of anxiety balled up like a leaden weight in Percy's gut. She needed to take herself in hand. There was nothing to be gained by ruining Saffy's evening—Lord knew, her twin had little enough opportunity to exercise her zest for entertaining. Oh, but Percy felt giddy at the ease with which she might. A sensation similar to that when a person stands right on the precipice overlooking a great height, when the knowledge that one must not jump is so strong that an odd compulsion almost overtakes one, whispering that to jump is the very thing that must be done.

God, she was a hopeless case. There was something fundamentally broken at the heart of Percy Blythe, something queer and defective and utterly unlikable. That she should contemplate, even for a second, the ease with which she might deprive her sister, her infuriating, beloved twin, of happiness. Had she always been so mired in perversity? Percy sighed deeply. She was ill, clearly, and it wasn't a recent condition. Throughout their lives it had been thus: the more enthusiasm Saffy showed for a person or an object or an idea, the less Percy was able to give. It was as if they were one being, split into two, and there was a limit to the amount of combined feeling they could exhibit at any one time. And at some point, for some reason, Percy had appointed herself the balance keeper: if Saffy were anguished, Percy opted for glib merriment; if Saffy were excited, Percy did her best to douse it with sarcasm. How bloody cheerless she was.

The gramophone had been opened and cleaned and a pile of records stacked beside it. Percy picked one up, a new album sent by Juniper from London. Obtained God knew where and by what means; Juniper, it might be guessed, had her ways. Music would surely help. She dropped the needle and Billie Holiday started to croon. Percy exhaled, whisky warm. That was better: contemporary music without previous associations. Many years ago, decades before, during one of the Blythe Family Evenings, Daddy had given the word "nostalgia" in a challenge. He'd read out the definition, "an acute homesickness for the past," and Percy had thought, with the gauche certainty of the young, what a very strange concept it was. She couldn't imagine why anyone would seek to reinhabit the past when the future was where all the mystery lay.

Percy drained her glass, tilted it idly this way and that, watching the remaining droplets congeal into a single entity. It was the meeting with Lucy that had her nerves prickling, she knew that, but a pall had spread across all the day's events and Percy found her thoughts drawn back again to Mrs. Potts in the post office. Her suspicions, her insistence almost, that Juniper was engaged to be married. Gossip attached itself to Juniper, but it was Percy's experience that where rumor nested there was always a shred of truth. Though not in this case, surely.

Behind her, the door sighed as it was opened and a cooler gust crept in from the passage.

"Well?" came her sister's breathless voice. "Where is she? I heard the door."

If Juniper were to speak of private matters it would be to Saffy. Percy tapped the rim of her glass thoughtfully.

"Is she upstairs already?" Saffy's voice dropped to a whisper as she said, "Or was it him? What's he like? Where is he?"

Percy straightened her shoulders. If she expected any cooperation from Saffy she needed to offer an unreserved mea culpa. "They're not here yet," she said, turning to her twin and smiling—she hoped—guilelessly.

"They're late."

"Only a little."

Saffy had that look, the transparent, nervous face she used to wear when they were children putting on plays for Daddy's friends and no one had yet arrived to fill out the chairs for the audience. "Are you sure?" she said. "I could have sworn I heard the door—"

"Check under the chairs if you like," said Percy lightly. "There's no one else here. It was just the shutter you heard, the one on the window over there. It came loose in the storm, but I fixed it." She nodded at the wrench on the sill.

Saffy's eyes widened as she took in the wet marks on the front of Percy's dress. "It's a special dinner, Perce. Juniper will—"

"Neither notice nor care," Percy finished. "Come on now. Forget about my dress. You look good enough for both of us. Sit down, won't you? I'll make us a drink while we wait."

EIGHT

GIVEN that neither Juniper nor her gentleman friend had arrived, what Saffy really wanted to do was scurry back downstairs, put the pieces of torn letter back together, and learn Percy's secret. To find her twin in such placatory spirits, though, was an unexpected boon and one she couldn't afford to squander. Not tonight, not with Juniper and the special guest expected any minute. On that note, it was as well to remain as close as possible to the front door, all the better to catch Juniper alone when she finally arrived. "Thank you," she said, accepting the proffered glass, taking a healthy sip to signal goodwill.

"So," said Percy, returning to perch on the edge of the gramophone table, "how was your day?"

Curiouser and curiouser, as Alice might have said. Percy, as a rule, did not peddle in small talk. Saffy hid behind another sip of her drink and decided it was wise to proceed with extreme caution. She fluttered her hand and said, "Oh, fine. Although I did fall over putting on my underwear."

"You didn't," said Percy, with a genuine crack of laughter.

"I most certainly did; I've got the bruise to prove it. I'll see every color of the rainbow before it's gone." Saffy prodded her bottom delicately, shifting her weight as she sat on the end of the chaise longue. "I suppose that means I'm getting old."

"Impossible."

"Oh?" Saffy perked up slightly, despite herself. "Do tell?"

"Simple. I was born first; technically I'll always be older than you are."

"Yes, I know, but I don't see—"

"And I can assure you I've never so much as teetered when getting dressed. Even during a raid."

"Hmm . . ." Saffy frowned, considering. "I see your point. Shall we ascribe my misadventure to a momentary lapse then, unrelated to age?"

"I expect we must; to do otherwise would be to script our own demise." It had been one of Daddy's favorite expressions, uttered in the face of many and varied obstacles, and they both smiled. "I'm sorry," Percy continued. "About before, on the stairs." She struck a match and lit her cigarette. "I didn't mean to quarrel."

"Let's blame the war, shall we?" Saffy said, twisting to avoid the oncoming smoke. "Everybody else does. Tell me, what's new in the big, wide world?"

"Not a lot. Lord Beaverbrook's talking about tanks for the Russians; there's no fish to be had in the village; and it appears that Mrs. Caraway's daughter is expecting."

Saffy inhaled greedily. "No!"

"Yes."

"But she'd be what, fifteen?"

"Fourteen."

Saffy leaned closer. "A soldier, was it?"

"Pilot."

"Well, well." She shook her head dazedly. "And Mrs. Caraway such a pillar. How terrible." It didn't pass beneath Saffy's notice that Percy was smirking around her cigarette, almost as if she suspected her twin of enjoying Mrs. Caraway's misfortune. Which she was, a little, but only because the woman was an eternal bossy-breeches who picked fault with everybody and everything, including, word had made its way to the castle, Saffy's very own stitching. "What?" she said, flushing. "It *is* terrible."

"But not surprising," said Percy, tapping away ash. "Girls these days and their missing morals."

"Things are different since the war," Saffy agreed. "I've seen it in the letters to the editor. Girls playing up while their husbands are away, having babies out of wedlock. It seems they barely have to know a fellow and they're walking down the aisle."

"Not our Juniper though."

Saffy's skin cooled. There it was, the snag she'd been waiting for: Percy knew. Somehow she knew about Juniper's love affair. That explained the sudden lightening of mood; this was a fishing expedition, a sneaky one, and Saffy had been caught on a hook threaded with tasty village gossip. Mortifying. "Of course not," she said as smoothly as she could manage. "Juniper's not like that."

"Of course not." They sat for a moment, each regarding the other, matching smiles applied to matching faces, sipping their drinks. Saffy's heart was ticking louder than Daddy's favorite clock and she wondered that Percy couldn't hear it; she knew now what it was to be an insect in a web, awaiting the great spider's approach.

"Although," Percy said, dropping ash into the crystal tray, "I did hear something funny today. In the village."

"Oh?"

"Yes."

Silence stretched uneasily between them as Percy smoked and Saffy concentrated on biting her tongue. How maddening it was, not to mention underhanded: her own twin, using her predilection for local chatter in hopes of tempting her to give away her secrets. Well, she refused to fall into line; what did Saffy need with Percy's village gossip anyway? She already knew the truth: it was she, after all, who had read Juniper's journal, and she wasn't about to be tricked into sharing its contents with Percy.

With as much poise as she could muster, Saffy stood, straightened her dress, and began an inspection of the table's setting, aligning knives and forks with assiduous care. She even managed to hum mindlessly beneath her breath and affect a small, blameless smile. Which was a comfort of sorts when the doubts came creeping from the shadows.

That Juniper had a lover was surprising, certainly, and it had been hurtful to Saffy not to have been told, but the fact itself didn't change things. Did it? Not things that Percy cared about; not things that mattered. Surely nothing ill could come from Saffy keeping the news to herself? Juniper had a lover, that was all. She was a young woman, it was natural; a small matter and one that was bound to be temporary. Like all of Juniper's various fascinations, this fellow would fade and thin and be blown away on the same breeze that brought the next attraction.

Outside, the wind had picked up and the claws of the cherry tree scratched against the loose shutter. Saffy shivered, though she was not cold; her own small movement was caught by the mirror above the hearth and she glanced to meet herself. It was a grand mirror, gilt framed, and hung on a chain from a hook at great height. It leaned, therefore, away from the wall, angling towards the ground, and the effect as Saffy looked up was of the glass glaring down, foreshortening her like a stumpy green dwarf beneath its thumb. She sighed, shortly and unintentionally, alone suddenly and tired of obfuscating. She was about to look away, to return her attention to the table, when she noticed Percy, hunched at the mirror's glass rim, smoking as she watched the green dwarf at its center. Not merely watched, scrutinized. Searching for evidence, for confirmation of something she already suspected.

The realization that she was being observed made Saffy's pulse quicken and she had the sudden urge to speak, to fill the room with conversation, with noise. She drew a short, cool breath and began. "Juniper's late, of course, and I suppose we shouldn't be surprised; no doubt it's the weather keeping her, some sort of holdup on the line; she was due off the five forty-five, and even allowing for the bus from the village I'd have expected her home by now . . . I do hope she packed an umbrella, only you know what she's like when it comes to—"

"Juniper's engaged," Percy interrupted sharply. "That's what they're saying. That she's engaged."

The entrée knife clinked high and metallic against its mate. Saffy's lips parted, she blinked: "Pardon, dearest?"

"To be married. Juniper's engaged to be married."

"But that's ridiculous. Of course she's not." Saffy was genuinely stunned. "Juniper?" She laughed a little, a tinny sound. "Married? Wherever did you hear such a thing?"

A stream of smoky exhalation.

"Well? Who's been talking such nonsense?"

Percy was busy rescuing a piece of stray tobacco from her bottom lip and for a moment said nothing. She frowned instead at the speck on her fingertip. Finally, she flicked her hand on its way to the ashtray. "It was probably nothing. I was just in the post office and—"

"Ha!" said Saffy, with rather more triumph than was perhaps warranted. Relief, too, that Percy's gossip was just that: village talk with no grounding in truth. "I might have known. That Potts woman! Really, she's an utter menace. We must all be thankful that she hasn't turned her loose talk yet to matters of state."

"You don't believe it then?" Percy's voice was woody, no modulation at all.

"Of course I don't believe it."

"Juniper hasn't said anything to you?"

"Not a word." Saffy came to where Percy was sitting, reached out, and touched her sister's arm. "Really, Percy dear. Can you imagine Juniper as a bride? Dressed all in white lace; agreeing to love and obey somebody else as long as they both shall live?"

The cigarette lay withered and lifeless in the ashtray now, and Percy steepled her fingers beneath her chin. Then she smiled slightly, lifting her shoulders, settling them again, shaking the notion away. "You're right," she said. "Silly gossip, nothing more. I only wondered . . ." But what precisely she wondered, Percy let taper to its own conclusion.

Although there was no music playing, the gramophone needle was still tracing dutifully around the record's center and Saffy put it out of its misery, lifting it back to the cradle. She was about to excuse herself to check on the rabbit pie, when Percy said, "Juniper would have told us. If it were true; she would've told us."

Saffy's cheeks warmed, remembering the journal on the floor upstairs, the shock of its most recent entry, the hurt at having been kept in the dark.

"Saffy?"

"Certainly," she said quickly. "People do, don't they? They tell each other things like that."

"Yes."

"Especially their sisters."

"Yes."

And it was true. Keeping a love affair secret was one thing, an engagement quite another. Even Juniper, Saffy felt sure, would not be so blind to the feelings of others, the ramifications that such a decision would have.

"Still," said Percy, "we should speak with her. Remind her that Daddy—"

"Isn't here," Saffy finished gently. "He isn't here, Percy. We're all of us free now to do exactly as we please." To leave Milderhurst behind, to set sail for the glamour and excitement of New York City and never look back.

"No." Percy said it so sharply that Saffy worried for a moment that she'd spoken her intentions out loud. "Not free, not completely. We each of us have duties towards the others. Juniper understands that; she knows that marriage—"

"Perce—"

"Those were Daddy's wishes. His *condition*."

Percy's eyes were searching her own and Saffy realized it was the first time in months that she'd had the opportunity to study her twin's face so closely; she saw that her sister wore new lines. She was smoking a lot and worrying, and no doubt the war itself was taking its toll, but whatever the cause the woman sitting before her was no longer young. Neither was she old, and Saffy understood suddenly—though surely she had known it before?—that there was something, someplace, in between. And that they were both in it. Maidens no more, but a way yet from being crones.

"Daddy knew what he was doing."

"Of course, darling," Saffy said tenderly. Why hadn't she noticed them before—all those women in the great in-between? They were not invisible surely, they were merely going about their business quietly, doing what women did when they were no longer young but not yet old. Keeping neat houses, wiping tears from their children's cheeks, darning the holes in their husband's socks. And suddenly Saffy understood why Percy was behaving this way, almost as if she were jealous of the possibility that Juniper, who was only eighteen, might someday marry. That she still had her entire adult life ahead of her. She understood, too, why tonight of all nights Percy should lose herself in such sentimental thoughts. Though driven by concern for Juniper, motivated by gossip in the village, it was the encounter with Lucy that had her behaving this way. Saffy was drenched then by a wave of crashing affection for her stoic twin, a wave so strong it threatened to leave her breathless. "We were unlucky, weren't we, Perce?"

Percy looked up from the cigarette she was rolling. "What's that?"

"The two of us. We were unfortunate when it came to matters of the heart."

Percy considered her. "I shouldn't think that luck had much to do with it. A basic matter of mathematics, wasn't it?"

Saffy smiled; it was just as the governess who replaced Nanny had told them, right before she went away, returning to Norway to marry her widower cousin. She'd taken them for a lesson by the lake, her habit when she wasn't in the mood for teaching but wanted to escape Mr. Broad's scrutiny; she'd looked up from where she was sunning herself to say, in that lazy, accented manner of hers, eyes glinting with malicious pleasure, that they'd do well to put all thought of marriage aside; that the same Great War that had wounded their father had also killed their chances. The thirteen-year-old twins had merely stared blankly, an expression they'd perfected, knowing it drove adults to agitation. What did they care? Marriage and suitors were the last things on their minds back then.

Saffy said softly, "Well, that's a sorry luck of sorts, isn't it? To have all one's future husbands die on the French battlefields?"

"How many were you planning on having?"

"What's that?"

"Husbands. You said, 'To have all one's future' . . ." Percy lit her cigarette and waved her hand. "Never mind," she said.

"Only one." Saffy felt suddenly light-headed. "There was only one I wanted."

The silence that followed was agonizing and Percy, at least, had the dignity to look uncomfortable. She didn't say anything though, offered no words of comfort or understanding, no kind gestures, merely pinched the tip of her cigarette, sending it to sleep, and made for the door.

"Where are you going?"

"A headache. It's come on quickly."

"Sit down then; I'll fetch you a couple of aspirin."

"No—" Percy refused to meet Saffy's gaze—"no, I'll fetch them myself from the medicine box. The walk will do me good."

NINE

PERCY hurried along the hallway, wondering how she could have been so bloody stupid. She'd meant to burn the pieces of Emily's letter immediately, and instead she'd allowed the encounter with Lucy to flummox her so that she'd left them in her pocket. Worse yet, she'd delivered them directly to Saffy, the very person from whom the correspondence must be kept concealed. Percy drummed down the stairs, through the door, and into the steam-filled kitchen. When, she wondered, might she have remembered the letter herself, if not for Saffy's allusion to Emily's husband, Matthew, just now? Was it too premature to lament the loss of her reliable mind, to wonder at the sorts of demonic deals she'd have to make to get it back?

Percy stopped abruptly before the table. Her trousers were no longer where she'd left them. Her heart lurched, a hammer against her ribs; she forced it back inside its cage where it belonged. Panic would not help; besides, this wasn't of itself a terrible thing. Percy was quite sure Saffy hadn't yet read the letter: her manner upstairs had been far too measured, too calm, for it to be otherwise. For, dear God, if Saffy knew that Percy was still in touch with their cousin, there'd be no masking that tantrum. Which meant all was not yet lost. Find the trousers, remove the evidence, and everything would be all right.

There had been a dress on the table too, she remembered, which meant there was a pile of laundry somewhere. How difficult could that be to find? More difficult, certainly, than if she had the vaguest notion how laundry was done, but unfortunately Percy had never paid much attention to Saffy's housekeeping routine, an oversight she promised silently to amend just as soon as the letter was safely in her possession.

She began with the baskets on the shelf beneath the table, rummaging through tea towels and baking trays, saucepans and rolling pins, one ear trained on the stairs in case Saffy should come searching. Which was unlikely, surely? With Juniper already late, Saffy would be loath to venture far from the front door. Percy wanted to get back there herself: as soon as Juniper arrived she intended to ask plainly about Mrs. Potts's rumor.

For although Percy had gone along with her twin's certainty that Juniper, if engaged, would have told them the news, in reality she had no such confidence. It was the sort of thing that people did tell one another, that was true enough, but Juniper wasn't like other people: she was beloved but she was also undeniably singular. And it wasn't only the lost time, the episodes: this was the little girl who'd comforted herself by rubbing objects on her naked eyeball—smooth stones, the end of Cook's rolling pin, Daddy's favorite fountain pen; who'd driven away countless nannies with her incurable obstinacy and refusal to abandon imaginary cohorts; who, on the rare occasions she was induced to wear shoes, insisted on wearing them wrong-footed.

Oddness, of itself, was of no concern to Percy: as the family argument went, which person of value didn't have a good pinch of strangeness in them? Daddy had his ghosts, Saffy had her panics, Percy herself made no claims on the pedestrian. No, oddness was neither here nor there; Percy cared only about doing her duty: protecting Juniper from herself. Daddy had given her the task. Juniper was special, he'd said, and it was up to all of them to keep her safe. And they had, so far, they had. They'd become expert at recognizing occasions when the very aspects that fueled her talent were at risk of tipping over into fearsome rage. Daddy, when he was alive, had allowed her to rampage without restraint: "It's passion," he'd said, admiration burnishing his voice, "unaffected, unbridled passion." But he'd made sure to talk to his lawyers. Percy had been surprised when she'd first discovered what he'd done; her immediate reaction had been the heat of betrayal, the sibling's mantra of "It isn't fair!" but she'd soon enough come to heel. She'd understood that Daddy was right, that what he proposed would work out best for all of them. And she adored Juniper, they all did. There was nothing Percy wouldn't do for her baby sister.

A noise from upstairs and Percy froze, scrutinizing the ceiling. The castle was full of noises so it was a matter of sorting through the usual suspects. Too loud for the caretakers, surely? There it was again. Footsteps, she figured; but were they getting closer? Was Saffy coming downstairs? A long, breath-held moment in which Percy remained absolutely still, motionless until she was satisfied, finally, that the footsteps were moving away.

She stood up then, carefully, and scanned the kitchen with rather more desperation than she had before; still no sign of the bloody laundry. Brooms and a mop in the corner, Wellington boots by the back door, the sink containing nothing more than soaking bowls, and on the stovetop a saucepan and a pot—

A pot! Of course. Surely she'd heard Saffy talking before about pots and washing right before the topic turned to immovable stains and a lecture on Percy's own lack of care. Percy hurried to the stove, peered inside the large steel container, and bingo! What relief—the trousers.

With a grin, she heaved out the sodden uniform, twisted it back and forth to find the collapsed pockets and squirrelled her hand into first one, then the other—

Blood drained instantly from her face: the pockets were empty. The letter was gone.

More noise from upstairs: footsteps again; Saffy pacing. Percy swore under her breath, berated herself again for her stupidity, then shut the hell up as she tracked her sister's whereabouts.

The footsteps were coming nearer. Then there was a banging sound. The footsteps changed direction. Percy strained harder. Was someone at the door?

Silence. In particular, no urgent call from Saffy. Which meant no one had knocked, for one thing was certain—Percy's absence would not be tolerated once guests arrived.

Perhaps it was the shutter again; she'd only tapped it lightly back into place with the small wrench—without a tool set handy there'd been little else she could do—and it was still blowing a gale outside. Add that to the list of things to mend tomorrow.

Percy took a deep breath and let out a dispirited sigh. She watched the trousers sink back inside the pot. It was after eight o'clock, Juniper was already late, the letter could be anywhere. Maybe—her spirits lifted—Saffy had taken it for rubbish? It was torn, after all; perhaps the letter had already been burned and was little more now than ashes in the Aga.

Short of running a fine-tooth comb over the entire house, or asking Saffy directly what had become of it—Percy winced just to imagine that conversation—she couldn't see that there was anything more she could do. Which meant she might as well go back upstairs and wait for Juniper.

A great crash of thunder then, loud enough that even in the bowels of the house Percy shivered. In its wake, another, softer noise, closer. Outside perhaps, almost like someone scratching along the wall, hammering periodically, looking for the back door.

Juniper's guest was due about now.

It was possible, Percy supposed, that a person unfamiliar with the castle, approaching it by night, during the blackout, in the midst of a great rainstorm, might find themselves seeking entrance elsewhere than the front door. Slim though the possibility was, once she'd considered it Percy knew she had to check. She couldn't jolly well leave him floundering out there.

Stitching her lips tight, she took a last glance about the kitchen—dry pantry goods ready for use on the bench, a scrunched tea towel, a saucepan lid: nothing even resembling a stack of torn paper—then she dug the battery torch from the emergency kit, pulled a mackintosh over her dress, and opened the back door.

Juniper was almost two hours late and Saffy was officially worried. Oh, she knew it was bound to be a delay on the train line, a punctured bus tire, a roadblock, something ordinary, and certainly there'd be no enemy planes complicating matters on a sodden night like this; nonetheless, sensible reasoning had no place in the worries of a big sister. Until Juniper walked through that front door, life and limbs intact, a significant part of Saffy's mind would remain encased by fear.

And what news, she wondered with a nibble on her bottom lip, would her baby sister bring with her when she did, finally, spill across the threshold? Saffy had believed it when she'd reassured Percy that Juniper wasn't engaged to be married, she really had, but in the time since Percy had disappeared so abruptly, leaving her alone in the good parlor, she'd grown less and less certain. The doubts had started when she'd joked about the dubious spectacle of Juniper in white lace. Even as Percy was nodding agreement, the froufrou image that had flashed into Saffy's mind was undergoing transmutation—a reflection in rippling water—into another, far less unlikely vision. One Saffy already held within her imagination and had done since she'd started work on the dress upstairs.

From there, the pieces had fallen quickly into place. Why else had Juniper asked her to alter the dress? Not for something as ordinary as a dinner, but for a wedding. Her own wedding, to this Thomas Cavill who was coming tonight to meet them. A man they hitherto had known nothing about. Indeed, the extent of their knowledge now was limited to the letter Juniper had sent advising that she'd invited him to dinner. They'd met during an air raid, they shared a mutual friend, he was a teacher and a writer; Saffy racked her brains to remember the rest, the precise words Juniper had used, the turn of phrase that had left them with the impression that the gentleman in question had been responsible, in some way, for saving her life. Had they imagined that detail, she wondered? Or was it one of Juniper's creative untruths, an embellishment designed to predispose their sympathies?

There had been a little more about him in the journal, but that information was not in a biographical vein. What had been written there were the feelings, the desires, the longings of a grown woman.

A woman Saffy didn't recognize, of whom she felt shy; a woman who was becoming worldly. And if Saffy found the transition difficult to reconcile herself to, Percy was going to need a great deal of coaxing. As far as her twin was concerned, Juniper would always be the baby sister who'd come along when they were almost fully grown, the little girl who needed spoiling and protecting. Whose spirits could be lifted, her loyalties won, with nothing more weighty than a bag of sweets.

Saffy smiled with sad fondness for her barnacled twin, who was, no doubt, even at this minute, arming herself so that their father's wishes might be respected. Poor, dear Percy: intelligent in so many ways, courageous and kind, tougher than leather, yet unable ever to unshackle herself from Daddy's impossible expectations. Saffy knew better; she'd stopped trying to please Himself a long time ago.

She shivered, cold suddenly, and rubbed her hands together. Then she crossed her arms, determined to find steel within them. Saffy needed to be strong for Juniper now; it was her turn. For she could understand, where Percy would not, the burden of romantic passion.

The door sucked open and Percy was there. A draft pulled the door closed with a slam behind her. "It's bucketing down." She chased a drip from the end of her nose, her chin, shook her wet hair. "I heard a noise up here. Before."

Saffy blinked, greatly perplexed. Spoke as if by rote: "It was the shutter. I think I fixed it, though of course I'm not much use with tools—Percy, where on earth have you been?" And what had she been doing? Saffy's eyes widened as she took in her twin's wet, muddy dress, the—were they leaves?—in her hair. "Headache gone then, has it?"

"What's that?" Percy had collected their glasses and was at the drinks table pouring them each another whisky.

"Your headache. Did you find the aspirin?"

"Oh. Thank you. Yes."

"Only you were gone a long time."

"Was I?" Percy handed a glass to Saffy. "I suppose I was. I thought

I heard something outside; probably Poe, frightened of the storm. I did wonder at first if it might be Juniper's friend. What's his name?"

"Thomas." Saffy took a sip. "Thomas Cavill." Did she imagine that Percy was avoiding her eyes? "Percy, I hope—"

"Don't worry. I'll be nice to him when he arrives." She swirled her glass. "*If* he arrives."

"You mustn't prejudge him for being late, Percy."

"Why ever not?"

"It's the fault of the war. Nothing runs on time anymore. Juniper's not here either."

Percy reclaimed the cigarette she'd left earlier, propped against the rim of the ashtray. "That's hardly a surprise."

"He'll be here eventually."

"If he exists."

What an odd thing to say; Saffy tucked a wayward curl behind her ear, confused, concerned, wondering if Percy was making some sort of joke, one of the trademark ironies that Saffy had a habit of taking literally. Though her stomach had begun to churn, Saffy ignored it, choosing to take the remark as humor. "I do hope so; such a great shame to learn he's a mere figment. The table will look terribly unbalanced minus a setting." She perched on the edge of the chaise longue, but no matter how she strove for ease, a peculiar nervousness seemed to have transplanted itself from Percy to her.

"You look tired," said Percy.

"Do I?" Saffy tried to affect an amiable tone. "I suppose I am. Perhaps activity will perk me up. I might just slip down to the kitchen and—"

"No."

Saffy's glass dropped. Whisky spilled across the rug, beading brown on the blue and red surface.

Percy picked up the glass. "I'm sorry," she said. "I just meant—"

"How silly of me." Saffy fussed at a wet spot on her dress. "Silly, silly . . ."

And then it came, a knock on the door.

They stood as one.

"Juniper," said Percy.

Saffy swallowed, noting the assumption. "Or Thomas Cavill."

"Yes. Or Thomas Cavill."

"Well," said Saffy with a stiff smile. "Whoever it is, I expect we'd better let them in."

PART TWO

PART TWO

The Book of Magical Wet Animals

I couldn't stop thinking about Thomas Cavill and Juniper Blythe. It was such a melancholy story; I made it *my* melancholy story. I returned to London, I got on with my life, but a part of me remained tethered to that castle. On the brink of sleep, in a moment of daydream, the whispers found me. My eyes fell closed and I was right back in that cool, shadowy corridor, waiting alongside Juniper for her fiancé to arrive. "She's lost in the past," Mrs. Bird had told me as we drove away, as I watched through the rearview mirror, the woods drawing their wings around the castle, a dark, protective shroud: "That same night in October 1941, over and over; a record player with a stuck needle."

The proposition was just so terribly sad—an entire life spoiled in an evening—and it filled me with questions. How had it been for her that night when Thomas Cavill failed to show for dinner? Had all three sisters waited in a room done up specially for the occasion? I wondered at what point had she begun to worry; whether she'd thought at first that he'd been injured, that there'd been an accident; or whether she'd known at once she'd been forsaken? "He married another woman," Mrs. Bird had told me when I asked, "engaged himself to Juniper, then ran off with someone else. Nothing but a letter to break off their affair."

I held the story in my hands, turned it over, looked at it from every angle. Envisaged, amended, replayed. I suppose the fact that I'd been similarly betrayed might have had a little to do with it, but my obsession—for I confess, that's what it became—was fed by more than

empathy. It concerned itself particularly with the final moments of
my encounter with Juniper; the transition I'd witnessed when I mentioned my return to London; the way the young woman waiting long-
ingly for her lover had been replaced by a tense and wretched figure,
begging me for help, berating me for having broken a promise. Most
of all, I fixated on the moment she'd looked me in the eye and accused
me of having failed her in some grave manner, the way she'd called me
Meredith.

Juniper Blythe was old, she was unwell, and her sisters had been
at great pains to warn me that she often spoke of things she didn't
understand. Nonetheless, the more I considered it the more awfully
certain I became that Mum had played some part in her fate. It was
the only thing, surely, that made any sense. It explained Mum's reaction to the lost letter, the cry—for it had been of anguish, hadn't it?—
when she saw from whom it came, the same cry I'd heard as we drove
away from Milderhurst when I was small. That secret visit, decades
before, when Mum had taken my hand and wrenched me from the
gate, forced me back into the car, saying only that she'd made a mistake, that it was too late.

But too late for what? To make amends, perhaps; to repair some
long-ago transgression? Had it been guilt that took her back to the
castle and then drove her away again before we passed through the
gates? It was possible. And if it were true it would certainly explain
her distress. It might also account for why she'd kept the whole thing
secret in the first place. For it was the secrecy as much as the mystery
that struck me then. I don't believe in an obligation of full disclosure,
yet in this case I couldn't shake off the sense that I'd been lied to. More
than that: that I was somehow affected directly. Something sat in my
mother's past, something she'd made every attempt to hide, and it refused to stay there. An action, a decision, a mere moment, perhaps,
when she was just a girl; something that had cast its shadow, long and
dark, into Mum's present, and therefore right across mine too. And,
not just because I was nosy, not just because I was coming to empa-

thize so strongly with Juniper Blythe, but because in some way that was difficult to explain, this secret had come to represent a lifetime's distance between my mother and me—I needed to know what had happened.

"I SHOULD say that you do," Herbert had agreed when I said as much to him. We'd spent the afternoon squeezing my boxes of books and other assorted household items into storage in his cluttered attic and had just headed out for a stroll through Kensington Gardens. The walks are a daily habit of ours, begun at the vet's behest; they're supposed to help with Jess's digestion, the regular activity giving her metabolism a little boost, but she approaches the event with spectacularly bad grace. "Come along, Jessie," said Herbert, tapping his shoe against a stubborn bottom, which had affixed itself rather firmly to the concrete. "We're nearly at the ducks, old lovely."

"But how am I going to find out?" There was Auntie Rita, of course, but Mum's fraught relationship with her elder sister made that idea seem particularly sneaky. I pushed my hands deep into my pockets, as if the answer might be found among the lint. "What should I do? Where should I start?"

"Well now, Edie." He handed over Jess's lead while he fussed a cigarette from his pocket and cupped his hand to light it. "It seems to me there's only one place *to* start."

"Oh?"

He exhaled a theatrical stream of smoke. "You know as well as I, my love; you need to ask your mother."

YOU WOULD be forgiven for thinking that Herbert's suggestion was obvious, and I must take some of the blame for that. I suspect I've given you entirely the wrong impression about my family, beginning as I did with that long-lost letter. It's where this story starts, but it's not where *my* story starts; or rather, it's not where the story of Meredith and Edie starts. Coming into our family that Sunday afternoon, you'd be forgiven for thinking we were a rather expansive pair, that we chatted and shared easily. However nice that might sound, it was not the case. There are any number of childhood experiences I could submit in evidence to demonstrate that ours was not a relationship marked by conversation and understanding: the unexplained appearance in my drawer of a military-style bra when I turned thirteen; my reliance on Sarah for all but the most basic information regarding birds and bees and everything in between; the ghostly brother my parents and I pretended not to see.

But Herbert was right: this was my mother's secret, and if I wanted to know the truth, to learn more about that little girl who'd shadowed me around Milderhurst Castle, it was the only proper place to begin. As good luck would have it, we'd arranged to meet for coffee the following week in a patisserie around the corner from Billing & Brown. I left the office at eleven o'clock, found a table in the back corner, and placed our order, as per habit. The waitress had just brought me a steaming pot of Darjeeling when there came a blurt of road noise and I looked up to see the patisserie door was open and Mum was standing tentatively just inside, bag and hat in hand. A spirit of defensive caution had taken hold of her features as she surveyed the unfamiliar, decidedly modern café, and I glanced away, at my hands, the table, fiddled with the zip on my bag, anything to avoid bearing witness. I've noticed that look of uncertainty more often lately, and I'm not sure whether it's because she's getting older, or because I am, or because the world really is speeding up. My reaction to it dismays me, for surely a glimpse of my mother's weakness should engender pity, make her more lovable to me, but the opposite is true. It frightens me, like a tear in the fabric of normality that threatens to render everything unlovely, unrecognizable, not as it should be. All my life my mother has been an oracle, a brick wall of propriety, so to see her unsure, particularly in a situation that I meet without a wrinkle, tilts my world and makes the solid ground swirl like clouds beneath me. So I waited, and only when enough time had passed did I look up again, catch her eye, sure again now, confident, and wave with candor, as if only in that moment had I realized she was there.

She negotiated the crowded café cautiously, guarding her bag from bumping people's heads in an ostentatious way that managed somehow to convey disapproval at the seating arrangements. I, meanwhile, busied myself making sure no one had left spilled sugar granules or cappuccino froth or pastry flakes on her side of the table. These semiregular coffee dates of ours were a new thing, instituted a few months after Dad's retirement started. They were a little awkward for both of us, even when I wasn't hoping to undertake a delicate excavation of Mum's life. I stood halfway out of my seat when she reached the table, my lips met the air near her proffered cheek, then we both sat down, smiling with excessive relief because the public greeting was over.

"Warm out, isn't it?"

I said, "Very," and we were back in motion down a comfortable road: Dad's current home-improvement obsession (tidying the boxes in the attic), my work (supernatural encounters on Romney Marsh), and Mum's bridge club gossip. Then a pause while we smiled at each other, both waiting for Mum to falter beneath the weight of her routine inquiry: "And how's Jamie?"

"He's well."

"I saw the recent write-up in *The Times*. The new play's been well received."

"Yes." I'd seen the review, too. I didn't go hunting, I really didn't; it just jumped out at me when I was looking for the letting pages. A *very* good review, as it happens. Damn paper; no suitable flats to rent either.

Mum paused while the cappuccino I'd ordered for her arrived at the table. "And tell me," she said, laying a paper napkin between her cup and saucer to soak up the slopped milk, "what's next on his agenda?"

"He's working on his own script. Sarah has a friend, a film director, who's promised to read it when he's done."

Her mouth formed a silent, cynical "Oh" before she managed to utter some positive noises. The last of these was drowned when she took a sip of coffee, flinched at the bitter taste, and, blessedly, changed the subject. "And how's the flat? Your father wants to know whether that tap in the kitchen's still giving you trouble. He's had another idea he thinks will fix it once and for all."

I pictured the cold and empty flat I'd left for the final time that morning, phantom memories sealed within the collection of brown cardboard boxes my life had become, then crammed into Herbert's attic. "It's fine," I said. "The flat's fine, the tap's fine. Tell him he really doesn't need to worry anymore."

"I don't suppose there's anything else that needs attention?" A faint pleading note had crept into her voice. "I thought I might send him around on Saturday to do some general maintenance."

"I told you. Everything's fine."

She looked surprised and hurt and I knew I'd spoken brusquely, only these dreadful conversations in which I pretended all was going swimmingly were wearing me down. Despite my willingness to disappear inside storybooks, I'm not a liar and I don't cope well with subterfuge. Under ordinary circumstances this might have been the perfect time for me to break the news about Jamie—but I couldn't, not when I wanted to steer us back to Milderhurst and Juniper Blythe. In any case, the man at the next table chose that very instant to turn around and ask whether he could borrow our salt shaker.

As I handed it to him, Mum said, "I have something for you." She pulled out an old M&S bag, folded over to protect whatever was inside. "Don't get too excited," she added, passing it to me. "It's nothing new."

I opened the bag, slipped out the contents, and stared in puzzlement for a moment. People are often giving me things they think are worth publishing, but I couldn't believe anyone could be that far off the mark.

"Don't you remember?" Mum was looking at me as if I'd forgotten my own name.

I gazed again at the stapled wad of paper, stapled together, the child's drawing on the front, the ill-formed words at the top of the page: *The Book of Wet Animals, Written and Illustrated by Edith Burchill.* A little arrow had been inserted between *of* and *Wet* and the word *Magical* added in a different-colored pen.

Mum said, "You wrote it. Don't you remember?"

"Yes," I lied. Something in Mum's expression told me it was important to her that I did, and besides—I ran my thumb over an inky blob made by a pen allowed to rest too long between strokes—I wanted to remember.

"You were so proud of it." She tilted her head to look at the little bundle in my hands. "You worked on it for days, crouched over on the floor beneath the dressing table in the spare room."

Now that *was* familiar. A delicious memory of being tucked in the warm, dark space withdrew itself from long-term storage and my body tingled with its release: the smell of dust in the circular rug, the crack in the plaster just large enough to store a pen, the hardness of wooden boards beneath my knees as I watched the sunlight sweep across the floor.

"You were always working on one story or another, scribbling away in the dark. Your father worried sometimes that you were going to turn out shy, that you'd never make any friends, but there was nothing we could do to dampen your enthusiasm."

I remembered reading but I didn't remember writing. Still, Mum's talk of dampening my enthusiasm struck a nerve. Distant memories of Dad shaking his head incredulously when I returned from the library, asking me over dinner why I wasn't borrowing from the nonfiction shelves, what I wanted with all that fairy nonsense, why I didn't want to learn about the real world.

"I'd forgotten that I wrote stories," I said, turning the book over and smiling at the pretend publisher's logo I'd drawn on the back.

"Well." She wiped an old crumb from the table. "Anyway, I thought you should have it. Your father's been pulling boxes down from the attic; that's how I came to find it. No point leaving it for the silverfish, is there? You never know, you may even have your own daughter to show it to one day." She straightened in her seat and the rabbit hole to the past closed behind her. "Tell me," she said. "How was your weekend? Did you do anything special?"

And there it was. The perfect window, curtains drawn wide. I couldn't have constructed a better opening for myself if I'd tried. And as I looked down at *The Book of Magical Wet Animals* in my hand, the time-dusted paper, the imprints from felt pens, the childish shading and coloring; as I realized that my mum had kept it all this time, that she'd wanted to save it despite her misgivings about my wasteful occupation, that she'd chosen today, of all days, to remind me of a part of myself I'd quite forgotten; I was overcome by a sudden swelling desire to share with her everything that had happened to me at Milderhurst Castle. A sweet sense that it would all work out for the best.

"Actually," I said. "I did."

"Oh?" She smiled brightly.

"Something very special." My heart had begun to gallop ahead; I was watching myself from the outside, wondering, even as I teetered on the cliff edge, whether I was really going to jump. "I went for a tour," said a faint voice rather like my own, "inside Milderhurst Castle."

"You . . . You what?" Mum's eyes widened. "You went to Milderhurst?" Her gaze held mine as I nodded, then it dropped. She shifted her cup on the saucer, swiveled it by its dainty handle, this way and that, and I watched with cautious curiosity, unsure what was about to happen, eager and loath, in equal measure, to find out.

I ought to have had more faith. Like a brilliant sunrise clarifying the clouded horizon, dignity reasserted itself. She lifted her head and smiled across the table as she set her saucer straight. "Well now," she said. "Milderhurst Castle. And how was it?"

"It was . . . big." I work with words and that was the best I could come up with. It was the surprise, of course, the utter transformation I'd just witnessed. "Like something out of a fairy tale."

"A tour, did you say? I didn't realize one could do such a thing. That's our modern times, I suppose." She waved a hand. "Everything for a price."

"It was informal," I said. "One of the owners took me. A very old lady called Persephone Blythe."

"Percy?" A tiny tremble in her voice, the only prick in her composure. "Percy Blythe? She's still there?"

"They all are, Mum. All three. Even Juniper, who sent you the letter."

Mum opened her mouth as if to speak; when no words came out she closed it again, tightly. She laced her fingers in her lap, sat as still and as pale as a marble statue. I sat too, but the silence took on weight and it became more than I could bear.

"It was eerie," I said, picking up my teapot. I noticed that my hands were shaking. "Everything was dusty and dim and to see them all sitting in the parlor together, the three of them in that big, old house—it felt a little like I'd stumbled inside a doll's—"

"Juniper, Edie"—Mum's voice was strange and thin and she cleared her throat—"how was she? How did she seem?"

I wondered where to start: the girlish joy, the disheveled appearance, the final scene of desperate accusations. "She was confused," I said. "She was wearing an old-fashioned dress and she told me she was waiting for someone, a man. The lady at the farmhouse where I stayed said that she isn't well, that her sisters look after her."

"She's ill?"

"Dementia. Sort of." I continued carefully: "Her boyfriend left her years ago and she never fully recovered."

"Boyfriend?"

"Fiancé to be precise. He stood her up and people say it drove her mad. Literally mad."

"Oh, Edie," said Mum. The slightly ill look on her face resolved into the sort of smile you might give a clumsy kitten. "Always so full of fancy. Real life isn't like that."

I bristled; it gets tiresome being treated like an ingénue.

"I'm just telling you what they said in the village. A lady there said Juniper was always fragile, even when she was young."

"I *knew* her, Edie; I don't need you telling me what she was like when she was young."

She'd snapped and it had caught me unawares. "I'm sorry," I said, "I—"

"No." She lifted a palm then pressed it lightly against her forehead and stole a surreptitious glance over her shoulder. "No, *I'm* sorry. I can't think what came over me." She sighed, smiled a little shakily. "It's the surprise, I expect. To think that they're all still alive, all of them at the castle. Why—they must be so *old*." She frowned, affecting great interest in the mathematical puzzle. "The other two were old when I knew them—at least they seemed that way."

I was still startled by her outburst and said guardedly, "You mean they looked old? Gray hair and all?"

"No. No, not that. It's hard to say what it was. I suppose they were only in their midthirties at the time, but of course that meant something different back then. And I was young. Children do tend to see things differently, don't they?"

I didn't answer; she didn't intend me to. Her eyes were on mine, but they had a faraway look about them, like an old-fashioned silver screen on which pictures were projected. "They behaved more like parents than sisters," she said, "to Juniper, I mean. They were a lot older than she was, and her mother had died when she was only a child. Their father was still alive, but he wasn't much involved."

"He was a writer, Raymond Blythe." I said it cautiously, wary that

I might be overstepping again, offering information that was hers firsthand. This time, though, she didn't seem to mind, and I waited for some indication that she knew all that the name meant, that she remembered bringing the book home from the library when I was a girl. I'd kept an eye out when I was packing up the flat, hoping I might be able to bring it to show her, but I hadn't found it. "He wrote a story called *The True History of the Mud Man*."

"Yes," was all she said, very softly.

"Did you ever meet him?"

She shook her head. "I saw him a few times, but only from a distance. He was very old by then and quite reclusive. He spent most of his time up in his writing tower and I wasn't allowed to go up there. It was the most important rule—there weren't many." She was looking down and a raised vein pulsed mauve beneath each eyelid. "They talked about him sometimes; he could be difficult, I think. I always thought of him as a little like King Lear, playing his daughters off, one against the other."

It was the first time I'd ever heard my mother reference a character of fiction, and the effect was to derail my train of thought entirely. I wrote my honors thesis on Shakespeare's tragedies and not once did she give any sign that she was familiar with the plays.

"Edie?" Mum, looked up sharply. "Did you tell them who you were? When you went to Milderhurst. Did you tell them about me? Percy, the others?"

"No." I wondered whether the omission would offend Mum, whether she'd demand to know why I hadn't told them the truth. "No, I didn't."

"Good," she said, nodding. "That was a good decision. Kinder. You'd only have confused them. It was such a long time ago and I was with them so briefly; they've no doubt quite forgotten I was there at all."

And here was my chance; I took it. "That's just it though, Mum. They hadn't, that is, Juniper hadn't."

"What do you mean?

"She thought I was you."

"She . . . ?" Her eyes searched mine. "How do you know?"

"She called me Meredith."

Mum's fingertips brushed her lips. "Did she . . . say anything else?"

A crossroads. A choice. And yet, it wasn't really. I had to tread lightly: if I was to tell Mum exactly what Juniper had said, that she'd accused her of breaking a promise and ruining her life, our conversation would most certainly be ended. "Not much," I said. "Were you close, the two of you?"

The man sitting behind stood up then, his considerable backside nudging our table so that everything upon it quivered. I smiled distractedly at his apology, focused instead on preventing our cups and our conversation from toppling. "Were you and Juniper friends, Mum?"

She picked up her coffee, seemed to spend a long time running her spoon around the inside of her cup to tidy the froth. "You know, it's so long ago it's difficult to remember the details." A brittle, metallic noise as the spoon hit the saucer. "As I said, I was only there a little over a year. My father came and fetched me home in early 1941."

"And you never went back?"

"That was the last I saw of Milderhurst."

She was lying. I felt hot, light-headed. "You're sure?"

A little laugh. "Edie—what a queer thing to say. Of course I'm sure. It's the sort of thing one would remember, don't you think?"

I would. I did. I swallowed. "That's just it. A funny thing happened, you see. On the weekend, when I first saw the entrance to Milderhurst—the gates at the bottom of the drive—I had the most extraordinary sense that I'd been there before." When she said nothing, I pressed: "That I'd been there with you."

Her silence was excruciating and I was aware suddenly of the murmur of café noise around us, the jarring thwack of the coffee basket being emptied, the grinder whirring, shrill laughter somewhere on the mezzanine. I seemed to be hearing it all at one remove, though, as if Mum and I were quite separate, encased within our own bubble.

I tried to keep the tremor from my voice. "When I was a kid. We drove there, you and I, and we stood at the gates. It was hot and there was a lake and I wanted to swim, but we didn't go inside. You said it was too late."

Mum patted her napkin to her lips, slowly, delicately, then looked at me. Just for a moment I thought I glimpsed the light of confession in her eyes, then she blinked and it was gone. "You're imagining things."

I shook my head slowly.

"All those gates look alike," she continued. "You've seen a picture somewhere, sometime—a film—and become confused."

"But I *remember*—"

"I'm sure it seems that way. Just like when you accused Mr. Watson from next door of being a Russian spy, or the time you became convinced you were adopted—we had to show you your birth certificate, do you remember?" Her voice had taken on a note I recalled only too well from my childhood. The infuriating certainty of someone sensible, respectable, powerful; someone who wouldn't listen no matter how loudly I spoke. "Your father had me take you to the doctor about the night terrors."

"This is different."

She smiled briskly. "You're fanciful, Edie. You always have been. I don't know where you get it from—not from me. *Certainly* not from your father." She reached down to reclaim her handbag from the floor. "Speaking of whom, I ought to be getting home."

"But, Mum—" I could feel the chasm opening between us. A gust of desperation spurred me on. "You haven't even finished your coffee."

She glanced at her cup, the cooling gray dribble at the bottom. "I've had enough."

"I'll get you another, my shout—"

"No," she said. "What do I owe you for the first?"

"Nothing, Mum. Please stay."

"No." She laid a five-pound note by my saucer. "I've been out all morning and your father's by himself. You know what he's like: he'll have the house dismantled if I don't get back soon."

A press of her cheek, clammy against mine, and she was gone.

A Suitable Strip Club and Pandora's Box

For the record it was Auntie Rita who made contact with me, not the other way round. It so happened that while I was floundering, trying without success to find out what had happened between Mum and Juniper Blythe, Auntie Rita was getting revved up to host a hen night for my cousin Samantha. I wasn't sure whether to be offended or flattered when she phoned the office to ask me the name of an upmarket male strip club, so I went with bemused, and ultimately, because I can't seem to help myself, useful. I told her I didn't know off the top of my head but that I'd do some research, and we agreed to meet in secret at her salon the following Sunday so I could pass on my reconnaissance. It meant skipping Mum's roast again, but it was the only time Rita was free; I told Mum I was helping with Sam's wedding and she couldn't really argue.

Classy Cuts squats behind a tiny shopfront on the Old Kent Road, breath held to fit between an indie record outlet and the best fish and chips shop in Southwark. Rita's as old-school as the Motown records she collects and her salon does a roaring trade specializing in finger waves, beehives, and blue rinses for the bingo set. She's been around long enough to be retro without realizing it and likes to tell anyone who'll listen how she started out at the very same salon as a skinny sixteen-year-old when the war was still raging; how she'd watched through those very front windows on VE Day when Mr. Harvey from the milliner's across the road stripped off his clothes and started dancing down the street, nothing to know him by but his finest hat.

Fifty years in the one spot. It's no wonder she's wildly popular in her part of Southwark, the busy chattering stalls set apart from the glistening dress circle of Docklands. Some of her oldest clients have known her since the closest she got to a pair of scissors was the broom cupboard out back, and now there's no one else they'd trust to set their lavender perms. "People aren't daft," Auntie Rita says, "give 'em a bit of love and they'll never stray." She has an uncanny knack for picking winners from the local racing form, too, which can't be bad for business.

I don't know much about siblings, but I'm quite sure no two sisters have ever been less alike. Mum is reserved, Rita is not; Mum favors neat-as-a-pin court shoes, Rita serves breakfast in heels; Mum is a locked vault when it comes to family stories, Rita is the willing font of all knowledge. I know this firsthand. When I was nine and Mum went to the hospital to have her gallstones removed, Dad packed me a bag and sent me to Rita's. I'm not sure whether my aunt somehow intuited that the sapling in the doorway was way out of touch with her roots, or whether I besieged her with questions, or whether she just saw it as a chance to aggravate Mum and strike a blow in an ancient war, but she took it upon herself that week to fill in many blanks.

She showed me yellowed photographs on the wall, told me funny stories of the way things had been when she was my age, and painted a vivid picture with colors and smells and long-ago voices that made me starkly aware of something I'd already opaquely known. The house where I lived, the family in which I was growing up, was a sanitary, lonely place. I remember lying on the small spare mattress at Rita's house as my four cousins filled the room with their soft snores and fidgety sleep noises, wishing she were my mother instead, that I lived in a warm, cluttered house stretching at the seams with siblings and old stories. I remember, too, the instant rush of liquid guilt as the thought formed in my mind, screwing my eyes tight shut and picturing my disloyal wish as a piece of knotted silk, untying it in my mind, then conjuring a wind to blow it away as if it had never been.

But it had.

Anyway. It was early July and hot the day I reported in, the sort of hot you carry in your lungs. I knocked on the glass door and, as I did so, caught a glimpse of my own tired reflection. Let me just say, carving out sofa real estate with a flatulent dog does nothing for one's complexion. I peered beyond the CLOSED sign and saw Auntie Rita sitting at a card table in the back, cigarette dangling from her bottom lip as she examined something small and white in her hands. She waved me in. "Edie, luvvie," she said over the welcome bell and the Supremes, "lend me your eyes, will you, poppet?"

It's a little like stepping back in time, visiting Auntie Rita's shop. The black-and-white checkerboard tiles, the bank of vinyl chairs with lime-green cushions, the old-fashioned cone-shaped hair dryers on retractable arms. Posters of Marvin Gaye and Diana Ross and the Temptations framed behind glass. The unchanging smell of peroxide and next door's chip grease, locked in mortal combat.

"I've been trying to thread this blasted thing through there and there," Rita said around her cigarette, "but as if it's not bad enough that my fingers have turned to thumbs, the bloody ribbon's upped and grown a mind of its own."

She thrust it towards me and with a bit of squinting I realized it was a small lacy bag with holes in the top where a drawstring should be.

"They're favors for Sam's hens," Auntie Rita said, nodding at a box of identical bags by her feet. "Well, they will be once we've made 'em up and filled 'em with goodies." She dumped the ash from her cigarette. "Kettle's just boiled, but I've got some lemonade in the fridge if you'd rather?"

My throat contracted at the mere suggestion. "I'd love one."

It's not a word you'd normally think to associate with your mother's sister, but it's true so I'll say it: she's saucy, my auntie Rita. Watching her as she poured our lemonades, rounded bottom stretching her skirt in all the right places, waist still small despite four babies more than thirty years ago, I could well believe the few anecdotes I'd gleaned from Mum over the years. Without exception these had been delivered in the form of warnings about the things good girls didn't do; however they'd had a rather unintended effect: cementing for me the admirable legend of Auntie Rita, rabble-rouser.

"Here you are then, luvvie." She handed me a martini glass spitting bubbles and harrumphed into her own chair, prodding at her beehive with both sets of fingers. "Phew," she said, "what a day. Lord—you look as tired as I feel!"

I swallowed a glorious lemon sip, fierce bubbles singeing my throat. The Temptations started crooning "My Girl" and I said, "I didn't think you opened Sundays."

"I don't, not as a habit, but one of my old dears needed a rinse and set for a funeral—not her own, mercifully—and I didn't have the heart to turn her away. You do what you must, don't you? Like family, some of them." She inspected the bag I'd threaded, tightened the drawstring, loosened it again, long pink fingernails clacking together. "Good girl. Only twenty more to go."

I saluted as she handed me another.

"Anyway, gives me a chance to get a bit of work in for the wedding, away from prying eyes." She widened her own briefly before narrowing them like shutters. "That Sam of mine's a nosy one, always was, even as a girl. Used to scale the cupboards looking for where I'd stashed the Christmas goodies, then she'd dazzle her brothers and sisters by guessing what was wrapped beneath the tree." She drew a fresh cigarette from the packet on the table, said, "Little beggar," and struck a match. The cigarette tip flared hopefully then settled. "How about you then? Young girl like you oughta have better things to be doing with her Sunday."

"Better than this?" I held up my second little white bag, ribbon in place. "What could be better than this?"

"Cheeky mare," she said, and her smile reminded me of Gran in a way that Mum's never does. I'd adored Gran with a might that belied any suspicions I'd had growing up that I must surely be adopted. She'd lived alone for as long as I'd known her, and though, as she was quick to point out, she'd had her share of offers, she refused to remarry and be an old man's slave when she knew what it was to be a young man's darling. There was a lid for each pot, she'd told me often and soberly, and she thanked God she'd found her lid in my grandfather. I never met Gran's husband, Mum's father, not that I remembered: he died when I was three and on the few occasions I thought to ask about him, Mum, with her distaste for rehashing the past, had always been quick to skim the subject's surface. Rita, thank goodness, had been more forthcoming. "So," she said, "how'd you get on then?"

"I got on very well." I rummaged inside my bag for my notes, unfolded them, and read out the name Sarah had given me: "The Roxy Club. Phone number's on here, too." Auntie Rita wriggled her fingers at me and I handed her the paper. She puckered her lips as tight as the top of the little drawstring bags. "The Roxy Club," she repeated. "And it's a nice place? Classy?"

"According to my sources."

"Good girl." She refolded the paper, tucked it into her bra strap, and winked at me. "Your turn next, eh, Edie?"

"What's that?"

"Down the aisle."

I smiled weakly, lifted a shoulder to flick away the comment.

"How long's it been now, you and your fellow—six, is it?"

"Seven."

"Seven years." She cocked her head. "He'd be wanting to make an honest woman of you soon else you'll be getting the itch and moving on. Doesn't he know what a fine catch he's got? You want me to have a good talk to him?"

Even if not for the fact that I was trying to conceal a breakup, it was a scary thought. "Actually, Auntie Rita"—I wondered how best to put her off without revealing too much—"I'm not sure either one of us is the marrying kind."

She drew on her cigarette, one eye narrowing slightly as she considered me. "That right?"

"Afraid so." This was a lie. Partly. I was, and remain, most definitely the marrying kind. My acceptance, throughout our relationship, of Jamie's sneering skepticism towards wedded bliss was at complete odds with my naturally romantic sensibilities. I offer no defense other than to say that, in my experience, when you love someone you'll do just about anything to keep them.

On the back of a slow exhalation Rita's gaze seemed to shift gears, from disbelief, through perplexity, arriving finally at weary acceptance. "Well, maybe you've got the right idea. It just happens to you, life, you know; happens while you're not watching. You meet someone, you go riding in his car, you marry him and have a batch of children. Then one day you realize you've got nothing in common. You know you used to, you must have—why else would you have married the fellow?—but the sleepless nights, the disappointments, the worry. The shock of having more life behind than in front. Well"—she smiled at me as if she'd given me a recipe for pie rather than the desire to stick my head in an oven—"that's life, isn't it?"

"That's glorious, Auntie Rita. Make sure you put that in your wedding speech."

"Cheeky thing."

With Auntie Rita's pep talk still hanging in the smoky haze, we each engaged in private struggle with a tiny white bag. The record player kept spinning, Rita hummed as a man with a molten voice urged us to take a good look at his smile, and finally I could stand it no longer. Much as I enjoy seeing Rita, I'd come with an ulterior motive. Mum and I had barely spoken since our meeting at the patisserie; I'd canceled our next scheduled coffee date, pleading a backlog at work, and even found myself screening her phone calls when she rang my machine. I suppose my feelings were hurt. Does it sound hopelessly juvenile to say so? I hope not, because it's true. Mum's continued refusal to trust me, her adamant denial that we'd visited the castle gates, her insistence that it was *I* who had invented the whole thing, caused a small spot inside my chest to ache and made me more determined than ever to learn the truth. And now I'd skipped the family roast again, put Mum's nose even further out of joint, ventured across town in shoe-melting heat: I wouldn't, I couldn't, I *mustn't* leave without some gold. "Auntie Rita?" I said.

"Hmm?" She scowled at the ribbon that had knotted itself in her fingers.

"There's something I wanted to talk to you about."

"Hmm?"

"About Mum."

A look so sharp it scratched. "She all right?"

"Oh yes, fine. It's nothing like that. I've just been thinking a bit about the past."

"Ah. That's different then, isn't it, the past. Which particular bit of the past were you thinking of?"

"The war."

She set down her little bag. "Well now."

I proceeded with caution. Auntie Rita loves to talk but this, I knew, was a touchy subject. "You were evacuated, you and Mum and Uncle Ed."

"We were. Briefly. Ghastly experience it was, too. All that talk of clean air? Load of bollocks. No one tells you about the stink of the countryside, the piles of steaming shite every place you care to tread. And they called us dirty! I've never been able to look at cows or country folk the same way since; couldn't wait to get back and take my chances with the bombs."

"How about Mum? Did she feel the same way?"

A swift, suspicious flicker. "Why? What's she told you?"

"Nothing. She's told me nothing."

Rita returned her attention to the little white bag, but there was a self-consciousness in her downturned eyes. I could almost see her biting her tongue to stop the flow of things she wanted to say but suspected she shouldn't.

Disloyalty burned in my veins but I knew it was my best chance. Each of my next words singed a little: "You know what she's like."

Auntie Rita sniffed sharply and caught the whiff of allegiance.

She pursed her lips and regarded me sidelong a moment before inclining her head towards mine. "She loved it, your mum. Didn't want to come home again." Bewilderment glistened in her eyes and I knew I'd struck an old and aching nerve. "What kind of a child doesn't want to be with her own parents, her own people? What kind of a child would rather stay with another family?"

A child who felt out of place, I thought, remembering my own guilty whispers into the dark corners of my cousins' bedroom. A child who felt as if they were stuck somewhere they didn't belong. But I didn't say anything. I had a feeling that for someone like my aunt who'd had the good fortune to find herself exactly where she fitted, no explanation would make sense. "Maybe she was frightened of the bombs," I said eventually. My voice was rocky and I coughed a little to clear the gravel. "The Blitz?"

"Pah. She wasn't frightened, no more than the rest of us. Other kids wanted to be back in the thick of things. All the kids in our street came home, went down into the shelters together. Your uncle?" Rita's eyes took on a reverence befitting the mention of my feted Uncle Ed. "Thumbed his way back from Kent, he did; he was that keen to get home once the action started. Arrived on the doorstep in the middle of a raid, just in time to shepherd the simple lad from next door to safety. But not Merry, oh no. She was the opposite. Wouldn't come home until our dad went down there himself and dragged her back. Our mum, your gran, she never got over it. Never said as much, that wasn't her way, she pretended like she was glad Merry was safe and sound in the countryside, but we knew. We weren't blind."

I couldn't meet my aunt's fierce gaze: I felt tarred by the brush of disloyalty, guilty by association. Mum's betrayal of Rita was real still, an enmity that burned across the fifty-year gulf between then and now. "When was that?" I said, starting on a new white bag, innocent as you please. "How long had she been away?"

Auntie Rita drilled her bottom lip with a long baby-pink talon, a butterfly painted on the tip. "Let me see now, the bombs had been going awhile but it wasn't winter because my dad brought primroses back with him; he was that keen to soften your gran up, make everything go as easy as it could. That was Dad." The fingernail tapped a thinking rhythm. "Must've been sometime in 1941. March, April, thereabouts."

She'd been honest in that, then. Mum had been gone for just over a year and had come home from Milderhurst six months before Juniper Blythe suffered the heartbreak that destroyed her, before Thomas Cavill promised to marry her, then left her stranded. "Did she ever—"

A blast of "Hot Shoe Shuffle" drowned me out. Auntie Rita's novelty stiletto telephone jittered away on the counter.

Don't answer it, I pleaded silently, desperate that nothing be allowed to disturb our conversation now that it was finally up and flying.

"That's as like to be Sam," said Rita, "spying on me."

I nodded and the two of us sat out the last few bars, after which I wasted no time steering us back on track. "Did Mum ever talk about her time at Milderhurst? About the people she'd been staying with? The Blythe sisters?"

Rita's eyes rolled like a pair of marbles. "It was all she'd talk about at first. Gave us the pip, I can tell you. Only time I saw her looking happy was when a letter arrived from that place. All secretive she was; refused to open them until she was alone."

I remembered Mum's account of being left by Rita in the evacuation line at the hall in Kent. "You and she weren't close as kids."

"We were sisters—there'd have been something wrong if we didn't fight now and then, living on top of each other like we did in Mum and Dad's little house . . . We got on all right, though. Until the war, that is, until she met that lot." Rita speared the last cigarette from the packet, lit up, and shot a jet of smoke doorwards. "She was different after she got back, and not just the way she spoke. She'd got all sorts of ideas, up there in her castle."

"What kind of ideas?" I asked, but I already knew. A defensiveness had crept into Rita's voice that I recognized: the hurt of a person who feels themselves to have suffered by unfair comparison.

"Ideas." The pink fingernails of one hand frisked the air near her beehive and I feared she'd said all she was going to. She contemplated the door, lips moving as they chewed over the various answers she could give. After what seemed an age, she met my eyes again. The cassette had finished and the salon was unusually quiet; rather, the absence of music gave the building space to hiss and creak, to complain wearily about the heat, the smell, the slow toll of the passing years. Auntie Rita set her chin and spoke in a slow, clear voice: "She came back a snob. There, I've said it. She went away one of us and she came back a snob."

Something I'd always sensed was made solid: my dad, the way he felt about my aunt and cousins and even my gran, hushed conversations between him and Mum, my own observations of the different ways things were done at our place and at Rita's. Mum and Dad were snobs and I felt embarrassed for them and embarrassed for me, and then, confusingly, angry with Rita for saying it and ashamed of myself for encouraging her to do so. My vision blurred as I pretended to focus on the white bag I was threading.

Auntie Rita, conversely, was lightened. Relief spilled across her face and seemed to radiate beyond. The untold truth was a wound that had waited decades for someone to lance. "Book learning," Rita spat, crushing her cigarette butt, "that's all she wanted to talk about once she got back. Walked into our house, turned her nose up at the small rooms and our dad's laboring songs, and took up residence at the lending library. Hid in corners with one book or another when she should've been helping out. Talked a lot of bosh about writing for the newspapers, too. Sent things off and all! Can you imagine?"

My mouth actually fell open. Meredith Burchill did not write; she certainly did not send things off to the newspapers. I'd have assumed Rita was embellishing, only the news was so perfectly confounding it simply had to be true. "Were they published?"

"Of course not! And that's just what I'm saying: that's the sort of mumbo jumbo they put in her head. Gave her ideas above her station, they did, and there's only one place those ideas take you."

"What were they like, the things she wrote? What were they about?"

"I wouldn't know. She never showed them to me. Probably thought I wouldn't understand. Anyway, I wouldn't have had the time: I'd met Bill by then, and I'd started here. There was a war on, you know." Rita laughed, but sourness deepened the lines around her mouth; I'd never noticed them before.

"Did any of the Blythes come to visit Mum in London?"

Rita shrugged. "Merry was awful secretive once she got back, ducking off on errands without saying where she was going. She could've been meeting anyone."

Was it something in the way she said it, the shadow of insinuation clinging to her words? Or was it the way she glanced away from me as she spoke? I'm not sure. Whatever the case, I knew immediately that there was more to her comment than met the eye. "Like who?"

Rita squinted at the box of lace bags, inclining her head as if there'd never been anything as interesting as the way they sat together in little white and silver rows.

"Auntie Ri-ta?" I dragged it out. "Who else would she have been meeting?"

"Oh, all right." She folded her arms so that her boobs perked together, then looked directly at me. "He was a teacher, or he had been before the war, back at Elephant and Castle." She made a show of fanning her peachy cleavage. "Ooh-la-la. Very good-looking, he was—he and his brother both: like film stars, those strong, silent types. His family lived a few streets over from us and even your gran used to find a reason to come out on the step when he was passing by. All the young girls had crushes on him, including your mum.

"Anyway," Rita continued with another shrug, "one day I saw them together."

You know that expression "her eyes goggled"? Mine did. "What?" I said. "Where? How?"

"I followed her." Justification trounced any embarrassment or guilt she might have felt. "She was my little sister, she wasn't behaving normally, it was a dangerous time. I was just making sure she was all right."

I couldn't have cared less *why* she followed Mum; I wanted to know what she'd seen. "But where were they? What were they doing?"

"I only saw from a distance but it was enough. They were sitting together on the grass in the park, side by side, tight as you please. He was talking and she was listening—real intent, you know—then she handed him something and he . . ." Rita rattled her empty packet of cigarettes. "Bloody things. I swear they smoke themselves."

"Auntie Ri-ta!"

A brisk sigh. "They kissed. She and Mr. Cavill, right there in the park for all the world to see."

Worlds collided, fireworks exploded, little stars shot up the black corners of my mind. "Mr. *Cavill*?"

"Keep up, Edie, luvvie: your mum's teacher, Tommy Cavill."

Words were beyond me, words that made any sense. I must've made some sort of noise because Rita held a hand to her ear and said, "What's that?" but I couldn't manage it a second time. My mother, my teenage mother, had sneaked away from home for secret meetings with her teacher, Juniper Blythe's fiancé, a man she'd had a crush on, meetings that involved the handing over of items and, more to the point, kissing. And all this had happened in the months leading up to his desertion of Juniper.

"You look peaky, love. Would you like another lemonade?"

I nodded; she fetched; I gulped.

"You know, if you're so interested you should read your mum's letters from the castle yourself."

"Which letters?"

"The ones she wrote back to London."

"She'd never let me."

Rita inspected a dye-stain on her wrist. "She wouldn't need to know."

My look, I'm sure, said, *Huh?*

"They were among Mum's things," Rita explained, "came to me after she passed away. Kept them all those years, the sentimental old girl, never matter that they hurt her so. Superstitious, she was, didn't believe in throwing letters away. I'll dig 'em out, eh?"

"Oh . . . I don't know, I'm not sure that I should—"

"They're letters," said Rita, with a dip of her chin that made me feel daft in a Pollyanna sort of way. "They were written to be read, weren't they?"

I nodded. Tentatively.

"Might help you to understand what it was your mum was thinking up there in her fancy castle."

The thought of reading Mum's letters without her knowledge plucked at my guilt strings, but I silenced them. Rita was right: the letters might have been written by Mum, but they'd been addressed to her family back in London. Rita had every right to pass them on to me, and I had every right to read them.

"Yes," I said, only it sounded more like a squeak. "Yes, please."

The Weight of the Waiting Room

AND because that's the way life seems to work sometimes, it was while I sat unpicking Mum's secrets with the sister from whom she most wished to keep them that my dad had his heart attack.

Herbert was waiting with the message when I got home from Rita's; he took both my hands and told me what had happened. "I'm terribly sorry," he said, "I'd have let you know sooner only I didn't know how."

"Oh . . ." Panic throbbed in my chest. I pivoted towards the door, then back. "Is he——?"

"He's at the hospital; stable, I believe. Your mother didn't say much."

"I should——"

"Yes. Come on; I'll hail you a cab."

I MADE small talk with the driver all the way. A short man with very blue eyes and brown hair beginning to rust towards silver, a father of three young children. And while he told stories of their mischief and shook his head with that mask of mock exasperation parents of small children adopt to degloss their pride, I smiled and asked questions, and my voice sounded ordinary, light even. We came closer to the hospital, and it wasn't until I'd handed him a tenner and told him to keep the change and to enjoy his daughter's dance recital that I realized it had started to rain and I was standing on the pavement outside the hospital in Hammersmith without an umbrella, watching a cab disappear into the dusk while my father lay somewhere inside, his heart all broken.

MUM LOOKED smaller than usual, alone at one end of a bank of plastic chairs, drab blue hospital wall glooming over her shoulder. She's always well turned out, my mum, dressing from a different age: hats and gloves that match, shoes kept swaddled in their shop boxes, a shelf full of different handbags jostling together, awaiting promotion to complete the day's outfit. She wouldn't dream of setting foot outside the house without her powder and lipstick in place, even when her husband's gone ahead in an ambulance. What a loping disappointment I must be, inches too tall, far too frizzy, lips stained with whichever gloss I happen to excavate first from the detritus of loose change, dusty breath mints, and random stuff that lives in the depths of my faded tote.

"Mum." I went straight to her, kissed a cheek made deathly cool by the air-conditioning, and slid into the bucket seat beside her. "How is he?"

She shook her head and fear of the worst lodged lumplike in my throat. "They haven't said. All sorts of machines, doctors coming and going." She let her lids fall briefly closed. She was still shaking her head, softly, from habit. "I don't know."

I swallowed hard and decided not knowing was preferable to knowing the worst, but I thought better of sharing this platitude. I wanted to say something original and reassuring, something to alleviate her worry, make it all okay, but Mum and I had no experience down this road of suffering and consolation, so I said nothing.

She opened her eyes and looked at me, reached to hook a fuzzy curl behind my ear, and I wondered whether perhaps it didn't matter, that she knew already what I was thinking, how earnestly I wanted to make it better. That there was no need to say anything because we were family, mother and daughter, and some things were understood without being spoken—

"You look dreadful," she said.

I stole a sideways glance and caught my shadowy reflection in a glossy National Health Service poster. "It's raining out."

"Such a big bag," she said with a wistful smile, "and no room for a little umbrella."

I shook my head lightly and it turned into a shiver, and I realized suddenly that I was cold.

YOU HAVE to do something in hospital waiting rooms or else you find yourself waiting, which can lead to thinking, which in my experience can be a bad idea. As I sat silently beside my mum, worrying about my dad, making a note to buy an umbrella, listening to the wall clock sweep away the seconds, a horde of lurking thoughts seeped along the wall to brush my shoulders with their tapered fingers. Before I knew what was happening, they'd taken my hand and led me places I hadn't been for years.

I was standing against the wall of our bathroom, watching my four-year-old self tightrope-walk along the bathtub. The little naked girl wants to run away with the Gypsies. She's not sure exactly who they are, or where to seek them, but knows they're her best bet for finding a circus to join. That's her dream and it's why she's practicing her balancing act. She's almost across to the other side when she slips. Falls forwards, winds herself, lands with her face beneath the water. Sirens, bright lights, strange faces . . .

I blinked and the image dispersed, only to be replaced by another. A funeral, my gran's. I'm sitting in the front pew beside my mum and dad, only half listening as the rector describes a different woman from the one I knew. I'm distracted by my shoes. They're new, and although I know I should be listening better, focusing on the casket, thinking serious thoughts, I can't stop looking at those patent leather shoes, turning them back and forth to admire the sheen. My dad notices, shoulders me gently, and I wrestle my attention forwards. There are two pictures on top of the coffin: one of the Gran I knew, the other of a stranger, a young woman sitting on a beach somewhere, leaning away from the camera, smile hooked as if she were about to open her mouth and make a quip at the cameraman's expense. The minister says something then and Auntie Rita starts to wail, mascara spilling black across her cheeks, and I watch my mum expectantly, waiting for a matched response. Her gloved hands are folded in her lap, her attention is fixed on the casket, but nothing happens. Nothing happens and I catch my cousin Samantha's eyes. She has been watching my mum too and I am suddenly ashamed . . .

I stood decisively, catching the black thoughts by surprise and sending them scuttling to the floor. My pockets were deep and I plunged my hands down to their seams firmly enough to convince myself I had a purpose, then I paced the corridor paying museum attention to the faded posters touting immunization schedules that were two years out of date; anything to stay here and now and far away from then.

I turned another corner into a brightly lit alcove and found a hot-drinks machine nudging the wall. The sort with a platform for the cup and a nozzle that shoots out chocolate powder, coffee granules, or boiling water, depending on your predilection. There were teabags in a plastic tray and I draped a couple into Styrofoam cups, one for Mum and one for me. I watched awhile as the bags bled rusty ribbons into the water, then took my time over stirring in the powdered milk, letting the grains dissolve fully before carrying them back down the corridor.

Mum took hers wordlessly, used an index finger to catch a drip as it rolled down the side. She held the warm cup between her hands but didn't drink. I sat beside her and thought about nothing. Tried to think about nothing while my brain ticked ahead of me, wondering how it was I had so few memories of my dad. Real ones, not the sort stolen from photographs and family stories.

"I was angry with him," Mum said finally. "I raised my voice. I'd finished the roast and laid it on the table for carving and even though it was getting cool sitting out, I decided that it would serve him right to eat a cold dinner. I thought about going to fetch him myself, but I was sick and tired of calling to no avail. I thought: see how you like a cold roast." She rolled her lips together the way people do when the threat of tears makes talking difficult and they're hoping to cover the fact. "He'd been up in the roof again all afternoon, pulling down boxes, cluttering the hallway—God knows how they'll get back up again, he'll be in no fit state—" She looked, unseeing, into her tea. "He'd gone into the bathroom to wash before dinner and that's where it happened. I found him lying beside the tub, right where you fainted that time, when you were small. He'd been washing his hands, there was soap all over them."

Silence ensued and I itched to fill it. There's something reassuring about conversation; its ordered pattern provides an anchor to the real world: nothing terrible or unexpected can happen, surely, when the rational exchange of dialogue is taking place. "And so you called the ambulance." I prompted her, my tone that of a nursery-school teacher.

"They came quickly; that was lucky. I sat with him and wiped the soap away, and then it seemed that they were there. Two of them, a man and a woman. They had to do CPR, and use one of those electric-shock machines."

"A defibrillator," I said.

"And they gave him something, some medicine to dissolve any clots." She studied her upturned hands. "He was still wearing his undershirt, and I remember thinking I should go and bring him a clean one." She shook her head and I wasn't sure whether it was with regret that she hadn't, or astonishment that such a thing had occurred to her while her husband lay unconscious on the floor, and I decided that it didn't really matter right now and that I was in no position to judge anyway. Don't think it had escaped my notice that I'd have been there to help if I hadn't been probing Auntie Rita at the time, lifting stories from my mum's past.

A doctor came down the corridor towards us and Mum knotted

her fingers. I half stood, but he didn't slow, striding across the waiting room to disappear through another door.

"Won't be long now, Mum." The weight of unspoken apology curled my words and I felt utterly helpless.

THERE'S ONLY one photograph from my mum and dad's wedding. I mean, presumably there are more, gathering dust somewhere in a forgotten white album, but there's only one image I know of that's survived the passage of years.

It's just the two of them in it, not one of those typical wedding photos where the bride and groom's families fan out in either direction providing wings to the couple in the center, unbalanced wings so you suspect the creature would never be able to fly. In this photo their mismatched families have melted away and it's just the two of them, and the way she's staring at his face it's like she's enraptured. As if he glows, which he sort of does: an effect of the old lights photographers used back then, I suppose.

And he's so impossibly young, they both are; he still has hair, right across the top of his head, and no idea that it's not going to stick around. No idea that he will have a son, then lose him; that his future daughter will so bewilder him and that his wife will come to ignore him, that one day his heart will seize up and he'll be taken to the hospital in an ambulance and that same wife will sit in the waiting room with the daughter he can't understand, waiting for him to wake up.

None of that is present in the photo, not even a hint. That photo is a frozen moment; their whole future lies unknown and ahead, just as it should. But at the same time, the future *is* in that photo, a version of it at any rate. It's in their eyes, hers especially. For the photographer has captured more than two young people on their wedding day, he's captured a threshold being crossed, an ocean wave at the precise moment before it turns to foam and begins its crash towards the ground. And the young woman, my mum, is seeing more than just the young man standing beside her, the fellow she's in love with, she's seeing their whole life together, stretching out ahead . . .

Then again, perhaps I'm romanticizing; perhaps she's just admiring his hair, or looking forward to the reception, or the honeymoon . . . You create your own fiction around photos like that, images that become iconic within a family, and I realized as I sat there in the hospital that there was only one way, of knowing for sure how she'd felt, what she'd hoped for when she looked at him that way, whether her life was more complicated, her past more complex, than her sweet expression suggests. And all I had to do was ask; strange that I'd never thought of it before. I suppose it's the light on my father's face that's to blame. The way Mum's looking at him draws the attention his way, so it's easy to dismiss her as a young and innocent girl of unremarkable origins whose life is only just now beginning. It was a myth Mum had done her best to propagate, I realized; for whenever she spoke of their lives before they met it was always my dad's stories she told.

But as I conjured the image to mind, fresh from my visit to Rita, it was Mum's face I brought into focus, back in the shadows, a little smaller than his. Was it possible that the young woman with the wide eyes had a secret? That a decade before her wedding to the solid, glowing man beside her, she'd enjoyed a furtive love affair with her schoolteacher, a man engaged to her older friend? She'd have been fifteen or so at the time, and Meredith Burchill was certainly not the kind of woman to have a teenage love affair, but what about Meredith Baker? When I was growing up, one of Mum's favorite lectures was on the sorts of things good girls did not do: was it possible she'd been speaking from experience?

I was sunk then by the sense that I knew everything and nothing of the person sitting next to me. The woman in whose body I had grown and whose house I'd been raised was in some vital ways a stranger to me; I'd gone thirty years without ascribing her any more dimension than the paper dollies I'd played with as a girl, with the pasted-on smiles and the folding-tab dresses. What was more, I'd spent the past few months recklessly seeking to unlock her deepest secrets when I'd never really bothered to ask her much about the rest. Sitting there in the hospital, though, as Dad lay in an emergency bed somewhere, it suddenly seemed very important that I learn more about them. About her. The mysterious woman who made allusions to Shakespeare, who'd once sent articles to newspapers for publication.

"Mum?"

"Hmm?"

"How did you and Dad meet?"

Her voice was brittle from lack of use and she cleared her throat before saying, "At the cinema. A screening of *The Holly and the Ivy*. You know that."

A silence.

"What I mean is, *how* did you meet? Did you see him? Did he see you? Who spoke first?"

"Oh, Edie, I can't remember. Him; no, me. I forget." She moved the fingers of one hand a little, like a puppeteer dangling stars on strings. "We were the only two there. Imagine that."

A look had come upon Mum's face as we spoke, a distance, but a fond one, a release almost from the discombobulating present, where her husband was clinging to life in a nearby room. "Was he handsome?" I prodded gently. "Was it love at first sight?"

"Hardly. I mistook him for a murderer at first."

"What? *Dad?*"

I don't think she even heard me, so lost was she in her own memory. "It's spooky being in a cinema by yourself. All those rows of empty seats, the darkened room, the enormous screen. It's designed to be a communal experience and the effect when it's not is uncannily detaching. Anything could happen when it's dark."

"Did he sit right by you?"

"Oh no. He kept a polite distance—he's a gentleman, your father—but we started talking afterwards, in the foyer. He'd been expecting someone to meet him—"

"A woman?"

She paid undue attention to the fabric of her skirt and said, with gentle reproach, "Oh, Edie."

"I'm only asking."

"I believe it was a woman, but she didn't show. And that"—Mum pressed her hands against her knees, lifted her head with a delicate sniff—"was that. He asked me out to tea and I accepted. We went to the Lyons Corner House in the Strand. I had a slice of pear cake and I remember thinking it was very fancy."

I smiled. "And he was your first boyfriend?"

Did I imagine the hesitation? "Yes."

"You stole another woman's boyfriend." I was teasing, trying to keep things light, but the moment I said it I thought of Juniper Blythe and Thomas Cavill and my cheeks burned. I was too flustered by my own faux pas to pay much attention to Mum's reaction, hurrying on before she had time to reply. "How old were you then?"

"Twenty-five. It was 1952 and I'd just turned twenty-five."

I nodded like I was doing the math in my head, when really I was listening to the little voice that whispered: *Might this not be a good time, seeing as we're on the subject, to ask a little more about Thomas Cavill?* Wicked little voice and shameful of me to pay it any heed; while I'm not proud of it, the opportunity was just too tempting. I told myself I was taking my mum's mind off Dad's condition, and with barely a pause, I said, "Twenty-five. That's sort of late for a first boyfriend, isn't it?"

"Not really." She said it quickly. "It was a different time. I had been busy with other things."

"But then you met Dad."

"Yes."

"And you fell in love."

Her voice was so soft I read her lips rather than heard her when she said, "Yes."

"Was he your first love, Mum?"

She inhaled a sharp little breath and her face looked as if I'd slapped her. "Edie—don't!"

So. Auntie Rita had been right; he wasn't.

"Don't talk about him in the past tense like that." Tears were brimming over the folds around her eyes. And I felt as bad as if I had slapped her, especially when she started to weep quietly against my shoulder, leaking more than crying, because crying isn't something she does. And although my arm was pressed hard against the plastic edge of the chair, I didn't move a muscle.

OUTSIDE, THE distant tide of traffic continued to drift, in and out, punctuated occasionally by sirens. There's something about hospital walls; though only made of bricks and plaster, when you're inside them the noise, the reality of the teeming city beyond, disappears; it's just outside the door, but it might as well be a magical land, far, far away. Like Milderhurst, it occurred to me; I'd experienced the same dislocation there, an overwhelming sense of envelopment as I passed through the front door, as if the world without had turned to grains of sand and fallen away. I wondered vaguely what the Sisters Blythe were doing, how they'd filled their days in the weeks since I'd left them, the three of them together in that great, dark castle. My imaginings came one after the other, a series of snapshots: Juniper drifting the corridors in her grubbied silk dress; Saffy appearing from nowhere to lead her gently back; Percy frowning by the attic window, surveying her estate like a ship's captain keeping watch . . .

Midnight passed, the duty nurses shuffled, new faces brought with them the same old banter. Laughing and bustling around the illuminated medical station: an irresistible beacon of normality, an island across an unpassable sea. I tried to doze, using my bag as a pillow, but it was no use. My mum, beside me, was so small and alone, and older somehow than the last time I'd seen her, and I couldn't stop my mind from racing ahead to paint detailed scenes of her life without Dad. I saw it so clearly: his empty armchair, the quiet meals, the cessation of all DIY hammering. How lonely the house would be, how still, how swamped by echoes.

It would be just the two of us if we lost my dad. Two is not a large number; it leaves no reserves. It's a quiet number that makes for neat and simple conversations where interruption is not required, is not really possible. Or necessary, for that matter. Was that our future, I wondered? The two of us passing sentences back and forth, speaking around our opinions, making polite noises and telling half-truths and keeping up appearances? The notion was unbearable and I felt, suddenly, very, very alone.

It's when I'm at my loneliest that I miss my brother most of all. He would be a man by now, with an easy manner and a kind smile and a knack for cheering our mother up. The Daniel in my mind always knows exactly what to say; not remotely like his unfortunate sister who suffers terribly with being tongue-tied. I glanced at Mum and wondered whether she was thinking of him, too, whether being in the hospital brought back memories of her little boy. I couldn't ask, though, because we didn't talk about Daniel, just as we didn't talk about her evacuation, her past, her regrets. We never had.

Perhaps it was my sadness that secrets had simmered for so long beneath our family's surface; perhaps it was a type of penance for upsetting her with my earlier probing; perhaps there was even a tiny part of me that wanted to provoke a reaction, to punish her for keeping memories from me and robbing me of the real Daniel: whatever the case, the next thing I knew I'd drawn breath and said, "Mum?"

She rubbed her eyes and blinked at her wristwatch.

"Jamie and I broke up."

"Oh?"

"Yes."

"Today?"

"Well, no. Not exactly. Around Christmastime."

A tiny utterance of surprise, "Oh," and then she frowned, confused, calculating the months that had passed. "But you didn't mention—"

"No."

This fact and its implications brought a sag to her face. She nodded slowly, remembering, no doubt, the fifty small and smaller inquiries she'd made after Jamie in that time; the answers I'd given, all lies.

"I've had to let the flat go," I said, clearing my throat. "I'm looking for a bedsit. A little place of my own."

"That's why I couldn't reach you; after your father—I tried all the numbers I could think of, even Rita's, until I got on to Herbert. I didn't know what else to do."

"Well," I said, a strange artificial brightness in my tone, "as it happens that was the perfect thing to do. I've been staying with Herbert."

She looked baffled. "He has a spare room?"

"A sofa."

"I see." Mum's hands were clasped in her lap, held together as if she sheltered a little bird inside, a precious bird she was determined not to lose. "I must post Herbert a note," she said, her voice threadbare. "He sent some of his blackberry jam at Easter and I can't think that I remembered to write."

And like that it was over, the conversation I'd been dreading for months. Relatively painless, which was good, but also somehow soulless, which wasn't.

Mum stood then, and my first thought was that I'd been wrong, it wasn't over and there was going to be a scene after all, but when I followed the direction of her eyes I saw that a doctor was coming towards us. I stood too, trying to read his face, to guess which way the penny was about to drop, but it was impossible. His expression was the sort that could be read to fit each scenario. I think they learn how to do that at medical school.

"Mrs. Burchill?" His voice was clipped, faintly foreign.

"Yes."

"Your husband's condition is stable."

Mum let out a noise, like air being pushed from a small balloon.

"It's a good thing the ambulance got there so soon. You did well to call it in time."

I was aware of soft hiccuping noises next to me and I realized Mum's eyes were leaking again.

"We'll see how his recovery progresses, but at this stage angioplasty is unlikely. He'll need to stay in for a few days longer so we can monitor him, but his recovery after that can be done at home. You'll have to watch him for moods: cardiac patients often struggle with feelings of depression. The nurses will be able to help you further with that."

Mum was nodding with grateful fervor. "Of course, of course," and scrabbling, as was I, for the right words to convey our gratitude and relief. In the end she went with plain old, "Thank you, doctor," but he'd already withdrawn behind the untouchable screen of his white coat. He merely bobbed his head in a disconnected way, as if he had another place to be, another life to save, both of which he no doubt did, and had already forgotten quite who we were and to which patient we belonged.

I was about to suggest that we go in and see Dad when she began to cry—my mother, who never cries—and not just a few tears wiped away against the back of her hand; great big racking sobs that reminded me of the time in my childhood when I was upset about one trifling thing or another and Mum told me that while some girls were fortunate to look pretty when they cried—their eyes widened, their cheeks flushed, their pouts plumped—neither she nor I were among them.

She was right: we're ugly criers, both of us. Too blotchy, too snarly, too loud. But seeing her standing there, so small, so impeccably dressed, so distressed, I wanted to wrap her in my arms and hold on until she couldn't help but stop. I didn't though. I dug inside my bag and found her a tissue.

She took it but she didn't stop crying, not right away, and after a moment's hesitation, I reached out to touch her shoulder, turned it into a sort of pat, then rubbed the back of her cashmere cardigan. We stood like that, until her body yielded a little, leaning in to me like a child seeking comfort.

Finally, she blew her nose. "I was so worried, Edie," she said, wiping beneath her eyes, one after the other, checking the tissue for mascara.

"I know, Mum."

"I just don't think that I could . . . if anything were to happen . . . if I lost him—"

"It's okay," I said firmly. "He's okay. Everything's going to be all right."

She blinked at me like a small animal for whom the light is too bright. "Yes."

I obtained his room number from a nurse and we negotiated the fluorescent corridors until we found it. As we drew close, Mum stopped.

"What is it?" I said.

"I don't want your father upset, Edie."

I said nothing, wondering how on earth she thought I might be planning to do such a thing.

"He'd be horrified to learn that you were sleeping on a sofa. You know how he worries about your posture."

"It won't be for long." I glanced towards the door. "Really, Mum, I'm working on it. I've been checking the rentals but there's nothing suitable—"

"Nonsense." She straightened her skirt and drew a deep breath. Didn't quite meet my eyes as she said, "You've a perfectly suitable bed at home."

HOME AGAIN, HOME AGAIN, JIGGETY JIG

WHICH is how, at the age of thirty, I came to be a single woman living with my parents in the house in which I'd grown up. In my very own childhood bedroom, in my very own five-foot bed, beneath the window that overlooked Singer & Sons Funeral Home. An improvement, one might add, on my most recent situation: I adore Herbert and I've a lot of time for dear old Jess, but Lord spare me from ever having to share her sofa again.

The move itself was relatively painless; I didn't take much with me. It was a temporary arrangement, as I told anyone who'd listen, so it made far more sense to leave my boxes at Herbert's. I packed myself a single suitcase and arrived back home to find everything pretty much as I'd left it a decade before.

Our family house in Barnes was built in the sixties, purchased brand-new by my parents when Mum was pregnant with me. What makes it particularly striking is that it's a house with no clutter. Really, none at all. There's a system for everything in the Burchill household: multiple baskets in the laundry; color-coded cloths in the kitchen; a notepad by the telephone with a pen that never seems to wander, and not one envelope lying around with doodles and addresses and the half-scribbled names of people whose calls have been forgotten. Neat as a pin. Little wonder I'd suspected adoption when I was growing up.

Even Dad's attic clear-out had generated a polite minimum of mess; two dozen or so boxes with their lists of contents taped on the lids, and thirty years' worth of superseded electronic appliances, still housed in their original packaging. They couldn't live in the hallway forever, though, and with Dad recuperating and my weekends tumble-weed clear, I was a natural to take over the job. I worked like a soldier, falling prey to distraction only once, when I stumbled upon the box marked EDIE'S THINGS and couldn't resist ripping it open. Inside lay a host of forgotten items: macaroni jewelry with flaking paint, a por-celain trinket box with fairies on the side, and, deep down, among assorted bits and bobs and books—I gasped—my illicitly kept, utterly cherished, hitherto misplaced copy of the *Mud Man*.

Holding that small, timeworn book in my grown-up hands, I was awash with shimmering memories; the image of my ten-year-old self, propped up on the lounge sofa, was so lucent I could almost reach across the years to poke ripples in it with my finger. I could feel the pleasant stillness of the glass-filtered sunlight and smell the reassur-ing warm air: tissues and lemon barley and lovely doses of parental pity. I saw Mum, then, coming through the doorway with her coat on and her string bag filled with groceries. Fishing something from within the bag, holding it out to me, a book that would change my world. A novel written by the very gentleman to whom she'd been evacuated during the Second World War . . .

I rubbed my thumb thoughtfully across the embossed type on the cover: Raymond Blythe. *Perhaps this will cheer you up,* Mum had said. *It's for slightly older readers, I think, but you're a clever girl; with a bit of effort I'm sure you'll be fine.* My entire life, I'd credited the librarian Miss Perry with setting me on my proper path, but as I sat there on the wooden floor of the attic, the *Mud Man* in my hands, another thought began to coalesce in a thin streak of light. I wondered whether it was possible that I'd been wrong all this time, whether perhaps Miss Perry had done little more than locate and lend the title and it had been my mother who'd known to give me the perfect book at the perfect time. Whether I dared ask.

The book had been old when it came to me, and passion-ately well loved since, so its state of déshabillé was to be expected.

Within its crumbling binding were stuck the very pages I'd turned when the world they described was new: when I didn't know how things might end for Jane and her brother and the poor, sad man in the mud.

I'd been longing to read it again, ever since I returned from my visit to Milderhurst, and with a swift intake of breath, I opened the book randomly, letting my eyes alight in the middle of one of the lovely old yellowing pages: *The carriage that took them to live with the uncle they'd never met set off from London in the evening and traveled through the night, arriving at last at the foot of a neglected drive while dawn was breaking.* I read on, bumping in the back of that carriage beside Jane and Peter. Through the weary, whiny gates we went, up the long and winding path, until finally, at the top of the hill, cold in the melancholy morning light, it appeared. Bealehurst Castle. I shivered with anticipation at what I might find inside. The tower broke through the roofline, windows dark against the creamy stone, and I leaned out with Jane, laid my hand beside hers on the carriage window. Heavy clouds fleeted across the pale sky, and when the carriage finally stopped with a clunk we clambered out to find ourselves standing by the rim of an ink-black moat. A breeze then, from nowhere, rippling the water's surface, and the driver gestured towards a wooden drawbridge. Slowly, silently, we walked across it. Just as we reached the heavy door, a bell rang, a real one, and I almost dropped the book.

I don't think I've mentioned the bell yet. While I was returning boxes to the attic, Dad had been set up to convalesce in the spare room, a pile of *Accountancy Today* journals on the bedside table, a cassette player loaded with Henry Mancini, and a little butler's bell for summoning attention. The bell had been his idea, a distant memory from a bout of fever as a boy, and after a fortnight during which he'd done little more than sleep, Mum had been so pleased to see a return of spirit that she'd happily gone along with the suggestion. It made good sense, she'd said, failing to anticipate for a moment that the small, decorative bell might be commandeered for such nefarious use. In Dad's bored and grumpy hands, it became a fearful weapon, a talisman in his reversion to boyhood. Bell in fist, my mild-mannered, number-crunching father became a spoiled and imperious child, full of impatient questions as to whether the postman had been, what Mum was doing with her day, what time he might expect his next cup of tea to be served.

On the morning that I found the box with the *Mud Man* inside, however, Mum was at the supermarket and I was officially on Dad-watch. At the sound of the bell, the world of Bealehurst withered, the clouds receded quickly in all directions, the moat, the castle vanished, the step on which I stood turned to dust so that I was falling, with nothing but black text floating in the white space around me, dropping through the hole in the middle of the page to land with a bump back in Barnes.

Shameful of me, I know, but I sat very still for a few moments, waiting it out in case I earned a reprieve. Only when the bell's tinkle came a second time did I tuck the book inside my cardigan pocket and clamber, with regrettable reluctance, down the ladder.

"Hiya, Dad," I said brightly—it is not kind to resent intrusions from a convalescent parent—arriving at the spare-room door. "Everything all right?"

He'd slumped so far he'd almost disappeared inside his pillows. "Is it lunchtime yet, Edie?"

"Not yet." I straightened him up a bit. "Mum said she'd fix you some soup as soon as she got in. She's made a lovely pot of—"

"Your mother's still not back?"

"Shouldn't be long." I smiled sympathetically. Poor Dad had been through an awful time: it isn't easy for anyone being bed-bound weeks on end, but for someone like him, with no hobbies and no talent whatsoever for relaxing, it was torture. I freshened his water glass, trying not to finger the top of the book protruding from my pocket. "Is there anything I can fetch you in the meantime? A crossword? A heat pad? Some more cake?"

He let out a forebearing sigh. "No."

"Are you sure?"

"Yes."

My hand was on the *Mud Man* again; my mind had taken guilty leave to debate the particular merits of the daybed in the kitchen and the armchair in the lounge, the one by the window that spends the afternoon drenched in sunlight. "Well then," I said sheepishly, "I guess I'll get back to it. Chin up, eh, Dad . . ."

I was almost at the door when he said, "What's that you've got there, Edie?"

"Where?"

"There, sticking out of your pocket." He sounded so hopeful. "Not the mail, is it?"

"This? No." I patted my cardigan. "It's a book from one of the attic boxes."

He pursed his lips. "The whole point is to stow things away, not to dig them out again."

"I know, but it's a favorite."

"What's it all about then?"

I was stunned; I couldn't think that my dad had ever asked me about a book before. "A pair of orphans," I managed to say. "A girl called Jane and a boy called Peter."

He frowned impatiently. "A little more than that, I should say. By the looks of it, there's a lot of pages."

"Of course—yes. It's about far more than that." Oh, where to start! Duty and betrayal, absence and longing, the lengths to which people will go to protect the ones they cherish, madness, fidelity, honor, love . . . I glanced again at Dad and decided to stick with the plot. "The children's parents are char-grilled in a ghastly London house fire and they're sent to live with their long-lost uncle in his castle."

"His castle?"

I nodded. "Bealehurst. Their uncle's a nice enough fellow, and the children are delighted by the castle at first, but gradually they come to realize that there's more going on than meets the eye, that there's a deep, dark secret lurking beneath it all."

"Deep *and* dark, eh?" He smiled a little.

"Oh yes. Both. Very terrible indeed."

I'd said it quickly, excitedly, and Dad leaned closer, easing himself onto his elbow. "What is it then?"

"What's what?"

"The secret. What is it?"

I looked at him, dumbfounded. "Well, I can't just . . . tell you."

"Of course you can."

He crossed his arms like a cranky child and I scrabbled for the words to explain to him the contract between reader and writer, the dangers of narrative greed. The sacrilege of just blurting out what had taken chapters to build, secrets hidden carefully by the author behind countless sleights of hand. All I managed was, "I'll lend it to you if you like."

He pouted unbecomingly. "Reading makes my head ache."

A silence settled between us, tending towards uncomfortable as he waited for me to concede and I—of course, for what choice did I have?—refused. Finally, he gave a forlorn sort of sigh. "Never mind," he said, waving his fingers disconsolately. "I suppose it doesn't matter."

But he looked so glum, and the memory came upon me so intensely of how I'd fallen into the world of the Mud Man when I was laid up with mumps or whatever it was, that I couldn't help saying, "If you really want to know, I suppose I could read it *to* you."

THE MUD *Man* became our habit, something I looked forward to every day. As soon as dinner was over, I helped Mum with the kitchen, cleared Dad's tray, then he and I would pick up wherever we'd left off. He couldn't fathom that a made-up story could interest him so avidly. "But it must be based on true events," he said repeatedly, "an old kidnapping case. Like that Lindbergh fellow, the child taken from his bedroom window?"

"No, Dad, Raymond Blythe just invented it."

"But it's so vivid, Edie; I can see it in my head when you're reading, as if I were watching it happen, as if I knew the story already." And he would shake his head with a wonder that made me warm to the tips of my toes with pride, even though I'd taken no part, myself, in the Mud Man's creation. On days when I stayed late at work he became fidgety, grouching at Mum all evening, listening for my key in the door, then ringing his little bell and feigning surprise when I answered: "Is that you, Edie?" he'd say, lifting his brows as if confused. "I was just going to ask your mother to plump my pillows. I say—seeing as you're here, we might as well take a look at what's happening at the castle."

And perhaps it was the castle, even more than the story, that had really won him over. His jealous respect for grand family estates was as close as Dad came to having a existing interest, and once I let slip that Bealehurst was based heavily on Raymond Blythe's real ancestral home, his interest was assured. He asked copious questions, some of which I could answer from memory or existing knowledge, others that were so specific I had no choice but to produce my copy of *Raymond Blythe's Milderhurst* for him to pore over, sometimes even reference books I'd borrowed from Herbert's enormous collection and brought home from work. Thus it was that Dad and I fanned each other's infatuation, and for the first time ever, the pair of us found ourselves with something in common.

There was only one sticking point in our happy formation of the Burchill family Mud Man fan club, and that was Mum. No matter that our Milderhurst habit had arisen quite innocently, the fact that Dad and I were sitting together behind closed doors, bringing to life a world Mum resolutely refused to speak about, and over which she had greater claim than either of us, felt sneaky. I knew I was going to have to talk to her about it; I also knew the conversation was going to be prickly.

Since I'd moved back home, things between Mum and me had continued as they always had. Somewhat naively, I think I'd half expected that the two of us might undergo a miraculous renaissance of affection; that we might slip into a routine together, fall easily and often into conversation; that Mum might even bare her soul and divulge her secrets to me. I suppose that's what I'd hoped might happen. Needless to say, it didn't. In fact, although I think Mum was pleased to have me there, grateful that I was helping out with Dad and far more tolerant of our differences than she had been in the past, in other respects she seemed more distant than ever, distracted and vague and very, very quiet. I'd assumed, at first, that it was a result of Dad's heart attack, that the worry followed hotly by relief had thrown her into a tumble of reevaluation; but as the weeks went by and things didn't improve, I began to wonder. I found her sometimes paused in the middle of an activity, standing with her hands in the sudsy kitchen sink, staring blankly through the window. And the expression on her face was so faraway, so knotted and confused, it was as if she'd forgotten where and who she was.

It was in just such inclination that I found her on the evening I came to fess up about the reading.

"Mum?" I said. She didn't seem to hear and I went a little closer, stopping by the corner of the table. "Mum?"

She turned from the glass. "Oh, hello, Edie. It's pretty this time of year, isn't it. The long, late sunsets."

I joined her by the window, watching the last glaze of peach darken from the sky. It *was* pretty, though perhaps not sufficiently to warrant the ardent attention she was paying it.

After a time, in which Mum said nothing further, I cleared my throat. I told her I'd been reading the *Mud Man* to Dad, then I very carefully explained the circumstances that had led to such a thing, in particular that it hadn't been planned. She barely seemed to hear me, a slight nod when I mentioned Dad's fascination with the castle the only sign that she was listening. When I'd reported everything I considered of consequence, I stopped and waited, steeled myself a little for whatever might be coming.

"It's kind of you to read to your dad, Edie. He's enjoying it." It was not exactly the response I'd expected. "That book is becoming something of a tradition in our family." The flicker of a smile. "A companion in times of ill health. You probably don't remember. I gave it to you when you were home with mumps. You were so miserable, it was all I could think to do."

So. It had been Mum all along. She, and not Miss Perry, had chosen the *Mud Man*. The perfect book, the perfect time. I found my voice. "I remember."

"It's good that your father has something to think about while he's lying in bed. Better still that he has you to share it with. He hasn't had many visitors, you know. Other people lead busy lives, the fellows from his work. Most of them sent cards, and I suppose since he retired . . . well, time marches on, doesn't it? It just . . . it isn't easy for a person to feel they've been forgotten."

She turned her face away then, but not before I'd noticed her lips pressed hard together. I had a feeling we were no longer speaking only of my dad, and because all roads of thought led me at that time to Milderhurst, to Juniper Blythe and Thomas Cavill, I couldn't help wondering whether Mum was mourning an old love affair, a relationship from long before she met my dad, when she was young and impressionable and easily wounded. The more I pondered it, the longer I stood there stealing glances at her pensive profile, the angrier I felt. Who was this Thomas Cavill who had skipped off during the war, leaving a spill of broken hearts behind him? Poor Juniper, wasting away in her family's crumbly castle, and my own mother, nursing her private sorrow decades after the fact.

"There's one thing, Edie"—Mum was back to facing me now, her sad eyes searching mine—"I'd rather your father didn't know about my evacuation."

"Dad doesn't know you were evacuated?"

"He knows that it happened, but not where I went. He doesn't know about Milderhurst."

She suddenly paid great attention to the back of her hands, lifting each finger in turn, adjusting her fine gold wedding band.

"You do realize," I said gently, "that he'd think you a person of inestimable fabulousness if he knew you'd lived there once?"

A slight smile ruffled her composure, but her attention didn't leave her hands.

"I'm serious. He's smitten with the place."

"Nevertheless," she said, "I'd prefer it this way."

"Okay. I understand." I didn't, but I think we've established that already, and the way the streetlight was now caressing her cheekbones made her look vulnerable, like a different kind of woman, younger and more breakable somehow, so I didn't press further. I continued to watch her, though; her attitude was one of such keen contemplation that I couldn't look away.

"You know, Edie," she said softly, "when I was a girl my mother used to send me out around this time of night to fetch your grandfather back from the pub."

"Really? By yourself?"

"It wasn't uncommon back then, before the war. I'd go and wait by the door of the local and he'd see me and wave and finish his drink and then we'd walk home together."

"The two of you were close?"

She tilted her head a little. "I perplexed him, I think. Your grandmother, too. Did I ever tell you that she wanted me to become a hairdresser when I left school?"

"Like Rita."

She blinked at the night-black street outside. "I don't think I'd have been much good at it."

"I don't know. You're pretty handy with the pruning shears."

There was a pause and she smiled sideways at me, but not completely naturally, and I had the feeling there was something more she wanted to say. I waited, but whatever it was, she decided against it, soon turning back to stare at the glass pane.

I made a halfhearted attempt to engage her in further conversation about her school days, hoping, I suppose, that it might lead to mention of Thomas Cavill, but she didn't take the bait. She said only that she'd enjoyed school well enough and asked me whether I'd like a cup of tea.

THE SINGLE virtue of Mum's abstraction at that time was that I was spared having to discuss my breakup with Jamie. Repression being something of a family hobby, Mum didn't ask for details; neither did she drown me in platitudes. She kindly let us both cling to the myth that I'd made a purely selfless decision to come home and help her with Dad and the house.

The same, I'm afraid, could not be said of Rita. Bad news travels swiftly and my aunt is nothing if not a foul-weather friend, so I expect I shouldn't have been surprised when I arrived at the Roxy Club for Sam's hen night only to be accosted at the door. Rita tucked her arm through mine and said, "Darling, I've heard. Now, don't you worry; you're not to think it means you're old and unattractive and destined to be alone for the rest of your life."

I waved to let the waiter know I was ready to place a rather stiff drink order and realized, with a vague sinking sensation, that I was actually envying my mother her evening at home with Dad and his bell.

"Lots of people meet 'the one' in their later years," she continued, "and they're made very happy indeed. Just look at your cousin over there." Rita pointed at Sam, who was grinning at me past the G-string of a bronzed stranger. "Your turn will come."

"Thanks, Auntie Rita."

"Good girl." She nodded in approval. "You have a good time now and put it all behind you." And she was about to move on to spread her cheer elsewhere when she grabbed my arm. "Almost forgot," she said. "I've brought something for you." She dug inside her tote and pulled out a shoebox. The picture on the side was of an embroidered pump slipper, the sort my gran would have cherished, and although it seemed rather an unlikely gift, I had to admit they looked comfy. And not impractical: I was, after all, spending a lot of nights in these days.

"Thank you," I said. "How kind." And then I lifted the lid and saw that the box didn't contain slippers at all, but was half-filled with letters.

"Your mum's," said auntie Rita with a devilish smile. "Just like I promised. You have a good old read of those, won't you? Cheer yourself up."

And although I was thrilled by the letters, I felt a curl of dislike for my auntie Rita then, on behalf of the small girl whose handwriting swirled and looped in earnest lines across the fronts of the envelopes. The young girl whose older sister had deserted her during the evacuation, slinking off to be housed with a friend, leaving little Meredith to fend for herself.

I put the lid back on, anxious suddenly to get the letters out of that club. They didn't belong there amid the bump and grind, the unedited thoughts and dreams of a little girl from long ago; the same young girl who'd walked beside me in the corridors of Milderhurst, whom I hoped to know better one day. When the novelty straws appeared I made my excuses and took the letters home to bed.

ALL WAS black as pitch when I arrived and I tiptoed carefully up the stairs, fearful of waking the sleeping bell-ringer. My desk lamp imparted a dusky glow, the house made queer nocturnal noises, and I sat on the edge of the bed, shoebox on my lap. This was the moment, I suppose, when I might have done things differently. Two roads forked away from me and I could have followed either. After the merest hesitation, I lifted the lid and pulled the envelopes from within, noticing as I leafed through that they were arranged carefully by date.

A photograph dropped loose onto my knees, two girls grinning at the camera. The smaller, darker one I recognized as my mother— earnest brown eyes, bony elbows, hair cut in the short, sensible style my gran favored—the other, an older girl with long blond hair. Juniper Blythe, of course. I remembered her from the book I'd bought in Milderhurst village; this was the child with the luminous eyes, all grown up. With a surge of determination, I put the photograph and letters safely back into the box, all except the first, which I unfolded. The letter was dated September 6, 1939; neat printing in the top right-hand corner.

> *Dear Mum and Dad,* it began, in large, rounded handwriting,

> *I miss you both lots and lots. Do you miss me? I'm in the country now and things are very different. There are cows for one thing—did you know they really do say "moo"? Very loudly. I almost jumped out of my skin, the first one I heard.*
>
> *I am living in a castle, a real one, but it doesn't look the way you might imagine. There is no drawbridge, but there is a tower, and three sisters and an old man who I don't see, ever. I only know he's there because the sisters talk about him. They call him Daddy and he's a writer of books. Real ones, like in the lending library. The youngest sister is called Juniper, she's seventeen and very pretty with big eyes. She's the one who brought me to Milderhurst. Did you know that's what gin is made from, by the way—juniper berries?*
>
> *There is a telephone here, too, so maybe if you have the time and Mr. Waterman at the shop doesn't mind, you could . . .*

I'd reached the end of the first page but didn't turn it over. I sat motionless, as if I were listening very carefully to something. And I was, I suppose; for the little girl's voice had drifted from the shoebox and was echoing now in the shadow-hung hollows of the room. *I'm in the country now . . . they call him Daddy . . . there is a tower, and three sisters . . .* Letters are special like that. Conversations waft away the moment they've been had, but the written word prevails. Those letters were little time travelers; fifty years they'd lain patiently in their box, waiting for me to find them.

The headlights from a car in the street outside threw slivers between my curtains, tinsel shards slid across the ceiling. Silence, dimness again. I turned the page and read on, and as I did so a pressure built behind my chest, as if a warm, firm object were being pushed hard from within against my ribs. The sensation was a little like relief and, oddly, the quenching of a strange sort of homesickness. Which made no sense, only that the girl's voice was so familiar that reading the letters was a little like re-meeting an old friend. Someone I'd known a long time ago . . .

ONE

MEREDITH had never seen her father cry. It wasn't something fathers did, not hers certainly (and he wasn't actually crying, not yet, but it was close), and that's how she knew for sure that it was wrong what they'd been saying, that this was no adventure they were going on and it wouldn't be over soon. That this train was waiting to take them away from London and everything was about to change. The sight of Dad's big, square shoulders shaking, the strong face knotted queerly, his mouth pulled so tight that his lips threatened to disappear, and she wanted to wail just as hard as Mrs. Paul's baby when he needed feeding. But she didn't, she couldn't, not with Rita sitting right there at her side just waiting for another reason to pinch her. Instead, she lifted a hand and her father did the same, then she pretended someone was calling her and turned around so that she didn't have to watch him any longer, so they could both stop being so horribly brave.

There'd been drills at school in the summer term and Dad had been talking the whole thing up at night, telling them over and over about the times he'd gone down to Kent as a boy, hop-picking with his family: the sunny days, the campfire songs in the evening, how beautiful the countryside was, how green and sweet and endless. But although Meredith had enjoyed his stories, she'd also thrown a glance or two Mum's way, and that had got the lump of foreboding roiling in her stomach. Mum had been hunched over the sink, all sharp hips and

224

knees and elbows, exercising the same fierce attention to scrubbing pans spotless that always presaged grim times ahead.

Sure enough, a few nights after the stories started, Meredith heard the first argument. Mum saying they were a family and they ought to stay together and take their chances as one, that a family broken apart could never be put back together quite the same. Dad had spoken then, calmer, telling her it was like the posters said, that kids had a better chance out of the city, that it wouldn't last for long and then they'd all be back together. Things had gone quiet for a moment after that, and Meredith had strained to hear, then Mum had laughed, but not happily. She hadn't come down in the last shower, she said; if there was one thing she knew it was that governments and men in fancy suits couldn't be trusted, that once the kids were taken God only knew when they'd get them back and in what sort of condition they'd be, and she'd shouted some of the words Rita got regular swipes for using, and said that if he loved her he wouldn't send her children away, and Dad had shushed her and there'd been sobbing and no more talking and Meredith had put her pillow over her head, as much to drown out Rita's snoring as anything else.

There'd been no more talk of evacuation after that, not for days, until one afternoon Rita came running home to tell them that the public swimming baths were closed and there were big new notices out front. "There's one on each side," she'd said, eyes widened by the press of portentous news: "The first says 'Women Contaminated,' the second says 'Men Contaminated.' " And Mum had knotted her hands and Dad had said only, "Gas," and that was that. Next day Mum pulled down the only suitcase they owned and any pillowcases she could spare and started filling them with things on the list from school—just in case: a change of knickers, a comb, handkerchiefs, and a brand-new nightdress each for Rita and Meredith, the necessity of which Dad had gently queried and Mum had justified with a fierce scowl. "You think I'm letting my children go with threadbare clothing into the homes of strangers?" Dad had stayed quiet after that and even though Meredith knew her parents would be paying for the new items until Christmas, she couldn't help taking guilty delight in the nightie, which was crisp and white and the first she'd ever owned that hadn't been Rita's first . . .

And now they *were* being sent away and Meredith would have done anything to take back her wish. Meredith wasn't brave, not like Ed, and she wasn't loud and confident like Rita. She was shy and awkward, and utterly different from everyone else in her family. She shifted in her seat, lined her feet up together on her suitcase, and considered the gleam of her shoes, then blinked away the image of Dad polishing them the night before, setting them down when he'd finished only to wander the room a few idle minutes, hands in pockets, before starting the whole process again. As if by applying polish, driving it deep into the leather and buffing until it shone, he could somehow ward off the untold dangers that lay ahead.

"Mu-mmy, Mu-mmy!"

The shriek came from across the carriage and Meredith glanced up to see a little boy, not much more than a baby, clinging to his sister and pawing the glass. Tears had snaked down his dirty cheeks and the skin beneath his nose was shiny. "I want to stay with you, Mummy," he cried. "I want to get killed with you!"

Meredith concentrated on her knees, rubbed at the red marks her gas-mask box had made as it banged against her legs on the walk from school. Then she looked again through the train's window, she couldn't help herself; peered up at the railing above the station where the adults were crowded together. He was still there, still watching them, the stranger's smile still twisting up his normal Dad-face, and Meredith found it difficult suddenly to breathe and her spectacles were starting to fog, and even as she wished the earth would open up and swallow her so it would all be over, a small part of her mind remained detached, wondering which words she'd use, if asked to describe the way fear was making her lungs constrict. As Rita squealed with laughter at something her friend Carol had whispered in her ear, Meredith closed her eyes.

IT HAD begun at precisely eleven fifteen the previous morning. She'd been sitting at the front of the house, legs stretched out along the top step, taking notes as she watched Rita across the road making eyes at that ghastly Luke Watson with his big yellow teeth. The announcement had come in distant strains from the wireless next door, Neville Chamberlain talking in that slow, solemn voice of his, telling them there'd been no response to the ultimatum and that they were now at war with Germany. Then had come the national anthem, after which Mrs. Paul appeared on the neighboring doorstep, spoon still dripping with Yorkshire pudding batter, with Mum close behind her, and householders all the way along the street doing the same. Everyone stood where they were, looking one to the other, bewilderment, fear, and uncertainty written loud on their faces, as mutterings of "It's happened" began to pass along the street in a great disbelieving wave.

Eight minutes later, the air-raid siren clattered and all hell broke loose. Old Mrs. Nicholson ran up and down the street in hysterics alternating the Lord's Prayer with panicked declarations of their impending doom; Moira Seymour, who was the local ARP warden, got excited and started twirling the heavy rattle signaling a gas attack and people scattered in the hunt for their masks; and Inspector Whitely wove his bicycle through the mayhem wearing a cardboard placard over his body that read TAKE COVER.

Meredith had watched, wide-eyed, drinking in the mayhem, then stared up at the sky, waiting for the enemy planes, wondering how they'd look, how their appearance might make her feel, whether she was able to write fast enough to jot it all down as it was happening, when all of a sudden Mum had clutched her arm and dragged her and Rita down the street towards the trench shelter in the park. Meredith's notebook had dropped in the rush and been trampled and she'd wrenched her arm free and stopped to pick it up, and Mum had shouted that there wasn't time and her face had been white, almost angry looking, and Meredith had known she'd get a tongue-lashing later, if not worse, but she'd had no choice. There'd been no question of leaving it behind. She'd run back, ducked beneath the crowd of frightened neighbors, seized her notebook—worse for wear, but still intact—and returned to her furious mother, face no longer white but red as Heinz tomato ketchup. By the time they got to the shelter and realized they'd forgotten their gas masks, the all-clear had sounded, Meredith had earned a smack across the legs, and Mum had resolved to evacuate them the next day.

"Hey there, kiddo."

Meredith opened moist eyes to see Mr. Cavill standing in the aisle. Her cheeks warmed instantly and she smiled, cursing the image that came to mind of Rita leering at Luke Watson.

"Mind if I take a look at your name tag?"

She wiped beneath her specs and leaned closer so he could read the cardboard tag around her neck. There were people everywhere, laughing, crying, shouting, swirling round and round, but for a moment she and Mr. Cavill were alone in the middle of it all. Meredith held her breath, conscious of the way her heart had started to hammer, watching his lips as he mouthed the words written there, her very own name, his smile when he'd verified they were all correct.

"You've got your suitcase, I see. Did your mother make sure to include everything on the list? Is there anything you need?"

Meredith nodded, then shook her head. Blushed as words she would never, *ever,* dare to speak popped into mind: *I need you to wait for me, Mr. Cavill. Wait for me to get a little older—fourteen maybe, fifteen—and then the two of us can get married.*

Mr. Cavill marked something down on his paper form and capped his pen. "We might be on the train awhile, Merry. Have you brought something to keep you busy?"

"I brought my notebook."

He laughed then, for he was the one who'd given it to her, a reward for doing so well in her exams. "Of course," he said. "That's perfect. Make sure you write it all down, now. Everything you see and think and feel. Your voice is your own; it matters." And he gave her a chocolate bar and a wink, and she smiled broadly as he continued up the aisle, leaving her heart swelling as big as a melon in her chest.

THE NOTEBOOK was Meredith's most treasured possession. The first proper journal she'd ever owned. She'd had it for twelve months now but she hadn't written a single word inside, not even her name. How could she? Meredith loved the smart little book so well, the smooth leather cover and the perfect neat lines across each page, the ribbon stitched into the binding for use as a bookmark, that to spoil it with her own penmanship, her own dull sentences about her own dull life, seemed too great a sacrilege. She'd pulled it from hiding many times only to sit with it on her knee for a while, drawing great pleasure simply from owning such a thing, before tucking it away again.

Mr. Cavill had tried to convince her that what she wrote about wasn't nearly as important as the way she wrote it. "No two people will ever see or feel things in the same way, Merry. The challenge is to be truthful when you write. Don't approximate. Don't settle for the easiest combination of words. Go searching instead for those that explain *exactly* what you think. What you feel." And then he'd asked if she understood what he meant, and his dark eyes had been filled with such intensity, such earnest desire that she should see things as he did, and she'd nodded and just for a moment it was as if a door had opened up to a place that was very different from the one in which she lived . . .

Meredith sighed fervently and sneaked a sideways glance at Rita, who was combing her fingers through her ponytail, pretending not to notice that Billy Harris was making moon eyes at her from across the aisle. Good. The last thing she needed was for Rita to guess how she felt about Mr. Cavill; thankfully, Rita was far too wrapped up in her own world of boys and lipstick to bother with anyone else's. A fact Meredith counted on in order to write her daily journal. (Not the real journal, of course; in the end, she'd struck a compromise, collecting spare paper from wherever she could find it and keeping it folded within the front cover of the precious book. She wrote her reports on that, telling herself that one day, maybe, she'd broach the real thing.)

Meredith risked another peek at her dad then, ready to look away before she caught his eye, but as she skimmed the faces, searched for his familiar bulk, cursorily at first, then with rising panic in her throat, she discovered he wasn't there. The faces had changed; mothers were still crying, some waved handkerchiefs, others smiled with grim determination, but there was no sign of him. Where he'd been standing was a gap that filled and shuffled as she watched, and as she searched the crowd she realized that he'd really gone. That she'd missed seeing him go.

And although she'd held it in all morning, although she'd schooled herself away from sadness, Meredith felt so sorry then, so small and frightened and alone, that she started to cry. A great rush of feeling rose from within her, warmly and wetly, and her cheeks were instantly drenched. The awful thought that he might have been standing there all that time, that he might have been watching her as she watched her shoes, spoke with Mr. Cavill, thought about her notebook, and willing her to look up, to smile, to wave good-bye; that eventually he must have given up and gone home, believing that she didn't care at all—

"Oh, shut up," said Rita beside her. "Don't be such a blubbering baby. For goodness' sake, this is fun!"

"My mum says not to look out the window or you'll get your head chopped off by a passing train." This was Rita's friend Carol, who was fourteen and as big a know-it-all as her mother. "And not to give anyone directions. They're just as likely to be German spies looking for Whitehall. They murder children, you know."

So Meredith hid her face behind her hand, allowed herself a few more silent sobs, then wiped her cheeks dry as the train jerked and they were off. The air filled with the shouts of parents outside and children inside and steam and smoke and whistles and Rita laughing beside her, and then they pulled out of the station. Rattled and clattered along the lines, and a group of boys, dressed in their Sunday best although it was Monday, ran up the corridor from window to window, drumming on the glass and whooping and waving, until Mr. Cavill told them to sit down and not to open the doors. Meredith leaned against the glass and, rather than meet the sad gray faces that lined the roadsides, weeping for a city that was losing its children, she watched with wonder as great silver balloons began slowly to rise all around, drifting in the light currents above London like strange and beautiful animals.

TWO

THE bicycle had been gathering cobwebs in the stables for almost two decades and Percy was in little doubt that she looked a sight riding it. Hair tied back with an elastic band, skirt gathered and tucked between locked knees: her modesty might have survived the ride intact, but she was under no illusion that she cut a stylish figure.

She had received the ministry warning about the risk of bicycles falling into enemy hands, but she'd gone ahead and resurrected the old thing anyway. If there was any truth to the rumors flying about, if the government really was planning for a three-year war, fuel was sure to be rationed and she'd need a way of getting about. The bicycle had been Saffy's once, long ago, but she had no use for it now; Percy had dug it out of storage, dusted it off, and ridden it round and round at the top of the driveway until she could balance with some reliability. She hadn't expected to enjoy it so much and couldn't for the life of her remember why she'd never got one of her own all those years ago, why she'd waited until she was a middle-aged woman with hair starting to gray before discovering the pleasure. And it *was* a pleasure, particularly during this remarkable Indian summer, to feel the breeze rush against her warm cheeks as she whizzed along beside the hedgerow.

Percy crested the hill and leaned into the next dip, a smile spreading wide across her face. The entire landscape was turning to gold, birds twittered in the trees, and summer's heat lingered in the air. September in Kent and she could almost convince herself she'd dreamed the announcement of the day before. She took the shortcut through Blackberry Lane, traced her way around the lake's edge, then jumped off to walk her bicycle through the narrow stretch bordering the brook.

Percy passed the first couple shortly after she'd started through the tunnel; a boy and girl, not much older than Juniper, matching gas masks slung over their shoulders. They held hands and their heads were bowed so close as they conferred in earnest, low voices that they barely registered her presence.

Soon a second, similarly arranged pair came into view, then a third. Percy nodded a greeting to the latter, then wished immediately that she hadn't; the girl smiled back shyly and leaned into the boy's arm and they exchanged a glance of such youthful tenderness that Percy's own cheeks flushed and she knew at once her blundering intrusion. Blackberry Lane had been a favorite spot for courting couples even when she was a girl, no doubt long before that. Percy knew that better than most. Her own love affair had been conducted for years beneath the strictest veil of secrecy, not least because there was no chance that it might ever be validated by marriage.

There were simpler romantic choices she could have made, suitable men with whom she might have fallen in love, with whom she could have conducted a courtship openly and without risk of exposing her family to derision, but love was not wise, not in Percy's experience: it was unmindful of social strictures, cared not for lines of class or propriety or plain good sense. And no matter that she prided herself on her pragmatism; Percy had been no more able to resist its call when it came than to stop herself from drawing breath. Thus, she had submitted, resigning herself to a lifetime of layered glances, smuggled letters, and rare, exquisite assignations.

Percy's cheeks warmed as she walked; it was little wonder she felt such special affinity with these young lovers. She kept her head down thereafter, focused on the leaf-strewn ground, ignoring all further passersby until she emerged at the roadside, remounted, and began to coast down into the village. She wondered, as she rode, how it was possible that the great machine of war might be grinding its wheels when the world was still so beautiful, when birds were in the trees and flowers in the fields, when lovers' hearts still heaved with love.

THE FIRST inkling that Meredith needed to wee came when they were still among the gray and sooty buildings of London. She pressed her legs together and shuffled her suitcase hard onto her lap, wondered where precisely they were going and how much longer they had to wait before they got there. She was sticky and tired; she'd already eaten her way through her entire packed lunch of marmalade sandwiches and wasn't remotely hungry, but she was bored and uncertain and she was sure she remembered seeing Mum tuck a pound of chocolate digestive biscuits into the suitcase that morning. She opened the spring locks and lifted the lid a crack, peered inside the dark cavity, then threaded her hands in so she could rummage about. She could have lifted the lid entirely, of course, but it was best not to alert Rita with any sudden movements.

There was the topcoat Mum had sat up nights finishing; further to the left a can of Carnation milk Meredith was under strict instructions to present to her hosts on arrival; behind it, a half-dozen bulky terry towels Mum had insisted she bring, in a mortifying conversation that had made Meredith cringe with embarrassment. "There's every chance you'll become a woman while you're away, Merry," her mum had said. "Rita will be there to help, but you need to be prepared." And Rita had grinned and Meredith had shuddered and wondered at the slim chance that she might prove a rare biological exception. She ran her fingers around her notebook's smooth cover, then—*bingo!* Beneath it she found the paper bag filled with biscuits. The chocolate had melted a little, but she managed to liberate one. Turned her back on Rita as she nibbled her way around the edges.

Behind her one of the boys had started singing a familiar rhyme—"*Under the spreading chestnut tree, Neville Chamberlain said*

to me: *If you want to get your gas mask free, join the blinking ARP!"*—
and Meredith's eyes dropped to her own gas mask. She stuffed the
rest of the biscuit in her mouth and brushed crumbs from the top of
the box. Stupid thing with its horrid rubbery smell, the ghastly ripping sensation as it pulled off her skin. Mum had made them promise
they'd wear their masks while they were away, that they'd carry them
always, and Meredith, Ed, and Rita had all given grudging agreement.
Meredith had later heard Mum confessing to Mrs. Paul next door that
she'd sooner die of a gas attack than bear the horrid feeling of suffoca-
tion beneath the mask, and Meredith planned to lose hers just as soon
as she was able.

There were people waving to them now, standing in their small
backyards watching as the train steamed past. Out of nowhere, Rita
pinched her arm and Meredith squealed. "Why'd you do that?" she
asked, slapping her hand over the stinging spot and rubbing it fiercely.

"All those nice people out there just lookin' for a show." Rita
jerked her head towards the window. "Be a sport now, Merry; give 'em
a few sobs, eh?"

EVENTUALLY, THE city disappeared behind them and green was everywhere. The train clattered along the railway line, slowing occasionally
to pass through stations, but the signs had all been removed so there
was no way of knowing where they were. Meredith must have slept
for a time because the next she knew the train was screeching to a
halt and she was jerked awake. There was nothing new to see, nothing
but more green, clumps of trees on the horizon, occasional birds cutting across the clear blue sky. For one brief elated moment after they'd
stopped, Meredith thought they might be turning around, going home
already. That Germany had recognized that Britain was not to be tri-
fled with after all, the war was over, and there was no longer any need
for them to go away.

But it wasn't to be. After another lengthy wait, during which Roy

Stanley managed to vomit yet more canned pineapple through the window, they were all ordered out of the carriage and told to stand in line. Everyone received an injection, their hair was checked for lice, then they were told to get back on board and sent on their way. There wasn't even an opportunity to use a toilet.

The train was quiet for a while after that; even the babies were too worn out to cry. They traveled and they traveled, on and on, for what seemed like hours and Meredith began to wonder how big England was, when, if ever, they'd reach a cliff. And it occurred to her that perhaps the whole thing was really a great big conspiracy, that the train driver was a German and it was all part of some devious plot to abscond with England's children. There were problems with the theory, holes in its logic—what, for instance, could Hitler possibly want with thousands of new citizens who couldn't be relied on not to wet their beds?—but by then Meredith was too tired, too thirsty, too utterly miserable, to fill them, so she squeezed her legs together even tighter and started counting fields instead. Fields and fields and fields, leading her to God knew what or where.

ALL HOUSES have hearts; hearts that have loved, hearts that have billowed with contentment, hearts that have been broken. The heart at the center of Milderhurst was larger than most and it beat more powerfully. It thumped and paused, raced and slowed, in the small room at the top of the tower. The room where Raymond Blythe's many-times-great-grandfather had sweated over sonnets for Queen Elizabeth; from which a great-aunt had escaped to sweet sojourn with Lord Byron; and upon whose brick ledge his mother's shoe had caught as she leaped from the little archer's window to meet her death in the sun-warmed moat below, her final poem fluttering behind her on a sheet of fine paper.

Standing at the great oak desk, Raymond loaded his pipe bowl with a fresh pinch of tobacco, then another. After his littlest brother, Timothy, died, his mother had retreated to the room, cloaked in the black singe of her own sorrow. He'd glimpsed her by the window when he was down at the grotto, or in the gardens, or on the edge of the woods, the dark shape of her small, neat head facing out towards the fields, the lake: the ivory profile, so like that on the brooch she wore, passed down from her mother before her, the French countess Raymond had never met. Sometimes he'd stayed outside all day, darting in and out of the hop vines, scaling the barn roof, in the hope that she would notice him, worry for him, shout him down. But she never did. It was always Nanny who called him in when the day was spent.

But that was long ago and he a foolish old man becoming lost amid fading memories. His mother was little more than a distantly revered poetess around whom myths were beginning to form as myths were wont to do—the whisper of a summer's breeze, the promise of sunlight against a blank wall—*Mummy* . . . He wasn't even sure he could still remember her voice.

The room belonged to him now: Raymond Blythe, king of the castle. He was his mother's eldest son, her heir and, along with the poems, her greatest legacy. An author in his own right, commanding respect and—it was only honest, he countered when a wave of humility threatened—a certain fame, just as she had done before him. Had she known, he often wondered, when she'd bequeathed the castle to him along with her passion for the written word, that he would rise to meet her expectations? That he would one day do his bit to further the family's reach in literary circles?

His bad knee seized suddenly and Raymond clutched it hard, stretching his foot in front of him until the tension eased. He hobbled to the window and leaned against the ledge while he struck a match. It was a damn near perfect day and as he sucked on his pipe to get it smoking, he squinted across the fields, the driveway, the lawn, the quivering mass of Cardarker Wood. The great wild woods of Milderhurst that had brought him home from London, that had called to him from the battlefields of France, that had always known his name.

What would become of it all when he was gone? Raymond knew

his doctor spoke the truth; he wasn't stupid, only old. And yet it was impossible to believe that a time was coming in which he would no longer sit by this window and look out across the estate, master of all that he surveyed. That the Blythe family name, the family legacy, would die with him. Raymond's thoughts faltered; the responsibility to avoid this had been his. He ought to have remarried, perhaps, tried again to find a woman who could deliver him a son. The matter of legacy had been very much on his mind of late.

Raymond drew on his pipe and puffed with soft derision, just as he might in company with an old friend whose familiar ways were becoming tiresome. He was being melodramatic, of course, a sentimental old fool. Perhaps every man liked to believe that without his presence the great foundations would crumble? Every man as proud as he, at any rate. And Raymond knew he ought to tread more carefully, that pride comes before a fall, as the Bible warned. Besides, he had no need of a son: he had a choice of successors, three daughters, none of them of the marriageable type; and then there was the church, his new church. His priest had spoken to him recently of the eternal rewards awaiting men who saw fit to honor the Catholic brethren in such a generous way. Canny Father Andrews knew Raymond could use all the heavenly goodwill he could arrange.

He took in a mouthful of smoke, held it a moment before exhaling. Father Andrews had explained it to him, the reason for the haunting, what must be done to exorcise Raymond's demon. He was being punished, he knew now, for his sin. His sins. To repent, to confess, even to self-flagellate had not been enough; Raymond's crime was greater than that.

But could he really hand his castle over to strangers, even to smite the wretched demon? What would become of all the whispering voices, the distant hours, caught within her stones? He knew what Mother would say: the castle must stay within the Blythe family. Could he really bear to disappoint her? Especially when he had such a fine natural successor: Persephone, the eldest and most reliable of his children. He'd watched her leave by bicycle that morning, watched as she stopped by the bridge to check its footings, just as he'd once shown her. She was the only one among them whose love for the castle came close to matching his own. A blessing that she'd never found a husband, and wouldn't now, certainly. She'd become a castle fixture, as much his own possession as the statues in the yew hedge; she could be trusted never to do wrong by Milderhurst. Indeed, Raymond sometimes suspected she, like he, would strangle a man with her bare hands if he so much as threatened to remove a stone.

He noticed then the noise of an engine, a motorcar, somewhere below. As quickly as it had started it stopped, a door slammed, heavy, metallic, and Raymond craned to see over the stone windowsill. It was the big old Daimler; someone had driven it from the garage to the top of the driveway, only to abandon it. His attention caught on a moving figment. A pale sprite, his youngest, Juniper, skipping from the front stairs to the driver's door. Raymond smiled to himself, bemusement and pleasure combined. She was a scatty waif, that was certain, but what that thin, loopy child could do with twenty-six simple letters, the arrangements she could make, were breathtaking. If he a were a younger man, he might have been jealous—

Another noise. Closer. Inside.

Hush . . . Can you hear him?

Raymond froze, listening.

The trees can. They are the first to know that he is coming.

Footsteps on the landing below. Climbing, climbing towards him. He laid his pipe down on the flat stone. His heart had begun to kick.

Listen! The trees of the deep, dark wood, shivering and jittering their leaves . . . whispering that soon it will begin.

He exhaled as steadily as he could; it was time. The Mud Man had come at last, seeking his revenge. Just as Raymond had known he must.

He couldn't escape the room, not with the demon on the stairs.

The only other option was through the window. Raymond glanced over the sill. Straight down like an arrow just as his mother had done.

"Mr. Blythe?" A voice drifted up the stairs. Raymond readied himself. The Mud Man could be clever; he had many tricks. Every inch of Raymond's skin crawled; he strained to hear over his own rough breaths.

"Mr. Blythe?" The demon spoke again, closer this time. Raymond ducked behind the armchair. Crouched, quivering. A coward to the very end. The footsteps came steadily. At the door. On the carpet. Closer, closer. He screwed shut his eyes, hands over his head. The thing was right above him.

"Oh, Raymond, you poor, poor man. Come along; give Lucy your hand. I've brought you some lovely soup."

ON THE outskirts of the village, either side of the High Street, the twin lines of poplars stood as ever, like weary soldiers from another time. They were back in uniform now, Percy noted as she whizzed by, new white stripes of paint around their trunks; the curbs had been painted, too, and the wheel rims of many cars. After much talk, the blackout order had finally come into effect the night before: half an hour past sundown the streetlights had been extinguished, no car headlights were allowed, and all windows had been curtained with heavy black cloth. After Percy had checked on Daddy, she'd climbed the stairs to the top of the tower and looked out across the village in the direction of the Channel. The moon had cast the only light and Percy had experienced the eerie sensation of feeling what it must have been like hundreds of years before, when the world was a far darker place, when armies of knights thundered across the land, horses' hooves thrummed the hard soil, castle guards stood poised and ready—

She swerved as old Mr. Donaldson drove along the street seemingly right at her, steering wheel gripped tight, elbows stuck out to the sides, face held in a grimace as he squinted through his specs at the road ahead. He brightened when he made out who she was, lifted his hand to wave, and dragged his car even closer to the road's edge. Percy waved back from the safety of the grass, following his progress with a barb of concern as he zigzagged towards his home at Bell Cottage. What would he be like once night fell? She sighed; bombs be damned, it was the darkness that was going to kill people around here.

To a casual observer, unaware of the previous day's announcement, it might have appeared that all was unchanged in the heart of Milderhurst village. People were still going about their business, shopping for groceries, chatting in small groups outside the post office, but Percy knew better. There was no wailing or gnashing of teeth; it was more subtle than that and perhaps the sadder for it. Impending war was evidenced by the faraway expression in the older villagers' eyes, the shadows on their faces, not of fear but of sorrow. Because they knew; they had lived through the last war and they remembered the generation of young men who had marched away so willingly and never come back. Those too, like Daddy, who had made it home but left in France a part of themselves that they could never recover. Who surrendered to moments, periodically, in which their eyes filmed and their lips whitened, and their minds gave over to sights and sounds they wouldn't share but couldn't shake.

Percy and Saffy had listened together to Prime Minister Chamberlain's announcement on the wireless the day before and had sat through the national anthem in deep thought.

"I suppose we shall have to tell him now," Saffy had said eventually.

"I suppose so."

"You'll do it, of course."

"Of course."

"Choose your moment carefully? Find a way to keep him sensible?"

"Yes."

For weeks they'd put off mentioning to Daddy the likelihood of war. His most recent descent into delusion had further ruptured the tissue connecting him to reality and he'd been left swinging between extremes like the pendulum in the grandfather clock. One moment he seemed perfectly reasonable, speaking to her intelligently of the castle and of history and the great works of literature, the next he was hiding behind chairs, sobbing in fear of imagined specters, or giggling like a cheeky schoolboy, begging Percy to come paddling with him in the brook, telling her he knew the best place for collecting frogspawn, that he'd show her if only she knew how to keep a secret.

When they were eight years old, in the summer before the Great War started, she and Saffy had worked with Daddy on making their own translation of *Sir Gawain and the Green Knight*. He would read the original Middle English poetry and Percy would close her eyes as the magical sounds, the ancient whispers, surrounded her.

"Gawain felt *etaynes that hym anelede,*" Daddy would say, "the giants blowing after him, Persephone. Do you know how that feels? Have you ever heard the voices of your ancestors breathing from the stones?" And she would nod, and curl up tighter beside him, and close her eyes while he continued . . .

Things had been so uncomplicated then, her love for Daddy had been so uncomplicated. He'd been seven feet tall and fashioned of steel and she'd have done and thought anything to be approved of by him. So much had happened since, though, and to see him now, his old face adopting the avid expressions of childhood, was almost too much for Percy to bear. She would never have confessed it to anyone, certainly not to Saffy, but Percy could hardly stand to look at Daddy when he was in one of what the doctor called his "regressive phases." The problem was the past. It wouldn't leave her alone. Nostalgia was threatening to be her ball and chain, which was an irony because Percy Blythe did not go in for sentimentality.

Nettled by unwanted melancholy, she wheeled her bicycle the final short distance to the church hall and propped it against the wooden face of the building, careful not to squash the vicar's garden bed.

"Good morning, Miss Blythe."

Percy smiled at Mrs. Collins. The old dear who, in some inexplicable curvature of time, had seemed ancient for at least three decades had a knitting bag strung over one arm and was clutching a fresh-baked Victoria sponge. "Oh, but Miss Blythe," she said with a woeful shake of her fine silvery curls, "did you ever think it would come to this? Another war?"

"I hoped it wouldn't, Mrs. Collins, I really did. But I can't say I'm surprised, human nature being what it is."

"But another war." The curls shivered again. "All those young boys."

Mrs. Collins had lost both her sons to the Great War, and although Percy had no children of her own, she knew what it was to love so fiercely that it burned. With a smile, she took the cake from her old friend's trembling grasp and hooked one of Mrs. Collins's arms over her own. "Come on, my dear. Let's go inside and find ourselves a seat, shall we?"

The Women's Voluntary Service had decided to meet in the church hall for their sewing bee after certain vocal members of the group had declared the larger village hall, with its wide wooden floor and lack of ornamental detail, a far more suitable site for the processing of evacuees. As Percy took in the huge crowd of eager women clustered around the assembled tables, however, setting up sewing machines, rolling out great swathes of fabric from which to make clothing and blankets for the evacuees, bandages and swabs for the hospitals, she thought that it might have been a foolish choice. She wondered too how many of this number would drop away after the initial excitement wore off, then chastised herself for being uncharitably sour. Not to mention hypocritical, for Percy knew she'd be the first to make her excuses just as soon as she found another way to contribute to the war effort. She was no use with a needle and had come today simply because while it was the duty of all to do what they could, it was the duty of Raymond Blythe's daughters to give what they couldn't a damn good go.

She helped Mrs. Collins into a seat at the knitting table, where conversation, as might be expected, was about the sons and brothers and nephews who were set to join up, then delivered the Victoria sponge to the kitchen, careful to avoid Mrs. Caraway, who was wearing the same dogged expression that always presaged delivery of a particularly nasty task.

"Well now, Miss Blythe." Mrs. Potts from the post office reached out to accept the offering, held it up for inspection. "And what a lovely rise you've managed here."

"The cake comes courtesy of Mrs. Collins. I'm merely its courier." Percy attempted a swift escape, but Mrs. Potts, practiced in conversational entrapment, cast her net too fast.

"We missed you at ARP training on Friday."

"I was otherwise engaged."

"What a pity. Mr. Potts always says what a wonderful casualty you make."

"How kind of him."

"And there's no one can wield a stirrup pump with quite so much verve."

Percy smiled thinly. Sycophancy had never been so tiresome.

"And tell me, how's your father?" A thick layer of hungry sympathy coated the question and Percy fought the urge to plant Mrs. Collins's marvelous sponge right across the postmistress's face. "I hear he's taken a bad turn?"

"He's as well as might be expected, Mrs. Potts. Thank you for asking." An image came to her of Daddy some nights ago, running down the hallway in his gown, cowering behind the stairs, and crying like a frightened child, sobbing that the tower was haunted, that the Mud Man was coming for him. Dr. Bradbury had been called in and had left stronger medicine for them to administer, but Daddy had quivered for hours, fighting against it with all he had, until finally he fell into a dead sleep.

"Such a pillar of the community." Mrs. Potts affected a sorrow-ful tremor. "Such a shame when their health begins to slide. But what a blessing he has someone like you to carry on his charitable works. Especially in a time of national emergency. People around here do look to the castle when times are uncertain—they always have."

"Very kind of you, Mrs. Potts. We all do our best."

"I expect we'll be seeing you over at the village hall this after-noon, helping the evacuation committee?"

"You will."

"I've already been over there this morning, arranging the cans of condensed milk and corned beef: we're sending one of each with every child. It isn't much, but with hardly a scrap of assistance from the authorities it was the best we could offer. And every little bit helps, doesn't it? I hear you're planning on taking in a child yourself. Very noble of you; Mr. Potts and I talked about it of course, and you know me, I'd dearly love to help, but my poor Cedric's allergies"—she raised an apologetic shoulder heavenwards—"well, they'd never stand it." Mrs. Potts leaned in closer and tapped the end of her nose. "Just a little warning: those living in the East End of London have entirely different standards from our own. You'd be well advised to get in some Keating's and a good-quality disinfectant before you let one of them set foot inside the castle."

And although Percy harbored her own grim fears as to the char-acter of their soon-to-be lodger, Mrs. Potts's suggestion was so dis-tasteful that she plucked a cigarette from the case in her handbag and lit it, just to be spared answering.

Mrs. Potts carried on undeterred. "And I suppose you've heard the other exciting news?"

Percy shifted her feet, keen to pursue alternative occupation. "What's that, Mrs. Potts?"

"Why, you must know all about it, up there at the castle. You probably have far more of the details than any of us."

Naturally at that moment silence had fallen and the entire group

245

turned to regard Percy. She did her best to ignore them. "The details of what, Mrs. Potts?" Irritation lengthened her spine a good inch. "I have no idea of what you're speaking."

"Why"—the gossip's eyes widened and her face brightened with the realization that she was a star performer with a new audience—"the news about Lucy Middleton, of course."

Three

EVIDENTLY there was a trick to applying the glue and plastering the fabric strip without gumming up the glass. The perky woman in the illustrated guide didn't seem to be having any difficulty reinforcing *her* windows; indeed she looked positively chipper about the whole prospect, tiny waist, neat haircut, bland smile. No doubt she'd be equal to the bombs, too, when they fell. Saffy, by contrast, was flummoxed. She'd started on the windows back in July when the pamphlets first arrived, but despite the sage advice in the ministry's pamphlet number two—"Do not leave things to the last!"—she'd slackened somewhat when it looked as if war might yet be averted. With Mr. Chamberlain's ghastly announcement, however, she was back at it. Thirty-two windows crisscrossed, a mere hundred left to go. Why she hadn't just used tape, she'd never know.

She pasted the last corner of cloth into place and climbed down off the chair, stepping back to observe her handiwork. Oh dear; she tilted her head a little and frowned at the skewed cross. It would hold, just, but it was no work of art.

"Bravo," said Lucy, coming through the door just then with the tray of tea. "X marks the spot, don't they say?"

"I certainly hope not. Mr. Hitler should be warned: he'll have Percy to answer to if his bombs so much as graze the castle." Saffy swiped the towel against her sticky hands. "I'm afraid this glue has quite set against me; I can't think what I've done to offend it, but offend it I have."

"Glue with a mood. How terrifying!"

"It's not the only one. Forget the bombs, I'm going to need a good nerve tonic after dealing with these windows."

"Tell you what"—Lucy was pouring from the pot and she let the phrase hang while she finished the second cup—"I've taken your father his lunch already; why don't I lend you a hand here?"

"Oh, Lucy darling, would you? What a brick! I could weep with gratitude."

"No need for all that." Lucy fought back a glad smile. "I've just finished my own house and it turns out I have a way with glue. Shall I paste while you cut?"

"Perfect!" Saffy tossed the towel back onto the chair. Her hands were still tacky but they'd do. When Lucy handed her a cup, she took it gratefully. They stood for a moment, sharing the companionable silence as each savored a first sip. It had become something of a habit, taking tea together like this. Nothing fancy: they didn't stop their daily tasks or lay the best silver; they just managed to be busy together in the same place at the right time of day. Percy, had she known, would've been horrified; she'd have come over all frowns and glowers, pursed her lips, and said things like "It isn't proper," and "Standards should be maintained." But Saffy liked Lucy—they were friends, after a fashion, and she couldn't see that sharing tea could do any harm at all. Besides, what Percy didn't know couldn't hurt her.

"And tell me, Lucy," she said, breaking the silence and thereby signaling that they might both resume their work, "how's the house going?"

"Very well indeed, Miss Saffy."

"You're not too lonely there by yourself?" Lucy and her mother had lived together always in the little cottage on the village's outskirts. Saffy could only imagine what a gap the old woman's death must have left.

"I keep myself busy." Lucy had balanced her teacup on the windowsill while she ran the glue-laden brush diagonally across the pane. For a moment Saffy thought she detected a sadness in the housekeeper's face, as if she'd been about to confess some deep feeling but had thought better of it.

"What is it, Lucy?"

"Oh, it's nothing." She hesitated. "Only that, I miss Mother, of course . . ."

"Of course." Lucy was discreet (to a fault, the nosier part of Saffy sometimes thought), but over the years Saffy had gleaned enough to know that Mrs. Middleton was not an easy person. "But?"

"But I do quite enjoy my own company." She glanced sideways at Saffy. "If that doesn't sound too awful?"

"Not awful at all," Saffy said with a smile. Truthfully, she thought it sounded wonderful. She began to picture her own little dream flatlet in London, then stopped herself. On a day when she was pillar to post with chores it was foolish to become distracted. She sat on the floor and set about running the scissors through the fabric, making strips. "Things all right upstairs, are they, Lucy?"

"The room looks lovely; I've aired it and changed the linens and I hope you don't mind"—she smoothed out a piece of fabric—"but I've put away your grandmother's Chinese vase. I can't think how I missed it when we were wrapping and storing the precious items last week. It's safe and sound now, tucked away in the muniment room with the others."

"Oh"—Saffy's eyes widened, searching Lucy's face—"but you don't think we'll get a little wretch, do you? Intent on breaking things and wreaking havoc?"

"Not at all. I just thought it was as well to be safe rather than sorry."

"Yes." Saffy nodded as the housekeeper took up a new piece of fabric. "Very wise, Lucy, and of course you're right. I should have thought of it myself. Percy will be pleased." She sighed. "All the same; I thought we might put a little bunch of fresh flowers on the nightstand. Raise the poor little mite's spirits? Perhaps a glass vase from the kitchen?"

"Far more suitable. I'll find one, shall I?"

Saffy smiled agreement, but as she pictured the child's arrival her smile staled and she shook her head. "Oh, but isn't it ghastly, Lucy?"

"I'm sure no one expects you to offer your best crystal."

"No, I mean the whole thing. The proposition itself. All those frightened children, their poor mothers back in London having to smile and wave as they watch their babies disappear into the great unknown. And for what? All to clear the stage for war. So young men can be forced to kill other young men in far-off places."

Lucy turned to look at Saffy, surprise in her eyes, some concern mixed in. "You mustn't go getting yourself all upset, now."

"I know, I know. I won't."

"It's up to us to keep morale high."

"Of course."

"It's lucky there are people like you willing to take the poor little wretches in. What time are you expecting the child?"

Saffy set down her empty teacup and took up the scissors again. "Percy says the buses arrive sometime between three and six; she couldn't be any more specific than that."

"She's making the selection then?" Lucy's voice had caught a little, and Saffy knew what she was thinking: Percy was hardly the obvious choice when it came to maternal matters.

As Lucy shifted the chair to the next window, Saffy scampered along the floor to keep up. "It was the only way I could get her to agree—you know how she is about the castle; she has images of some unholy terror snapping curlicues off the banisters, scribbling on the wallpaper, setting the curtains on fire. I have to keep reminding her that these walls have stood for hundreds of years, that they've survived invasions by the Normans, the Celts, and Juniper. One poor child from London isn't going to make any difference."

Lucy laughed. "Speaking of Miss Juniper, will she be in for lunch? Only I thought I saw her leaving in your father's car earlier?"

Saffy waved the scissors in the air. "Your guess is as good as mine. The last time I knew Juniper's mind was . . ." She thought for a moment, chin on her knuckles, then released her arms theatrically. "You know, I can't remember a single time."

"Miss Juniper has talents other than predictability."

"Yes," said Saffy with a fond smile. "She certainly has."

Lucy hesitated then, climbed back down to the ground and drew slim fingers across her forehead. A funny, old-fashioned motion, a little like a damsel contemplating a fainting spell; it amused Saffy and she wondered whether she could incorporate the endearing habit into her novel—it seemed just the sort of thing that Adele might do when made nervous by a man . . .

"Miss Saffy?"

"Mmm?"

"There is something rather serious I wanted to talk to you about."

Lucy exhaled but didn't continue and Saffy wondered for a terrible, hot instant whether she might be ill. Whether there'd been bad news from the doctor: it would explain Lucy's reticence and, come to think of it, her recent habit of distraction. Why, just the other morning, Saffy had come into the kitchen to see Lucy watching unseeingly from the back door, across the kitchen garden and beyond, while Daddy's eggs continued to boil far beyond his usual soft preference.

"What is it, Lucy?" Saffy stood up, gesturing that Lucy should join her in the sitting area. "Is everything all right? You're peaky. Shall I fetch you a glass of water?"

Lucy shook her head but glanced about for something to lean on, choosing the back of the nearest armchair.

Saffy sat on the chaise longue and waited; and in the end, when Lucy's news finally burst forth, she was glad that she was seated.

"I'm going to be married," said Lucy. "That is, someone has asked me to marry him and I've said yes."

For a moment Saffy wondered if the housekeeper was delusional, or at least playing a trick. Quite simply, it made no sense: Lucy, dear reliable Lucy, who had never once in all the years she'd worked at Milderhurst so much as mentioned a male companion, let alone stepped out with a fellow, was to be married? Now, out of the blue like this, and at her age? Why, she was a few years older than Saffy, surely nearing forty years old.

Lucy shifted where she stood and Saffy realized that silence had fallen rather heavily between them and it was her turn to speak. Her tongue moved around some words, but she couldn't seem to utter them.

"I'm getting married," said Lucy again, more slowly this time, and with the sort of caution that suggested she was still getting used to the notion herself.

"But, Lucy, that's wonderful news," said Saffy, all in a rush. "And who is the lucky fellow? Where did you meet him?"

"Actually—" Lucy flushed. "We met here, at Milderhurst."

"Oh?"

"It's Harry Rogers. I'm marrying Harry Rogers. He's asked me and I've said yes."

Harry Rogers. The name was familiar, vaguely; Saffy felt sure she should know the gentleman, but she couldn't find a face to match the name. But how embarrassing! Saffy could feel her cheeks reddening and she covered her dilemma by planting a broad smile on her face, hoped it was sufficient to convince Lucy of her delight.

"We'd known one another for years, of course, what with him visiting so regularly at the castle, but we only started walking out together a couple of months ago. It was right after the grandfather clock began playing up, back in spring."

Harry Rogers. But not, surely, the hirsute little clock man? Why, he was neither handsome nor gallant nor, from what Saffy had observed, remotely witty. He was a common man, interested only in chatting with Percy about the state of the castle and the inside workings of clocks. Obliging enough, as far as Saffy could tell, and Percy had always spoken kindly of him (until Saffy chided that he'd be sweet on her if she weren't careful); nonetheless, he wasn't at all the right man for Lucy with her pretty face and easy laugh. "But how did this happen?" The question had risen and bubbled out before Saffy could even think to stem it. Lucy didn't appear to take offense, answering directly, almost too quickly, Saffy thought; as if she herself needed to hear the words spoken in order to understand how such a thing could have occurred.

"He'd been up to see about the clock and I was leaving early on account of Mother being poorly, and it just so happened that we bumped into one another on our way out of the door. He offered me a lift home and I took it. We struck up a friendship and then, when Mother passed away . . . Well, he was very kind. Quite a gentleman."

There fell then a pall of silence in which the scenario played out variously in each of their minds. Saffy, though surprised, was also curious. It was the writer in her, she supposed: wondering at the type of conversation the two might have had in Mr. Rogers's little motorcar, how, exactly, one thoughtful lift home had blossomed into a love affair. "And you're happy?"

"Oh yes." Lucy smiled. "Yes, I'm happy."

"Well." Saffy forced strength into her own smile. "Then I'm enormously happy *for* you. And you must bring him up for tea. A little celebration!"

"Oh no." Lucy shook her head. "No. It's kind of you, Miss Saffy, but I don't think that would be wise."

"Why ever not?" said Saffy, though as she said it she knew perfectly well why not, and suffered a wave of embarrassment for not having found a smarter way to extend the invitation. Lucy was far too proper to entertain the notion of dining with her employers. With Percy, especially.

"We'd rather not make a fuss," she said. "We're neither of us young. There won't be a long engagement; there's no point in waiting, what with the war."

"But surely at his age Harry won't be going—?"

"Oh no, nothing like that. He'll be doing his bit though, with Mr. Potts's mob. He was in the first war, you know; at Passchendaele. Alongside my brother—alongside Michael."

There was a new expression on Lucy's face then—a type of pride,

Saffy realized, a tentative pleasure shot through with mild self-consciousness. It was the novelty, of course, the recent change in circumstance. Lucy was still becoming used to this new persona, that of a woman soon to be married, a woman who was part of a couple, who had a male counterpart through whom she might be clothed in reflected glory. Saffy warmed a little vicariously; she couldn't think of anyone she knew who deserved happiness as much as Lucy. "Well, of course, that all makes very good sense," she said. "And you must certainly take a few days for yourself either side of the wedding. Perhaps I could—"

"Actually . . ." Lucy pressed her lips together and concentrated on the patch of space above Saffy's left shoulder. "That's the thing I really must talk to you about."

"Oh?"

"Yes." Lucy smiled, but not easily and not happily, then the smile fell away leaving only a slight sigh in its place. "It's rather awkward you see, but Harry would prefer . . . that is, he thinks that once we're married it would be best if I stay at home, look after his house, and do my bit for the war effort." Perhaps Lucy felt as keenly as Saffy that further explanation was required for she went on to say, quickly, "And in case we should be blessed with children."

And then Saffy understood; it was as if a great veil had been lifted. Everything that had been blurred came into focus: Lucy wasn't in love with Harry Rogers any more than Saffy was, she merely yearned for a baby. It was a wonder Saffy hadn't figured it out straightaway; it was so plain now that she knew. It was, in fact, the only explanation. Harry had offered her that one last chance; what woman in Lucy's position wouldn't make the same decision? Saffy fingered her locket, ran a thumb over the snib, and felt a surge of kinship with Lucy, a flush of sisterly affection and understanding so strong that she was overcome with a sudden desire to tell Lucy everything, to explain that she, Saffy, knew exactly how she felt.

She opened her mouth to do just that, but found no words had come. She smiled slightly, blinked and was astonished to feel a wave of warm tears threatening to spill. Lucy, meanwhile, had turned away, was searching her pockets for something, and Saffy, recovering her composure as best she could, glanced surreptitiously towards the window, watching as a single black bird sailed an invisible current of warm air.

She blinked again and everything took on a misty veneer. But how ridiculous it was to cry! It was the war of course, the uncertainty, the wretched, hateful windows!

"I'm going to miss you too, Miss Saffy. All of you. I've spent over half my life here at Milderhurst; I always assumed I'd end my days here too." A slight hesitation. "If that doesn't sound too morbid?"

"Terribly morbid." Saffy smiled through tears, pinching the locket again beneath her fingers. Lucy would be dreadfully missed, but that wasn't the only reason Saffy wept. She didn't open the locket anymore; she didn't need the photograph to see his face. The young man with whom she'd been in love, who'd been in love with her. The future had stretched ahead, anything had been possible, everything. Before it was all stolen from her—

But Lucy knew none of that, and if she did, if over the years she'd gathered threads here and there, connected them to form a rueful picture, she was polite enough never to mention it. Even now. "The wedding will be in April," she continued softly, handing Saffy an envelope she'd drawn from her pocket. Her letter of resignation, Saffy realized. "Spring. In the village church, just a small wedding. Nothing fancy. I'd be very happy to stay on until then, but I understand if . . ." There were tears in her eyes now. "I'm so sorry, Miss Saffy, not to give you more notice. Especially at a time like this, with help so difficult to find."

"Nonsense," said Saffy. She shivered, aware suddenly of a draft, crisp against her damp cheeks. She pulled out her handkerchief and dabbed, noticed the smudges of face powder on the cloth. "Oh goodness," she said, pulling a face of mock horror, "what a mess I must look." She smiled at Lucy. "Now, never mind your apologies. You're not to give it another thought, and you're certainly not to do any more crying. Love is a thing to be celebrated, not wept over."

"Yes," said Lucy, looking anything but a woman in love. "Well then."

"Well then."

"I should get on."

"Yes." Saffy didn't smoke, she couldn't stand the smell or the taste of tobacco, but at that moment she wished she did. Something settling to do with her hands. She swallowed, straightened a little, drew strength as she often did by pretending to be Percy . . .

Oh dear. Percy.

"Lucy?"

The housekeeper turned from where she was collecting the empty teacups.

"What about Percy? Does she know about Harry? That you're leaving us?"

The housekeeper's face paled as she shook her head.

Unease set up camp in Saffy's stomach. "Perhaps I ought to—?"

"No," said Lucy, with a small, brave smile. "No. It's something I must do."

FOUR

PERCY didn't go home. Neither did she go on to the village hall to assist with the arrangement of corned beef tins. Saffy would later accuse her of forgetting to collect an evacuee on purpose, of never having wanted one in the first place; but although there was an element of truth in the latter accusation, Percy's failure to show up at the hall had nothing to do with Saffy and everything to do with Mrs. Potts's gossip. Besides, as she reminded her twin, everything had worked out in the end: Juniper, unpredictable, beloved Juniper, had happened by the village hall quite by chance and Meredith had thus been plucked for the castle. Percy, meanwhile, having left the WVS meeting in something of a daze, had forgotten about her bicycle, turning to walk instead along the High Street, head held high, gait assured, looking for all the world like someone with a list in her pocket of a hundred tasks to be met by dinnertime. Giving no hint at all that she was the walking wounded, a ghostly echo of her former self. How she found herself at the hair salon she would never know, but that is precisely where her numb feet took her.

Percy's hair had always been long and blond, though never so long as Juniper's nor so golden as Saffy's. Percy didn't mind either of these things; she'd never been the sort to pay much attention to her crowning glory. While Saffy left her hair long because she was vain and Juniper ignored hers because she wasn't, Percy kept it that way for the simple reason that Daddy preferred it. He believed that girls should be pretty, that his daughters, especially, should have long fair hair that fell in waves down their backs.

Percy flinched as the hairdresser wetted and combed her hair until it was dishwater-dark and lank. Metal blades whispered cool against the back of her neck and the first hank dropped to the floor, where it lay still, a dead thing. She felt light.

The hairdresser had been shocked when Percy made the request, had asked her over and again if she were sure. "But your curls are so pretty," she'd said sadly; "do you really want them all off?"

"All of them."

"But you won't recognize yourself."

No, Percy thought, and the notion had pleased her. When she'd sat in the chair, still in something of a dream, Percy had looked and met her own image in the mirror, caught herself in a moment of introspection. What she'd seen had disquieted her. A woman of increasing years, still wrapping her hair in rags at night to affect the girlish curls that nature had forgotten. Such fussing was all well and good for Saffy, who was a romantic, refusing even now to let go of old dreams and accept that her knight in shining armor was not coming, that her place was, and would always be, at Milderhurst; but it was laughable in Percy. Percy the pragmatist, Percy the planner, Percy the protector.

She should have cut off her hair years ago. The new style was trim and spare and although she couldn't claim to look better, it was enough to know that she looked different. With each snip something inside her released, an old idea to which she'd been clinging without knowing it, so that finally, when the young hairdresser lay down the scissors and said, a little greenly, "There you are then, dear. Don't you look neat?" Percy had ignored the infuriating condescension to agree with some surprise that yes, she did indeed look neat.

MEREDITH HAD been waiting for hours, first standing, then sitting, now slouching on the wooden floor of the Milderhurst village hall. As time stretched out, and the stream of farmers and local ladies dried completely, and the dark started to hover outside the windows, Meredith let herself wonder what dreadful fate might await her if she weren't chosen at all, if *nobody* wanted her. Would she spend the next few weeks living here, alone, in the drafty hall? The very thought made her spectacles mist so that everything was blurred.

And it was then, at that precise moment, that *she* arrived. Swept in, like a resplendent angel, like something out of a made-up story, and rescued Meredith from the cold, hard floor. As if she knew somehow, through some sort of magic or sixth sense—something science was yet to explain—that she was needed.

Meredith didn't see the actual entrance, she was too busy cleaning her spectacle lenses on the hem of her skirt but she did feel a crackle in the air and perceived the unnatural silence when it fell among the chirruping women.

"Why, Miss Juniper," one of them said, as Meredith fumbled her spectacles back onto her nose and blinked towards the refreshments table. "What a surprise. And how may we be of assistance? Are you looking for Miss Blythe, because it's quite a curious thing, but we haven't seen her since midday—"

"I've come for my evacuee," said the girl who must be Miss Juniper, cutting the woman off with a wave of her hand. "Don't get up. I see her."

And she started walking, passing the children in the front row and Meredith blinked a few more times, looked over her shoulder and realized there was no one remaining there, then turned back just in time to find that splendid person standing directly above her. "Ready?" the stranger said. Casually, lightly, as if they were old friends and the whole thing had been planned in advance.

LATER, AFTER Percy had lost hours somehow by the brook, sat cross-legged on a smooth-washed stone, built childish boats from whatever came to hand, she returned to the church hall to collect her bicycle. After such a warm day the evening had come in cool, and by the time Percy started for the castle, the falling dusk had shadowed the hills.

Despair had tangled Percy's thoughts and she tried, as she pedaled, to straighten them. The engagement itself was devastating, but it was the duplicity that cut deepest. All this time—for there must have been a period of courtship leading to the proposal—Harry and Lucy had been sneaking behind her back, conducting their affair beneath her nose as if she were nothing to either of them, neither lover nor employer. The betrayal was like a hot iron to her chest; she wanted to scream, to tear at her own face, and his, and hers, to scratch and harm them both as they had wounded her. To bellow until her voice failed, to be beaten until she no longer felt pain, to close her eyes and never have to open them again.

But she would do none of those things. Percy Blythe did not behave in such a way.

Over the treetops, the oncoming darkness continued to bruise the distant fields and a flock of black birds took flight towards the Channel. The moon's pale casing, as yet unlit, hung lifeless in the shadows. Percy wondered, idly, whether the bombers would come tonight.

With a short sigh she lifted one hand to press the newly exposed skin at the nape of her neck, then, as the breath of evening brushed her face, she pedaled harder. Harry and Lucy were to be married and nothing Percy did or said would change that fact. Crying would not help, neither would reproach. What was done was done. All that remained was for Percy to formulate and follow a new plan. To do what needed to be done, just as she always had.

When finally she reached the gates of Milderhurst, she swerved across the road and the rickety footbridge and jumped off her bicycle. Although she'd done little more than sit all day, she was tired, and strangely so. Tired to the ends of her fingers. Her bones, her eyes, her arms, all airy, as if they were made up of grains. Like a rubber band that had been wound too tightly and unraveled now to find itself stretched and frayed, weak and shapeless. She fumbled with her handbag until she found a cigarette.

Percy walked the final mile, pushed the bicycle beside her as she smoked, stopping only when the castle came into view. Barely visible, a black armory against the navy sky, not a chink of light showed. The curtains were drawn, the shutters were closed, the blackout was being followed to the letter. Good. The last thing she needed was for Hitler to set his sights on her castle.

She rested her bicycle on the ground and lay beside it on the night-cooled grass. Smoked another cigarette. Then another, her last. Percy curled onto her side and pressed her ear to the ground, listened as Daddy had shown her. Her family, her home, was built on a foundation of words, he'd said, time and again, the family tree laced together with sentences in place of limbs. Layers of expressed thought had soaked into the soil of the castle gardens so that poems and plays, prose and political treatises, would always whisper to her when she needed them. Ancestors she would never meet, who had lived and died before her birth, left behind them words, words, words, chattering to one another, to her, from beyond the grave, so she was never lonely, never alone.

After a time Percy stood, picked up her things, and continued in silence towards the castle. Dusk had been swallowed by dark and the moon had arrived, the beautiful, traitorous moon, stretching her pale fingers over the landscape. A brave harvest mouse fled across a silver spill of lawn, fine grass quivered on the gentle rises of the fields, and beyond the woods shrugged blackly.

She could hear voices inside as she drew nearer: Saffy's and Juniper's, and another, a child's voice, a girl. Allowing herself a moment's hesitation, Percy climbed the first step, then the next, remembering the thousands of times she'd run through the door, in a hurry to get to the future, to whatever was coming next, to this moment.

As she stood there, hand poised to open the door of her home, as the tallest trees of Cardarker Wood bore witness, she made a promise: she was Persephone Blythe of Milderhurst Castle. There were other things in life she loved—not many, but there were some: her sisters, her father, and their castle, of course. She was the eldest—if only by a matter of minutes—she was Daddy's heir, the only one of his children who shared his love for the stones, the soul, the secrets of their home. She would pick herself up and carry on. And she would make it her duty, from this moment forth, to ensure no harm befell any of them, that she did whatever was necessary to keep them all safe.

PART THREE

PART THREE

KIDNAPPINGS AND RECRIMINATIONS

1992

MILDERHURST Castle was almost lost to the Sisters Blythe in 1952. The castle needed urgent repair, the Blythe family finances were dire, and the National Trust was keen to acquire the property and begin its restoration. It seemed that the sisters had little choice but to move somewhere smaller, sell the estate to strangers, or sign it over to the trust so they might get on with "preserving the crowning glory of the building and gardens." Only they did none of those things. Percy Blythe opened the castle to visitors instead, sold a few parcels of surrounding farmland, and somehow managed to scrape together sufficient funds to keep the old place standing.

I know this because I spent the better part of a sunny weekend in August trawling through the local library's microfilm records of the *Milderhurst Mercury*. In retrospect, telling my dad that the origin of *The True History of the Mud Man* was a great literary mystery was a little like putting a box of chocolates on the floor beside a toddler and expecting him not to touch it. He's rather results-based, my dad, and he liked the idea that he might be able to solve a mystery that had plagued academics for decades. He had his theory: the real-life kidnapping of a long-ago child lay at the novel's gothic heart; all he needed to do was prove it and the fame, the glory, the personal satisfaction, would be his. Confinement to bed, however, is no friend to the sleuth, so an agent was necessarily enlisted and dispatched in his place. Which was where I figured. I humored him for three reasons: partly because he was recuperating from a heart attack, partly because his theory wasn't completely ridiculous, but most of all because reading my mother's letters had stretched my fascination with Milderhurst to pathological proportions.

I started my inquiries, as I usually do, by asking Herbert whether he knew anything about unsolved kidnapping cases from the early part of the century. One of my hands-down favorite things about Herbert—and the list is long—is his ability to find precisely the information he's after in the face of apparent chaos. His house is tall and skinny to start with, four onetime flats patched back together: our office and printing press take up the first two levels, the attic's been sacrificed to storage, and the basement flat is where he lives with Jess. Every wall of every room is lined with books: old books, new books, first editions, signed editions, twenty-third editions, stacked together on mismatched, improvised sets of shelves, in a glorious, healthy disregard for display. And yet the entire collection is catalogued in his brain, his very own reference library, so that he has every reading experience of his life at his fingertips. To see him home in on a target is a thing of beauty: first, his impressive brow furrows as he takes in the query, then a single finger, delicate and smooth as a candlestick, rises and he hobbles, wordlessly, to a distant wall of books, where the finger is given free rein to hover, as if magnetized, above the spines, leading him, finally, to slide the perfect book from its place.

Asking Herbert about the kidnapping was a lazy long shot, so I wasn't really surprised when it yielded little of use. I told him not to feel bad and headed to the library, where I befriended a delightful old lady in the basement who'd apparently been waiting there all her life on the off chance I'd show up. "Just sign in over here, my dear," she said eagerly, pointing to a clipboard and pen, and shadowing me closely as I filled in the requisite columns. "Oh, Billing & Brown, how lovely. My dear old friend, may he rest in peace, published his memoirs with B&B some thirty years ago."

There weren't many other folk spending that gorgeous summer's day in the bowels of the library, so I was easily able to co-opt Miss Yeats to my purpose. We passed a lovely time together, trawling through the archives, turning up three unsolved kidnapping cases in and around Kent during the Victorian and Edwardian periods, then plenty of newspaper reports concerning the Blythe family of Milderhurst Castle. There was a charming, semiregular column of housekeeping advice written by Saffy Blythe throughout the fifties and sixties; numerous articles about Raymond Blythe's literary success; and some headlining reports of the family's near loss of Milderhurst in 1952. At the time Percy Blythe had given an interview in which she made an emphatic case: "A place is more than the sum of its physical parts; it's a repository for memories, a record and retainer of all that has happened within its boundaries. This castle belongs to my family. It belonged to my ancestors for centuries before I was born, and I won't see it passed into the hands of people who wish to plant conifers in its ancient woods."

A rather pernickety representative of the National Trust had also been interviewed for the article, lamenting the lost opportunity for their new garden scheme to restore the property to its former glory: "It's a tragedy," he began, "to think that the great properties of our nation will be lost to us over the coming decades, through the sheer bloody-mindedness of those who cannot see that in these lean and austere times, individual residence in such national treasures is tantamount to sacrilege." When asked about the trust's plans for Milderhurst Castle, he outlined a program of works including "the structural repair of the castle itself, and a complete garden restoration." An aim, I'd have thought, that was very much in line with Percy Blythe's wishes for her family estate.

"There was a lot of ambivalence about the trust at the time," said Miss Yeats, when I ventured as much. "The fifties were a difficult period: the cherry trees were taken out at Hidcote, the avenue at Wimpole was cut down, all in the service of a sort of all-purpose historical prettiness."

The two examples meant little to me, but all-purpose historical prettiness certainly didn't sound like much of a match for the Percy Blythe I'd met. As I read further, matters became clearer still. "It says here that the trust planned to restore the moat." I looked up at Miss Yeats, who inclined her head, awaiting explanation. "Raymond Blythe had the moat filled in after the twins' mother's death: a sort of symbolic memorial. They wouldn't have been happy with the trust's plans to dig it out again." I leaned back in my chair, stretching my lower back. "What I don't understand is how they could've hit such hard times in the first place. The *Mud Man* is a classic, a bestseller, even today. Surely the royalties would have been enough to keep them out of trouble?"

"One would think so," Miss Yeats agreed. Then she frowned and turned her attention to the rather large stack of printouts on the table before us. "You know, I'm sure I . . ." She shuffled the pages back and forth until one was chosen and held right by her nose. "Yes! Here it is." She handed me the newspaper article dated May 13, 1941, and peered over the top of her half-moon glasses. "Apparently Raymond Blythe left a couple of large bequests when he died."

The article was entitled "Generous Gift from Literary Patron Saves Institute" and was accompanied by a picture of a grinning, dungaree-clad woman clutching a copy of the *Mud Man*. I scanned the text and saw that Miss Yeats was right: the majority of the royalties were divided after Raymond Blythe's death between the Catholic Church and another group. "The Pembroke Farm Institute," I read slowly. "It says here that they're a conservation group based in Sussex. Committed to the promotion of sound ecological practice."

"Rather ahead of their time," said Miss Yeats.

I nodded.

"Shall we check the reference files upstairs? See what else we can find?"

Miss Yeats was so buoyed by the prospect of a new research tangent that her cheeks had taken on a rosy sheen and I felt really rather cruel when I said, "Not today, no. I'm afraid I haven't the time." She looked crestfallen, so I added, "I'm so sorry. But my dad's expecting a report on my research."

WHICH WAS true, and yet I didn't go straight home. When I said there were three reasons I was happy to give up my weekend to my dad's library task, I'm afraid I was a little disingenuous. I wasn't lying, they were all true, however there was also the small matter of a fourth and more pressing reason. I was avoiding my mother. It was all the fault of those letters, more accurately, of my inability to leave the damned shoebox closed once Rita had given it to me.

I read them all, you see. The night of Sam's hen party, I took them home and devoured them, one by one, beginning with Mum's arrival at the castle. I endured with her the freezing early months of 1940, witnessed the Battle of Britain raging above my head, the nights spent shivering in the Anderson shelter. Over the course of eighteen months, the handwriting grew neater, the expression more mature, until finally, in the wee hours, I reached the last letter, the one sent home just before her father came to fetch her back to London. It was dated February 17, 1941, and read as follows.

> *Dear Mum and Dad,*
>
> *I'm sorry that we argued on the telephone. I was so pleased to hear from you both and I feel terrible about the way it ended. I don't think I explained myself very well at all. What I meant to say is that I understand that you just want the best for me, and I'm grateful, Dad, that you've been to speak with Mr. Solley on my behalf. I can't agree, however, that my coming home and finding typing work with him is "best."*
>
> *Rita is different from me. She hated it here in the country and has always known what she wanted to do and be. For my entire life I've felt that there was something wrong with me, that I was "other" in some important way I couldn't explain, that I couldn't even understand myself. I love to read books, I love to watch people, I love to capture the things I see and feel by ar-*

ranging words on paper. Ridiculous, I know! Can you imagine what an odd, black sheep I've felt my entire life?

Here, though, I've met people who enjoy these things, too; and I realize that there are others who see the world as I do. Saffy believes that when the war ends, which it must do soon, I have a good chance of getting a place at one of the grammar schools; after that—who knows? Perhaps even university?! I must keep up with my schooling though, if I am to stand a chance of transferring to grammar school.

So I beg you—please don't make me come home! The Blythes are happy for me to stay and you know that I'm well cared for here. You haven't "lost" me, Mum; I wish you wouldn't put it like that. I'm your daughter—you couldn't lose me if you tried. Please, though, please let me stay.

With much love and heaps of hope,
Your daughter, Meredith

I dreamed of Milderhurst that night. I was a girl again, dressed in a school uniform I didn't recognize, and standing at the tall iron gates at the bottom of the driveway. They were locked and far too high to scale, so high that when I looked up at where their tops should be they seemed to disappear into the swirling clouds above. I tried to climb them but my feet kept slipping, they'd gone all jellylike, the way they often do in dreams: the iron was icy beneath my hands, yet I was filled with a deep longing, a fierce desire to know what lay beyond.

I looked down and saw that a large key, rusting around the edges, lay across my palm. Next thing I knew, I was beyond the gates and sitting in a carriage on the other side. In a scene borrowed directly from the *Mud Man*, I was being drawn up the long and winding drive, past the dark and shivering woods, across the bridges, until finally the castle loomed above me at the top of the hill.

And then, somehow, I was inside. The whole place felt abandoned. Dust coated the corridor floors, the paintings hung crooked on the walls, the curtains had all faded, but it was more than just the way it looked. The air was stale, cloying, and I felt as if I'd been locked within a box inside a dark and musty attic.

A noise then, a whispery rustling sound, and the merest suggestion of movement. At the end of the hall was Juniper, dressed in the same silky dress she'd been wearing when I visited the castle. I was aware of a strange sense within me, the dream's pervasive mood of profound and troubled longing. I knew, although she didn't say a word, that this was October 1941 and she was waiting for Thomas Cavill to arrive. A door appeared behind her, the entrance to the good parlor. There was music, a tune I felt I knew.

I followed her into the room, where a table had been set. The room was thick with anticipation, and I drifted around the table, counting the places, knowing, though I'm not sure how, that one was set for me and another for my mum. Juniper was saying something then; that is, her lips were moving but I couldn't make out any words.

Then, suddenly, I was at the parlor window, only, in a strange dream twist of logic, it was my mother's kitchen window too, and I was staring at the glass pane. I looked outside and it was stormy and I realized there was a glistening, black moat. Movement and a dark figure began to emerge; my heart struck like a bell. I knew it was the Mud Man and I was frozen where I stood. My feet had become one with the floor, but just when I was about to scream, my fear suddenly disappeared. I was filled instead with a flood of yearning and sorrow and, quite unexpectedly, desire.

I woke with a start, catching my dream in the process of dissolving. Tattered fancies hung like ghosts in the room's corners and I lay very still for a time, willing them not to dissipate. It seemed to me that even the slightest movement, the merest hint of morning sunlight, would burn the imprints off like fog. And I didn't want to lose them yet. The dream had been so vivid, the heaviness of longing so real that when I pressed my hand against my chest I half expected to find the skin bruised.

271

After a time, the sun rose high enough to slide across the roof-top of Singer & Sons and pry through the gaps in my curtains and the dream's spell was broken. I sat up with a sigh and noticed Gran's shoebox on the end of the bed. At the sight of all those envelopes addressed to Elephant and Castle, details of the night before came rushing back and I was hit by the sudden, clear-light-of-day guilt of someone who'd glutted on a feast of fat and sugar and someone else's secrets. No matter how glad I was to have acquired the voice, the pictures, the small sense of my mum, and no matter how convincing my justifications (the letters were written long ago; they were intended for an audience; she'd never have to know), I couldn't erase the expression on Rita's face as she'd given me the box and told me to have a good old read; the hint of triumph, as if we two shared a secret now, a bond, a connection that excluded her sister. The warm feeling of holding the little girl's hand had gone, leaving only the sneak's remorse in its place.

I would have to confess my crime, that much was certain, but I made a deal with myself. If I managed to leave the house without running into Mum, I could have a day's grace to consider how best to do it. On the other hand, if I ran into her before I reached the door, I would confess all, then and there. I dressed quickly and quietly, took stealthy care of all additional grooming needs, rescued my tote from the lounge—all was going brilliantly until I reached the kitchen. Mum was standing by the kettle, robe fastened around her middle, a little higher than it should be, giving her an odd snowmanlike shape.

"Morning, Edie," she said, glancing over her shoulder.

Too late to backtrack. "Morning, Mum."

"Sleep well?"

"Yes, thanks."

I was rustling up an excuse for skipping breakfast when she put a cup of tea on the table in front of me and said, "And how was Samantha's party?"

"Colorful. Noisy." I gave her a quick smile. "You know Sam."

"I didn't hear you come in last night. I left you some supper."

"Oh . . ."

"I wasn't sure, but I see you didn't—"

"I was pretty tired—"

"Of course."

Oh, but I felt like a heel! And the unfortunate pudding effect of Mum's robe made her seem more vulnerable than ever, which made me feel even worse. I sat where she'd put the tea, drew a decisive breath, and said, "Mum, there's something I need to—"

"*Ah!*" She winced, sucked her finger, then shook it quickly. "Steam," she said, blowing lightly across her fingertip. "It's this silly new kettle."

"Can I fetch you some ice?"

"I'll just run it under cold water." She turned on the tap. "It's something in the shape of the spout. I don't know why they keep redesigning things that work perfectly well already."

I took another breath but let it out again as she continued talking.

"I wish they'd just focus their attention on something useful. A cure for cancer, perhaps." She turned off the tap.

"Mum, there's something I really need—"

"I'll be right back, Edie; let me take your father his tea lest the bell begin to toll."

She disappeared upstairs and I waited, wondering what I was going to say, how I was going to say it, whether it was possible to phrase my sin in such a way that she might understand. A fond hope, but I dismissed it swiftly. There is no kind way of telling someone you've been peeking through the keyhole at them.

I could hear the edges of the low conversation Mum was having with Dad, then his door closing, then footsteps. I stood quickly. What was I thinking? I needed more time; it was foolish just to rush in; a little thought would make all the difference—but then she was in the kitchen saying, "That ought to keep His Nibs happy for the next fifteen minutes," and I was still standing somewhat awkwardly behind my chair, as natural as a bad actor in a play.

273

"You're off already?" she said, surprised. "You haven't even had your tea."

"I, ah . . ."

"You were saying something, weren't you?"

I picked up my teacup and studied the contents closely. "I . . ."

"Well?" She tightened the belt of her robe, waiting for me, the merest hint of concern narrowing her eyes. "What is it?"

Who was I kidding? More thought, a few additional hours: none of it was going to change the facts. I let out a sigh of resignation. "I have something for you."

I went back up to my room and collected the letters from beneath my bed.

Mum watched my return, a slight crease in her brow, and I laid the box on the table between us.

"Slippers?" She frowned lightly, first at her slipper-clad feet, then at me. "Well, thank you, Edie. One can never have too many pairs."

"No, but you see, they're not—"

"Your gran." She smiled suddenly, a distant memory firing. "Your gran used to wear this type." And the look she gave me then was so unguarded, so unexpectedly pleased, that it was all I could do not to seize the lid from the box and declare myself the ghastly traitor that I was. "Did you know that, Edie? Is that why you bought them? It's a wonder you could still find the old—"

"They're not slippers, Mum. Open the box; please, just open it."

"Edie?" An uncertain smile as she sat in the nearest chair and pulled the box towards her. She offered me a last wavering glance before turning her attention to the lid, lifting it and frowning at the pile of discolored envelopes within.

My blood ran hot and thin, like gasoline beneath my skin, as I watched the emotions flit across her face. Confusion, suspicion, then the intake of breath heralding recognition. Later, as I ran the memory over in my mind, I could pinpoint the precise instant at which the scrawled handwriting on the top envelope metamorphosed into a lived experience. I saw her face change, her features adopting, once more, those of the almost-thirteen-year-old girl who'd written the first letter to her parents, telling them about the castle in which she'd found herself; she was there again, caught in the original moment of composition.

Mum's fingers rested on her lips, her cheek, then hovered above the soft indentation at the base of her throat, until finally, after what seemed an age, she reached tentatively into the box, withdrew the pile of envelopes, and sat holding them in both hands. Hands that were shaking. She spoke without meeting my eyes. "Where did you . . . ?"

"Rita."

She released a slow sigh, nodded as if she'd been given the answer to something she should have guessed. "How did she come by them? Did she say?"

"They were with Gran's things, after she died."

A noise that might have been the start of a laugh, wistful, surprised, a little bit sad. "I can't believe she kept them."

"You wrote them," I said softly. "Of course she kept them."

Mum was shaking her head. "But it wasn't like that . . . my mother and I, we weren't like that."

I thought of *The Book of Magical Wet Animals*. My mother and I weren't like that either, or so I'd thought. "I suppose that's what parents do."

Mum fumbled envelopes from the pile, fanning them out in her hands. "Things from the past," she said, more to herself than to me. "Things I'd worked so hard to put behind me." Her fingers lightly traced the drift of envelopes. "Now it seems no matter where I turn . . ."

My heart had begun to race at the promise of revelation. "Why do you want to forget the past, Mum?"

But she didn't answer, not right then. The photograph, smaller than the letters, had fallen loose from the pile, just as it had the night before, slipping onto the table. She inhaled, before lifting it higher, rubbing her thumb across its surface; the expression on her face was vulnerable, pained. "Such a long time ago, yet sometimes . . ."

She seemed to remember then that I was there. Made a show of tucking the photograph back among the letters, casually, as if it meant little to her. She looked directly at me. "Your gran and I . . . it was never easy. We were very different people, we always had been, but my evacuation brought certain things to the fore. We fought and she never forgave me."

"Because you wanted to transfer to grammar school?"

Everything seemed to freeze then; even the natural circulations in the air stopped their swirling.

Mum looked as if she'd been struck. She spoke quietly, a quaver in her voice: "You read them? You read my letters?"

I swallowed, nodded jerkily.

"How could you, Edith? These are private."

All my earlier justifications dissolved like flecks of tissue in the rain. Shame made my eyes water so that everything seemed bleached, including Mum's face. Color had dissolved from her skin, leaving only a splatter of small freckles across her nose so that she looked like her thirteen-year-old self. "I just . . . I wanted to know."

"It's none of your *business* to know," Mum hissed. "It's got nothing to do with you." She seized the box, clutched it tightly to her chest, and after a moment's indecision hurried towards the door.

"But it does," I said to myself, then louder, my voice trembling, "you lied to me."

A stumble in her step—

"About Juniper's letter, about Milderhurst, about everything; we *did* go back—"

The slightest hesitation in the doorway, but she didn't turn and she didn't stop.

"—I *remember* it."

And I was alone again, surrounded by that peculiar glassy silence that follows when something fragile has been broken. At the top of the stairs a door slammed shut.

A FORTNIGHT had passed since then, and even by our standards relations were icy. We'd maintained a ghastly civility, for Dad's sake as much as because it was our style, nodding and smiling but never speaking a word that wasn't of the "Please pass the salt" variety. I felt guilty and self-righteous in turn; proud and interested in the girl who loved books as much as I did, angry and hurt by the woman who refused to share the merest part of herself with me.

Most of all though, I regretted having told her about the letters. I cursed whoever it was that said honesty was the best policy, turned a keen eye back to the letting pages, and fed our cold war by making sure I was barely around. It wasn't difficult: the edits for *Ghosts of Romney Marsh* were under way so I had a perfectly valid reason for putting in long hours at the office. Herbert, for his part, was pleased to have the company. My industry, he said, reminded him of the "good old days" when the war had finally ended, England was getting back on its feet, and he and Mr. Brown were rushing about acquiring manuscripts and filling orders.

So it was, on the Saturday of the library visit, when I tucked my file of newspaper printouts beneath my arm, checked my watch, and realized it had only just gone one, I didn't head for home. Dad was sweating on his kidnapping research, but he'd wait until our *Mud Man* session that evening. I started for Notting Hill instead. Swept along by the promise of good company, welcome distraction, and maybe even a little something for lunch.

THE PLOT BECOMES RATHER THICK

I had forgotten that Herbert was away for the weekend, delivering the keynote address at the annual meeting of the Bookbinders Association. The shades at Billing & Brown were down and the office was somber and lifeless. As I stepped across the threshold and was met by utter stillness, I felt a deflation out of all proportion.

"Jess?" I called hopefully. "Jessie girl?"

There came no grateful padding, no labored clamber up the stairs from the basement, just ripples of silence rolling towards me. There is something deeply disquieting about a beloved place relieved of its rightful occupants, and at that moment I'd never been so eager to jostle with Jess for room on the sofa.

"Jessie?" Still nothing. Which meant that she had gone to Shrewsbury, too, and I really was alone.

Never mind. I jollied myself along; there was plenty of work to keep me busy all afternoon. *Ghosts of Romney Marsh* was going to proof on Monday and although circumstances had already gifted it my close attention, there was always room for improvement. I lifted the blinds, switched on my desk lamp, making as much incidental noise as I could, then sat down and leafed through the manuscript pages. I shifted commas, I put them back again. I vacillated over the merits of using "however" in place of "but" without drawing any conclusion and marked the spot for further thought. I similarly failed to reach a firm decision on the next five stylistic queries before deciding it had been madness to attempt concentration on an empty stomach.

Herbert had been cooking and there was fresh pumpkin lasagna in the fridge. I removed a slice, heated it up, and took my plate back to my desk. It felt wrong to eat over the ghost whisperer's manuscript, so I slid across my file of *Milderhurst Mercury* printouts instead. I read bits and pieces, but most of all I looked at the pictures. There's something deeply nostalgic about black-and-white photographs, the absence of color a visual rendering of the deepening funnel of time. There were lots of shots taken of the castle itself at various periods, some of the estate, a very old one of Raymond Blythe and his twin daughters on the occasion of the publication of the *Mud Man*. Photos of Percy Blythe looking stiff and uncomfortable at the wedding of a local couple called Harold and Lucy Rogers, Percy Blythe cutting the ribbon at the opening of a community center, Percy Blythe presenting a signed copy of the *Mud Man* to the winner of a poetry competition.

I flicked back through the pages: Saffy was in none of them, and the fact struck me as rather unusual. Juniper's absence I could understand, but where was Saffy? I picked up an article celebrating the end of the Second World War, highlighting the involvement of various villagers. Yet another photograph of Percy Blythe, this time in ambulance uniform. I stared at it thoughtfully. It was possible, of course, that Saffy didn't like having her photo taken. It was possible, too, that she was staunchly opposed to involvement in the wider community. More likely, though, I felt certain, having seen the pair in action, she was a twin who knew her place. With a sister like Percy, filled with the steel of resolution and a fierce commitment to her family's good name, what hope had poor Saffy of getting her smile in the newspaper?

It was not a good photograph, very unflattering. Percy was in the foreground and the photo had been taken from below, no doubt in order to capture the castle behind her. The angle was unfortunate, making Percy seem looming and rather severe; the fact that she wasn't smiling didn't help matters.

I looked closer. There was something in the background that I hadn't noticed before, just beyond Percy's tightly cropped hair. I dug in Herbert's drawer until I found the magnifying glass, held it over the photograph, and squinted. Drew back in amazement. It was just as I had thought. There was someone on the castle roof. Sitting on a ridge by one of the peaks, a figure in a long white dress. I knew at once that it must be Juniper. Poor sad, mad Juniper.

As I looked at the tiny speck of white up by the attic window, I was overcome by a wave of indignant sadness. Anger, too. My feeling that Thomas Cavill was the root of all evil reawakened and I let myself sink once more into my imaginings of the fateful October night on which he'd broken Juniper's heart and ruined her life. The fantasy was well developed, I'm afraid; I'd been there many times before, and it played like a familiar film, moody soundtrack and all. I was with the sisters in that perfectly set parlor, listening as they wondered what could be keeping him so long, watching as Juniper began to fall victim to the madness that would consume her, when something happened. Something that had never happened before.

I'm not sure why or how, only that clarity, when it came, was sudden and fevered. The dream soundtrack screeched to a halt and the vision dissolved leaving only one fact behind: there was more to this story than met the eye. There had to be. For people didn't go mad simply because their lover stood them up, did they? Even if they did have a history of anxiety or depression or whatever Mrs. Bird had meant when she spoke of Juniper's episodes.

I let the *Mercury* drop and sat up very straight. I'd taken the sad story of Juniper Blythe at face value because Mum was right: I'm terribly fanciful and tragic tales are my favorite type. But this wasn't fiction, this was real life, and I needed to look at the situation more critically. I'm an editor, it's my job to examine narratives for plausibility, and this one was lacking in some way. It was oversimplified. Love affairs disintegrate, people betray one another, lovers part. Human experience is littered with such personal tragedies; ghastly, but surely, in the greater scheme, minor? *She went mad*: the words rolled off the tongue well enough, but the reality seemed thin, like something out of a penny dreadful. Why, I had been replaced in similar fashion myself recently and had not gone mad. Not even skirted close.

My heart had started to tick along rather quickly and I was already reaching for my bag, shoving my newspaper file back inside, gathering my dirty plate and cutlery for the kitchen. I needed to find Thomas Cavill. Why hadn't I thought of it before? Mum wasn't going to talk to me, Juniper couldn't; he was the key, the answer to everything lay at his feet, and I needed to know more about him.

I switched off the lamp, dropped the blinds, and locked the front door behind me. I'm a book person, not a people person, so it didn't occur to me to do it any other way: with a skip in my step, I hurried back in the direction of the library.

Miss Yeats was delighted to see me. "Back so soon," she said, with the sort of enthusiasm you might expect from a long-lost friend. "But you're all wet! Don't tell me the weather's come in again."

I hadn't even noticed. "I don't have an umbrella," I said.

"Well, never mind. You'll dry off soon enough, and I'm very glad you've come." She gathered a thin pile of papers from her desk and brought it to me with a reverence befitting transportation of the holy grail itself. "I know you said you hadn't time, but I did a little sleuthing anyway—the Pembroke Farm Institute," she said, having noticed, perhaps, that I hadn't a clue what she was talking about. "Raymond Blythe's bequest?"

"Oh," I said, remembering. The morning seemed an awfully long time ago. "Terrific. Thanks."

"I've printed out everything I could find. I was going to ring you at work and let you know, but now you're here!"

I thanked her again and gave the documents a cursory glance, flicking through pages detailing the institute's history of conservation, making a small show of considering the information, before tucking them inside my bag. "I'm really looking forward to exploring them properly," I said, "but there's something I need to do first." And I explained then that I was looking for information about a man. "Thomas Cavill is his name. He was a soldier during the Second World War and a teacher before that. He lived and worked near Elephant and Castle."

She was nodding. "Is there anything in particular you were hoping to uncover?"

Why he failed to arrive at Milderhurst Castle for dinner in October 1941, why Juniper Blythe was plunged into a madness from which she never recovered, why my mother refused to talk to me about any aspect of her past. "Not really," I said. "Whatever I can find."

Miss Yeats was a wizard. While I battled the microfilm machine solo, cursing the dial, which refused to perform small incremental shifts and flew instead through weeks at a time, she darted about the library accumulating odd bits of paper from here and there. When we reconvened after half an hour, I brought a worse-for-wear newsreel and a crushing headache to the table, while she'd assembled a small but decent dossier of information.

There wasn't much, certainly nowhere near the reams of local press concerning the Blythe family and their castle, but it was a start. There was a small birth notice from a 1916 *Bermondsey Gazette* that read *CAVILL—Feb. 22, at Henshaw St., the wife of Thomas Cavill of a son, Thomas*, an effusive report in the *Southwark Star* from 1937, entitled "Local Teacher Wins Poetry Prize," and another from 1939 with a similarly unambiguous title, "Local Teacher Joins War Effort." The second article contained a small photograph labeled "Mr. Thomas Cavill," but the copy was of such poor quality that I could tell little more about him than that he was a young man with a head, shoulders, and a British army uniform. It seemed rather a small collection of public information to show for a man's life and I was extremely disappointed to see that there was nothing at all from after 1939.

"That's it," I said, trying to sound philosophical rather than ungrateful.

"Almost." Miss Yeats handed me another clutch of papers.

They were advertisements, all dated March 1981, all taken from the bottom corner of *The Times, Guardian,* and *Daily Telegraph* classifieds. Each one bore the same message:

> Would Thomas Cavill, once of Elephant and Castle,
> please telephone Theo on the following number as a
> matter of urgency: (01) 394 7521

"Well," I said.

"*Well*," Miss Yeats concurred. "Rather curious, wouldn't you agree? Whatever could they mean?"

I shook my head. I had no idea. "One thing's certain: this Theo, whoever he might be, was pretty keen to get in touch with Thomas."

"May I ask, dear—I mean, I certainly don't like to pry, but is there anything here that helps you with your project?"

I took another look at the classifieds, pushed my hair behind my ears. "Perhaps."

"Because you know, if it's his service record you're interested in, the Imperial War Museum has a wonderful archive collection. Or else there's the General Register Office for births, deaths, and marriages. And I'm sure with just a little more time I could . . . oh dear," she said, flushing as she glanced at her watch, "but what a shame. It's almost closing time. And right when we were getting somewhere. I don't suppose there's anything more I could do to help before they lock us in?"

"Actually," I said, "there is one little thing. Do you think I could use your telephone?"

IT HAD been eleven years since the advertisements were placed so I'm not sure what I expected; I know only what I hoped: that a fellow by the name of Theo would pick up at the other end and happily fill me in on the past fifty years of Thomas Cavill's life. Needless to say, it's not what happened. My first attempt was met by the rude insistence of a disconnection tone and I was so utterly frustrated that I couldn't help but stamp my foot like a spoiled Victorian child. Miss Yeats was kind enough to ignore the tantrum, reminding me gently to convert the area code to 071 in line with the recent changes, then hovering very closely as I dialed the number. Under scrutiny I grew clumsy and had to try a second time, but finally—success!

I gave the receiver a quick tap to signal that the number had begun to ring, touched Miss Yeats's shoulder excitedly when the line picked up. It was answered by a kindly lady who told me, when I asked for Theo, that she'd bought the house from an elderly man by that name the year before. "Theodore Cavill," she said, "that's who you're after, isn't it?"

I could barely contain myself. Theodore *Cavill*. A relative, then. "That's him."

Beneath my nose, Miss Yeats clapped the heels of her hands like a seal.

"He went to live in a nursing home in Putney," said the lady on the phone, "right by the river. He was very happy about that, I remember. Said he used to teach at a school across the way."

I WENT to visit him. I went that very evening.

There were five nursing homes in Putney, only one of which was on the river, and I found it easily. The drizzle had blown away and the evening was warm and clear; I stood at the front like someone in a dream, comparing the address of the plain brick building before me to that in my notepad.

As soon as I set foot inside the foyer, I was accosted by the nurse on duty, a young woman with a pixie haircut and a way of smiling so that one side of her mouth rose higher than the other. I told her who I'd come to see and she grinned.

"Oh, how lovely! He's one of our sweetest is Theo."

I felt my first pang of doubt then and returned her smile a little queasily. It had seemed like a good idea at the time, but now, beneath the stark fluorescent light of the hallway we were fast approaching, I wasn't so sure. There was something not terribly likable about a person prepared to impose upon an unsuspecting old gentleman, one of the nursing home's sweetest. An arrant stranger with designs on the fellow's family history. I considered backing out, but my guide was surprisingly invested in my visit and had already railroaded me through the foyer with breathtaking efficiency.

"It's lonely for them when they get near the end," she was saying, "especially if they never married. No kids or grandkids to think about."

I agreed and smiled and trailed her at a skip along the wide, white corridor. Door after door, the spaces between punctuated by wall-hung vases. Purple flowers, just this side of fresh, poked their heads over the top, and I wondered absently whose job it was to change them. I didn't ask, though, and we didn't stop, continuing right down the corridor until we reached a door at the very end. Through its glass panel, I could see that a neat garden lay on the other side. The nurse held open the door and tilted her head, indicating that I should go first, then followed closely on my heel.

"Theo," she said, in a louder-than-normal voice, though to whom she spoke I couldn't tell. "Someone here to see you. I'm sorry"—she turned to me—"I don't remember your name."

"Edie. Edie Burchill."

"Edie Burchill's here to visit, Theo."

I saw then an iron bench seat just beyond a low hedge, and an old man standing. It was evident from the way he stooped, the hand holding the back of the seat, that he'd been sitting until the moment we arrived, that he'd clambered to his feet out of habit, a vestige of the old-fashioned manners he'd no doubt been using all his life. He blinked through bottle-thick glasses. "Hello there," he said. "Join me, won't you?"

"I'll leave you to it," said the nurse. "I'm just inside. Give me a yell if there's anything you need." She bobbed her head, crossed her arms, and disappeared sprucely back along the red-brick path. The door closed behind her and Theo and I were left alone in the garden.

He was tiny, five feet tall if he was lucky, with the sort of portly body you might draw, if you were so inclined, by starting with a rough eggplant shape and strapping a belt across the widest point. He gestured away from me with a tufted head. "I've been sitting here watching the river. It never stops, you know."

I liked his voice. Something in its warm timbre reminded me of being a very little child, of sitting cross-legged on a dusty carpet while a blurry-faced grown-up intoned reassuringly and my mind took leave to wander. I was aware suddenly that I had no idea how to begin speaking with this old man. That coming here had been an enormous mistake and I needed to leave immediately. I'd opened my mouth to tell him so when he said, "I've been stalling. I'm afraid I can't place you. Forgive me, it's my memory . . ."

"It's quite all right. We haven't met before."

"Oh?" He was silent and his lips moved slowly around his thoughts. "I see . . . well, never mind, you're here now, and I don't have a lot of visitors . . . I'm terribly sorry, I've forgotten your name already. I know Jean said it, but . . ."

Run, said my brain. "I'm Edie," said my mouth. "I've come about your advertisements."

"My . . . ?" He cupped his ear as if he might have misheard. "Advertisements, did you say? I'm sorry, but I think you might've confused me with someone else."

I reached inside my bag and found the printout page from *The Times*. "I've come about Thomas Cavill," I said, holding it so he could see.

He wasn't looking at the paper though. I'd startled him and his whole face changed, confusion swept aside by delight. "I've been waiting for you," he said eagerly. "Come, sit down, sit down. Who are you with then, the police? The military police?"

The *police*? It was my turn for confusion. I shook my head.

He'd become agitated, clasping his small hands together and speaking very quickly: "I knew if I just lasted long enough, someone, someday would show a bit of interest in my brother. Come." He waved impatiently. "Sit down, please. Tell me—what is it? What have you found?"

I was utterly flummoxed; I had no idea what he meant. I went closer and spoke gently. "Mr. Cavill, I think there's been some sort of misunderstanding. I haven't found anything and I'm not with the police. Or with the military for that matter. I've come because I'm trying to find your brother—to find Thomas—and I thought you might be able to help."

His head inclined. "You thought I might . . . That I could help *you* . . . ?" Realization drained the color from his cheeks. He held the back of the seat for support and nodded with a bitter dignity that made me ache, even though I didn't understand its cause. "I see . . ." A faint smile. "I see."

I'd upset him and although I'd no idea how, or what the police might have to do with Thomas Cavill, I knew I had to say something to explain my presence. "Your brother was my mother's teacher, back before the war. We were talking the other day, she and I, and she was telling me what an inspiration he was. That she was sorry to have lost contact with him." I swallowed, surprised and disturbed in equal measure by how easy it was for me to lie like this. "She was wondering what became of him, whether he kept teaching after the war, whether he got married."

As I spoke, his attention had drifted back towards the river, but I could tell by the glaze of his eyes that he wasn't seeing anything. Nothing that was there, at any rate; not the people strolling across the bridge, or the small boats bobbing on the distant bank, or the ferry-load of tourists with pointed cameras. "I'm afraid I'm going to disappoint you," he said finally. "I don't have any idea what happened to Tom."

Theo sat down, easing his back against the iron rails and picking up his story. "My brother disappeared in 1941. The middle of the war. First we knew was a knock at my mum's door and the local bobby standing there. Wartime reserve policeman, he was—friend of my dad's when he was alive, fought alongside him in the Great War. Ah"— Theo flapped his hand as if he were swatting a fly—"he was embarrassed, poor fellow. Must've hated delivering that sort of news."

"What sort of news?"

"Tom hadn't reported for duty and the bobby'd come to bring him in." Theo sighed with the memory. "Poor old Mum. What could she do? She told the fellow the truth: that Tom wasn't there and she had no idea where he was staying, that he'd taken to living alone since he was wounded. Couldn't settle back into the family home after Dunkirk."

"He was evacuated?"

Theo nodded. "Almost didn't make it. He spent weeks in the hospital afterwards; his leg mended up all right, but my sisters said he came out different to when he went in. He'd laugh in all the same places but there'd be a pause beforehand. Like he was reading lines from a script."

A child had begun to cry nearby and Theo's attention flickered in the direction of the river path; he smiled faintly. "Ice cream dropped," he said. "It wouldn't be a Saturday in Putney if some poor kid didn't lose his ice cream on that path."

I waited for him to continue and when he didn't, prompted him as gently as I could. "And what happened? What did your mother do?"

He was still watching the path, but he tapped his fingers on the back of the seat and said, in a quiet voice, "Tom was absent without leave in the middle of a war. The bobby's hands were tied. He was a good man though, showed some leniency out of respect for Dad; gave Mum twenty-four hours to find Tom and have him report for duty before it all went official."

"But she didn't? She didn't find him."

He shook his head. "Needle in a haystack. Mum and my sisters went to pieces. They searched everywhere they could think but . . ." He shrugged weakly. "I was no help, I wasn't there at the time—I've never forgiven myself for that. I was up north, training with my regiment. First I knew was when Mum's letter arrived. By then it was too late. Tom was on the absconders' list."

"I'm so sorry."

"He's on it to this day." His eyes met mine and I was dismayed to see that they were glassy with tears. He straightened his thick spectacles, hooked the arms over his ears. "I've checked every year since because they told me once that some old fellows turn up decades later. Front up at the guardroom with their tail between their legs and a string of bad decisions behind them. Throw themselves on the mercy of the officer on duty." He lifted a hand and let it fall, helplessly, back to his knee. "I only check because I'm desperate. I know in my heart that Tom won't be showing up at any guardroom." He met my concern, searched my eyes, and said, "Dishonorable bloody discharge."

There was chatter behind us and I glanced over my shoulder to see a young man helping an elderly woman through the door and into the garden. The woman laughed at something he'd said as they walked together slowly to look at the roses.

Theo had seen them, too, and he lowered his voice. "Tom was an *honorable* man." Each word was a struggle, and as he held his lips tight against the quiver of strong emotion, I could see how much he needed me to believe the best of his brother. "He never would've done what they said, run away like that. Never. I told them so, the military police. No one would listen. It broke my mother's heart. The shame, the worry, wondering what had really happened to him. Whether he was out there somewhere, lost and alone. Whether he'd come to some harm, forgotten who he was and where he belonged—." He broke off, rubbed at his bowed brow as if abashed, and I understood that these were heartbreaking theories for which he'd been castigated in the past. "Whatever the case," he said, "she never got over it. He was her favorite, though she'd never have admitted such a thing. She didn't have to; he was everybody's favorite, Tom."

Silence fell and I watched as two rooks twirled across the sky. The rose couple's stroll brought them close and I waited for them to reach the riverbank before turning to Theo and saying, "Why wouldn't the police listen? Why were they so sure that Tom had run away?"

"There was a letter." A nerve in his jaw flickered. "Early 1942 it arrived, a few months after Tom went missing. Typed and very short, saying only that he'd met someone and run off to get married. That he was lying low but would make contact later. Once the police saw that, they weren't interested in Tom or us. There was a war on, didn't we know? There wasn't time to be looking for a fellow who'd deserted his nation."

His hurt was still so raw, fifty years later. I could only imagine what it must have been like at the time. To be missing a loved one and unable to convince anyone else to help in the search. And yet . . . In Milderhurst village I'd been told that Thomas Cavill failed to show up at the castle because he'd eloped with another woman. Was it only family pride and loyalty that made Theo so certain the elopement was a lie? "You don't believe the letter?"

"Not for a second." His vehemence was a knife. "It's true that he'd met a girl and fallen in love. He told me that himself, wrote long letters about her—how beautiful she was, how she made everything right with the world, how he was going to marry her. But he wasn't about to elope—he couldn't wait to introduce her to the family."

"You didn't meet her?"

He shook his head. "None of us did. It was something to do with her family and keeping it secret until they'd broken the news to them. I got the feeling her people were rather grand."

My heart had started to race as Theo's story overlay so neatly with the cast of my own. "Do you remember the girl's name?"

"He never told me."

The frustration winded me.

"He was adamant that he had to meet her family first. I can't tell you how it's plagued me over the years," he said. "If I'd only known who she was, I might've had a place to start searching. What if she went missing too? What if the pair of them were in an accident together? What if her family has information that might help?"

It was on the tip of my tongue then to tell him about Juniper, but I thought better of it at the last. I couldn't see that there was any point in raising his hopes when the Blythes had no additional information on the whereabouts of Thomas Cavill, when they were as convinced as the police that he'd eloped with another woman. "The letter," I said suddenly, "who do you think sent it, if it wasn't Tom? And why? Why would somebody else do such a thing?"

"I don't know, but I'll tell you something. Tom didn't marry anyone. I checked with the Register Office. I checked the death records, too; I still do. Every year or so, just in case. There's nothing. No record of him after 1941. It's like he just disappeared into thin air."

"But people don't just disappear."

"No," he said with a weary smile. "No, they don't. And I've spent my whole life trying to find him. I even hired a fellow some decades ago. Waste of money that was. Thousands of quid just to have some idiot tell me that wartime London was an excellent place for a man who wanted to go missing." He sighed roughly. "No one seems to care that Tom *didn't* want to go missing."

"And the advertisements?" I gestured to the printout, still on the seat between us.

"I ran those when our little brother Joey took his turn for the worse. I figured it was worth a shot, just in case I'd been wrong all along and Tom was out there somewhere, looking for a reason to come back to us. Joey was simple, poor kid, but he adored Tom. Would've meant the world to him to see him one more time."

"You didn't hear anything though."

"Nothing but some lads making prank calls."

The sun had slipped from the sky and early dusk was sheer and pink. A breeze brushed my arms and I realized we were alone again in the garden, remembered that Theo was an old man who ought to be inside contemplating a plate of roast beef and not the sorrows of his past. "It's getting cool," I said. "Shall we go in?"

He nodded and tried to smile a little, but as we stood I could tell that the wind had left his sails. "I'm not stupid, Edie," he said as we reached the door. I pulled it open, but he insisted on holding it for me to pass through first. "I know I won't be seeing Tom again. The ads, checking the records each year, the file of family photographs and other odds and sods I keep to show him, just in case—I do all that because it's habit, and because it helps to fill the absence."

I knew exactly what he meant.

There was noise coming from the dining room—chairs scraping, cutlery clanging, the mumbles of congenial conversation—but he stopped in the middle of the corridor. A purple flower wilted behind him, a humming came from the fluorescent tube above, and I saw what I hadn't outside. His cheeks shone with the spill of old tears. "Thank you," he said quietly. "I don't know how it is you chose today to come, Edie, but I'm glad you did. I've been blue all day—some are like that—and it's good to talk about him. I'm the only one left now: my brothers and sisters are in here." He pressed a palm against his heart. "I miss them all, but there's no way to describe Tom's loss. The guilt"—his bottom lip quivered and he fought to wrest it back under control—"knowing that I failed him. That something terrible happened and no one knows it; the world, history, considers him a traitor because I couldn't prove them wrong."

Every atom of my being ached to make things right for him. "I'm sorry I didn't bring news of Tom."

He shook his head, smiled a little. "It's all right. Hope's one thing, expectation's quite another. I'm not a fool. Deep down I know I'll go to my grave without setting Tom to rest."

"I wish there were something I could do."

"Come back and visit me some afternoon," he said. "That'd be marvelous. I'll tell you some more about Tom. Happier days next time, I promise."

ONE

THERE was a war on and he had a job to be doing, but the way the sun beat hard and round in the sky, the silver dazzle of the water, the hot stretch of tree limbs above him; well, Tom figured it would've been wrong in some indescribable way not to stop for a moment and take a plunge. The pool was circular and handsomely made, with stones rimming the outside and a wooden swing suspended from an enormous branch, and he couldn't help laughing as he dropped his satchel onto the ground. What a find! He unstrapped his wristwatch and laid it carefully on the smooth leather bag he'd bought the year before, his pride and joy, kicked off his shoes and started unbuttoning his shirt.

When was the last time he'd been swimming? Not through all of the summer, that was certain; a group of friends had borrowed a car and taken off for the sea, a week in Devon during the hottest August any of them could remember, and he'd been all set to join them until Joey took his fall and the nightmares started and the poor kid wouldn't go to sleep unless Tom sat by the bed and made up stories about the Underground. He'd lain in his own narrow bed afterwards, heat thickening in the room's corners as he dreamed of the sea, but he hadn't minded; not really, not for long. There wasn't much he wouldn't do for Joey—poor kid, with his big man's body turning to flab and his little-boy laugh; the cruel music of that laugh made Tom ache and knot inside for the kid Joey'd been, the man he ought to have become.

He shrugged out of his shirtsleeves and slipped his belt free, shed the sad old thoughts, then his trousers too. A big black bird coughed above him and Tom stood for a moment, craned to glimpse the clear blue sky. The sun blazed and he squinted, following the bird as it glided in graceful silhouette towards a distant wood. The air was sweet with the scent of something he stood no chance of recognizing but knew he liked. Flowers, birds, the distant burble of water scooting over stones; pastoral smells and sounds straight from the pages of Hardy, and Tom was high on the knowledge that they were real and he was among them. That this was life and he was in it. He laid a hand flat on his chest, fingers spread; the sun was warm on his bare skin, everything was ahead of him, and it felt good to be young and strong and here and now. He wasn't religious, but this moment certainly was.

Tom checked over his shoulder, but lazily and without expectation. He wasn't a rule breaker by nature; he was a teacher, he owed his students an example, and he took himself seriously enough to attempt to set them one. But the day, the weather, the newly arrived war, the smell he couldn't name that sat on the breeze like that, all of it made him bold. He was a young man, after all, and it didn't take much for a young man to find himself infused with a fine, free sense that the earth and its pleasures were his to be taken where found; that rules of possession and prevention, though well intentioned, were theoretical dictates that belonged only in books and on ledgers and in the conversations of dithering white-bearded lawyers at Lincoln's Inn Fields.

Trees encircled the clearing, a changing room stood silent nearby, and the hint of a stone staircase led somewhere beyond. Across it all lay a spill of sunlight and birdsong. With a deep, contented sigh, Tom decided the time was upon him. There was a diving board and the sun had warmed the wood so that as he stepped onto it his feet burned; he stood for a moment, enjoying the pain, letting his shoulders bake, the skin tighten, until finally he could stand it no longer and took off with a grin, jumping at the end, drawing his arms back and launching, cutting like an arrow through the water. The cold was a vise around his chest and he gasped as he came to the surface, his lungs as grateful for air as a baby's on drawing first breath.

He swam for some minutes, dived deeply, emerged again and again, then he lay on his back and let his limbs drift out from his body to form a star. This, he thought, is *it,* perfection. The moment Wordsworth and Coleridge and Shelley were on about: the sublime. If he were to die right now, Tom was sure, he would die content. Not that he wanted to die, not for at least seventy years. Tom calculated quickly: the year 2009, that would do nicely. An old man living on the moon. He laughed, backstroked idly, then resumed his floating, closed his eyes so that his lids warmed. The world was orange and star-shot, and within it he saw his future glowing.

He would be in uniform soon; the war was waiting for him and Thomas Cavill couldn't wait to meet it. He wasn't naive, his own father had lost a leg and parts of his mind in France and he entertained no illusions as to heroics or glory; he knew war was a serious matter, a dangerous one. Neither was he one of those fellows keen to escape his present situation, quite the opposite: as far as Tom could see, the war offered a perfect opportunity for him to better himself, as a man and as a teacher.

He'd wanted to be a teacher ever since he realized he'd grow up one day to be an adult, and had dreamed about working in his old London neighborhood. Tom believed he could open the eyes and minds of kids like he'd once been, to a world far beyond the grimy bricks and laden laundry lines of their daily experience. The goal had sustained him right through teacher-training college and into the first years of Prac until finally, through some silver-tongued talking and good old-fashioned luck, he'd arrived exactly where he wanted to be.

As soon as it had become clear that war was coming, Tom had known he'd sign up. Teachers were needed at home, it was a reserved occupation, but what sort of an example would that set? And his reasoning was more selfish too. John Keats had said that nothing became real until it was experienced and Tom knew that to be true. More than that, he knew it was precisely what he was missing. Empathy was all well and good, but when Tom spoke of history and sacrifice and nationality, when he read to his students the battle cry of Henry V, he scraped against the shallow floor of his own limited experience. War, he knew, would give him the depth of understanding he craved, which was why as soon as he was sure his evacuees were safely settled with their families he was heading back to London; he'd signed up with the 1st Battalion of the East Surrey regiment and with any luck he'd be in France by October.

He turned his fingers idly in the warm surface water and sighed so deeply that he sank a little lower. Perhaps it was the awareness that he would be in uniform next week that made this day somehow more vivid, more real than those that fanned out on either side. For there was definitely some unreal force at work. It wasn't a simple matter of the warmth or the breeze itself, or the smell he couldn't name, but a strange blend of condition, climate, and circumstance; and although he was keen to line up and take his turn, although his legs ached sometimes at night with impatience, right now, at this very moment, he wished only for time to slow, that he might remain here floating like this forever . . .

"How's the water?" The voice when it came was startling. Perfect solitude, shattered like a golden eggshell.

Later, on the many occasions he was to replay the memory of their first meeting, it was her eyes he would remember clearest of all. And the way she moved—be honest: the way her hair hung long and messy around her shoulders, the curve of her small breasts, the shape of her legs, oh God, those legs. But before and above all those, it was the light in her eyes, those cat's eyes. Eyes that knew things and thought things that they shouldn't. In the long days and nights that were to come, and when he finally reached the end, it was her eyes he would see when he closed his own.

She was sitting on the swing, bare feet on the ground, watching him. A girl—a woman? He wasn't sure; not at first—dressed in a simple white sundress, watching him while he floated in the pool. Any number of casual rejoinders came to mind, but something in the quality of her expression tied his tongue and all he managed was, "Warm. Perfect. Blue." Her eyes were blue, almond shaped, a little too far apart, and they widened slightly when he uttered his three words. No doubt wondering what sort of simpleton she'd stumbled across making free with her pool.

He paddled awkwardly, waited for her to ask him who he was, what he was doing, what business he had swimming there at all, but she didn't, she asked none of those questions, merely pushed off lazily so the swing traveled in a shallow arc across the edge of the pool and back. Keen to establish himself as a man of more than three words, he answered them anyway: "I'm Thomas," he said, "Thomas Cavill. Sorry to use your pool like this but the day was so hot. I couldn't help myself." He grinned up at her and she leaned her head against the rope, and he half wondered whether she might be trespassing as well. Something in the way she looked, a cutout quality as if she and the environment in which he found her were not natural companions. He wondered vaguely where it was she might fit, a girl like this, but he drew a blank.

Wordlessly she stopped swinging, stood, and let go of the seat. The ropes slackened and it lassoed back and forth. He saw that she was rather tall. She sat then on the stone edge, gathered her knees close to her chest so that her dress bunched high around her legs, and dipped in her toes, peering over the tops of her knees to watch the ripples as they ran away from her.

Tom felt the rise of indignation in his chest. He'd trespassed but he hadn't done any real harm, nothing to earn this sort of silent treatment. She was behaving now as if he weren't there at all, though she was sitting right by him, her face was fixed in an attitude of deep, distracted thought. He decided she must be playing some sort of game, one of those games that girls—that women—liked to play, the sort that confused men and thereby, in some strange counteractive fashion, kept them in line. What other reason had she for ignoring him? Unless she was shy. Perhaps that was it; she was young, there was every chance she found his boldness, his maleness, his—let's face it—near nakedness confronting. He felt sorry then—he'd not intended anything like that, had only fancied a swim after all—and he adopted his most casual, friendly tone: "Look here. I'm sorry to surprise you like this; I don't mean any harm. My name's Thomas Cavill. I've come to—"

"Yes," she said, "I heard you." She looked at him then as if he were a gnat. Wearily, mildly annoyed, but otherwise unaffected. "There's really no need to trumpet on and on about it."

"Now, hang on a minute. I was only trying to assure you that . . ."

But Tom let his assurances trail off. For one thing, it was evident that this strange person was no longer listening, for another he was far too distracted. She'd stood up while he was speaking and was now lifting her dress to reveal a swimsuit beneath. Just like that. Not a glance his way, no peeping beneath her eyelashes or giggling at her own forwardness. She tossed her dress behind her, a small pile of discarded cotton, and stretched like a sun-warmed cat, yawned a little, bothering herself with none of the female fripperies of covering her mouth or excusing herself or blushing in his direction.

With no fanfare at all she dived from the side and as she hit the water Tom hurried to climb out. Her boldness, if that's what it was, alarmed him in some way. His alarm frightened him and his fear was compelling. It made *her* compelling.

Tom hadn't a towel, of course, nor any other way of drying himself quickly enough to get dressed, so he stood out in a sunny patch and tried to look as if he were relaxed about doing so. It was no mean feat. His ease had deserted him and he knew now what it was to be one of his bumbling friends who fell to shuffling their feet and confusing their words when faced with a pretty woman. A pretty woman who had swum to the pool's surface and was floating lazily on her back, long wet hair fanning out like seaweed from her face, unalarmed, unaffected, seemingly unaware of his intrusion.

Tom tried to find some dignity, decided trousers would help and pulled them over his wet shorts. He aimed for authority, tried not to let nervousness tip him over into cockiness. He was a teacher, for God's sake, he was a man about to become a soldier; it shouldn't be so hard. Professionalism, though, wasn't an easy thing to exude when one was standing barefoot and seminaked in someone else's garden. All earlier epiphanies regarding the foolishness of property law were revealed now as crude, if not delusional, and he swallowed before saying as calmly as he could, "My name is Thomas Cavill. I'm a teacher. I've come here to check on a pupil of mine I believe has been evacuated here." He was dripping water, a rivulet ran warm down the center of his stomach, and he winced when he added, "I'm her teacher." Which, of course, he'd already said.

She'd rolled over and was watching him now from the center of the pool, studying him as if she might be making mental notes. She swam beneath the water, a silvery streak, and emerged at the edge, pressed her arms flat against the stones, one hand on top of the other, and rested her chin on them. "Meredith."

"Yes." A sigh of relief. At last. "Yes, Meredith Baker. I'm here to see how she's doing. To check that she's all right."

Those wide-apart eyes were on him, her feelings impossible to read. Then she smiled and her face was transformed in some transcendent way and he drew breath as she said, "I suppose you'd better ask her that yourself. She'll be along soon. My sister's measuring her for dresses."

"Good then. That's good." Purpose was his life raft and he clung to it with gratitude and a total lack of shame. He put his arms back through his shirtsleeves and sat down on the end of a nearby sun lounger, pulling the folder and its checklist from his satchel. With a pretense of composure he performed great interest in its information, never mind that he could have recited it if pressed. It was as well to read it through again: he wanted to be sure that when any of his pupils' parents saw him back in London, he'd be able to answer their questions with honesty and certainty. Most of his kids had been accommodated in the village, two with the vicar at the vicarage, another at a farmhouse down the way; Meredith, he thought, glancing over his shoulder at the army of chimney pots above the distant trees, had scattered the farthest. A castle, according to the address on his checklist. He'd hoped to see inside, not just to see but to explore a little; so far the local ladies had been very welcoming, asking him in for tea and cake, fussing over whether he'd had enough.

He risked another glance at the creature in the pool and figured that an invitation here was decidedly unlikely. Her attention was elsewhere, so he let his focus rest on her awhile. This girl was perplexing: she seemed blind to him and blind to his charm. He felt ordinary next to her and that was something he wasn't used to. From this distance, however, and with his pride somewhat smoothed, he was able to put his vanity aside long enough to wonder who she was. The officious lady from the local WVS had told him that the castle was owned by one Mr. Raymond Blythe, a writer ("*The True History of the Mud Man*—why, surely you've read it?") who was old now and unwell, but that Meredith would be in good hands with his twin daughters, a pair of spinsters perfectly suited to the care of a poor, homeless child. No other occupant had been mentioned and he had assumed, if indeed he'd given it much thought at all, that Mr. Blythe and the twin spinsters would be the full complement at Milderhurst Castle. He certainly hadn't expected this girl, this woman, this young and ungraspable woman who was certainly no spinster. He wasn't sure why, but it felt incredibly urgent all of a sudden that he know more about her.

She splashed and he looked away, shook his head, and smiled at his own regrettable conceit; Tom knew enough of himself to realize that his interest in her was in direct proportion to her lack of interest in him. Even as a child he'd been driven by that most senseless of all motivators: the desire to possess precisely what he couldn't. He needed to let it go. She was just a girl. An eccentric girl at that.

A rustle then and a bonny Labrador charged honey blond through the foliage, chasing its wagging tongue; Meredith appeared on its heels, a smile on her face that told him all he needed to know about her condition. Tom was so pleased to see her, a little piece of normality in spectacles, that he grinned and stood, almost tripping over himself in his hurry to greet her. "Hey there, kiddo. How's tricks?"

She stopped dead, blinked at him, confounded, he realized, to see him so decidedly out of context. As the dog ran circles around her and the blush in her cheeks spread to her neck, she shuffled her shoes and said, "Hello, Mr. Cavill."

"I've come to see how things are going."

"Things are going well, Mr. Cavill. I'm staying in a castle."

He smiled. She was a sweet kid, timid but clever with it. A quick mind and excellent skills of observation, a habit of noticing hidden details that made for surprising and original descriptions. She had little to no belief in herself unfortunately, and it wasn't hard to see why: her parents had looked at Tom as if he'd lost his mind when he suggested she might sit the grammar school entry a year or two back. Tom was working on it though. "A castle! That's a piece of luck. I don't think I've ever been inside a castle."

"It's very large and very dark, with a funny smell of mud and lots and lots of staircases."

"Have you climbed them all yet?"

"Some, but not the stairs that lead to the tower."

"No?"

"I'm not allowed up there. That's where Mr. Blythe works. He's a writer, a real one."

"A real writer. He might offer you some tips if you're lucky." Tom reached to give the side of her shoulder a playful tap.

She smiled, shy but pleased. "Maybe."

"Are you still writing your journal?"

"Every day. There's a lot to write about." She sneaked a glance at the pool and Tom followed it. Long legs drifted out behind the girl as she held on to the edge. A quote came unexpectedly into his head: Dostoevsky, "Beauty is mysterious as well as terrible." Tom cleared his throat. "Good," he said. "That's good then. The more you practice, the better you'll become. Don't let yourself settle for less than your best."

"I won't."

He smiled at her and nodded at his clipboard. "I can mark down that you're happy then? Everything's all right?"

"Oh yes."

"You're not missing your mum and dad too much?"

"I'm writing them letters," said Meredith. "I know where the post office is and I've already sent them the postcard with my new address. The nearest school is in Tenterden, but there's a bus that goes."

"And your brother and sister, they're near the village, too, aren't they?"

Meredith nodded.

He laid his palm on her head; the hair on top was hot from the sun. "You're going to be all right, kiddo."

"Mr. Cavill?"

"Yes?"

"You should see the books inside. There's a room just filled, every wall lined with shelves, all the way to the ceiling."

He smiled broadly. "Well, I feel a whole lot better knowing that."

"Me too." She nodded at the figure in the water. "Juniper said I could read any of them that I wanted."

Juniper. Her name was Juniper.

"I'm already three-quarters through *The Woman in White* and then I'm going to read *Wuthering Heights*."

"Are you coming in, Merry?" Juniper had swum back to the side and was beckoning to the younger girl. "The water's lovely. Warm. Perfect. Blue."

Something about his words on her lips made Tom shiver. Beside him Meredith shook her head as if the question had caught her off guard. "I don't know how to swim."

Juniper climbed out, slipped her white dress over her head so that it stuck to her wet legs. "We'll have to do something about that while you're here." She pulled her wet hair into a messy ponytail and tossed it over her shoulder. "Is there anything else?" she said to him.

"Well, I thought I might . . ." He exhaled, collected himself, and started again. "Perhaps I ought to come up with you and meet the other members of your household?"

"No," said Juniper without flinching. "That's not a good idea."

He felt unreasonably affronted.

"My sister doesn't like strangers, particularly male strangers."

"I'm not a stranger, am I, Merry?"

Meredith smiled. Juniper did not. She said, "It isn't personal. She's funny that way."

"I see."

She was standing close to him, drips sliding into her lashes as her eyes met his; he read no interest in them yet his pulse quickened. "Well then," she said.

"Well then."

"If that's it?"

"That's it."

She lifted her chin and considered him a moment longer before nodding. A short flick that ended their interaction absolutely.

"Good-bye, Mr. Cavill," said Meredith.

He smiled, reached out to shake her hand. "Good-bye, kiddo. You take care now. Keep up your writing."

And he watched them go, the two of them disappearing into the greenery, heading towards the castle. Long blond hair dripping down her back, shoulder blades that sat like hesitant wings on either side. She reached out an arm and put it lightly around Meredith's shoulders and hugged her close, and although Tom lost sight of them then, he thought he heard a giggle as they continued up the hillside.

Over a year would pass before he saw her again, before they met again quite by chance on a London street. He would be a different person by then, inexorably altered, quieter, less cocksure, as damaged as the city around him. He would have survived France, dragged his injured leg to Bray Dune, been evacuated from Dunkirk; he would have watched friends die in his arms, survived a bout of dysentery, and he would know that while John Keats was correct, that experience was indeed truth, there were some things it was as well not to know firsthand.

And the new Thomas Cavill would fall in love with Juniper Blythe for precisely the same reasons he'd found her so odd in that clearing, in that pool. In a world that had been grayed by ash and sadness, she would now seem wonderful to him; those magical unmarked aspects that remained quite separate from reality would enchant him, and in one fell swoop she would save him. He would love her with a passion that both frightened and revived him, a desperation that made a mockery of his neat dreams for the future.

But he knew none of that then. He knew only that he could check the last of his students off his list, that Meredith Baker was in safe hands, that she was happy and well cared for, that he was free now to hitch a ride back to London and get on with his education, his life's plan. And although he wasn't yet dry he buttoned up his shirt, sat to tie his shoelaces, and whistled to himself as he left the pool behind him, lily pads still bobbing over the ripples she'd left in the surface, that strange girl with the unearthly eyes. He started back down the hill, walking along the shallow brook that would lead him towards the road, away from Juniper Blythe and Milderhurst Castle, never—or so he thought—to see either one of them again.

TWO

OH—but things were never to be the same afterwards! How could they be? Nothing in the thousand books she'd read, nothing she'd imagined, or dreamed, or written, could have prepared Juniper Blythe for the meeting by the pool with Thomas Cavill. When first she'd come upon him in the clearing, glimpsed him floating on the water's surface, she'd presumed she must have conjured him herself. It had been some time since her last "visitor," and it was true there'd been no thrumming in her head, no strange, displaced ocean whooshing in her ears to warn her; but there was a familiar aspect to the sunshine, an artificial, glittering quality that made the scene less real than the one she'd just left. She'd stared up at the canopy of trees, and when the uppermost leaves moved with the wind, it appeared that flakes of gold were falling down to earth.

She'd sat on the pool swing because it was the safest thing to do when a visit was upon her. *Sit somewhere quiet, hold something firmly, wait for it to pass:* the three golden rules that Saffy had devised when Juniper was small. She'd lifted Juniper onto the table in the kitchen to tend her latest bleeding knee and said very softly that the visitors were indeed a gift, just as Daddy said, but nonetheless she must learn to be careful.

"But I love to play with them," Juniper had said. "They're my friends. And they tell me such interesting things."

"I know, darling, and that's wonderful. All I ask is that you re-member that you're not one of them. You are a little girl with skin, and blood beneath it, and bones that could break, and two big sisters who very much want to see you reach adulthood!"

305

"And a daddy."

"Of course. And a daddy."

"But not a mother."

"No."

"But a puppy."

"Emerson, yes."

"And a patch on my knee."

Saffy had laughed then, and given her a hug that smelled like talcum and jasmine and ink, and set her back down on the kitchen tiles. And Juniper had been very careful not to make eye contact with the figment at the window that was beckoning her outside to play.

JUNIPER DIDN'T know where the visitors came from. All she knew was that her earliest memories were of figures in the streams of light around her crib. They'd been there before she'd understood that others couldn't see them. She had been called fey and mad, wicked and gifted; she'd driven away countless nannies who wouldn't abide imaginary friends. "They're not imaginary," Juniper had explained, over and over again, with as reasonable a tone as she could muster; but it seemed there were no English nannies prepared to accept this assertion as truth. One by one they'd packed their bags and demanded an audience with Daddy; from her hiding spot in the castle's veins, the little nook by the gap in the stones, Juniper had cloaked herself in a whole new set of descriptions: "She's impertinent . . . ," "She's obstinate . . . ," and even, once, "Possessed!"

Everybody had a theory about the visitors. Dr. Finley believed them to be "fibers of longing and curiosity," projected from her own mind and linked in some way to her faulty heart; Dr. Heinstein argued they were symptoms of psychosis and had provided a raft of pills he promised would end them; Daddy said they were the voices of her ancestors and that she had been chosen specially to hear them; Saffy insisted she was perfect as she was, and Percy didn't mind much either way. She said that everyone was different and why on earth must things be categorized, people labeled normal or otherwise?

ANYWAY. JUNIPER had not really sat on the swing seat because it was the safest thing to do. She'd sat there because it afforded her the best view of the figment in the pool. She was curious and he was beautiful. The smoothness of his skin, the rise and fall of muscles on his bare chest as he breathed, his arms. If she had conjured him herself, then she had done a bloody brilliant job; he was exotic and lovely and she wanted to observe for as long as it took him to turn back into dappled light and leaves before her eyes.

Only that wasn't what had happened. As she sat with her head resting against the swing's rope, he'd opened his eyes, met hers, and begun to speak.

This, of itself, was not unprecedented; the visitors had spoken to Juniper before, many times, but this was the first time they'd taken the shape of a young man. A young man with very little clothing on his body.

She'd answered him, but shortly. Truthfully, she'd been irritated; she hadn't wanted him to speak; she'd wanted him just to close his eyes again, to float upon the shimmering surface, so she could play voyeur. So she could watch the dance of sunlight on his limbs, his long, long limbs, his quite beautiful face, and concentrate on the queer sensation, like a plucked string humming, way down deep within her belly.

She hadn't known many men before. There was Daddy, of course—but he hardly counted; her godfather, Stephen; a few ancient gardeners who'd worked on the estate over the years; and Davies, who'd babied the Daimler.

But this was different.

Juniper had tried ignoring him, hopeful that he might get the idea and stop trying to make conversation, but he'd persisted. He'd told her his name, Thomas Cavill. They didn't usually have names. Not normal ones.

She'd dived into the pool herself, and he had made a hasty exit. She'd noticed then that there were clothes on the sun bed; his clothes, which was very strange indeed.

And then, the most peculiar thing of all. Meredith had come—released at last from Saffy's sewing room—and she and the man had begun to converse.

Juniper, watching them from the water, had almost drowned in shock, for one thing was certain: her visitors could not be seen by others.

JUNIPER HAD lived at Milderhurst Castle all her life. She had been born, like her father and her sisters before her, in a room on the second floor. She knew the castle and its woods as one might be expected to know the only world one had met. She was safe and loved and indulged. She read and she wrote and she played and she dreamed. Nothing was expected of her other than to be precisely as and who she was. Sometimes, more so.

"You, my little one, are a creature of the castle," Daddy had told her often. "We are the same, you and I." And for a long time Juniper had been perfectly content with this description.

Lately, though, in ways she couldn't properly explain, things had begun to change. She woke at night sometimes with an inexplicable tugging in her soul; a desire, like hunger, but for what she couldn't say. Dissatisfaction, longing, a deep and yawning absence, but no idea of how to fill it. No idea of what it was she missed. She'd walked and she'd run; she'd written with speed and fury. Words, sounds, had pressed against her skull, demanding release, and to put them on paper was a relief; she didn't agonize, she didn't ponder, she never reread; it was enough just to free the words so that the voices in her head were stilled.

Then one day an urge had taken her to the village. She didn't drive often, but she'd steered the big old Daimler into the High Street. As if in a dream, a character in someone else's story, she'd parked it and gone inside the hall; a woman had spoken at her but by then Juniper had already seen Meredith.

Later, Saffy would ask her how she'd chosen, and Juniper would say: "I didn't choose."

"I don't like to disagree, lamb, but I'm quite sure it was you who brought her home."

"Yes, of course, but I didn't *choose*. I just knew."

Juniper had never had a friend before. Other people, Daddy's pompous friends, visitors to the castle, just seemed to take up more air than they should. They squashed one with their blustering and their posturing and their constant talking. But Meredith was different. She was funny and she saw things her own way. She was a bookish person who'd never been exposed to books; she was gifted with astute powers of observation, but her thoughts and feelings weren't filtered through those that she'd read, those that had been written before. She had a unique way of seeing the world and a manner of expressing herself that caught Juniper unawares and made her laugh and think and feel things anew.

Best of all, though, Meredith had come laden with stories of the outside world. Her arrival had made a small tear in the fabric of Milderhurst. A tiny, bright window to which Juniper could press her eye and glimpse what lay beyond.

AND NOW just look what she had brought! A man, a real man of flesh and blood. A young man from the outside, the real world, had appeared in the pool. Light from the outside world had shone through the veil, brighter now that a second hole was torn, and Juniper knew that somehow she must see more.

He'd wanted to stay, to come with them up to the castle, but Juniper had told him no. The castle was all wrong. She wanted to watch him, to inspect him like a cat—carefully, slowly, unnoticed as she drifted past his skin; if she couldn't have that, it was better to have nothing. He would remain that way a sunlit, silent moment; a breeze against her cheek as the swing tilted back and forth across the warming pool; a new, low pull within her stomach.

He went. And they stayed. And she draped her arm over Meredith's shoulder and laughed as they returned up the hill; joked about Saffy's habit of sticking pins into legs as well as fabrics; pointed out the old fountain, no longer working; paused a moment to inspect the stagnant green water sulking inside, the dragonflies hovering fitfully about its rim. But all the while her thoughts drew out behind her like a spider's thread, following the man as he made his way toward the road.

She began to walk, faster now. It was hot, so hot, her hair was already drying, sticking to the sides of her face; her skin seemed tighter than usual. She felt oddly animated. Surely Meredith could hear her heart, hammering away against her ribs?

"I have a grand idea," she said. "Have you ever wondered what France looks like?" And she took her little friend's hand and together they ran, up the stairs, through the briars, beneath the long row of tunneled trees. Fleeting—the word came into her head and made her feel lighter, like a deer. Faster, faster, both of them laughing, and the wind tore at Juniper's hair, and her feet rejoiced against the baking, hard earth, and joy ran with her. Finally, they reached the portico, tripped up the stairs, panting, both of them, through the open French doors and into the cool stillness of the library.

"June? Is that you?"

It was Saffy, sitting at her writing desk. Dear Saffy, looking up from behind the typewriter in the way that was habit with her; always just a little bewildered, as if she'd been caught in the middle of a rose-petal, dewdrop dream and reality was a slightly dusty surprise.

Whether it was the sunlight, the pool, the man, the clear blue of the sky, Juniper couldn't resist planting a kiss on the top of her sister's head as they hurried by.

Saffy beamed. "Did Meredith— Oh yes, she did. Good. Oh, I see you've been swimming; be careful that Daddy . . ."

But whatever the warning, Juniper and Meredith had gone before it was finished. They ran along looming stone corridors, up narrow flights of stairs, level by level, until finally they reached the attic at the very top of the castle. Juniper went swiftly to the open window, eased herself onto the bookcase, and swiveled so that her feet were on the roof outside. "Come," she said to Meredith, who was still standing by the door, a strange look on her face. "Quickly now."

Meredith let out a tentative sigh, propped her spectacles back on the bridge of her nose, then followed, did exactly as Juniper had done. Inched her way along the steep roof until they came upon the ridge that pitched south like a ship's prow.

"There, see?" said Juniper, when they were seated side by side, settled on the flat behind the edging tiles. She pointed, a scribble on the far horizon. "I told you. All the way to France."

"Really? That's it?"

Juniper nodded, but she paid the coastline no more heed. Squinted instead at the wide field of long, yellow grass skirting Cardarker Wood; scanning, scanning, hoping for just one final glimpse . . .

A jolt. She saw him then, a tiny figure, crossing the field by the first bridge. His shirtsleeves were rolled to his elbows, she could tell that much, and he had his palms out flat beside him, brushing the tops of the long grass. He stopped as she watched, lifted and bent his arms so that his hands rested on the back of his head, seemed to embrace the sky. She realized he was turning; had turned. Was looking back now at the castle. She held her breath, wondered how it was that life could change so much in half an hour when nothing much had changed at all.

"The castle wears a skirt." Meredith was pointing at the ground below.

He was walking again, and then he disappeared behind the fold of the hill and everything was still. Thomas Cavill had slipped through the crack and into the world beyond. The air around the castle seemed to know it.

"Look," said Meredith, "just down there."

Juniper took her cigarettes from her pocket. "There used to be a moat. Daddy had it filled in when his first wife died. We're not supposed to swim in the pool either." She smiled as Meredith's face became a study in anxiety. "Don't look so worried, little Merry. No one's going to be cross when I teach you to swim. Daddy doesn't leave his tower, not anymore, so he's not to know whether we use the pool or not. Besides, when the day's as warm as this it's a crime not to have a swim."

Warm, perfect, blue.

Juniper struck the match hard. With a long, drawing breath, she leaned a hand back against the sloping roof and squinted at the clear, blue sky. The ceiling of her dome. And words came into her head, not her own.

> *I, an old turtle,*
> *Will wing me to some wither'd bough; and there*
> *My mate, that's never to be found again,*
> *Lament till I am lost.*

Ridiculous, of course. Utterly ridiculous. The man was not her mate; he was no one for her to lament till she was lost. And yet the words had come.

"Did you like Mr. Cavill?"

Juniper's heart kicked; she burned with instant heat. She'd been discovered! Meredith had intuited the secret workings of her mind. She thumbed her damp dress strap back onto her shoulder, was stalling, returning the matches to her pocket when Meredith said, "I do."

And by the pinkness on her cheeks, Juniper perceived that Meredith liked her teacher very much indeed. She was torn between relief that her own thoughts were still private and a wild, crushing envy that her feelings should be shared. She looked at Meredith and the latter sensation passed as fast as it had flared. She strove for nonchalance. "Why? What do you like about him?"

Meredith didn't answer at first. Juniper smoked and stared at the spot where the man had breached the Milderhurst dome.

"He's very clever," she said at last. "And handsome. And he's kind, even to people who aren't easy to be with. He has a simple brother, a great big fellow who acts like a baby, cries easily, and shouts sometimes in the street, but you should see how patient and gentle Mr. Cavill is with him. If you saw them together, you'd say he was having the best time of his life, and not in that overdone way that people have when they know they're being watched. He's the best teacher I've ever had. He gave me a journal as a present, a real one with a leather cover. He says that if I work hard I could stay at school longer, maybe even go to a grammar school or university, write properly one day: stories or poems, or articles for the newspaper"—there was a pause as she drew breath, then—"nobody ever thought I was good at anything before."

Juniper leaned to bump shoulders with the skinny sapling beside her. "Well, that's just madness, Merry," she said. "Mr. Cavill is right, of course, you're good at a great many things. I've only known you a matter of days and I can see that much—"

She coughed against the back of her hand, unable to continue. She'd been overcome by an unfamiliar feeling as she'd listened to Meredith describe her teacher's attributes, his kindnesses, as the girl spoke nervously of her own aspirations. A heat had started to build in her chest, growing until it could no longer be contained then spreading like treacle beneath her skin. When it reached her eyes it had grown points and threatened to turn to tears. She felt tender and protective and vulnerable, and as she saw the beginnings of a hopeful smile stir on the edges of the young girl's mouth, she couldn't help wrapping her arms around Merry and squeezing hard. The girl tensed beneath the embrace, gripping the shingles tight.

Juniper sat back. "What is it? Are you all right?"

"Just a little frightened of heights, is all."

"Why—you didn't say a word!"

Meredith shrugged, focused on her bare feet. "I'm frightened of a lot of things."

"Really?"

She nodded.

"Well, I suppose that's pretty normal."

Meredith turned her head abruptly. "Do you ever feel frightened?"

"Sure. Who doesn't?"

"What of?"

Juniper dipped her head, drew hard on her cigarette. "I don't know."

"Not ghosts and scary things in the castle?"

"No."

"Not heights?"

"No."

"Drowning?"

"No."

"Being unloved and alone forever?"

"No."

"Having to do something you can't stand for the rest of your life?"

Juniper pulled a face. "Ugh . . . no."

And then Meredith had looked so downhearted that she couldn't help saying, "There is one thing." Her pulse began to race, even though she had no intention of confessing her great, blank fear to Meredith. Juniper had little experience with friendship, but she was quite sure telling a new and treasured acquaintance that you feared yourself capable of great violence was inadvisable. She smoked instead and remembered the wild rush of passion, the anger that had threatened to rip her apart from the inside. The way she'd charged towards him, picked up the spade without a second thought, and then—

—woken up in bed, her bed, Saffy by her side and Percy at the window.

Saffy had been smiling, but there'd been a moment, before she saw Juniper was awake, in which her features told a different story. An agonized expression, lips taut, brow creased, that belied her later assurances that all was well. That nothing untoward had happened—why, of course it hadn't, dearest! Just a small case of lost time, no different than before.

They'd kept it from her out of love; they kept it from her still. She'd believed them at first; of course she had. What reason, after all, did they have to lie? She'd suffered lost time before. Why should this be any different?

Only it had been. Juniper had found out what it was they hid. They still didn't know that she knew. In the end it had been a matter of pure chance. Mrs. Simpson had come to the house to see Daddy, and Juniper had been following the brook by the bridge. The other woman had leaned over the railing and thrust a shaking finger, saying at her, "You!" and Juniper had wondered what she meant. "You're a wild thing. A danger to others. You ought to be locked away for what you did."

Juniper hadn't understood, hadn't known what the woman was talking about.

"My boy needed thirty stitches. Thirty! You're an animal."

An animal.

That had been the trigger. Juniper had flinched when she heard it and a memory had dislodged. A fragmented memory, ragged around the edges. An animal—Emerson—crying out in pain.

Though she'd tried her hardest, forced her mind to focus, the rest had refused to clarify. It remained hidden in the dark wardrobe of her mind. Wretched, faulty brain! How she despised it. She'd give up the other things in a flash—the writing, the giddy rush of inspiration, the joy of capturing abstract thought on a page; she'd even give up the visitors if it meant she could keep all her memories. She'd worked on her sisters, pleaded eventually, but neither would be drawn; and in the end Juniper had gone to Daddy. Up in his castle tower, he had told her the rest—what Billy Simpson had done to poor, ailing Emerson, the dear old dog who'd wanted little more than to while away his final days by the sunlit rhododendron—and what Juniper had done to Billy Simpson. And then he'd said that she wasn't to worry. That it wasn't her fault. "That boy was a bully. He deserved everything he got." And then he'd smiled, but behind his eyes the haunted look was lurking. "The rules," he'd said, "they're different for people like you, Juniper. For people like us."

"WELL?" SAID Meredith. "What is it? What do you fear?"

"I'm frightened, I suppose," said Juniper, examining the dark edge of Cardarker Wood, "that I'll turn out like my father."

"How do you mean?"

There was no way to explain, no way that wouldn't burden Merry with things she mustn't know. The fear that held tight as elastic bands round Juniper's heart; the horrid dread that she'd end her days a mad old lady, roaming the castle corridors, drowning in a sea of paper and cowering from the creatures of her very own pen. She shrugged, made light of her confession. "Oh, you know. That I'll never escape this place."

"Why would you want to leave?"

"My sisters smother me."

"Mine would *like* to smother me."

Juniper smiled and tapped some ash in the gutter.

"I'm serious. She hates me."

"Why?"

"Because I'm different. Because I don't want to be like her even though it's what everyone expects."

Juniper drew long on her cigarette, tilted her head and watched the world beyond. "How can a person expect to escape their destiny, Merry? That is the question."

A silence, then a small, practical voice. "There's always the train, I guess."

Juniper thought at first she'd misheard; she glanced at Meredith and realized that the child was completely serious.

"I mean, there are buses, too, but I think the train would be faster. A smoother ride, as well."

Juniper couldn't help it; she started to laugh, a great hulking laugh that rose up from very, very deep within her.

Meredith smiled uncertainly and Juniper gave her an enormous hug. "Oh, Merry," she said, "did you know you're really, truly, and utterly perfect?"

Meredith beamed and the two lay back against the roof tiles, watching as the afternoon stretched its film across the sky.

"Tell me a story, Merry."

"What sort of story?"

"Tell me more about your London."

THE LETTING PAGES

DAD was waiting when I got in from visiting Theo Cavill. The front door hadn't even latched behind me when the bell tinkled from his room. I went straight up and found him propped against his pillows, holding the cup and saucer Mum had brought him after dinner and feigning surprise. "Oh, Edie," he said, glancing at the wall clock, "I wasn't expecting you. Time quite got away from me."

A very unlikely assertion. My copy of the *Mud Man* was lying facedown on the blanket beside him and the spiral notepad he had taken to calling his "casebook" was propped against his knees. The whole scene smacked of an afternoon spent musing on the *Mud Man*'s mysteries, not least the way he was hungrily surveying the printouts peeping from the top of my tote. Although I can't say why, the devil entered into me at that moment and I yawned widely, patting my mouth and making my way slowly to the armchair on the other side of his bed. I smiled when I was comfy and finally he could stand it no longer. "I don't suppose you had any luck at the library? Old kidnappings at Milderhurst Castle?"

"Oh," I said. "Of course. I quite forgot." I took the file from my bag and sorted through the pages, presenting the kidnap articles for his keen perusal.

He skimmed them, one after the other, with an eagerness that made me feel cruel for having made him wait. The doctors had talked to us more about the risk of depression for cardiac patients, especially in a man like my dad, who was accustomed to being busy and important and was already on shaky ground dealing with his recent retirement. If he saw a future for himself as a literary sleuth, I wasn't going to be the one to stop him. Never mind that the *Mud Man* was the first book he'd read in roughly forty years. Besides, it seemed to me a far better purpose in life than the endless mending of household items that weren't broken to begin with. I resolved to make more of an effort. "Anything pertinent, Dad?"

His fervid expression, I noticed, had begun to droop. "None of these is about Milderhurst."

"I'm afraid not. Not directly anyway."

"But I was sure there'd be something."

"Sorry, Dad. It was the best I could do."

He grimaced bravely. "Never mind, not your fault, Edie, and we mustn't let ourselves become discouraged. We just need to think laterally." He knocked his pen against his chin then pointed it at me. "I've been going over the book all afternoon, and I'm positive it's something to do with the moat. It has to be. It says in your book about Milderhurst that Raymond Blythe had the moat filled in just before he wrote the *Mud Man*."

I nodded with all the conviction I could muster and decided against reminding him of Muriel Blythe's death and Raymond's subsequent show of grief.

"Well, there you are then," he said brightly. "It must mean something. And the child in the window, stolen while her parents slept? It's all in there, I just need to make the right connection."

He turned his attention back to the articles, reading them slowly and carefully jotting notes in a quick, stabbing hand. I tried to concentrate, but it was difficult when a real mystery was preying on my mind. Eventually I fell to staring through the window at the dusky evening light; the crescent moon was high in the purple sky and thin sheets of cloud drifted across its face. My thoughts were with Theo and the brother who'd disappeared into thin air fifty years ago when he failed to arrive at Milderhurst Castle. I'd gone searching for Thomas Cavill in the hope I might find something that would help me better understand Juniper's madness, and although that hadn't happened, my meeting with Theo had certainly changed the way I thought of Tom. Not a cheat at all, but a fellow, if his brother was correct, who had been much maligned. Certainly by me.

"You're not listening."

I glanced back from the window, blinked: Dad was watching me reproachfully over the top of his reading glasses. "I've been outlining a very sensible theory, Edie, and you haven't heard a word."

"Yes, I have. Moats, babies . . ." I winced, took a crack. "Boats?"

He huffed indignantly. "You're as bad as your mother. The two of you are downright distracted these days."

"I don't know what you're talking about, Dad. Here." I leaned my elbows on my knees and waited. "Look, I'm all ears. Lay the theory on me."

His chagrin was no match for his enthusiasm and he proceeded to do so at a skip. "It's this report here that's got me thinking. An unsolved kidnapping of a young lad from his bedroom in a manor house near Milderhurst. The window was left wide open, even though the nurse insisted she checked it when the children went to sleep, and there were marks on the ground that seemed to indicate a stepladder. It was 1872, so Raymond would've been six years old. Old enough for the whole event to have left quite an impression, don't you think?"

It was possible, I supposed. It wasn't *impossible*. "Definitely, Dad. That sounds very likely."

"The real clincher is that the boy's body was found after an extensive search"—he grinned, proud of himself and stretching the suspense—"at the bottom of the muddy estate lake." His eyes scanned mine, his smile faltered. "What is it? Why do you look like that?"

"I . . . because it's rather awful. That poor little boy. His poor family."

"Well yes, of course, but it was a hundred years ago and they're all long gone now, and that's just what I'm saying. It must've been an awful thing for a little boy living in a nearby castle to hear his parents talking about."

I remembered the locks on the nursery window, Percy Blythe telling me that Raymond was funny about security because of something in his childhood. Dad actually had a point. "That's true."

He frowned. "But I'm still not sure what it all has to do with the moat at Milderhurst. Or how the boy's muddy body turned into a man who lives at the bottom of a mudded moat. Or why the description of the man emerging would be so vivid—"

A soft knock at the door and we both looked up to see Mum. "I don't mean to interrupt. I'm just checking whether you've finished with your teacup."

"Thank you, dear." He held it out and she hesitated before coming to collect it.

"You're very busy in here," she said, pretending great interest in a tea drop on the cup's outer curve, blotting it with her finger and making every effort not to look in my direction.

"We're working on our theory." Dad winked at me, blissfully unaware that a cold front had cut his room in two.

"I expect you'll be a while then. I'll say my good-nights and turn in. It's been a rather tiring day." She kissed Dad on the cheek then nodded my way without actually making eye contact. "Good night, Edie."

"Night, Mum."

Oh Lord, but it was so stiff between us! I didn't watch her leave, pretending great interest instead in the printout on my lap. It happened to be the stapled set of pages Miss Yeats had sourced on the Pembroke Farm Institute. I glanced through the introduction, which gave the group's history: started in 1907 by a guy called Oliver Sykes—the name was familiar and I racked my brain before remembering it was the fellow architect who'd designed the circular pool at Milderhurst. It figured; if Raymond Blythe was going to leave money to a group of conservationists, they must've been people he had reason to admire. Ergo, he'd have employed the same people to work on his prized estate . . . Mum's bedroom door closed and I breathed a sigh of something like relief. I laid down the papers and tried to act normally for Dad's sake.

"You know, Dad," I said, my throat gritty, "I think you might be on to something, that thing about the lake and the little boy."

"That's what I'm talking about, Edie."

"I know. And I definitely think it could've been the inspiration for the novel."

He rolled his eyes. "Not that, Edie; forget about the book. I'm referring to your mother."

"To Mum?"

He pointed at the closed door. "She's unhappy and I don't like to see her that way."

"You're imagining things."

"I'm not daft. She's been moping about the house for weeks, then today she mentioned that she'd found the letting pages in your room and she started to cry."

Mum had been in my room? "Mum cried?"

"She feels things deeply, she always has. Wears her heart on her sleeve. You're similar that way, the two of you."

And I'm not sure whether the comment was calculated to knock me off guard, but the very notion of Mum wearing her heart on her sleeve was so confounding that I lost all ability to insist that he was totally and utterly incorrect about us being similar. "What do you mean?"

"It was one of the things I most liked about her. She was different from all the stiff upper lips I'd come across before. The first time I laid eyes on her she was having a good old cry."

"Really?"

"We were at the pictures. By chance we were the only ones there. It wasn't a particularly sad film, not that I could see, but your mum spent the whole time weeping in the dark. She tried to hide it, but when we got out into the foyer her eyes were as red as your T-shirt. I felt so sorry for her I took her out for cake."

"What was she crying about?"

"I was never sure exactly. She cried rather easily in those days."

"No . . . really?"

"Oh yes. She was very sensitive—funny, too; clever and unpre-dictable. She had a way of describing things that made you see them as if for the first time."

I wanted to ask, "What happened?" but the insinuation that she was no longer any of those things seemed cruel. I was glad when Dad continued anyway.

"Things changed," he said, "after your brother. After Daniel. Things were different then."

I couldn't be certain I'd ever heard my dad say Daniel's name and the effect was to freeze me. There were so many things I wanted to say, to ask, that they swamped one another and I managed only, "Oh."

"It was a terrible thing." His voice was slow and even, but his bot-tom lip betrayed him, a strange, involuntary mobility that made my heart constrict. "A terrible thing."

I touched his arm lightly, but he didn't seem to notice. His eyes were fixed on a patch of carpet by the door; he smiled wistfully at something that wasn't there, before saying, "He used to jump. He loved it. 'I jump!' he'd say. 'Look, Daddy, I jump!' "

I could picture him then, my little big brother, beaming with pride while he took clumsy frog leaps around the house. "I would have liked to know him."

Dad planted his hand on top of mine. "I'd have liked that, too."

The night breeze toyed with the curtain by my shoulder and I shivered. "I used to think we had a ghost. When I was little. I some-times heard you and Mum talking; I heard you say his name, but whenever I came into the room you stopped. I asked Mum about him once."

He looked up and his eyes searched mine. "What did she say?"

"She said I was imagining things."

Dad lifted one of his hands and frowned at it, spidered his fingers into a loose fist, scrunching an invisible piece of paper as he gave a rumpled sigh. "We thought we were doing the right thing. We did the best we could."

"I know you did."

"Your mum . . ." He tightened his lips against his sorrow and a part of me wanted to put him out of his misery. But I couldn't. I'd waited such a long time to hear this story—it described my absence, after all—and I was greedy for any crumb he might share. He chose his next words with a care that was painful to watch. "Your mother took it especially badly. She blamed herself. She couldn't accept that what happened"—he swallowed—"what happened to Daniel was an accident. She got it into her head that she'd brought it on herself somehow, that she deserved to lose a child."

I was speechless, and not just because what he described was so horrid, so sad, but because he was telling me at all. "But why would she think such a thing?"

"I don't know."

"Daniel's condition wasn't hereditary."

"No."

"It was just . . ." I struggled for words that weren't "one of those things," but failed.

He folded over the cover of his spiral notebook, laid it evenly on top of the *Mud Man,* and set them on the bedside table. Evidently, we wouldn't be reading tonight.

"Sometimes, Edie, a person's feelings aren't rational. At least, they don't seem that way on the surface. You have to dig a little deeper to understand what lies at the base."

And I could only nod because the day had already been so bizarre and now my father was reminding me about the subtleties of the human condition and it was all just too topsy-turvy to compute.

"I've always suspected it had something to do with her own mother, a fight they'd had years before, when your mum was still a teenager. They became estranged afterwards. I never knew the details, but whatever your gran said, Meredith remembered it when she lost Daniel."

"But Gran would never have hurt Mum, not if she could help it."

He shook his head. "You never can tell, Edie. Not with people.

I never liked the way your gran and Rita used to gang up on your mother. It used to leave a bad taste in my mouth. The two of them setting against her, using you to create a wedge."

I was surprised to hear his reading of the situation, touched by the care in his voice as he told me. Rita had implied that Mum and Dad were snobs, that they'd looked down on the other side of the family, but to hear Dad tell it—well, I began to wonder whether things weren't quite as clear as I'd supposed.

"Life's too short for rifts, Edie. One day you're here, the next you're not. I don't know what's happened between you and your mum, but she's unhappy and that makes me unhappy, and I'm a not-*quite*-old-yet chap, recovering from a heart attack, whose feelings must be taken into account."

I smiled, and he did, too.

"Patch it up with her, Edie love."

I nodded.

"I need my mind clear if I'm to sort out this *Mud Man* business."

I sat on top of my bed later that night with the letting pages spread out before me, doodling circles around flats I hadn't a hope of affording and wondering about the sensitive, funny, laughing, crying young woman I'd never had the chance to know. An enigma in one of those dated photographs—the square ones with the rounded corners and the soft, sun-shadowed colors—wearing faded bell-bottoms and a floral blouse, holding the hand of a little boy with a bowl haircut and leather sandals. A little boy who liked to jump, and whose death would soon despoil her.

I thought, too, about Dad's suggestion that Mum had blamed herself when Daniel died. Her conviction that she'd deserved to lose a child. Something in the way he'd said it, his use of the word *lost* perhaps, his suspicion that it had something to do with a fight she'd had with Gran, made me think of Mum's final letter home to her parents.

Her pleas to be allowed to remain at Milderhurst, her insistence that she'd finally found the place where she belonged, her reassurances that her choice didn't mean Gran had "lost" her.

Links were being made, I could feel them, but my stomach didn't care one whit. It issued an unceremonious interruption, reminding me that I hadn't eaten a bite since Herbert's lasagne.

The house was quiet and I went carefully along the dark corridor towards the stairs. I'd almost made it when I noticed the thin strip of light issuing from beneath Mum's bedroom door. I hesitated, the promise I'd made to Dad ringing in my ears; the small matter of patching things up. I didn't like my chances—there's no one quite like Mum for skating airily along the surface of a frost—but it was important to Dad, so I drew a deep breath and knocked, ever so lightly, on the door. Nothing happened and for a moment I thought I might be spared, but then a soft voice came from the other side: "Edie? Is that you?"

I opened the door and saw Mum sitting up in bed beneath my favorite painting of the full moon turning a licorice black sea to mercury. Her reading glasses were balanced on the tip of her nose and a novel called *The Last Days in Paris* leaned against her knees. Her expression as she blinked at me was one of strained uncertainty.

"I saw the light under the door."

"I couldn't sleep." She tilted the book towards me. "Reading helps sometimes."

I nodded agreement and neither of us spoke further; my stomach noticed the silence and took the opportunity to fill it. I was making movements to excuse myself and escape back towards the kitchen when Mum said, "Close the door, Edie."

I did as she said.

"Please. Come and sit down." She took off her glasses and hung them by the chain over her bedpost. I sat carefully, leaning against the wooden end-rail in the same place I'd occupied as a kid on birthday mornings.

"Mum," I started, "I—"

"You were right, Edie." She slid the bookmark into her novel, closed its cover but didn't relinquish it to the bedside table. "I did take you back to Milderhurst. Many years ago now."

I was seized by a sudden urge to cry.

"You were just a little girl. I didn't think you'd remember. We weren't there for long. As it happens, I lacked the courage to go any further than the front gates." She didn't meet my eyes, hugging her novel firmly to her chest. "It was wrong what I did, pretending that you'd imagined the whole thing. It was just . . . such a shock when you asked. I was unprepared. I didn't mean to lie about it. Can you forgive me?"

Is it possible not to wilt before a request like that? "Of course."

"I loved that place," she said, lips drawing. "I never wanted to leave it."

"Oh, Mum." I wanted to reach out and touch her.

"I loved her, too: Juniper Blythe." And then she looked up and the expression on her face was so lost, so forlorn, that my breath caught in my throat.

"Tell me about her, Mum."

There was a pause, an enduring pause, and I could see by her eyes that she was far away and long ago. "She was . . . like no one else I'd ever met." Mum brushed a phantom strand of hair from her forehead. "She was enchanting. And I say that quite earnestly. She enchanted me."

I thought of the silver-haired woman I'd met within the shadowy corridor of Milderhurst; the utter transformation of her face when she smiled; Theo's account of his brother's love-mad letters. The little girl in the photograph, caught unawares and staring at the camera with those wide-apart eyes.

"You didn't want to come home from Milderhurst."

"No."

"You wanted to stay with Juniper."

She nodded.

"And Gran was angry."

"Oh, yes. She'd wanted me home for months, but I'd . . . I'd managed to persuade her that I should stay. Then the Blitz happened and they were pleased, I think, that I was safe. She sent my father to get me in the end, though, and I never went back to the castle. But I always wondered."

"About Milderhurst?"

She shook her head. "About Juniper and Mr. Cavill."

My skin actually tingled and I held the bed rail very tightly.

"That was my favorite teacher's name," she continued. "Thomas Cavill. They became engaged, you see, and I never heard from either one of them again."

"Until the lost letter arrived from Juniper."

At the mention of the letter, Mum flinched. "Yes," she said.

"And it made you cry."

"Yes." And for a long moment I thought she might do so again. "But not because it was sad, not the letter itself. Not really. All that time, you see, all the time that it was lost, I thought that she'd forgotten."

"Forgotten what?"

"Why, me, of course." Mum's lips were trembling. "I thought that they'd got married and forgotten all about me."

"But they hadn't."

"No."

"They hadn't even got married, for that matter."

"No, but I didn't know that then. I didn't realize until you told me. All I knew was that I never heard from either one of them again. I'd sent something to Juniper, you see, something very important to me, and I was waiting to hear back from her. I waited and waited and checked the mail twice every day, but nothing came."

"Did you write back to her? To find out why, to check that she'd received it?"

"I almost did a number of times but it seemed so needy. Then I bumped into one of Mr. Cavill's sisters at the grocery shop and she told me that he'd run off to get married without telling any of them."

"Oh, Mum. I'm sorry."

She set her book down on the quilt beside her and said softly, "I hated them both after that. I was so hurt. Rejection is a cancer, Edie. It eats away at a person." I shifted closer and took her hand in mine; she held on tightly. There were tears on her cheeks. "I hated her and I loved her and it hurt so very deeply." She reached into the pocket of her dressing gown and handed me an envelope. "And then this. Fifty years later."

It was Juniper's lost letter. I took it from Mum, unable to speak, uncertain whether she meant for me to read it. I met her eyes and she nodded slightly.

Fingers trembling, I opened it and began.

Dearest Merry,

My clever, clever chicken! Your story arrived safely and soundly and I wept when I read it. What a beautiful, beautiful piece! Joyous and terribly sad, and oh! so beautifully observed. What a clever young miss you are! There is such honesty in your writing, Merry; a truthfulness to which many aspire, but which few attain. You must keep on; there is no reason why you shouldn't do exactly what you wish with your life. There is nothing holding you back, my little friend.

I would love to have been able to tell you this in person, to hand your manuscript back to you beneath the tree in the park, the one with the little diamonds of sunlight caught within its leaves, but I'm sorry to say that I won't be back in London as I thought. Not for a time, at any rate. Things here have not worked out as I'd imagined. I can't say too much, only that something has happened and it's best for me to stay at home for now. I miss you, Merry. You were my first and only friend, did I ever tell you

that? I think often of our time here together, especially that af-
ternoon on the roof—do you remember? You'd only been with us
a few days and hadn't yet told me you were frightened of heights.
You asked me what I was frightened of and I told you. I'd never
spoken of it to anyone else.

> *Good-bye, little chicken,*
> *Much love always, Juniper x*

I read it again, I had to, tracing the scratchy, cursive handwriting with my eyes. There was so much within the letter that made me curious, but one thing in particular to which my focus returned. Mum had shown it to me so I'd understand about Juniper, about their friendship, but all I could think of was Mum and me. My whole adult life had been spent happily immersed in the world of writers and their manuscripts: I'd brought countless anecdotes home to the dinner table even though I knew they were falling on deaf ears and I'd presumed myself since childhood an aberration. Not once had Mum even hinted that she'd harbored literary aspirations of her own. Rita had said as much, of course, but until that moment, with Juniper's letter in hand and my mother watching me nervously, I don't think I'd fully believed her. I handed the letter back to Mum, swallowing the clot of aggrievement that had settled in my throat. "You sent her a manuscript? Something you'd written?"

"It was a childish fancy, something I grew out of."

But I could tell by the way she wouldn't meet my eyes that it had been far more than that. I wanted to press harder, to ask if she ever wrote now, if she still had any of her work, if she'd ever show it to me. But I didn't. She was gazing at the letter again, her expression so sad that I couldn't. I said instead, "You were good friends."

"Yes."

I loved her, Mum had said; *my first and only friend,* Juniper had written. And yet they'd parted in 1941 and never made contact again. I thought carefully before saying, "What does Juniper mean, Mum? What do you think she means, when she says that something happened?"

Mum smoothed the letter. "I expect she means that Thomas ran off with another woman. You're the one who told me that."

Which was true, but only because that's what I'd thought at the time. I didn't think it anymore, not after speaking with Theo Cavill. "What about that bit at the end," I said, "about being frightened? What does she mean there?"

"That is a bit odd," Mum agreed. "I suppose she was remembering that conversation as an instance of our friendship. We spent so much time together, did so many things—I'm not sure why she'd mention that especially." She looked up at me and I could tell that her puzzlement was genuine. "Juniper was an intrepid sort of person; it didn't occur to her to fear the things that other people do. The only thing that scared her was some notion she had that she'd turn out like her father."

"Like Raymond Blythe? In what way?"

"She never told me, not exactly. He was a confused old gentleman, and a writer, as was she—but he used to believe that his characters had come to life and were going to come after him. I ran into him once, by mistake. I took a wrong turn and wound up near his tower—he was rather terrifying. Perhaps that's what she meant."

It was certainly possible; I cast my mind back to my visit to Milderhurst village and the stories I'd been told about Juniper. The lost time that she couldn't account for later. Watching her father lose his mind in old age must have been particularly scary for a girl who suffered her own episodes. As it turned out, she'd been right to be afraid.

Mum sighed and ruffled her hair with one hand. "I've made a mess of everything. Juniper, Thomas—now you're looking at the letting pages because of me."

"Now, that's *not* true." I smiled. "I'm looking at the letting pages because I'm thirty years old and I can't stay at home forever, no matter how much better the tea tastes when you make it."

She smiled too then, and I felt a tug of deep affection, a stirring sensation of something profound that had been sleeping for a very long time.

"And I'm the one who made a mess. I shouldn't have read your letters. Can *you* forgive *me*?"

"You don't need to ask."

"I just wanted to know you better, Mum."

She brushed my hand with a featherlight touch and I knew she understood. "I can hear your stomach grumbling from here, Edie," was all she said. "Come down to the kitchen and I'll make you something nice to eat."

An Invitation and a New Edition

AND right when I was puzzling over what had gone on between Thomas and Juniper and whether I'd ever have the chance to find out, something completely unexpected happened. It was Wednesday lunchtime and Herbert and I were returning with Jess from our constitutional around Kensington Gardens. Returning with a lot more fuss than that description suggests, mind you: Jess doesn't like to walk and she has no difficulty making her feelings known, registering protest by stopping every fifty feet or so to snout about in the gutters, chasing one mysterious odor after another.

Herbert and I were cooling our heels during one such rummaging session, when he said, "And how's life on the home front?"

"Beginning to thaw, actually." I proceeded to give him the summary version of recent events. "I don't want to speak too soon, but I believe we might've reached a new and brighter dawn."

"Are your plans to move on hold, then?" He steered Jess away from a patch of suspiciously odorous mud.

"Lord, no. My dad's been making noises about buying me a personalized robe and putting a third hook in the bathroom once he's able. I fear if I don't make the break soon, I'll be lost forever."

"Sounds dire. Anything in the letting pages?"

"Loads. I'm just going to need to hit my boss for a significant pay rise to afford them."

"Fancy your chances?"

I shifted my hand like a puppeteer.

"Well," said Herbert, passing me Jess's lead while he dug out his cigarettes. "Your boss may not be able to stretch to a pay rise, but he might have had an idea."

I raised a brow. "What sort of an idea?"

"Rather a good one, I should think."

"Oh?"

"All in good time, Edie, my love." He winked over the top of his cigarette. "All in good time."

We turned the corner into Herbert's street to find the postman poised to feed some letters through the door. Herbert tipped his hat and took the clutch of envelopes beneath his arm, unlocking the door to let us in. Jess, as per habit, went straight for the cushioned throne beneath Herbert's desk, arranging herself artfully before fixing us with a look of wounded indignation.

Herbert and I have our own post-walk habit, so when he closed the door behind him and said, "Potlatch or post, Edie?" I was already halfway to the kitchen.

"I'll make the tea," I said. "You read the mail."

The tray had been set up earlier in the kitchen—Herbert is very fastidious about such things—and a fresh batch of scones was cooling beneath a checkered tea towel. While I scooped cream and homemade jam into small ramekins, Herbert read out snippets of import from the day's correspondence. I was juggling the tray into the office when he said, "Well, well."

"What is it?"

He folded the letter in question towards him and peered over its top. "An offer of work, I believe."

"From whom?"

"A rather large publisher."

"How cheeky!" I handed him a cup. "I trust you'll remind them that you already have a perfectly good job."

"I would, of course," he said, "only the offer isn't for me. It's you they want, Edie. You and no one else."

THE LETTER, as it turned out, was from the publisher of Raymond Blythe's *Mud Man*. Over a steaming cup of Darjeeling and a jam-laden scone, Herbert read it aloud to me; then he read it again. Then he explained its contents in rather basic terms because, despite a decade in the publishing industry, the surprise had rendered me temporarily incapable of understanding such things myself: to wit, there was a new edition of the *Mud Man* being printed the following year to coincide with its seventy-fifth anniversary. Raymond Blythe's publishers wanted me to write a new introduction to celebrate the occasion.

"You're having a joke . . ." He shook his head. "But that's just . . . far too unbelievable," I said. "Why me?"

"I'm not sure." He turned over the letter, saw that the other side was blank. Gazed up at me, eyes enormous behind his glasses. "It doesn't say."

"But how peculiar." A ripple beneath my skin as the threads that had tied themselves to Milderhurst began to tremble. "What shall I do?"

Herbert handed me the letter. "I should think you might start by giving this number a ring."

MY CONVERSATION with Judith Waterman, publisher at Pippin Books, was short and not unsweet. "I'll be honest with you," she said, when I told her who I was and why I was calling, "we'd employed another writer to do it and we were very happy with him. The daughters, though, Raymond Blythe's daughters, were not. The whole thing's become rather a grand headache; we're publishing early next year, so time is of the essence. The edition's been in development for months: our writer had already conducted preliminary interviews and got some way into his draft, then out of the blue we received a phone call from the Misses Blythe letting us know they were pulling the plug."

That I could imagine. It was not difficult to envisage Percy Blythe taking great pleasure in such contrary behavior.

"We're committed to the edition, though," Judith continued.

"We've a new imprint starting, a series of classics with memoiresque opening essays, and *The True History of the Mud Man,* as one of our most popular titles, is the ideal choice for summer publication."

I realized I was nodding as if she were with me in the room. "I can understand that," I said, "I'm just not sure how I can—"

"The problem," Judith pressed on, "would appear to be with one of the daughters in particular."

"Oh?"

"Persephone Blythe. Which is an unexpected nuisance seeing as the proposal came to us in the first instance from her twin sister. Whatever the case, they weren't happy, we can't do anything without permission due to a complicated copyright arrangement, and the whole thing is teetering. I went down there myself a fortnight ago and mercifully they agreed to allow the project to go ahead with a different writer, someone of whom they approved—" She broke off and I heard her gulping a drink at the other end of the line. "We sent them a long list of writers, including samples of their work. They sent them all back to us unopened. Persephone Blythe asked for you instead."

A hook of niggling doubt snagged my stomach lining. "She asked for me?"

"By name. Quite assuredly."

"You know I'm not a writer."

"Yes," said Judith. "And I explained that to them, but they didn't mind at all. Evidently they already know who you are and what you do. More to the point, it would appear you're the only person they'll tolerate, which reduces our options rather dramatically. Either you write it, or the entire project collapses."

"I see."

"Look"—the busy sound of papers being moved across a desk— "I'm convinced you'll do a good job. You work in publishing, you know your way around sentences. I've contacted some of your former clients and they all spoke very highly of you."

"Really?" Oh, frightful vanity, fishing for a compliment! She was right to ignore me.

"And all of us at Pippin are looking at this as a positive. We're wondering whether perhaps the sisters have been so specific because they're ready, finally, to talk about the inspiration behind the book. I don't need to tell you what a terrific coup that would be, to discover the true history behind the book's creation!"

She did not. My dad was doing a brilliant job of that already.

"Well then. What do you say?"

What did I say? Percy Blythe had requested me personally. I was being asked to write about the *Mud Man*, to speak again with the Sisters Blythe, to visit them in their castle. What else was there to say? "I'll do it."

"I WAS at the opening night of the play, you know," said Herbert when I'd finished relaying the conversation.

"The *Mud Man* play?"

He nodded as Jess took up her position on his feet. "Have I never mentioned it?"

"No." That he hadn't was not as strange as it might seem. Herbert's parents were theater people and much of his childhood had been spent knocking about behind the proscenium arch.

"I was twelve, or thereabouts," he said, "and I remember it because it was one of the most astonishing things I'd ever seen. Marvelous in many ways. The castle had been constructed in the center of the stage, but they'd built it on a disc, raised and inclined, so that the tower pointed towards the audience and we could look right through the attic window into the room where Jane and her brother slept. The moat was on the very rim of the disc and the lights came from behind, so that when the Mud Man finally emerged, when he began his climb up the stones of the castle, long shadows fell into the audience, as if the mud of the story, the damp and the dark and the monster himself, were reaching out to touch one."

I shivered theatrically and earned a suspicious look from Jess. "Sounds the stuff of nightmares. No wonder you remember it so well."

"Quite, although there was more to it than that. I remember that night specially because of the kerfuffle in the audience."

"Which kerfuffle?"

"I was watching from the wings, so I was well placed to see it when it happened. A commotion, up in the writer's box, people standing, a small child crying, someone ailing. A doctor was called and some of the family retired backstage."

"The Blythe family?"

"I suppose it must have been, although I confess to having lost interest once the disturbance was over. The show went on, as it must— I don't think the incident rated as much as a mention in the papers the following day. But for a young lad like myself it was all a bit of excitement."

"Did you ever find out what it was that happened?" I was thinking of Juniper, the episodes I'd heard so much about.

He shook his head and drained the last of his tea. "Just another colorful theater moment." He fumbled a cigarette into his mouth, grinned around it as he drew. "But enough about me. How about this summons to the castle for young Edie Burchill? What a lark, eh?"

I beamed, I couldn't help it, but the expression staled a little as I reflected on the circumstances of my appointment. "I don't feel great about the other writer, the fellow they engaged first."

Herbert waved his hand and ash sifted to the carpet.

"Not your fault, Edie love. Percy Blythe wanted you—she's only human."

"Having met her, I'm not so sure of that."

He laughed and smoked and said, "The other fellow will get over it: all's fair in love, war, and publishing."

I was quite certain the displaced writer bore me no love, but I hoped it wasn't a case of war either. "Judith Waterman says he's offered to hand over his notes. She's sending them this afternoon."

"Well, then. That's very decent of him."

It most definitely was, but something else had occurred to me. "I won't be leaving you in the lurch when I go, will I? You'll be all right here by yourself?"

"It will be difficult," he said, furrowing his brow with mock perseverance. "Still, I suppose I must bear it bravely."

I made a face at him.

He stood up and patted his pockets, feeling for his car keys. "I'm only sorry we've got the vet's appointment and I won't be here when the notes arrive. Mark the best bits, won't you?"

"Of course."

He called Jess to heel then leaned over to hold my face in his two hands, so firmly I could feel the tremors that lived inside them as he planted a whiskery kiss on each cheek. "Be *brilliant,* my love."

THE PACKAGE from Pippin Books arrived by courier that afternoon, just as I was closing up shop. I debated taking the whole lot home, opening it in a steady, professional manner, then thought better of it. I jiggled the key in the lock, fired up the lights again, and hurried back to my desk, tearing the parcel open as I went.

Two cassette tapes fell free as I fumbled an enormous stack of papers from inside. There were over a hundred pages, fastened neatly with a pair of bulldog clips. On top was a cover letter from Judith Waterman including a project brief, the crux of which read as follows:

> NEW PIPPIN CLASSICS is an exciting new imprint of PIPPIN BOOKS that will bring a selection of our favorite classic texts to new readers and old. Rejacketed with beautiful matching bindings, assorted decorative endpapers, and all-new biographical introductions, the NPC titles promise to be a dynamic publishing presence in coming years. Beginning with Raymond Blythe's *The True History of the Mud Man,* NPC titles

will be numbered so that readers can enjoy collecting
them all.

There was an asterisked handwritten note from Judith at the bottom of the letter:

Edie, what you write is, of course, up to you; however, in our initial briefing discussions we wondered whether, seeing as so much is already known about Raymond Blythe and because he was so reticent about his inspiration, it might be interesting to write the piece with a particular eye to the three daughters, posing and answering the question of what it was like to grow up in the place from which the Mud Man came.

You'll see in the interview transcripts that our original writer, Adam Gilbert, has included detailed descriptions and impressions of his visits to the castle. You are most welcome to work from these, but you'll no doubt wish to conduct your own research. In fact, Persephone Blythe was surprisingly amenable on that count, suggesting that you pay them a visit. (And it goes without saying that if she should choose to let slip the origins of the story we'd love for you to write that up for us!)

The budget isn't huge but there's sufficient remaining to fund a short stay in the village of Milderhurst. We have made an arrangement with Mrs. Marilyn Bird at the nearby Home Farm Bed and Breakfast. Adam was pleased with the standard and cleanliness of the room, and the tariff includes meals. Mrs. Bird has advised of a four-night vacancy beginning October 31, so when next we speak please let me know whether you'd like us to make a reservation.

I flipped over the letter, ran my hand across Adam Gilbert's cover sheet, and sank into this most thrilling moment. I believe I may actually have smiled as I turned the page; I certainly bit my lip. Rather too hard, which is how I remember it so well.

FOUR HOURS later I'd read it all and I was no longer sitting in a quiet office in London. I was, of course, but also I was not. I was many miles away inside a dark and knotty castle in Kent, with three sisters, their larger-than-life daddy, and a manuscript that was yet to become a book that was yet to become a classic.

I laid down the transcripts, pushed back from my desk, and stretched. Then I stood and stretched some more. A kink had tied itself at the base of my spine—I'm told reading with one's feet crossed atop the desk can do that—and I struggled to dislodge it. Time and a little space allowed certain thoughts to rise from the ocean floor of my mind, and two things in particular floated to the surface. First up, I was awestruck by Adam Gilbert's workmanship. The notes had clearly been transcribed verbatim from taped interviews and prepared on an old-fashioned typewriter, with impeccable handwritten annotations where necessary, and a level of detail so that they read more like play scripts than interviews (complete with bracketed stage directions if any of his subjects so much as scratched), which is probably why the other thought struck me so strongly: there had been a notable omission. I knelt on my chair and leafed again through the stack to confirm, checking both sides of the paper to confirm. There was nothing from Juniper Blythe.

I drummed my fingers slowly on the stack of notes: there were perfectly good reasons why Adam Gilbert might have passed her over. There was more than enough material without additional comment, she hadn't even been alive when the *Mud Man* was first published, she was Juniper . . . Nonetheless, it niggled. And when things niggle, the perfectionist in me starts to fret. And I don't much like to fret. There were three Sisters Blythe. Their story, therefore, should not—could not—be written without Juniper's voice.

Adam Gilbert's contact details were typed at the bottom of his cover sheet and I deliberated for around ten seconds—just long enough to wonder whether nine thirty was too late to ring somebody whose home address was Old Mill Cottage, Tenterden—before reaching for the phone and dialing his number.

A woman picked up and said: "Hello. Mrs. Button speaking."

Something about the slow, melodic tone of her voice reminded me of those wartime movies with the vows of phone operators working the switchboard. "Hello," I said. "My name's Edie Burchill, but I'm afraid I might have called the wrong number. I was looking for Adam Gilbert."

"This is Mr. Gilbert's residence. This is his nurse speaking, Mrs. Button."

Nurse. Oh dear. He was an invalid. "I'm so sorry to bother you this late. Perhaps I ought to call back another time."

"Not at all. Mr. Gilbert is still in his study; I see the light beneath the door. Quite against doctor's orders, but so long as he keeps off his bad leg there's not much I can do. He's rather stubborn. Just a minute and I'll transfer your call."

There was a heavy plastic clunk as she laid down the receiver, and the steady sound of footsteps retreating. A knock on a distant door, a murmured exchange, then a few seconds later, Adam Gilbert picked up.

There was a pause after I introduced myself and my purpose, in which I apologized some more for the awkward way in which we'd entered each other's orbit. "I didn't even know about the Pippin Books edition until today. I've no idea at all why Percy Blythe would put her foot down like that."

Still he didn't speak.

"I'm really very, very sorry. I can't explain it; I've only met her once before and then only briefly. I certainly never meant for this to happen." I was jabbering, I could hear it, so with great force of will I stopped.

Finally he spoke, in a world-weary sort of voice. "All right, then, Edie Burchill. I forgive you for stealing my job. One condition, though. If you find out anything to do with the *Mud Man*'s origins you tell me first."

My dad would not be pleased. "Of course."

"Right, then. What can I do for you?"

I explained that I'd just read through his transcript, I complimented him on the thoroughness of his notes, and then I said, "There's one little thing I'm wondering, though."

"What's that?"

"The third sister, Juniper. There's nothing here from her."

"No," he said. "No, there's not."

I waited, and when nothing followed I said, "You didn't speak with her?"

"No."

Again I waited. Again nothing followed. Apparently this was not going to be easy. At the other end of the line he cleared his throat and said, "I proposed to interview Juniper Blythe but she wasn't available."

"Oh?"

"Well, she was available in a bodily sense—I don't think she leaves the castle much—but the older sisters wouldn't permit me to speak with her."

Comprehension dawned. "Oh."

"She's not well, so I expect that's all it was, but . . ."

"But what?"

A break in conversation during which I could almost see him grabbing for the words to explain himself. Finally, a brambly sigh. "I got the feeling they were trying to protect her in some way."

"Protect her from what? From whom? From *you*?"

"No, not from me!"

"Then what?"

"I don't know. It was just a feeling. As if they were worried about what she might say. How it might reflect."

"On them? On their father?"

"Maybe. Or else on her."

I remembered then the strange feeling I'd got when I was at Milderhurst, the glance that had passed between Saffy and Percy when Juniper shouted at me in the yellow parlor; Saffy's concern when she discovered that Juniper had wandered off, that she'd been talking to me in the passage. That she might have said something she shouldn't. "But why?" I said, more to myself than to him, thinking about Mum's lost letter, the trouble hinted at between its lines. "What could Juniper possibly have to hide?"

"Well," said Adam, lowering his voice a little, "I must admit to having done a bit of digging. The more adamant they were about keeping her out of it, the more interested I got."

"And? What did you find?" I was glad he couldn't see me. There was no dignity in the way I was practically swallowing the telephone receiver in my eagerness.

"An incident in 1935; I guess you could call it a scandal." He let the final word hang between us with a sort of mysterious satisfaction, and I could just picture him: leaning back against his bentwood desk chair, smoking jacket drawn taut against his belly, warm pipe clamped between his teeth.

I matched his hushed tone. "What sort of scandal?"

"Some 'bad business' is what I was told, involving the son of an employee. One of the gardeners. The details were all rather imprecise and I couldn't find anything of an official nature to verify it, but the story goes that the two of them were involved in some sort of a scrap and he came out of it beaten black and blue."

"By *Juniper*?" An image came to mind of the wisp of old woman I'd met at Milderhurst, the slender girl in the old photos. I tried not to laugh. "When she was thirteen years old?"

"That was the implication, though saying it out loud like that makes it seem rather far-fetched."

"But that's what he told people? That Juniper did it?"

"Well, *he* didn't say any such thing. I can't imagine there are too many young fellows who'd admit freely to being bested by a slim young girl like her. It was his mother who went up to the castle making claims. From what I hear, Raymond Blythe paid them off. Dressed up as a bonus for his father, apparently, who'd worked his whole life on the estate. The rumor didn't go away, though, not completely; there was still talk in the village."

I got the feeling Juniper was the sort of girl people liked to talk about: her family was important, she was beautiful and talented—in Mum's words, enchanting—but still: Juniper the Teenage Man-Beater? It seemed unlikely, to say the very least.

"Look, it's probably just groundless old talk." Adam's tone was breezy again as he echoed my thoughts. "Nothing at all to do with why her sisters vetoed our interview."

I nodded slowly.

"More likely, they just wanted to spare her the stress. She's not well, she's certainly not good with strangers, she wasn't even born when the *Mud Man* was written."

"I'm sure you're right," I said. "I'm sure that's all it was."

But I wasn't. I didn't really imagine that the twins were fretting over a long-forgotten incident with the gardener's son, but I couldn't rid myself of the certainty that there was something else behind it. I put down the phone and I was back in that ghostly passage, looking between Juniper and Saffy and Percy, feeling like a child who is old enough to recognize nuance at play but hopelessly ill-equipped to read it.

THE DAY that I was due to leave for Milderhurst, Mum came early to my bedroom. The sun was still hiding behind the wall of Singer & Sons, but I'd been awake for an hour or so already, as excited as a kid on her first day of school.

"There's something I wanted to give you," she said. "To lend you, at any rate. It's rather precious to me."

I waited, wondering what it might be. She reached inside her dressing-gown pocket and took an object out. Her eyes searched mine for a moment, then she handed it over. A little book with a brown leather cover.

"You said you wanted to know me better." She was trying hard to be brave, to keep her voice from shaking. "It's all in there. *She's* in there. The person that I used to be."

I took the journal, as nervous as a novice mother with a brand-new baby. Awed by its preciousness, terrified of doing it damage, amazed and touched and gratified that Mum would trust me with such a treasure. I couldn't think what to say; that is, I could think of lots of things I wanted to say, but there was a lump in my throat, years in the making, and it wasn't about to budge. "Thank you," I managed to say before I began to cry.

Mum's eyes misted in instant response and at the very same moment each of us reached for the other and held on tight.

THREE

IT was typical. After a terribly cold winter, spring had arrived with a great big smile and the day itself was perfect, a fact Percy couldn't help but take as a direct slight from God. Then and there she became a nonbeliever, standing in the village church, at the far end of the family pew her grandmother had designed and William Morris had carved, watching as Mr. Gordon, the vicar, pronounced Harry Rogers and Lucy Middleton man and wife. The entire experience had the vaguely spongy feeling of a nightmare, though it was possible the quantity of bolstering whisky she'd consumed beforehand was playing its part.

Harry smiled at his new bride and Percy was struck again by how handsome he was. Not in the conventional sense, neither devilish nor suave nor clean-cut, rather he was handsome because he was good. She had always thought so, even when she was a little girl and he a young fellow who came to the house to attend the clocks for Daddy. There was something about the way he carried himself, the unassuming set of his shoulders, that marked him as a man whose self-opinion was not unduly inflated. Moreover he was possessed of a slow, steady nature, which might not have been dynamic but spoke of care and tenderness. She used to watch him from between the banisters, coaxing life back into the oldest and crossest of the castle's clocks, but if he'd noticed he'd never let on. He didn't see her now, either. He only had eyes for Lucy.

For her part, Lucy was smiling, giving an excellent performance of one who was pleased to be marrying the man she loved above all

347

others. Percy had known Lucy for a long time but had never thought her such a very good actress. An ill feeling shifted in the pit of her stomach and she longed again for the whole ordeal to be ended.

She could have stayed away, of course—feigned illness or pleaded essential war work—but there'd have been talk. They'd employed Lucy at the castle for over twenty years: it was unthinkable that she might be married without a Blythe standing witness in the congregation. Daddy, for obvious reasons, made a poor choice; Saffy was preparing the castle for Meredith's mother and father; and Juniper—never an ideal candidate—had retreated to the attic with her pen in a frenzy of inspiration; thus the duty had fallen to Percy. To shirk the responsibility wasn't an option, not least because Percy would've had to explain her absence to her twin. Crushed to be missing the wedding herself, Saffy had demanded a report of every last detail.

"The dress, the flowers, the way they look at one another," she'd said, listing them on her fingers as Percy tried to leave the castle. "I want to hear it all."

"Yes, yes," Percy had said, wondering whether her whisky flask would fit inside the fancy little handbag Saffy had insisted she carry. "Don't forget Daddy's medicine, will you? I've left it out on the table in the entrance hall."

"The hall table. Right."

"It's important he has it on the hour. We don't want a repeat of last time."

"No," Saffy agreed, "we certainly do not. Poor Meredith thought she was seeing a ghost, poor lamb. A very rambunctious ghost."

Percy had almost been at the bottom of the front stairs when she'd turned back. "And, Saffy?"

"Mmm?"

"Let me know if anyone comes to call."

Ghastly death merchants preying on an old man's confusion. Whispering in his ear, playing up to his fears, his ancient guilt. Rattling their Catholic crucifixes and muttering their Latin into the castle corners; convincing Daddy that the specters of his imagination were bona fide demons. All, she was sure, so they could get their hands on the castle when he died.

Percy picked at the skin around her fingernails, wondered how much longer it would be before she could get outside for a cigarette, whether it was possible for her to slip out unnoticed if she affected the perfect attitude of authority. The vicar said something then and everybody stood; Harry took Lucy's hand in his to walk her back down the aisle, holding it with such tenderness that Percy realized she couldn't hate him, even now.

Joy animated the married couple's features and Percy did her best to match it. She even managed to join in the applause as they made their way along the narrow aisle and out into the sunshine. She was aware of her limbs, the unnatural claw she'd made with her hand on the back of the pew, the lines of her face sitting in forced merriment that made her feel like a clockwork puppet. Someone hidden high above in the raked church ceiling jerked an invisible wire and she seized her handbag from beside her. Laughed a little and pretended to be a living, feeling thing.

THE MAGNOLIAS were out, just as Saffy had hoped and prayed and crossed her fingers for, and it was one of those rare but precious days in April when summer begins to advertise itself. Saffy smiled just because she couldn't help it.

"Come on, slowpoke," she called, turning to hurry Meredith along. "It's Saturday, the sun is shining, your mother and father are on their way to visit; there's no excuse for dragging your feet." Really, the child was in a most cheerless mood. One would've thought she'd be delighted at the prospect of seeing her parents, yet she'd been moping all morning. Saffy could guess why, of course.

"Don't worry," she said, as Meredith reached her side. "Juniper won't be much longer. It never lasts more than a day or so."

"But she's been up there since dinnertime. The door's locked, she won't answer. I don't understand . . ." Meredith squinted in an unflattering way, a habit that Saffy found frightfully endearing. "What's she doing?"

"Writing," said Saffy simply. "That's how it is with Juniper. That's how it's always been. It won't last long and then she'll be back to normal. Here"—she handed Meredith the small stack of cake plates—"why don't you help by laying these out? Shall we sit your mother and father with their backs to the hedge so they can see the garden?"

"All right," said Meredith, cheering up.

Saffy smiled to herself. Meredith Baker was delightfully compliant—an unexpected joy after raising Juniper—and her residency at Milderhurst Castle had been a resounding success. There was nothing like a child for forcing life back into tired, old stones, and the infusion of light and laughter had been just what the doctor ordered. Even Percy had taken a shine to the girl, relieved, no doubt, at having found the curlicues intact.

The greatest surprise, though, had been Juniper's reaction. The evident affection she felt for the young evacuee was the closest Saffy had ever seen her come to caring for another person. Saffy heard them sometimes, talking and giggling in the garden, and was confounded, but pleasantly so, by the genuine geniality in Juniper's voice. *Genial* was not a word Saffy had ever thought to use when describing her little sister.

"Let's lay a place here for June," she said, indicating the table, "just in case, and you beside, I think . . . and Percy over there . . ."

Meredith had been following, laying down the plates, but she stopped then. "What about you?" she said. "Where will you sit?" And perhaps she read the apology forming in Saffy's face, for she went on quickly. "You are coming, aren't you?"

"Now, my dear." Saffy let the clutch of cake forks fall limp against her skirt, "I'd love to, you know I would. But Percy's very traditional about such matters. She's the eldest, and in the absence of Daddy that makes her the host. I know it must all sound terribly silly and formal to you, very old-fashioned indeed, but that's the way things are done here. It's the way Daddy likes to entertain at Milderhurst."

"But I still don't see why you can't both come."

"Well, one of us has to stay inside should Daddy need help."

"But Percy—"

"Is so looking forward to it. She's very keen to meet your parents."

Saffy could see that Meredith was unconvinced; more than that, the poor child looked so bitterly disappointed that Saffy would have done just about anything to cheer her up. She prevaricated, but only briefly and not with any real strength, and when Meredith let out a long, dispirited sigh, Saffy's remaining resolve collapsed. "Oh, Merry," she said, sneaking a glance over her shoulder, "I shouldn't say anything, I really shouldn't, but there *is* another reason I have to stay indoors."

She slid to one end of the rickety garden seat and indicated Meredith should join her. Took a deep, cool breath and released it decidedly. Then she told Meredith all about the telephone call she was expecting that afternoon. "He's a very important private collector in London," she said. "I wrote to him after a small advertisement appeared in the newspaper seeking an assistant to catalogue his collection. And he wrote back recently to tell me that mine was the successful application, that he would telephone me this afternoon so we might work out the details together."

"What does he collect?"

Saffy couldn't help clasping her hands together beneath her chin. "Antiquities, art, books, beautiful things—what *heaven*!"

Excitement brightened the tiny freckles across Meredith's nose and Saffy thought again what a lovely child she was and how far she'd come in six short months. When one considered the poor skinny waif she'd been when Juniper first brought her home! Beneath the pale London skin and ragged dress, though, there lurked a quick mind and a delightful hunger for knowledge.

"Can I visit the collection?" said Meredith. "I've always wanted to see a real, live Egyptian artifact."

Saffy laughed. "Of course you shall. I'm certain Mr. Wicks would be delighted to show his precious things to a clever young lady like you."

Meredith really did appear to glow then and the first barb of regret poked holes in Saffy's pleasure. Was it not just a little unkind to fill the girl's head with such grand imaginings only to then expect her to keep quiet about them? "Now, Merry," she said, sobering, "it's very exciting news, but you must remember that it's a secret. Percy doesn't know yet, and nor shall she."

"Why not?" Meredith's eyes widened further. "What will she do?"

"She won't be happy, that's for certain. She won't want me to go. She's rather resistant to change, you see, and she likes things the way they are, all three of us here together. She's very protective like that. She always has been."

Meredith was nodding, absorbing this detail of the family dynamic with so much interest that Saffy half expected her to pull out that little journal of hers and take down notes. Her interest was understandable, though: Saffy had heard sufficient of the child's own older sister to know that notions of sibling protectiveness would be unfamiliar to her.

"Percy is my twin and I love her dearly, but sometimes, Merry dear, one has to put one's own desires first. Happiness in life is not a given, it must be seized." She smiled and resisted adding that there had been other opportunities, other chances, all lost. It was one thing to feed a child a confidence, quite another to burden her with adult regrets.

"But what will happen when it's time for you to go?" said Meredith. "She'll find out then."

"Oh, but I'll tell her before that!" Saffy said with a laugh. "Of course I will. I'm not planning to abscond in the black of night, you know! Certainly not. I just need to find the perfect words, a way of ensuring that Percy's feelings aren't hurt. Until such time, I think it best that she not hear a thing about it. Do you understand?"

"Yes," said Meredith, somewhat breathlessly.

Saffy bit down on her bottom lip; she had the uneasy sense that she'd made an unfortunate error of judgment, that it had been unfair to put a child in such an awkward position. She'd only meant to take Meredith's mind off her own miserable mood.

Meredith misunderstood Saffy's silence, taking it for a lack of faith in her ability to keep a confidence. "I won't say anything, I promise. Not a word. I'm very good at secrets."

"Oh, Meredith." Saffy smiled ruefully. "I don't doubt it. That's not it at all— Oh, dear, I'm afraid I must apologize. It was wrong of me, asking you to keep a secret from Percy—will you forgive me?"

Meredith nodded solemnly and Saffy detected a glimmer in the girl's face; pride at having been treated in such an adult manner, she supposed. Saffy remembered her own childish eagerness to grow up, how she'd waited impatiently on the cliff edge, pleading with adulthood to claim her, and she wondered whether it was possible ever to slow another's journey. Was it even fair to try? Surely there could be nothing wrong in wanting to save Meredith, just as she'd tried to save Juniper, from reaching adulthood and its disappointments too fast?

"There now, lovely one," she said, taking the last plate from Meredith's hands, "why don't you leave me to finish here? Go and have some fun while you wait for your parents to arrive. The morning's far too brilliant to be spent doing chores. Just try not to get your dress too dirty."

It was one of the pinafores Saffy had sewn when Merry first arrived, made from a lovely piece of Liberty fabric ordered years ago, not because Saffy had a project in mind, but because it was simply too beautiful not to possess. It had languished ever since in the sewing cupboard, waiting patiently for Saffy to find it a purpose. And now she had. As Meredith dissolved into the horizon, Saffy returned her attention to the table, making sure everything was just so.

MEREDITH WANDERED aimlessly through the long grass, swishing a stick from side to side, wondering how it was that one person's absence could rob the day so wholly of its shape and meaning. She rounded the hill and met the stream, then followed it as far as the bridge carrying the driveway.

She considered going further. Across the verge and into the woods. Deep enough that the light sifted, the spotted trout disappeared, and the water ran thick as molasses. All the way until she crossed into the wild woods and reached the forgotten pool at the base of the oldest tree in Cardarker Wood. The place of insistent blackness that she'd hated when she'd first come to the castle. Mum and Dad weren't due for an hour or so yet, there was still time, and she knew the way, it was only a matter of sticking by the burbling brook, after all . . .

But without Juniper, Meredith knew, it wouldn't be so much fun. Just dark and damp and rather smelly. "Isn't it wonderful?" Juniper had said the first time they'd explored together. Meredith had been uncertain. The log they were sitting on was cool and damp and her shoes wet from where she'd slid off a rock. There was another pool on the estate, teeming with butterflies and birds, and a rope swing that lazed back and forth in the dappled sunlight, and she'd wished, wished, wished they'd decided to spend the day there instead. She didn't say as much, though; the force of Juniper's conviction was such that Meredith knew the fault was her own, that her tastes were too juvenile, that she just wasn't trying hard enough. Screwing her determination to the sticking place, she'd smiled and said, "Yes." And again, with feeling, "Yes. It is. Wonderful."

In a single, fluid motion, Juniper had stood, arms extended to the sides, and tiptoed across a fallen log. "It's the shadows," she'd said, "the way the reeds slip down the banks, almost slyly; the smell of mud and moisture and rot." She smiled sideways at Meredith. "Why, it's almost prehistoric. If I told you we'd crossed an invisible threshold into the past, you'd believe me, wouldn't you?"

Meredith had shivered then, just as she did now, and a small, smooth magnet within her child's body had thrummed with inexplicable urgency, and she'd felt the pull of longing, though for what she did not know.

"Close your eyes and listen," Juniper had whispered, finger to her lips. "You can hear the spiders spinning . . ."

Meredith closed her eyes now. Listened to the chorus of crickets, the occasional splashing of trout, the distant drone of a tractor somewhere . . . There was another sound, too. One that seemed distinctly out of place. It was an engine, she realized, close by and coming nearer.

She opened her eyes and saw it. A black motorcar, winding down the graveled driveway from the castle. Meredith couldn't help but stare. Visitors were rare at Milderhurst, motorcars even rarer. Few people had the petrol for making social calls, and from what Meredith could tell, those who did were hoarding it so they could flee north when the Germans invaded. Even the priest who called on the old man in the tower arrived on foot these days. This visitor must be someone official, Meredith decided, someone on special war business.

The motorcar passed and the driver, a man she did not recognize, touched his black hat, nodding sternly at Meredith. She squinted after him, watching the car as it continued warily along the gravel. It disappeared behind a wooded bend only to reappear sometime later at the foot of the driveway, a black speck turning onto the Tenterden Road.

Meredith yawned and promptly forgot all about it. There was a patch of violets growing wild near the bridge and she couldn't resist picking some. When her posy was lovely and thick, she climbed up to sit on the railing of the bridge and divided her time between daydreaming and dropping the flowers, one by one, into the stream, watching as they turned purple somersaults in the gentle current.

"Morning."

She looked up to see Percy Blythe pushing her bicycle up the driveway, an unflattering hat on her head, requisite cigarette in hand. The stern twin, as Meredith usually thought of her, though today there was something else in her face, something beyond stern and a little more like sad. It might just have been the hat. Meredith said, "Hello," and clutched the railing to save herself from falling.

"Or is it afternoon already?" Percy slowed to a stop and flicked her wrist, reading the small watch-face that sat against the inside. "Just gone half past. You won't forget we have a tea engagement, will you?" She glanced over the end of her cigarette as she drew long and hard, then exhaled slowly. "Your parents would be rather disappointed, I imagine: to travel all this way only to miss you."

It was a joke, Meredith suspected, but there was nothing jovial about Percy's expression or her manner, so she couldn't be sure. She hedged her bets, smiling politely; at the very least, she figured, Percy might assume she hadn't heard.

Percy gave no indication that she'd noticed Meredith's response, let alone given it further thought. "Well," she said, "things to do." And she nodded bluntly, continuing on towards the castle.

FOUR

WHEN Meredith finally caught sight of her parents, walking together up the driveway, her stomach flip-flopped. For a split second she felt as if she was watching the approach of two dream people, familiar yet entirely out of place here, in the real world. The sensation lasted only a moment before something inside her, some disc of perception, turned over and she saw properly it was Mum and Dad and they were here at last and she had so much to tell them. She ran forwards, arms wide, and Dad knelt, mirroring her posture, so she could leap into his big, wide, warm embrace. Mum planted a kiss on her cheek, which was unusual but not unpleasant, and although she knew herself to be far too old for it, neither Rita nor Ed was there to tease her, so Meredith let her dad hold hands with her all the rest of the way, as she talked without pause about the castle and its library and the fields and the brook and the woods.

Percy was already waiting by the table, smoking another cigarette, which she extinguished when she saw them. She smoothed the sides of her skirt, held out a hand, and with a bit of fussing the greeting was effected. "And how was your train trip? Not too unpleasant I hope?" The question was perfectly ordinary, polite even, but Meredith heard the upper-class clip of Percy's voice through her parents' ears and wished it were Saffy's soft welcome instead.

Sure enough, Mum's voice was thin and guarded: "It was long. Stopping and starting all the way, letting the troop trains pass. We spent more time in the sidings than we did on the track."

"Still," said Dad, "our boys have gotta get themselves to war somehow. Show Hitler Britain can take it."

357

"Just so, Mr. Baker. Sit down, won't you, please?" said Percy, indicating the prettily laid table. "You must be famished."

Percy poured tea and offered slices of Saffy's cake, and they spoke, somewhat stiltedly, about the crowding on the trains, the state of the war (Denmark had toppled, would Norway be next?), predictions for its progress. Meredith nibbled a piece of cake and watched. She'd been convinced that Mum and Dad would take one look at the castle, then another at Percy Blythe, with her plummy accent and broomstick spine, and adopt defensive maneuvers, but so far things were going smoothly enough.

Meredith's mum was very quiet, it was true. She kept one hand holding tightly on to the handbag on her lap in a nervous, stiff sort of way, which was a little disquieting given that Meredith couldn't think that she'd ever seen her mother nervous before: not of rats, or spiders, or even Mr. Lane from across the road when he'd spent too long in the pub. Dad seemed to be a bit more at ease, nodding as Percy described the Spitfire drive and the care packages for soldiers in France, and sipping tea from a hand-painted porcelain teacup as if he did so every day. Well, almost. He did manage to make it look rather like a doll's house tea set. Meredith didn't think she'd ever realized quite how enormous his fingers were and an unexpected wave of affection washed over her. She reached out beneath the table to lay her palm on his other hand. They weren't a family who expressed themselves physically and he glanced up, surprised, before squeezing hers in return.

"How's your schoolwork going, my girl?" He leaned his shoulder a little closer and looked up to wink at Percy: "Our Rita might have got the looks, but young Merry here took all the brains."

Meredith warmed with pride. "I'm doing lessons here, Dad, at the castle, with Saffy. You should see the library, there are more books even than at the circulating library. Every wall covered with shelves. And I'm learning Latin . . ." Oh, how she loved Latin. Sounds from the past, imbued with meaning. Ancient voices on the wind. Meredith pushed her spectacles higher up the bridge of her nose; they often slipped with excitement. "And I'm learning the piano, too."

"My sister Seraphina is very pleased with your daughter's progress," said Percy. "She's come along rather well, considering she'd never seen a piano before."

"Is that right?" said Dad, hands jiggling in his pockets so that his elbows moved most peculiarly above the tabletop. "My girl can play tunes?"

Meredith smiled proudly and wondered if her ears were glowing. "Some."

Percy topped up everybody's tea. "Perhaps you'll take your parents inside later, Meredith; into the music room, where you might play one of your pieces for them?"

"You hear that, Mum?" Dad nodded his chin. "Our Meredith is playing real music."

"I heard." Something seemed to set then in Mum's face, though Meredith wasn't sure exactly what it was. It was the same look she got when she and Dad were fighting over something and he made a small but fatal error ensuring that victory would be hers. Her voice tight, she spoke to Meredith as if Percy wasn't there. "We missed you at Christmas."

"I missed you too, Mum. I did really want to come and visit. Only there were no trains. They needed them all for the soldiers."

"Rita's coming home with us today." Mum set her teacup on its saucer, straightened the teaspoon decisively, and pushed it away. "Found her a position with a hairdressing salon we have, down on the Old Kent Road. Starts on Monday. Cleaning at first, but they'll teach her how to do sets and cuts, too." Gratification brought a glimmer to Mum's eyes. "There's opportunities at the moment, Merry, what with so many of the older girls joining the Wrens or going to the factories. Good opportunities for a young girl without other prospects."

It made sense. Rita was always fussing with her hair and her prized collection of beauty aids. "Sounds good, Mum. Nice to have someone in the family who can set your hair for you." That didn't seem to please her mum.

Percy Blythe took a cigarette from the silver case Saffy insisted she use in company and felt about in her pocket for matches. Dad cleared his throat. "The thing is, Merry," he said, and his awkwardness was no consolation to Meredith for the terrible thing he said next: "your Mum and me—we thought it might be time for you, too."

And then Meredith understood. They wanted her to go home, to become a hairdresser, to leave Milderhurst. Deep inside her stomach panic formed a ball and started rolling back and forth. She blinked a couple of times, straightened her specs, then stammered, "But, but, I don't want to be a hairdresser. Saffy says it's important I finish my education. That I might even get a place at grammar school when the war is over."

"Your mum was just thinking of your future with the hairdressing; we can talk about something else if you like. An office girl maybe. One of the ministries?"

"But it's not safe in London," said Meredith suddenly. It was a stroke of genius: she wasn't really remotely frightened of Hitler or his bombs, but perhaps this was a way to convince them.

Dad smiled and patted her shoulder. "There's nothing to worry about, my girl. We're all doing our bit to ruin Hitler's party: Mum's just started in a munitions factory and I'm working nights. There's no bombs been dropped, no poison gas, the old neighborhood looks just the same as always."

Just the same as always. Meredith pictured the grimy old streets and her grim place in them, and with a bolt of sickening clarity admitted then how desperate she was to stay on at Milderhurst. She turned towards the castle, knotting her fingers, wishing she could summon Juniper with nothing more than the intensity of her need; wishing that Saffy might appear and say the perfect thing, make Mum and Dad see that taking her home was the wrong thing to do, that they must let her stay.

Perhaps by some strange twin communication, Percy chose that moment to wade in. "Mr. and Mrs. Baker," she said, tapping the end of her cigarette on the silver case and looking like she'd rather be anywhere else, "I can understand that you'd very much like to have Meredith home with you, but if the invasion should—"

"You're coming with us this afternoon, young miss, and that's final." Mum's hackles had risen like a set of quills. She didn't so much as glance at Percy, fixing Meredith with a look that promised fierce punishment later.

Meredith's eyes watered behind her spectacles. "I'm not."

Dad growled, "Don't you talk back to your mother—"

"Well," said Percy abruptly. She'd lifted the lid on the teapot and was scrutinizing its contents. "The pot's empty; excuse me while I refill it, won't you? We're rather short on help at the moment. Wartime economies."

They all three watched her retreat, then Mum hissed at Dad, "Rather short on help. You hear that?"

"Come on, Annie." Confrontation was not something Dad enjoyed. He was the sort of man whose impressive bulk was enough of a deterrent that he rarely needed to come to blows. Mum, on the other hand . . .

"That woman's been looking down her nose at us since we arrived. Wartime economies indeed—in a place like this." She tossed her hand in the direction of the castle. "Probably thinks we ought to be in there fetching after her."

"She does not!" said Meredith. "They're not like that."

"Meredith." Dad was still staring at a fixed point on the ground, but his voice rose, almost pleading, and he shot a glance at her from beneath his knotted brow. Ordinarily, she knew, he relied on her to stand silently beside him when Mum and Rita started screaming. But not today, she couldn't just stand by today.

"But, Dad, look at the lovely tea they put on specially—"

"That's enough lip from you, miss." Mum was on her feet now and she jerked Meredith up by the sleeve of her new dress, harder than she might otherwise have. "You get on inside and fetch your things. Your *real* clothes. The train's leaving soon and we're all going to be on it."

"I don't want to go," said Meredith, turning urgently to her father. "Let me stay, Dad. Please don't make me go. I'm learning—"

"Pah!" Mum swiped her hand dismissively. "I can see well enough what you've been learning here with your Lady Muck; learning to cheek your parents. I can see what you're forgetting, too: who you are and where you come from." She shook her finger at Dad. "I told you we were wrong to send them away. If we'd only kept them home like I wanted—"

"Enough!" Dad's top had finally blown. "That's enough, Annie. Sit down. There's no need for all this; she's coming home now."

"I'm not!"

"Oh yes you are," said Mum, pulling back her flattened hand. "And there's a good clip round the ear waiting for you when you get there."

"That's enough!" Dad was on his feet now, too; he grabbed hold of Mum's wrist. "For Christ's sake, that's enough, Annie." His eyes searched hers and something passed between them; Meredith saw her mother's wrist go limp. Dad nodded at her. "We've all become a bit hot and bothered, that's all."

"Talk to your daughter . . . I can't stand to look at her. I only hope she never knows what it is to lose a child." And she walked away, arms folded stubbornly across her body.

Dad looked tired suddenly, old. He ran a hand over his hair. It was thinning on top, so that Meredith could see the marks that the comb had made that morning. "You mustn't mind her. She's fiery, you know how she gets. She's been worried about you, we both have." He glanced again at the castle, looming above them. "Only we've heard stories. From Rita's letters and from some of the kids who've come home, terrible stories about how they were treated."

Was that all? Meredith felt the bubbling delirium of relief; she knew there had been evacuees less fortunate than her, but if that was all they were worried about, then surely all she had to do was reassure her dad. "But there's nothing to worry about, Dad. I told you in my letters: I'm happy here. Didn't you read my letters?"

" 'Course I did. We both did. Brightest spot in our day, your mum and me, getting a letter from you."

The way he said it, Meredith knew that it was true and something inside her panged, imagining them at the table, poring over the things she'd written. "Well then," she said, unable to meet his eyes, "you know that everything's all right. *Better* than all right."

"I know that's what you said." He looked towards Mum, checking she was still a fair distance away. "That was part of the problem. Your letters were so . . . cheerful. And your mother heard from one of her friends that there were foster families changing the letters that the boys and girls were writing home. Stopping them from saying anything that might reflect badly. Making things seem better than they really were." He heaved a sigh. "That's not how it is, though, is it, Merry? Not for you."

"No, Dad."

"You're happy here, happy as your letters make out?"

"Yes." Meredith could see that he was wavering. Possibility shot like fireworks through her limbs, and she spoke quickly. "Percy's a bit stiff, but Saffy's wonderful. You could meet her if you come inside; I could play you a song on the piano."

He looked up at the tower, sunlight sweeping across his cheeks. Meredith watched as his pupils shrank; she waited, trying to read his wide, blank face. His lips moved as if he were taking measurements, memorizing figures, but it was impossible for her to see which way the sums might lead him. He glanced, then, at his wife, fuming by the fountain, and Meredith knew that it was now or never. "Please, Dad." She grabbed the fabric of his shirtsleeve. "Please don't make me go back. I'm learning so much here, far more than I could learn in London. Please make Mum see that I'm better off here."

A light sigh and he frowned at Mum's back. As Meredith watched his face changed, fell along lines of tenderness, so that Meredith's heart turned a somersault. But he didn't look down at her and he didn't speak. Finally, she followed his sight line and noticed that Mum had twisted a bit, was standing now with one hand on her hip, the other fidgeting lightly by her side. The sun had crept up behind her and found glints of red in her brown hair, and she looked pretty and lost and unusually young. Her eyes were locked with Dad's, and in a dull thudding moment, Meredith saw that the tenderness in his face was for Mum, and not for her at all.

"I'm sorry, Merry," he said, covering her fingers, still clutching at his shirt, with his. "It's for the best. Go and fetch your things. We're going home."

And that's when Meredith did the very wicked thing, the betrayal for which her mother would never forgive her. Her only excuse that she was robbed entirely of choice; that she was a child and would be for years to come, and nobody cared what she wanted. She was tired of being treated like a parcel or a suitcase, shunted off here or there depending on what the adults thought was best. All she wanted was to belong somewhere.

She took her dad's hand and said, "I'm sorry, too, Dad."

And as bewilderment was still settling on his lovely face she smiled apologetically, avoided her mum's furious glare, and ran as fast as she could down the grassy lawn. Leaped across the verge and into the cool, dark safety of Cardarker Wood.

PERCY FOUND out about Saffy's plans for London quite by chance. If she hadn't absented herself from tea with Meredith's parents, she might never have known. Not until it was too late. It was fortunate, she supposed, that the public airing of dirty laundry was something she found both embarrassing and drear, and that she'd made her excuses and gone inside, intending only to allow the requisite time to pass before returning to stilled waters. She'd expected to find Saffy crouched by the window, spying on proceedings from afar and demanding a report—What were the parents like? How did Meredith seem? Had they enjoyed the cakes?—so it had been somewhat surprising to find the kitchen empty.

Percy remembered she was still carrying the teapot and, following her rather feeble ruse, returned the kettle to the stove. Time passed slowly and her attention drifted away from the flames, and she started wondering instead what dreadful thing she'd done to deserve both a wedding and a tea engagement on the same day. And that's when it came, a shrill clattering from the butler's pantry. Telephone calls had become rare after the post office warned that social chatter over the networks could delay important war talks, so it took a moment for Percy to realize the cause of the indignant racket.

As a consequence, when she did finally lift the receiver, she succeeded in sounding both fearful and suspicious: "Milderhurst Castle. Hello?"

The caller identified himself at once as Archibald Wicks of Chelsea and asked to speak to Miss Seraphina Blythe. Taken aback, Percy offered to jot down a message, and that's when the gentleman told her he was Saffy's employer, calling with revised advice regarding her accommodation in London as of the following week.

"I'm sorry, Mr. Wicks," said Percy, blood vessels dilating beneath her skin, "I'm afraid there must have been a misunderstanding."

An airy hesitation. "A misunderstanding, did you say? The line—it's rather difficult to hear."

"Seraphina—my sister—will be unable to take up a position in London."

"Oh." There was another pause, during which the line crackled across the distance and Percy couldn't help picturing the telephone wires, strung from post to post, swaying in the wuthering breeze. "Oh, I see," he continued. "But that is odd, only I have her letter accepting the position right here in my hand. We'd corresponded quite reliably on the topic."

That explained the frequency of mail Percy had been carrying to and from the castle of late, Saffy's determination to stay within reach of the telephone "in case an important call should come through regarding the war." Percy cursed herself for having been distracted by her WVS duties, for not having paid closer attention. "I understand," she said. "And I'm certain that Seraphina had every intention of honoring her agreement. But the war, you see, and now our father has been taken ill. I'm afraid she'll be needed at home for the duration."

Though disappointed and understandably confused, Mr. Wicks was mollified somewhat by Percy's promise to send him a signed first edition of the *Mud Man* for his collection of rare books and rang off in relatively good spirits. There would be no question, at least, of his suing them for breach of contract.

Saffy's disappointment, Percy suspected, would not be so easily managed. A toilet flushed somewhere in the distance, then the pipes gurgled in the kitchen wall. Percy sat on the stool and waited. Within minutes, Saffy hurried in from upstairs.

"Percy!" She stopped still, glanced towards the open back door. "What are you doing here? Where's Meredith? Her parents haven't left already, surely? Is everything all right?"

"I came to fetch more tea."

"Oh." Saffy's face relaxed into a faltering smile. "Then let me help. You don't want to be away from your guests too long." She fetched the jar of tea leaves and lifted the pot's lid.

Percy considered obfuscation but the conversation with Mr. Wicks had so surprised her that she drew a blank. In the end, she said simply, "There was a telephone call. While I was waiting for the kettle."

Only the faintest tremor, a fine drift of tea leaves from the sides of the spoon. "A telephone call? When?"

"Just now."

"Oh." Saffy brushed the loose leaves into the palm of one hand; they lay together like a pile of dead ants. "Something to do with the war, was it?"

"No."

Saffy leaned against the bench top and clenched a nearby tea towel in her hand as if trying to avoid being pulled out to sea.

The kettle chose that moment to spit, hissing through its spout before winding itself up to a menacing whistle. Saffy took it off the heat, remained at the stove with her back to Percy, her breath stilled.

"It was a fellow by the name of Mr. Archibald Wicks," Percy said then. "Calling from London. A collector, he said."

"I see." Saffy didn't turn. "And what did you tell him?"

A shout from outside and Percy moved swiftly to the open door.

"What did you tell him, Percy?"

A breeze, and on it the yellowing scent of cut grass.

"Percy?" Barely a whisper.

"I told him that we needed you here."

Saffy made a sound that might have been a sob.

Percy spoke carefully then, slowly. "You know you can't go, Saffy. That you mustn't mislead people like that. He was expecting you in London next week."

"Expecting me in London because that's where I'm going to be. I applied for a position, Percy, and he chose me." She did turn then. Lifted her clenched hand, elbow bent, a strangely theatrical gesture made more so by the scrunched tea towel still in her grasp. "He *chose* me," she said, shaking her fist for emphasis. "He collects all sorts of things, beautiful things, and he's hired me—*me*—to assist him with his work."

Percy dug a cigarette from her case, had to fight the match, but eventually she struck it.

"I'm going, Percy, and you can't stop me."

Damn Saffy; she wasn't going to make things easy. Percy's head was already throbbing; the wedding had left her spent, then playing hostess to Meredith's parents. This was the last thing she needed; Saffy was being purposely obtuse, goading her into spelling things out. Well, if that was how she wanted to play it, Percy wasn't afraid to lay down the law. "No," she exhaled smokily, "you're not. You're not going anywhere, Saff. You know it, I know it, and now Mr. Wicks knows it, too."

Saffy's arms slackened beside her, the tea towel fell to the flag-stones. "You told him I wasn't coming. Just like that."

"Someone had to. He was about to wire you the fare."

Saffy's eyes were brimming now, and although Percy was

367

angry with her she was pleased too, to see that her sister was fighting the rush of tears. Perhaps a scene would be avoided this time, after all.

"Come along now," she said, "I'm sure you'll see eventually that it's for the best—"

"You're really not going to let me go."

"No," said Percy, firmly but kindly, "I'm not."

Saffy's bottom lip trembled and her voice when finally she managed to speak was little more than a whisper. "You can't control us forever, Percy." Her fingers were scrabbling together against her skirt, gathering invisible sticky threads into a tiny ball.

The gesture was one from childhood and Percy was overwhelmed by déjà vu and a fierce urge to hold her twin close and never let her go, to tell her she was loved, that Percy didn't mean to be cruel, that she was doing it for Saffy's own good. But she didn't. She couldn't. And it wouldn't have made any difference if she had, because nobody wants to be told that sort of thing, even when they know, in their heart of hearts, that it's true.

She settled instead for softening her own voice and saying, "I'm not trying to control you, Saffy. Maybe some other day, in the future, you'll be able to leave." Percy gestured at the castle walls. "But not now. We need you here now, what with the war and Daddy as he is. Not to mention the severe shortage of staff: have you considered what would happen to the rest of us if you left? Can you see Juniper or Daddy or—Lord help us—*me* staying on top of the laundry?"

"There's nothing you can't do, Percy." Saffy's voice was bitter. "There's never been anything *you* couldn't do."

Percy knew then that she'd won; more importantly, that Saffy knew it, too. But she felt no joy, only the familiar burden of responsibility. Her whole being ached for her sister, for the young girl she'd once been with the world at her feet.

"Miss Blythe?" Percy looked up to see Meredith's father at the door, his thin little wife by his side, and an air of complete perturbation surrounding them both.

She'd forgotten them completely. "Mr. Baker," she said, ruffling the back of her hair. "I apologize. I've taken an age with the tea—"

"That's all right, Miss Blythe. We're about done with tea. It's Meredith, you see." His shoulders seemed to sink a little. "My wife and I planned to take her home with us but she's that set on staying—I'm afraid the little devil's given us the slip."

"Oh." It was the last thing Percy needed. She glanced behind her, but Saffy had performed her own escape act. "Well. I expect we'd better take a look then, hadn't we?"

"That's just it," Mr. Baker said unhappily. "My wife and I have to be back on the three twenty-four to London. It's the only service today."

"I see," said Percy. "Then of course you must go. The trains are terrible these days. If you miss today's, you're as likely still to be waiting this time Wednesday."

"But my girl . . ." Mrs. Baker looked as if she might be about to cry and the prospect didn't sit comfortably on her tough, pointy face. Percy knew the feeling.

"You're not to worry," she said with a short nod. "I'll find her. Is there a number in London where I can reach you? She won't have gone far."

From a branch in the oldest oak of Cardarker Wood, Meredith could just make out the castle. The pointed turret of the tower and its needlelike spire piercing the sky. The tiles glowed crimson with the afternoon light, and the silver tip shone. On the lawn at the top of the driveway Percy Blythe was waving her parents good-bye.

Meredith's ears burned with the thrilling wickedness of what she'd done. There'd be repercussions, she knew, but she'd had no other option. She'd run and she'd run until she could run no further, and when her breath was finally caught, she'd scaled the tree, alive with the strange, humming energy of having acted impetuously for the very first time in her life.

At the top of the driveway, Mum's shoulders sagged and Meredith thought for a moment she was crying, then her arms flew out to the sides, hands like startled starfish. Dad flinched backwards and Meredith knew that Mum was shouting. She didn't need to hear what Mum was saying to know that she was in big trouble.

Meanwhile, still standing in the castle yard, Percy Blythe was smoking, one hand on her hip as she watched the woods, and Meredith felt a whisper of doubt grow wings within her stomach. She had presumed she'd be welcome to stay on at the castle, but what if she weren't? What if the twins were so shocked by her disobedience that they refused to look after her any longer? What if following her own desires had led her into terrible trouble? As Percy Blythe finished her cigarette and turned back towards the castle, Meredith felt suddenly very alone.

Movement drew her gaze to the castle roof and Meredith's heart turned like a Catherine wheel. Someone in a white summer dress was climbing there. *Juniper.* Finished at last! Back in the outside world. As Meredith watched, she reached the flattened edge and sat, long legs dangling over the side. She'd be lighting a cigarette now, Meredith knew, leaning back, looking up at the sky.

But she didn't. She stopped abruptly instead and looked towards the woods. Meredith held tightly to the branch; excitement had brought on a funny sort of laugh that caught in her throat. It was almost as if Juniper had heard her, as if the older girl had somehow sensed her presence. If anyone could do such a thing, Meredith knew, it was Juniper.

She couldn't go back to London. She wouldn't. Not now, not yet.

Meredith watched her mum and dad walk down the drive away from the castle, Mum's arms folded over her middle, Dad's limp by his sides. "I'm sorry," she whispered under her breath, "I didn't have a choice."

FIVE

THE water was tepid and shallow, but Saffy didn't mind. A long soak in a hot bath was a pleasure of the past, and it was enough just to be alone with Percy's ghastly betrayal. She eased her bottom forward so she could lie flat on her back, knees bent towards the ceiling, head submerged, and ears underwater. Her hair floated like seaweed around the island of her face and she listened to the eddies and gurgles of the water, the clanking of the plug chain against the enamel, and other strange languages of the watery world.

For their entire adult life, Saffy had known herself to be the weaker twin. Percy liked to pooh-pooh such talk, insisting there was no such thing, not with them, that there was only a sunlight and a shadow position, between which they alternated so that things were always in perfect balance. Which was kind of her, but no more accurate for being well intentioned. Quite simply, Saffy knew that the things for which she had a superior talent were those that did not matter. She wrote well, she was a fine dressmaker, she could cook (passably) and lately even clean; but what use were such skills when she remained enslaved? Worse, a willing slave. Because for the most part, it shamed her to admit, Saffy didn't mind the role. There was an ease, after all, that came with being subordinate, a release of burden. And yet, there were times, like today, when she resented the expectation that she ought to fall into line without argument, no matter her own preference.

Saffy lifted her body and leaned against the tub's smooth end, swiped the wet washcloth against her anger-warmed face. The enamel was cool on her back and she arranged the washcloth like a shrunken

371

blanket across her breasts and stomach, watched it tighten and release with her breaths, a second skin; then she closed her eyes. How dare Percy presume to speak *for* her? To make decisions on Saffy's behalf, to determine her future without consultation?

But Percy did, just as she always had, and today, as ever, there'd been no arguing with her.

Saffy exhaled, long and slow, in an attempt to control her anger. The sigh caught on a sob. She supposed she should be pleased, flattered even, that Percy needed her so fiercely. And she was. But she was tired, too, of being powerless; more than that, she was sick at heart. For as long as she could remember, Saffy had been stuck in a life that ran parallel to the one of which she'd dreamed, the one she'd had every reasonable expectation to believe would be hers.

This time, however, there was one little thing she *could* do—Saffy brushed each cheek, enlivened by the creep of determination—a small way in which she might exercise her own feeble power against Percy. It would be a strike of omission rather than commission; Percy would never even know the blow had been struck. The only spoil of war would be a slight return of Saffy's self-respect. But that was enough.

Saffy was going to keep something to herself, something that Percy would prefer to know: all about the unexpected visitor who'd arrived at the castle that day. While Percy was at Lucy's wedding, Juniper was in the attic and Meredith was stalking the estate, Daddy's solicitor, Mr. Banks, had arrived in his black motorcar, accompanied by two dour little women in plain suits. Saffy, who'd been making adjustments to the tea table outside, had first considered hiding, pretending there was no one at home—she didn't particularly like Mr. Banks, and she certainly didn't like answering the door to unexpected callers—but the old man had been known to her since she was a small girl, he was a friend to Daddy, and therefore she'd been bound in some way she couldn't easily explain.

She'd run through the kitchen entrance, straightened herself in the oval mirror by the larder, then hurried upstairs, just in time to greet him at the front door. He'd been surprised, almost displeased, when he saw her, wondering aloud what times were coming to when somewhere as grand as Milderhurst was without a proper housekeeper, then instructing her to take him to her father. For all that Saffy longed to embrace society's changing mores, she harbored an old-fashioned reverence for the law and its officers, so she'd done precisely as he said. He was a man of few words (that is, he was a man not disposed to making idle chitchat with the daughters of his clients); their climb was silent, and for that she'd been glad; men like Mr. Banks always made her tongue-tied. When they finally reached the top of the winding staircase, he'd given her a curt nod before showing himself and his two officious companions through the doorway and into Daddy's tower room.

Saffy's intention hadn't been to snoop; indeed, she'd resented the intrusion on her time almost as much as she resented any task that took her up to the ghastly tower with its smell of impending death, the monstrous framed print on the wall. If the tortured struggle of a butterfly trapped in a web between the banisters hadn't caught her eye, she'd no doubt have been halfway down the stairs and well out of earshot. But she had and she wasn't and so, while she carefully unthreaded the insect, she heard Daddy say: "That's why I called you, Banks. Damned nuisance, death. Have you made the amendments?"

"I have. I've brought them to be signed and witnessed, along with a copy for your records, of course."

The details thereafter Saffy hadn't heard, nor had she wanted to. She was the second daughter of an old-fashioned man, a spinster in her middle years: the masculine world of property and finance neither interested nor concerned her. She wanted only to free the weakened butterfly and get away from the tower, to leave the stale air and stifling memories behind her. She hadn't been inside the little room for over twenty years, she intended never to set foot inside again, ever. And as she hurried down and away, she'd tried to elude the cloud of memories that pressed upon her as she went.

For they'd been close once, she and Daddy, a long time ago, but the love had spoiled. Juniper was the better writer and Percy the better daughter, which left very little room for Saffy in their father's affections. There had been only the one brief, glorious moment in which Saffy's usefulness had outshone that of her sisters. After the Great War, when Daddy had returned to them, all bruised and broken, it was she who had been able to bring him back, to give him the very thing he needed most. And it had been seductive, the force of his fondness, the evenings spent in hiding, where no one else could find them . . .

Suddenly there was bedlam and Saffy's eyes snapped open. Someone was shouting. She was in the tub but the water was icy; the light had disappeared through the open window leaving dusk in its place. Saffy realized that she'd slipped into a doze. She was fortunate that was all the slipping she'd done. But who was shouting? She sat up, straining to hear. Nothing, and she wondered whether she'd imagined the noise.

Then it came again. And the din of a bell. The old man in the tower, off on one of his rants. Well, let Percy see to him. They deserved each other.

With a shiver, Saffy peeled back the cold washcloth and stood, sending the water buckling back and forth. She stepped, dripping, onto the mat. There were voices downstairs now, she could hear them. Meredith, Juniper—and Percy, too; they were all there, all of them in the yellow parlor together. Waiting for their dinner, she supposed, and she would fetch it for them as she always did.

Saffy tugged her dressing gown from the hook on the door, fought with the sleeves and fastened it over her cool, wet skin, then she started down the hallway, her wet footsteps echoing along the flagstones. Nursing her little secret close.

"You wanted something, Daddy?" Percy pushed open the heavy door to the tower room. It took her a moment to spot him, tucked in the alcove by the fireplace, beneath the Goya print; and, when she did, he looked frightened to see her and she knew immediately that he'd suffered another of his delusions. Which meant that when she went downstairs she'd more than likely find his daily medicine sitting on the hall table where she'd left it that morning. It was her own fault for having expected too much, and she cursed herself for not having thought to check on him as soon as she'd arrived home from the church.

She softened her voice, spoke to him the way she imagined she might to a child, had she ever had the chance to know one well enough to love them: "There now. Everything's all right. Would you like to sit down? Come along, I'll help you get settled here by the window. It's a lovely evening."

He nodded jerkily, started towards her outstretched arm, and she knew that the delusion had ended. She knew, too, that it hadn't been a bad one because he'd managed to recover himself sufficiently to say, "I thought I told you to wear a hairpiece."

He had, many times now, and Percy had dutifully purchased one (not an easy thing to do in a time of war), only to leave the wretched thing lying like a severed fox's tail on her bedside table. There was a crocheted blanket draped over the arm of the chair, a small, brightly colored thing that Lucy had made for him some years ago, and Percy straightened it over his knees when he sat down, saying, "I'm sorry, Daddy. I forgot. I heard the bell and I didn't want to leave you waiting."

"You look like a man. Is that what you want? People to treat you like a man?"

"No, Daddy." Percy's fingertips went to the nape of her neck, centered on the little velvety coil that dipped lower than the rest of her hairline. He'd meant nothing by it and she wasn't offended, only a little startled by the suggestion. She sneaked a sideways glance at the glass-fronted bookcase, caught her image rippling in the dimpled surface; a rather severe-looking woman, sharp angles, a very straight spine, but a pair of not ungenerous breasts, a definite curve at the hips, a face that wasn't primped with lipstick and powder but that she didn't think was manly. That she hoped was not.

Daddy, meanwhile, had turned his head to look out across the night-draped fields, blissfully unaware of the line of thinking he had sparked. "All of this," he said without shifting his gaze. "All of this."

She leaned against the side of the chair, rested an elbow on its top. He didn't need to say more. She understood as no one else the way he felt as he looked out across the fields of his ancestors.

"Did you read Juniper's story, Daddy?" It was one of the few topics that could be relied upon to brighten his spirits, and Percy deployed it carefully, hoping she might thereby pull him back from the edges of the black mood she knew was still hovering.

He waved his hand in the direction of his pipe kit and Percy handed it to him. Rolled herself a cigarette as he was feeding tobacco into the bowl. "She's a talent. There's no doubt about it."

Percy smiled. "She gets it from you."

"We must be careful with her. The creative mind needs freedom. It must wander at its own pace and in its own patterns. It's a difficult thing to explain, Persephone, to someone whose mind works along more stolid lines, but it is *imperative* that she be freed from practicalities, from distractions, from anything that might steal her talent away." He grabbed at Percy's skirt. "She hasn't got a fellow chasing her, has she?"

"No, Daddy."

"A girl like Juniper needs protection," he continued, setting his chin. "To be kept somewhere safe. Here at Milderhurst, within the castle."

"Of course she will stay here."

"It's up to you to make sure. To take care of both your sisters." And he launched into his familiar spiel about legacy and responsibility and inheritance.

Percy waited a time, finished smoking her cigarette, and only when he was reaching the end said, "I'll take you to the lavatory before I go, shall I, Daddy?"

"Go?"

"I've a meeting this evening, in the village—"

"Always rushing off." Displeasure pulled at his bottom lip and

Percy had a very clear picture of what he might have looked like as a boy. A spoiled child accustomed to having things as he wished.

"Come along now, Daddy." She walked the old man to the lavatory and reached for her tobacco tin as she waited in the cooling corridor. Patting her pocket and remembered she'd left it in the tower room. Daddy would be a time, so she hurried back to fetch the tin.

She found them on his desk. And that's where she also found the parcel. A package from Mr. Banks but with no stamp affixed. Meaning it had been delivered personally.

Percy's heart beat faster. Saffy had not mentioned a visitor. Was it possible Mr. Banks had come from Folkestone, sneaked into the castle, and made his way up to the tower without announcing himself to Saffy? Anything was possible, she supposed, but it was surely unlikely. What reason would he have for doing such a thing?

Percy stood for a moment, undecided, fingering the envelope as heat collected along the back of her neck and beneath her arms so that her blouse stuck.

With a glance over her shoulder, even though she knew herself to be alone, she unsealed it and shimmied the folded papers from inside. A will. The date was today's; she straightened the letter and skimmed it for meaning. Experienced the strange, oppressive gravity of having her worst suspicions confirmed.

She pressed the fingers of one hand against her forehead. That such a thing should have been allowed to happen. Yet here it was; in black and white, and blue where Daddy had slashed his agreement. She read the document again, more closely, checking it for loopholes, for a missing page, for anything that might suggest she'd misunderstood, read too quickly.

She hadn't.

Oh Christ, she hadn't.

PART FOUR

BACK TO MILDERHURST CASTLE

HERBERT lent me his car to drive to Milderhurst, and as soon as I was off the motorway I wound down the window and let the breeze buffet my cheeks. The countryside had changed in the months between my visits. Summer had come and gone, and autumn was now in its final days. Enormous dried leaves lay in golden piles by the side of the road, and as I slipped deeper and deeper into the weald of Kent, great tree branches reached across the road to meet at its center. Every time the wind blew, a fresh layer was shed; lost skin, an ended season.

There was a note waiting for me when I arrived at the farmhouse.

> *Welcome, Edie. I had some errands that couldn't wait and Bird's laid up with the flu. Please find attached a key and settle yourself into Room 3 (first floor). So sorry to miss you. Will see you at dinner, seven o'clock in the dining room.*
> *Marilyn Bird.*
> *PS I had Bird move a better writing desk into your room. It's a little cramped, but I thought you might appreciate being able to spread out with your work.*

A little cramped was putting it mildly, but I've always had a thing for small, dark spaces and I set about immediately making an artful arrangement of Adam Gilbert's interview transcripts, my copies of *Raymond Blythe's Milderhurst* and the *Mud Man*, and assorted notebooks and pens; then I sat down, running the fingers of each hand

Kate Morton

along the table's smooth edge. A small sigh of satisfaction escaped as I leaned my chin on my hands. It was that first-day-of-school feeling, but a hundred times better. The four days stretched ahead and I felt infused with enthusiasm and possibility.

I noticed the telephone then, an old-fashioned Bakelite affair, and was possessed by an unfamiliar urge. It was being back at Milderhurst, of course, in the very same location where my mum had found herself.

The phone rang and rang, and just as I was about to hang up, she answered, somewhat breathlessly. There was a moment's pause after I said hello.

"Oh, Edie, sorry. I was looking for your father. He got it into his head to— Is everything all right?" Her tone had sharpened like a pencil.

"Everything's fine, Mum. I just wanted to let you know that I'd arrived."

"Oh." A pause as she caught her breath. I'd surprised her: the safe-arrival phone call was not a part of our usual routine; it hadn't been for around a decade, since I convinced her that if the government trusted me to vote, perhaps it was time she trusted me to take the tube without calling in my successful journey. "Well. Good. Thank you. That's very kind of you to let me know. Your father will be pleased to hear it. He misses you; he's been moping since you left." Another pause, a longer one this time in which I could almost hear her thinking, and then, all in a rush:

"You're there, then? Milderhurst? How—how is it? How does it look?"

"It looks glorious, Mum. Autumn's turning everything to gold."

"I remember. I remember how it looked in autumn. The way the woods stayed green for a time but the outer tips burned red."

"There's orange, too," I said. "And the leaves are everywhere. Seriously, everywhere, like a thick carpet covering the ground."

"I remember that. The wind comes in off the sea and they fall like rain. Is it windy, Edie?"

"Not yet, but it's forecast to come in blustery during the week."

382

"You wait. The leaves fall like snow then. They crunch beneath your feet when you run across them. I remember."

And her last two words were soft, somehow fragile, and I don't know where it came from but I was overwhelmed by a rush of feeling, and I heard myself say: "You know, Mum—I finish here on the fourth. You should think about driving down for the day."

"Oh, Edie, oh no. Your father couldn't—"

"*You* should come."

"By myself?"

"We could get lunch somewhere nice, just the two of us. Go for a walk around the village." The suggestion was met with the eerie whistling of the telephone line. I lowered my voice. "We don't have to go near the castle, not if you don't want to."

Silence, and I thought for a moment she was gone, then a small noise and I knew that she wasn't. I realized, as it continued, that she was crying, very lightly, against the phone.

I WASN'T due up at the castle to meet with the Sisters Blythe until the following day, but the weather was predicted to turn and it seemed wasteful to spend a clear afternoon sitting at my desk. Judith Waterman had suggested that the article include my own sense of the place, so I decided to go for a walk. Once again, Mrs. Bird had left a fruit basket on the bedside table and I selected an apple and a banana, then tossed a notebook and pen into my tote. I was surveying the room, about to leave, when Mum's journal caught my eye, sitting small and quiet to one side of the desk. "Come on then, Mum," I said, snatching it up. "Let's take you back to the castle."

WHEN I was a child, on the rare occasions that Mum wasn't going to be waiting for me at home after school, I caught the bus instead to my dad's office in Hammersmith. There I was supposed to find a patch of carpet—a desk, if I was lucky—in one of the junior partners' rooms, a place to do my homework, or decorate my school planner, or practice signing the surname of my most recent boy-crush; anything really, so long as I stayed off the telephone and didn't get in the way of industry.

One afternoon I was sent to a room I'd not been inside before, through a door I'd never noticed, right at the end of the very long hallway. It was small, little more than a cupboard with lighting, and although it was painted beige and brown, there were none of the glitzy copper-tone mirror tiles and glass bookshelves of the other corporate rooms. Instead, there was a small wooden table and chair, and a thin, towering bookcase. On one of the shelves, beside the jowly accounting tomes, I spied something interesting. A snow globe: you know the sort, a wintry scene in which a small stone cottage stood bravely on a pine-planted hill, flakes of white dusting the ground.

The rules of Dad's workplace were clear. I wasn't supposed to touch anything, and yet I couldn't help it. The globe transfixed me: it was a tiny splinter of whimsy in a beige-brown world, a doorway at the back of the cupboard, an irresistible emblem of childhood. Before I knew it I was on the chair, dome in hand, tipping and righting it, watching as the snowflakes fell, over and over, the world within oblivious to that without. And I remember feeling a curious longing to be inside that dome, to stand with the man and woman behind one of the gold-lit windows, or with the pair of tiny children pushing a maroon sleigh, in a safe place that knew nothing of the hustle and the noise outside.

That's what it felt like to approach Milderhurst Castle. As I walked up the hill, nearer and nearer, I could almost feel the air changing around me, as if I were crossing an invisible barrier into another world. Sane people do not speak of houses having forces, of enchanting people, of drawing them closer, but I came to believe that week, as I still do now, that there was some indescribable force at work, deep within Milderhurst Castle. I'd been aware of it on my first visit, and I felt it again that afternoon. A sort of beckoning, as if the castle itself were calling to me.

I didn't go the same way as before; I cut across the field to meet the driveway and followed it over a small stone bridge, then a slightly larger one, until finally the castle itself came into view, tall and imposing at the peak of the hill. I walked on and I didn't stop until I reached the very top. Only then did I turn to view the direction from which I'd come. The canopy of the woods was spread out beneath me and it looked as if autumn had taken a great torch to the trees, burnishing them gold, red, and bronze. I wished I'd brought a camera so I could take a shot back for Mum.

I left the driveway and skirted along a large hedge, looking up as I went at the attic window, the smaller one attached to the nurse's room with the secret cupboard. The castle was watching me, or so it seemed, all its hundred windows glowering down from beneath their drooping eaves. I didn't look at it again, continuing along the hedge until I reached the back.

There was an old chicken coop, empty now, and on the other side a domelike structure. I went closer, and that's when I recognized what it was. The bomb shelter. A rusty sign had been planted nearby— from the days of the regular tours, I supposed—labeling it THE ANDERSON, and although the writing had faded over time, I could make out enough to see that it contained information about the role of Kent in the Battle of Britain. A bomb had landed only a mile away, it said, killing a young boy on his bicycle. This sign said that the shelter had been constructed in 1940, which meant, surely, that it was the very one in which my mum must have crouched when she was at Milderhurst during the blitz.

There was no one around to ask, so I figured it would be okay to take a look inside, climbing down the steep stairs and beneath the corrugated iron arch. It was dim, but sufficient light slanted through the open doorway for me to see that it had been decorated like a stage set with paraphernalia from the war. Cigarette cards with Spitfires and Hurricanes on them, a small table with a vintage wood-paneled wireless in the center, a poster with Churchill's pointed finger warning me to "Deserve Victory!" just as if it were 1940 again, the alarm had panicked, and I was waiting for the bombers to fly overhead.

I climbed out again, blinked into the glare. The clouds were skimming fast across the sky, and the sun was covered now by a bleak white sheet. I noticed then a little nook in the hedge, a raised hillock that I couldn't resist sitting on; I pulled Mum's journal from my bag, leaned back, and opened to the first page. It was dated January 1940.

Dearest and most lovely notebook! I have been saving you for such a long time—a whole year now, even a little bit longer— because you were a gift to me from Mr. Cavill after my examinations. He told me that I was to use you for something special, that words lasted forever, and that one day I would have a story that warranted such a book. I didn't believe him at the time: I've never had anything special to write about—does that sound terribly sad? I think it might and I really don't mean it that way, I wrote it only because it's true: I've never had anything special to write about and I didn't imagine that I would. But I was wrong. Terribly, totally, wonderfully wrong. For something has happened and nothing will ever be the same again.

I suppose the first thing I should tell you is that I'm writing this in a castle. A real castle, made of stone, with a tower and lots of winding staircases, and enormous candleholders on all the walls with wax mounds, decades and decades of blackening wax, drooping from their bases. You might think that this, my living in a castle, is the "wonderful" thing, and that it's greedy to expect anything more on top, but there is more.

I'm sitting on the windowsill in the attic, the most marvelous place in the whole castle. It is Juniper's room. Who is Juniper, you might ask, if you were able? Juniper is the most incredible person in the world. She is my best friend and I am hers. It was Juniper who encouraged me finally to write in you. She said she was tired of seeing me carrying you around like a glorified pa-

*perweight and that it was time I took the plunge and marked
your beautiful pages.*

*She says there are stories everywhere and that people who
wait for the right one to come along before setting pen to paper
end up with very empty pages. That's all writing is, apparently,
capturing sights and thoughts on paper. Spinning, like a spider
does, but using words to make the pattern. Juniper has given me
this fountain pen. I think it might have come from the tower, and
I'm a little frightened that her father will decide to go looking
for whoever stole it, but I use it nonetheless. It is truly a glorious
pen. I think it is quite possible to love a pen, don't you?*

*Juniper suggested that I write about my life. She is always
asking me to tell her stories about Mum and Dad, Ed and Rita,
and Mrs. Paul next door. She laughs very loudly, like a bottle
that's been shaken then opened, bubbles exploding everywhere:
alarming, in a way, but lovely, too. Her laugh is not at all how
you might expect. She's so smooth and graceful, but her laugh
is throaty like the earth. It's not only her laugh that I love; she
scowls, too, when I tell her the things that Rita says, scowls and
spits in all the right places.*

*She says that I am lucky—can you imagine? Someone like
her saying that of me?—that all my learning has been done in
the real world. Hers, she says, was acquired from books. Which
sounds like heaven to me, but evidently was not. Do you know,
she hasn't been to London since she was tiny? She went with her
entire family to see the premiere of a play from the book that her
father wrote,* The True History of the Mud Man. *When Juniper
mentioned that book to me, she said its name as if, surely, I
would be familiar with it, and I was very embarrassed to admit
that I was not. Curses on my parents for having kept me in the
dark about such things! She was surprised, I could tell, but she
didn't make me feel bad. She nodded, as if she quite approved,
and said that it was no doubt only because I was far too busy*

in my real world with real people. And then she got the sad look that she gets sometimes, thoughtful and a bit puzzled, as if trying to work out the answer to a complex problem. It is the look, I think, that my mother despises when it sets in on my own face, the one that makes her point her finger and tell me to shake off the gray skies and get on with things.

Oh, but I do enjoy gray skies! They're so much more complex than blue ones. If they were people, those are the ones I'd make the time to learn about. It's far more interesting to wonder what might be behind the layers of clouds than to be presented always with a simple, clear, bland blue.

The sky outside today is very gray. If I look through the window it's as if someone has stretched a great, gray blanket over the castle. It's frosty on the ground, too. The attic window looks down upon a very special place. One of Juniper's favorites. It's a square plot, enclosed by hedges, with little gravestones rising from beneath the brambles, all stuck out at odd angles like rotting teeth in an old mouth.

Clementina Blythe
1 year old
Taken cruelly
Sleep, my little one, sleep

Cyrus Maximus Blythe
3 years old
Gone too soon

Emerson Blythe
10 years old
Loved

The first time I went there, I thought it was a graveyard for children, but Juniper told me they were pets. All of them. The

Blythes care very much for their animals, especially Juniper, who cried when she told me about her first dog, Emerson.

Brrr . . . But it's freezing cold in here! I've inherited an enormous assortment of knitted socks since I arrived at Milderhurst. Saffy is a great one for knitting but a terrible one for counting, the upshot of which is that a third of the socks she's made for the soldiers are far too tight to cover so much as a burly man's big toe, but perfect for my twiglet ankles. I have put three pairs on each foot, and another three singletons on my right arm, leaving only my left exposed so that I might hold a pen. Which explains the state of my writing. I apologize for that, dear journal. Your beautiful pages deserve better.

So here I am, alone in the attic room, while Juniper is busy downstairs reading to the hens. Saffy is convinced that they lay better when they're stimulated; Juniper, who loves all animals, says that there is nothing so clever or soothing as a hen; and I enjoy eggs very much indeed. So there. We are all happy. And I am going to start at the beginning and write as quickly as I can. For one thing, it will keep my fingers warm

Fierce barking, of the sort that makes one's heart contract like a slingshot, and I almost jumped out of my skin.

A dog appeared above me, Juniper's lurcher; lips pulled back, teeth bared, a low growl emanating from deep within him.

"There, boy," I said, my voice tight with fear. "There now."

I was debating whether to reach out and stroke him, whether he might that way be calmed, when the end of a stick appeared in the mud. A pair of brogue-clad feet followed, and I looked up to see Percy Blythe glaring at me. I'd quite forgotten how thin and severe she was. Hunched over her cane, peering down, and dressed in much the same fashion as the last time we'd met, pale trousers and a well-cut shirt that might have seemed manly if not for her incredibly narrow frame and the dainty watch that hung loosely around her gaunt wrist.

"It's you," she said, clearly as surprised as I was. "You're early."

"I'm so sorry. I didn't mean to disturb you, I—"

The dog growled again and she made an impatient noise, waving her fingers. "Bruno! That's enough." He whimpered and slunk back to her side. "We were expecting you tomorrow."

"Yes, I know. Ten in the morning."

"You're still coming?"

I nodded. "I arrived from London today. The weather was clear and I know it's expected to come in rainy over the next few days, so I thought I'd take a walk, make some notes, I didn't think you'd mind, and then I found the shelter and—I didn't mean to be a nuisance."

At some point during my explanation her attention had waned. "Well," she said, without a whiff of gladness, "you're here now. I suppose you might as well come in for tea."

A Faux Pas and a Coup

THE yellow parlor seemed more down-at-heel than I remembered. On my previous visit I had thought the room a warm place, a patch of life and light in the middle of a dark, stone body. It was different this time, and perhaps the change of seasons was to blame, the loss of summer's brilliance, the sneaking chill that presaged winter, for it wasn't only the alteration in the room that struck me.

The dog was panting hard and he collapsed against the tattered screen. He, too, had aged, I realized, just as Percy Blythe had aged since May, just as the room itself had faded. The notion popped into my head then that Milderhurst really was somehow separate from the real world, a place outside the usual bounds of space and time. That it was under some enchantment: a fairy-tale castle in which time could be slowed down, speeded up, at the whim of an unearthly being.

Saffy was standing in profile, her head bent over a fine porcelain teapot. "Finally, Percy," she said as she tried to replace the lid. "I was beginning to think we might need to gather a search— Oh!" She'd looked up and seen me at her sister's side. "Hello there."

"It's Edith Burchill," said Percy matter-of-factly. "She's arrived rather unexpectedly. She's going to join us for tea."

"How lovely," said Saffy, and her face lit up so fully that I knew she wasn't just being polite. "I was about to pour, if only I could get this lid to sit as it should. I'll lay another setting—I say, what a treat!"

Juniper was by the window, just as she had been when I'd come in May, but this time she was asleep, snoring lightly with her head tucked into the pale green wing of the velvet chair. I couldn't help but think, when I saw her, of Mum's journal entry, of the enchanting young woman whom Mum had loved. How sad it was, how terrible, that she should have been reduced to this.

"We're so glad you could come, Miss Burchill," said Saffy.

"Please call me Edie—it's short for Edith."

She smiled with pleasure. "Edith. What a lovely name. It means 'blessed in war,' doesn't it?"

"I'm not sure," I said apologetically.

Percy cleared her throat and Saffy continued quickly. "The gentleman was very professional, but"—she shot a glance at Juniper—"well. One finds it so much easier to speak with another woman. Isn't that so, Percy?"

"It is."

Seeing them together like that, I realized that I hadn't imagined the passing of time. On my first visit, I'd noticed that the twins were the same height, even though Percy's authoritative character added stature. This time, however, there was no mistaking it, Percy was smaller than her twin. She was frailer, too, and I couldn't help thinking of Jekyll and Hyde, the moment in which the good doctor encounters his smaller, darker self.

"Sit, won't you," said Percy tartly. "Let's all sit and get on with it."

We did as she said, and Saffy poured the tea, conducting a rather one-sided conversation with Percy about Bruno, the dog—where had she found him? How had he been? How had he managed the walk? And I learned that Bruno wasn't well, that they were worried about him, very worried. They kept their voices low, sneaking glances at the sleeping Juniper, and I remembered Percy telling me that Bruno was her dog, that they always made sure she had an animal, that everybody needed something to love. I studied Percy over the top of my teacup; I couldn't help it. Although she was prickly, there was something in her bearing that I found fascinating. As she gave short answers to Saffy's questions, I watched the tight lips, the sagging skin, the deep lines etched by years of frowning, and I wondered whether she'd been speaking, in some part, of herself when she said that everybody needed something to love. Whether she, too, had been robbed of someone.

I was so deep in thought that when Percy turned to look directly at me, I worried for an instant that she'd somehow read my mind. I blinked and heat rushed to my cheeks, and that's when I realized Saffy was speaking to me, that Percy had looked up only to see why I hadn't answered.

"I'm sorry?" I said. "I was somewhere else."

"I was just asking about your journey from London," said Saffy; "it was comfortable, I hope?"

"Oh, yes—thank you."

"I remember when we used to go up to London as girls. Do you remember that, Percy?"

Percy gave a low noise of acknowledgment.

Saffy's face had come alive with the memory. "Daddy used to take us every year; we went by train at first, sitting in our very own little compartment with Nanny, and then Daddy purchased the Daimler and we all went up by motorcar. Percy preferred it here at the castle, but I adored being in London. So much happening, so many glorious ladies and handsome gentlemen to watch; the dresses, the shops, the parks." She smiled, sadly, though, it seemed to me. "I always assumed . . ." The smile flickered, and she looked down at her teacup. "Well. I expect all young women dream of certain things. Are you married, Edie?" The question was unexpected, causing me to draw breath, at which she held out a fine hand. "Forgive me for asking. How impertinent I am!"

"Not at all," I said. "I don't mind. And no, I'm not married."

Her smile warmed. "I didn't think so. I hope you don't think I'm prying, but I noticed that you don't wear a ring. Though perhaps young people don't these days. I'm afraid I'm rather out of touch. I don't get away often." She glanced, almost imperceptibly, at Percy. "None of us does." Her fingers fluttered a little before coming to rest on an antique locket that hung on a fine chain around her neck. "I was almost married, once."

Beside me, Percy shifted in her seat. "I'm sure Miss Burchill doesn't need to hear our tales of woe—"

"Of course," said Saffy, flushing. "How foolish of me."

"Not at all." She looked so embarrassed I was anxious to offer reassurance; I had a feeling she'd spent much of her long life doing just as Percy bade her. "Please, do tell me about it."

A sizzle as Percy struck a match and lit the cigarette she'd trapped between her lips. Saffy was torn, I could see; a blend of timidity and longing playing on her face as she watched her twin. She was reading a subtext to which I was blind, assessing a battleground scored with the blows of previous scuffles.

She returned her attention to me only when Percy stood up and took her cigarette to the window, switching on a lamp as she went. "Percy's right," she said tactfully, and I knew then that she had lost this skirmish. "It's self-indulgent of me."

"Not at all, I—"

"The article, Miss Burchill," Percy interrupted. "How is it progressing?"

"Yes," said Saffy, recovering herself, "tell us how it's going, Edith. What are your plans while you're here? I expect you'll want to start with interviews."

"Actually," I said, "Mr. Gilbert did such a thorough job that it won't be necessary for me to take up too much of your time."

"Oh—oh, I see."

"We've spoken of this already, Saffy," said Percy, and I thought I detected a note of warning in her voice.

"Of course." Saffy smiled at me, but there was sadness behind her eyes. "Only sometimes one thinks of things . . . later."

"I'd be very happy to speak with you if there's something you've thought of that you might not have told Mr. Gilbert," I said.

"That won't be necessary, Miss Burchill," said Percy, returning to the table to tip some ash from her cigarette. "As you said, Mr. Gilbert has amassed quite a dossier."

I nodded, but her adamant stance perplexed me. Her position

that further interviews were unnecessary was so emphatic, it was clear that she didn't want me to speak alone with Saffy, and yet it was Percy who'd dropped Adam Gilbert from the project and insisted that I replace him. I wasn't vain or mad enough to believe it had anything to do with my writing prowess or the fine rapport we'd struck up on my previous visit. Why, then, had she asked for me? And why was she so determined that I should not speak with Saffy? Was it about control? Was Percy Blythe so accustomed to ordering the lives of her sisters that she couldn't permit so much as a conversation to be carried on without her? Or was it more than that? Was she concerned about whatever it was Saffy wanted to tell me?

"Your time here will be better spent seeing the tower and getting a feel for the castle itself," continued Percy. "The way Daddy worked."

"Yes," I said, "of course. That's certainly important." I was disappointed in myself, unable to shake the feeling that I, too, was submitting myself meekly to Percy Blythe's direction. Deep inside me, a small pigheaded something stirred. "All the same," I heard myself say, "there seem to be a few things that weren't covered."

The dog whimpered from the floor and Percy's eyes narrowed. "Oh?"

"I noticed that Mr. Gilbert hadn't interviewed Juniper and I thought I might—"

"No."

"I understand that you don't want her disturbed, and I promise—"

"Miss Burchill, I assure you there is nothing to be gained in speaking with Juniper about our father's work. She wasn't even born when the *Mud Man* was written."

"That's true, but the article is supposed to be about the three of you and I'd still like to—"

"Miss Burchill." Percy's voice was cold. "You must understand that our sister is not well. I told you once before that she suffered a great setback in her youth, a disappointment from which she never recovered."

"You did, and I would never dream of mentioning Thomas to her—"

I broke off as Percy's face blanched. It was the first time I could think of that I'd seen her rattled. I hadn't meant to say his name and it hung like smoke in the air around us. She snatched up a new cigarette. "Your time here," she repeated with a stern, slow finality, belied by the quivering matchbox in her hand, "would be best spent seeing the tower. Gaining an understanding of the way Daddy worked."

I nodded, and a strange unsettled weight shifted in the pit of my stomach.

"If there are any questions you still need answered, you will ask them of me. Not my sisters."

Which was when Saffy intervened, in her own inimitable fashion. She'd kept her head down during my exchange with Percy, but she looked up then, a pleasant, mild expression arranged on her face. She spoke in a clear voice, perfectly guileless. "Which means, of course, that she must take a look at Daddy's notebooks."

Was it possible that the whole room chilled when she said it? Or did it only seem that way to me? *Nobody* had seen Raymond Blythe's notebooks; not when he was alive, and not in the fifty years of post-humous scholarship. Myths had begun to form around their very existence. And now, to hear them mentioned like this, so casually; to glimpse a possibility that I might touch them, might read the great man's handwriting and run my fingertip, ever so lightly, over his thoughts, right as they were forming— "Yes," I managed to say, in little more than a whisper, "yes, please."

Percy, meanwhile, had turned to look at Saffy, and although I had no more hope of understanding the dynamics that stretched between them and back over nearly nine decades than I did of untangling the undergrowth of Cardarker Wood, I knew that a blow had been struck. A fierce blow. I knew, too, that Percy did not want me to see those notebooks. Her reluctance only fed my desire, my need, to take them in my hands, and I held my breath as the twins continued their dance.

"Go on, Percy," said Saffy, blinking widely and allowing her smile to wilt a little at the corners, as if perplexed, as if she couldn't understand why Percy needed prodding. She sneaked the briefest glance at me, sufficient only for me to know that we were allies. "Show her the muniment room."

The muniment room. Of course that's where they were! It was just like a scene from the *Mud Man* itself: Raymond Blythe's precious notebooks, concealed within the room of secrets.

Percy's arms, the cage of her torso, her chin: all were rigid. Why didn't she want me to see those books? What was inside them that she feared?

"Percy?" Saffy softened her tone the way one might with a child who needs cajoling to speak up. "Are the notebooks still there, then?"

"I expect so. I certainly haven't moved them."

"Well then?" The tension between them was so thick I could barely stand to breathe as I watched and hoped. Time stretched painfully; a gust of wind outside made the shutters vibrate against the glass. Juniper stirred. Saffy spoke again. "Percy?"

"Not today," Percy said finally, driving her spent cigarette into the little crystal ashtray. "The dark comes in quickly now. It's almost evening."

I glanced at the window and saw that she was right. The sun had slid away quickly and the cool night air was sifting into place. "When you come tomorrow, I'll show you the room." Her eyes were hard on mine. "And, Miss Burchill?"

"Yes?"

"I'll hear no more from you about Juniper or *him*."

ONE

IT was a small flat, little more than a pair of tiny rooms at the top of a Victorian building. The roof sloped on one side until it met the wall that someone, at some time, had erected so that one drafty attic might become two, and there was no kitchen to speak of, only a small sink beside an old gas burner. It wasn't Tom's flat, not really; he hadn't a place of his own because he'd never needed one. He'd lived with his family near the Elephant and Castle until war began, and then with his regiment as it dwindled to a small band of stragglers on their way to meet the coast. After Dunkirk, he'd slept in a bed at Chertsey Emergency Hospital.

Since his discharge, though, he'd been drifting from this spare room to that, waiting for his leg to heal and his unit to recall him. There were places empty all over London so it was never hard to find a new abode. It seemed that everything had been shuffled by the war—people, possessions, affections—and there was no longer one right way of doing things. This particular flat, this plain room that he would remember specially to his dying day, that was soon to become the repository for his life's best and brightest memories, belonged to a friend with whom he'd studied at teacher training college, in a different version of his life, long ago.

It was early still, but Tom had already walked to Primrose Hill and back. He didn't sleep late anymore, nor deeply. Not after the months in France, living by his wits, in retreat. He woke with the birds, the sparrows in particular, a family of whom had taken up digs on his sill.

It had been a mistake, perhaps, to feed them, but the bread had been moldy to begin with and the fellow down at the Salvage Department fierce that it shouldn't be thrown away. It was the heat of the room and the steam from the boiler turning Tom's bread to mold. He kept the window open, but the day's sun accumulated in the flats beneath, spread up the staircase and shrugged through the floorboards, before hitting his ceiling and stretching out with proprietorial ease to shake hands with the steam. It had been just as well to accept it: the mold was his, as were the birds. He woke early, he fed them, he walked.

The doctors had said that walking was the best thing for his leg, but Tom would've done so regardless. There was something restless living inside him now, something he'd gained in France that needed to be exorcised daily. Each footfall on the pavement helped a little, and he was glad for the release, even though he knew it to be temporary. That morning, as he'd stood at the top of Primrose Hill and watched the dawn roll up its sleeves, he'd picked out the zoo and the BBC and, in the distance, the dome of St. Paul's, rising clear of its blitzed surroundings. Tom had been in the hospital during the worst of the raids and Matron had arrived on December 30, the *Times* in hand (he'd been allowed the newspaper by then). She'd stood beside the bed, stern-faced but not unkind, as he began to read, and before he'd finished the headline, she'd declared it an act of God. Although Tom had agreed that the dome's survival was a wonder, he'd thought it had a bit more to do with luck than Lord. He had trouble with God, with the notion that a divine being might save a building when all of England was bleeding to death. To Matron, however, he'd nodded agreement: blasphemy would've been just the sort of thing to get her whispering to the doctor about worrying states of mind.

A MIRROR HAD been propped on the ledge of the narrow casement window and Tom, dressed in his undershirt and trousers, leaned towards it, rolling the stub of shaving soap across his cheeks. He watched dispassionately the mottled reflection in the stippled glass, the young man, cocking his head so that milky sunlight lay across his cheek, running the razor carefully along his jaw, stroke by stroke, flinching as he negotiated the territory around his earlobe. The fellow in the mirror rinsed the razor in the shallow water, shook it a little, and started on the other side, just as a man might when he was tidying himself up to visit his mother on her birthday.

Tom caught himself drifting and sighed. He laid the razor gently on the sill and rested both hands on the outer curve of the basin. Screwed his eyes shut, beginning the familiar count to ten. This dislocation had been happening a lot lately, since he returned from France but even more so after leaving the hospital. It was as if he were outside himself, watching, unable quite to believe that the young man in the mirror with the amiable face, the mild expression, the day stretching ahead, could possibly be him. That the experiences of the past eighteen months, the sights and sounds—that child, dear God, lying dead, alone, on the road in France—could possibly live behind that still-smooth face.

You are Thomas Cavill, he told himself firmly when he'd reached ten; *you are twenty-five years old, you are a soldier. Today is your mother's birthday and you are going to visit her for lunch.* His sisters would be there, the eldest with her baby son, Thomas—named for him—and his brother Joey, too; though not Theo, who'd been sent up north with his regiment for training and wrote cheery letters home about butter and cream and a girl named Kitty. They would be their usual rowdy selves, the wartime version of themselves, at any rate: never questioning, hardly complaining, and then only ever in a jocular fashion about the difficulties of obtaining eggs and sugar. Never doubting that Britain could take it. That they could take it. Tom could vaguely remember feeling the same way himself.

JUNIPER TOOK out the piece of paper and checked the address once more. Turned it sideways, twisted her head, then cursed herself for her appalling handwriting. Too quick, too careless, too eager always to move on to the next idea. She looked up at the narrow house, spotted the number on the black front door. Twenty-six. This was it. It had to be.

It was. Juniper decisively shoved the paper in her pocket. Number and street name aside, she recognized this house from Merry's stories as vividly as she would Northanger Abbey or Wuthering Heights. With a skip in her step, she climbed the concrete stairs and knocked on the door.

She had been in London for exactly two days and still she couldn't quite believe it. She felt like a fictional character who'd escaped the book in which her creator had carefully and kindly trapped her; taken a pair of scissors to her outline and leaped, free, into the unfamiliar pages of a story with far more dirt and noise and rhythm. A story she adored already: the shuffling, the mess, the disorder, the things and people she didn't understand. It was exhilarating, just as she'd always known it would be.

The door opened and a scowling face caught her off guard, a person younger than she was but also somehow older. "What do you want?"

"I've come to see Meredith Baker." Juniper's voice was strange to her own ears, here in this other story. An image came to her of Percy, who always knew precisely how to behave out in the world, but it merged with another more recent memory—Percy, red-faced and angry after a meeting with Daddy's solicitor—and Juniper let it turn to sand and scatter to the ground.

The girl—with those pursed and grudging lips she could only be Rita—looked Juniper up and down before arriving at an expression of haughty suspicion and, oddly, for they had never met before, strong dislike. "Meredith!" she called finally from the side of her mouth. "Get yourself out here now."

Juniper and Rita observed one another as they waited, neither speaking, and a host of words appeared in Juniper's mind, knitting themselves together to form the beginning of a description she would later write back to her sisters. Then Meredith appeared with a clatter, spectacles on her nose and a tea towel in her hand, and the words seemed unimportant.

Merry was the first friend Juniper had made and the first she'd had occasion to miss, so the immense weight of her friend's absence had been totally unexpected. When Merry's father had arrived without notice at the castle in March, insisting that his daughter return home this time, the two girls had clung to one another and Juniper had whispered in Merry's ear, "I'm coming to London. I'll see you soon." Merry had cried but Juniper hadn't, not then, she'd waved and returned to the attic roof and tried to remember how it was to be alone. Her whole life had been spent that way—though in the silences left by Merry's departure, there'd been something new. A clock was softly ticking, counting down the seconds to a fate that Juniper was stubbornly determined to outrun.

"You came," said Meredith, nudging her spectacles with the back of her hand and blinking as if she might be seeing things.

"I told you I would."

"But where are you staying?"

"With my godfather."

A grin broke across Meredith's face and turned into a laugh. "Let's get out of here then," she said, gripping Juniper's hand tightly in her own.

"I'm telling Mum you didn't finish the kitchen like you were s'posed to," the sister shouted after them.

"Don't mind her," said Meredith. "She's in a snit because they won't let her out of the broom cupboard at work."

"It's a great pity no one's thought to lock her in it."

In the end, Juniper Blythe had taken herself to London. By train, just as Meredith had suggested when they sat together on the Milderhurst roof. Escaping hadn't been nearly as hard as she'd expected. She'd simply walked across the fields and refused to stop until she reached the railway station.

She'd been so pleased with herself when she did, that it skipped her attention for a moment that she'd need to do anything further. Juniper could write, she could invent grand fictions and capture them within an intricacy of words, but she knew herself to be perfectly hopeless at everything else. Her entire knowledge of the world and its operation had been deduced from books and the conversations of her sisters—neither of whom was particularly worldly—and the stories Merry had told her of London. It wasn't a surprise, therefore, as she stood outside the station, to realize she had no idea what to do next. Only when she noticed the kiosk labeled TICKET OFFICE did she remember that, of course, she would need to purchase one of those.

Money. It was something Juniper had never known or needed, but there had been a small sum left when Daddy died. She hadn't concerned herself with the details of the will and the estate—it was enough to know that Percy was angry, Saffy concerned, and Juniper, herself, the unwitting cause—but when Saffy mentioned a parcel of actual money, the sort that could be folded and held and exchanged for things, and offered to put it away safely, Juniper had said no. That she preferred to keep it, just to look at for a while. Saffy, dear Saffy, hadn't blinked, accepting the odd request as perfectly reasonable because it had come from Juniper, whom she loved and therefore would not question.

The train when it arrived was full, but an older man in the carriage had stood and tipped his hat and Juniper had understood that he meant for her to slide into the seat he'd vacated. A seat by the window. How charming people were out here! She smiled and he nodded, and she sat with her suitcase on her lap, waiting for whatever might come. IS YOUR JOURNEY REALLY NECESSARY? the sign on the platform demanded. *Yes,* thought Juniper. *Yes, it is.* To remain at the castle, she knew with more certainty now than ever, would have been to submit herself to a future she refused to meet. The one she'd seen reflected in her father's eyes when he took her shoulders between his hands and told her they were the same, the two of them, the same.

Steam swirled and eddied along the platform and she felt as excited as if she'd climbed onto the back of a great huffing dragon who was about to launch into the sky, carrying her with him as he flew away to a place of fascination and fancy. A shrill whistle sounded, making the hairs on Juniper's arms stand up, and they were off, moving, the train lurching in mighty heaves. Juniper couldn't help but laugh against the glass then, because she'd done it. She'd really done it.

Over time, the window misted with her breath and unnamed, unknown stations, fields and villages and woods, skimmed by: a blur—pastels of green and blue and streaky pink, run through with a watery brush. The skidding colors stopped sometimes, clarifying to form a picture, framed like a painting by the window's rectangle. A Constable, or one of the other pastorals Daddy had admired. Renderings of a timeless countryside that he'd eulogized with the familiar sadness clouding his eyes.

Juniper had no patience for the timeless. She knew that there was no such thing. Only the here and now, and the way her heart was beating in its too-fast way, though not dangerously so, because she was sitting inside a train on her way to London while noise and movement and heat surrounded her.

London. Juniper said the word once beneath her breath, then again. Relished its evenness, its two balanced syllables, the way it felt on her tongue. Soft but weighted, like a secret, the sort of word that might be whispered between lovers. Juniper wanted love, she wanted passion, she wanted complications. She wanted to live and to love and to eavesdrop, to learn secrets and know how other people spoke to one another, the way they felt, the things that made them laugh and cry and sigh. People who weren't Percy or Saffy or Raymond or Juniper Blythe.

Once, when she was a very small girl, a hot-air balloonist had launched from one of the Milderhurst fields; Juniper couldn't remember why, whether he'd been a friend of Daddy's or a famous adventurer, only that there'd been a breakfast picnic on the lawn to celebrate and they'd gathered, all of them, the northern cousins too, and a select few guests from the village, to watch the great event. The balloon had been tethered to the ground by ropes and as the flame leaped and the basket strained to follow it, men stationed at the base of each cord had worked to effect its release. Ropes screamed with tension, the flames raged higher, and for a moment, as all eyes widened, disaster had seemed imminent.

A single rope came loose while the others remained, and the whole contraption lurched to the side, flames licking perilously close to the fabric of the balloon. Juniper had glanced at Daddy. She was only a child and hadn't then known the full horror of his past—it would be some time yet before he burdened his youngest daughter with his secrets—but she had known, even then, that he feared fire above all else. His face as he watched events unfold had been a sheet of white marble with dread cut clear upon it. Juniper had found herself adopting his expression, curious to know what it might feel like to be turned to stone and scored by fear. Just in time, the final ropes had released and the balloon had righted itself, jerked free and aimed for the sky, rising high into the blue beyond.

For Juniper, Daddy's death had been like the release of that first rope. She had felt the liberation as her body, her soul, her whole being shifted sideways, and a significant portion of the weight that had shackled her fell away. The last ropes she'd cut herself: packing a small suitcase with a few mismatched clothes and the two addresses she had for people in London, and waiting until a day when both her sisters were busy so she could set off unobserved.

There remained now only a single piece of rope stretching between Juniper and her home. It was the hardest to sever, tied neatly in a careful knot by Percy and Saffy. And yet it had to be done, for their love and concern entrapped her just as surely as Daddy's expectations. As Juniper had reached London, and the smoke and the bustle of Charing Cross Station had enwrapped her, she'd imagined herself a shining pair of scissors and leaned to slice the rope right through. She'd watched as it fell back upon itself, hesitated for an instant like an excised tail, before receding fast into the distance, gaining speed as it slithered back towards the castle.

Free at last, she'd asked directions to a mailbox and sent the letter home, explaining briefly what she'd done and why. It would reach her sisters before they'd time to worry too deeply or send out search parties to bring her back. They would fret, she knew; Saffy in particular would be waylaid by fear, but what else could Juniper have done?

One thing was certain. Her sisters would never have agreed to let her go alone.

Juniper and Meredith lay side by side on the sun-bleached grass of the park, slivers of light playing hide and seek within the glancing leaves above. They'd hunted for deck chairs but most had been broken, left to lean against tree trunks in the hope that someone might find and fix them. Juniper didn't mind: the day was sweltering and the cool of the grass, the earth beneath it, was a welcome pleasure. She lay with one arm folded behind her head. In the other hand she held a cigarette, smoking slowly, closing her left eye in a wink, then her right, watching as the foliage shifted against the sky, listening as Meredith outlined the progress of her manuscript.

"So," she said, when her friend had finished, "when are you going to show it to me?"

"I don't know. It's nearly ready. Nearly. But . . ."

"But what?"

"I don't know. I feel so . . ."

Juniper turned her head sideways, sliding her palm flat across her eyes to block the glare. "So what?"

"Nervous."

"Nervous?"

"What if you hate it?" Meredith sat up suddenly.

Juniper did the same, crossing her legs. "I'm not going to hate it."

"But if you do, I'll never, *ever* write another thing again."

"Well then, little chicken"—Juniper pretended to be stern, furrowing her brow and feeling like Percy—"if that's the case you might just as well stop immediately."

"Because you think you *will* hate it!" Meredith's face took on the shadows of despair and Juniper was caught unawares. She'd only been fooling, making fun as they always had. She'd expected Merry to laugh and adopt the same strict tones, to say something equally meaningless. Met with such a confusing response, Juniper's own expression faltered and she let the imperious facade drop away.

"That's not what I mean at all," she said, laying a hand flat on her friend's blouse, near enough her heart that she could feel its beat beneath her fingertips. "Write what's in here because you must, because it pleases you, but never because you want someone else to like what you've said."

"Even you?"

"Especially me! God, Merry—what on earth would I know?"

Meredith smiled and the desolation faded, and she began to speak with abrupt energy about a hedgehog that had turned up in her family's Anderson shelter. Juniper listened and laughed and left only the smallest part of her attention free to circle the strange new tension in her friend's face. Had she been a different sort of person, someone for whom made-up people and places didn't present so easily, for whom words sometimes refused to form, she might have understood Merry's anxiety better. But she wasn't, and she didn't, and after a time she let it go. To be in London, to be free, to be sitting on the grass with the sun now creeping up her back, was all that mattered.

Juniper extinguished her cigarette and saw that a button had loosened on Meredith's blouse. "Here," she said, reaching out, "you're coming all undone, chicken. Let me get you sorted."

Two

Tom decided to walk towards the Elephant and Castle. He didn't like the tube; the trains traveled too deeply underground and made him feel nervous and enclosed. It seemed a lifetime ago that he'd taken Joey to sit on the platform and listen for the oncoming roar. He unballed the fists that hung now by his sides and remembered how it had felt to hold that plump little hand—sweating, always sweating, with the thrill and the heat—as they peered into the tunnel together, awaiting the glow of headlights, the stale and dusted fist of wind that announced the train's arrival. He remembered especially looking down at Joey's face, as joyous each time as it had been the first.

Tom paused a moment and closed his eyes, letting the memory fray and fade. When he opened them again he almost stepped into the path of three young women, younger than him, surely, but so neat in their utility suits, walking with such smart purpose, that they made him feel foolish and wrong-footed by comparison. They smiled as he stepped aside and each girl lifted a hand to form a victory sign with her fingers as she passed. Tom smiled back, a little too stiffly, a little too late, and then continued on towards the bridge. Behind him the girls' laughter, coy and bubbling like a cool drink before the war, the brisk tapping of their shoes, receded, and Tom had the vague sense that he'd missed an opportunity, though for what he couldn't say. He didn't stop and he didn't see them glance over their shoulders, heads close together as they sneaked another look at the tall young soldier, commented on his handsome face and serious dark eyes. Tom was too busy walking, one foot after the other—just as he'd done in

France—and thinking about that symbol. The V sign. It was everywhere, and he wondered where it had started, who had decided what it meant, and how everyone seemed to know to do it.

As he crossed Westminster Bridge and came closer to his mother's house, Tom allowed himself to notice something he'd been trying to avoid. The restless feeling was back again, the gnawing absence beneath his rib cage. It had been smuggled in on the back of his memories of Joey. Tom drew a deep breath and walked faster, though he knew he had more chance that way of outrunning his shadow. It was strange, the experience of something that was missing; odd that a vacancy might exert as much pressure as a solid object. The effect was a little like homesickness, a fact that perplexed him; first, because he was a grown man and should surely be beyond such feelings; second, because he *was* at home.

He had thought—lying on the wet wooden boards of the boat that brought him back from Dunkirk, in the crisp-sheeted hospital bed, in the first borrowed flat in Islington—that the sensation, the dull, unquenchable ache, would be alleviated when he set foot again inside his family home; the instant his mother wrapped her arms around him and wept against his shoulder and told him that he was home now and everything would be all right. It hadn't, though, and Tom knew why. The hunger wasn't really homesickness at all. He'd used the term lazily, perhaps even hopefully, to describe the feeling, the awareness that something fundamental had been lost. It wasn't a place that he was missing, though; the reality was far worse than that. Tom was missing a layer of himself.

He knew where he'd left it. He'd felt it happen on that field near the Escaut Canal, when he'd turned and met the eyes of the other soldier, the German fellow with his gun pointed straight at Tom's back. He'd felt panic, a hot liquid surge, and then his load had lightened. A layer of himself, the part that felt and feared, had peeled away like a piece of tobacco paper in his father's tin and fluttered to the ground, been left discarded on the battlefield. The other part, the hard remaining kernel called Tom, had put his head down and run, thinking nothing, feeling nothing, aware only of the rasping breaths, his own, in his ears.

The separation, Tom knew, the dislocation, had made him a better soldier but it had left him an insufficient man. It was the reason he no longer lived at home. He looked at things and people now as if through smoky glass. He could see them, but not clearly, and he certainly couldn't touch them. The doctor had explained it to him in the hospital, told him that he'd seen other fellows with the same complaint, which was all very well, but didn't make it any less terrifying when Tom's mum smiled at him as she had when he was a boy, when she insisted that he pull off his socks and let her at them with her needle, and all he felt was emptiness. When he drank from his pa's old cup; when his little brother Joey—a large man now, yet always his little brother Joey—let out a yelp and came at him with a clumsy gallop, the tattered copy of *Black Beauty* clutched to his chest; when his sisters arrived and started fussing over how much weight he'd lost and how they were going to pool their rations and fatten him up. Tom felt nothing and the fact made him want to—

"Mr. Cavill!" His father's name, and Tom's heart skipped a beat. In the electric instant that followed, he sickened with relief because it meant his father was still alive and well and things might therefore be mended. These past weeks, when he'd glimpsed the old man walking down the London street towards him, waving across the battlefield, reaching down to grip Tom's hand on that boat crossing the channel, he hadn't been imagining things at all. That is, he had, but not the things he'd thought: this world, this place of bombs and bullets, and a gun in his hands, leaky boat trips across the sly, dark Channel, and months languishing in hospitals where excessive cleanliness masked the smell of blood, of children left dead on blast-scorched roads; this was the horrid invention. In the *real* world, he realized with the swelling, sudden, giddy gladness of a boy, everything was well because his father was still alive. He must be, for someone was calling him. "Mr. Cavill!"

Tom turned and saw her then, a girl, waving her hand; a familiar face coming towards him. A girl walking in the way of young girls who long to be older—shoulders back, chin set, wrists turned out—yet hurrying like an excited child from a seat in the park, through the barrier where the iron railings used to stand, railings that were being turned now into rivets and bullets and airplane wings.

"Hello, Mr. Cavill," she said breathlessly, arriving right before him. 'You're back from the war!'

The expectation of meeting his father deflated; hope, joy, relief leaked like air from a thousand pin pricks in his skin. Tom perceived with a winded sigh that *he* was Mr. Cavill, and this girl in the middle of the pavement, blinking through her spectacles, expecting something from him, was a pupil of his, had been a pupil of his, once. Before, when he'd had such things, when he'd spoken with trite authority of grand concepts he hadn't begun to understand. Tom winced to remember himself back then.

Meredith. It came to him suddenly and certainly. That was her name, Meredith Baker, but she'd grown since last they met. She was less of a girl, taller, stretched, anxiously filling her extra inches. He felt himself smile, managed the word *hello,* and was visited by a pleasant sensation he couldn't immediately place, something connected to the girl, to Meredith, and to the last time he'd seen her. Just as he was beginning to frown, to wonder, the memory to which the feeling was attached surfaced: a hot day, a circular pool, a girl.

And then he saw her. The girl from the pool, right there in the London street, plain as day, and for a moment he knew he must be imagining things. How could it be otherwise? The girl from his dreams, whom he'd seen sometimes while he was away, radiant, hovering, smiling, as he traipsed across France; when he'd collapsed beneath the weight of his mate Andy—dead over his shoulder for how long before Tom knew?—as the bullet struck and his knee gave way and his blood began to stain the soil near Dunkirk—

Tom stared and then shook his head a little, beginning the silent count to ten.

411

"This is Juniper Blythe," said Meredith, fingering a button near her collar as she grinned up at the girl; Tom followed her gaze. Juniper Blythe. Of course that was her name.

She smiled then with astonishing openness, and her face was utterly transformed. It made *him* feel transformed, as if, for a split second, he really was that young man again, standing by a glittering pool on a hot day before the war got started. "Hello," she said.

Tom nodded in reply, words still too slippery to manage.

"Mr. Cavill was my teacher," said Meredith. "You met him once at Milderhurst."

Tom sneaked another glance while Juniper's attention was on Meredith. She was no Helen of Troy; it wasn't the face itself that drove him to distraction. On any other woman the features would've been considered pleasant but flawed: the too-wideset eyes, the too-long hair, that gap between her front teeth. On her, though, they were an abundance, an extravagance of beauty. It was her peculiar form of animation that distinguished her, he decided. She was an unnatural beauty, and yet she was entirely natural. Brighter, more lustrous than everything else.

"By the pool," Meredith was saying. "Remember? He came to check where I was living."

"Oh, yes," said the girl, said Juniper Blythe, turning back to Tom so that something inside him folded over. His breath snagged when she smiled. "You were swimming in my pool." She was teasing and he longed to say something light in return, to banter as he might once have done.

"Mr. Cavill is a poet, too," said Meredith, her voice seeming to come from somewhere else, a long way away.

Tom tried to focus. A poet. He scratched his forehead. He no longer thought of himself as that. He distantly remembered going to war to gain experience, believing he might unlock the secrets of the world, see things in a new, more vivid way. And he had. He did. Only the things he saw, the things that he had seen, did not belong in poems.

"I don't write much anymore," he said. It was the first sentence he'd managed and he felt bound to improve it. "I've been busy. With other things." He was looking only at Juniper now. "I'm in Notting Hill," he said.

"Bloomsbury," she answered.

He nodded. Seeing her here, like this, after imagining her so many times and in so many different ways, was almost embarrassing.

"I don't know many people in London," she continued, and he couldn't decide whether she was artless or entirely aware of her charm. Whatever the case, something in the way she said it made him bold.

"You know me," he said.

She looked at him curiously, inclined her head as though listening to words he hadn't said, and then smiled. She took a notepad from her bag and wrote something. When she handed it to him her fingers brushed his palm and he experienced a jolt, as if from electricity. "I know you," she agreed.

And it seemed to him then, and every time thereafter that he replayed the conversation, that no three words had ever been finer, contained more truth, than those.

"Are you going home, Mr. Cavill?" This was Meredith. He'd forgotten she was there.

"That's right," he said, "it's Mum's birthday." He glanced at his wristwatch, the numbers made no sense. "I should be getting on."

Meredith grinned and held up two fingers in the V symbol; Juniper only smiled.

Tom waited until he was on his mother's street before opening the piece of paper, but by the time he reached the front door he'd committed the Bloomsbury address to memory.

NOT UNTIL late that night was Meredith finally alone and able to write it all down. The evening had been torturous: Rita and Mum had argued all through dinner, Dad had made them sit together and listen to Mr. Churchill's announcement on the wireless about the Russians, and then Mum—still punishing Meredith for her betrayal at the castle—had found a huge pile of socks that needed darning. Consigned to the kitchen, which always sweltered in summer, Meredith had run the day over and over in her mind, determined not to forget a single detail.

And now, at long last, she'd escaped to the quiet of the room she shared with Rita. She was sitting on the bed, her back against the wall; her journal, her precious journal, resting on her knees as she scribbled furiously across its pages. It had been wise to wait, torture or not; Rita was particularly obnoxious at the moment and the consequences if she were to find the journal would be dire. Thankfully, the coast was clear for the next hour or so. Through some black magic Rita had managed to get the assistant from the butcher's across the way to pay her notice. It must be love: the fellow had taken to putting sausages aside and giving them to Rita on the sly. Rita, of course, considered herself the bee's knees and was quite convinced that marriage would be next.

Love, unfortunately, had not softened her. She'd been waiting when Meredith got home that afternoon, demanding to know who the woman was at the door that morning, where they'd gone in such a hurry, what Meredith was up to. Meredith hadn't told her, of course. She hadn't wanted to. Juniper was her own secret.

"Just someone I know," she'd said, trying not to seem at all mysterious.

"Mum won't be happy when I tell her you've been shirking your chores and walking about with Lady Muck."

But Meredith, for once, had possessed her own shot to fire. "Nor Dad when I tell him what you and the sausage man have been doing in the Anderson."

Rita's face had flushed with indignation and she'd thrown something, which turned out to be her shoe, and left a nasty bruise above Meredith's knee, but she hadn't mentioned Juniper to Mum.

Meredith finished her sentence, made an emphatic full stop, and then sucked thoughtfully on the end of her pen. She'd reached the moment in which she and Juniper had come across Mr. Cavill, walking along the pavement, frowning at the ground with as much concentration as if he'd been counting his footsteps. From across the park Meredith's body had known that it was him before her brain caught up. Her heart had lurched inside her, as if spring-loaded, and she'd remembered at once the childish crush she used to harbor. The way she'd watched him and hung on his every word and imagined that one day they might even be married. It made her cringe to remember! Why, she'd only been a kid back then. What on earth had she been thinking?

How strange it was, though, how unfathomable, how wonderful, that Juniper and he should both rematerialize on a single day; the two people who had been most instrumental in helping her discover the path she wished to follow through life. Meredith knew herself to be fanciful, her mum was always accusing her of daydreaming, but she couldn't help but feel it meant something. That there was an element of fate in their twined arrival back in her life. Of destiny.

Seized by an idea, Meredith leaped off the bed and pulled her collection of cheap notebooks out from the hiding spot at the bottom of the wardrobe. Her story didn't have a title yet, but she knew it must be given one before she handed it over to Juniper. Typing it up like a proper manuscript wouldn't hurt either—Mr. Seebohm at number fourteen had an old typewriter; perhaps if Meredith were to offer to fetch him lunch he might be induced to let her use it?

Kneeling on the floor, she hurried her hair behind her ears and flicked through the books, reading a few lines here, a few there, tensing as even those she'd been most proud of wilted under the imagined scrutiny of Juniper. She deflated. The whole story was too starchy by half, Meredith could see that now. Her characters spoke too much and felt too little and didn't seem to know what it was they wanted from life. Most importantly, there was something vital missing—an aspect of her heroine's existence, that she suddenly understood must be fleshed out. What a wonder that she hadn't realized it before!

Love, of course. That's what her story needed. For it was love, wasn't it—the glorious lurching of a spring-loaded heart—that made the world go round?

THREE

LONDON, OCTOBER 17, 1941

THE windowsill in Tom's attic was wider than most, which made it perfect for sitting on. It was Juniper's favorite place to perch, a fact that she refused to believe had anything to do with her missing the attic roof at Milderhurst. Because she didn't. She wouldn't. In fact, during the months that she'd been gone, Juniper had resolved never to go back.

She knew now about her father's will, the things he'd wanted for her and the lengths to which he'd been prepared to go to get his way. Saffy had explained it all in a letter, her intention not to make Juniper feel bad, only to agonize about Percy's ill humor. Juniper had read the letter twice, just to make sure she properly understood its meaning, and then she'd drowned it in the Serpentine, watching as the fine paper submerged and the ink ran blue and her temper finally subsided. It was precisely the sort of thing Daddy had always done, she could see that clearly from this distance, and it was just like the old man to try to pull his daughters' strings from beyond the grave. Juniper, though, refused to let him. She wasn't prepared to let even *thoughts* of Daddy bring black clouds upon her day. Today of all days was to be only sunshine—even if there wasn't much of the real thing about.

Knees drawn up, back arched against the render, smoking contentedly, Juniper surveyed the garden below. It was autumn and the ground was thick with leaves, the little cat in raptures. He'd been busy for hours down there, stalking imaginary foes, pouncing and disappearing beneath the drifts, hiding in the dusk of dappled shadows. The lady from the ground-floor flat, whose life had gone up in flames in Coventry, was there too, putting down a saucer of milk. There wasn't much to spare these days, not with the new register, but between them there was always enough to keep the stray kitten happy.

A noise came from the street and Juniper craned her neck to see. There was a man in uniform walking towards the building and her heart began its race. Only a second passed before she knew it wasn't Tom, and she drew on her cigarette, suppressing a pleasant shiver of anticipation. Of course it wasn't him, not yet. He'd be another thirty minutes at least. He was always an age when he visited his family, but he'd be back soon, full of stories, and then she would surprise him.

Juniper glanced inside at the small table by the gas cooker, the one they'd bought for a pittance and convinced a taxi driver to help them transport back to the flat in exchange for a cup of tea. Spread across its top was a feast fit for a king. A king on rations, anyway. Juniper had found the two pears at Portobello Market. Lovely pears, and at a price they'd been able to pay. She'd polished them carefully and set them out alongside the sandwiches and the sardines and the newspaper-wrapped parcel. In the center, standing proud atop an up-turned bucket, was the cake. The first that Juniper had ever baked.

The idea had come to her weeks ago that Tom must have a birthday cake and that she ought to make it for him. The plan had faltered, though, when Juniper realized that she hadn't a clue how to go about doing such a thing. She'd also come to entertain serious doubts about the ability of their tiny gas cooker to cope with such a mighty task. Not for the first time, she'd wished that Saffy were in London. And not only to help with the cake; although Juniper didn't mourn the castle, she found she missed her sisters.

In the end, she'd knocked on the door of the basement flat, hoping to find that the man who lived there—whose flat feet had kept him out of the army, much to the local canteen's gain—would be at home. He was, and when Juniper explained to him her plight, he'd been de-

lighted to lend a hand, drawing up a list of things they'd need to pro-
cure, almost seeming to relish the restraints that rationing imposed.
He'd even donated one of his very own eggs to the cause, and as she
was leaving, handed her something wrapped in newspaper, tied with
twine—"A present for the two of you to share." There'd been no sugar
for icing, of course, but Juniper had written Tom's name on top with
spearmint toothpaste and it really didn't look half bad.

He'd been trying to leave for forty minutes, politely of course, and
it wasn't proving easy. His family were so happy to see him returned
somewhat to normal, acting like "our Tom," that they'd taken to direct-
ing each morsel of conversation his way. Never mind that his mother's
tiny kitchen was stretched to the seams with assorted Cavills, every
question, every joke, every statement of fact hit Tom right between the
eyes. His sister was talking now about a woman she knew, killed during the blackout by a double-decker bus. Shaking her head at Tom and
tutting, "Such a shock, Tommy. Only stepped out to deliver a bundle
of scarves for the servicemen."

Tom agreed that it was awful; it *was* awful; and he listened as his
uncle Jeff related a neighbor's similar run-in with a bicycle, then he
shuffled his feet a little before standing. "Look, thank you, Mum—"

"You're leaving?" She held up the kettle. "I was just about to put it
on to boil again."

He planted a kiss on her forehead, surprised to notice how far
down he had to lean. "There's no one brews tea better, but I really have
to go."

His mum raised a single brow. "When are we going to meet her
then?"

Little brother Joey was pretending to be a train and Tom gave him
a playful pat, avoiding his mother's eyes. "Ah, Mum," he said as he
swung his bag over his shoulder, "I don't know what you mean."

HE WALKED briskly, keen to get back to the flat, to her; keen to get out of the thickening weather. It didn't matter how fast he went, though, his mother's words kept pace. They had claws because Tom longed to tell his family about Juniper. Every time he saw them he had to fight the urge to grab hold of their shoulders and exclaim like a child that he was in love and that the world was a wonderful place, even if young men were shooting one another and nice ladies—mothers with small children at home—were being killed by double-decker buses when they'd only set out to deliver scarves for soldiers.

But he didn't because Juniper had made him promise not to. Her determination that nobody should know they were in love confounded Tom. The secrecy seemed an ill fit for a woman who was so forthright, so unequivocal in her opinions, so unlikely to apologize for anything she felt or said or did. He'd been defensive at first, wondering that perhaps she thought his people were beneath her, but her interest in them had quashed that notion. She talked about them, asked after them, like somebody who'd been friendly with the Cavills for years. And he'd since learned that she didn't discriminate. Tom knew for a fact that the sisters she professed to adore were being kept just as deeply in the dark as his own family. Letters from the castle always came via her godfather (who seemed remarkably unfazed by the deception), and Tom had noticed her replies gave Bloomsbury as the return address. He'd asked her why, indirectly at first, then outright, but she'd refused to explain, speaking only vaguely about her sisters being protective and old-fashioned, and saying that it was best to wait until the time was right.

Tom didn't like it, but he loved her so he did as she asked. For the most part. He hadn't been able to stop himself from writing to Theo. His brother was in the north with his regiment, which seemed to make it somehow all right. Besides, Tom's first letter about the strange and beautiful girl he'd met, the one who'd managed to mend his emptiness, had been written long before she'd asked him not to.

420

TOM HAD known from that first meeting in the street near Elephant and Castle that he must see Juniper Blythe again. He'd walked to Bloomsbury at dawn the very next day, just to look, he told himself, just to see the door, the walls, the windows behind which she was sleeping.

He'd watched the house for hours, smoking nervously, and finally she'd come out. Tom followed her a little way before he found the courage to call her name.

"Juniper."

He'd said it, thought it, so many times, but it was different when he called it out loud and she turned.

They spent the whole sunlit day together, walking and talking, eating the blackberries they found growing over the cemetery wall, and when evening came, Tom wasn't ready to let her go. He suggested that she might like to come to a dance, thinking that was the sort of thing girls enjoyed. Juniper, it seemed, did not. The look of distaste that crossed her face when he said it was so guileless that Tom was momentarily stunned. He regained his composure sufficiently to ask whether there was something else she'd rather do, and Juniper replied that of course they should keep walking. Exploring, she had called it.

Tom was a fast walker but she kept up, skipping from one side of him to the other, ebullient at times, silent at others. She reminded him in certain ways of a child; there was that same air of unpredictability and danger, the uneasy but somehow seductive sense that he had joined forces with someone for whom the ordinary rules of conduct had no pull.

She stopped to look at things then ran to catch up, completely heedless, and he began to worry that she'd trip on something in the blackout, a hole in the pavement or a sandbag.

"It's different to the country, you know," he said, an old teacherly note creeping into his voice.

Juniper only laughed and said, "I certainly hope so. That's exactly why I've come." She went on to explain that she had especially good eyesight, like a bird; that it was something to do with the castle and her upbringing. Tom couldn't remember the details, he'd stopped listening by then. The clouds had shifted, the moon was almost ripe, and her hair had turned to silver in its glaze.

He'd been glad she hadn't caught him staring. Lucky for Tom, she'd crouched on the ground and started digging about in the rubble. He went nearer, curious as to what had claimed her focus, and saw that somehow, in the jumble of London's broken streets, she'd found a tangle of honeysuckle, fallen to the ground after its fence railings were removed but growing still. She picked a sprig and threaded it through her hair, humming a strange and lovely tune as she did so.

When the sun had begun its rise and they'd climbed the stairs to his flat, she'd filled an old jam jar with water and put the sprig in it, on the sill. For nights after, as he lay alone in the warm and the dark, unable to sleep for thoughts of her, he'd smelled its sweetness. And it had seemed to Tom, as it still seemed now, that Juniper was just like that flower. An object of unfathomable perfection in a world that was breaking apart. It wasn't only the way she looked, and it wasn't only the things she said. It was something else, an intangible essence, a confidence, a strength, as if she were connected somehow to the mechanism that drove the world. She was the breeze on a summer's day, the first drops of rain when the earth was parched, light from the evening star.

SOMETHING, THOUGH Juniper wasn't certain what, made her glance towards the pavement. Tom was there, earlier than she'd expected, and her heart skipped a beat. She waved, almost falling from the window in her gladness to see him. He hadn't noticed her yet. His head was down, checking the mail, but Juniper couldn't take her eyes from him. It was madness, it was possession, it was desire. Most of all, though, it was love. Juniper loved his body, she loved his voice, she loved the way his fingers felt upon her skin and the space beneath his collarbone where her cheek fitted perfectly when they slept. She loved that she could see in his face all the places that he'd been. That she never needed to ask him how he felt. That words were unnecessary. Juniper had discovered she was tired of words.

It was raining now, steadily, but nothing like the way it had rained the day she fell in love with Tom. That had been summer rain, one of those sudden, violent storms that sneak in on the back of glorious heat. They'd spent the day walking, wandering through Portobello Market, climbing Primrose Hill, and then winding back to Kensington Gardens, wading in the shallows of the Round Pond.

The thunder when it came was so unexpected that people stared into the sky, fearing a brand-new form of weapon was upon them. And then had come the rain, great big sobbing drops that brought an immediate sheen to the world.

Tom grabbed Juniper's hand and they ran together, splashing through the instant puddles, and laughing from the shock of it, all the way back to his building, up the stairs and into the dim and the dry of his room.

"You're wet," Tom had said, his back against the door he'd just slammed shut. He was staring at her flimsy frock, the way it clung to her legs.

"Wet?" she said. "I'm soaked enough to benefit from a good wringing."

"Here," he slid his spare shirt from the hook behind the door and tossed it to her, "put this on while you dry."

And she'd done as he suggested, pulling off her dress and slipping her arms inside his sleeves. Tom had turned away, pretending business at the small porcelain sink, but when she'd looked, interested to know what he was doing, she'd caught his eyes in the mirror. She'd held them just a moment longer than was usual, long enough to notice when something in them changed.

The rain continued, the thunder too, and her dress dripped in the corner where he'd hung it to dry. The two of them gravitated towards the window and Juniper, who didn't usually suffer from shyness, said something pointless about the birds and where they went in the rain.

Tom didn't answer. He reached out his hand, bringing his palm to rest on the side of her face. The touch was only light, but it was enough. It silenced her and she inclined towards it, turning just enough so that her lips grazed his fingers. Her eyes remained on his, she couldn't have moved them if she'd tried. And then his fingers were on the shirt buttons, her stomach, her breasts, and she was aware, suddenly, that her pulse had shattered into a thousand tiny balls, all of them spinning now in concert, right throughout her body.

THEY'D SAT together on the windowsill afterwards, eating the cherries they'd bought at the market and dropping the stones onto the puddled ground below. Neither of them spoke, but they caught one another's attention occasionally, smiling almost smugly, as if they, and they alone, had been let in on a mighty secret. Juniper had wondered about sex, she'd written about it, the things she'd imagined she might do and say and feel. Nothing, though, had prepared her for the fact that love might follow it so closely.

To fall in love.

Juniper understood why people referred to it as a fall. The brilliant, swooping sensation, the divine imprudence, the complete loss of free will. It had been just like that for her, but it had also been much more. After a lifetime spent shrinking away from physical contact, Juniper had finally connected. When they lay together in that sultry dusk, her face pressed warm against his chest, and she listened to his heart, absorbed its regular beat, she'd felt her own, calming to meet it. And Juniper had understood, somehow, that in Tom she'd found the person who could balance her, and that more than anything, to fall in love was to be caught, to be saved . . .

The front door shut with a bang, and there was noise then on the stairs, Tom's footfalls winding up and up towards her, and with a sudden rush of blinding desire Juniper forgot about the past, she turned away from the garden, from the stray cat with his leaves and the sad old lady crying for Coventry Cathedral, the war outside the window, the city of stairs that led to nowhere, portraits on walls without ceilings, and kitchen tables of families who no longer needed them, and she flitted across the floor and back to bed, shedding Tom's shirt on the way. In that moment, as his key turned in the door, there was only him and her and this small, warm flat with a birthday dinner laid out.

THEY'D EATEN the cake in bed, two enormous slices each, and there were crumbs everywhere. "It's because there's not a lot of egg," said Juniper, sitting with her back against the wall and surveying the mess with a philosophical sigh. "It isn't easy to make things stick together, you know."

Tom grinned up at her from where he lay. "How knowledgeable you are."

"I am, aren't I?"

"And talented, of course. A cake like that one belongs in Fortnum & Mason."

"Well, I can't tell a lie, I did have a little help."

"Ah, yes," said Tom, rolling onto his side, stretching as far as he could towards the table and capturing the newspaper-wrapped parcel—just—within his fingertips. "Our resident cook."

"You know he's not a cook, really, he's a playwright. I heard him speaking with a man the other day who's going to put on one of his plays."

"Now, Juniper," said Tom, carefully unwrapping the paper to reveal a jar of blackberry jam inside. "What business does a playwright have making anything as beautiful as this?"

"Oh lovely! How heavenly," said Juniper, lunging for the jar. "Think of the sugar! Shall we have some now with toast?"

Tom pulled his arm back, holding the jam out of reach. "Is it possible," he said incredulously, "that the young lady is still hungry?"

"Well no. Not exactly. But it isn't a matter of hunger."

"It isn't?"

"It's a matter of a new option presenting itself after the fact. A sweet and glorious new option."

Tom turned the jar round in his fingers, paying close attention to the delicious red-black spoils inside. "No," he said at length, "I think we should save it for a special occasion."

"More special than your birthday?"

"My birthday's been special enough. This we should keep for the next celebration."

"Oh, all right," said Juniper, nestling in against his shoulder so his arm contained her, "but only because it's your birthday, and because I'm far too full to get up."

Tom smiled around his cigarette as he lit it.

"How was your family?" said Juniper. "Is Joey over his cold?"

"He is."

"And Maggie? Did she make you listen as she read the horoscopes?"

"Very kind of her it was, too. How else am I supposed to know how to behave this week?"

"How else indeed?" Juniper took his cigarette and drew slowly. "Was there anything interesting, pray tell?"

"Marginally," said Tom, sneaking his fingers beneath the sheet. "Apparently I'm going to propose marriage to a beautiful girl."

"Oh, really?" She squirmed when he tickled her side and a smoky exhalation became a laugh. "That is interesting."

"I thought so."

"Though of course the real question is what the young lady is forecast to say by way of reply. I don't suppose Maggie had any insight into that?"

Tom pulled his arm back, rolling onto his side to face her. "Unfortunately, Maggie couldn't help me there. She said I had to ask the girl myself and see what happened."

"Well, if that's what Maggie says . . ."

"So?" said Tom.

"So?"

He propped himself up on an elbow and adopted a posh voice. "Will you do me the honor, Juniper Blythe, of becoming my wife?"

"Well, kind sir," said Juniper, in her best impersonation of the Queen, "that depends on whether one might also be permitted three fat babies."

Tom took the cigarette back and smoked it casually. "Why not four?"

His manner was light still, but he'd dropped the accent. It made Juniper uneasy and somehow self-conscious and she couldn't think of anything to say.

"Come on, Juniper," he pressed. "Let's get married. You and I." And there was no doubting now that he was serious.

"I'm not expected to get married."

He frowned. "What does that mean?"

A silence fell between them, remaining unbroken until the kettle whistled in the flat downstairs. "It's complicated," said Juniper.

"Is it? Do you love me?"

"You know I do."

"Then it isn't complicated. Marry me. Say yes, June. Whatever it is, whatever you're worried about, we can fix it."

Juniper knew there was nothing she could say that would please him, nothing except yes, and she wasn't able to do that. "Let me think about it," she said finally. "Let me have some time."

He sat abruptly, with his feet on the floor and his back to her. His head was bowed; he was leaning forwards. He was upset. She wanted to touch him, to run her fingers down the center of his back, to go back in time so that he'd never asked her. As she was wondering how such a thing might be done, he reached into his pocket and pulled out an envelope. It was folded in half, but she could see there was a letter inside. "Here's your time," he said, handing it to her. "I've been recalled to my unit. I report in a week."

Juniper made a noise, almost a gasp, and scrambled to sit beside him. "But how long . . . ? When will you be back?"

"I don't know. When the war is over, I suppose."

When the war is over. He was leaving London and suddenly Juniper understood that without Tom this place, this city, would cease to matter. She might as well be back at the castle. She felt her heart speeding up at the thought, not with excitement like an ordinary person's, but with the reckless intensity she'd been taught to watch for all her life. She closed her eyes, hoping that it might improve matters.

Her father had told her she was a creature of the castle, that she belonged there and it was safest not to leave, but he'd been wrong. She knew that now. The opposite was true: away from the castle, away from the world of Raymond Blythe, the terrible things he'd told her, his seeping guilt and sadness, she was free. In London, there'd been none of her visitors, there'd been no lost time. And although her great fear—that she was capable of harming others—had followed her, it was different here.

Juniper felt a pressure on her knees and blinked open. Tom was kneeling on the floor before her, concern flooding his eyes. "Hey, sweetheart," he said. "It's all right. Everything's going to be all right."

She'd had no need to tell Tom any of it and for that she'd been glad. She hadn't wanted his love to change, for him to become protective and concerned like her sisters. She hadn't wanted to be watched, her moods and silences measured. She hadn't wanted to be loved carefully, only well.

"Juniper," Tom was saying. "I'm sorry. Please, don't look like that. I can't bear to see you look like that."

What was she thinking, turning him away, giving him up? Why on earth would she do such a thing? To follow the wishes of her father?

Tom stood, began to walk away, but Juniper grabbed his wrist. "Tom—"

"I'm getting you a glass of water."

"No," she shook her head quickly, "I don't want water. I just want you."

He smiled and a stubbled dimple appeared in his left cheek. "Well, you already have me."

"No," she said, "I mean yes."

He cocked his head.

"I mean I want us to get married."

"Really?"

"And we'll tell my sisters together."

"Of course we will," he said. "Whatever you want."

And then she laughed, and her throat ached but she laughed despite it and felt lighter in some way. "Thomas Cavill and I are getting married."

Juniper lay awake, her cheek on Tom's chest, listening to his steady heartbeat, his steady breaths, trying to match her own to his. But she couldn't sleep. She was trying to word a letter in her mind. For she'd have to write to her sisters, to let them know that she and Tom were coming, and she had to explain it in a way that would please them. They mustn't suspect a thing.

There was something else she'd thought of, too. Juniper had never been interested in clothing, but she suspected that a woman getting married ought to have a dress. She didn't care about such things, but Tom might and his mother certainly would, and there was nothing Juniper wouldn't do for Tom.

She remembered a dress that had belonged once to her own mother: pale silk, a full skirt. Juniper had seen her wear it, a long time ago. If it were somewhere in the castle still, Saffy would be able to find it and she would know just what was needed to resurrect it.

Four

MEREDITH hadn't seen Mr. Cavill—Tom, as he'd insisted that she call him—in weeks, so it was a tremendous surprise when she opened the front door to find him standing on the other side.

"Mr. Cavill," she said, trying not to sound excited. "How are you?"

"Couldn't be better, Meredith. And it's Tom, please." He smiled. "I'm not your teacher anymore."

Meredith blushed, she was sure she did.

"Mind if I come inside for a moment?"

She shot a glance over her shoulder, through the other doorway and into the kitchen, where Rita was scowling at something on the table. Her sister had recently fallen out with the young butcher's assistant and been terribly sour since. As far as Meredith could tell, it was Rita's plan to ameliorate her own disappointment by making her little sister's life every bit as miserable.

Tom must have sensed her reservation for he added, "We could go for a walk, if you prefer?"

Meredith nodded gratefully, closed the door quietly behind her as she made her getaway.

They went together down the road and she kept a small distance, arms crossed, head bowed, trying to seem as if she were listening to his good-natured talk of school and writing, the past and the future, when really her brain was scurrying ahead, trying to guess at the purpose of his visit. Trying very hard not to think about the schoolgirl crush she'd once nursed.

They came to a stop at the same park where Juniper and Meredith had conducted their fruitless search for deck chairs back in June when the weather had been hot. The contrast between that warm memory and the gray skies now made Meredith shiver.

"You're cold. I should have thought to remind you about a coat." He shrugged his arms from the sleeves of his own, handed it to Meredith.

"Oh no, I—"

"Nonsense. I was getting hot anyway."

He pointed at a spot on the grass and Meredith followed readily, sitting cross-legged beside him. He spoke some more, asked her about her writing and listened closely to her reply. He told Meredith that he remembered giving her the journal, that he was delighted to think that she was using it still; all the while he plucked strands from the grass, rolling them into small spirals. Meredith listened and nodded and she watched his hands. They were lovely, strong but fine. A man's hands, but not thick or hairy. She wondered what they would feel like to touch.

A pulse in her temple began to throb and she felt dizzy thinking about how easily such a thing might be done. All she had to do was reach out a little further with her own hand. Would his be warm, she wondered, would they be smooth or rough? Would his fingers startle then tighten around her own?

"I have something for you," he said. "It was mine, but I've been recalled to my unit so I need to find it a good home."

A gift before he went back to the war? Meredith's breath caught and all thought of hands dissolved. Wasn't this the very sort of thing that sweethearts did? Exchanged gifts before the hero marched away?

She jumped as Tom's hand brushed her back. He retracted it immediately, held his palm before her and smiled, embarrassed. "I'm sorry. It's just that the gift, it's in my coat pocket."

Meredith smiled too, relieved but also somehow disappointed. She returned his coat to him and he withdrew a book from its pocket.

"*The Last Days of Paris, a Journalist's Diary,*" she read, turning it over. "Thank you . . . Tom."

His name on her lips made Meredith shudder. She was fifteen now, and although perhaps only passably pretty, she was no longer a flat-chested child. It was possible, wasn't it, that a man might fall in love with her?

She was aware of his breath close to her neck as he reached over to touch the book's cover.

"Alexander Werth kept this diary while Paris was falling. I'm giving it to you because it shows how important it is for people to write what they see. Particularly in days like ours. Otherwise people don't know what's really happening, do you see that, Meredith?"

"Yes." She glanced sideways and found him looking at her with such intensity that she was overcome. It happened in a matter of seconds, but for Meredith, stuck in the moment's middle, everything moved like a film reel on slow motion. It was like watching a stranger as she leaned closer, drew breath, closed her eyes and pressed her lips to his in an instant of sublime perfection . . .

Tom was very gentle. He spoke kindly to her, even as he removed her hands from his shoulders, even as he gave them a squeeze, unmistakably of the friendly sort, and told her not to be embarrassed.

But Meredith *was* embarrassed; she wished only to melt into the ground. To dissolve into the air. Anything but to be still sitting beside him in the stark glare of her horrible mistake. She was so mortified that when Tom began to ask questions about Juniper's sisters—what they were like, the sorts of things they enjoyed, whether there were any particular flower they favored—she answered as if by rote. And she certainly didn't think to ask him why he cared.

O N   T H E day Juniper left London, she met Meredith at Charing Cross Station. She was glad of the company, not only because she was going to miss Merry, but because it kept her mind from Tom. He'd gone the day before to rejoin his regiment—for training first, before being sent back to the front—and the flat, the street, the city of London itself, was unbearable without him. Which is why Juniper had decided to take an early train east. She wasn't going back to the castle though, not yet: the dinner wasn't until Wednesday, she still had money in her suitcase, and she had an idea that she might spend the next three days exploring some of those swirling paintings she'd spied from the window of the train that had brought her to London.

A familiar figure appeared at the top of the concourse, breaking into a grin when she spotted Juniper's eager wave. Meredith scuttled through the crowd to where Juniper was standing, directly beneath the clock as they'd arranged.

"Well, now," said Juniper, after they'd embraced, "Where is it then?"

Meredith held her thumb and forefinger very close together and winced. "Just a few last-minute corrections."

"You mean I won't have it for the train ride?"

"A few more days, honest."

Juniper stepped aside for a porter pushing an enormous pile of suitcases. "All right," she said. "A few more days. No more, mind!" She shook a finger with mock sternness. "I'll be expecting it in the post by the end of the week. Agreed?"

"Agreed."

They smiled at one another as the train let out a mighty whistle. Juniper glanced over and saw that most of the passengers had boarded. "Well," she said, "I suppose I should be—"

The rest of her sentence was smothered by Meredith's embrace. "I'm going to miss you, Juniper. Promise you'll come back."

"Of course I'll come back."

"No more than a month?"

Juniper smoothed a fallen eyelash from her young friend's cheek. "Any longer and you're to presume the worst and mount a rescue mission!"

Merry grinned. "And you'll let me know as soon as you've read my story?"

433

"By return mail, the very same day," Juniper said with a salute. "Take care of yourself, little chicken."

"You take care, too."

"As always." Juniper's smile straightened and she hesitated, flicking a stray hair from her eyes. She was deliberating. The news ballooned inside her, pressing for release, but a little voice urged restraint.

The guard blew his whistle, blocking out the voice, and Juniper was decided. Meredith was her best friend, she could be trusted. "I have a secret, Merry," she said. "I haven't told anyone, we said we wouldn't until later, but you're not just anyone."

Meredith nodded keenly and Juniper leaned in towards her friend's ear, wondering if the words would feel as strange and wonderful as they had the first time: "Thomas Cavill and I are getting married."

MRS. BIRD'S SUSPICIONS

1992

DARKNESS had fallen by the time I reached the farmhouse, and with it a fine drizzle was settling, netlike, across the landscape. There were still a couple of hours until dinner would be served and I was glad. After an unexpected afternoon in the company of the sisters, I was in need of a hot bath and time alone to shake off the cloying atmosphere that had trailed me home. I wasn't sure what it was exactly, only that there seemed to be so much unfulfilled longing within those castle walls, frustrated desires that had soaked inside the stones only to seep back out with time so that the air was stale, almost stagnant.

And yet the castle and its three gossamer inhabitants held an inexplicable fascination for me. No matter the moments of discomfort I experienced when I was there; as soon as I was away from them, from their castle, I felt compelled to return and found myself counting the hours until I could go back. It makes little sense; perhaps madness never does. For I was mad about the Sisters Blythe, I see that now.

As soft rain began to fall on the farmhouse eaves, I lay curled up on my bedspread, a blanket draped across my feet, reading and dozing and thinking, and by dinnertime I felt much restored. It was natural that Percy should wish to spare Juniper pain, that she should leap to stop me when I threatened to open old wounds; it had been insensitive of me to mention Thomas Cavill, particularly with Juniper sleeping nearby. And yet the fire of Percy's reaction had piqued my interest . . . Perhaps if I was lucky enough to find myself alone with Saffy, I might probe a little further. She had seemed agreeable, eager even, to help me with my research.

Research that now included rare and special access to Raymond Blythe's notebooks. Even saying the words beneath my breath was enough to send a shiver of delight rippling down my spine. I rolled onto my back, thrilled to the tips of my toes, and gazed up at the joist-crossed ceiling, envisaging the very moment when I would glimpse inside the writer's mind, see precisely the things he'd thought and the way he'd thought them.

I ate dinner at a table by myself in the cozy dining room of Mrs. Bird's farmhouse. The whole place smelled warmly of the vegetable stew that had been served, and a fire crackled in the grate. Outside, the wind continued to build, buffeting the glass panes, gently for the most part, but with occasional sharper bursts, and I thought—not for the first time—what a true and simple pleasure it was, to be inside and sated when the cold and the starless dark spread out across the world.

I'd brought my notes to begin work on the Raymond Blythe article, but my thoughts would not behave themselves, drifting back, time and again, to his daughters. It was the sibling thing, I suppose. I was fascinated by the intricate tangle of love and duty and resentment that tied them together. The glances they exchanged; the complicated balance of power established over decades; the games I would never play with rules I would never fully understand. And perhaps that was key: they were such a natural group that they made me feel remarkably singular by comparison. To watch them together was to know strongly, painfully, all that I'd been missing.

"Big day?" I looked up to see Mrs. Bird standing above me. "And another tomorrow, I don't doubt?"

"I'm going to see Raymond Blythe's work notebooks in the morning." I couldn't help myself; the excitement just bubbled up and out of its own volition.

Mrs. Bird was nonplussed, but in a kind sort of way. "Well, that's nice, dear. You don't mind if I . . . ?" She laid a hand on the chair across from me.

"Of course not."

She sat with a heavy lady's huff, flattening a hand across her stomach as she righted herself against the table edge. "Well now, that feels a bit better. I've been run off my feet all day." She nodded at my notes. "But I see you're working late, too."

"Trying. I'm a bit distracted, though."

"Oh." Her eyebrows arrowed. "Handsome fellow, is it?"

"Something like that. Mrs. Bird, I don't suppose there were any phone calls for me today?"

"Phone calls? Nothing I can think of. Were you expecting one? The young fellow you're mooning over?" Her eyes brightened as she said, "Your publisher, perhaps?"

She looked so hopeful that it felt rather cruel to disappoint her. Nonetheless, for clarity's sake: "My mum, actually. I had hoped she might make it down for a visit."

A particularly large gust of wind rattled along the window locks and I shivered, from pleasure more than chill. There was something about the atmosphere that night, something enlivening. Mrs. Bird and I were the only two remaining in the dining room, and the log in the fire had been honeycombed so that it glowed red, popping occasionally and spitting bits of gold against the bricks. I'm not sure whether it was the warm, smoky room itself, its contrast with the wet and the wind outside; or a reaction to the pervasive atmosphere of knots and secrets I'd encountered at the castle; or even just a sudden desire to have a normal conversation with another human being. Whatever the case, I felt expansive. I closed my notebook and pushed it aside. "My mother came here as an evacuee," I said. "During the war."

"To the village?"

"To the castle."

"No! Really? Stayed there with the sisters?"

I nodded, pleased out of all proportion by her reaction. Wary, too, as a little voice inside my head whispered that my pleasure stemmed from the sense of possession Mum's link with Milderhurst conferred onto me. A sense of possession that was most misplaced, and one that I'd thus far failed to mention to the Misses Blythe themselves.

"Goodness!" Mrs. Bird was saying, clapping her fingertips together. "What a lot of stories she must have! The mind boggles."

"Actually, I have her war journal here with me—"

"War journal?"

"Her diary from the time. Bits and pieces about how she felt, the people she met, the place itself."

"Why then, there's probably mention of my own mum in there," said Mrs. Bird, straightening proudly.

It was my turn to be surprised. "Your mum?"

"She worked at the castle. Started as a maid when she was sixteen; finished up as head housekeeper. Lucy Rogers, though it was Middleton back then."

"Lucy Middleton," I said slowly, trying to recall any mention in Mum's journal. "I'm not sure; I'll have to check." Mrs. Bird's shoulders had slumped a little under the weight of her disappointment and I felt personally responsible, clutching at ways to make it better. "She hasn't told me much about it, you see; I only found out about her evacuation recently."

I regretted saying it immediately. Hearing myself speak the words made me more acutely aware than ever how strange it was for a woman to have kept such a thing secret; and I felt implicated somehow, as if Mum's silence might be due to a personal failing of mine. And I felt foolish, too, because if I'd been a little more circumspect, a little less eager to absorb Mrs. Bird's interest, I wouldn't be in this predicament. I prepared myself for the worst, but Mrs. Bird surprised me. With a knowing nod, she leaned a little closer and said, "Parents and their secrets, eh?"

"Yes." A lump of charcoal popcorned in the hearth and Mrs. Bird lifted a finger, signaling that she'd be back in just a minute; she squeezed herself out of her chair and disappeared through a concealed exit in the papered wall.

Rain blew softly against the wooden door, filling the pond outside, and I pressed my palms together, held them prayerlike against
my lips, before tilting them to lean my cheek on the back of my fire-
warmed hand.

When Mrs. Bird returned with a bottle of whisky and two cut-
glass tumblers, the suggestion so suited the moody, inclement evening
that I smiled and accepted gladly.

We clinked glasses across the table.

"My mother nearly didn't marry," said Mrs. Bird, pressing her lips
and savoring the whisky warmth. "What do you think of that? I almost didn't exist." She laid a hand against her brow in a performance
of *quelle horreur!*

I smiled.

"She had a brother, you see, an adored older brother. The way
she tells it, he was responsible for making the sun rise each morning.
Their father died young and Michael—that was his name—stepped
in and took over. Real man about the house, he was; even as a boy
he used to work after school and on weekends, cleaning windows for
tuppence. Giving the coins to his mum so she could keep the house
nice. Handsome, too—hang on! I've a photograph." She hurried to
the hearth, wriggled her fingers above the host of frames cluttering
the mantelpiece, before diving in and fishing out a small brass square.
She used the plumped-out front of her tweed skirt to wipe dust from
its face before handing it to me. Three figures caught in a long-ago
instant: a young man whose destiny made him handsome, an older
woman on one side, a pretty girl of about thirteen on the other.

"Michael went with all the rest of them to fight in the Great War."
Mrs. Bird was standing behind me, peering heavily over my shoulder.
"His last request, when my mum was seeing him off on the train, was
that if anything happened to him she should stay at home with their
mother." Mrs. Bird took back the photo and sat again, straightening
her glasses on her nose to look at it further as she spoke. "What was
she to say? She assured him she'd do as he asked. She was young—I
don't suppose she thought it would come to anything. People didn't,

not really. Not at the start of the Great War. They didn't know then." She pulled out the frame's cardboard stand and set it on the table by her glass.

I sipped my whisky and waited, and at length she sighed. She met my eyes, opened her hand upwards in a sudden motion, as if to toss invisible confetti. "Anyway," she said, "history happened. He was killed and poor old Mum resigned herself to doing as he'd asked. Can't say I'd have been so obliging, but people were different back then. They stuck by their word. Grandmother was a right old harridan, to be honest, but Mum supported them both, gave up hopes of marriage and children, accepted her lot."

A flurry of heavy raindrops spat against the nearby window and I shivered into my cardigan. "And yet, here you are."

"Here I am."

"So what happened?"

"Grandmother died," said Mrs. Bird, with a matter-of-fact sort of nod, "very precipitously in June 1939. She'd been ill for a time, something to do with her liver, so it was no surprise. Rather a relief, I've always gathered, though Mum was far too kind to admit such a thing. By the time the war was nine months old, Mum was married and expecting me."

"A whirlwind romance."

"Whirlwind?" Mrs. Bird bunched her lips, considering. "I suppose so, by today's standards. Not at the time, though, not in a war. I'm not so sure about the 'romance' part, either, to be honest. I've always suspected it was a practical decision on Mum's part. She never said as much, not in so many words, but children know such things, don't they? No matter that we'd all prefer to believe we were the product of grand love affairs." She smiled at me, but in a tentative way, as if she were sizing me up, wondering whether she could trust me further.

"Did something happen?" I asked, edging closer. "Something to make you feel like that?"

Mrs. Bird drained the rest of her whisky and twisted the glass back and forth, making rings on the tabletop. She frowned then at the bottle, seemed to be engaged in some deep and silent debate; I can't say whether she won or lost, but she took the top off and poured us each another.

"I found something," she said. "A few years back. After Mum passed away and I was taking care of her affairs."

Whisky hummed warm in my throat. "What was it?"

"Love letters."

"Oh."

"Not from my father."

"Oh!"

"Hidden in a can at the back of her dressing-table drawer. I almost didn't find them, you know. It wasn't until an antiques dealer came to see about buying some of the furniture. I was showing him the pieces and I thought the drawer was stuck, so I pulled it, rather harder than I needed to, and the can came scuttling to the front."

"Did you read them?"

She wouldn't meet my eyes. "I opened the can later. Terrible, I know." She flushed and began smoothing the hair by her temples, hiding, it seemed, behind her curled hands. "I just couldn't help it. By the time I realized what I was reading, well, I had to keep on with it, didn't I? They were lovely, you see. Heartfelt. To the point, but almost the more meaningful for their brevity. And there was something else, an air of sadness in those letters. They were all written before she married my dad—Mum wasn't the type to play up once she was wed. No, this was a love affair from back when her own mother was still alive, when there was no chance that she might marry or move away."

"Who was it, do you know? Who wrote the letters?"

She left her hair alone then, flattened her hands on the table. The stillness was arresting, and when she leaned towards me, I felt myself incline to meet her. "I really shouldn't say," she whispered. "I don't like to gossip."

"Of course not."

She paused and a thread of excitement plucked at her lip; she shot a surreptitious glance over each shoulder in turn. "I'm not one hundred percent certain; they weren't signed with a full name, just a single initial." She met my eyes, blinked, then smiled, almost slyly. "It was an R."

"An R." I echoed her accentuated pronunciation of the letter, thought about it a moment, chewed the inside of my cheek, and then I gasped. "Why, you don't think . . . ?" But why not? She meant R for Raymond Blythe. The king of the castle and his longtime housekeeper: it was almost a cliché, and clichés only got that way because they happened all the time. "That would explain the secrecy in the letters, the impossibility of being open about their relationship."

"It would explain something else, too."

I looked at her, still dazed by the whole proposition.

"There's a coldness in the eldest sister, Persephone; a coldness towards *me*. It's nothing I've done, certainly, and yet I've always felt it. Once, when I was a girl, she caught me playing by the pool, the circular one with the swing. Well—the look in her eyes; it was as if she'd seen a ghost. I half believed she might be going to throttle me, then and there. Since I found out about my mum's affair, though, the likelihood that it was with Mr. Blythe, well, I've wondered whether Percy might not have known; whether she might not have found out somehow and taken umbrage. Things were different back then, between the classes. And Percy Blythe is a rigid sort of person, one for rules and traditions."

I was nodding, but slowly; it certainly didn't sound implausible. Percy Blythe didn't strike me as the type ever to be warm and fuzzy, but I'd noticed on my first visit to the castle that she was particularly short with Mrs. Bird. And there was definitely some sort of secret being kept at the castle. Was it possible that this love affair was the very thing Saffy had wanted to tell me about, the detail she hadn't felt comfortable discussing with Adam Gilbert? And was that why Percy was so adamant that Saffy should not be interviewed further? Because she sought to stop her twin from giving up their father's secret, from telling me about Raymond Blythe's long-standing relationship with his housekeeper?

But why would Percy care so much? Not from loyalty to her own mother, surely: Raymond Blythe had married more than once, so presumably Percy had come to terms with the realities of the human heart. And even if it were as Mrs. Bird proposed, that Percy was old-fashioned and didn't approve of the classes mingling romantically, I was doubtful as to whether she would care so deeply after all these decades, especially when so much else had happened to bring perspective to their lives. Could she really consider it such a travesty that her father had once been in love with his long-term housekeeper that she would fight to keep the fact forever hidden from public record? I just couldn't see it. Whether Percy Blythe was old-fashioned or not was neither here nor there: she was a pragmatist; I had seen enough of her to realize that a flint of steely realism lay within Percy's heart. If she was keeping secrets, it wasn't for reasons of prudery or social morality.

"Even more than that," said Mrs. Bird, sensing perhaps my wavering opinion, "I've sometimes wondered whether—I mean, Mum never so much as hinted at it, but—" She shook her head and flapped her fingers forward. "No—no, it's silly."

She was now holding her hands clutched against her chest almost coyly, and it took me a confused moment to make out why, what it was she wanted me to think. I picked my way slowly along the prickly notion and said, "You believe he might have been your father?"

Her eyes met mine and I knew I'd guessed correctly. "Mum loved that house, the castle, all of the Blythe family. She talked about old Mr. Blythe sometimes, about how clever he was, how proud she was to have worked for such a famous writer. But she was funny about it, too. Didn't like to drive past if we could help it. Clammed up right in the middle of a story and refused to go any further, got this sad, wistful look in her eyes."

It would certainly explain a lot of things. Percy Blythe might not have minded that her father carried on a relationship with his housekeeper, but for him to have fathered another child? A younger daughter, another half sister for his girls? There would be implications if that was so, implications that had nothing to do with prudery or morality, implications that Percy Blythe, defender of the castle, protector of her family legacy, would do anything to avoid.

And yet, even as I thought such things, acknowledged the possibilities and drew quite tangible connections, there was something in Mrs. Bird's suggestion that I just could not accept. My resistance wasn't rational and I would have struggled to explain it if asked; nonetheless, it was fierce. Loyalty, however misguided, to Percy Blythe, to the three old ladies on the hill who were such a closed coterie that it was impossible for me to imagine there might be any addition to their number.

The clock above the fireplace chose that moment to announce our arrival at the hour, and it was as if an enchantment had been broken. Mrs. Bird, her burden lightened for having been shared, began to clear the salt and pepper shakers from the tables. "The room isn't going to do itself, I expect," she said. "I keep hoping, but I've been disappointed thus far."

I stood, too, gathering our empty tumblers.

Mrs. Bird smiled at me as I arrived at her side. "They can surprise us, can't they, our parents? The things they got up to before we were born."

"Yes," I said. "Almost like they were real people once."

THE NIGHT HE DIDN'T COME

ON my first day of official interviews, I started early for the castle. It was cold and gray, and although the previous night's drizzle had lifted, it had taken much of the world's vitality with it and the landscape looked to have been bleached. There was something new in the air, too, a bitter chill that made me drive my hands deep into my pockets as I walked, cursing myself because I'd forgotten to bring gloves.

The Sisters Blythe had told me not to knock, but to come in directly when I arrived and make my way to the yellow parlor. "It's on Juniper's account," Saffy had explained discreetly as I left the day before. "A knock at the door and she thinks it's *him,* arrived at last." She didn't explain further the identity of *him;* she didn't have to.

The last thing I wanted to do was upset Juniper, so I was on guard, particularly after my faux pas the day before. I did as I'd been told, pushed open the front door, stepped into the stone entrance hall, and followed the dark corridor. Holding my breath, for some reason, as I went.

When I reached the parlor, no one was there. Even Juniper's green velvet chair was empty. I stood for a moment, wondering what to do next, whether I'd somehow got the timing wrong. Then I heard footsteps and turned to see Saffy at the door, dressed in her usual pretty fashion, but with an air of fuss about her, as if I'd caught her unawares.

"Oh!" She stopped abruptly at the edge of the rug. "Edith, you're here. But of course you are"—a glance at the mantel clock—"it's almost ten o'clock." She brushed a fine hand against her forehead and attempted a smile. It refused to form easily or fully and she dropped it.

"I'm so sorry if I've kept you waiting. Only, we've had rather an eventful morning and time quite slipped away."

A creeping sense of dread had followed her into the room and it settled now around me. "Is everything all right?" I asked.

"No," she said, and she wore a pallor of such utter bereavement on her face that my first shocking thought, given the empty chair, was that something had happened to Juniper. It was almost a relief when she said, "It's Bruno. He's disappeared. He'd gone from Juniper's room when I went to help her dress this morning and we've seen neither hide nor hair since."

"Perhaps he's playing somewhere," I suggested. "In the woods or the gardens?" Even as I said it, I remembered the way he'd looked the day before, the shortness of breath, the sagging shoulders, the ridge of gray along his spine, and I knew it wasn't so.

Sure enough, Saffy shook her head. "No. No, he wouldn't, you see. He rarely strays from Juniper, and then only ever to sit by the front stairs, watching for visitors. Not that we ever have any. Present company excepted." She smiled slightly, almost apologetically, as if she feared I might have taken offense. "This is different, though. We're all terribly worried. He hasn't been well and he's not been acting himself. Percy had to go looking for him yesterday, and now this." Her fingers knotted together at her belt, and I wished there was something I could do to help. There are certain people who exude vulnerability, whose pain and discomfort are particularly difficult to witness, and for whom you would endure almost any inconvenience if it promised to ease their suffering. Saffy Blythe was one of them.

"Why don't I go and have a look at the spot where I saw him yesterday?" I said, starting for the door. "Perhaps he's gone back there for some reason."

"No—"

She said it so sharply that I turned immediately; one of her hands reached out to me, the other worried the neckline of her knitted cardigan against her fragile skin.

"What I mean is"—her outstretched arm dropped to her side— "how kind it is of you to offer, but that it's unnecessary. Percy's on the telephone right now, calling Mrs. Bird's nephew so that he might come around and help us search . . . I'm sorry. I'm not being very clear. Forgive me, but I'm rather flummoxed, only"—she glanced beyond me, at the door—"I had hoped that I might catch you like this."

"You had?"

She pressed her lips together, and I saw that she wasn't merely worried for Bruno's safety, she was nervous about something else. "Percy will be along in a minute," she said softly. "She's going to take you to see the notebooks, just as she promised—but before she comes, before you go with her, there's something I need to explain."

Saffy looked so serious then, so vexed, that I went to her, placed a hand on the side of her birdlike shoulder. "Here," I said, leading her to the sofa, "come and sit down. Is there something I can get for you? A cup of tea while we wait?"

Her smile was lit with the gratitude of a person unused to being the recipient of kindness. "Bless you, but no. There isn't time. Sit with me, please."

A shadow shifted by the doorway and she stiffened slightly, listening. There was nothing but silence. Silence and the odd corporeal noises to which I was growing accustomed: the gurgle of something behind the pretty ceiling cornice, the gentle breathing of the shutters against the windowpane, the grinding of the house's bones.

"I feel I must explain," she said in an undertone, "about Percy, about yesterday. When you asked about Juniper, when you mentioned *him,* and Percy was such a tyrant."

"You really don't need to explain."

"But I do, I must, only it isn't easy to find a private moment"— a grim smile—"such an enormous house and yet one is never really alone."

Her nervousness was contagious, and although I was doing nothing wrong, a strange feeling came over me. My heart had started to race and I matched her subdued voice. "Is there somewhere else we could meet? The village perhaps?"

"No." She said it quickly, shook her head. "No. I couldn't do that. It isn't possible." Another glance at the empty doorway and she said, "It's best if we speak here."

I nodded agreement and waited as she gathered her thoughts carefully, like a person collecting scattered pins. When she had them together, she told her story quickly, in a low, determined voice. "It was a terrible thing," she said. "A terrible, terrible thing. Over fifty years ago now, yet I remember the evening as if it were yesterday. Juniper's face as she came through the door that night. She was late, she'd lost her key, so she knocked and we answered and in she came, dancing across the threshold—she never walked, not like an ordinary person—and her face—I'll never stop seeing it when I close my eyes at night. That instant. It was such a relief to see her. A terrible storm had blown up during the afternoon, you see. It was raining and the wind was howling, the buses were running late . . . We'd been so worried.

"We thought it was him when we heard the knock. I was nervous about that, too; worried about Juniper, nervous about meeting him. I'd guessed, you see, that they were in love, that they planned to marry. She hadn't told Percy—Percy, like Daddy, had rather fixed opinions about such things—but Juniper and I were always very close. And I desperately wanted to like him; I wanted him to be worthy of her love. I was curious, too, on that count: Juniper's love was not easily won.

"We sat together for a time in the good parlor. We talked at first, of trivial things, Juniper's life in London, and we told each other that he'd been held up on the bus, that transport was the culprit, the war was to blame, but at some point we stopped." She glanced sideways at me and memory shadowed her eyes. "The wind was blowing, the rain was hammering against the shutters, and the dinner was spoiling in the oven . . . the smell of rabbit"—her face turned at the thought—"it was everywhere. I've never been able to stomach it since. It tastes like fear to me. Lumps of horrid, charred fear . . . I was so frightened, seeing Juniper like that. It was all we could do to stop her from running out into the storm, searching for him. Even when midnight passed and it was clear he wasn't coming, she wouldn't give up. She became hysterical, we had to use Daddy's old sleeping pills to calm her—"

Saffy broke off; she'd been speaking very quickly, trying to get her story told before Percy arrived, and her voice had dwindled. She coughed against a delicate lace handkerchief she'd pulled from her sleeve. There was a jug of water on the table near Juniper's chair and I poured her some. "It must have been awful," I said, handing her the glass.

She sipped gratefully, then cradled the glass in both hands on her lap. Her nerves were stretched taut it seemed; the skin around her jaw appeared to have contracted during the telling and I could see the blue veins beneath.

"And he never came?" I prompted.

"No."

"And you never knew why? There was no letter? No telephone call?"

"Nothing."

"And Juniper?"

"She waited and waited. She waits still. Days went by, then weeks. She never gave up hope. It was dreadful. Dreadful." The last word Saffy allowed to hang between us. She was lost in that time, all those years ago, and I didn't probe further.

"Madness isn't sudden," she said eventually. "It sounds so simple—'she fell into madness'—but it isn't like that. It was gradual. First she withdrew. She showed signs of recovery, she talked about going back to London, but only vaguely, and she never went. She stopped writing, too; that's when I knew that something fragile, something precious, had been broken. Then one day she threw everything out of the attic window. All of it: books, papers, a desk, even the mattress . . ." She trailed off and her lips moved silently around things she thought better of adding. With a sigh, she said, "The papers blew far and wide, down the hillsides, into the lake, like discarded leaves, their season ended. Where did they all go, I wonder?"

I shook my head: she was asking the whereabouts of more than papers, I knew, and there was nothing I could think to say. I couldn't imagine how difficult it must have been to see a beloved sibling regress in such a way, to watch countless layers of potential and personality, talent and possibility, disintegrate, one by one. How hard it must have been to witness, especially for someone like Saffy, who, according to Marilyn Bird, had been more like a mother to Juniper than a sister.

"The furniture remained in a broken heap on the lawn. We none of us had the heart to carry it back upstairs, and Juniper didn't want it. She took to sitting by the cupboard in the attic, the one with the hidden doorway, convinced that she could hear things on the other side. Voices calling to her, though of course they were in her head. The poor love. The doctor wanted to send her away when he heard that, to an *asylum* . . ." Her voice caught on the ghastly word, her eyes implored me to find in it the same horror she did. She'd started kneading the white handkerchief with a balled hand, and I reached out to touch her forearm very gently.

"I'm so sorry," I said.

She was trembling with anger, with distress. "We wouldn't hear a word of it; *I* wouldn't hear a word of it. There was no way I was letting him take her from me. Percy spoke to the doctor, explained that such things were not done at Milderhurst Castle, that the Blythe family looked after its own. Eventually he agreed—Percy can be very persuasive—but he insisted on leaving stronger medicine for Juniper." She pressed the painted fingernails of her hand against her legs, like a cat, releasing tension, and I saw in the set of her features something I hadn't noticed before. She was the softer twin, the submissive twin, but there was strength there, too. When it came to Juniper, when it came to fighting for the little sister whom she loved, Saffy Blythe was rock hard. Her next words shot like steam from a kettle, so hot they scalded: "Would that she'd never gone to London, never met that fellow. The greatest regret of my life is that she went away. Everything was ruined afterwards. Nothing was ever the same; not for any of us."

And that's when I began to glimpse her purpose in telling me this story, why she thought it might help to explain Percy's brusqueness; the night Thomas Cavill failed to arrive had been life-altering for all of them. "Percy," I said, and Saffy gave a slight nod. "Percy was different afterwards?"

There came a noise then in the corridor, the deliberate gait, the unmistakable beating of Percy's cane, as if she'd heard her name, intuited somehow that she was the subject of an illicit conversation.

Saffy used the arm of the sofa to push herself to standing. "Edith has just arrived," she said quickly as Percy appeared at the door. She gestured towards me with the hand that held her handkerchief. "I was telling her about poor Bruno."

Percy looked between us: from me, still seated on the sofa, to Saffy, standing right beside me.

"Did you reach the young man?" Saffy pressed on, her voice wavering a little.

A short nod. "He's on his way. I'm going to meet him at the front door, give him some idea of where to look."

"Yes," said Saffy, "good. Good."

"Then I'll take Miss Burchill downstairs." She met my unspoken query. "The muniment room. As promised."

I smiled, but instead of continuing the search for Bruno, as I'd expected, Percy walked into the parlor and went to stand by the window. She made a show of scrutinizing its wooden frame, scratching at a mark on the glass, leaning closer, but it was apparent that the impromptu inspection was a ruse so she might remain in the room with us. I realized then that Saffy had been right. For some reason Percy Blythe didn't want me to be alone with her twin, and I returned to my suspicion of the day before—that Percy was worried Saffy might tell me something she shouldn't. The control Percy wielded over her sisters was astonishing; it intrigued me, it caused a small voice inside my head to urge prudence, but more than anything it made me greedy to hear the conclusion of Saffy's story.

451

The five or so minutes that followed, in which Saffy and I made small talk about the weather, and Percy continued to glare at the glass and prod at the dusty sill, were among the longest I'd experienced. At last, relief, as the sound of a car motor came closer. We all gave up our performances, falling instead into stillness and silence.

The motor grew very near and stopped. A heavy clunk as the car door closed. Percy exhaled. "That will be Nathan."

"Yes," said Saffy.

"I'll be back in five minutes."

And then, finally, she left. Saffy waited, and only when the footsteps had receded completely did she sigh, once, shortly, and swivel in her seat to face me. She smiled, and in it I read apology and discomfort. When she picked up the thread of her story, there was a new determination to her voice. "Perhaps you can tell," she began, "Percy is the strongest of us. She's always seen herself as a protector, even when we were girls. For the most part I've been glad. A champion can be a very fortunate thing to have."

I couldn't help but notice the way her fingers were moving against one another, the way she continued to glance towards the doorway. "Not always, though," I said.

"No. Not always. Not for me, and not for her either. The attribute has been a great burden in her life, not least after Juniper was . . . after it happened. We both took it hard; Juniper was our baby sister, is still our baby sister, and to see her like that"—her head was shaking as she spoke—"it was unspeakably difficult. But Percy"—Saffy's gaze picked at the space above my head, as if she might find there the words she sought to explain—"Percy was in such a black mood afterwards. She'd been crotchety in the lead-up—my twin was one of those women who found purpose during the war, and when the bombs stopped falling, when Hitler turned his sights on Russia, she was rather disappointed—but after that evening, it was different. She took the young man's desertion of Juniper personally."

This was a curious turn. "Why would that have been?"

"It was strange, almost as if she felt responsible in some way. She wasn't, of course, and there was nothing she could have done that would have made things turn out differently. But that's Percy: she blamed herself because that's what Percy does. One of us was hurt and there was nothing she could do to fix it." She sighed, folding her handkerchief over and over to form a small, neat triangle. "And I suppose that's why I'm telling you all this, though I fear I'm doing it all wrong. I want you to understand that Percy's a good person, that despite the way she is, the way she comes across, she has a good heart."

It was important to Saffy, I could tell, that I should not think poorly of her twin, so I returned the smile she'd given me. But she was right—there was something about her story that didn't make sense. "Why, though?" I said. "Why would she have felt responsible? Did she know him? Had she met him before?"

"No, never." She looked at me searchingly. "He lived in London; that's where he and Juniper met. Percy hadn't been to London since before the war."

I was nodding, but I was thinking, too, about my mum's journal, the entry she'd made in which she mentioned that her teacher, Thomas Cavill, had come to visit her at Milderhurst in September 1939. That was the first time Juniper Blythe had met the man she would one day fall in love with. Percy might not have been to London, but there was every possibility that she'd met Thomas Cavill while he was here, in Kent. Though Saffy, it was evident, had not.

A cool gust crept into the room and Saffy pulled her cardigan closer. I noticed that the skin across her collarbone had reddened, she was flushed; she regretted saying as much as she had, and she moved quickly now to sweep her indiscreet comments back beneath the rug. "My point is only that Percy took it very hard, that it changed her. I was glad when the Germans started with the doodlebugs and V2s because it gave her something new to worry about." Saffy laughed, but it had a hollow ring. "She'd have been happiest, I sometimes think, had the war continued indefinitely."

She was uncomfortable and I felt bad for her; sorry, too, that it was my probing that had caused her this new worry. She'd only meant to assuage any bruised feelings I'd suffered the day before and it seemed cruel to saddle her with a new social anxiety. I smiled and tried to change the subject. "And what about you? Did you work during the war?"

She cheered up a little. "Oh, we all did our bit; I didn't do anything as exciting as Percy, of course. She's the better suited to heroics. I sewed and cooked and made do; knitted a thousand socks. Though not particularly well in some cases." She was poking fun at herself and I smiled with her, an image coming to mind of a young girl shivering in the castle's attic, shrunken socks layering both ankles and the hand that didn't hold her pen. "I almost spent it employed as a governess, you know."

"Really?"

"Yes. A family of children who went to America for the duration. I received the offer of employment but had to turn it down."

"Because of the war?"

"No. The letter arrived at the same time as Juniper's great disappointment. Now, don't you look like that. No need for a long face on my account. I don't believe in regrets, not generally, there's not much point, is there? I couldn't have taken it, not then. Not when it took me so far away, not with Juniper. How could I have left her?"

I didn't have siblings; I wasn't sure how these things worked. "Percy couldn't have—?"

"Percy has many gifts, but caring for children and invalids has never been among them. It takes a certain"—her fingertips fussed, and she searched the antique fire screen as if the words she sought might be written there—"softness, I suppose. No. I couldn't have left Juniper with only Percy to care for her. So I wrote a letter, turning the position down."

"It must have been very difficult."

"One doesn't have a choice when it comes to family. Juniper was my baby sister. I wasn't about to leave her, not like that. And besides, even if the fellow had come as he was supposed to, if they'd married and moved away, I probably wouldn't have been able to leave anyway."

"Why not?"

She turned her elegant neck, didn't meet my eye.

A noise in the corridor, just as before, a muffled cough and the sharp beat of a cane coming towards us.

"Percy . . ." And in the moment before she smiled I glimpsed the answer to my question. I saw in her pained expression a lifetime of entrapment. They were twins, two halves of a whole, but where one had longed for escape, to lead a single existence, the other had refused to be left alone. And Saffy, whose softness made her weak, whose compassion made her kind, had been unable ever to wrest herself free.

THE MUNIMENT ROOM AND A DISCOVERY

I followed Percy Blythe along corridors and down sets of stairs into the increasingly dim depths of the castle. Never chatty, that morning she was resolutely stony. Stony and coated with stale cigarette smoke; the smell was so strong I had to leave a pace between us as we walked. The silence suited me, at any rate; after my conversation with Saffy, I was in no mood for awkward chatter. Something in her story, or perhaps not in the story itself so much as the fact that she'd told it to me, was disquieting. She'd said it was an attempt to explain Percy's manner, and I could well believe that both the twins had been shattered by Juniper's abandonment and subsequent collapse, but why had Saffy been so adamant that it was harder for Percy? Especially when Saffy herself had taken on the maternal role with her wounded little sister. She'd been embarrassed by Percy's discourtesy the day before, I knew, and she'd sought to show her twin's human face; yet it was almost as if she protested too much, was *too* determined that I should see Percy Blythe in a saintly light.

Percy stopped at a juncture of corridors and took a packet of cigarettes from her pocket. Gristly knuckles balled as she fidgeted with a match, finally bringing it to life; in the flame's light I glimpsed her face and I saw there proof that she was shaken by the morning's events. As the sweet, smoky smell of fresh tobacco mushroomed around us, and the silence deepened, I said, "I'm really sorry about Bruno. I'm sure Mrs. Bird's nephew will find him."

"Are you?" Percy exhaled and her eyes scanned mine without kindness. A twitch on one side of her lip. "Animals know when their end is coming, Miss Burchill. They do not wish to be a burden. They are not like human beings, seeking always to be comforted." She inclined her head, indicating that I should follow her around the corner, and I felt foolish and small and resolved to offer no further words of sympathy.

We stopped again at the first door we came to. One of the many we'd passed during the tour all those months ago. Cigarette resting on her lip, she pulled from her pocket a large key and rattled it in the lock. After a moment's difficulty, the old mechanism turned and the door creaked open. It was dark inside, there were no windows, and from what I could make out the walls were lined with heavy wooden filing cabinets, the sort you might find in very, very old legal firms in the City. A single lightbulb hung from a fine, frail wire, drifting a little back and forth in the new breath of air from the open door.

I waited for Percy to lead the way, and when she didn't I looked at her, uncertain. She drew on her cigarette and said only, "I don't go in there."

Perhaps my surprise showed, for she added, with a tremor so slight I almost missed it, "I don't enjoy small spaces. There's a paraffin lamp around that corner. Pull it out and I'll light it for you."

I glanced back into the room's dark depths. "Does the lightbulb not work?"

She regarded me a moment, then pulled a string and the bulb flared then dulled, settling at a low level, so that the shadows shifted. The light penetrated only far enough to illuminate a patch three feet in diameter. "I'd suggest you take the lamp too."

I smiled grimly and found it easily enough, tucked around the corner just as she'd said it would be. There was a sloshing sound as I retrieved it, at which Percy Blythe said, "That's promising. Not much good without paraffin inside." As I held the base, she removed the glass flue, fiddled with a coin-sized dial to lengthen the fabric wick before lighting it. "I've never enjoyed the smell," she said, restoring the flue. "It signals bomb shelters to me; ghastly places. Filled with fear and helplessness."

"And safety, I'd have thought. Comfort?"

"Perhaps for some, Miss Burchill."

She said no more, and I found occupation familiarizing myself with the thin metal handle at the top, testing it to make sure it would hold the lamp's weight.

"No one's been inside for an age," said Percy Blythe. "There's a desk at the back. You'll find the notebooks in boxes beneath. I wouldn't imagine that they're in good order: Daddy died during the war, there were other things to contend with. No one had much time for filing." She said it defensively, as if I might be about to take her to task for slovenly housekeeping.

"Of course."

A flicker of doubt crossed her face but dissolved when she coughed heavily into her hand. "Well then," she said, once recovered. "I'll be back in an hour."

I nodded, keen suddenly that she might stick around just a little longer. "Thank you," I said, "I'm really very grateful for the opportunity—"

"Be careful with the door. Don't let it close behind you."

"Okay."

"It's self-locking. We lost a dog that way." Her lips distorted, a grimace that didn't quite become a smile. "I'm an old lady, you know. I can't be relied upon to remember where I left you."

THE ROOM was long and thin, and low brick arches spanned the width, holding up the ceiling. I clutched the lamp tightly, lifting it out ahead of me so that light flickered against the walls as I took slow, cautious steps deeper inside. Percy had told the truth when she said that no one had been inside for a long time. The room bore an unmistakable signature of stillness. There was silence, too, church silence; and I had the uncanny sense that something greater than me was watching.

You're being fanciful, I told myself sternly. *There is no one here but you and the walls.* But that was half my problem. These weren't just any walls, these were the stones of Milderhurst Castle, beneath whose skin the distant hours were whispering, watching. The further into the room I went, the more aware I was of a strange, heavy feeling. A depth of aloneness—loneliness, almost—cloaking me. It was the dark, of course, my recent interaction with Saffy, Juniper's melancholy story.

But this was my one and only opportunity to see Raymond Blythe's notebooks. I had only a single hour, and then Percy Blythe would be back to collect me. Chances were, I wouldn't be permitted a second visit to the muniment room, so it was as well to pay close attention now. I made a mental checklist as I walked: wooden filing cabinets lining both walls; above them—I lifted the lamp to see—maps and architectural plans of all vintages. A little further along was hung a collection of tiny framed daguerreotypes.

It was a series of portraits, the same woman in each: in one she was reclined along a chaise longue in a state of some deshabille, in the others she was facing the camera directly, Edgar Allan Poe–style, dressed in a high-necked Victorian collar. I leaned closer, brought my lamp high to observe the face within the bronze, blowing once to scatter some of the layered dust. I felt an odd coldness creep up my spine as the face was revealed. She was beautiful, but in a vaguely nightmarish way. Smooth lips; perfect, poreless skin stretched taut along high cheekbones; teeth large and polished. I held the lamp near enough to read the name engraved in cursive writing at the bottom of the picture: *Muriel Blythe*. Raymond's first wife, the twins' mother.

How strange that all her portraits had been relegated to the muniment room. Had it been the result of Raymond Blythe's grief, I wondered, or the jealous decree of his second wife? Whatever the case, and although I can't say what made me so pleased to do it, I shifted the lamp then, casting her back into darkness. There wasn't time to explore each and every hollow of the room. I resolved to find Raymond Blythe's notebooks, absorb as much from them as I could in the hour allotted, then leave behind this strange, stale place. I held the lamp before me and kept on walking.

But then the pictures on the walls gave way to shelves, stretching from floor to ceiling, and despite myself I slowed. It was like being inside a treasure trove; all manner of items had been stacked along them: books—lots of books—vases and Chinese porcelain, and even crystal jugs. Precious things, from what I could tell, not junk or detritus. What they were doing, languishing on shelves in the muniment room, I could not begin to guess.

Beyond them was something interesting enough to make me stop: a collection of forty or fifty boxes, all of the same size, covered in pretty paper—floral for the most part. There were little labels on some of them and I went close enough to read one. *Heart Reclaimed: A Novel by Seraphina Blythe.* I lifted the lid and peeked inside: a stack of paper with typewritten text all over it, a manuscript. I remembered Mum telling me that the Blythes had all been writers, all except Percy. I held the lamp higher so that I could take in the entire collection of boxes, smiling in wonder. These were Saffy's stories. She was so prolific. It oppressed me, in some way, to see them all huddled down here together: stories and dreams, people and places invested at one time with great energy and industry, only to be left in the dark over years to turn back into dust. Another label read MARRIAGE TO MATTHEW DE COURCY. The publisher in me couldn't help it; I lifted the lid and pulled the papers from inside. This one didn't contain a manuscript, though; it was a collection of assorted papers—research, I supposed. Old sketches—wedding dresses, floral arrangements—newspaper clippings describing various society weddings, scribbled notes as to orders of service, and then, further down, a 1924 notice of the engagement of Seraphina Grace Blythe and Matthew John de Courcy.

I set the papers down. This was research, but not for a novel. This box contained the planning for Saffy's own wedding that never was. I put the lid back on and stepped away, guilty suddenly for my intrusion. It struck me then that every item in this room was the remnant of a bigger story, the lamps, the vases, the books, Saffy's floral boxes. The muniment room was a tomb, just like those in ancient times. A pharaoh's dark, cool tomb where precious things went to be forgotten.

By the time I reached the table at the very end, I felt as if I'd walked a marathon through Alice's Wonderland. It was a surprise, then, when I turned around, to see that the swaying lightbulb, the door—carefully propped open with a wooden box—was only forty-five feet or so behind me. I found the notebooks just where Percy had said they'd be and, just as she'd said, piled into boxes, as if someone had walked along Raymond Blythe's study shelves and desk, swept everything in together, then left them here. I understood that there were other concerns during the war; nonetheless, it seemed odd that neither of the twins had found time to return in the decades since. Raymond Blythe's notebooks, his journals and letters, deserved to be on display in a library somewhere, protected and valued, available for scholars to access for many years to come. Percy, in particular, I'd have thought, with her keen eye to posterity, would have sought to protect her father's legacy.

I set my lamp at the back of the desk, far enough away so that I wouldn't accidentally knock it, and slid the boxes from beneath the table, lifting them one by one onto the chair and rummaging until I found the journals spanning 1916 to 1920. Raymond Blythe had helpfully labeled each with the year, and it didn't take long before I had 1917 spread out before me. I took my notebook from my bag and began jotting down anything I could think of that might be helpful for the article. Every so often I paused, just so that I could appreciate again that these were actually his journals, that this looping script, these ideas and sentiments, had originated with the great man himself.

Can I possibly convey here, with only words at my disposal, the incredible moment when I turned that fateful page and sensed a shift in the scrawl beneath my fingers? The handwriting was heavier, more purposeful; the script looked to have been written faster: lines and lines, filling each page, and when I bent closer, began to decipher the rough scrawl, I realized, with a thrill that started deep inside my heart, that this was the first draft of the *Mud Man*. Seventy-five years later, I was witnessing the birth of a classic.

Page after page I turned, scanning the text, devouring it, delighting in the small changes as I compared what was written with my memories of the published text. At length, I reached the end, and although I knew I shouldn't, I laid my open palm across the final page, closed my eyes, and focused on the pen marks beneath my skin.

And that was when I felt it: the small ridge running down the side of the page, about an inch from the outer margin. Something had been tucked between the journal's leather cover and its final page. I turned it over, and there it was, a stiff piece of paper with scalloped serrations around the rim, the sort found in an expensive correspondence set. It had been folded in half.

Was there ever any chance I wasn't going to open it? I doubt it. I didn't have a very good track record with leaving letters unread, and the moment I saw it something began to caper beneath my skin. I felt eyes upon me, eyes in the dark, urging me to look inside.

It was neatly handwritten but faded, and I had to hold it close to the lamp to make out the words. It picked up midsentence, a single sheet in a longer letter:

> . . . *don't need me to tell you that it's a wonderful story. Never before has your writing taken the reader on such a vivid journey. The writing is rich and the tale itself captures, with an almost eerie prescience, Man's eternal quest to shed the past and move beyond old, regrettable actions. The girl, Jane, is a particularly moving creature, her situation on the verge of adulthood perfectly rendered.*
>
> *I couldn't help noticing, however, as I read the manuscript, deep similarities to another story with which we're both familiar. For that reason, and knowing you to be a fair and a kind man, I must beseech you, as much for your own sake as for the other, not to publish* The True History of the Mud Man. *You know as well as I do that it is not your story to tell. It is not too late to withdraw the manuscript. I fear that if you do not, the consequences will be of a most distressing*

I turned it over but there was nothing further. I searched the notebook for the rest. Flicked back through the pages, even held it by the spine and shook it very carefully. Nothing.

But what could it mean? Which similarities? Which other story? What consequences? And who had seen fit to deliver such a warning?

A shuffling in the corridor. I sat stone-still, listening. Someone was coming. My heart hammered in my chest; the letter shook between my fingertips.

A split second of indecision, then I stuffed it inside my notebook and pressed the cover flat. I glanced over my shoulder in time to see Percy Blythe and her cane silhouetted in the doorway.

A LONG WAY TO FALL

How I made it back to the farmhouse I cannot tell you; I don't remember a second of the walk. Presumably I managed to say farewell to Saffy and Percy, then stumble back down the hill without doing myself bodily harm. I was in a daze, completely unaware of anything that took place between leaving the castle and arriving back at my room; I couldn't stop thinking about the contents of the letter, the letter I had stolen. I needed to speak to someone immediately. If I were reading its contents correctly—and the wording wasn't especially complicated—someone had accused Raymond Blythe of plagiarism. Who was this mystery person, and to which earlier story were they referring? Whoever it was had specified having read Raymond Blythe's manuscript, which meant that they'd read the story and written the letter before the book was published in 1918; that fact narrowed the possibilities but was still no real help. I didn't have a clue as to whom the manuscript might have been sent to. Well, I had a clue: I work in publishing, I knew it would have been read by editors, proofreaders, a few trusted friends. But those were general terms; I needed names, dates, specifics before I could ascertain how seriously I should take the letter's claims. For if they were true, if Raymond Blythe had misappropriated the story of the Mud Man, the ramifications were enormous.

It was the sort of discovery scholars and historians—convalescent fathers in Barnes—dreamed of, a career-making scoop, yet all I felt was nauseated. I didn't want it to be true, I longed for it to be some sort of joke, a misunderstanding even. My own past, my love of books and reading, was inextricably linked with Raymond Blythe's *Mud Man*. To accept that it had never been his story, that he had pinched it from somewhere else, that it didn't have its roots in the fertile soil of Milderhurst Castle, was not only the breaking apart of a literary legend, it was a brutal, personal blow.

Be that as it may, I *had* found the letter, and I *was* being paid to write about Raymond Blythe's composition, specifically the origins, of the *Mud Man*. I couldn't just ignore a claim of plagiarism because I didn't like it. Particularly when it seemed to explain so much of Raymond Blythe's reticence about discussing his inspiration.

I needed help, and I knew just the person to give it to me. Back at the farmhouse, I avoided Mrs. Bird and made a beeline for my room. I'd picked up the telephone receiver before I'd even sat down. My fingers tripped over themselves in their rush to dial Herbert's number.

The phone rang out.

"No!" I grouched at the receiver. It stared back blankly.

I waited impatiently, then tried again, listened and listened to the faraway lonely ring. I chewed my nails and read my notes and tried again, with no more satisfaction. I even considered calling my dad, stopped only by fears of what the excitement might do to his heart. And that's when my gaze fell upon Adam Gilbert's name on the original interview transcript.

I dialed, I waited; no answer. I tried again.

The click of someone picking up. "Hello, Mrs. Button speaking."

I could have wept with joy. "This is Edith Burchill. I'm ringing to speak with Adam Gilbert."

"I'm sorry, Miss Burchill. Mr. Gilbert's gone up to London for a hospital appointment."

"Oh." A trembly deflation rather than a word.

"He's due back in the next day or two. I could leave a message and have him telephone you when he returns at the end of the week, if you'd like?"

"No," I said; it was too late, I needed help now—and yet, it was better than nothing. "Yes, all right. Thank you. If you could let him know that it's rather important. That I think I might have stumbled on something related to the mystery we were discussing recently."

I spent the rest of the evening staring at the letter, scribbling indecipherable patterns in my notebook, and dialing Herbert's number, listening to the phantom voices trapped inside that empty phone line. At eleven o'clock I accepted finally that it was too late to continue stalking Herbert's empty house, that, for now at any rate, I was alone with my problem.

As I headed for the castle next morning, exhausted and bleary-eyed, I felt as if I'd spent the night tumbling through the wash. I had the letter concealed within the inside pocket of my jacket and I kept slipping my hand in to check it was still there; I can't explain why exactly, but as I left my room I'd been compelled to retrieve it, to tuck it away safely and carry it on my person. To leave the letter behind on the desk was unthinkable, somehow. It wasn't a rational decision; it wasn't through fear that someone else might happen upon it during the day. It was a strange and burning conviction that the letter belonged with me, that it had presented itself to me, that we were attached in some way now and I had been entrusted with unraveling its secrets.

When I arrived Percy Blythe was waiting for me, pretending to pull weeds from a plant pot by the entrance stairs. I saw her before she noticed me, which is how I know she was pretending. Right up until the moment some creeping sixth sense made her aware of my presence, she'd been standing upright, leaning against the stone of the stairs, arms wrapped across her middle, attention fixed on something in the distance. She'd been so still, so pale, that she'd looked like a statue. Though not the sort of statue most people would choose to stand in front of their house.

"Any sign of Bruno?" I called, wondering at my ability to sound normal.

She made a small performance of surprise at my arrival and I rubbed her fingers together so that tiny pieces of dirt sifted to the ground. "I don't hold out high hopes. Not with the cold come in as it has." She waited for me to reach her, then, extending her arm, invited me to follow. "Come."

It was no warmer inside the castle than out. Indeed, the stones seemed somehow to trap the cold air, making the whole place grayer, darker, more bleak than before.

I expected that we would follow the usual corridor towards the yellow parlor, but Percy led me instead to a small hidden doorway, tucked behind an alcove within the entrance hall.

"The tower," she said.

"Oh."

"For your article."

I nodded, and then, because she'd started up the narrow, winding staircase, I began to follow.

With each step, my sense of unease grew. It was true what she had said—seeing the tower was important for my article—and yet there was something indefinably strange in Percy Blythe suggesting that she should show it to me. She'd been so reticent thus far, so reluctant that I should speak to her sisters or see her father's notebooks. To find her waiting for me this morning, outside in the cold, for her to propose showing me the tower room without my having to ask first—well, it was unexpected, and I am not made comfortable by unexpected things.

I told myself I was reading too much into it: Percy Blythe had selected me for the task of writing about her father, and she was nothing if not proud of her castle. Perhaps it was as simple as that. Or perhaps she'd decided that the sooner I saw what I needed to, the sooner I'd be on my way and they would be left once more to their own devices. But no matter how much sense I made, the niggling had started. Was there any way, I wondered, that she knew what I had found?

We'd reached a small platform of uneven stone; a narrow archer's window had been cut into the dusky wall and I was able to glimpse through it a thick sweep of Cardarker Wood, so glorious when seen in full, yet ominous somehow in section.

Percy Blythe pushed open the narrow round-topped door. "The tower room."

Once again, she stepped aside so that I might go first. I went gingerly, stopping in the center of the small, circular room on a faded rug of sooty shades. The first thing I noticed was that the fire had been freshly set, in preparedness for our visit, I supposed.

"There," she said, closing the door behind us. "Now we are alone."

Which set my heart to racing, though why precisely I could not say. My fear made little sense. She was an old lady, a frail old lady who'd just employed what scant energy she had in climbing the stairs. If the two of us were to engage in a physical tussle, I was pretty sure I'd hold my own. And yet . . . There was something in the way her eyes still shone, a spirit that was stronger than her body. And all I could think was that it was an awfully long drop from here to the ground and that a lot of people already had died plummeting from that window right there . . .

Happily, Percy Blythe was unable to read my mind and see written there the sorts of horrors that belonged only in melodramatic fiction. She rolled a wrist slightly and said, "This is it. This is where he worked."

And hearing her say it, I was able finally to creep out from beneath my own clouded thoughts and appreciate that I was standing in the middle of Raymond Blythe's tower. These bookshelves, built to mold against the curving walls, were where he'd kept his favorites; the fireplace had been that by which he'd sat, day and evening, working on his books. My fingers ran along the very desk at which he'd written the *Mud Man*.

The letter whispered against my skin. *If indeed he wrote the book himself.*

"There's a room," said Percy Blythe as she struck a match and set the fire burning, "behind the tiny door in the entrance hall. Four stories below, but right beneath the tower. We used to sit there sometimes, Saffy and I. When we were young. When Daddy was working." It was a rare moment of expansiveness, and I couldn't help but watch her as she spoke. She was tiny, thin and wan, and yet there was something deep inside Percy Blythe, a strength—of character perhaps?—that drew one like a moth. As if sensing my interest, she withdrew her light, that twist of a smile breezed across her face, and she straightened. Nodded at me as she tossed the spent matchstick into the flames. "Please yourself," was all she said. "Have a look around."

"Thank you."

"Don't go too near the window, though. It's a long way to fall."

Giving her what little smile I could manage, I began to take in the details of the room. The shelves were quite empty now; most of their former contents, I supposed, were lining the walls of the muniment room; but there were still framed pictures on the wall. One in particular caught my eye. It was an image with which I was familiar: Goya's *Sleep of Reason*. I paused before it, taking in the foreground human figure, slumped—in despair it seemed—over his writing desk, while a host of batlike monsters flurried above, arising from and feeding on his sleeping mind.

"That was my father's," said Percy. Her voice made me jump, but I didn't turn, and when I looked again at the picture my perception had changed, so that I saw my own shadowy reflection, and hers behind me, in the glass. "It used to frighten us terribly."

"I can understand why."

"Daddy said to fear was foolish. That we'd do better to draw a lesson."

"Which lesson was that?" I turned now to face her.

She touched the chair by the window.

"Oh no, I"—another weak smile—"I'm happy to stand."

Percy blinked slowly and I thought for a moment that she might insist. She didn't, though, saying only, "The lesson, Miss Burchill, was that when reason sleeps, the monsters of repression will emerge."

My hands were clammy and a spreading heat was climbing up my arms. But surely she had not read my mind. She couldn't possibly know the monstrous things I'd been imagining since I found the letter, my morbid fantasies of being pushed from the window.

"Goya anticipated Freud by some time, in that respect."

I smiled somewhat sickly, and then the fever hit my cheeks and I knew that I could stand the suspense, the subterfuge, no longer. I was not formed for games like these. If Percy Blythe knew what I had found in the muniment room, if she knew that I had taken it with me and that I was bound to investigate further; if this was all an elaborate ploy to have me admit to my deception, and for her to try, by whatever means she could, to prevent me from exposing her father's lie, then I was ready. What was more, I was going to strike the first blow. "Miss Blythe," I said, "I found something yesterday. In the muniment room."

A dreadful look came over her, a leaching of color that was instant and absolute. As quickly as it had appeared she managed to conceal it again. She blinked. "Well? I'm afraid I'm not going to be able to guess, Miss Burchill. You're going to have to tell me what it was."

I reached into my jacket and retrieved the letter, tried to steady my fingers as I handed it to her. I watched as she dug reading glasses from her pocket, held them before her eyes, and scanned the page. Time slowed interminably. She shifted her fingertips lightly over its surface. "Yes," she said, "I see." She seemed almost relieved, as if my discovery was not what she'd feared.

I waited for her to continue, and when it was clear she had no intention of doing so, I said, "I'm rather worried—" It was, without doubt, the most difficult conversation I'd ever had to initiate. "If there's any question, you see, that the *Mud Man* was—" I couldn't bring myself to say *stolen*. "If there's any chance at all that your father might have read it elsewhere first"—I swallowed; the room was swimming a little before my eyes—"as this letter seems to suggest, the publishers will need to know."

She was folding the letter very carefully and crisply, and only when she'd finished did she say, "Let me set your mind at ease, Miss Burchill. My father wrote every word of that book."

"But the letter—are you sure?" I had made a huge mistake in telling her. What had I expected her to do? Speak honestly with me? Give me her blessing while I made inquiries that stood to strip her father of his literary credibility? It was natural, of course, for his daughter to support him, especially a daughter like Percy.

"I am very sure, Miss Burchill," she said, meeting my gaze. "It was I who wrote that letter."

"*You* wrote it?"

A curt nod.

"But why? Why did you write such a thing?" Especially if it was true that every word was his.

There was fresh color in her cheeks and her eyes were bright, her energy much improved, almost as if she were feeding in some way on my confusion. Enjoying it. She looked at me slyly, a look to which I was becoming accustomed, a look that suggested she had something more to tell me than what I'd thought to ask. "There comes a time in the lives of all children, I expect, when the shutters are lifted and they become aware that their parents are not immune to the worst of human frailties. That they are not invincible. That sometimes they will do things to suit themselves, to feed their own monsters. We are a selfish species by nature, Miss Burchill."

My thoughts were swimming in a deep and clouded soup. I wasn't quite sure how one thing related to the other, but assumed it must have something to do with the distressing consequences that her letter had prophesied. "But the letter—"

"That letter is nothing," she snapped with a wave of her hand. "Not anymore. It's an irrelevance." She glanced at it briefly and her face seemed to flicker like a projection screen, a film running backwards across seventy-five years. In a single sudden motion she tossed it onto the fire, where it sizzled and burned and made her flinch. "As it happens, I was wrong. It *was* his story to tell." She smiled then, wryly, a little biliously. "Even if he didn't know it at the time."

I was utterly confused. How could he not know that it was his story, and how could she have thought it otherwise? It made no sense.

"I knew a girl once, in the war." Percy Blythe had gone to sit on the chair behind her father's desk and she leaned back into the chair's arms as she continued. "She worked in the cabinet rooms, met Churchill a number of times in the corridors. There was a sign they had hanging, one that he'd put there. It said, 'Please understand there is no depression in this house, and we are not interested in the possibilities of defeat. They do not exist.'" She sat for a moment, her chin lifted and her eyes slightly narrowed, her own words hanging still around her. Through the wash of smoke, with her neat haircut, her fine features, the silk blouse, she almost looked as if she were back in the Second World War. "What do you think of that?"

I do not do well with these sorts of games; I never have, particularly riddles without even the most tenuous link to the rest of the conversation. I shifted my shoulders miserably.

"Miss Burchill?"

A statistic came to me then, something I'd read or heard once about the way suicide rates plummet during times of war; people are too busy trying to survive to give much thought to how miserable they are. "I think wartime is different," I said, unable to avoid the rising tone that betrayed my discomfort. "I think the rules are different. I imagine depression is probably akin to defeat during war. Maybe that's what Churchill meant."

She nodded, a slow smile playing at her lips. She was making things difficult for me on purpose, and I didn't understand why. I'd come to Kent at her behest, but she wouldn't let me interview her sisters, she wouldn't answer any of my questions directly, she preferred to play cat-and-mouse games in which I was cast always as the quarry. She might just as easily have let Adam Gilbert continue with the project. He'd done his interviews, he needn't have bothered them again. You may take it as an indication of my profound discomfort and frustration that I said then, "Why did you ask me to come, Miss Blythe?"

A single scarlike brow shot up like an arrow. "What's that?"

"Judith Waterman from Pippin Books told me you rang. That you asked specifically for me."

A twitch at the corner of her mouth and she looked straight at me; you don't realize how rare that is until someone actually does it. Stares, unflinchingly, right down deep into your soul. "Sit," she said, just as you might instruct a dog or a disobedient child, and the word was so brittle in her mouth that this time I did not argue; I spotted the nearest chair and did precisely as I was told.

She tapped a cigarette on the desk, then lit it. She drew hard, eyeing me as she exhaled. "There's something different about you," she said, resting her other wrist across her body, leaning back into the chair. All the better to appraise me.

"I'm not sure what you mean."

She squinted then, dissecting, watery eyes looking me up and down with an intensity that made me shiver. "Yes. You're less chirpy than you were before. The last time you came."

I couldn't argue with that, so I didn't. "Yes," I said. My arms were threatening to flail around, so I crossed them. "Sorry about that."

"Don't be," said Percy, lifting her cigarette and her chin. "I like you better this way."

Of course she did. And, happily, before I was faced with the impossibility of formulating a reply, she returned to my initial question: "I asked for you, in the first instance, because my sister wouldn't tolerate an unknown man in the house."

"But Mr. Gilbert had already finished his interviews. There was no need for him to come back to Milderhurst if Juniper didn't like it."

That sly smile reappeared. "You're astute. Good. I had hoped you might be. I wasn't entirely sure after our first meeting and I didn't fancy dealing with an imbecile."

I was torn between "Thank you" and "Sod off" and elected to compromise with a cool smile.

"We don't know many people," she continued on an exhalation, "not anymore. And then when you came to visit, and that Bird woman told me that you worked in publishing. Well, I began to wonder. Then you told me that you hadn't any siblings."

I nodded, trying to follow the logic in her explanation.

"And that's when I decided." She drew again on her cigarette, performed a piece of fussy stage business in retrieving an ashtray. "I knew you wouldn't be biased."

I was feeling less and less astute by the second. "Biased about what?"

"About us."

"Miss Blythe, I'm afraid I don't understand what any of this has to do with the article I've been commissioned to write, with your father's book and your memories of its publication."

She waved her hand impatiently and ash fell to the floor. "Nothing. Nothing. It has nothing at all to do with any of that. It has to do with what I'm going to tell you."

Was that when I felt it, the ominous creeping beneath my skin? Perhaps it was only that a gust of autumn chill came then, blustering beneath the door, angering the lock so that the key fell to the floor. Percy ignored it and I tried to do the same. "With what you're going to tell me?"

"Something that needs to be set right, before it's too late."

"Too late for what?"

"I'm dying." She blinked with customary cold frankness.

"I'm so sorry—"

"I'm old. It happens. Please don't patronize me with unnecessary sympathy." A change came over her face, like clouds scudding across the wintry sky, covering the last of the sun's feeble light. She looked old, tired. And I saw that what she said was true—she was dying. "I was dishonest when I telephoned that woman, that publisher, and asked for you. I regret any inconvenience caused to the other fellow. I've little doubt he'd have done an excellent job. He was nothing if not professional. Nonetheless, it was all I could think to do. I wanted you to come and I didn't know how else to make that happen."

"But why?" There was something new in her manner, an urgency that made my breathing grow shallow. The back of my neck prickled, with cold but with something else, too.

"I have a story. I am the only one who knows it. I am going to tell it to you."

"Why?" It came out little louder than a whisper and I coughed, then asked again. "Why?"

"Because it needs to be told. Because I value accurate records. Because I cannot carry it further." Did I imagine that she glanced then at Goya's monsters?

"But why tell me?"

She blinked. "Because of who you are, of course. Because of who your mother was." The slightest of smiles and I glimpsed that she was taking certain pleasure from our conversation, from the power, perhaps, that she wielded over my ignorance. "It was Juniper who picked it up. She called you Meredith. That's when I realized. And that's when I *knew* you were the one."

The blood drained from my face and I felt as shameful as a child caught telling lies to their teacher. "I'm so sorry I didn't say anything earlier, I only thought—"

"Your reasons don't interest me. We all have secrets."

I caught the rest of my apology before it tumbled from my lips.

"You are Meredith's daughter," she continued, her pace quickening, "which means you are like family. And this is a family story."

It was the last thing I'd expected her to say and I was floored; something inside me beat with glad empathy for my mother, who had loved this place and long believed herself so poorly used. "But what do you want me to do?" I said. "With your story, I mean."

"Do with it?"

"Do you want me to write it down?"

"I shouldn't think so. Not write it down, just set it right. I need to trust you to do that . . ." She pointed a sharp finger but the stern gesture was weakened when the face behind it fell to repose. "Can I trust you, Miss Burchill?"

I nodded, even though her manner gave me grave misgivings as to precisely what it was she asked of me.

She seemed relieved, but her guard dropped only for an instant before she picked it up again. "Well then," she said bluntly, turning her gaze towards the window from which her father had fallen to his death. "I hope you're able to go without lunch. I haven't time to waste."

PERCY BLYTHE'S STORY

PERCY Blythe began with a disclaimer. "I am not a storyteller," she said, striking a match, "not like the others. I only have one tale to tell. Listen carefully; I won't be telling it twice." She lit her cigarette and leaned back in her chair. "I told you that this has nothing to do with the *Mud Man*, but I was wrong. In one way or another, this story begins and ends with that book."

An arm of wind reached down the chimney to tease the flames and I opened my notebook. She'd said it wasn't necessary, but I nursed a strange feeling of disquiet and it soothed me in some way to hide behind the purpose of my creamy black-lined pages.

"My father told us once that art was the only form of immortality. That was the sort of thing he used to say; something, I imagine, that his own mother told him. She was a gifted poet and a great beauty, but she was not a warm woman. She could be cruel. Not intentionally; her talent made her cruel. She gave my father all sorts of odd ideas." Percy's mouth twisted and she paused to smooth the hair at the nape of her neck. "He was wrong, anyway. There is another type of immortality, far less sought or celebrated."

I leaned forward a little, waiting for her to tell me what it was, but she didn't. I would become used to her sudden shifts of topic that stormy afternoon, the way she shone a spotlight on a certain scene, brought it to life only to turn her abrupt attention to another.

"I'm quite sure my parents were happy once," she said, "before we were born, but there are two types of people in this world. Those who enjoy the company of children and those who don't. My father was of the former type. I think he surprised even himself with the force of his affection when Saffy and I were born." She glanced at the Goya painting and a muscle twitched in her neck. "He was a different man when we were young, before the Great War, before he wrote that book. He was an unusual man for his time and class. He adored us, you see—never mere fondness; he delighted in us and we in him. We were spoiled. Not with objects, though there was no shortage of those, but with his attention and his faith. He thought that we could do no wrong and indulged us accordingly. I don't imagine it is ever good for children to find themselves the subject of such idolatry. Would you like a glass of water, Miss Burchill?"

I blinked. "No. No, thank you."

"I will, if you don't mind. My throat—" She set her cigarette in the ashtray and took up a jug from a set of low shelves, filling a cut-glass tumbler. She gulped, and I noticed that despite her clear, flat tone, those piercing eyes, her fingers were shaking. "Did your parents spoil you when you were small, Miss Burchill?"

"No," I said. "No, I don't think they did."

"I don't think they did either. You don't carry the sense of entitlement of a child who's been placed front and center." Her gaze drifted again to the window, where the weather was gathering grayly. "Daddy used to put the two of us in an old baby carriage that had been his when he was small and take us on long walks about the village. When we got older he'd have Cook make up elaborate picnics and the three of us would explore the woods, stroll across the fields, and he would tell us stories, speaking to us about matters that seemed grave and wonderful. That this was our home, that our ancestors' voices would always speak to us, that we could never be alone as long as we were within reach of our castle." A faint smile tried to settle on her lips. "At Oxford, he'd been a great one for languages, the old tongues, and bore a particular fondness for Anglo-Saxon. He used to do translations for his own pleasure, and from a very early age we were allowed to help. Up here in the tower, usually, but sometimes in the gardens. One afternoon we lay together, the three of us on a picnic rug, looking back towards the castle on the hilltop, and he read to us from 'The Wanderer.' It was a perfect day. Those are rare and it's as well to remember them." She paused then, her face relaxing somewhat as she slipped deeper into memory. When finally she spoke again, her voice was reedy. "The Anglo-Saxons had a gift for sadness and longing, and heroics, of course; children, I suspect, are predisposed to all three. *Seledreorig*." The word was like an incantation in the round stone room. "Sadness for the lack of a hall," she said. "There's no word like it in the English language, and yet there ought to be, don't you think? . . . There now. I've drifted off track."

She straightened in her chair, reached for her cigarette only to find it fallen to ash. "The past is like that," she said as she battled another from the pack. "Always waiting to lure you away." She struck the match, drew impatiently, and squinted at me through the haze. "I'll be more careful from here on." The flame extinguished swiftly, as if to underline the intention. "My mother had struggled to have children and when she did she was waylaid with a depression so strong she could barely raise herself from her bed. When she finally recovered, she found that her family were no longer waiting for her. Her children hid behind her husband's legs when she tried to hold them, cried and fought if she came too close. We took to using words from other languages, too, those that Daddy had taught us, so she wouldn't understand. He would laugh and encourage us, delighting in our precocity. How ghastly we must have been. We hardly knew her, you see. We refused to be with her, we only wanted to be with Daddy and he with us, and so she grew lonely."

Lonely. I wasn't certain that a word had ever sounded quite as ominous as that one did on Percy Blythe's lips. I remembered the daguerreotype images of Muriel Blythe I'd seen in the muniment room. I'd thought it odd then that they'd been hung in such a dark, forgotten place; now it seemed positively menacing. "What happened?" I asked.

She looked at me sharply. "All in good time."

An explosion of thunder sounded outside and Percy glanced towards the window. "A storm," she said with disgust. "Just what we need."

"Would you like me to close the window?"

"No, not yet. I enjoy the air." She frowned at the floor as she pulled on her cigarette; she was collecting her thoughts and when she found them she met my eyes. "My mother took a lover. Who could blame her? It was my father who brought them together—not intentionally. This isn't that type of story—he was trying to make amends. He must've known he was ignoring her, and he arranged for extensive improvements to the castle and gardens. Shutters were added to the downstairs windows to remind her of those she'd admired in Europe, and work was carried out on the moat. The digging went on for such a long time, and Saffy and I used to watch from the attic window. The architect's name was Sykes."

"Oliver Sykes."

She was surprised. "Well done, Miss Burchill. I knew you were astute; I didn't suspect you of great powers of intuition."

I shook my head and explained about *Raymond Blythe's Milderhurst*. What I didn't tell her was that I also knew of Raymond Blythe's bequest to the Pembroke Farm Institute. Which meant, of course, that he hadn't known of the affair.

"Daddy didn't know," she said, as if reading my thoughts. "But we did. Children know such things. It never occurred to us to tell him, though. As far as we were concerned, we were his world and he cared as little about Mother's activities as we did." She shifted slightly and her blouse rippled. "I do not hold stock with regrets, Miss Burchill, nonetheless we are all accountable for our actions and I've wondered many times since whether that was the moment when the cards fell ill for the Blythes, even those not yet born. Whether it all might have turned out differently had Saffy and I told him about Mother."

"Why?" Foolish of me to break her train of thought, but I couldn't help myself. "Why would it have been better if you'd told him?" I should have remembered that the stubborn streak in Percy Blythe took interruption hard.

She stood, pressed her palms against the small of her narrow back, and bowed her pelvis forward. Took a last draw on her cigarette stub, then tapped it out in the ashtray and walked stiffly to the window. I could see from where I sat that the sky hung dark and heavy, but her eyes narrowed at the distant glare still quavering on the horizon. "That letter you found," she said as thunder rumbled closer, "I didn't realize Daddy had kept it, but I'm glad he did. It took a lot for me to write it—he was so excited by the manuscript, the story. When Daddy returned from the war he was a shadow of himself. Skinny as a stovepipe with a horrid glassy shallowness to his eyes. We were kept from visiting much of the time—too disruptive, the nurses said—but we sneaked in anyway, through the castle veins. He'd be sitting by this window, looking out yet seeing nothing, and he'd speak of a great absence within him. His mind itched, he said, to be put to creative use, yet when he held a pen nothing came. 'I am empty,' he said, over and over, and he was right. He was. You can imagine, then, the restorative thrill when he began work on the notes that would become the *Mud Man*."

I nodded, remembering the notebooks downstairs, the changed handwriting, heavy with confidence and intent from first line until last.

Lightning struck and Percy Blythe flinched. She waited out the answering thunder. "The words in that book were his, Miss Burchill; it was the idea he stole."

From whom? I wanted to shout, but I bit my tongue this time.

"It pained me to write that letter, to dampen his enthusiasm when the project so sustained him, but I had to." Rain began to fall, an instant sheen. "Soon after Daddy returned from France, I contracted scarlet fever and was sent away to recover. Twins, Miss Blythe, do not do well with solitude."

"It must have been awful—"

"Saffy"—she continued as if she'd forgotten I were there—"was always the more imaginative. We were a balanced pair in that way; illusion and reality were kept in check. Separated, though, we each sharpened to opposing points." She shivered and stepped back from the window; spots of rain were falling on the sill. "My twin suffered terribly with nightmare. The fanciful among us often do." She glanced at me. "You will notice, Miss Burchill, that I did not say night*mares*. There was only ever one."

The glowering storm outside had swallowed the day's last light and the tower room fell to darkness. Only the fire's orange flicker provided jagged relief. Percy returned to the desk and switched on its lamp. Light shone greenly through the colored glass shade, casting dark shadows beneath her eyes. "She'd been dreaming about him since she was four years old. She would wake in the night screaming, bathed in sweat, convinced that a man coated in mud had climbed from the moat to claim her." A slight tilt of the head and Percy's cheekbones leaped into relief. "I always soothed her. I told her it was just a dream, that no harm could come while I was there." She exhaled thornily. "Which was all well and good until July 1917."

"When you went away with the fever."

A nod, so slight I might have imagined it.

"So she told your father instead."

"He was hiding from his nurses when she found him. She was no doubt in quite a state—Saffy was never one for reserve—and he asked her what was wrong."

"And then he wrote it down."

"Her demon was his savior. In the beginning, anyway. The story fired him: he sought her out, hungry for details. His attention flattered her, I'm sure, and by the time I returned from hospital things were very different. Daddy was bright, recovered, delirious almost, and he and Saffy shared a secret.

"Neither of them mentioned the Mud Man to me. It wasn't until I saw proof copies of *The True History of the Mud Man*, on this desk right here, that I guessed what had happened."

The rain was teeming now, and I got up to close the window so that I could hear. "And so you wrote the letter."

"I knew, of course, that for him to publish such a thing would be terrible for Saffy. He wouldn't be convinced, though, and he lived with the consequences for the rest of his life." Her attention drifted to the Goya again. "The guilt of what he'd done, his sin."

"Because he'd stolen Saffy's nightmare," I said. Sin was taking it a bit far, perhaps, but I certainly understood how such a thing might impact upon a young girl, particularly one with a bent for the fantastic. "He sent it out into the world and gave it new life. He made it real."

Percy laughed then, a wry, metallic sound that made me shiver. "Oh, Miss Burchill, he did more than that. He inspired it. He just didn't know that then."

A growl of thunder rolled up the tower and the lamplight dulled; Percy Blythe, however, did not. She was possessed by her story's purpose, and I leaned closer, desperate to know just what she meant, what Raymond Blythe could possibly have done to spark Saffy's nightmare. Another cigarette was lit; her eyes shone, and perhaps she smelled my interest, for she shifted the spotlight. "Mother kept her affair secret for the better part of a year."

The change of subject was a physical blow and I deflated. Rather obviously, I'm afraid, for it did not escape my host's attention. "Am I disappointing you, Miss Burchill?" she snapped. "This is the story of the Mud Man's birth. It's quite a scoop, you know. We all played our part in his creation, even Mother, though she was dead before dream was dreamed or book was writ." She brushed a trail of ash from the front of her blouse and picked up her story. "Mother's affair carried on and Daddy had no idea. Until one night when he came home early from a trip to London. He'd had good news—a journal in America had published an article of his, to great acclaim—and he was of a mind to celebrate. It was late. Saffy and I, just four years old, had been put to bed hours before, and the lovers were in the library. Mother's lady's maid tried to stop Daddy, but he'd been drinking whisky all afternoon and he wouldn't be calmed. He was jubilant; he wanted his wife to share in his good mood. He burst into the library, and there they were." Her mouth darted to form a grimace, for she knew what was coming. "Daddy was enraged and a terrible fight ensued. He and Sykes, then when the other man lay injured on the floor, he and Mother. Daddy berated her, called her names, and then he shook her, not hard enough to hurt but with sufficient force that she fell against the table. A lamp toppled to the ground and broke, the flames catching the hem of her dress.

"The fire was immediate and fierce. It raced up the chiffon of her dress and within an instant she was engulfed. Daddy was horrified, of course, dragging her to the curtains, trying to smother the flames. It only made matters worse. The curtains caught, the whole room soon after; fire was everywhere. Daddy ran for help; he dragged Mother out of the library, saved her life—albeit briefly—but he didn't go back for Sykes. He left him there to die. Love makes people do cruel things, Miss Burchill.

"The library burned completely but when the authorities arrived, no other body was found. It was as if Oliver Sykes had never existed. Daddy supposed that the body had disintegrated under such intense heat, Mother's maid never spoke of it again for fear of tarnishing her mistress's good name, and no one came looking for Sykes. In a great gift of fortune for Daddy, the man was a dreamer who'd spoken often of his desire to escape to the continent and slip from the world."

What she'd told me was awful, that the fire that killed their mother had been caused in such a way, that Oliver Sykes had been left to die in the library, yet I knew I was missing something, for I still couldn't see what it had to do with the *Mud Man*.

"I saw none of this myself," she said. "But someone did. High up in the attic, a small girl had woken from her sleep, left her twin alone in bed, and climbed up on the bookcase to see the strange and golden sky. What she saw was fire, leaping from the library, and, down on the ground, a man all black and charred and melted, screaming in agony as he tried to climb out of the moat."

Percy refilled her water and drank shakily. "Do you remember when you first visited, Miss Burchill, and you mentioned the past singing in the walls?"

"Yes." The tour that seemed a lifetime ago.

"I told you it was nonsense, the distant hours. That the stones were old but that they didn't tell their secrets."

"I remember."

"I was lying." She lifted her chin and set her eyes on mine, a challenge. "I do hear them. The older I get, the louder they become. This has not been an easy story to tell, but it's been necessary. As I said, there is another type of immortality, a far more lonely one."

I waited.

"A life, Miss Burchill, a human life, is bracketed by a pair of events: one's birth and one's death. The dates of those events belong to a person as much as their name, as much as the experiences that happen in between. I am not telling you this story so that I might feel absolved. I am telling you because a death should be recorded. Do you understand?"

I nodded, thinking of Theo Cavill and his obsessive checking of his brother's records, the ghastly limbo of not knowing.

"Good," she said. "There must be no confusion on that count."

Her talk of absolution reminded me of Raymond's guilt, for that was why he'd converted to Catholicism, of course. Why he'd left a great deal of his wealth to the Church. The other recipient had been Sykes's Farm Institute. Not because Raymond Blythe admired the group's work, but because he was guilty. I thought of something. "You said before that your father didn't know that he'd inspired the dream at first; did he realize later?"

She smiled. "He received a letter from a doctoral student in Norway writing a thesis on physical injury in literature. He was interested in the Mud Man's blackened body because at times, the student felt, the descriptions painted him in a way that mirrored other representations of burn victims. Daddy never wrote back, but he knew then."

"When was that?"

"The midthirties. That's when he began to see the Mud Man in the castle."

And when he added a second dedication to his book: MB and OS. Not the initials of his wives, but an attempt to atone in some way for

485

the deaths he'd caused. Something struck me: "You didn't see it happen. How do you know about the fight in the library? Oliver Sykes being there that night?"

"Juniper."

"What?"

"Daddy told her. She suffered a traumatic event of her own when she was thirteen. He was always on about how similar they were: I expect he thought it would comfort her to know that we are all capable of behaving in ways we might regret. He could be grand and foolish like that."

She fell silent then, reaching for her glass of water, and the room itself seemed to exhale. Relief, perhaps, that the truth had finally been disclosed. Was Percy Blythe relieved? I wasn't so sure. Glad that her duty had been discharged, no doubt, but there was nothing in her bearing that seemed lightened by the telling. I had a feeling I knew why: any comfort she might have drawn was far exceeded by her grief. *Grand and foolish.* They were the first words I'd heard her speak ill about her father and on her lips, she who was so fiercely protective of his legacy, they'd weighed especially heavily.

And why shouldn't they? What Raymond Blythe had done was wicked, no one could argue with that and it was little wonder he'd been driven mad by guilt. I remembered that photograph of the elderly Raymond in the book I'd bought from the village shop: the fearful eyes, the contracted features, the sense that his body was burdened by black thoughts. A similar appearance, it occurred to me, to the one his eldest daughter presented now. She had shrunk into the chair and her clothing seemed oversized, draping from one bone to the next. Her story had left her spent, her eyelids sagging and the fragile skin shot through with blue; it struck me as wretched that a daughter should have to suffer the sins of her father in such a way.

Rain was falling hard outside, beating against the already sodden ground, and inside the room had darkened with the passing afternoon. Even the fire, which had flickered alongside Percy's story, was dying now, taking the last of the study's warmth with it.

I closed my notebook. "Why don't we finish up for the after-noon?" I said, with what I hoped was kindness. "We can pick up again tomorrow, if you like."

"Almost, Miss Burchill, I'm almost done."

She rattled her cigarette box and tipped a final stick onto the desk. Fiddled with it a bit before her match took and the cigarette end glowed. "You know now about Sykes," she said, "but not about the other one."

The other one. My breath caught.

"I see by your face, you know of whom I speak."

I nodded, stiltedly. There was an enormous crack of thunder and I shivered where I sat. Let my notebook fall open again.

She drew hard on her cigarette, coughed as she exhaled. "Juniper's friend."

"Thomas Cavill," I whispered.

"He did arrive that night. October 29, 1941. Write that down. He came as he'd promised her. Only she never knew it."

"Why? What happened?" Perched on the fringes of enlighten-ment, I almost didn't want to know.

"There was a storm, rather like this one. It was dark. There was an accident." She spoke so softly I had to lean very close to hear. "I thought he was an intruder."

There was nothing I could think to say.

Her face was ashen and in its lines I read decades of guilt. "I never told anyone. Certainly not the police. I was concerned they might not believe me. That they might think I was covering for someone else."

Juniper. Juniper with the violent incident in her past. The scandal with the gardener's son.

"I took care of it. I did my best. But nobody knows and that, fi-nally, must be set to rights." I was shocked then to see that she was weeping, tears rolling freely down her old, old face. Shocked, be-cause it was Percy Blythe, but not surprised. Not after what she'd just confessed.

Two men's deaths, two concealments; there was much to

process—so much that I could neither see nor feel distinctly. My emotions had run together like the colors in a set of waterpaints so that I didn't feel angry or frightened or morally superior, and I certainly wasn't feverish with glee at having learned the answers to my questions. I just felt sad. Upset and concerned for the old woman sitting across from me, who was weeping for her life's spiny secrets. I wasn't able to alleviate her pain, but I couldn't just sit there staring either. "Please," I said, "let me help you downstairs."

And this time, she wordlessly agreed.

I kept a gentle hold of her as we went. Slowly, carefully, winding down the stairs. She insisted on carrying the walking cane herself and it dragged behind, marking our progress, step-by-step, with a drear tattoo. Neither of us spoke; we were both too tired.

When finally we reached the closed door behind which was the yellow parlor, Percy Blythe stopped. By sheer force of will she composed herself, drawing her frame erect and finding an extra inch of height. "Not a word to my sisters," she said. Her voice was not unkind, but its sinew caused me to startle. "Not a word, do you hear?"

"STAY FOR dinner, won't you, Edith?" said Saffy brightly as we came through the door. "I prepared extra when it got so late and you were with us still." She glanced at Percy, a pleasant expression on her face, yet I could tell she was perplexed, wondering what it was her sister had been saying that had taken the whole day.

I demurred, but she was already laying a place and it was pouring with rain outside.

"Of course she'll stay," said Percy, letting go of my arm and making her way slowly but certainly to the far side of the table. She turned to regard me when she reached it and beneath the room's electric light I could see how thoroughly, how astonishingly, she'd managed to resurrect her spirits for the benefit of her sisters. "I kept you working over lunch. The least we can do is feed you dinner."

We ate together, all four of us, a meal of smoked haddock—bright yellow in color, slimy in consistency, lukewarm in preparation—and the dog, who'd been found, finally, holed up in the butler's pantry, spent most of the time lying across Juniper's feet as she fed him pieces of fish from her plate. The storm did not let up, in fact it gained in strength. We ate a dessert of toast and jam; we drank tea, and then more tea, until finally we ran out of amiable chat. At irregular intervals the lights flickered, signaling the likelihood of power outage, and each time they revived we exchanged smiles of reassurance. All the while, rain sluiced over the eaves and swept across the windows in great sheets.

"Well," said Saffy eventually, "I don't see that there's any choice about it. We'll make you up a bed and you can stay here the night. I'll telephone the farmhouse and let them know."

"Oh no," I said, with more alacrity than was perhaps polite. "I don't want to impose." I *didn't* want to impose—neither did I fancy the idea of staying in the castle overnight.

"Nonsense," said Percy, turning from the window. "It's as black as pitch. You're as likely to fall into the brook and be swept away like a piece of driftwood." She straightened. "No. We don't want any accidents. Not when we have room to spare here."

A Night at the Castle

It was Saffy who showed me to my bedroom. We walked quite a distance from the wing in which the Sisters Blythe now lived, and although our passage was long and dark, I was grateful that I wasn't being led downstairs. It was enough that I was staying in the castle overnight; I didn't fancy sleeping anywhere near the muniment room. We each carried a paraffin lamp up a set of stairs to the second floor and along a wide, shadowy corridor. Even when the electric bulbs weren't flickering, the glow was a peculiar sort of half-light. Finally, Saffy stopped.

"Here we are," she said, opening the door. "The guest chamber."

She—or perhaps it had been Percy—had put sheets on the bed and arranged a small pile of books by the pillow. "It's rather cheerless, I'm afraid," she said, glancing about the room with an apologetic smile. "We don't entertain often; we're rather out of the habit. It's been such a long time since anybody came to stay."

"I'm sorry to have put you to the trouble."

She was shaking her head. "Nonsense. It's no trouble at all. I always loved having guests. Entertaining was one of the things I found the most fulfilling in life." She started towards the bed and set her lamp down on the side table. "Now, I've laid out a nightgown and found some books, too. I can't imagine facing the end of the day without a story to drop into on my way towards sleep." She fingered the book on top of the pile. "*Jane Eyre* was always a favorite of mine."

"Of mine, too. I always carry a copy, though my edition's not nearly as beautiful as yours."

She smiled, pleased. "You remind me a little of myself, you know,

490

Edith. The person I might have become if things had been different. If times had been different. Living in London, working with books. When I was young, I dreamed of becoming a governess. Traveling and meeting people, working in a museum. Meeting my own Mr. Rochester perhaps."

She became shy then, and wistful, and I remembered the floral boxes I'd found in the muniment room, in particular the one marked MARRIAGE TO MATTHEW DE COURCY. I knew Juniper's tragic love story well enough, but very little of Saffy's and Percy's romantic pasts. Surely they, too, had once been young and filled with lust; yet both had been sacrificed to Juniper's care. "You mentioned that you were engaged once?"

"To a man called Matthew. We fell in love when we were very young. Sixteen." She smiled softly, remembering. "We planned to marry when we were twenty-one."

"Do you mind me asking what happened?"

"Not at all." She began folding down the bed, smoothing back the blanket and sheet at a neat angle. "It didn't work out; he married someone else."

"I'm sorry."

"Don't be. So much time has passed. Both of them have been dead for years." Perhaps she was uncomfortable that the conversation had taken a self-pitying turn, for she made a joke then: "I was fortunate, I suppose, that my sister was kind enough to let me live on at the castle for such a bargain rate."

"I can't imagine Percy would have minded that at all," I said lightly.

"Perhaps not, though it was Juniper I meant."

"I'm afraid I . . . ?"

Saffy blinked at me, surprised. "Why, the castle is hers. Didn't you know? We'd always supposed that it would pass to Percy, of course— she was the eldest and the only one who loved it as he did—but Daddy changed his will at the last."

"Why?" I was thinking aloud; I hadn't really expected her to answer, but she appeared to be wrapped up in the telling of her story.

"Daddy was obsessed with the impossibility of creative women being able to continue with their art once saddled with the burden of marriage and children. When Juniper showed such promise, he became fixated on the idea that she might marry and waste her talent. He kept her here, never let her go out to school or to meet other people, and then had his will changed so that the castle was hers. That way, he reasoned, she would never have to concern herself with the business of making a living, nor with marrying a man who'd keep her. It was terribly unfair of him, though. The castle was always meant to be Percy's. She loves this place as other people love their sweethearts." She gave the pillows a final plump before collecting her lamp from the table. "I suppose in that respect it's fortunate that Juniper *didn't* marry and move away."

I failed to make the connection. "But wouldn't Juniper have been happy in that case to have a sister who cared so much for the old place living here and looking after it?"

Saffy smiled. "It wasn't so simple. Daddy could be cruel when it came to getting his own way. He put a condition on the will. If Juniper were to marry, the castle would no longer be hers, passing instead to the Catholic Church."

"The Church?"

"He suffered with guilt, did Daddy."

And after my meeting with Percy, I knew exactly why that would be. "So if Juniper and Thomas had married, the castle would have been lost?"

"Yes," she said, "that's right. Poor Percy would never have borne it." She shivered then. "I am sorry. It's so cold in here. One never realizes. We have no need to use the room ourselves. I'm afraid there's no heating along this wing, but there are extra blankets in the bottom of the wardrobe."

A spectacular bolt of lightning struck then, followed by a crack of thunder. The feeble electric light wavered, flickered, then the bulb went dark. Saffy and I both raised our lamps, as if puppets drawn by the same string. We gazed together at the cooling bulb.

"Oh dear," she said, "there goes our power. Thank goodness we thought to bring the lamps." She hesitated. "Will you be all right, alone up here?"

"I'm sure I will."

"Well then," she said with a smile. "I'll leave you to it."

NIGHTTIME IS different. Things are otherwise when the world is black. Insecurities and hurts, anxieties and fears grow teeth at night. Particularly when one is sleeping in a strange, old castle with a storm outside. Even more particularly when one has spent the afternoon listening to an elderly lady's confession. Which is why, when Saffy left, closing the door behind her, I didn't even consider snuffing my lamp's flame.

I changed into the nightdress and sat, white and ghostlike, on the bed. Listened as the rain continued to pour and the wind rattled the shutters, just as if someone were on the other side, struggling to get in. No—I pushed the thought aside, even managed to smile at myself. I was thinking of the *Mud Man*, of course. Understandable when I was spending the night in the very place in which the novel was set, on a night that might have materialized from its pages.

I tucked myself under the covers and turned my thoughts to Percy. I'd brought my notebook with me and now I opened it, jotting down ideas as they came to me. Percy Blythe had given me the story of the *Mud Man*'s genesis, which was a great coup. She'd also answered the mystery of Thomas Cavill's disappearance. I should have felt relieved, and yet I was unsettled. The sensation was recent, something to do with what Saffy had told me. As she'd spoken of her father's will, unpleasant connections were being made in my mind, little lights turning on that made me feel increasingly uncomfortable: Percy's love for the castle, a will that specified its loss if Juniper should marry, Thomas Cavill's unfortunate death . . .

But no. Percy had said it was an accident and I believed her.

I did. What reason did she have to lie? She might just as well have kept the whole thing to herself.

And yet . . .

Round and round the snippets went: Percy's voice, then Saffy's, and my own doubts thrown in for good measure. Not Juniper's voice, though. I only ever seemed to hear *about* the youngest Blythe, never from her. Finally, I closed my notebook with a slap.

That was enough for one day. I heaved a sigh and glanced through the books that Saffy had provided, seeking something that might still my mind: *Jane Eyre, The Mysteries of Udolpho, Wuthering Heights*. I grimaced—good friends, all, but not the sort with whom I felt like keeping company on this cold and stormy night.

I was tired, very tired, but I warded off the moment of sleep, loath to blow out the lamp and submit myself finally to the dark. Eventually, though, my eyelids began to droop, and after I'd jerked myself awake a few times, I figured I was tired enough for sleep to claim me quickly. I blew out the flame, closed my eyes as the smell of dying smoke thinned in the cold air around me. The last thing I remember is a rush of rain slipping down the glass.

I woke with a jolt, suddenly and unnaturally at an unknown hour. I lay very still, listening. Waiting, wondering what it was that had woken me. The hairs on my arms were standing on end and I had the strongest, eeriest sense that I was not alone, that there was someone in the room with me. I scanned the shadows, my heart hammering, dreading what I might see.

I saw nothing, but I knew. Someone was there.

I held my breath and listened, but it was still raining outside and with the howling wind rattling the shutters, its wraiths gliding along the stone corridor, there was little chance of hearing anything else. I had no matches and no means of relighting my lamp, so I talked myself back to a state of comparative calm. I told myself it was my pre-sleep thoughts, my obsession with the *Mud Man*. I'd dreamed a noise. I was imagining things.

And just when I had myself almost convinced, there was a huge lightning flash and I saw that my bedroom door was open. Saffy had closed it behind her. I'd been right. Someone *had* been in the room with me, was still there, perhaps, waiting in the shadows—

"*Meredith . . .*"

Every vertebra in my body straightened. My heart pounded, my pulse ran electric in my veins. That wasn't the wind or the walls; someone had whispered Mum's name. I was petrified and yet a strange energy gripped me. I knew I had to do something. I couldn't sit the entire night out, wrapped in my blanket, wide eyes scanning the dark room.

The last thing I wanted to do was get out of bed, but I did. I slid across the sheet and made my way on tiptoe to the door. The handle was cool, smooth beneath my hand, and I pulled it lightly, noiselessly towards me, stepping out to scan the corridor.

"*Meredith . . .*"

I almost screamed. It was right behind me.

I turned, slowly, and there was Juniper. She was wearing the same dress she'd put on during my first visit to Milderhurst, the dress—I knew now—that Saffy had made for her to wear when Thomas Cavill came to dinner.

"Juniper," I whispered. "What are you doing here?"

"I've been waiting for you, Merry. I knew you'd come. I have it for you. I've been keeping it safe."

I had no idea what she meant, but she handed me something rather bulky. Firm edge, sharp angles, not too heavy. "Thank you," I said.

In the half-light, her smile faltered. "Oh, Meredith," she said, "I've done a terrible, terrible thing."

Which was precisely what she'd said to Saffy in the corridor at the end of my tour. My pulse began to beat a little faster. It was wrong to question her, but I couldn't help saying, "What is it? What did you do?"

"Tom is coming soon. He's coming for dinner."

I felt so sad for her then; she'd been waiting for him fifty years, convinced she'd been abandoned. "Of course he is," I said. "Tom loves you. He wants to marry you."

"Tom loves me."

"Yes."

"And I love him."

"I know you do."

And just as I was enjoying the warm, pleased feeling of having swept her mind back to a happy place, her hands leaped to her mouth in horror and she said, "But there was blood, Meredith . . ."

"What?"

". . . so much blood; all over my arms, all over my dress." She looked down at her dress then up at me and her face was a picture of misery. "Blood, blood, blood. And Tom didn't come. But I don't remember. I can't remember."

Then, with a swooping certainty, I understood.

Everything shifted into place and I saw what they were hiding. What had really happened to Thomas Cavill. Who had been responsible for his death.

Juniper's habit of blacking out after traumatic events; the episodes after which she couldn't recall what she'd done; the hushed-up incident in which the gardener's son had been beaten. With dawning horror, I remembered too the letter she'd sent to Mum in which she'd mentioned her one fear: that she might turn out like her father. And she had.

"I can't remember," she was saying still. "I can't remember." Her face was pathetically confused, and although what she was telling me was ghastly, in that moment I wanted only to embrace her, to release her in some small way from the terrible burden she'd been carrying for fifty years. She whispered again, "I've done a terrible, terrible thing," and before I could say anything to calm her, she darted past me towards the door.

"Juniper," I called after her. "Wait."

"Tom loves me," she said, as if the happy thought had just occurred to her. "I'm going to go and look for Tom. He must be coming soon."

And then she disappeared into the dark corridor.

I threw the boxy object towards the bed and followed her. Round a corner, along another short corridor until she reached a small landing from which a staircase fell away. A biting gust of wind blew up damp from below and I knew she must have opened a door, that she was planning to disappear into the cold, wet night.

A split second's indecision and I started down after her. I couldn't just leave her to the elements. For all I knew, she was intending to follow the drive all the way to the road, looking for Thomas Cavill. I reached the bottom of the stairs and saw there was a door leading the way through a small antechamber that connected the castle to the outside world.

It was still raining heavily, but I could see it was a garden of sorts. Not much seemed to be growing there, a few odd statues were dotted about, the whole was enclosed by massive hedges—I drew breath. It was the garden I'd seen from the attic on my first visit, the square enclosure Percy Blythe had been at great pains to tell me was not a garden at all. And she was right. I'd read about it in Mum's journal. This was the pets' graveyard, the place that was special to Juniper.

Juniper had stopped at the center of the garden, a frail old lady in a ghostly pale dress, drenched and wild looking. And suddenly it made sense to me what Percy had said earlier, about stormy weather adding to Juniper's agitation. It had been stormy that night in 1941, just as it was now . . .

It was odd, but the storm appeared to calm around her as she stood there. I was transfixed for a short time, before realizing that of course I had to go outside and bring her in, that she couldn't stay out in the weather. At that moment, I heard a voice and saw Juniper look to her right. Percy Blythe appeared from a gate in the hedge, dressed in a mackintosh and Wellington boots, approaching her little sister, calling her back inside. She held out her arms and Juniper stumbled into her embrace.

I suddenly felt like an intruder, a stranger observing a personal moment. I turned to leave.

Someone was behind me. It was Saffy, her hair brushed over her shoulders. She was wrapped in a dressing gown and her face was all apology. "Oh, Edith," she said, "I'm terribly sorry for the disturbance."

"Juniper—" I started, gesturing over my shoulder, trying to explain.

"It's all right," she said, a kind smile on her face. "She wanders sometimes. There's nothing to worry about. Percy's bringing her inside. You can go back to bed now."

I hurried back up the stairs, along the corridor, and into my room, closing the door carefully behind me. I leaned against it, catching breaths that continued to run away from me. I flicked the electric switch, in the hope that power had been restored, but alas: a dull plastic clunk and no reassuring spill of light.

I tiptoed back to bed, shifted the mysterious box onto the floor, and wrapped myself in the blanket. I lay with my head on the pillow, listening to my pulse race in my ear. I couldn't stop replaying the details of Juniper's confession, her confusion as she struggled to put the pieces of her fragmented mind together, the embrace she'd shared with Percy in the pets' graveyard. And I knew then why Percy Blythe had lied to me. I had no doubt that Thomas Cavill had indeed died on a stormy October night in 1941, but it wasn't Percy who'd done it. She'd merely been protecting her little sister to the last.

The Day After

I MUST finally have slept because the next I knew, a weak misty light was stealing through the gaps in the shutters. The storm had passed, leaving only weary morning in its place. I lay for a time, blinking at the ceiling, sifting through the previous night's events. By the welcome light of day I was more certain than ever that it was Juniper who'd been responsible for Thomas's death. It was the only thing that made sense. I knew, too, that Percy and Saffy were anxious no one should ever learn the truth.

I hopped out of bed and almost tripped over a box on the floor. Juniper's gift. With everything else that had happened, I'd completely forgotten. It was the same shape and size as those in Saffy's collection in the muniment room, and when I opened it, a manuscript lay within, but it wasn't one of Saffy's. The cover page read: *Destiny: A Love Story, by Meredith Baker, October 1941.*

WE'D ALL overslept and it was midmorning. The breakfast table was laid in the yellow parlor when I came downstairs and all three sisters were seated, the twins chatting away as if nothing out of the ordinary had happened in the night. And perhaps it hadn't; perhaps I'd witnessed only one upset of many. Saffy smiled and offered me a cup of tea. I thanked her and glanced at Juniper, sitting blankly in the armchair, none of the night's excitement evident in her demeanor. Percy, I thought, watched me a little more closely than usual as I drank my tea, but that might have been the result of her confession, false or otherwise, the day before.

After I'd said my good-byes, she walked me to the entrance hall and we spoke pleasantly enough of trivial matters until we reached the door. "With regard to what I told you yesterday, Miss Burchill," she said, planting her cane firmly. "I wanted to reiterate that it was an accident."

She was testing me, I realized; this was her way of ascertaining whether I still believed her story. Whether Juniper had told me anything in the night. This was my chance to reveal what I had learned, to ask her outright who had really killed Thomas Cavill. "Of course," I said. "I understand completely." To what end would I have told her? To satisfy my own curiosity at the expense of the sisters' peace of mind? I couldn't do it.

She was visibly relieved. "I've suffered endlessly. I never intended for it to happen."

"I know. I know you didn't." I was touched by her sisterly sense of duty, a love so strong that she would confess to a crime she didn't commit. "You must put it out of your mind," I said as kindly as I could. "It wasn't your fault."

She looked at me then with an expression I'd never seen before, one that I am hard-pressed to describe. Part anguish, part relief, but with hints of something else mixed in as well. She was Percy Blythe, though, and she didn't go in for sentiment. She coolly composed herself and nodded sharply. "Don't forget your promise, now, Miss Burchill. I'm relying on you. I am not the sort who likes to trust to chance."

THE GROUND was wet, the sky was white, and the entire landscape had the blanched look of a face in the aftermath of a hysterical rage. A little the way I imagined my own face might be looking. I went carefully, keen to avoid being swept away like a log downstream, and by the time I reached the farmhouse Mrs. Bird had already moved on to lunch preparation. The strong, dense smell of soup hung thickly in the air, a simple but tremendous pleasure for someone who'd spent a night in company with the castle's ghosts.

Mrs. Bird herself was setting tables in the main room and her plump, apron-wrapped figure was such an ordinary, comforting sight that I felt possessed by a strong urge to hug her. I might have, too, had I not then noticed that we weren't alone.

There was someone else, another guest, leaning forward to pay close attention to the black-and-white photographs on the wall.

A very familiar person.

"Mum?"

She looked up and offered me a tentative smile. "Hello, Edie."

"What are you doing here?"

"You said I should come. I wanted to surprise you."

I don't think I'd ever been so pleased or relieved to see another person in my life. I gave *her* my hug instead. "I'm so glad you're here."

Perhaps my vehemence showed, perhaps I held on just a mite too long, for she blinked at me and said, "Is everything all right, Edie?"

I hesitated as the secrets I'd learned, the grim truths I'd witnessed, shuffled like cards in my mind. Then I folded them away and smiled. "I'm fine, Mum. Just a bit tired. There was quite a storm last night."

"Mrs. Bird was telling me, she said you'd been rained in at the castle." The buckle in her voice was only slight. "I'm glad I didn't set off in the afternoon as I'd planned."

"Have you been here long?"

"Only twenty minutes or so. I've been looking at these." She pointed to a nearby photograph, one of the *Country Life* pictures from 1910. It was the circular pool, when it was still under construction. "I learned to swim in that pool," she said, "when I was living at the castle."

I bent closer to read the annotation beneath the photo: *Oliver Sykes, overseeing the construction, shows Mr. and Mrs. Raymond Blythe the work on their new pool.* There he was, the handsome young architect, the Mud Man who would end his days buried beneath the moat he was restoring. The brush of prescience swept across my skin and I felt heavily the burden of having learned the secret of that young man's fate. Percy Blythe's entreaty came drifting back to me: *Don't forget your promise. I'm relying on you.*

"Can I get you ladies some lunch?" Mrs. Bird said.

I turned away from Sykes's smiling face. "What do you say, Mum? You must be hungry after the drive."

"Soup would be lovely. Is it all right if we sit outside?"

WE SAT at a table in the garden from which we could glimpse the castle; Mrs. Bird had made the suggestion, and before I could demur, Mum had declared it perfect. As the farmhouse geese kept busy in the nearby puddles, ever hopeful that a crumb might fall their way, Mum began to talk about her past. The time she'd spent at Milderhurst, the way she'd felt about Juniper, the crush she'd had on her teacher, Mr. Cavill; finally, she told me of her dreams of being a journalist.

"What happened, Mum?" I said, spreading butter on my bread. "Why did you change your mind?"

"I didn't change my mind. I just—" She shifted a little in the white iron seat that Mrs. Bird had towel-dried— "I suppose I just . . . In the end I couldn't . . ." She frowned at her inability to find the words she needed, then continued with new determination. "Meeting Juniper opened a door for me and I desperately wanted to belong on the other side. Without her, though, I couldn't seem to keep it open. I tried, Edie, I really did. I dreamed of going to university, but so many schools were closed in London during the war and in the end I applied for work as a typist. I always believed that it was temporary, that one day I would go on and do what I'd intended. But when the war ended I was eighteen and too old for school. I couldn't go to university without my diploma."

"So you stopped writing?"

"Oh no." She drew a figure eight in her soup with the tip of the spoon, round and round again. "No, I didn't. I was rather stubborn back then. I set my mind to it and decided I wasn't going to let a small matter like that stop me." She smiled a little without looking up. "I was going to write for myself, become a famous journalist."

I smiled too, unfeasibly pleased by her description of the intrepid young Meredith Baker.

"I embarked on a program of my own, reading whatever I could find in the library, writing articles, reviews, stories sometimes, and sending them off."

"Was anything published?"

She shifted coyly in her seat. "A few small pieces here and there. I got some encouraging letters from the editors of the bigger journals, gentle but firm, telling me that I needed to learn more about their house style. Then, in 1952, a job came up." Mum glanced over to where the geese were flapping their wings and something in her bearing changed, some of the air went out of her. She set down her spoon. "The job was with the BBC, entry-level, but exactly what I wanted."

"What happened?"

"I saved up and bought myself a smart little outfit and a leather satchel so I'd look the part. I gave myself a stern talking-to about acting confidently, speaking clearly, not letting my shoulders slouch. But then"—she inspected the backs of her hands, rubbed a thumb across her knuckles—"then there was a mix-up with the buses and instead of taking me to Broadcasting House, the driver let me off down near Marble Arch. I ran most of the way back, but when I got to the top of Regent Street, I saw all these girls sallying out of the building, laughing and joking, so smart and together, so much younger than I was, and looking as if they knew the answers to all life's questions." She swept a crumb from the table to the ground before meeting my eyes. "I caught sight of myself then in a department store window and I looked such a fraud, Edie."

"Oh, Mum."

"Such a bedraggled fraud. I despised myself and I was embarrassed that I'd ever thought I might belong in such a place. I don't think I'd ever felt so lonely. I turned away from Portland Place and walked in the other direction, tears streaming. What a mess I must've looked. I felt so desolate and sorry for myself and strangers kept telling me to keep my chin up, so when I finally passed a cinema I ducked inside to be miserable in peace."

I remembered Dad's account of the girl who'd cried the whole way through a film. "And you saw *The Holly and the Ivy*."

Mum nodded, drew a tissue from somewhere, and dabbed at her eyes. "And I met your father. And he took me to tea and bought me pear cake."

"Your favorite."

She smiled through tears, fond of the memory. "He kept asking what the matter was and when I told him that the film had made me cry he looked at me with total disbelief. 'But it's not real,' he said as he ordered a second slice of cake. 'It's all made up.' "

We both laughed then; she'd sounded just like Dad.

"He was so firm, Edie, so solid in his perception of the world and his place in it. Astonishingly so. I'd never met anyone quite like him. He didn't see things unless they were there, he didn't worry about them until they happened. That's what I fell in love with, his assurance. His feet were planted firmly in the here and now and when he spoke I felt enveloped in his certainty. Happily, he saw something in me too. It may not sound exciting, but we've been very happy together. Your father's a good man, Edie."

"I know he is."

"Honest, kind, reliable. There's a lot to be said for that."

I agreed, and as we fell to sipping our soup a picture of Percy Blythe came into my mind. She was a bit like Dad in that respect: the sort of person who might be overlooked among more vibrant company, but whose sturdiness, steeliness even, was the foundation upon which everybody else could shine. Thoughts of the castle and the Sisters Blythe reminded me of something.

"I can't believe I forgot!" I said, reaching for my bag and pulling out the box that Juniper had given me in the night.

Mum laid down her spoon and wiped her fingers on the napkin in her lap. "A present? You didn't even know that I was coming."

"It's not from me."

"Then who?"

I was about to say, "Open it and find out," when I remembered that the last time I'd presented her with a box of memories and said the same thing it hadn't worked out so well. "It's from Juniper, Mum."

Her lips parted and she made a tiny winded noise, fumbled with the box, trying to get it open. "Silly me," she said in a voice I didn't recognize, "I'm all thumbs." Finally, the lid came off and her hand went to her mouth in wonder. "Oh my." She took the delicate sheets of austerity paper from inside and held them, as if they were the most precious items in the world.

"Juniper thought I was you," I said. "She'd been keeping this for you."

Mum's eyes darted to the castle on the hill and she shook her head with gentle disbelief. "All this time . . ."

She turned over the typewritten pages, scanning as she read bits here and there, her smile flickering. I watched her, enjoying the evident pleasure the manuscript was giving her. There was something else, too. A change had come over her, subtle but certain, as she realized that her friend had not forgotten her: the features of her face, the muscles in her neck, even the blades of her shoulders seemed to soften. A lifetime's defensiveness fell away and I could glimpse the girl within as if she'd just been woken from a long, deep sleep.

I said gently, "What about your writing, Mum?"

"What's that?"

"Your writing. You didn't continue?"

"Oh, no. I gave up on all that." She wrinkled her nose a little and her expression cast a sort of apology. "I suppose that sounds very cowardly to you."

"Not cowardly, no." I continued carefully. "Only, if something gave you pleasure, I don't understand why you would stop."

The sun had broken through the clouds, skating off puddles to throw a layer of dappled shadow across Mum's cheek. She readjusted her glasses, shuffled slightly in her chair, and pressed her hands delicately on the manuscript. "It was such a big part of my past, of who

I'd been," she said. "The whole lot got all wrapped up together. My distress at having thought myself abandoned by Juniper and Tom, the feeling that I'd let myself down by missing the interview . . . I suppose I stopped finding pleasure in it. I settled down with your father and concentrated on the future instead."

She glanced again at the manuscript, held a sheet of paper aloft, and smiled fleetingly at whatever was written there. "It *was* such a pleasure," she said. "Taking something abstract, like a thought or a feeling or a smell, and capturing it on paper. I'd forgotten how much I enjoyed it."

"It's never too late to start again."

"Edie, love." She smiled with fond regret. "I'm sixty-five years old. I haven't written more than a shopping list in decades. I think it's safe to say that it's too late."

I was shaking my head. I met people of all ages, every day of my working life, who were writing just because they couldn't stop themselves.

"It's never too late, Mum," I said again, but she was no longer listening. Her attention had drifted over my shoulder and back towards the castle. With one fine hand she drew her cardigan closed across her breasts. "You know, it's a funny thing. I wasn't sure quite how I'd feel, but now that I'm here, I don't know that I can go back. I don't know that I want to."

"You don't?"

"I have a picture in my mind. A very happy picture; I don't want for that to change."

Perhaps she thought I might try to convince her otherwise, but I didn't. The castle was a sad place now, fading and falling to pieces, a little like its three inhabitants. "I can understand that," I said. "It's all looking a bit tired."

"*You're* looking a bit tired, Edie." She frowned at my face as if she'd only just noticed.

As she said it, I began to yawn. "Well, it *was* an eventful night. I didn't get much sleep."

"Yes, Mrs. Bird mentioned there was quite a storm—I'm very content to stroll around the garden. I've lots to keep me busy." Mum fingered the edge of her manuscript. "Why don't you go and have yourself a little lie-down?"

I was halfway up the first flight of stairs when Mrs. Bird caught my attention. Standing on the next landing, waving something over the rail, and asking whether she could borrow me for a minute. She was so emphatically eager that, although I agreed, I couldn't help but feel a certain amount of trepidation.

"I have something to show you," she said, darting a glance over her shoulder. "It's a bit of a secret."

After the twenty-four hours I'd had, this did not thrill me.

She pressed a grayish envelope into my hands when I reached her and said, in a stage whisper, "It's one of the letters."

"Which letters?" I'd seen a few over the past few months.

She looked at me as if I'd forgotten which day of the week it was. Which, come to think of it, I had. "The letters I was telling you about, of course, the love letters sent to Mum by Raymond Blythe."

"Oh! Those letters."

She nodded eagerly, and the cuckoo clock hanging on the wall behind her chose that moment to spit out its pair of dancing mice. We waited out the jig, then I said, "You want me to look at it?"

"You needn't read it," said Mrs. Bird, "not if you feel uncomfortable. It's just that something you said the other evening got me thinking."

"It did?"

"You said that you were going to be seeing Raymond Blythe's notebooks and it occurred to me that you'd probably have a very good idea by now of what his handwriting looks like." She drew breath and then said, all in a rush, "I wondered, that is, I hoped . . ."

"That I could take a look and let you know."

"Exactly."

"Sure, I guess—"

"Wonderful!" She clapped her hands together lightly beneath her chin as I slid the sheet of paper from within its envelope.

I knew at once that I was going to disappoint her, that the letter hadn't been written by Raymond Blythe at all. Reading his notebook so closely, I'd become very familiar with his sloping handwriting, the long looping tails when he wrote *G* or *J*, the particular type of *R* he used to sign his name. No, this letter had been written by someone else.

Lucy, my love, my one, my only.

Have I ever told you how I fell in love? That it happened in the first instant that I saw you? Something in the way you stood, in the set of your shoulders, in the wisps of hair that had come loose to brush against your neck; I was yours.

I've thought of what you said when last we met. I've thought of little else. I wonder whether perhaps you might be right; that it is not a mere fancy. That we might just forget everything and everybody else and go far away together.

I didn't read the rest. I skipped over the next few paragraphs and arrived at the single initial, just as Mrs. Bird had said. But as I looked at it, variables shifted by degrees and a number of things slipped into alignment. I had seen this person's handwriting before.

I knew who had written the letter and I knew who it was that Lucy Middleton had loved above all others. Mrs. Bird had been right— it was a love that flew in the face of their society's conventions—but it hadn't been between Raymond and Lucy. It wasn't an *R* at the end of those letters, it was a *P*, written in an old-fashioned hand so that a small tail emerged from the curve of the letter. Easy to confuse with an *R*, especially if that's what one was looking for.

"It's lovely," I said, tripping over my words because I felt forlorn suddenly, thinking of those two young women and the long lives they'd spent apart.

"So sad, don't you think?" She sighed, tucking the letter back inside her pocket, then she looked at me hopefully. "Such a beautifully *written* letter."

WHEN I'D finally extricated myself from Mrs. Bird, having been as noncommittal as I could, I made a beeline for my room and collapsed sideways across the bed. I closed my eyes and tried to relax my mind, but it was no use. My thoughts remained tethered to the castle. I couldn't stop thinking of Percy Blythe, who had loved so well and so long ago; who people thought of as stiff and cold; who had spent most of her life keeping a terrible secret to protect her little sister.

Percy had told me about Oliver Sykes and Thomas Cavill on condition that I did "the right thing." She'd spoken a lot about people's closing dates, but what I couldn't work out was why she'd needed to tell me at all; what she wanted me to do with the information that she couldn't do herself. I was too tired that afternoon. I needed a sleep and then I was looking forward to spending the evening with Mum. So I resolved to visit the castle the following morning, to see Percy Blythe one final time.

AND IN THE END

ONLY I never got the chance. After dinner with Mum I fell asleep quickly and soundly, but, just past midnight, I woke with a start. I lay for a moment in my bed at the farmhouse, wondering why I'd emerged from sleep, whether it was something I'd heard, some nocturnal sound that had since subsided, or whether I'd somehow dreamed myself awake. One thing I did know: the sudden wakefulness didn't feel anywhere near as frightening as it had the previous night. I had no sense this time that there was anyone with me in the room, and I could hear nothing untoward. Yet that pull I've spoken of, the connection I felt towards the castle, was tugging at me. I slid out of bed and went to the window, drew aside the curtains. And that's when I saw it. Shock buckled my knees, and I was hot and cold at once. Where the dark castle should have sat, all was bright: orange flames licking at the low and heavy sky.

The fire at Milderhurst Castle burned most of the night. By the time I called the fire brigade they were already on their way, but there was little they could do. The castle might have been built of stone but there was so much wood within, all that oak paneling, the struts, the doors, the millions of sheets of paper. As Percy Blythe had warned, one spark and the whole lot went up like a tinderbox.

The old ladies inside never stood a chance. So said one of the firemen next morning, at the breakfast Mrs. Bird supplied. They'd all three been sitting together, he said, in a room on the first floor. "It looked as if they'd been caught unawares while dozing by the fire."

"Is that what started it?" asked Mrs. Bird. "A spark from the fire—just like what happened to the twins' mother." She shook her head, tutting at the tragic parallel.

510

"It's hard to say," said the fireman, before proceeding to say much more. "It could've been anything, really. A stray ember from the fireplace, a dropped cigarette, an electrical fault—the wiring in those places is older than me, most times."

THE POLICE or the fire brigade, I'm not sure which, had put barriers around the outside of the smoldering castle, but I knew the garden pretty well by now and was able to climb up the back way. It was grisly, perhaps, but I needed to have a closer look. I'd known the Sisters Blythe only briefly, but had come to feel such strong possession of their stories, their world, that to wake and find it all turned into ash provoked in me a feeling of deep bereavement. It was the loss of the sisters, of course, and their castle, but it was something more, as well. I was overcome by a sense that I'd been left behind. That a door so recently opened to me had closed again, swiftly and completely, and I would never step through it again.

I stood for a time, taking in the black and hollowed shell, remembering my first visit, all those months before, the sense of anticipation as I'd made my way past the circular pool and towards the castle. Everything I'd learned since.

Seledreorig . . . The word came into my head like a whisper. Sadness for the lack of a hall.

A small castle stone lay loose on the ground by my feet, and it made me more melancholy still. It was just a bit of rock. The Blythes were no more and their distant hours were silent.

"I can't believe it's gone."

I turned to see a young man with dark hair standing beside me. "I know," I said. "Hundreds of years old and it was destroyed in hours."

"I heard on the radio this morning and I had to come and see it for myself. I was hoping to see you, too."

Perhaps I looked surprised, for he held out a hand and said, "Adam Gilbert."

That name should have meant something, and it did: an elderly chap in tweeds and an antique office chair. "Edie," I managed. "Edie Burchill."

"I thought as much. The very same Edie who stole my job."

He was joking and I needed a witty rejoinder. I came up instead with muddleheaded gibberish: "Your knee . . . Your nurse . . . I thought—"

"All better now. Or very nearly." He indicated the walking stick in his other hand. "Would you believe a rock-climbing incident?" A crooked smile. "No? Oh, all right. I tripped over a pile of books in the library and shattered my knee. These are the dangers of the writing life." He dipped his head towards the farmhouse. "Heading back?"

A final glance at the castle and I nodded.

"May I walk with you?"

"Of course."

We walked for a time, slowly due to Adam's stick, talking over our memories of the castle and the Sisters Blythe, our mutual passion for the *Mud Man* when we were kids. When we reached the field that led to the farmhouse he stopped. I did the same.

"God, I feel crass to ask this now," he said, gesturing at the distant smoking castle. "And yet . . ." He seemed to listen to something I couldn't hear. Nodded. "Yes, it appears I'm going to ask you anyway. Mrs. Button gave me your message when I got in last night. Is it true? Did you find something out about the *Mud Man*'s origins?"

He had kind brown eyes, which made it hard for me to look at them and lie. So I didn't. I looked at his forehead instead. "No," I said, "unfortunately not. It was a false alarm."

He held aloft a palm and sighed. "Ah well. Then the truth dies with them, I suppose. There's a certain poetry to that. We need our mysteries, don't you think?"

I did, but before I could say so, something caught my attention, back at the farmhouse. "Will you excuse me just a minute?" I said. "There's something I need to do."

I'M NOT sure what Chief Inspector Rawlins thought when he saw a wild-haired, washed-out woman hurrying across the field towards him, and even less when I began telling him my stories. To his credit, he managed to keep an extraordinarily straight expression when I suggested over the breakfast table that he might want to extend his investigation, that I had it on good authority that the remains of two bodies lay buried beneath the earth around the castle. He merely slowed his stirring spoon a fraction and said, "Two men, you say? I don't s'pose you'd be knowing their names."

"I do, actually. One was called Oliver Sykes, the other Thomas Cavill. Sykes died in the 1910 fire that killed Muriel Blythe, and Thomas died by accident during a storm in October 1941."

"I see." He swatted a fly by his ear, without taking his eyes from mine.

"Sykes is buried on the western side, where the old moat used to be."

"And the other one?"

I remembered the night of the storm, Juniper's terrible flight down the corridors and into the garden; Percy knowing just where to find her. "Thomas Cavill is in the pets' graveyard," I said. "Right in the center, near the headstone marked Emerson."

A slow appraisal as he sipped from his tea then added another half spoonful of sugar. Regarded me with slightly narrowed eyes as he stirred again.

"If you check the records," I continued, "you'll see that Thomas Cavill was reported as missing and that neither man's death was ever recorded." And a person needed their set of dates, just as Percy Blythe had told me. It wasn't enough to retain only the first. A person without a closed bracket could never rest.

I DECIDED not to write the introduction for the Pippin Books edition of the *Mud Man*. I explained to Judith Waterman that I had a scheduling clash, that I'd barely had a chance to meet with the Sisters Blythe anyway before the fire. She told me that she understood; that she was sure Adam Gilbert would be happy enough to pick up where he'd left off. I had to agree that it made sense: he was the one who'd compiled all the research.

And I couldn't have written it. I knew the answer to a riddle that had plagued literary critics for seventy-five years, but I couldn't share it with the world. To do so would have felt like a tremendous betrayal of Percy Blythe. "This is a family story," she'd said, before asking whether she could trust me. It would also have made me responsible for unveiling a sad and sordid story that would overshadow the novel forever. The book that had made me a reader.

To write anything else, though, to rehash the same old accounts of the book's mysterious origins, would have been utterly disingenuous. Besides, Percy Blythe had hired me under false pretenses. She hadn't wanted me to write the introduction, she'd wanted me to set the official records straight. And I'd done that. Rawlins and his men broadened the investigation into the fire and two bodies were found in the castle grounds, right where I'd said they'd be. Theo Cavill finally learned what had become of his brother Tom: that he'd died on a stormy night at Milderhurst Castle in the middle of the war. Chief Inspector Rawlins pressed me for any further details I might have, but I told him nothing more. And it was true, I didn't *know* more. Percy had told me one thing, Juniper another. I believed that Percy was covering for her sister, but I couldn't prove it. And I wasn't going to tell, either way. The truth had died with the three sisters, and if the foundation stones of the castle whispered still about what had happened that night in October 1941, I couldn't hear them. I didn't want to hear them. Not anymore. It was time for me to go back to my own life.

PART FIVE

ONE

THE STORM that had pushed its way in from the North Sea on the afternoon of October 29, 1941, had rolled and groaned, thickened and furrowed, before settling finally over the tower of Milderhurst Castle. The first reluctant raindrops broke through the clouds at dusk and many more would follow before the night was done. It was a stealthy storm, the sort of rain that eschews clatter in favor of constancy; hour by steady hour fat drops pounded, poured down the roof tiles and sheeted over the castle eaves. Roving Brook began to rise, the dark pool in Cardarker Wood grew darker, and the skirt of soft ground around the castle, a little lower than that beyond, became sodden, collecting water so that a shadow of the long-ago moat appeared in the darkness. But the twins inside knew none of that; they knew only that after hours of anxious waiting a knock had finally come at the castle door.

SAFFY GOT there first, laid a hand on the jamb, and drove the brass key into the lock. The fit was tight, it had always been tight, and she struggled for a moment, noticed that her hands were shaking, that her nail polish was chipped, that her skin was looking old; then the mechanism gave way, the door opened, and such thoughts flew away into the dark, wet night, for there was Juniper.

"Darling girl." Saffy could have wept to see her little sister, safe and well and home at last. "Thank God! We've missed you so!"

517

"I lost my key," said Juniper. "I'm sorry."

Despite the grown-up raincoat, the grown-up haircut revealed beneath her hat, Juniper looked such a child in the half-light of the doorway that Saffy couldn't help but take her sister's face between her hands and plant a kiss upon her forehead as she'd used to do when June was small. "Nonsense," she said, gesturing at Percy, whose dark mood had retreated into the stones. "We're just so glad to have you home, to see you in one piece. Let me look at you . . ." She held her sister at arm's length, and her chest swelled with a wave of gladness and relief she knew would be impossible to express with words; she drew Juniper into an embrace instead. "When you were so late we began to worry—"

"The bus. We were stopped, there was some kind of . . . incident."

"An incident?" Saffy stepped back.

"Something with the bus. A roadblock, I suppose; I'm not exactly sure . . ." She smiled and shrugged, let her sentence trail off, but a thread of perplexity tugged briefly at her features. Only a moment's shift, but it was enough; the unspoken words echoed in the room as clearly as if she'd said them. *I can't remember.* Three simple words, innocent when uttered by anyone but Juniper. Unease dropped clean as a sinker through Saffy's stomach. She glanced at Percy, noticed that same familiar anxiety settling on her too.

"Well, come on inside," said Percy, reviving her smile. "There's no need for us to stand out in the weather."

"Yes!" Saffy matched her twin's cheer. "You poor dear; you'll catch a chill if we're not careful—Percy, go downstairs, will you, and fetch a hot-water bottle?"

As Percy disappeared along the darkened hall towards the kitchen, Juniper turned to Saffy, took her wrist, and said, "Tom?"

"Not yet."

Her face fell. "But it's late. *I'm* late."

"I know, darling."

"What could be keeping him?"

"The war, darling; the war's to blame. Come and sit by the fire. I'll fix you a lovely drink and he'll be right along, you'll see."

They reached the good parlor and Saffy allowed herself a moment's pleasure at the pretty scene before leading Juniper to the rug by the hearth. She gave the largest log a prod as her sister produced a case of cigarettes from her coat pocket.

The fire sparked and Saffy flinched. She straightened, leaned the poker back where it belonged, and dusted her hands, even though there was nothing on them to clean. Juniper struck a match, drew hard. "Your hair," said Saffy softly.

"I had it cut." Anyone else's hand might have gone to their neck, but not Juniper's.

"Well, I like it."

They smiled at one another, Juniper a little skittishly, it seemed to Saffy. Though, of course, that made no sense; Juniper did not get nervous. Saffy pretended not to watch as her sister wrapped an arm across her middle and continued to smoke.

London, Saffy wanted to say. *You've been to London! Tell me about it; paint me pictures with words so that I might see and know everything that you do. Did you dance? Did you sit by the Serpentine. Did you fall in love?* The questions lined up, one behind the other, begging to be spoken, and yet she said nothing. She stood instead like a ninny, as the fire warmed her face and the minutes ticked by. It was ridiculous, she knew; Percy would be back at any moment and the opportunity to speak alone with Juniper would be gone. She ought just to leap in, to demand outright: *Tell me about him, darling; tell me about Tom, about your plans.* This was Juniper, after all, her own, her dearest little sister. There was nothing they couldn't talk about. And yet . . . Saffy thought of the journal entry and her cheeks warmed. "Here," she said. "How remiss of me! Let me take your coat."

She took up position behind her sister like a housemaid might, unthreaded first one arm, then, when Juniper shifted her cigarette, the other; slipped the brown coat from the thin shoulders and took it to the chair beneath the Constable. It wasn't ideal to let it drip all over the floor, but there wasn't time to do otherwise. She fussed a bit, straightening the fabric, noting the needlework of the hem, as she wondered at her own reticence. Chastised herself for letting ordinary familial inquiries stale on her tongue, as if the young woman standing by the fire were a stranger. It was Juniper, for God's sake; home at last, and likely with a rather important secret up her sleeve.

"Your letter," Saffy prompted, smoothing out the coat's collar, wondering vaguely, in the random fleeting manner of thought, where her sister had acquired such an item. "Your most recent letter."

"Yes?"

Juniper had crouched before the fire as she'd liked to as a child and didn't even turn her head. Saffy realized with a thud that her sister was not going make it easy. She hesitated, steeled herself, then the slam of a distant door reminded her that time was of the essence. "Please, Juniper," she said, hurrying to stand closer. "Tell me about Tom; tell me everything, darling."

"About Tom?"

"Only that, I couldn't help but wonder whether there was something between you—something more serious than you suggested in your letter."

A pause, silence, as the walls strained to hear.

Then came a small noise from Juniper's throat, a breath. "I wanted to wait," she said softly. "We decided to wait till we were together."

"Wait?" Saffy's heart was flickering like a captured bird's. "I'm not sure what you mean, darling."

"Tom and I." Juniper dragged hard on her cigarette then leaned her cheek against the heel of her hand. On an exhalation: "Tom and I are going to be married. He's asked me and I've said yes, and oh, Saffy"—for the first time she looked behind to meet her sister's gaze—"I love him. I can't be without him. I won't."

Though the news itself was just as she'd supposed, Saffy was bruised by the force of the confession. The speed of its delivery, its potency, its repercussions. "Well," she said, heading to the drinks table, remembering to smile. "How wonderful, dearest; then tonight is a celebration."

"You won't tell Percy, will you? Not until—"

"No. No, of course not." Saffy eased the stopper from the whisky.

"I don't know how she'll . . . Will you help me? Help me make her see?"

"You know I will." Saffy concentrated on the drinks that she was pouring. It was true. She would do whatever she could, there was nothing she wouldn't do for Juniper. But Percy was never going to see. Daddy's will was clear: if Juniper were to marry, the castle would be lost. Percy's love, her life, her very reason . . .

Juniper was frowning at the fire. "She'll come round, won't she?"

"Yes." Saffy lied, then drained her glass. Topped it up again.

"I know what it means, I do know that, and I regret it absolutely; I wish that Daddy had never done what he did. I never wanted any of this." Juniper gestured at the stone walls. "But my heart, Saffy. My heart."

Saffy held out a glass to Juniper. "Here darling, have a—" Her other hand clapped against her mouth as her sister stood and turned to take it.

"What is it?"

She couldn't speak.

"Saffy?"

"Your blouse," she managed, "it's—"

"It's new."

Saffy nodded. It was a trick of the light, nothing more. She took her sister by the hand and pulled her swiftly towards the lamp.

Then buckled.

It was unmistakable. Blood. Saffy urged herself not to panic, told herself there was nothing to fear, not yet, that they had to remain calm. She searched for suitable words to say as much, but before she found them Juniper had followed her gaze.

She pulled at the fabric of her shirt, frowned an instant, then she screamed. Brushed frantically at her blouse. Stepped back as if the horror might that way be escaped.

"Shh," said Saffy, flapping her hand. "There now, dearest. Don't be frightened." She could taste her own panic, though, her shadow companion. "Let me take a look at you. Let Saffy take a look."

Juniper stood inert and Saffy undid the buttons, fingers shaking. She opened the blouse, ran her fingertips over her sister's smooth skin—shades of tending Juniper as a child—scanning her chest, her sides, her stomach for wounds. Breathed a great sigh of relief when none was found. "You're all right."

"But whose?" said Juniper. "Whose?" She was shivering. "Where did it come from, Saffy?"

"You don't remember?"

Juniper shook her head.

"Nothing at all?"

Juniper's teeth were chattering; she shook her head again.

Saffy spoke calmly, softly, as if to a child. "Dearest, do you think you might have lost some time?"

Fear lit Juniper's eyes.

"Is your head aching? Your fingers—are they tingling?"

Juniper nodded slowly.

"All right." Saffy smiled as best she could, helped Juniper out of the spoiled blouse, then draped her arm around her sister's shoulders, almost wept with fear and love and anguish when she felt the narrow bones beneath her arm. They should have gone to London, Percy should have gone and brought June back. "It's all right," she said firmly, "you're home now.

"Everything's going to be all right."

Juniper said nothing; her face had glazed over.

Saffy glanced at the door; Percy would know what to do. Percy always knew what to do. "Shh," she said, "shh," but more for herself than for Juniper, who was no longer listening.

They sat together on the end of the chaise longue and waited. Fire crackled in the grate, wind scurried along the stones, and rain lashed the windows. It felt as if a hundred years had passed. Then Percy appeared at the door. She'd been running and held the hot-water bottle in her hand. "I thought I heard a scream—" She stopped, registered Juniper's state of undress. "What is it? What's happened?"

Saffy gestured towards the bloodstained blouse and said, with ghastly cheer, "Come and help me, Perce. Juniper's traveled all day and I thought we might draw her a lovely warm bath."

Percy nodded grimly, and one on either side, they helped their little sister towards the door.

The room settled around their absence; the stones began to whisper.

The loose shutter fell off its hinge, but nobody saw it slip.

"Is she sleeping?"

"Yes."

Percy exhaled relief and stepped further into the attic room to observe their little sister where she lay. She stopped beside Saffy's chair. "Did she tell you anything?"

"Not a lot. She remembered being on the train and then the bus, that it stopped and she was crouched down on the roadside; next thing she knew she was on her way up the drive, almost at the door, her limbs all tingly. The way they get—you know, afterwards."

Percy knew. She reached to run the backs of two fingers down Juniper's hairline towards her cheek. Their little sister looked so small, so helpless and harmless, when she was sleeping.

"Don't wake her."

"Not much chance of that." Percy indicated the bottle of Daddy's pills beside the bed.

"You've changed your clothes," said Saffy, tugging lightly on Percy's trouser leg.

"Yes."

"You're going out."

Percy nodded shortly. If Juniper had left the bus but still found her way home, it meant, presumably, that whatever it was that had caused her to lose time, that was responsible for the blood on her clothing, had happened close to home. Which meant that Percy had to check immediately, take the torch, walk down the drive and see what she could find. She refused to speculate as to what that might be, knew only that it was her duty to remove it. In truth, she was grateful for the task. A solid purpose with a clear objective would help keep the fears at bay, stop her imagination from running ahead unchecked. The situation was troubling enough without that. She looked down at Saffy's head, the pretty curls, and frowned. "Promise me you'll do something while I'm gone," she said, "something other than sitting here, worrying."

"But, Perce—"

"I mean it, Saffy. She'll be out for hours. Go downstairs; do some writing. Keep your mind busy. We don't need a panic."

Saffy reached up to knit fingers with Percy. "And you look out for Mr. Potts. Keep your torchlight low. You know what he's like about the blackout."

"I will."

"Germans too, Perce. Be careful."

Percy took her hand back for herself, softened the fact by driving both inside her pockets and answering wryly, "On a night like this? Any brains and they're all at home tucked up warm in bed."

Saffy attempted a smile but couldn't quite complete it. And who could blame her? The room was hanging with old ghosts. Percy stymied a shiver and headed for the door, saying, "Right, well, I'll—"

"Do you remember when we slept up here, Perce?"

Percy paused, felt for the cigarette she'd rolled earlier. "Distantly."

"It was nice, wasn't it? The two of us."

"As I remember it, you couldn't wait to get downstairs."

Saffy did smile then, but it was full of sadness. She avoided Percy's gaze, kept her eyes on Juniper. "I was always in a hurry. To grow up. To get away."

Percy's chest ached. She steeled herself against the pull of sentiment. She didn't want to remember the girl her twin had been, back before Daddy broke her, when she'd had talent and dreams and every chance of fulfilling them. Not now. Not ever, if she could help it. It hurt too much.

In her trouser pocket were the scraps of paper she'd found quite by chance in the kitchen while preparing the hot-water bottle. She'd been hunting for matches, had lifted a saucepan lid on the bench, and there they'd been, the torn pieces of Emily's letter. Thank God she'd found them. The last thing they needed was to lose Saffy to old despair. Percy would take them downstairs now, burn them on her way outside. "I'm going now, Saff—"

"I think Juniper will leave us."

"What?"

"I think she plans to fly away."

What would make her twin say such a thing? And why now? Why tonight? Percy's pulse began to race. "You asked her about him?"

Saffy's hesitation was long enough for Percy to know that she had.

"She intends to marry?"

"She says she's in love." Saffy spoke on a sigh.

"But she's not."

"She believes that she is, Perce."

"You're wrong." Percy set her chin. "She wouldn't marry. She won't. She knows what Daddy did, what it would mean."

Saffy smiled sadly. "Love makes people do cruel things."

Percy's matchbox slipped from her fingers and she reached to collect it from the floor. When she straightened, she saw that Saffy was watching her with an odd expression on her face, almost as if she were trying to communicate a complex idea or find the solution to a plaguing puzzle. "Is he coming, Percy?"

Percy lit her cigarette and started down the stairs. "Really, Saffy," she said. "How am I supposed to know?"

THE POSSIBILITY had crept up on Saffy softly. Her twin's glowering mood all evening had been unfortunate but not without precedent, thus she'd given it little thought other than to attempt its management so the dinner event wouldn't be spoiled. But then there'd been the lengthy disappearance down to the kitchen, ostensibly to obtain aspirin, the return with a marked dress and a story about noises outside. The blank expression when Saffy asked her whether she'd found the aspirin, as if she'd quite forgotten having needed it in the first place . . . Now Percy's determination, her insistence almost, that Juniper would not be marrying—

But no.

Stop.

Percy could be hard, she could even be unkind, but she wasn't capable of that. Saffy would never believe such a thing. Her twin loved the castle with a passion, but never at the expense of her own humanity. Percy was brave and decent and honorable; she climbed into bomb craters to save lives. Besides, it wasn't Percy who'd been covered in someone else's blood . . .

Saffy trembled, stood suddenly. Percy was right: there was little to be gained by keeping silent vigil while Juniper slept. It had taken three of Daddy's pills to calm her into slumber, poor lamb, and there was little chance she'd surface now for hours.

To leave her as she lay like this, small and vulnerable, went against every maternal instinct Saffy had, and yet . . . To remain, she knew, was to invite descent into abject panic. Already her mind was addled by ugly possibilities: Juniper didn't lose time unless she'd suffered trauma of some sort, unless she'd seen or done something to excite her senses, something to set her heart racing faster than it should. Combined with the blood on her blouse, the general air of unease that had followed her into the house—

No.

Stop.

Saffy pressed the heels of her hands hard against her chest. Tried to ease the knot that fear was tying there. Now was not the time to succumb to one of her panics. She had to stay calm. So much was still unknown, yet one thing was certain. She would be of little use to Juniper if she couldn't keep her own jagged fears in check.

She would go downstairs and she would write her novel, just as Percy had suggested. An hour or so in Adele's lovely company was just the thing. Juniper was safe, Percy would find whatever there was to be found, and Saffy Would. Not. Panic.

She *must* not.

Resolved, she straightened the blanket and smoothed it gently across Juniper's front. Her little sister didn't flinch. She was sleeping so still: like a child, spent from a day beneath the sun; the clear, blue sky; a day beside the sea.

Such a special child she'd been. A memory came, instant and complete, a flash: Juniper as a girl, matchstick legs with white hairs shining in the sunlight. Crouching so her haunches supported her, knees with scabs, bare feet flat and dusty on the scorched summer earth. Perched above an old drain, scrabbling in the dirt with a stick, looking for the perfect stone to drop through the grille—

A sheet of rain slid across the window, and the girl, the sun, the smell of dry earth turned to smoke and blew away. Only the dim, musty attic remained. The attic where Saffy and Percy had been children together; within whose walls they'd grown from mewling babies into moody young ladies. Little evidence of their tenure remained, the sort that could be seen. Only the bed, the ink stain on the floor, the bookcase by the window that she'd—

No!

Stop!

Saffy clenched her fists. She noticed the bottle of Daddy's pills. Considered a moment, then unscrewed the lid and shook one into her hand. It would take the edge off, help her to relax.

She left the door ajar and crept carefully down the narrow stairs. Behind her in the attic room the curtains sighed.

Juniper flinched.

A long dress shimmered against the wardrobe like a pale, forgotten ghost.

IT WAS moonless, it was wet, and despite her raincoat and boots, Percy was drenched. To make matters worse, the torch was being temperamental. She planted her feet on the muddied drive and gave the torch a whack against her palm; the battery rattled, light flickered, and hope rose. Then it died. All of it.

Percy swore beneath her breath and swiped with her wrist at the hair that clung to her forehead. She wasn't sure what she'd been expecting to find, only that she'd hoped to have found it by now. The longer it took, the further from the castle she traveled, the less likely it was that the matter could be contained. And it must be contained.

She squinted through the rain, trying to make out what she could.

The brook was running high; she could hear it somersaulting, roaring on its way towards the wood. At this rate, the bridge would be out by morning.

She turned her head a little more to the left, sensed the glowering battalions of Cardarker Wood. Heard the wind skulking in the treetops.

Percy gave the torch another try. Damned thing ignored her still. She kept walking in the direction of the road, slowly, cautiously, scanning the way ahead as best she could.

A shard of lightning and the world was white, the sodden fields rolling away from her, the wood recoiling, the castle, its arms crossed in disappointment. A frozen moment in which Percy felt entirely alone, the cold, wet white within as well as without.

She saw it as the light's last echo died. A shape on the drive beyond. Something lying very still.

Dear God: the size, the shape, of a man.

TWO

TOM had brought flowers from London, a small bunch of orchids. They'd been hard to find, fiendishly expensive, and as day had dragged into night he'd come to regret the decision. They looked rather the worse for wear, and he'd started to wonder whether Juniper's sisters would like shop-bought flowers any more than she did. He'd brought the birthday jam, too. Christ, he was nervous.

He checked his watch, then resolved not to do so again. He was beyond late. It couldn't be helped: the train had been stopped, then he'd needed to find another bus and the only one heading east had gone from a nearby town, so he'd had to run cross-country for miles only to find it was out of service that afternoon. This bus had come along three hours later to replace it, just as he was about to set out on foot and see if he could hitch himself a ride.

He'd worn his uniform; he was heading back to the front in a few days, and besides, he was used to it now, but his nerves made him stiff and the jacket caught on his shoulders in a way that was unfamiliar. He'd worn his medal, too, the one they'd given him for the business on the Escaut Canal. Tom wasn't sure how he felt about receiving it—he couldn't feel it there against his chest without remembering the boys they'd lost as they scrambled madly out of hell—but it seemed to matter to others, his mother, for one, and seeing as it was his first time meeting Juniper's family, he supposed it was best.

He wanted them to like him, for everything to go as well as possible. For her sake more than his; her ambivalence confused him. She'd spoken of her sisters and her childhood often, and always with affection. Listening to her, and recalling what he could of his own glimpse of the castle, Tom had begun to envisage an idyll, a rural fantasy; more than that, a fairy tale of sorts. And yet, for a long time she hadn't wanted him to visit; had been almost wary if he so much as hinted at the possibility.

Then, not two weeks before—with characteristic suddenness—Juniper had changed her mind. While Tom was still reeling from the shock of her having accepted his proposal, she'd announced that they must visit her sisters and break the news together. Of course they must. So here he was. And he knew he must be getting close because they'd stopped a number of times already and he was one of the only passengers remaining. It had been overcast when he left London, a mask of white cloud covering the sky, gathering more darkly in the corners as he approached Kent, but now it was raining hard and the windshield wipers were shushing in a way that would have made him sleepy if he wasn't so nervous.

"Going home, then, are you?"

Tom searched the dark for the person attached to the voice, saw a woman sitting across the aisle. Fifty or so years old—it was difficult to know for sure—a kind enough face, the way his mother might have looked if her life had been an easier one. "Visiting a friend," he answered. "She lives on the Tenterden Road."

"She, eh?" The woman wore a knowing smile. "A sweetheart, I think?"

He smiled because it was true, then let it drop again because it also wasn't. He was going to marry Juniper Blythe, but she was not his sweetheart. "Sweetheart" was the girl a fellow met when he was home between postings, the pretty girl with the pout and the legs and the empty promises of letters at the front; the girl with a taste for gin and dancing and late-night groping.

Juniper Blythe was none of those things. She was going to be his wife, he would be her husband, but Tom knew, even as he clutched at absolutes, that she would never belong to him. Keats had known women like Juniper. When he wrote of his lady in the meads, the beautiful fairy's child with the long hair, the light foot, and the wild, wild eyes, he might have been describing Juniper Blythe.

The woman across the aisle was still awaiting confirmation, and Tom smiled. "Fiancée," he said, enjoying the word's pregnant expectation of solidity, even as he cringed beneath its unsuitability.

"Well now. Isn't that lovely. So nice to hear happy stories at a time like this. Meet around here, did you?"

"No—well, yes, but not properly. London, that's where we met."

"London." She smiled sympathetically. "I go up to visit my friend sometimes, and when I last hopped off at Charing Cross . . ." She shook her head. "Brave old London. Terrible, what's happened. Any damage to you or yours?"

"We've been lucky. So far."

"Taken you long to get here?"

"I left on the nine twelve. It's been a comedy of errors since."

She was shaking her head. "The stopping and starting. The overcrowding. The identity checks—still, you're here now. Almost at the end of your journey. Pity about the weather. Hope you've got an umbrella with you."

He hadn't, but he nodded and smiled and went back to thinking his own thoughts.

SAFFY TOOK her writing journal to the good parlor. Its fire was the only one they'd lit that evening, and despite everything, the room's delicate arrangement still gave her some small pleasure. She didn't like to feel enclosed, so she eschewed the armchairs in favor of the table. Cleared away one place setting. She did it neatly, careful not to disturb the other three—it was mad, she knew, but a tiny part of her still clung to the hope that they might yet dine, the four of them together.

She poured herself another whisky then sat and opened her notebook to the most recent page, read it through, reacquainting herself with Adele's tragic love story. She sighed as the secret world of her book stretched out its arms to welcome her home.

A tremendous clap of thunder made Saffy jump and reminded her that she'd wanted to see about rewriting the scene in which William broke off his engagement to Adele.

Poor, dear Adele. Of course her world should be broken apart during a storm in which the heavens themselves seemed likely to be rent asunder! It was only right. All life's tragic moments should be granted such elemental emphasis.

It ought to have stormed when Matthew broke off his engagement to Saffy, but it hadn't. They'd been seated, side by side, in the love seat by the library's French doors, sunlight streaming across their caps. Twelve months since the ghastly trip to London, the play's premiere, the dark theater, the hideous creature emerging from the moat, climbing up the wall, bellowing with hideous pain . . . Saffy had just poured tea for two when Matthew spoke.

"I believe the best thing now would be for us to release one another."

"To release . . . ? But I don't . . . ?" She blinked. "You no longer love me?"

"I'll always love you, Saffy."

"Then . . . why?" She'd changed into the sapphire blue dress when she knew that he was coming. It was her best: it was the one she'd worn to London; she'd wanted him to admire her, to covet her, to want her as he had that day by the lake. She felt foolish. "Why?" she said again, despising the weakness in her voice.

"We can't marry; you know that as well as I. How can we live as man and wife when you refuse to leave the castle?"

"Not refuse; I don't refuse, I *long* to leave—"

"Then come, come with me now—"

"I can't . . ." She stood. "I've told you."

A change came upon him then; a bitter knife twisting his features. "Of course you can. If you loved me, you would come. You'd climb into my motorcar and we'd drive away from this ghastly, mildewed place." He stood beside her, implored her. "Come on, Saffy," he said, all trace of resentment dropping away. He gestured with his hat to the top of the drive where his car was parked. "Let's go. Let's drive away this instant, the two of us together."

She'd wanted to say again, "I can't," to beg him to understand, to be patient, to wait for her; but she hadn't. A moment of clarity, a struck match, and she'd known that there was nothing she could say or do to make him comprehend. The crippling panic that crept upon her if she tried to leave the castle; the black and groundless fear that dug its claws into her, wrapped her in its wings and made her lungs constrict, her vision blur that kept her prisoner in this cold, dark place, as weak and helpless as a child.

"Come," he said again, reaching for her hand. "Come." He said it so tenderly that sitting in the castle's good parlor sixteen years later, Saffy would feel its echo trickling down her spine and settling warm beneath her skirt.

She'd smiled, she hadn't been able to help it, even though she'd known herself to be standing at the top of a great cliff, dark water swirling beneath her, the man she loved urging her to let him save her, unaware that she couldn't be saved, that his adversary was so much stronger than he was.

"You were right," she'd said, leaping from the cliff, falling away from him. "The best thing for us both would be to release each other."

She'd never seen Matthew again, nor her cousin Emily, who'd been lurking in the wings, waiting for her chance, always coveting that which Saffy wanted . . .

A LOG. Nothing but a piece of driftwood, washed downstream by the fast-rising current. Percy pulled it off the drive, cursing the weight, the branch that snagged her shoulder, and wondering whether she was relieved or dismayed that the search must now continue. She was about to press on down the drive when something stopped her. A strange sense, not a presentiment exactly, rather one of those odd twin things. A swirl of misgiving. She wondered whether Saffy had taken her advice and found some occupation.

Percy stood in the rain, undecided, looked down the hill towards the road, then back at the blackened castle.

The not completely blackened castle.

There was a light, small but bright, shining from one of the windows. The good parlor.

The bloody shutter. If she'd only fixed it properly in the first place.

It was the shutter that decided her absolutely. The last thing they needed tonight was the attention of Mr. Potts and his Home Guard platoon.

With a last backward look at the Tenterden Road, Percy turned and headed for the castle.

THE BUS stopped at the side of the road and Tom hopped out. It was raining hard and his flowers lost their valiant bid for life the moment he disembarked; he debated for a second, whether ruined flowers were better than no flowers at all, before tossing the stems into the overflowing ditch. The mark of a good soldier was knowing when to call retreat, and he still had the jam, after all.

Through the dense, wet night he glimpsed a set of iron gates and laid his hand on one, pushing it open. As it gave way with a shriek beneath his weight, he tilted his face towards the black, black sky. He closed his eyes and let the rain slide clean across his cheeks; it was a bugger, but without a raincoat or umbrella, he had little choice but to surrender. He was late, he was wet, but he was here.

He closed the gate behind him, hoisted his duffel bag over his shoulder, and started up the drive. By God, it was dark. The blackout was one thing in London, but in the country, and with foul weather having switched off all the stars, it was like walking through pitch. There was a looming mass to his right, blacker somehow than the rest, that he knew must be Cardarker Wood. The wind had picked up and the treetops gnashed their teeth as he watched. He shivered and turned away, thought of Juniper, waiting for him in the warm, dry castle.

One drenched foot after another, he kept on. He rounded a bend, crossed a bridge, water gushing fast beneath it, and still the drive wound on ahead.

A flash of jagged lightning then, and Tom stopped in wonder. It was magnificent. The world was drenched in silvery white light—a great heaving wrangle of trees, a pale stone castle on the hill, the winding driveway carving on ahead through shivering fields—before falling unevenly back to black. Imprints of the lit-up image remained, like a photographic negative, and that's how Tom knew he was not alone in the dark and the wet. Someone else, a thin but mannish figure, was making its way up the driveway ahead of him.

Tom wondered idly why anyone else would venture out in such a night, whether perhaps there was another guest expected at the castle, someone else as late as he was, also caught in the rain. His spirits rose on the back of such a notion, and he considered calling out—it was better, surely, to arrive in tandem with another tardy fellow?—but the clap of murderous thunder decided him against trying. He pressed on, eyeing the spot in the darkness where he knew the castle stood.

Tom saw it only when he drew near, a tiny relief in the darkness. He frowned, then blinked, realized he wasn't imagining things. There was a small patch of golden light ahead, a chink in the fortress wall. He pictured it as Juniper waiting for him, like a mermaid in one of the old stories, holding out a lantern to bring her lover in from the storm. Filled with ardent determination, he walked towards it.

As Percy and Tom climb through the rain, deep within Milderhurst Castle all is still. High in the attic room, Juniper is darkly dreaming; down in the good parlor, her sister Saffy reclines on the chaise longue, drifting on the verge of sleep. Behind her, a room with a crackling fire; before her, a door opening onto a picnic by the lake. A perfect day in the late spring of 1922, warmer perhaps than expected, the sky as blue as fine Venetian glass. People have been swimming and are sitting now on blankets, drinking cocktails and eating dainty sandwiches.

A few young people break away and the dreaming Saffy follows, watches in particular the young pair at the back, the boy called Matthew and a pretty girl of sixteen whose name is Seraphina. They have known one another since they were children, he is a family friend of her strange cousins from the north and has thus been deemed acceptable by Daddy; over the years they have chased one another through countless fields, fished generations of trout from the brook, sat wide-eyed by annual harvest bonfires; something, though, has changed between them. She has found herself on this visit tongue-tied in his presence; has caught him watching her, eyes heavy with something like intent; has felt her own cheeks warming in response. They haven't exchanged more than three words since he arrived.

The group the pair are trailing stop, blankets are spread with an extravagant lack of care beneath the trees, a ukulele is produced, cigarettes and banter lit; he and she remain on the fringe. They neither speak nor look at one another. Each sits, pretending interest in the sky, the birds, the sunlight playing on the leaves, while thinking only of the inch between her knee and his thigh. The pulse of electricity that fills the space. Wind whispers, leaves spiral, a starling calls . . .

She gasps. Covers her mouth lest anyone else should notice.

His fingertips have grazed the very edge of her hand. So lightly she mightn't have felt them had her attention not been focused with mathematical precision on the distance between them, his breath-stopping proximity . . . At this moment, the dreamer merges with her young self. She no longer watches the lovers from afar, but sits cross-legged on the blanket, arm stretched out behind her, heart pounding in her chest with all the unblemished joy and expectation of youth.

Saffy doesn't dare look at Matthew. She glances quickly around the group, shocked that no one else appears to have noticed what is happening, that the world has swung on its pendulum and everything is different, yet nothing around them seems to have been altered.

She lets her gaze drop then, lets it skim down the length of her arm, past her wrist, and onto her supporting hand. There. His fingertips. His skin on hers.

She is gathering the courage to lift her eyes, to cross the bridge he's made between them and allow her gaze to complete its journey, to trace its way along his hand, across his wrist, and all the way up his arm to where she knows his eyes will be waiting to meet her own, when something else catches her attention. A darkness on the hill behind them.

Her father, always protective, has followed and is watching now from the crest. She feels his eyes on her, knows that he is watching her especially; knows, too, that he has seen Matthew's fingers move against her own. She lets her gaze drop; her cheeks flare, and something moves deep and low within her belly. Somehow, though she's not at all sure why, Daddy's expression, his presence on the hill, bring her recent feelings into sharp focus. She realizes that her love for Matthew, for that, of course, is what she feels—love—is curiously similar to her passion for Daddy; the desire to be treasured, to captivate, the fierce need to be thought amusing and clever . . .

SAFFY WAS fast asleep on the chaise longue by the fire, an empty glass on her lap, a small, sleepy smile on her lips, and Percy breathed a sigh of relief. That was something; the shutter was hanging loose, there'd been no sign yet of whatever it was that had caused Juniper to lose time, but all was at least quiet on the domestic front.

She climbed down from the window ledge and jumped the final distance off the capping stones, bracing for the sodden landing, the old moat, drenched through and rising fast, well over her ankles already. It was as she'd thought; she would need the correct tools to secure the shutter properly.

Percy trudged around the side of the castle to the kitchen door, heaved it open, and fell through, out of the rain. The contrast was breathtaking. The warm, dry kitchen with its meaty steam, its humming electric light, was a picture of such easy domesticity that she was almost winded by a desire to shed her soaked clothing, the rubber boots and slimy socks, and curl up on the mat by the stove, leaving all that had to be done undone. To sleep with the childlike certainty of knowing that there was someone else to do them.

She smiled, catching such serpentine thoughts by the tail and tossing them aside. This was no time to be fantasizing about sleep and certainly not about curling up on the kitchen floor. She blinked widely as drips rolled down her face and started for the toolbox. She'd hammer the shutter closed tonight and make proper repairs by daylight.

SAFFY'S DREAM has twisted like a ribbon; the place, the time, have changed but the central image remains, like a dark shape on the retina when one's eyes are closed against the sun.

Daddy.

Saffy is younger now, a girl of twelve. She is climbing a set of stairs, stone walls rise on either side of her, and she is glancing over her shoulder because Daddy has told her that the nurses will stop the visits if they find out. It is 1917 and there's a war on; Daddy has been away but now he's back from the front and also, as they've been told by countless nurses, from the brink of death. Saffy is walking up the stairs because she and Daddy have a new game. A secret game in which she tells him things that frighten her when she's alone but that make his eyes light up with glee. They've been playing it for five days now.

Suddenly, within the dream, it is days before. Saffy is no longer climbing the cold stone stairs, but lying in her bed. She wakes with a start. Alone and afraid. She reaches for her twin, as she always does when the nightmare comes, but the sheet beside her is bare and cold. She spends the morning drifting through the corridors trying to fill days that have lost all shape and meaning, trying to escape the nightmare.

And now she sits with her back against the wall in the chamber beneath the spiral stairs. It is the only place where she feels safe. Sounds waft down from the tower, the stones sigh and sing, and as she closes her eyes she hears it. A voice, whispering her name.

For a single joyous instant she thinks it is her twin returned. Then, through the haze, she sees him. Sitting on a wooden bench by the far window, a cane across his lap. Daddy, though, much changed, no longer the strong young man who went away to war three years ago.

He beckons her and she is helpless to refuse.

She goes slowly, wary of him and his new shadows.

"I've missed you," he says as she reaches his side. And something in his voice is so familiar that all the longing she's bottled up while he was gone begins to swell. "Sit beside me," he says, "and tell me why it is you look so scared."

And she does. She tells him everything. All about the dream, the man who is coming for her, the fearsome man who lives in the mud.

FINALLY, TOM reached the castle and saw that it wasn't a lamp at all. The glow he had been following, the beacon bringing sailors safely home, was actually electric light, spilling from a window in one of the castle's rooms. A shutter, he noticed, was hanging loose, breaking the blackout.

He'd offer to fix it when he went inside. Juniper had told him that her sisters were keeping the whole place running themselves, having lost what little help they'd had to the war. Tom wasn't much when it came to mechanics, but he knew his way around a hammer and nails.

Feeling a little brighter, he waded across a patch of water in the low-lying land around the castle and climbed the front stairs. Stood a moment by the entrance taking stock. His hair, his clothes, his feet could not be wetter had he swum the channel to get there, but get there he had. He slid his duffel bag off his shoulder and dug inside, looking for the jam. There it was. Thomas pulled the glass jar clear and held it close, ran his fingers over it to check there'd been no breakage.

It felt perfect. Perhaps his luck was on the rise. With a smile, Tom ran a palm across his hair in an attempt to order it, knocked on the door, and waited, jam in hand.

PERCY CURSED and brought her palm down hard on the toolbox lid. For the love of God, where was the bloody hammer? She racked her brain, trying to remember the last time she'd used it. There'd been the repair work on Saffy's chicken run; the boards that had come loose on the sill in the yellow parlor; the balustrade on the tower staircase . . . She didn't have a clear memory of returning the hammer to the box, but Percy was sure she must have. She was mindful of that sort of thing.

Damn it.

Percy felt her sides, fiddled a path between the buttons of her raincoat to dig inside her trouser pocket, clutched the pouch of tobacco with relief. She stood and smoothed out a cigarette paper, held it clear of the drips that were falling still from her sleeves, her hair, her nose. She sprinkled tobacco along its crease, then licked and sealed it; rolled the cylinder between her fingers. She struck a match and drew hard. Breathed in glorious tobacco, breathed out frustration.

A missing hammer was the last thing she needed tonight. On top of Juniper's return, the mysterious blood all over her shirt, the news that she intended marriage, not to mention the afternoon's encounter with Lucy . . .

Percy drew again, wiped something from her eye as she exhaled. Saffy didn't mean it, she knew nothing of what had happened with Lucy, of the love and the loss that Percy had endured. Percy had been careful about that. It was always possible, she supposed, that her twin had heard or seen or somehow intuited that which she should not, but even so. Saffy surely wasn't one to rub Percy's nose in her misery. She, of all people, knew how it felt to be robbed of one's love.

A noise and Percy drew breath, listened hard. Heard nothing more. She had an image of Saffy, asleep in the chair, the empty whisky glass precarious on her lap. She'd moved, perhaps, and it had fallen to the ground. Percy scanned the ceiling, waited another half a minute, then decided that was all it had been.

Regardless, there was no time to be standing around lamenting what had been and gone. Cigarette clamped between her lips, she returned to digging through the tools.

TOM KNOCKED again, and set the jar down by the door so he could rub his hands together. It was a big place, he supposed; who knew how long it might take a person to get from top to bottom? A minute or so passed and he turned away from the door, watching the rain tumble over the eaves, wondering at the odd fact that one might feel colder being wet and sheltered than when one was standing beneath the rain's full force.

His attention fell to the ground and he noticed the way water was gathering deeper round the castle rim than it was further out. One day in London, when they were lying in bed together and he was asking all about the castle, Juniper had told him there had once been a moat at Milderhurst, that their father had ordered it filled in after his first wife died.

"It must have been grief," Tom had said, well able to understand when he looked across at Juniper, allowed himself to imagine the gaping horror of her loss, what such an absence might drive a man to do.

"Not grief," she'd replied, threading the end of her hair through her fingers. "More like guilt."

He'd wondered what she'd meant, but she'd smiled and swiveled to sit on the side of the bed, her naked back smooth and just begging him to stroke it, and his questions had fallen away. It hadn't occurred to him again until now. Guilt—for what? He made a mental note to ask her later; when he'd met the sisters, when Juniper and he had broken their news, when they were together, alone.

A triangle of light caught Tom's attention then, shining on the watery surface. It was coming from the window with the broken shutter. Tom wondered whether the repair might be a simple matter of hooking it up on an existing catch, and whether he ought to attempt it now.

The window wasn't high. He could be up and down in no time. It would save him coming out again once he was clean and dry, and it might just win the sisters' hearts.

With a grin, Tom set his bag down by the door and headed back out into the rain.

SINCE THE moment she turned her back on the crackling fire of the good parlor, Saffy has been dreaming her way inwards along the ripples of her mind's pool. Now she reaches its center. The place of stillness from which all dreams flow, to which all return. The site of her old familiar.

She has dreamed it countless times before, has been dreaming it since she was a child. It never changes, like an old piece of film footage, the spool rewound, ready to play again. And no matter that she's been there before, the dream is always fresh, the terror as raw as ever.

The dream begins with her waking, thinking that she's woken to the real world, then noticing the strange quality of silence that surrounds her. It is cold and Saffy is alone; she slides across the white sheet and puts her feet on the wooden floor. Her nurse is sleeping in the little room nearby, slow, steady breaths that should suggest safety but in this world signal only unbridgeable distance.

Saffy walks slowly to the window. She is drawn there.

She climbs atop the bookcase, gathers her nightdress round her legs against a sudden deathly chill. Lifts a hand to touch the misted glass and peers out into the night . . .

PERCY FOUND the hammer. It took much hunting and a fair amount of cursing, but finally her hand closed round the smooth wooden handle that years of varied use had rubbed clean of splinters. With a huff of jubilant frustration, she yanked it from among the wrenches and screwdrivers and laid it on the floor beside her. Opened the glass jar of nails and shook a dozen or so into her hand. She held one up against the light, studied it, and figured two and a half inches in length had to be enough to do the trick, at least for the night. She tucked the clutch of nails inside the pocket of her raincoat, snatched up the hammer, and stalked back across the kitchen to the door.

He hadn't got off to the best of starts and that was a fact. Misjudging a stone and slipping back into the muddy moat had been a rude shock and certainly not part of the plan, but after swearing like a soldier—which, of course, he was—Tom had picked himself up, dragged the back of his wrist across his eyes so he could see, and attacked the wall with more determination than ever.

Never say die, as his commanding officer had shouted at them when they were fighting their way across France. *Never say die.*

Now, finally, he'd reached the window ledge. By happy chance, there was a groove between two stones where mortar had long since dropped away, leaving the perfect cavity for him to wedge his boots. The light from the room was a blessing and it didn't take long for Tom to see that the shutter was going to need more than he could offer it right now.

He'd been so intent on the shutter that he'd paid no attention to the room inside. But now he looked through the window and saw that the scene was one of quintessential warmth and comfort. A pretty woman, asleep by the fire. He thought at first that it was Juniper.

The woman flinched, though, and her features tightened, and he knew then that it wasn't Juniper but one of the sisters: Saffy, he guessed, based on the stories Juniper had told him; the maternal one, the twin who Juniper said had stepped in when her mother died to raise her, the one who suffered with panic and wasn't able to leave the castle.

She opened her eyes as he watched, a sudden movement, and he almost lost his grip with surprise. She turned her head towards the window and their gazes met.

PERCY SAW the man at the window as soon as she turned the corner. The light from the window illuminated him; a dark figure, like a gorilla, climbing the wall, clinging to the stones, peering into the good parlor. The room in which Saffy was sleeping. Something inside Percy began to pulse; all her life she had known it her duty to protect her sisters, and her hand tightened around the hammer's wooden handle. Nerves on fire, she began to run through the rain towards the man.

TO APPEAR like a mud-bathed Peeping Tom at the window was about as far from the impression he'd hoped to make on Juniper's sisters as was possible.

But Tom had been seen now. He couldn't just jump down and hide, pretend it hadn't happened. He smiled tentatively; lifted a hand to wave, to signal good intentions, but dropped it again when he realized it was coated in mud.

Oh God. She was standing; she wasn't smiling.

She was coming towards him.

A small part of him could see beyond the mortification, could glimpse that by sheer virtue of its preposterousness, this moment was destined to become a favorite anecdote. *Remember the night we met Tom? He appeared at the window covered in mud and waved hello?*

But not yet. For now, he had little choice but to watch as she walked towards him, slowly, almost as if in a dream, shaking a little, as if she were as icy cold as he had been in the rain.

She reached to unlatch the window, he searched for words to explain, and then she picked something up from the sill.

PERCY STOPPED dead. The man was gone. Right before her eyes, he'd toppled and fallen to the ground. She glanced up at the window and saw Saffy, shaking, the wrench held tightly in her hands.

A SHARP crack, and he wondered what it was. Movement, his own, sudden and surprising.

Falling.

Something cold against his face, wet.

Noises, birds perhaps, crying, shrieking. He flinched and tasted mud. Where was he? Where was Juniper?

Raindrops pounded his head; he felt each one separately, like music, strings being plucked, a complex tune being played. They were beautiful, and he wondered why he'd never known that before. Individual drops, perfect, each one of them. Falling to earth and soaking into the ground, so that rivers could form, and oceans could fill, and people, animals, plants, might have water to drink—it was all so simple.

He remembered a rainstorm when he was a boy, when his father was still alive. Tom had been frightened. It was dark and loud and he'd hidden under the table in the kitchen. He'd cried and screwed shut his eyes and his fists. He'd been crying so hard, his own sorrow so loud in his ears that he hadn't noticed when his father came into the room. The first he'd known was when the great bear scooped him up and lifted him into his big, broad arms and held him close; and then he told Tom that everything was all right, and the sweet, sour, lovely smell of tobacco on his breath had made it so. On his father's lips those words had been an incantation. A promise. And Tom had not been frightened anymore . . .

Where had he put the jam?

The jam was important. The man in the basement flat had said it was his best batch yet, that he'd gathered the blackberries himself and used months of rationed sugar. But Tom couldn't remember where he'd put it. He'd had it, he knew that. He'd brought it from London in his bag, but then he'd taken it out and put it down. Had he left it under the table? When he hid from the rain, had he taken the jam jar with him? He supposed he should get up and look for it, and he would. He had to, the jam was a gift. He'd go and find it in just a minute, and then he'd laugh that he could have lost it at all. He'd just take a little rest first.

He felt tired. So tired. It had been such a long journey. The stormy night, the trudge up the drive, the day of trains and buses and near misses, but more than that, the journey that had led him to her. He'd walked so far; he'd read and taught and dreamed and wished and hoped so much. It was natural that he should need to rest, that he might just close his eyes now and take a moment; just rest a little, so that when he saw her again, he would be ready . . .

Tom closed his eyes and there were millions of tiny stars, twinkling, shifting, and they were so beautiful and he wanted only to watch them. It seemed to him that there was nothing he wanted more in the world than to lie there and watch those stars. So he did, he watched them as they drifted and sifted, he wondered if he might even be able to reach them, to hold out a finger and catch one on it, and then finally he saw there was something hiding among them. A face, Juniper's face. His heart shook its wings. She had arrived, then, after all. She was close by, leaning to lay her hand on his shoulder, to speak softly against his ear. Words that described it all so perfectly that when he tried to clutch them, to repeat them to himself, they turned to water in his hands, and there were stars in her eyes and stars on her lips and little shimmery lights hanging in her hair; and he couldn't hear her anymore, even though her lips were moving and the stars were winking, because she was fading now, turning into black; and he was fading, too.

"June—" he whispered as the last little lights began to tremble, to switch off one by one, as thick mud filled his throat and his nose and his mouth, as the rain beat down on his head, as his lungs were finally starved of air; he smiled as her breath caressed his neck . . .

THREE

JUNIPER woke with a start to a throbbing headache and the muddy mouth of unnatural sleep. The surface of her eyes felt grazed. Where was she? It was dark, nighttime, but a faint light crept in from somewhere. She blinked and registered a ceiling high above her. Its marks, its rafters, were familiar, and yet it wasn't right somehow. It didn't fit. What had happened?

Something, she knew that; she could feel it. But what?

I can't remember.

She turned her head—slowly—letting the clutter of loose, nameless objects inside tumble over. She scanned the space beside her for clues, saw nothing but an empty sheet, a jumbled shelf beyond, the merest strip of light spilling in from a door that was ajar.

Juniper knew this place. This was the attic at Milderhurst. She was lying in her own bed. She hadn't been here in a long time. There had been another attic, a sunny place, not like this at all.

I can't remember.

She was alone. The thought came to her as solidly as if she'd read it in, black text on white paper, and the absence was a pain, an aching wound. She'd expected there to be someone else with her. A man, she realized. She'd expected a man.

A strange wave of misgiving then; not to remember what had happened during the lost time was normal, but there was something else. Juniper was lost within the dark wardrobe of her mind, but although she couldn't see what lay around her, she was filled with a certainty, a heavy dread, that there was something terrible locked inside there with her.

I can't remember.

She closed her eyes and strained to hear, cast about for anything that might help. There was none of the bustle of London, the buses, the people on the street below, the murmurs from other flats; but the veins of the house were creaking, the stones were sighing, and there was another persistent noise. Rain—it was light rain on the roof.

Her eyes opened. She remembered rain.

She remembered a bus stopping.

She remembered blood.

Juniper sat up suddenly, too focused on this fact, this small glimmer of light, of remembrance, to mind the pain in her head. She remembered blood.

But whose blood?

The dread shifted, stretched out its legs.

She needed air. The attic was stifling, suddenly, warm and moist and thick.

She placed her feet on the wooden floor. Things, her things, lay everywhere, yet she felt disconnected from them. Someone had attempted to clear a space, a passage through the jumble.

She stood. She remembered blood.

What made her look at her hands then? Whatever it was, she recoiled. There was something on them. She brushed quickly on her shirt and the gesture caused a rippling of familiarity beneath her skin. She lifted her palms closer to her face and the marks fled. Shadows. They were only shadows.

Disconcerted, relieved, she went shakily to the window. Pulled aside the blackout curtain and opened the sash. A light cool film of fresh air brushed her cheeks.

The night was moonless, starless too, but Juniper didn't need light to know what lay beyond. The world of Milderhurst pressed upon her. Unseen animals shivering in the underbrush, Roving Brook laughing in the woods, a faraway bird lamenting. Where did the birds go when it rained?

There was something else, directly below. A small light, she realized, a lamp hanging from a stick. Someone was down there in the rain, working in the pets' graveyard.

Percy.

Percy holding a shovel.

Digging.

Something lay on the ground behind her. A mound. Large. Still.

Percy stepped aside then and Juniper's eyes widened. They fired a message to her beleaguered brain, and the light in the dark wardrobe flickered, and she saw clearly, just for a moment, the terrible, terrible thing that was hiding there, the evil that she'd sensed but hadn't seen, that had filled her with fear. She saw it, she named it, and horror fired every nerve within her body. *You're just like me,* Daddy had said, before he confessed his grisly tale—

The circuit blew and the lights went out.

Damned hands.

Percy recovered the dropped cigarette from the kitchen floor, wedged it between her lips, and struck the match. She'd been counting on the familiar action to return her some steel, but she'd been too hopeful. Her hand shook like a leaf in the wind. The flame extinguished and she tried again. Concentrated on striking firmly; on holding the bloody thing still as it sizzled and caught, as the flame leaped; on bringing it to meet the end of her cigarette. Closer, closer, closer— something caught her eye, a dark smear on her inner wrist, and, with a start she dropped the box of matches, the flame.

Matchsticks lay spilled across the flagstones and she got down on her knees to pick them up. One by one, side by side, into the box; Percy took her time, disappeared inside the simple task, wrapped it round her shoulders like a cloak and did up all the buttons.

It was mud on her wrist. Only mud. A small mark she'd missed when she came inside, when she'd stood at the sink and scrubbed the mud from her hands, her face, her arms, scrubbed until she thought her skin would bleed.

Percy held a matchstick between her thumb and forefinger. Looked beyond it but saw nothing. It fell again to the ground.

He'd been heavy.

She'd lifted bodies before, she and Dot; they'd rescued people from bomb-blasted houses, loaded them into the ambulance, carried them again at the other end. She knew that the dead weighed more than the friends they left behind. But this had been different. He'd been heavy.

She'd known he was dead as soon as she pulled him from the moat. Whether from the blow itself or the inches of mudded water into which he'd fallen, she couldn't say. But he was already dead; she knew that. She'd tried to revive him anyway, an instinct born of shock more than hope; she'd tried everything they had taught her in the ambulance brigade. And it had rained and she'd been glad because it meant she could deny the damned tears when they dared to fall.

His face.

She closed her eyes, clenched them tight; saw it still. Knew that she always would.

Her forehead met her knee and the solidity of the contact was a relief. The hardness of her kneecap, its cool certainty when pressed against her hot and racing head, was reassuring, almost like contact with another person, a calmer person than she was, older and wiser and more suited to the tasks that lay ahead.

For things would have to be done. Other things, more than what she'd done already. A letter would have to be written, she supposed, telling his family; though telling them what, she wasn't sure. Not the truth. Things had gone too far for that. There'd been an instant, a flame's-tip moment when she might have done things differently, telephoned Inspector Watkins and laid the whole mess out before him, but she hadn't. What could she have said to make him understand? To make him see that it wasn't Saffy's fault? And so a letter must be written to the man's family. Percy had no instinct for stories, but necessity was the mother of invention and she would think of something.

She heard a noise and jumped. It was someone on the stairs.

Percy collected herself, swiped her palm across wet cheeks. Angry with herself, with him, the world. Anyone but her twin.

"I've put her back to bed," said Saffy on her way through the door. "You were right, she was up again and terribly—Perce?"

"Over here." Her throat ached with tension.

Saffy's head appeared over the top of the table. "What are you doing down—oh, dear. Let me help."

While her twin crouched beside her, gathering matches, jumbling them into the box, Percy hid behind her unlit cigarette and said, "She's back to bed, then?"

"She is now. She'd got up—the pills mustn't be as strong as we'd thought. I've given her another."

Percy wiped at the mud smear on her wrist and nodded.

"She was in quite a state, the poor darling. I've done my best to reassure her that all will work out, that the young man's only been detained and that he's bound to be along tomorrow. That's all it is, isn't it, Percy? He'll be along? Perce? What is it? Why do you look that way?"

Percy shook her head.

"You're frightening me."

"I'm sure he'll come," said Percy, placing a hand on her sister's arm. "You're right. We just have to be patient."

Saffy's relief was evident. She handed over the full box of matches and nodded at the cigarette in Percy's hand. "There you are, then; you'll be needing these if you plan on smoking that." She stood, straightening the green dress that was too tight. Percy fought an urge to tear the thing to shreds, to weep and wail and rip. "You're right, of course. We just need to be patient. Juniper will be better in the morning. People always seem to be, don't they? In the meantime I suppose I should put the table settings away."

"It would be best."

"Of course. There's nothing so sad as a table set for a dinner party that never was—oh my!" She was by the door now, looking down on the mess there. "What's happened here?"

"I was careless."

"Why . . ." Saffy went closer. "That looks like jam, a whole jar. Oh, what a shame!"

Percy had found it by the front door when she was returning with the shovel. The worst of the storm had passed by then, clouds had begun to blow themselves apart, and a few eager stars had broken sharply through the sheet of night. She'd seen his duffel bag first, then the glass jar beside it.

"If you're hungry, Perce, I could fetch you some rabbit." Saffy was bent over cleaning up the shards of glass.

"I'm not hungry."

She'd come inside and sat at the kitchen table, put the jam and the bag on top and stared at them. An age had passed before the message had made it from brain to hand, telling her to open the bag and see to whom it belonged. She'd known, of course, that it had to be him she'd buried, but it was as well to be sure. Fingers trembling, heart thumping like a wet dog's tail, she'd reached for it, knocking the jam jar to the floor. A waste, such a waste.

There hadn't been much inside the bag. A change of underclothes, a wallet with very little money and no address, a leather notebook. It was inside that notebook that she'd found the letters. One from Juniper, which she could never bring herself to open, another from a fellow called Theo, a brother, she'd gathered as she read.

For she did read that one. She let herself sink inside the ghastly fact of reading a dead man's letter, of learning more than she ever wanted to about his family—the mother who was a widow, the sisters and their babies, the brother who was simple and loved especially. She forced herself to read every word twice; a half-formed notion that in such a way, by punishing herself thus, she might somehow make amends. A stupid notion. There would be no atoning now for what had happened. Except, perhaps, by way of honesty.

But was there any way she could write and tell them the truth? Any chance that they might be made to understand how it had happened, that it was an accident, a terrible accident, and not Saffy's fault at all? That Saffy, poor Saffy, was the person on earth least capable of desiring or doing harm to someone else. That she'd been blighted, too; that despite her fantasies of London, the elaborate dreams of leaving the castle (she thought Percy didn't know), she'd been unable ever to break the boundaries of Milderhurst, not since that first attack of hysteria in the theater; that if anyone were to blame for the young man's death, it was their father, Raymond Blythe—

No. No one else could be expected to look at things that way. They couldn't know what it was to grow up in the shadows of that book. Percy felt great bitterness as she thought about the ghastly legacy of the *Mud Man*. This—what had happened tonight, the damage poor Saffy had unwittingly caused—this was the legacy of what he'd done. He used to read Milton to them when they were small—*Evil on itself shall back recoil*—and Milton had been right, for they were paying still for Daddy's evil act.

No. There would be no honesty. She would write something else to the family, to this address she'd found in the bag, Henshaw Street, London. The bag itself she would destroy; if not destroy, then hide. The muniment room, perhaps, would be the best place for it—what a sentimental fool she was, to bury a man but be unable to throw away his personal items—the truth, and her defiance of it, would be Percy's burden to carry. Whatever else Daddy had done, he was right in one thing: it was her responsibility to look after the others. And she would make sure they all three stuck together.

"Are you coming upstairs soon, Perce?" Saffy had cleaned up the jam and was standing with a jug of water in her hands.

"Just a few more things to take care of down here. The torch needs batteries . . ."

"I'll take this up to Juniper, then. The poor love's thirsty. See you soon?"

"I'll look in on my way up."

"Don't be too long, Perce."

"I won't. I'll be with you soon."

Saffy hesitated at the bottom of the stairs, turned back to Percy, and smiled softly, a little nervously. "The three of us together," she said. "That's something, isn't it, Perce? The three of us back together again?"

THEREAFTER, SAFFY stayed all night on the chair in Juniper's room. Her neck grew stiff and she was cold despite the blanket draped across her knees. She didn't leave, though; she wasn't tempted by her own warm bed downstairs, not when she was needed here. Saffy sometimes thought that the happiest moments of her life had been when she was tending Juniper. She'd have liked children of her own. She'd have liked that very much indeed.

Juniper stirred and Saffy stood up immediately, stroked her little sister's damp forehead and wondered at the mists and demons that were swarming there.

The blood on her shirt.

Now that *was* a worry, but Saffy refused to think too much upon it. Not now. Percy would make it right. Thank God for Percy. Percy the fixer, who always knew just what to do.

Juniper had settled again, she was breathing deeply, and Saffy sat down. Her legs ached with the day's tension and she felt unusually tired. Still, she didn't want to sleep: it had been a night of odd imaginings. She should never have taken that pill of Daddy's; she'd had the most ghastly dream when she dozed off in the parlor. She'd been having the very same one since she was small, but it had been so vivid this time. It was the pill, of course, and the whisky, the upset of the evening, the storm outside. She'd been a girl again, alone in the attic. Something had woken her, in the dream, a noise by the window, and she'd gone to take a look. The man clinging to the stones outside had been as black as sealing wax, like someone charred by fire. A flash of lightning and Saffy had seen his face. The graceful, dashing youth beneath the Mud Man's wicked mask. A look of surprise, a smile beginning on his lips. It was just as she had dreamed when she was young, just as Daddy had written. The Mud Man's gift was his face. She'd lifted something, she couldn't remember what, and she'd brought it down hard upon his head. His eyes had widened with surprise and then he'd fallen. Slid against the stone and down, finally down, into the moat where he belonged.

FOUR

ELSEWHERE that night, in a neighboring village, a woman held her hours-old baby close, running her thumb against the tiny child's peachy cheek. Her husband would arrive home many hours later, tired from his night-watch duties, and the woman, still dazed from the unexpected and traumatic birth, would recount the details over tea, the way she'd gone into labor on the bus, the pain, the sudden, plunging pain, the bleeding and the savage fear that her baby would die, that she would die, that she would never hold her newborn son; and then she'd smile wearily, devotedly, and pause to press the tears that warmed her face, and she'd tell him about the angel who'd appeared beside her on the roadside, knelt at her knees, and saved her baby's life.

And it would become a family story, retold, passed down, resurrected on rainy nights by the fire, invoked as a means to quell disputes, recited at family events. And time would gallop on, month by year by decade, until on that baby's fiftieth birthday his widowed mother would watch from her cushioned chair at the end of the restaurant table as his children made a toast, reciting the family story of the angel who'd saved their father's life, and without whom none of them would exist.

THOMAS CAVILL didn't go with his regiment when they headed into the slaughter of North Africa. He was already dead by then. Dead and buried, cold beneath the ground of Milderhurst Castle. He died because the night was wet. Because a shutter was loose. Because he wanted to make a good impression. He died because many years before a jealous husband had found his wife with another man.

For a long time, though, nobody knew. The storm cleared, the floodwater receded, and the protective wings of Cardarker Wood spread out around Milderhurst Castle. The world forgot about Thomas Cavill, and any questions of his fate were lost beneath the destruction and debris of war.

Percy sent her letter, the final, rotten untruth that would plague her all her life; Saffy wrote to decline the governess position—Juniper needed her, what else could she have done? Planes flew overhead, war ended, the sky peeled back to reveal one new year after another. The Sisters Blythe grew old; they became objects of quaint curiosity in the village, the subjects of myth. Until one day, a young woman came to visit. She had ties to another who had come before and the castle stones began to whisper with recognition. Percy Blythe saw that it was time. That after fifty years of carrying her burden, she could finally take it from her shoulders and return to Thomas Cavill his closing date. The story could come to an end.

So she did, and she charged the girl to do the right thing with it.

Which left only one remaining task.

She gathered her sisters, her beloved sisters, and made sure they were fast asleep and dreaming. And then she struck a match, in the library where it had all begun.

EPILOGUE

For decades the attic has been used as storage. Nothing but boxes and old chairs and superseded printing materials. The building itself is home to a publishing house, and the faint smell of paper and ink has impregnated the walls and floors. It is rather pleasant, if you like that sort of thing.

It is 1993; the renovation has taken months but it is finally complete. The clutter has been cleared, the wall that someone, sometime, erected so that one drafty attic might become two, is gone, and for the first time in fifty years, the attic at the top of Herbert Billing's Victorian house in Notting Hill has a new tenant.

A knock at the door and a young woman skips across the floor from the windowsill. It's a particularly wide sill, perfect for perching, which is just what she's been doing. The girl is drawn to the window. The flat faces south so there is always sun, particularly in July. She likes to look out across the garden, along the street, and to feed the sparrows who have started to visit her for bread crumbs. She wonders, too, at the strange dark patches on the sill, almost like cherry stains, that refuse to remain hidden beneath the coat of fresh white paint.

Edie Burchill opens the door and is surprised and pleased to see her mother standing there. Meredith hands her a sprig of honeysuckle and says, "I saw it growing on a fence and couldn't resist bringing you some. Nothing brightens a room quite like honeysuckle, don't you think? Have you a vase?"

Edie hasn't, not yet, but she does have an idea. A glass jar, the sort that might once have been used to hold jam, was turned up during the renovation and is sitting now by the sink. Edie fills it with water and puts the sprig inside, pops it on the windowsill where it will catch some sun. "Where's Dad?" she says. "He didn't come with you today?"

"He's discovered Dickens. *Bleak House.*"

"Ah, well then," says Edie. "I'm afraid you've really lost him now." Meredith reaches inside her bag and pulls a pile of paper from within, shakes it above her head.

"You've finished it!" says Edie, clapping her hands.

"I have."

"And this is my copy?"

"I've had it bound especially."

Edie grins and takes the manuscript from her mother. "Congratulations—what a feat!"

"I was going to wait until we saw you tomorrow," Meredith says, flushing, "but I couldn't help myself. I wanted you to be the first to read it."

"I should think so! What time's your class?"

"Three."

"I'll walk with you," says Edie. "I'm on my way to visit Theo."

Edie opens the door and holds it for her mother. She's about to follow when she remembers something. She's meeting Adam Gilbert later for a drink to celebrate the publication of Pippin Books' *Mud Man* and has promised to show him her first edition *Jane Eyre,* a gift from Herbert when she agreed to take over at Billing & Brown.

She turns quickly and for a split second sees two figures on the sill. A man and a woman, close enough that their foreheads might be touching. She blinks and they're gone. Nothing left to see but the spill of sunlight across the sill.

It is not the first time. It happens occasionally, the shift in her peripheral vision. She knows it's just the play of sunshine on the whitewashed walls but Edie is fanciful and lets herself imagine that it's something more. That once upon a time, a happy couple lived together in the flat that is now hers. That they were the ones who left the cherry stains on her sill. That it was their happiness that soaked into the walls of the flat.

For everyone who visits says the same thing, that the room has a good feeling about it. And it's true. Edie can't explain it, but there is a good feeling in the attic; it is a happy place.

"Are you coming, Edie?"

It's Meredith, poking her head around the door, anxious not to be late for the writing class she loves so much.

"Coming." Edie snatches up *Jane Eyre,* checks her reflection in the little mirror propped above the porcelain sink, and runs after her mother.

The door closes behind her, leaving the ghostly lovers alone once more in the quiet and the warm.

ACKNOWLEDGMENTS

MY sincere thanks to everyone who read and commented on early drafts of *The Distant Hours,* particularly Davin Patterson, Kim Wilkins, and Julia Kretschmer; to my friend and agent, Selwa Anthony, for taking such great care of me; to Diane Morton for speed-reading the final pages; and to all my family—Mortons, Pattersons, and especially Oliver and Louis—and friends, for allowing me to abscond so often to Milderhurst Castle, and for putting up with me when I stumbled back down the hill, dazed, distracted, and sometimes even a tad displaced.

I am fortunate to work with a brilliant continent-spanning editorial team, and for their tireless work and unending support in getting *The Distant Hours* to the printer on time, I'd like to offer heartfelt thanks to Annette Barlow and Clara Finlay at Allen & Unwin, Australia; Maria Rejt, Eli Dryden, and Sophie Orme at Mantle, UK; and Liz Cowen, whose knowledge of all things continues to amaze me. Great thanks, too, is due to Lisa Keim, Judith Curr, and staff at Atria Books, U.S.; as it is to all my publishers, for their continued dedication to me and my books.

Thank you also to Robert Gorman at Allen & Unwin for his commitment; to Sammy and Simon from Bookhouse, who were incredibly patient with me and meticulous when it came to typesetting my words; to Clive Harris, who showed me that the blitz can still be found in London if you know where to look; to the artists and designers who worked on creating such beautiful jackets for *The Distant Hours;* to booksellers and librarians everywhere for understanding that stories are special things; and in memory of Herbert and Rita Davies.

Finally, a big thank-you to my readers. Without you, it would only be half the pleasure.

THE DISTANT HOURS started as a single idea about a set of sisters in a castle on a hill. I drew further inspiration from a great many sources, including illustrations, photographs, maps, poems, diaries, Mass Observation journals, online accounts of the Second World War, the Imperial War Museum's *Children's War* exhibition, my own visits to castles and country houses, novels and films from the 1930s and 1940s, ghost stories, and gothic novels of the eighteenth and nineteenth centuries. While it's impossible to list all of the nonfiction consulted, the following are some of my favorites: Nicola Beauman, *A Very Great Profession* (1995); Katherine Bradley-Hole, *Lost Gardens of England* (2008); Richard Broad and Suzie Fleming (eds.), *Nella Last's War: The Second World War Diaries of 'Housewife, 49'* (1981); Ann De Courcy, *Debs at War* (2005); Mark Girouard, *Life in the English Country House* (1979); Juliet Gardiner, *Wartime Britain 1939–1945* (2004); Juliet Gardiner, *The Children's War* (2005); Susan Goodman, *Children of War* (2005); Vere Hodgson, *Few Eggs and No Oranges: The Diaries of Vere Hodgson 1940–45* (1998); Gina Hughes, *A Harvest of Memories: A Wartime Evacuee in Kent* (2005); Norman Longmate, *How We Lived Then: A History of Everyday Life in the Second World War* (1971); Raynes Minns, *Bombers & Mash: The Domestic Front 1939–45* (1988); Jeffrey Musson, *The English Manor House* (1999); Adam Nicolson, *Sissinghurst* (2008); Virginia Nicolson, *Singled Out* (2007); Miranda Seymour, *In My Father's House* (2007); Christopher Simon Sykes, *Country House Camera* (1980); Ben Wicks, *No Time to Wave Goodbye* (1989); Sandra Koa Wing, *Our Longest Days* (2007); Mathilde Wolff-Mönckeberg, *On the Other Side: Letters to My Children from Germany 1940–1946* (1979); Philip Ziegler, *London at War 1939–1945* (1995).

THE
DISTANT
HOURS

KATE MORTON

A READERS CLUB GUIDE

Suggested Discussion Points

- Edie is passionate about reading and holds some novels close to her. Juniper, Saffy, and Meredith are passionate about writing. What would you say about the power of words in your life?
- In *The Distant Hours,* Milderhurst Castle takes on a life of its own. You can almost hear the stones murmuring. Can an inanimate object work as an important character in a novel? Perhaps there are other novels you've read where this occurs? Examine the way in which the author builds the atmosphere to transform the stones of Milderhurst into a character with moods. Is it successful?
- Would you say that the mysterious Milderhurst Castle reflects its hoary inhabitants? Does it also repel outsiders?
- Juniper was afraid of only one thing—following the emotional morass of her father's breaking sanity. What do you think of her story?
- What would you say are the major themes of *The Distant Hours*?
- Percy and Saffy both made it their lives' mission to protect their little sister, Juniper, from all outside influences. Was this the right thing to do? And for whom?
- World War II saw the introduction of large changes to English society across the class divisions. Can you imagine a life where, as a woman, it was controversial to be seen wearing pants?
- There are many secrets being kept hidden away within the pages of *The Distant Hours*. Percy, particularly, has had many foisted upon her that she has spent much of her life hiding. But she wanted to tell Edie everything as Percy saw how her and her sisters' story would end. Is it harder to be a secret-keeper or to reveal everything?
- The bond between mothers and daughters seems significant in the relationship between Meredith and Edie. Discuss the way their relationship played out in *The Distant Hours*.